SORCERY
AGAINST
CAESAR

The Complete Simon of Gitta Short Stories

by

RICHARD L. TIERNEY

AND DIVERS HANDS

Edited by Edward Stasheff

COPYRIGHT INFORMATION

Dedicated to

ROBERT E. HOWARD

Special thanks to Charles Danny Lovecraft of P'rea Press.

TABLE OF CONTENTS

INTRODUCTION:
SWORD OF THE AVATAR
by Robert M. Price

To Mount Sinai

Grim mountain, on your lowering slopes I stand,
Cowed by the sound of thunder in the skies,
While your dark crown of cloud spreads o'er the land
And stirs my mind to yet more dark surmise…

Cowed by the sound of thunder in the skies,
I sense beneath your flanks those monstrous Things
That shall one day awaken and arise
And—oh, to stifle these mad visionings!

I sense beneath your flanks those monstrous Things,
Grim with a hatred vast as cosmic space,
That lurk and strain to burst their prisonings
And rise in power to smite the human race.

Grim with a hatred vast as cosmic space,
Those sleeping Powers shall one day wake and rise
To smash this earth as with a giant mace
And strew its shards across the darkened skies.

— Richard L. Tierney

The Tierney Mythos

Richard L. Tierney is best known for his heroic fantasy, his tales of Simon of Gitta, and his novels, cowritten with David C. Smith, of the Robert E. Howard/Roy Thomas character Red Sonja, as well as his and Smith's able pastiche of Howard's hero Bran Mak Morn, *For the Witch of the Mists*. He is nearly unique in his ability to invoke both the colorful action that foregrounded Howard's fiction and the tragic, bloody-sunset grandeur that backgrounded it.

But in the circles of Lovecraft scholarship Tierney is best remembered for his epoch-making 1972 essay "The Derleth Mythos" (initially in Meade and Penny Frierson's *HPL*, now available in my collection *The Horror of It*

All, as well as Darrell Schweitzer's *Discovering H. P. Lovecraft)*. In this essay, Tierney clearly distinguished between the Cthulhu Mythos framework superimposed by August Derleth and Lovecraft's originally rather different vision. Lovecraft had painted a narrative universe in which humanity was a joke or a mistake, a bit of flotsam inevitably to be trodden underfoot by great cosmic forces indifferent to our puny existence. Derleth introduced a more conventional good-versus-evil schema. Lovecraft had figurally rendered his nihilism in the form of the Great Old Ones, but to these Derleth added a pantheon of Elder Gods friendly to man, and he made the Old Ones their rebellious servants, drawing explicit parallels with the Christian drama of salvation. Cthulhu and Azathoth were Satan and Beelzebub. Nodens was Jehovah. Derleth also compromised the utter alienness of Lovecraft's Old Ones by associating them with not only Christian but also other myth cycles, especially the Polynesian. Against these innovations, Tierney sought to restore Lovecraft's fearful nihilism and the Wholly Other character of his Old Ones. Dirk W. Mosig followed up Tierney's insights in another landmark article, "H. P. Lovecraft: Myth-Maker" (in S. T. Joshi, *H. P. Lovecraft: Four Decades of Criticism*, 1980). The whole critical movement of which *Lovecraft Studies* has been the flagship was the result.

Even the greatest discoverers often have their anticipators, and many Mythos fans and Lovecraftian scholars seem not to have noticed that the first to drive the wedge between Lovecraft and Derleth was actually Lin Carter in his book *Lovecraft: A Look behind the Cthulhu Mythos*. Perhaps this tree fell in a forest with no one to hear it, because Carter also went on in his own fiction to ignore the very differences he had so carefully delineated. He recognized Derleth as an innovator, but he *liked* the innovations! Carter was not hag-ridden with the conviction that only Lovecraft was orthodox. When Tierney axed the tree, there were ears to hear, but it was really Mosig's shot that was heard round the world (the world of "Lovecraftianity", anyway). Maybe this was due to the fact that Tierney, too, decided, once he had cleft the Lovecraft-Derleth gap, to leap over it!

Like Lin Carter, Richard Tierney thought that, handled rightly, Derleth's new elements could be made to work better than Derleth himself had done in stories which, as he himself admitted, he had tossed off carelessly as filler for *Weird Tales*. For example, take the supposed continuity between the Cthulhu Mythos and the Christian Mythos. The problem in Derleth's tales was his tendency to assimilate the Cthulhu Mythos to the Christian Mythos, featuring *deus ex machina* rescues by the angelic "star warriors" and the Elder Gods shaped like biblical pillars of fire. So, Tierney reasoned, why not do the opposite? Why not assimilate the Christian Mythos to the Cthulhu Mythos? As a rationalist skeptic and freethinker, Tierney already considered early Christianity to be simply one more of the ancient mystery religions, sprung from the same rich mulch of antique myth and superstition, so the transition was a natural one. You will find many examples of the Lovecraftian take on Christianity and the Bible in the stories in this volume, but perhaps the most dramatic and shocking instances occur in Tierney's novels *The Winds of Zarr* and *The Drums of Chaos*, where the biblical Yahweh is equated with Yog-Sothoth, and Jesus is made an avatar of the Old Ones like unto Wilbur Whateley.

The good-versus-evil framework imposed by Derleth? Tierney saw that all one needed to do was shift the weight from a Christian determinism, in which the victory of Light is fore-ordained, to more of a Manichean dualism, in which there is a real struggle between Light and Darkness, with no guaranteed outcome. This puts the teeth back in the beast—no safety net anymore. Even Derleth's association of the Lovecraftian Old Ones with the conventional scheme of elemental spirits (a feature borrowed from Francis T. Laney) did not seem so trite if only one viewed it as Tierney did, from the perspective of Zoroastrianism, which loaded the elements with theological importance, and of Gnosticism, where the elements, the *stoicheia*, were perceived as malicious minions of the Demiurge, powers oppressing the elect. In short, Tierney managed to transmute Derleth back into Lovecraft!

Simon's Scribe

I recall reading many years ago that when a local California TV station announced that it would be showing Paul Newman's early flick *The Silver Chalice*, Newman took out a full-page ad pleading with his public not to watch the damn thing. Newman, it seems, was ashamed of the old movie, essentially little more than a glorified sword and sandal flick reflective of the same sentimental 1950's "religion boom" devotionalism that also gave us *Slaves of Babylon* and *Demetrius and the Gladiators*. Heck, *The Silver Chalice* wasn't *that* bad. Nowhere near as bad as that *Plan 9* of religious flicks, *Salome*, the absolute nadir of Bible bombs.

It's a good thing that Richard Tierney happened to catch *The Silver Chalice* some years before Newman tried to cover his butt, because Tierney was intrigued and impressed, not with Newman, but with Jack Palance's portrayal of the inspired charlatan Simon Magus, Simon the Sorcerer, who was finally sucked in by his own scam and perished with the hubris of Icarus when he tried to impress Emperor Nero by flying through the air. When one day Tierney decided to use the mysterious Simon as the basis for a series of sword and sorcery adventures, Palance's Simon still loomed large enough that Tierney could think of him in no other way. Thus the Simon you will meet in the following pages is described in terms meant subtly to suggest the angular, strong-boned, and almost Asian features of the young Jack Palance.

The next two sections of introductory matter deal in some detail with the historical background of the Simon character as well as the Gnostic doctrines he is said to have espoused. You may wish to skip these sections, because Tierney's tales make plenty of sense on their own, but if you are intrigued by the hints he drops of higher truths, you might want to read on.

I. The Historical Simon Magus

The Legend

The Arab chiefs had warned me of the place
I meant to seek; they spoke in accents dire
Of some great Thing that lived within the fire
Upon the summit—something with a face
No man could bear—a Thing of alien race
That crept by night from out its molten mire
To perch upon some black granitic spire
Or ooze in hunger to the mountain's base.

The Thing, the Arabs claimed, was not of Earth
Nor yet of any world that man could know;
More ancient than Allah, its monstrous birth
Had taken place beyond the Time-stream's flow.
"In aeons past some black fate brought it here,"
They said, "and left it for all men to fear."

            — Richard L. Tierney

Simon the Samaritan

Who is, or was, Simon Magus? He is a prominent figure in the Western esoteric tradition, or at least in the Western esoteric legend. He appears suddenly as an already notorious figure in a number of second-century A.D. documents, including the Acts of the Apostles, the writings of Justin Martyr, and the Clementine *Homilies* and *Recognitions*. Later heresiologists make him the father of the Gnostic "heresy."

Simon is depicted as a Samaritan. Samaritans were descendants of the old tribes of the northern Hebrew kingdom of Israel and were named for their capital, Samaria. Following the death of the tyrant Solomon, the northern tribes seceded from the Davidic confederation of Israel (in the north), Judah (in the south), and Jerusalem (on the border). They'd had enough of the dynasty of David and Solomon, and for ever after, Israelites/Samaritans had little use for the traditions of Judah (or Judaism). This meant that their form of the Yahwist religion evolved parallel to the Judaism of the south, as the latter developed in the hands of Ezra, the Pharisee sect, and their successors, the rabbis. Thus both Samaritans and Jews condemned each other as heretics. The Hasmonean kings, having won a century's worth of freedom from the Seleucid Empire of Antiochus IV

Epiphanes, turned inward, converting "Galilee of the Gentiles" to Judaism at swordpoint and bulldozing the Samaritan temple atop Mt. Gerizim.

Jews claimed that after Israel had been absorbed by the Assyrian Empire in the seventh century B.C., the conquerors shipped in a number of foreign colonists who intermarried with Israelites and mixed their polytheism with Yahweh-worship. This provided an excuse to reject Samaritans as non-Jews, the same way the Orthodox rabbis in modern Israel deny that Reform Jews are Jews. Was there anything to this cavil? Probably not. It represents history in hindsight, since no doubt in the seventh century both Israel and Judah were predominantly polytheistic anyway. Hebrew monotheism was a late development, appearing for the first time with Jeremiah and the Second Isaiah in the sixth and fifth centuries. It remained a minority view for a long time thereafter (see Margaret Barker, *The Great Angel: A Study of Israel's Second God*, 1992). Thus Samaritan polytheism need have been no import. Both feuding sister faiths eventually became genuinely monotheistic, probably at more or less the same time, by the late first century A.D., though you still would have found some hold-outs for that old-time, polytheistic religion.

How did Samaritanism differ from emerging Judaism? One of the major points was that of the coming deliverer. While not all Jews expected a king (a Messiah, or "anointed", i.e., royal, one) to resume David's dynasty (James H. Charlesworth, ed., *The Messiah*, 1992), *no* Samaritans did. They had repudiated the house of David; why would they dream of its resumption? Instead, they awaited the appearance of the Taheb, the "restorer" (see John 4:25), a prophet like unto Moses, whom they saw predicted in Deuteronomy 18:15. In later centuries, this expectation would mutate into the hope for a second advent of the original Moses himself (John MacDonald, *The Theology of the Samaritans*, 1964).

The two faiths differed also on the extent of the canon of scripture. The Jewish list of officially approved writings eventually grew to the large list which also happens to serve as the Protestant Old Testament (the Catholic and Orthodox O.T. is longer, reflecting the contents of the Septuagint, the Greek translation of the Jewish scriptures used by Hellenized Jews outside of Palestine). The Samaritans, on the other hand, accepted only the Pentateuch, the so-called Books of Moses (Genesis, Exodus, Leviticus, Numbers and Deuteronomy). Joshua was almost as important to them. Once you get beyond Joshua, though, most everything in the Old Testament stems in some way from the royal court and the temple hierarchy of Jerusalem, hence all southern stuff and of no interest to Samaritans up north. Protestants don't spend a heck of a lot of time studying Papal Encyclicals either, in case you hadn't noticed.

In his version of Simon, Richard Tierney puts him at a double distance from Judaism, making him not only a Samaritan, but having him hail from Gitta, the old Gath, one of the five great Philistine city-states which had earlier produced another great epic hero, the towering "mighty man", Goliath. (Ironically, it is only in cheesy sword and sandal flicks that Goliath has regained some measure of his prebiblical hero status!)

The Samaritan sect still exists in the modern state of Israel, though it is a tiny group of only a few hundred, a cherished living fossil.

Simon the Holy God

The New Testament mentions the Samaritans in a few places, accounting for why most of us have heard of them at all. Matthew 10:5 warns missionaries not to set foot on Samaritan territory, while Luke has composed the splendid parable of the Good Samaritan (10:29-37) and attributed it to Jesus (likewise the episode of the Grateful Samaritan, Luke 17:11-19), an unambiguously positive portrayal that is single-handedly responsible for the fact that "Samaritan" has come to be synonymous for someone who goes out of their way to help another in trouble. John 4.7-9, 20-24 mentions and lampoons the childish spite that separated Jews and Samaritans to such an extent that they considered each other's dinnerware to be ritually unclean!

The sequel to Luke's gospel, the Acts of the Apostles, has Philip, one of the Seven who led the Hellenistic Christians, preach in Samaria and convert the whole capital city to faith in Jesus (Acts 8:5-8 ff). This is where Simon comes in. Luke, the narrator of Acts, tells us that when Philip came into town he found a religious revival already underway. The whole place was absolutely captivated by one Simon, a magician, who claimed to be the Great Power, i.e., the Godhead, made manifest in the flesh, a claim he validated by producing astonishing miracles (Acts 8:9-11). Luke seems to start rewriting the traditional story right at this point.

Other Christian sources preserve more of the original form of the legend. Various heresiologists tell us that Simon traveled with a woman named Helen, whom he had rescued from a brothel. She was his eternal soul mate, having existed in the divine Pleroma, the heavenly world of Light and Spirit, as the Ennoia or Epinoia, the First Thought (pretty much the same idea as the personified Lady Wisdom in Proverbs 8, Sirach 1, and Wisdom of Solomon 7). As such, she and the Great Power formed a syzygy (a "yoked" pair). She had been lost in the swamp of the world of matter (the sinister creation of the pernicious Archons, "Rulers") since the beginning, and it was only her spiritual wisdom which kept the world running. It was to rescue her that the Great Power had condescended to enter the dark world of matter.

This salvation myth, quite typical of Gnosticism in general, implied that those who followed Simon and learned his secret knowledge (*gnosis*) would be saved after death. You see, Helen's soul was symbolic of the divine Light of Wisdom that had been shattered into a million sparks and scattered throughout the material world. The ex-harlot Helen embodied, one supposes, the greatest single concentration of this Wisdom, but many other sparks lurked around, dazed and amnesiac, inside the souls of a certain chosen few, those who had ears to hear the gnosis of Simon. The pious ones know themselves to contain a latent spark of the divine glory, and they seek to liberate it from fleshly reincarnation by means of meditative exercises and asceticism, denial of fleshly pleasures. Some rare Gnostics took the left-handed path and sought liberation by libertine antinomianism: "Do as thou wilt shall be the whole of the law." In either case, the point was to proclaim and live out one's independence from the worldly laws of government and religion, since these were but the creations of the unknown Rulers of this world, the evil Archons, one of whom was the Yahweh ("Jehovah") of the Old Testament.

Love Stronger Than Death

Why had the Great Power repeatedly incarnated himself? After all, the divine sparks had to reincarnate because they were sunk in ignorance of their true heavenly origin and destiny. Being by nature divine, they could not really die, but until they were enlightened, neither could they slough off the defilement of the flesh and return to the Pleroma. But Simon certainly did not share that ignorance. In the manner of the Bodhisattvas of Mahayana Buddhism, he voluntarily undertook countless births in the world to seek out and to save that which was lost: Helen, the Ennoia, the symbol of the soul of the Elect Ones.

It must have been a wink to the knowing reader, but by the same token, like other second-century heresiologists, Luke has chosen to sink to the level of scurrilous mud-slinging instead of rational refutation. The author of John 4:16-18 also seems willfully to misunderstand when he depicts the Samaritan woman as having had five husbands and now to be living with someone who is no husband at all. The reference seems to be to the Simonian Helen, her sexual exploitation in at least five previous incarnations and to her association with Simon Magus in the present. The insinuations of Helen still being a whore and Simon openly living with her in sin are readily recognizable as typical polemical vilification. It is for the same reason that Mary Magdalene was depicted as both demoniac and prostitute by early church fathers who considered her a heretic (see my "Mary Magdalene: Gnostic Apostle?", *Grail*, vol. 6, #2, June 1990).

You will see that Richard Tierney has taken this theme of Simon seeking his soul-mate Helen on a will-o'-the-wisp chase through incarnation after incarnation and has made it central to his epic of Simon.

Sinful Simon

Speaking of vilification, we may pause to note that the very appellation, Simon "Magus", the magician, is another example. As anthropologists have shown, "magic" differs in no essential point from "miracle" in cultures that believe in both. The difference is rather one of evaluation: "My supernatural feat is a miracle; your supernatural feat is magic." Thus to call Simon a magician simply means that he had a reputation as a miracle-worker, and that someone wanted to portray that reputation in an invidious light. In exactly the same way, Jesus is depicted as a magical trickster in the various *Toledoth Jeschu* gospels of Jewish anti-Christian polemic. As you will see, Tierney makes Simon an escaped gladiator who has picked up some showman's stage illusions and Houdini tricks, but who does actually deal with Great Powers, too.

If "magician" was an undercutting term of reproach, so was the epithet "Samaritan", which had become synonymous with "heretic", as when John has the opponents of Jesus insult him: "Are we not right in saying you are a Samaritan and that you have a demon [at your disposal—i.e., a magician, too]?" (John 8:48).

Similarly, for Simon to have been called a Samaritan very likely means simply "Simon the heretic." What heresy? We have already seen that various second-century writers attribute to him claims to be the embodied Great Power. Michael Goulder accepts this and even argues that the whole notion of God incarnate was borrowed by Christians from Simonians.

II. Gnosticism

Yahweh

"The place is death!" the Arab chief had warned,
But, heedless, I approached with growing wonder
The mountain grim with cloud and muttered thunder
That rose before me steep and granite-horned.
Here where old Horeb's legends had their source
I now ascended, pausing not to rest
Till, when I gained at last the granite crest,
A hissing brimstone crater barred my course.

I watched as boiling clouds about me loomed
Like sulphurous serpents churning sluggishly,
When suddenly a Voice titanic boomed:
"Put off thy shoes—bow down and worship Me!"
I turned to flee—but, glancing backward, froze
As from the pit a monstrous head arose.

— Richard L. Tierney

Strangers in a Strange Land

Gnosticism was a pessimistic world view embraced by those who felt themselves to be strangers in a strange land, isolated and superior to the slobs and fools around them (on this see Hans Jonas, *The Gnostic Religion*, Epilogue to the 1963 edition, and E. R. Dodds, *Pagan and Christian in an Age of Anxiety*, 1970). It was also an ingenious answer to the perennial problem of theodicy, getting God off the hook for all the evil in the world. How can the world have been the creation of a righteous God and be ruled by his justice? Whence all the tragedy and evil? Gnostics chose to resolve the dilemma by positing that the true God, the unknown one, hidden away within the fullness (*pleroma*) of unapproachable light (1 Timothy 6:16), did not create the world. Instead, he emanated from himself a whole series of paired divine beings (syzygies). At the end of this process there emerged a single divinity, Sophia (Wisdom). She felt alienated from the Godhead, from which of all the divine entities (Aions) she was furthest removed. She was also frustrated for having no partner with whom to beget further Aions.

The divine essence was running out by this point, like a tenth-generation videotape, so when Sophia contrived to bear offspring by herself, a virgin conception and birth, the result was a brutish and malign entity called the Demiurge, i.e., the Creator, Carpenter, or Craftsman. This character was borrowed from Plato, who had posited him as a mythic link between philosophical categories of eternal matter and eternal spirit. The celestial gods were too aloof to get involved in creation, leaving it to the Demiurge, whose job it is to impose ceaselessly the likenesses of the eternal Forms, the spiritual prototypes of all things, onto hunks of unstable, shifting matter for as long as they can hold it.

The Gnostics, heavily influenced by the allegorical Hellenistic Judaism of Alexandria, interpreted the Genesis accounts of the creation and the fall in Platonic categories, even as Philo of Alexandria did. Their shocking result was to identify the Demiurge as both evil and as the same as the Hebrew God Yahweh/Jehovah!

Schizoid Creator

The Demiurge, imitating the ultimate Godhead, of whom he was nonetheless ignorant, proceeded to create matter and a series of material beings, a kind of mud-pie substitute for the Pleroma of Light. He created a world, but it was inert and chaotic ("without form and void"). To get some action going, he managed to steal some of the spiritual light from the Pleroma. According to whichever Gnostic text you choose, this might have been accomplished by waylaying and dismembering another Aion, the Man of Light, Son of Man, or Primal Man (= the Zoroastrian Gayomard, the Upanishadic Purusha, the Man of IV Ezra 13:1-4). Or the light may have been taken from the reflected image of Sophia, who had stooped over to look into the dark pool of the newly created abyss of matter. In any case, the Demiurge and his evil lieutenants, the Archons (based on the fallen Sons of God or angels from Jewish apocryphal versions of Genesis 6:1-6) used these sparks of alien light as something like DNA to program self-replicating order into the otherwise stillborn cosmos of matter.

The trick worked. Just as it says in that old song by the Demiurges, I mean the Carpenters: "On the day that you were born the angels got together and decided to create a dream come true, so they sprinkled moon dust in your hair of gold and starlight in your eyes of blue." But they still couldn't get the damn thing to move. This is where some stolen light came in handy. Light stolen from the Heavenly Eve (Eve was already a goddess in Jerusalem, Greece, and Phrygia and among the Hittites long before Genesis demoted her to a primordial Lucy Ricardo) animated the inert Pinocchio. The Archons then got the hots for Eve and tried to gang rape her. They did rape her shadowy physical counterpart, the earthly Eve, and then presented her to the now-awake Adam in only slightly used condition. All of this reflects very ancient variants, alternative versions, of the Eden story which people continued to remember and to pass down in defiance of the official canonical version in Genesis chapters 2 and 3.

Of the subsequent children of Adam and Eve, the descendants of Seth possessed the divine spark of light inherited from the Heavenly Eve, while the descendants of Cain were the bastard spawn of the Archon rapists. This is at least the version of events put forth by the Sethian sect, who regarded Seth as a messianic revealer and redeemer and who later, upon assimilation into Christianity, reinterpreted Seth as a previous incarnation of Christ (or, more to the point, Christ as the second coming of Seth). Others, like the Ophites or Naasenes, rightly understood Adam and Eve to be a local variant of the myth of Attis and Cybele, and thus made Jesus a later incarnation of the slain and resurrected Attis. Whatever name they might use, the various Gnostic sects believed their doctrine, their *gnosis*, had come to them from a heavenly revealer who had come to Earth in human flesh or at least in the likeness thereof, to awaken those possessing the divine spark to their true origin and destiny. This would enable them to escape the vicious cycle of rebirth and ascend once and for all to the Pleroma, to rejoin the Godhead.

Know Thyself

As Walter Schmithals (*Gnosticism in Corinth*, Eng. trans. 1971) speculated, "pure" Gnosticism must have understood the sheer fact of self-knowledge as enough to effect postmortem liberation. Later, more corrupt, superstitious forms of the doctrine pictured Jesus or Seth or Melchizedek providing not only self-knowledge but also a set of magical formulae, passwords, that would enable the elect soul to slip unnoticed through the cosmic checkpoints in each of the crystal spheres concentrically encasing our world. At each sphere there waited its ruling Archon (playing the role of the old Babylonian planetary gods), ready to turn back any escaping soul, like marksmen posted along the old Berlin Wall. A fictive account of this version of the heavenly ascent through the stations of the Archons, as well as a dramatized version of the myth of the Fall of Sophia, is provided in the Simon of Gitta tale "The Throne of Achamoth."

Often this revealer was himself an aspect of the Primal Man of Light whose sparks were scattered among the elect. He was on a mission to save himself! Thus he is called the Redeemed Redeemer. Simonian gnosis was a bit different at this point, since the revealer/redeemer Simon was not rescuing himself but rather his mate, the Ennoia. But since she was his own syzygy, his counterpart, what's the difference?

What happened to Gnosticism? Most of the early Gnostic Christians were members of the churches of emerging Catholicism, but they knew their doctrines could get them into trouble and so spoke of them only to fellow Gnostics (= "those in the know") or to likely recruits. From the mid-second century onward the Marcionites (sort of theological first cousins to Gnostics) were organized into fast-growing congregations all over the Roman Empire and beyond. A century later, Manichean Gnosticism formed its own congregations and rapidly spread into a genuine world religion. Hard times came once Constantine, a Catholic Christian himself, came to power and allowed his bishops to persecute other types of Christians, killing adherents and burning their scriptures. The imperial church killed far more fellow Christians than the pagan Romans ever had. Marcionism and Manicheism continued to exist for some centuries to the east of the empire, but the death blow had been dealt; eventually they faded away, though Manicheism survived till the eleventh century in China. The Middle Ages saw either a resurgence of Gnosticism (as Steven Runciman sees it in *The Medieval Manichee*) or a spontaneous rediscovery of the same themes (the view of Ioan Couliano in *The Tree of Gnosis*) in the form of the Bogomil and Catharist movements. These, too, were bloodily stamped out by Christian authorities. The Albigensian Crusade was aimed at wiping out the Catharists.

But that is not dead which can eternal lie, and interest in Gnosticism has again been fanned into flame in our own time by the recovery in Nag Maddami, Egypt, of a library of Gnostic gospels, epistles, revelations, and acts. It turns out that the monks of St. Pachomius had received advance word that their bishop, the famous St. Athanasius, would be sending inquisitors to examine the contents of their library, and they knew many of their most precious manuscripts would not stand the scrutiny. They hastened to bury them, and the books drowsed sixteen centuries till their accidental discovery in 1945, just a year or so before the discovery of the Dead Sea Scrolls not far away in Palestine. The translation and publication of these scriptures has aroused a good deal of popular curiosity about Gnosticism. Carl Jung studied the first of the texts to become available and ventured the opinion that the Gnostics were the first great psychoanalysts, that they had mapped out the process of psychic individuation better than anyone else in history. Today we are witnessing a revival of Gnostic spirituality and psychology, often interpreted through Jungian categories (see Stephan S. Hoeller, *Jung and the Lost Gospels*, 1989).

H. P. Lovecraft knew about Gnosticism, and thus I think it no accident that several prominent Gnostic themes appear in his Mythos tales. I set forth this case in the introduction to *The Azathoth Cycle*. I first came to know Richard Tierney after he had read my essay "The Old Ones' Promise of Eternal Life" (reprinted in *The Azathoth Cycle*). He, too, had seen the Gnostic connection and recognized me, I guess you'd say, as a fellow illuminatus. There is one major difference between his approach to Gnosticism and the Mythos and mine—my presentation suffers from reducing the Gnostic mythemes to a bloodless system of abstractions, an occupational hazard of academics, while Tierney follows the old and authentic path of setting forth the Gnosis in the living form of myth and story. The difference is well illustrated by a comparison of Talbot Mundy's Theosophist novels (including *Om: The Secret of Ahbor Valley*, *The Thunder Dragon Gate*, and *Old Ugly Face*) and his sole nonfiction book, *I Say Sunrise*, in which he lays out his beliefs in a didactic fashion. The former convey the reader to the Inner Sanctum of the Numinous in hushed tones of awe, while the latter falls as flat as an auto repair manual. Tierney has followed the former path, and the result has the authentic ring of the Mysteries.

— Robert M. Price

About "The Sword of Spartacus"

This rousing tale, which first appeared in Andrew J. Offutt's anthology *Swords Against Darkness #3*, Zebra Books, 1978, relates events in the career of Simon of Gitta occurring early in the summer of A.D. 27. In it we meet not only Simon but also his mentor and his fellow apprentice, Dositheus and Menander, respectively. Neither is wholly the creation of Richard Tierney. Both are based on legendary characters associated with Simon Magus in early Christian writings. Dositheus, too, was a Samaritan and a Gnostic mystagogue who reportedly declared himself to be a messiah. In the Clementine *Homilies* and *Recognitions,* one of Tierney's acknowledged sources, Dositheus and Simon Magus are said to have been disciples of John the Baptist. After the Baptist's execution by Herod Antipas, we are told, Simon and Dositheus engaged in a magic duel to determine who should succeed their master. Dositheus won and took charge of the small sect of thirty men.

As David Friedrich Strauss (*The Life of Jesus Critically Examined*, 1835) noticed, the Gospels preserve certain loose ends betraying the fact that John the Baptist headed a sect that continued parallel to Jesus' during the career of the latter, and then for as much as a century after. The Mandaean (or Nasorean) sect, which continues to this day, still venerates John as a true prophet, while vilifying Jesus as the Antichrist. Their Messiah is a Gnostic redeemer called Enosh-Uthras.

Robert Eisler *(The Messiah Jesus and John the Baptist*, 1931) believed that the Clementine narratives preserve some genuine information, and speculated that John the Baptist identified himself with this Messianic Enosh. Eisler also remarked on the similarity between the depiction of John (Ioannes in Greek) as preaching and teaching from the shallows of the Jordan and the mythic deity Oannes the fish-god, who emerged from the sea to teach human beings.

This all begins to explain why some Christians condemned John as the fountainhead of all heresies. The chain of heretical succession supplied us by the early Catholic writers like Eusebius of Caesarea may be an artificial and polemical one, linking figures that were actually independent teachers and messiahs. Thus, the attempt to blame John for the heresies of both Simon Magus and Dositheus may be fictive, but the very attempt attests to the fact that all three were remembered in some quarters as analogous figures, all rivals of Jesus as man-god and messiah.

Josephus reports a number of incidents regarding Pontius Pilate, to whom we shall return in connection with "The Dragons of Mons Fractus." Eventually Pilate, a nasty anti-Semite, finally went a step too far in outraging the sensibilities of his subjects. Upon learning of a planned gathering of

Samaritans led by a supposed Taheb (the Samaritan messiah/restorer) on the slopes of Mount Gerizim, the site of the old Samaritan temple, Pilate sent troops to disperse the crowd—by killing them all! This massacre was reported to Rome, and Pilate was recalled from office. Tierney speculates that the Samaritan messiah in question was none other than Dositheus. This provides him one of the markers in his chronology of the Simon tales, since the incident at Gerizim occurred in 36 A.D.

As for Menander, Irenaeus, second-century bishop of Lyons, Gaul, makes him a successor of Simon Magus, hence Tierney's depiction of the young Menander as Simon's junior partner. It is worth noting that one modern scholar has nominated Menander as the original author of the Gnostic-leaning Fourth Gospel (anonymous, and attributed only by tradition to John, son of Zebedee). This is due to the report that Menander promised his disciples eternal life in the flesh, recalling John 8:51.

THE SWORD OF SPARTACUS

by Richard L. Tierney

It is well known that the vital forces of a dead animal may continue to permeate its dwelling-place and the environs it was wont to inhabit while alive, bringing benefit or ill to those who come after. In the case of a man, this permeation may extend even to the objects he used in life. And especially is this true of weapons which have been wielded in the fury of battle with the most intense emotions of which man is capable, and for which the wielders come therefore to hold great affection, inasmuch as their lives depend on them.

— Ostanes, *Sapientia Magorum* (Dryden translation)

I

"See, good Dositheus!" exclaimed Atilius the contractor, gesturing at the towering walls of the new amphitheater, "the soundest board-and-timber arena in all the empire, I'll warrant, and mayhap the largest. It will seat fifty thousand. It cost me a fortune, by Pollux, but tomorrow it will earn me a greater!"

Dositheus the Samaritan stroked his short beard thoughtfully and gazed past the looming structure, to where the myriad houses of Fidenae clustered, receding away down the gentle slope to the banks of the muddy Tiber, their red-tiled roofs baking under the westering Italian sun. Already the outskirts of the town were dotted with the tents of travelers who had come up from Rome and elsewhere to attend the spectacle.

"My master will add somewhat to that fortune, Atilius, if you'll procure him the seat he wants and the gladiators to fight for him."

"As good as done." The contractor used a fold of his tunic to wipe the sweat from his broad, shaven face. "I've purchased the seat already—front row, middle of the west side. It cost me a pretty penny, too, by Hercules! But before we dicker further, good Dositheus," the contractor glanced at the large, drab-colored tent that stood nearby, "can we not get in out of this infernal sun?"

"Not in there, I fear." Atilius thought the Samaritan's voice held a trace of unease. "My master sleeps in the heat of the day. He is very old and it is not good for him to be disturbed."

"Well, then, let's walk around to the west of the amphitheater where it's shady, and I'll see about introducing you to Marius Pugio, the *lanista*. If it's gladiators you want, he's the man to see."

"Good. Wait just one moment." Dositheus turned aside and called out sharply: "Menander—bring Carbo out to me."

An instant later a boy perhaps ten years of age emerged from a small tent set close to the larger one where the master slept. Atilius judged him to be a Samaritan also, for he wore the same sort of brown robe emblazoned with unknown symbols as did Dositheus. The lad's dark eyes were large and intelligent in his olive face, and upon his extended right arm perched a great black raven. The contractor felt an uneasy qualm as the bird croaked and flapped over to settle on Dositheus' wrist; these Samaritans were all sorcerers, or so he had heard, and he hoped these two would not be performing any of their foreign blasphemies around him. Probably their unseen master was the blackest wizard of the lot. Still, as long as the old coot had money to throw around, he, Atilius, would be glad to cater to his crazy whims and trust afterward in a prayer to Jupiter and a demijohn of Bacchus' best wine to cleanse himself…

"Now, Menander, tend the camp like a good apprentice," said Dositheus, "while I go see about some gladiators for our master."

Several of the larger gladiator schools had set up temporary training camps to the east of the new amphitheater. It turned out that Marius Pugio, the man in charge of the camp for the Julius Caesar School, was not the head *lanista* but rather a subtrainer in charge of the impending games at Fidenae. Yet he was an impressive man indeed, every inch a gladiator—a giant, bronzed Hercules with curling black hair and a scarred face. His broken aquiline nose made him resemble a battered Roman eagle.

"You come to me late in the day, Samaritan," said Pugio. His voice had a metallic ring that made him sound more like a military officer than a gladiator. There was an air of hard discipline about him; his lined face was set in an expression that somehow combined contempt and cruelty with moral indignation. "Most of my fighters have already been spoken for. I hope your master realizes he'll have to pay high."

"He does, and he will," said Dositheus. "He wants only two fighters, but he'll pay well for them. However, he stipulates that his own agent do the choosing. How about fifty thousand *sestertii* for the first one?"

Atilius whistled and set down the cup from which he had been sipping snow-cooled Falernian wine. "By Pollux—that's high, all right!"

Marius Pugio nodded. "Come with me."

They left the awning-shaded area that served the trainer as an office and entered a wide courtyard walled like a stockade. The sun had declined far enough to the west that its heat was now mellow rather than blistering, and a faint breeze was now and then gently stirring the dust. More than a score of gladiators stopped in the middle of their mock combat at Pugio's barked command and stood at attention. Their chests heaved and sweat ran down their muscled limbs. Dositheus regarded their silent, sullen faces rather uneasily.

"You've bought one," snapped Pugio. "Now take your pick."

Dositheus extended his arm. "Carbo—choose!"

The raven croaked gutturally and flapped into the air, then began to circle above the crowd of gladiators—who, in turn, seemed to follow its flight with some slight apprehension. Atilius squawked an oath to Hercules, then gulped the rest of his wine.

"Here, now—let's have no wizard's tricks!" growled Pugio. "Who is this master of yours, anyway, who sends such an agent to do his choosing?"

"Tages of Rasena. Perhaps you've heard of him."

Pugio scowled with incomprehension, but Atilius swore another of his oaths. "Tages—aye, the Etrurian sorcerer! So he really does exist? I've heard it said he's well over a century old and has journeyed to all parts of the world in search of magic secrets."

"Well, just so he pays me solid money that won't vanish. … But, here!—what's that crazy bird doing?"

The raven had ceased to circle the gladiators and suddenly swooped across the courtyard to vanish through an open gate. Dositheus nodded in satisfaction and hurried after it, ignoring the protests of the trainer. When he stepped through the gateway he found himself in a much smaller court. The raven was sitting atop an iron cage that rested in one corner, and in this cage crouched a man who wore naught but a ragged tunic on his body and a feral snarl on his face.

"This is the man I want," said Dositheus as Pugio and Atilius caught up with him.

"This scoundrel?" The trainer shook his head. "You don't want him. He's not to be allowed to fight anymore. Tomorrow before the games he'll be hamstrung and thrown to the beasts."

"Why? He's a gladiator, isn't he?"

"Not anymore! This morning the Furies possessed him to attack me— and now he pays the price. By Pallas, his fury was excelled only by his stupidity! He went for my throat with his *sica*, but I disarmed him with my bare hands and beat him senseless."

"Then he's not a very good fighter?"

Pugio's condescending scowl grew withering in its intensity. "One of the best! He has survived two years of arena fighting because he is as quick as a striking serpent—as a *sica*-man *must* be. But I've survived *twelve* years, and not for nothing!"

"And why did he attack you?"

Pugio shrugged. "I found these gladiators soft and decided to toughen them up. This one couldn't take it."

"Let's see why Carbo chose him." Dositheus advanced a pace and stooped to peer in at the captive, being careful to stay beyond arm's reach. The man's body was well muscled and smoothly proportioned, suggestive of that of a panther crouched to spring. Had he been able to stand upright, Dositheus guessed, he would be somewhat taller than average. Yet in spite of the stubble on his face it was clear that he was little more than a youth. That face, immobile in a watchful rictus of hate, was strikingly unique with its high, prominent cheek bones and the black bangs spilling in tangles over the wide forehead. But there was also something generally familiar about it—

"I am a Samaritan, like yourself," said Dositheus suddenly, speaking rapidly in Aramaic. "Tomorrow you will fight for my master—and I think you will win." Then, rising, he turned to the trainer and said in Latin: "This is the man I want. My offer still stands—fifty thousand."

"For such a sum—very well. I see you recognized him as one of your kind. Is that why you want him?"

"I want him because I can see he hates."

Pugio's sharp bark seemed meant for a laugh. "They all hate. All good gladiators hate. If they do not, I soon see to it that they do."

"This one hates more than most."

The trainer shrugged again. "Perhaps, for he talks less. I know little of him, save that he comes from a town called Gitta and that he murdered a tax-gatherer who slew his parents. For this he would have been crucified had he not fought his captors so well that they decided to sell him to a gladiator school instead. His name is Simon. But, enough—let us seal our bargain. The sum must be paid now, of course, and in cash."

"Of course. And you, good Marius Pugio, must in turn have this man taken from his cage and given a proper supper. See that he has one of the cells beneath the arena in which to sleep the night undisturbed—for he must be able to fight well tomorrow."

Pugio nodded. "And now, what of the other gladiator?"

Dositheus glanced sidelong at a slight ruffling of black feathers. The raven, still perched atop the prisoner's cage, had turned so that its black beak now pointed straight at Marius Pugio. But of this the trainer took no notice.

"Yes—my master wants two. And they are to fight one another, of course. But as to the second, my master requires that he be a Roman citizen."

There was a long silence. Finally Pugio said, "These stipulations of your wizard-master are strange indeed."

Dositheus shrugged. "He has his peculiarities. But of course he is prepared to pay well for their indulgence."

"He'll need a fortune!" blurted Atilius. "What free citizen of Rome would ever be mad enough to face a beast of a gladiator in the arena—?"

"Some gladiators are free citizens," snapped Pugio; then he turned back to Dositheus and said: "How much is Tages of Rasena willing to pay for a Roman to fight your gladiator?"

"Five hundred thousand *sestertii*."

Atilius' empty wine cup clattered to the ground. "By Hercules," he stammered finally. "I could build another arena for that!"

Pugio's face worked. Though he prided himself on his self-discipline, he did have a weakness for gambling and his luck had taken a bad turn of late—so bad, in fact, that he was now suddenly overcome with a desire to praise whatever gods caused senile wizards to go mad.

"By Pallas, I'll do the choosing this time!" he shouted at last. "I'm your man—I've been a Roman citizen five years now, and have the papers to prove it. But in fairness I'd better warn you there's no man in this school who can best me—I'll break that callow *sica*-man like a stick. You still want us matched? Very well, then—and if your patron can make money by arranging bets on such a match, I'll admit he's a wizard indeed! Now, let's have at least a hundred thousand of that money handed over in advance."

II

The night was well advanced; the moon, perhaps a day past the full, was declining toward the west while the waters of the Tiber took on a silvery sheen beneath her rays. There was a stirring at the entrance of one of the larger tents, hitherto dark and silent, that had been pitched near the arena, and a figure in a cowled cloak stepped forth—a figure tall, lean, and slightly stooped. In its bony left hand, which was startlingly pale, it clutched a long wooden staff.

For a moment the figure stood motionless, seeming to stare at a smaller tent that stood near the one from which it had emerged; then a rasping half-whisper issued from the dark hollow of the cowl:

"Sleep well, good servants, for after tomorrow's dawn I shall see you no more."

The figure then turned and stood motionless for some time, facing the arena. The night was still save for small, occasional sounds—the crying of a babe from one of the tents, or the bark of a dog from the town. At length the hooded one stirred, reached under his robe with his right hand, and drew something forth. It was a small image—a wizard figure crouching on a pedestal, with snaky appendages sprouting from its head and a cruel beak curving from amid them. The dark substance of this image seemed to reflect the light of the moon and stars with a strange scintillation, as if it were somehow tenuously linked to them by their rays.

"Hear me, O Great Tuchulcha," the dark figure intoned softly. "Now at last is come the hour of my vengeance, and the day of thy feasting. Guide thou therefore my steps, and becloud the minds of any who would otherwise seek to stay me."

So saying, he replaced the image within his cloak and began to walk quietly toward the arena, weaving amid the tents. At length he stopped some thirty feet from the arena's towering wall, where a cleared space had been left between the tents of the travelers and the makeshift structures which shopkeepers had erected against its base, hoping for good business on the morrow. Here and there a bracketed torch burned in the still air, alleviating the gloom but little and making the shadows seem darker still.

Turning, the night-walker began to pace along the cleared space, dragging the tip of his wooden staff in the dust as he proceeded, so that it left a light furrow behind him. And as he paced he muttered a strange chant in time to his steps:

"O wand from out the Druid oak,
"Grown from the ashes of the dead,
"Mark now the boundaries of the Gate—
"The Master comes, the feast is spread."

Over and over he chanted thusly, while his steps carried him farther and farther around the circumference of the amphitheater. Occasionally he passed a strolling insomniac, or a watchful guardsman set to guard the shops, but these few merely eyed the strange, muttering figure warily and made no move to interfere with his progress. Now and then a watchdog slunk from his path with a low growl.

When at last the great circuit was completed and the staff had linked the end of its fine furrow with the beginning, the night-walker returned silently among the tents and paused before the one from which he had first emerged. Then he again reached his right hand into his robe and drew forth another object. It was a short Roman sword whose blade glinted coldly in the rays of the waning moon.

"O sword of him who fought and fell," the figure intoned, "drink now Selene's light which bathes thy blade. Soon shalt thou drink likewise the blood of thine enemies!"

Simon of Gitta woke from a fitful sleep with the uneasy feeling that someone was standing near him in the darkness of his cell. Immediately he told
himself that this was impossible. He wished he could see more, but the
moonlight from the high, iron-grated hole that passed for a window was
too scant to aid his eyes much. He rose with supple ease, crouching in the
stance of the trained fighter, and began to move about. A very few steps
were enough to reassure him that the small room was as empty as it should
be.

He settled back with a sigh on his thin straw pallet—so thin, in fact,
that the chill of the earthen floor came through it. Not comfortable, yet it
was luxurious compared to the cage of punishment they had put him in the
day before. He supposed he should thank the gods for his good fortune—
for the good meal that had restored him and the chance to fight and die
with honor on the morrow. But he felt thankful to no one, save perhaps
that strange Samaritan wizard who had given him the chance and had even
visited him briefly in this cell after he had been fed.

"I am Dositheus," the man had told him. "If you survive tomorrow's
games, come to the Caelian Hill in Rome and inquire for me at the house
of the senator Junius, who is henceforth my patron. If anyone asks, tell
them you are my freed servant—I shall have the papers to prove it."

"Why are you doing this for me?"

"Because you are about to perform a great and dangerous service for
my master and me—and for all who suffer at the hands of Rome. But ask
no more—I must leave now. My master shall come to you later and explain
all."

No one had come, however, and Simon now lay in the darkness devoid of any hope of surviving tomorrow's combat. Hope did not come easily any more—two years of the arena had steeled him against it and the
pain its inevitable disappointment brought. But now he dared to hope that
he might at least take an enemy or two with him when he died, as he had
attempted to do the day before....

Suddenly the hair prickled on his neck. The feeling that someone was
with him was stronger than ever. He turned—and caught his breath. Surely
he was dreaming! For the moonlight from the hole seemed to have intensified and in its dim light Simon thought he saw a cloaked form whose face
was shadowed by a cowl.

"Simon of Gitta—hear me now, and attend closely to my words."

For an instant Simon felt the strange horror of nightmare. He tensed,
ready to spring and fight to the death.

"Do not fear me," the voice continued. It seemed as faint as the shape
itself, as if it came from far away.

"Who are you?" Simon whispered.

"Men call me Tages of Rasena, and think me an Etruscan sorcerer; but I was born Trogus the Gaul. Listen, and you shall hear my tale, and know why I came to hate Rome."

Simon relaxed a trifle; no enemy of Rome could be completely an enemy to him. Once again he wondered if he dreamed. Surely there seemed to be a soft stupor enfolding him, subtly lulling his fears. And could he not now sense eyes far back within that shadowy cowl?—eyes old and intense and full of dark wisdom....

"I was born to slavery," the voice whispered. "My parents were captives brought down from the forests of Narbonensis; they were of the proud Druid blood, but were made to labor on the great orchard-farms of Campania. Our life was hard and bitter. Yet I was not always unhappy, for I knew no other life, and often did my parents contrive to teach me the Druidic lore of our people, and the secret runes of magic.

"Then, when I was twelve years old, Spartacus came with his great slave-army and set us free, together with all the other slaves who toiled with us—Spartacus, the escaped Thracian gladiator who gathered about him a mighty host that shook Rome to her rotten foundations and nigh caused her ruin!

"Never in my long life have I known greater excitement, greater joy, than I did in those far-off days. We joined the thousands of slaves who were flocking to Spartacus' banner, thirsting for vengeance and freedom. And for nearly two years we fought up and down this land of Italy, destroying Roman armies from the valley of the Po to the hills of Calabria, even as did Hannibal in centuries gone by. Rome trembled in terror, while all who had suffered her oppression exulted, hoping soon to see her toppled and the slavery whereby she maintained herself destroyed for aye.

"Yet this was not to be, for there came an ill day when treacherous allies betrayed our host into the hands of the Romans. Then did Rome send up against us a mighty army of many legions, the greatest they had yet gathered together, led by Marcus Crassus, their wealthiest commander. And in one last holocaust of desperate battle we went down in defeat. Spartacus himself died bravely, slaying Romans in battle to the very end, till the legionnaires gave over trying to take him alive and hacked him to pieces.

"When the carnage was over there remained six thousand of our soldiers who had thrown down their arms in hope of clemency. Better had they fought to the end with their leader! The Romans nailed them all on crosses to die, as a warning to all slaves who in future might think to rebel against the power that ruled the world. My father was among the crucified; my mother was torn from me and given to the soldiers, and I saw her no more.

"Because of my youth, they spared me and sold me once more into slavery. For two years more I labored in the iron mines of Noricum, nursing my hate; then the gods favored me with a chance of escape, and I fled to the hills. For a time I lived like a beast, often near to death, traveling westward by hill and fen and forest, till at last I came to Gaul and found kinsmen to aid me.

"That was nigh one hundred years ago, but the fire of hate in my breast is no less now than when it was first kindled. That hate is what has sustained me in my purpose, and kept me alive beyond my time. It has driven me over all the earth in search of secrets most men shun. In all the world there is no man more learned in sorcery than I!

"For many years I abode in Gaul, learning all the Druids could teach me. But this was not enough—I sought darker magic still. I journeyed to Britain, to Iberia, to Africa and Egypt, and even to Parthia and far-off Seen, studying ways and lore of the priests, the sages, the magi of those lands. And as I journeyed my power grew, and with it my wealth, so that when after two score years I returned to Italy, I was a rich man. And finally I came to dwell in Rasena and study the darkest magic of all, that of the Etruscans, which stems from Sumer and Akkad and those who came before.

"Once I returned to Campania, and on nights when the moon waxed I delved often in the earth, recovering the bones of many of those soldiers of Spartacus who had been crucified and buried by the roadsides. These I reduced to ashes, and when I returned at last to Rasena I planted an oak and nourished its roots with the substance of those who had perished fighting Rome. Behold, Simon of Gitta—this staff I hold in my left hand was hewn just last autumn from that tree, in the light of a waning moon!"

Simon shuddered. He had learned enough growing up in his own sorcery-riddled Samaria to know the implications of such things.

"Now my life is near its end," continued the voice of Tages, "and it is well, for during this last decade it has been sustained by magic alone, so that I cannot bear the direct light of the sun. I have invoked the darkest of all the Etruscan demons to my aid, even Great Tuchulcha; and in the hour of my triumph he shall slay me, even as of old he slew with lightning that King Hostilius who dared invoke him. But for death I care nothing; for vengeance alone have I lived these five score years, and now is the day of that vengeance at hand. Behold, Simon of Gitta!"

Simon watched in fascinated silence as the figure drew forth an object from beneath its dark robe. It was a Roman sword whose blade glimmered with a soft light, as of reflected moonbeams.

"It was on this very day, one hundred years ago," continued the hollow, whispering voice, "that Spartacus fought free of his gladiator school, together with many of his fellow prisoners. This sword I hold is the one he captured from his Roman foes for his own use. It is the sword he wielded when at last he was cut down, staining its blade with the blood of his enemies even as he fell. Ah, no man ever fought Rome's tyranny with greater fury than Spartacus!

"Crassus took up that blade and kept it for his own, as a memento of his victory. It was with him when years later he led another great army on an expedition of conquest into Parthia. But this time the gods looked not with favor on Marcus Crassus; the Parthians defeated him, took him prisoner and beheaded him. And for many years the sword of Spartacus lay in the possession of the Parthian kings, who were ignorant of its nature.

"A year ago I sent Dositheus, the Samaritan magician, to the Parthian court to divine the blade's whereabouts and purchase it. He was successful—and now, Simon of Gitta, this very day you shall hold this sword in hand, that it may strike its final blow against Rome!

"Sleep, now, for you will need strength. When you enter the arena, you will hear my voice. Come then to me, and receive from my hand this sword."

A great weariness swept over Simon; the figure before him seemed to be fading and vanishing away. Once more he felt himself to be alone, and his last thought as he lay back on his pallet was that surely it was all naught but a dream—a dream....

III

Dositheus paused in the roadway and glanced back as a roar went up from the distant arena. The sun was now high in the east. The great crowds that had earlier cluttered the Via Salaria, surging up from Rome to see the blood spectacle, had dwindled to a mere trickle of late-comers.

"That will be the end of the beast-killings and the announcement of the gladiatorial contests," Dositheus mused. He glanced at his apprentice, noting the boy's worried frown. "Fret not your heart for that mad crowd, Menander—they howl for blood, and now they shall reap as they sow. As the poet of the Book has written: 'Give them according to the wickedness of their endeavors; give them after the work of their hands; render to them their desert.' "

"Not for them am I concerned, sir," said Menander, "but for the brave Samaritan gladiator you told me of. Will he live to join us?"

"Baal alone knows. His danger is great. Yet Carbo flew straight to him without hesitation. I almost feel he is a man of destiny, and toward such the gods—"

"Ho, good Dositheus—wait!"

A heavy-set figure was hurrying after them on foot. As the man drew closer Dositheus saw that it was Atilius. He motioned to the two slaves accompanying Menander and himself, and they brought the four mules they were leading to a halt.

"Why do you not attend the games?" panted the contractor when he had caught up with them. "And where is your employer, the good Tages?"

"Tages is no longer my master. When I finished conducting him to his seat in the amphitheater an hour ago, he informed me that my services toward him were at an end. So now, since such spectacles as the one just beginning are not to my taste, I return to Rome."

"How curious. Not a falling-out, I hope…?"

"No, good Atilius—we parted amicably. And I may say that my former master greatly appreciates all the services you have rendered him, as do I. Good health to you, my friend—and to that end, might I suggest that you follow my example and stay away from bloody spectacles today. Farewell."

Atilius, standing in the middle of the Via Salaria and watching the Samaritan wizard and his companions resume their journey southward, felt suddenly a strange chill in spite of the hot morning sun.

"Perhaps I'll follow that advice," he muttered. "Aye—the arena will be sweltering today. No sense in suffering there with the noisy crowds when Fidenae has so many cool wine shops, by Bacchus!"

A dream—that was all it could have been, that insubstantial vision in the night. Simon realized that fully now as he stood surrounded by harsh reality—his last reality.

Reality was a huge oval of glaring sunlight on bright sand. Simon stood at the center of this oval, clad only in a dark breechcloth, a small, round buckler was strapped to his left forearm, a curved *sica* clutched in his right fist. Beyond the oval, shaded by the tremendous awning that protected them from the sun, he sensed the stirring of the vast crowd that waited to see him spill his blood. A moment before, when he had entered the arena, they had hooted and shouted their derision, for the caller had announced him not as a gladiator but as a disobedient slave who was to be given the unusual opportunity of dying with a weapon in his hand, as a preliminary to the real combats to follow. Amid the jeers there had been a few cries of approval; a discerning minority had recognized in the youth's carriage and compact muscularity a trained fighter, and a few had even taken up the challenge of those who felt they had a sure thing by betting their *denarii* on Marius Pugio.

But now the crowd had grown hushed. By raising his buckler to shade his eyes, Simon could see them dimly—row upon row of them, diminish-

ing away to where the high rim of the arena rose to support the gently billowing canopy. Fifty thousand they numbered, or so he had been told—the
greatest crowd that had ever gathered to see him strive for his life. They
seemed to surround him like the curled body of some vast, suspirating
beast, so that he felt like some insect held in the circle of a watchful cat's
paws—a cat that waited for him to make a move....

Suddenly a roar went up from the throng as a second figure strode into the sunlight. It was Marius Pugio, like Simon dressed only in a dark
breechcloth and bearing knife and buckler. Nearly four fifths of the crowd
rose to salute him, save the women at the back, who were furnished no
seats and were therefore standing already. Even most of the white-togaed
nobles rose in salute from their places of superior vantage, for this was a
rare treat for all. Pugio was one of the greatest fighters the arena had ever
known, and it had been some years since the mob had seen him in action.

The gladiator raised his weapon hand aloft to return the crowd's salute, his features set in an expression of scornful self-confidence. Simon
gripped the hilt of his *sica* more tightly as he saw that Pugio's knife was not
a fighting weapon at all but a kind of dirk used to dispatch wounded and
defeated gladiators. The insult caused Simon to feel a surge of hatred, but
he stifled it so that his only reaction was a narrowing of the eyes, a tightening of the muscles about his mouth. He knew that he was probably about
to die, that he was no match for a fighter such as Pugio, but the only important thing now was to stay cool enough to take his foe down to death
with him if possible.

A hush had again descended over the crowd. Simon crouched in a
fighting stance as Pugio began to stride across the sand toward him—

Simon—do not fight him. Come to me.

He whirled, startled. The voice was not vocal—it seemed to come
from inside his head. It was clear, demanding, compelling.

Come to me—quickly!

Then in the front row of the crowd, on the west side of the arena, Simon saw a dark form standing—a tall, cowled figure holding an oblong
bundle of cloth in its lean hands. Suddenly he realized that his dream of the
previous night had *not* been a dream.

Simon—come!

Abruptly Simon sheathed his *sica* and sprinted to the wall of the arena,
directly to the spot beneath the standing figure. The crowd howled in derision at what they considered his cowardice—then howled even louder in
protest as the cowled man unfurled the bundle he held, releasing a short
Roman sword which fell to the sand. This was not in the rules!

Now, Simon, take up the sword—and fight!

Simon snatched up the weapon and whirled—to see Pugio bearing down on him. Expertly he fended off the dagger with his buckler, and thrust. Pugio evaded the point barely in time and crouched back in a defensive stance; a trickle of blood began to run down his breast where the sword had nicked him. A surprised scowl had replaced the calm arrogance in his features. Simon felt a surge of power run through his body, a fighting madness fire his blood. It seemed to him in that instant that he was surrounded by foes in Roman armor hacking and thrusting at him.

"Roman pigs!" he roared—in a language he had never spoken before—and charged.

Pugio leaped back again, startled to realize that the man he had bested with relative ease the day before had suddenly become a foe of tremendous power and skill, apparently berserk with rage. The master gladiator continued to fall back on the defensive before the whirlwind fury of his attacker's sword-strokes, countering with thrusts of his dagger when he was able. Blades rang and grated against bucklers for a brief, furious moment, during which the action was too swift for the crowd to follow. Simon roared a Thracian oath, feinted, then slashed with lightning speed. An instant too late Pugio tried to fend off the sword with his round buckler—and then his left arm plopped to the sand while blood gushed from the numbed stump of his elbow.

"Foul play!" someone screamed. "Foul!"

Pugio, knowing in that instant that he was both doomed and dishonored, cast all defensive measures to the winds and thrust. The dagger-point grazed Simon's cheek as he barely evaded it. Again he slashed with the sword—and Pugio's right hand, still clutching the knife, leapt from his wrist and joined his severed arm upon the arena floor. The gladiator stumbled to the sand and strove feebly to rise, weakening swiftly as blood spurted from both limbs.

"Foul! Foul!" Every person in the crowd was now on their feet, screaming, gesturing with upraised thumbs. "Spare him!" "Spare Pugio!" "He'd have bested you in a fair fight, craven!"

Simon waved his blood-slimed sword aloft and snarled defiantly in the teeth of the howling mob. "*No*, you Roman butchers!" he screamed—wondering even as he did so how he had come to know the Thracian tongue so well. "Did you spare my six thousand when they were fools enough to surrender to you? Did you ever spare any man who dared fight for freedom against your bloody rule? It's blood you came here to see, you howling swine, and it's blood you'll have!"

Simon plunged his sword savagely between the ribs of the fallen gladiator, then ripped it forth in an arc of crimson droplets and waved it in the faces of the mob. The crowd yelled more loudly than ever, enraged at the thwarting of its will even more than at the flouting of the rules. Simon roared his rage back at them, feeling a savage exultation, wishing he could leap the wall and charge into their midst, slashing and slaying—

Simon—plunge now the sword once more into his breast, and rip forth his heart.

Snarling, Simon turned, stooped, and drove his blade into the body beneath the ribs, then withdrew it in a slashing cut that left a great cavity gaping. Hardly realizing what he did, he reached in with his left hand and clutched about in the wet gore till his fingers closed upon the still-pulsing heart, then with a snapping of fibers and vessels he savagely wrenched it forth and held it aloft while the bright blood rilled down his arm and side.

The crowd gasped, then slowly grew silent in horror at the sight. Simon felt his rage flowing out of him like a dark tide. Somehow this seemed more like a strange ritual than a gladiatorial combat—

And why not? For was not the spectacle of the arena originally a ritual of sacrifice to dark gods, practiced by Etruscan priests long before the Romans adopted and made a game of it? Suddenly Simon's rage abated, and he flung the heart and the sword from him in revulsion.

"O Spartacus!" screamed the cloaked figure. "Spartacus—now in this moment art thou avenged upon Rome!"

Simon realized the old man was now screaming in his own voice. His dark cowl had fallen back, and the face thereby disclosed was like that of a skeleton whose dark eyes flashed with an unearthly light—a light of glaring hate. Those nearest him in the crowd shrank back appalled.

"Sorcerer!" someone cried out. Others took up the cry: "Slay him! Slay him!"

But now the old man had drawn a dark, greenish object from the folds of his robe. He held it aloft and Simon saw that it was the image of some winged, tentacled being.

"Come, then, O Great Tuchulcha!" the sorcerer cried out in a voice of surprising power. *"The feast is spread!"*

Suddenly from the cloudless sky a titanic bolt of lightning crashed, shaking the earth and the heavens. The old man's form blazed instantly to nothingness and the crowd screamed and went to its knees. Simon sprawled to the sand, shaken from his feet by the awful concussion. He sensed the light of midday suddenly dimming. Glancing upward, he saw that the great canopy was rent asunder, blazing at its edges—and beyond it was something blotting out the sky, something shadowy and insubstantial, suggestive of a monstrous beaked face framed in writhing tentacles....

There was a great rending and cracking of wooden beams. Simon leaped up in terror and raced to the center of the arena. The rending sound grew louder, and a great wail of fear went up from the crowd. As he came to a stop in the center, Simon felt the sand tremble beneath his feet; the side of the arena before him seemed to be tossing and crumpling like a foundering ship. The scream of the crowd rose to an unbearable volume. Simon flung himself face down on the sand and covered his head with his hands.

There was a prolonged, roaring crash that mingled with the despairing shriek of fifty thousand doomed souls.

Simon rose slowly to his feet, coughing, for dust still swirled and billowed all about him in the air. As it slowly settled and cleared he stared, humbled and aghast, at the huge circle of destruction and carnage that ringed him. A swelling groan rose up from the countless throats of the dying.

Simon shuddered. He glanced up at the sky, relieved to see that it had resumed its unobstructed blue. Somehow, he realized, a Gate had been made to open for an instant; the stars must not have been right, for it had closed again. Yet that instant had been enough to accomplish the purpose of Tages—Tages, whose undying hatred for Rome had led him at the last to sacrifice his own life in order to bring about the destruction of his enemies....

" 'And Samson said, "Let me die with the Philistines," ' " muttered Simon, recalling the words of the ancient Book. " 'And the house fell upon the lords, and upon all the people that were therein.' "

Then he steeled himself to do what he knew he must in order to leave this place alive and anonymous.

About "The Fire of Mazda"

Simon didn't get much of a rest after the events of the previous story. Early autumn of A.D. 27 finds him with trouble on his hands again in "The Fire of Mazda" (first published in the first and only issue of *Orion's Child*, May-June, 1984).

Though Tierney has said "the flavor of the tale owes much more to E. R. Eddison than to Gnosticism" (Letter, June 1, 1984), the Gnosticism in the tale rings true. There is at least as much homage paid to Zoroastrianism, the great dualistic religion of ancient Iran. Zoroastrianism has often been considered one of the important roots of Gnosticism. In particular, Richard Reitzenstein (*Hellenistic Mystery Religions: Their Basic Ideas and Significance*, Eng. trans., 1978), makes a good case for a direct connection between Judaism and Zoroastrianism, forged during the Babylonian/Persian Exile, on into Jewish Apocalyptic and Gnosticism (see also, more recently, Norman Cohn, *Cosmos, Chaos and the World to Come: The Ancient Roots of Apocalyptic Faith*, 1993). The resemblance between Zoroastrianism and the third-century Gnosis of Manicheism is especially striking, as both are dualisms of Light versus Darkness, coordinated with Good versus Evil.

The eponymous Mazda is the chief deity of the Prophet Zoroaster (or Zarathustra, or Zardusht). He is usually called Ahura Mazda, the "Wise Lord" or the "Lord of Light." As such he appears to be the same as the Vedic god Varuna. Zoroaster, a Vedic priest in Iran, rejected the deities (*devas*) of Vedic Brahmanism as devils and restored Varuna the Wise Lord to primacy, retaining the Vedic Mitra and Atar (Agni) in various subordinate capacities.

We also hear an invocation of a demonic entity called Azdahak. Azi Dahaka is a hideous dragon in ancient Iranian religion "who has three mouths, three heads, six eyes, a thousand perceptions, the very powerful demonic liar, the evil deceiver of the world, the most powerful liar which Angra Mainyu [= Ahriman] brought forth... to destroy the world of Truth" (*Aradwi Sura Anahita* IX:4). This powerful being was given to rule the world for a thousand years, after which the hero Feridun bound him in a deep pit. Thus, with his infernal master Ahriman, Azdahak would seem to have been a major inspiration for the Jewish and New Testament transformation of Satan from the servant of God into his archenemy, especially as reflected in Revelation 20:1-3. Recalling the Gnostic reduction of the biblical Yahweh to the arrogant Demiurge who gave the Torah to Moses, Azdahak is said to have composed the Torah and established the city of Jerusalem. Finally, the *Arabian Nights* character Afrasiab with his boatload of demons, alluded to by Lovecraft in "The Nameless City", forms part of the myth-cycle of Azdahak.

THE FIRE OF MAZDA

by Richard L. Tierney

I

A lovely lady garmented in light
From her own beauty—deep her eyes, as are
Two openings of unfathomable night
Seen through a Temple's cloven roof—her hair
Dark—the dim brain whirls dizzy with delight,
Picturing her form; her soft smiles shone afar,
And her low voice was heard like love, and drew
All living things towards this wonder new.

— Shelley, "The Witch of Atlas"

"Magic," said Dositheus, "is but the method whereby the Mind of the World induces itself to change its own images. And each man possessing a True Spirit is a fragment of the great World-Mind. Therefore—"

"Stop!" cried Simon, rising. He stood trembling, one hand over his eyes, the other outstretched as if to grasp at something intangible.

The lecturer—a lean man in the robes of a Samaritan wizard—bent forward with an expression of concern. So did the two others present in the dim, torch-lit room; a pudgy, balding man clad in the garb of a Roman patrician, and a lad perhaps eleven years of age. This lad wore the same sort of brown, symbol-decorated robe as the lecturer, and upon his right shoulder perched a large, jet-black raven.

"What is it?" demanded Dositheus. "Speak, Simon. Have my words evoked aught in your mind?"

The man called Simon stood silent for a moment, while his trembling quieted. He was a tall young man of athletic build; his face, strikingly unique in its high-cheekboned angularity, yet seemed racially akin to those of the speaker and the eleven-year-old lad. He wore a dark tunic and high-strapped sandals. At his side hung sheathed a *sica*, or curved gladiatorial knife.

"Your words…." he muttered, his voice strangely tense. "They evoked an image—a vision…."

The young lad stared intently; the raven on his shoulder fluttered its wings uneasily. The pudgy Roman leaned forward, his lips agape. Dositheus drew himself erect, his face grave.

"A vision? Tell me of it, Simon."

"I saw a woman." Simon absently brushed back the black bangs that spilled over his wide forehead; immediately they fell back into place. "A young woman, with hair and eyes dark as night. Yet, as in the night, stars gleamed in her hair and eyes...."

He fell silent and bent forward, staring pensively at the backs of his hands.

Dositheus, the old Samaritan sorcerer, rose and smiled. "You have had a true vision, Simon of Gitta," he said smoothly. "Seldom have I witnessed its like. Of a surety you are a True Spirit, even as I suspected." Simon did not answer; he looked up and gazed ahead, as if to capture a vanishing image; then, with an expression of disappointment, he turned to Dositheus.

"Tell me, my mentor—who was she?"

Dositheus regarded Simon levelly, but there was a sadness in his eyes. "She is the sacrifice, Simon—the one you must slay. I told you this vision might come to you, and now it has."

Simon scowled thoughtfully. "So lovely—" he muttered.

"No!" Dositheus stood tall; the astrological symbols emblazoned on his dark robe seemed almost to glow, and his craggy face grew as stern as that of an olden prophet. "Think not thusly. Harden your mind and your heart, Simon, for she is the sacrifice whose death will bring about our vengeance upon Rome—the vengeance we have all so long desired."

Simon shook his head vigorously, as if to clear his mind, then drew himself up as a diver emerging from the water into clean air. "What do you say? You speak, Dositheus, as if this woman—this vision of mine—truly exists."

"She does." Again the sadness flashed briefly in Dositheus' eyes. "She is here, in the very house of our patron, Senator Junius." He nodded briefly at the pudgy, balding Roman. "And now—"

Simon scowled darkly. "You say she's the—the one I must slay?"

"Aye!" exclaimed Dositheus, his eyes gleaming suddenly as if with a dark fanaticism. "And you *shall* slay her, Simon, for your hatred of Rome is as great as ours. Did not the Romans slay your parents in their home in Samaria when they could not pay the tax? And did not Rome make of you a slave, a gladiator, to fight and shed blood for her amusement, until after two years my patron Junius and I finally freed you?" Simon glared at the floor; his hands, clenched at his sides, trembled.

"You remember!" Dositheus went on, his voice intense. "And you shall have your revenge—you, and all of us. Revenge upon Rome! Listen, Simon!" The Samaritan sorcerer bent forward, his eyes glaring intently. "Rome is the greatest evil in all this material world. You have experienced that evil, yet you know not whence it comes. Now I shall tell you.

"Magic, as I have said, is the way the World-Mind changes itself, and each True Spirit is a fragment of that Mind. Every one of us in this room is such a fragment, Simon. Contemplate that well—for it means that you are a part of the sundered soul of the Ultimate God."

"What nonsense is this?" demanded Simon. "If I am a fragment of this God-Mind, why do I have no power—?"

Dositheus raised a hand. "Listen. The Ultimate God is above materiality, but long ago He fell under the power of the evil demiurge Achamoth, whom the ancient Persians called Azdahak and the Stygians Azathoth. Thus was the One made to suffer pain and restriction in many fleshly bodies… and therefore, we are here.

"Now, Rome is the latest and most monstrous earthly manifestation of Achamoth, but on the spiritual plane he also commands the Primal Gods whose minions pervade all the matter of the universe with the intent of inducing all possible pain. That pain ascends to the stars as spiritual energy to nourish the Primal Gods and, ultimately, Achamoth himself.

Simon reflected on Dositheus' words. He thought of all the monstrous, unnecessary pain he had experienced and witnessed in his life, the slaying of his parents by Roman tax-gatherers—his brutal enslavement and training as a gladiator—the recent sorcerous destruction of the arena in which he had fought and the consequent deaths of many thousands of spectators….

Yet, surely Dositheus' talk of monstrous gods could be nothing but wild imaginings. And why, Simon wondered, had the Samaritan wizard gone to so much trouble to rescue him, only to keep him hidden these several months in the cellars of the house of the Senator Junius?

"I told you once, Simon," said Dositheus, as if he had read his mind, "that I sensed you to be a man of destiny. My divinations have confirmed this. You are not only a True Spirit, but one of the High Ones—one of the greatest soul-fragments of the One who was sundered and then trapped by Achamoth in this material world of his making. You scowl with doubt, Simon, yet hear me: You are indeed an incarnation of the One. And now you sense the presence of your counterpart, the Other—for a girl containing one of Her great soul-fragments was brought into this very house only yesterday."

"Are you mad?" muttered Simon, glaring at Dositheus.

"I sought her for a long time," continued the wizard, unperturbed, "by spells and divinations, and by means of spies hired by our patron, Senator Junius." He nodded again toward the stout Roman, who was sitting on a wine keg, a stern look on his heavy features.

"It cost a good deal, too," said Junius, "but at last we found her—in the Ionian city of Ephesus. She is the daughter of a slave woman and her noble master. Her name is Helen, and she is now quartered in the upper rooms of my house. Dositheus tells me it was quite a task to steal her away, for her father was beginning to conceive an incestuous liking for her and would accept no monetary offer. Fortunately our hired kidnappers succeeded before his lusts could be gratified, for Dositheus tells me that only a virgin will do for the sacrifice we must perform."

"Sacrifice?" Simon was facing the Roman senator squarely; for some reason, his fists were clenched so tightly at his sides that his arms trembled. Then he felt Dositheus' lean hand laid upon his shoulder.

"Simon, it is now the time for me to instruct you in your duties. Senator Junius, would you allow me to speak privately with my pupil?"

"Aye." The Roman rose to his feet. "Instruct him well, that he may do his part to rid Rome of its oppressors. I have paid you well for your sorcerous knowledge, Dositheus, and you have performed well. A little more effort and we may see the cruel tyrants overthrown, and the Republic restored." So saying, he turned and ascended the stone steps that led from the cellars.

"May Carbo and I stay?" asked the lad on whose shoulder perched the raven.

Dositheus nodded. "Aye, Menander. It may advance your apprenticeship. Come with me—and you also, Simon."

He lifted a torch from its bracket and led them into a farther chamber of the basement. It was a small room, completely empty save for a large, cubical block of stone in its center and, behind it, a statue of grayish stone.

"It is upon this altar, Simon, that you will perform the sacrifice." Simon stared at the statue, which was somewhat less than four feet in height and appeared to be completely conventional in nature—a toga-clad Roman with one arm upraised and a wreath of laurel about his locks.

"That's nothing but an image of Tiberius, the Emperor," he growled. "You'd have me sacrifice to *him*—?"

"Peace, Simon. Not *to* him, but *against* him. When you perform the ritual, and plunge your Thracian dagger into the heart of the sacrifice, the offended gods shall stir and smite Tiberius with lightning, even as of old they smote King Hostilius. Then Sejanus, who is supported by Senator Junius and many others, shall take power and restore the old Republican order. The reign of tyrants shall end."

Simon had started at the mention of Sejanus, who was reputed to be in the complete confidence of Tiberius and one of the most powerful men in Rome. Now he knew where Junius had gotten the money to finance his expensive enterprises.

"You gamble for big stakes," said Simon. "How did you convince these powerful Romans that your magic will not fail them?"

"Did it fail *you*, Simon? I went to Parthia and brought back the sword of Spartacus, which enabled you to slay the mightiest gladiator of Rome.

That deed released magic which destroyed the great amphitheater at Fidenae and slew nearly fifty thousand blood-mad Roman spectators. That was your first sacrifice, Simon, and it brought gladness to all who hate Rome and its oppression. Now is the time for your second sacrifice, and its results shall be even greater, for it shall overthrow the very government of Rome itself, and all the conquered nations shall rise up free from its yoke."

"A ritual of power," muttered Simon. "A blow of my hand shall free many lands, including ours, from Rome? Yet, to do this I must plunge my blade into the breast of an innocent girl.... Look you, Dositheus, how can you know such things?"

"I have journeyed far," said the Samaritan wizard, "and have learned much. I brought back the sword of Spartacus from Parthia, that with it you might strike a blow against Rome. But that sword was not the only item I brought. Look—," he gestured toward the gray statue of Tiberius behind the stone altar, "I had that image carved from the rock of the mountain of Zavalon, whereon dwelt Zarathustra, the first great prophet to recognize that this world is a stage for the struggle between good and evil. Zarathustra fought evil till the end, when at last he was struck down by the swords of the human servitors of Azdahak, the Evil One. Yet Mazda, the Lord of Light, lives on—and you, Simon of Gitta, are His latest fragmentary incarnation and champion, and you shall strike soon on His behalf."

Simon felt his head swim. He looked about the cellar, noticing the dank stones of the walls and floors, the wine kegs and amphorae, the spider webs and wooden beams highlighted by the torch in Dositheus' hand—anything that would help keep his mind in touch with material, prosaic reality.

Suddenly he turned to face Dositheus. "You are mad!" he snarled.

Then he turned and ran out of the room, through the cellar, and up the steps that would take him to the outer gardens of Senator Junius' property and the sane light of day.

No one stopped Simon as he hurried out of the garden into the narrow, cobbled street, for he had often been allowed out before to shop for goods or to walk for exercise.

He strode along rapidly for several minutes, until he suddenly remembered that he was not in disguise.

Stopping, he rubbed a hand over his shaven face. This was the first time since he had been in Junius' house that he had ventured outside without an artificial beard and mustache to hide his identity—not to mention a hooded cloak....

He shrugged and continued on his way. It was months since he had fought in the arena at Fidenae—the arena that had collapsed, killing most of the thousands of spectators. He was not going to worry about being recognized; that was unlikely. Besides, he now had other things to think about.

He walked aimlessly, down the northeastern slope of the Caelian Hill, through narrow and winding lanes. The district was a mixed one; Senator Junius' mansion was only one of several stately residences in the area, but there were many middle- and lower-class dwellings as well. Rome, as Simon had noticed already, was a mixture of extreme wealth, abject poverty, and everything in between, and the various elements had seemingly made little effort to separate themselves.

He neared the base of the hill and the end of the residential area, then turned into narrow Mercury Street and continued on. The raucous voices of vendors and beggars assailed him; the odors of sweat, dung and overripe fruits and meat hung like a wet cloth over his face in the warmth of the late afternoon. Mercury Street! How dared they name this filthy lane after a god, without fear of being struck down for their blasphemy...?

He turned left, onto a wider avenue of the Subura, then hurried on till at last he reached a less wretched section, finally emerging into an open space surrounded by stately, columned temples and government buildings—the grandiose area of the Forum. As always, Simon paused and marveled. No matter how often he had seen these sweeps of gleaming walls and pillars, he could not help but feel awe; no matter how much he hated Rome, he could not help but know that she was indeed ruler of the world.

He continued on, glimpsing to his left between the temples the white, distant porticoes of mansions and palaces on the slope of the Palatine—shrines of the Roman nobility, embedded like bright pearls in the surrounding greenery. Ahead of him rose the grandest structure of all—the fane of Jupiter, mightiest of all Rome's gods, looming in imposing, columned grandeur atop the steep Capitoline Hill.

"Rome!" muttered Simon, feeling the hate stir in him even as he said it.

Yet he continued on, up the winding path and numerous stone stairways that led to the top of the Capitoline, till at last he stood upon the wide steps that led up to the columned portico of Jupiter's temple. Below him Rome lay outspread, dim under a haze of humid air mingled with the smoke of innumerable cooking-fires. To the west, just above the southern ridge of Janiculum, the sun was going down, a rayless ball of ruddy fire; eastward, great masses of cloud were advancing—towering billows of cottony luminescence—and beneath them the Alban Hills were lost in deep shadow. A feel of impending rain was in the air.

Simon climbed the stair, but then, feeling a reluctance to enter what he felt was a fane of idolatry, he turned left and walked along the lip of the columned portico till he reached its edge. Below him dropped the Tarpein scarp, down which countless criminals had been hurled—enemies of

Rome. For an instant he seemed to feel that downward gulf plucking at him, like a dark vacuum. Snarling, he turned away. The clouds seemed to be advancing, darkening, in silent grandeur; below, a procession was winding up the pathway—a small group of worshipers with a white bullock to sacrifice to Capitoline Jupiter....

Then, suddenly Simon seemed to see a face in the darkening clouds— the same face he had glimpsed in his mind in the dim, torch-lit cellar of Senator Junius scarcely an hour ago.

"Baal!" he gasped. "What—?"

It was the face of a woman, towering in its hugeness, seeming to loom over him, over the entire world. Yet it was at the same time delicate, ephemeral, fragile—something that could pervade all things, yet vanish at a too-quick movement. Somehow he knew that he saw clouds and nothing more, that no one else in all this great city of Rome could see what he saw—and yet he also knew that what he saw was a great Reality, and Rome naught but a dream.

"I know you," muttered Simon.

And I know you.

The thought was powerful in his mind, like a distant thunder, yet soft, like the whisper of a loved one in the scented dark. The clouds grew darker as the sun declined. Their billowing folds were like the coils of dark tresses gleaming in the light of dimming tapers; their highlights were like the ivory features of a lovely goddess; and two regions of shadow were like pools of stars gleaming from the ultimate reaches of space: dark, reflecting pools— like eyes....

"I know you!" cried Simon suddenly, stretching forth his arms as if he were a supplicant. "I saw you, but an hour ago, in my mind—in the cellar of Junius—"

Even as he said it, he felt foolish. The words rang harshly on the air— too real, too physical—and surely the clouds were but clouds, dissolving, changing—

Then he seemed to hear again the voice, more clearly than ever:

I know you, Simon of Gitta; for aeons I have known you. You have forgotten me, and I you; yet never do we truly forget one another. The Aeons have trapped us in time and materiality, yet without us no time or materiality would exist. I am Hera, and you are Jupiter—aye, even the same as these Romans worship here on this darkening hill. I am foam-born Aphrodite, and you Hermes, that god of Magic who once embraced and conquered me with your spells. And once I was Helen, and you that one who held and loved me when the walls of Troy were assailed and shattered. Oft have we loved and been torn asunder since this world began, and now we draw close again. Hear me, Simon of Gitta....

The clouds, advancing, boiled and lost their shape. The wind rose. Simon cried out despairingly:

"What must I do? Tell me! *Tell me!*"

You must be true, Simon—true to me and to yourself....

The clouds rolled in overhead; lightning flashed, and fat drops of rain began to fall. Distant thunder sounded. Simon cried out; his despair sought a name, and his tongue found it.

"Helen!" he cried. "Helen!"

Then the storm burst. Simon raised his face from his cupped hands, realized that he had been crying. A veil had briefly lifted, revealing vistas of unthinkable landscapes—cosmic memories of power and pleasure, longing and love—

"Helen!"

Cupping his face in his hands once more, Simon blundered down the stairs of the temple. Thunder crashed and rain fell. Shaking his fists at the glaring sky, Simon hurried on, staggering, slipping often in the mud, cursing the gods, wondering if he were mad.

II

> Lo! in yon brilliant window-niche
> How statue-like I see thee stand,
> The agate lamp within thy hand!
> Ah, Psyche, from the regions which
> Are Holy-Land!
>
> — Poe, "To Helen"

He found himself standing against a brick wall, gasping for breath, with only a vague memory of having run through many streets and alleys. Evidently the storm had been as quick in passing as in coming, for the rain no longer fell and the sky had brightened a bit. His hair and tunic were soaked, his sandals and legs spattered with mud. Looking about him, he saw that he was in narrow Mercury Street once more.

"Hermes, God of Magic," he muttered, "save me from madness! What spells has Dositheus put upon me? What ill rite would he have me partake in? Does that—that woman really dwell at this time in the house of Senator Junius? I must know!"

By now he had regained his breath—despite the recent weeks of comparative inactivity, Simon's training as a gladiator had given him great reserves of stamina. Quickly he continued on through the jumble of narrow streets and alleys, now relatively deserted because of the recent downpour. At length he was ascending the lanes that led up amid the residences of the Caelian Hill, jogging in his haste; the sun was down now, but the sky had cleared and there was still plenty of light for him to see his way—

"*Stop!* Hold on, there!"

Simon paused and turned—to see three men bearing down on him. They carried long, iron-tipped staves and wore short swords at their sides. Seeing their richly designed cloaks and tunics, Simon guessed they were not regulars of the City Patrol, but rather mercenaries such as were often hired by some of the richer citizens to patrol their immediate neighborhoods.

"What do you want?" he demanded.

"Don't get churlish with us," snarled one of the men. "We want to know why you're dashing about the streets with a knife at your side. Have you robbed someone, or are you an escaped slave?"

Simon scowled in anger. "I am neither thief nor slave."

"Can you prove it?"

Reaching into a pouch at his belt, Simon drew forth a folded parchment and handed it over. The guardsman took it, unfolded it, and squinted carefully at the writing. "What does it say?" he asked suspiciously.

"It is a writ of manumission from my former master, the Senator Junius. I am his freedman."

The guard handed back the parchment. "What you say may be true," he said, his tone now a shade less belligerent, "but it is well to be sure. Come with us. Our patron's lector shall examine your writ and tell us if it is valid."

"I—I'm in a hurry," said Simon, stuffing the parchment back into his pouch.

"So? You excite my suspicion!" The guard motioned to his two companions. "Surround the dog! We'll beat some politeness into him before we—"

"By Pallas!" exclaimed one of them suddenly as he moved to a position that enabled him to see Simon's face more clearly. "It's *him*—the gladiator who fought at Fidenae when the arena was destroyed by sorcery! I was there—I barely escaped with my life—!"

Simon roared and struck out; his fist cracked sharply against the face of the nearest guard, who flopped to the cobbles without a cry. Quick as a panther he crouched and whirled, barely in time to avoid a murderous blow from a second guard's staff; his sharp-bladed *sica*, already in hand, shore through the guard's neck as Simon completed his whirl, and the man went down with a dying gurgle.

The remaining guard turned and ran off, throwing away his staff and bellowing in terror, lurching downhill over the cobbles in long, grotesque strides. Simon cursed. There were people in the streets; he could not pursue the man. Quickly he sheathed his Thracian knife and hurried on up the narrow lanes, hoping that the shadows of the deepening twilight would be enough to shield him from pursuit.

"He has fled!" said Junius angrily as he and Dositheus stood in the peristyle of the Senator's house. "Some of my slaves saw him run off."

"He has *not* fled," Dositheus assured him smoothly, "and he will shortly return to us, after he has had time to settle his mind. Besides his ties of gratitude to us, he is bound by the spells of the preparatory rituals we have performed."

Not far from them lingered the young lad Menander, disquiet and doubt mingling with curiosity in his face as he listened. The raven, still perched on his shoulder, also seemed to be listening, so intent was its beady gaze.

"Rituals." Junius shook his head slowly. "So many rituals—and now, you say the final one must be performed. I know you can invoke great powers, Dositheus, for I have heard all Rome speak of the destruction of the amphitheater at Fidenae. Yet sometimes I wonder if you really know what you are doing."

"Wherein lie your doubts, good Junius?"

The Roman scowled thoughtfully. "That girl—the one you say must be sacrificed. She has done harm to no one. Is there really no other way—?"

"Aye, it is a heavy thing that we do. Yet remember, Junius, that Tiberius and his agents daily slay innocents without number and his legions oppress all the provinces and nations. This act we are about to perform may seem to you an abomination before the gods. Well, it is—and it will cause the gods to *strike!* When the sacrifice is offered up to Tiberius' image, the offended Powers above the Sphere of Achamoth shall send down wrathful lightnings to blast the Emperor, wherever he may be."

"Let their aim be true!" growled Junius. "Still, I'm glad I need not be present at the ceremony. Tell me truly, Dositheus—will there be any danger?"

"Not if all goes well. Still, it would be well for you and your household to retire to the cellars during the ceremony, and hold yourselves ready to escape by the secret passage if necessary."

"Indeed?" Junius rubbed his heavy chin nervously with one thick hand. "Tell me all, wizard. Hold nothing back."

"The chance of danger is very slight. The stars are right, and all the preparatory rituals up to this point have been performed flawlessly. Yet, should anything go wrong at the sacrifice itself, the Powers might interfere. Then Atar, the fire-minion of Great Mazda, would wake and come forth from the four-dimensioned Varena, leading his legions of flame, seeking out the source of our rites in order to slay his enemies, the earth-bound followers of Azdahak the Corrupt. So, at any rate, has written the ancient Persian fire-priest, Ostanes—"

"Enough!" muttered Junius. "Though what you say is strange, I have seen too much to doubt. I will follow your instructions."

"Good. Now, send some of your stoutest slaves to the cellar; have them fetch the stone altar and statue, and set them up here in the peristyle near the pool. Sunset approaches, and I must perform the last preparatory rite even as the fiery symbol of Mazda is occulted by the earth's horizon. Menander, you and Carbo may assist me if you wish—"

As he turned to confront the lad, Dositheus found that his young apprentice was gone. He and the raven had slipped unnoticed from the peristyle.

Menander paused at the top of the marble stairway. The house of Senator Junius was perhaps the largest on the Caelian Hill, and its upper apartments gave promise of being as extensive as its lower ones; yet, never during the many weeks he had lived here had the young lad ventured to explore them. Now a qualm of uneasiness dampened his curiosity.

The raven on his shoulder rustled its feathers restlessly and softly croaked: *"Qua!"*

"Be quiet, Carbo," whispered Menander. "We won't find her if they catch us and kick us out—"

Even as he spoke he rounded the corner leading into a long, torch-lit hall—and saw, flanking a closed door at its opposite end, two burly guards. The guards saw him at the same time. They did not seem like either slaves or soldiers, Menander thought, but were lean and hard like professional fighters. Each wore a dark cloak and tunic, and bore a short sword on his hip.

One of them strode forward and stared down at Menander. The lad felt a pang of fear as the man's face twisted with a sinister, lopsided grin.

"Begone, runt!" he growled. "No one's allowed here."

Menander obeyed hastily. In a moment he was out of the hall and down the stairway.

"That must be where they're keeping her, Carbo," he muttered. "Come on—let's see if we can find out."

He moved through the shadowed atrium and out one of its side doors into a narrow strip of garden, then along the wall toward the back of the house. The light was starting to dim with the approach of sunset. After some distance, Menander stopped and looked up. There was a lit window above, but the space between the house and its surrounding wall was small and the lad could not back up far enough to see much of the room's interior.

"Carbo, will you fly up there, please?" he whispered. "Fly up, and see if she is there."

The raven spread its large wings, flapped them heavily, and rose up to the second-story window. For a moment it rested on the sill, then turned and flapped down to its original perch.

"Did you see her, Carbo?"

"*Ita!*" croaked the bird, bobbing its head.

Menander nodded. "Good. Go back up, and wait for me."

As the bird complied, the boy gripped a trellis-work of vines that wove its way up the rough side of the house to a projecting ledge that divided the two stories. Deciding that it would support his weight, he began to ascend with agility. In a moment he was just below the window. Cautiously he thrust his head over the sill and peered within. He saw a small, furnished room illuminated with hanging oil lamps. The only inhabitant was a young, dark-haired woman who was reclining on a couch, apparently asleep.

Feeling his heart beating, Menander slid over the sill; the raven resumed its place on his shoulder as he did so. For a moment the lad stood quietly, staring at the sleeper. She was younger than he had first thought, he realized, probably only a few years older than himself—no more than a girl. Her sleeping face seemed exquisitely beautiful in the soft lamplight, and Menander suddenly felt a pang of compassion for her.

"Oh, Carbo," he whispered, "we *can't* let them do it—!"

Suddenly the room darkened slightly. Menander turned to the window, was relieved to see that it was only a cloud blotting out some of the waning daylight. He leaned out the window. A cool breeze had begun to blow, and a towering cloud-mass was moving in from the east with surprising swiftness. Lightning was flashing distantly beneath it, briefly illuminating the far-off hills and the walls of nearby houses. Thunder rolled, muted with distance. The sky darkened still more, and though Menander's view was partly cut off by the back corner of the mansion he sensed that the storm was going to miss the Caelian Hill, was probably bursting even now over the Forum, the Palatine, and the great temple of Capitoline Jupiter—

"Simon! *Simon!*"

Fear jolted Menander at the sound of the girl's outcry. He whirled—and saw that she was sitting up on the couch, staring wildly into space. Then her eyes alighted on him; she started in surprise and opened her mouth as if to cry out again. Hastily Menander stepped forward with a finger to his lips. "Please—don't," he whispered.

"Who—who are you?"

"My name is Menander, and this is Carbo. We want to be your friends, but you must let us help you. Tell me, why did you cry out the name of Simon?"

The girl glanced doubtfully at the raven, then back to the face of the strange lad who wore a wizard's robe. "Why? Do you know a Simon?"

"Yes. He is my fellow apprentice, and my friend. You would like him. I wish he were here to help us."

The girl stared at the floor and frowned slightly. "I dreamed I was in danger, but that someone was near who could aid me—someone I knew from long, long ago. I spoke to him. His name was Simon, but I knew him by many other names as well. I—I can't remember—the vision fades so fast...."

"Tell me—what is *your* name?"

"I am Helen, of the house of Prodikos in Ionia." The girl's voice was bitter; she raised her eyes to the closed portal, and there was fear in them. "Those two brutes who guard my door—they kidnapped me and brought me here. Now I fear for myself even more than I did in the house of my father and master. Tell me, Menander, what is going to happen to me? Why am I here?"

"I can't tell you—there is no time. But Simon will help us, I know he will. Don't be afraid. I must leave now. I'll steal some money for you so that you can go far away from Rome and find good people to live with, and I'll find Simon and bring him here and we'll both help you escape."

So saying, Menander turned to the window and climbed through. His last glimpse of the girl was from the window ledge, just before he began to let himself down the vines. Her beautiful face registered a mixture of bewilderment and hope.

"Be careful, Menander," she whispered anxiously.

Then she returned to her couch and tried to sit and wait calmly, feeling a mounting suspense that promised to soon become agonizing.

Simon paused in the shadows of the narrow lane, breathing hard from his uphill run. He forced himself to stand still for a few moments, listening, while his breathing quieted and his heartbeat slowed. There was no sound of pursuit, yet he thought he dimly heard a distant tumult back the way he had come, as of many angry voices. Simon cursed. The wolves were roused, but he hoped they would not find his trail.

A few strides more brought him to the back wall of Junius' garden. In the dusk he could just make out the gate. It was open. That was unusual, considering the hour, and Simon guessed that the guards had orders to leave it open till his return and were probably waiting for him just within.

Then he heard a low, droning chant issuing forth. That would be Dositheus, he realized, intoning his last preparatory ritual from the peristyle where the statue and the altar would now be awaiting the sacrifice. The few words he caught were Persian ones, unintelligible to him, but more than once he heard the name *Azdahak*, and shuddered as he remembered what it signified. Despite his hatred for Rome and his gratitude toward

Dositheus, Simon felt a revulsion sweep over him and knew he could never take part in the impending blasphemy.

"Helen!" he muttered. "If I am not mad and you are indeed here, they shall not have you for their purpose!"

Carefully he skirted the gate and hurried around a corner of the wall into a narrow alley. Here the shadows were even deeper. For a moment Simon groped carefully along the wall toward the front of the mansion. Suddenly he heard a slight rustling of feathers just above him; then:

"Simon! Simon!"

Startled, he yet recognized instantly the low, guttural croak. Peering up, he saw the large bird perched atop the wall, silhouetted against the darkening sky.

"Carbo! What are you doing here? Damn you, did Dositheus set you to watch for me?"

The bird shook its head. *"Menander! Menander!"* it croaked.

Simon crouched, then leaped and clutched the top of the wall. Easily he drew himself up and over, then dropped softly to the ground inside. The raven fluttered down and perched on his shoulder.

"Qua!" it croaked, pointing its beak toward the nearest upper window of the house. *"Qua!"*

"What is it, Carbo? What's there?"

"Elán!"

"Elán—'light,' " muttered Simon, scowling with incomprehension. Then: "Wait! You mean—Helen?"

"Ita!"

Suddenly a light appeared in the window, and Simon saw that it was an oil lamp, held in the hand of a slender young woman who was leaning slightly outward from the sill. She seemed to be listening, or trying to peer into the night. Her face, framed by long tresses darker than the night itself, was pale in the lamplight; her eyes, wide with what seemed a touch of anxiety, reflected the small flame like dark pools.

Simon gasped. It was—*her!*

Then, crouching motionless in the shadow of the wall, he found himself forming her name with his lips—but so silently that not even the raven on his shoulder heard him.

"Menander? Carbo?" The girl's voice was little more than a cautious whisper. "Is that you?"

Simon could not move or answer, but Carbo, uttering a low croak, flapped upward and came to rest on the sill beside the young woman, who seemed somewhat relieved upon seeing him.

"Hurry, Menander," she said, looking down the wall.

With an effort, Simon shook off the fascination that had held him motionless and hurried to the side of the house. Quickly he climbed up to the casement. It was no effort for his trained muscles, yet he felt the vines give slightly and knew that they would not support a greater weight than his. In another moment he had drawn himself over the sill and stood upon the marble-tiled floor of the chamber.

The woman had drawn back to the center of the room and was regarding him intently but without fear. There seemed to be a strange wonderment in her gaze. Simon saw now, at this close range, that she was not a woman at all but a girl of perhaps no more than fifteen years of age—yet he sensed also that she was more ageless than the nations. Though he knew he had never before seen her in his life, he seemed to know every line of her beautiful form and face.

"You!" he muttered softly. "You—!"

"Simon! I knew you would come."

She set her lamp on a low table and came toward him, and Simon moved to meet her. Strange, contradictory emotions swept through him. He felt exultation and fear entwined in one, and somehow properly so; he felt like the Lord of the World, advancing to receive the World's submission, yet at the same time like a powerless supplicant approaching the altar of One whose approval would give his lordly power its only life and meaning....

Then, suddenly, he was holding a young, slender, human girl in his arms, and she was sobbing on his breast, clinging to him desperately as to a rock in a storm.

"Oh, Simon! Who am I? And who are you?"

"I do not know," he said, soothingly. "I had a vision of you—"

"And I had a dream of *you*. Simon—who are we?"

He held her away from him, his hands gentle on her shoulders as he gazed into her dark eyes. He did not reply, for there was no need. It seemed in that moment that his mind and hers were somehow one, not in unity but in profound, reciprocal understanding. He had always known her, and she him, and so it would always be throughout all the future cycles of the great Illusion of Change, losing and finding one another in dreams of love and pain, horror and ecstasy, until that final Union at the end of time....

Then the vision was gone, but not the understanding, and Simon knew that the girl had shared it all with him.

"How strange!" she murmured. "And yet, we are only human—a man and a woman. How can it be, that all things should have their only meaning in and through us...?"

"I—I don't know, Helen. Dositheus, the sorcerer, says that some people are True Spirits—fragments of the God-soul, trapped in the material world created by the mad demon Achamoth."

"Oh, Simon! What you say is surely true, for I used to hear the priestesses of Artemis at Ephesus speak of such things—"

"Wait—*listen!*"

Helen ceased speaking, suddenly fearful because of the tension in Simon's voice—and then heard, through the window, the distant hum of many angry voices.

III

> The wine of life is spilt upon the sand,
> My heart is as some famine-murdered land
> Whence all good things have perished utterly,
> And well I know my soul in Hell must lie
> If I this night before God's throne should stand.
>
> — Wilde, "E Tenebris"

Simon turned suddenly toward the window, then strode to it and leaned out into the night. "They are gathering—I think they're coming this way. That damned guardsman! I should never have mentioned the name of Senator Junius—"

Helen, hurrying to his side, listened to what seemed the distant babble of many voices, as if a crowd were gathering. The raven, perched by her on the sill, stirred and croaked uneasily; she absently stroked it and it grew quiet, as if comforted.

"What is it, Simon?" Her voice was quiet but anxious.

At that instant, before he could answer, the door of the room rattled open. Simon and the girl both turned abruptly. The two brutal-faced guards were entering, and between them—

"Dositheus!" snarled Simon. His Thracian dagger, already drawn, quivered in his hand.

The wizard regarded him, then glanced at Helen. Again there was a trace of sadness on his stern features.

"I divined your presence here, Simon. You must come with me. It is the time."

Simon shook his head grimly. "I owe you much, Dositheus—my very life, in fact. Yet I'll spill your guts on this floor before I'll perform your damned sacrifice!"

"It is no use, Simon. You are bound to the service of Azdahak, by reason of the rites in which you have taken part. Behold." The Samaritan wizard advanced a pace, and Simon saw in the palm of his outstretched hand an object about the size and shape of a pigeon's egg, jet black in color. On it there glowed the outline of some strange being—a monstrous, dragon-headed creature with two serpents springing from its shoulders in lieu of arms. Simon felt an intense revulsion, even as he wondered how he was able to discern at a glance the details of such a diminutive figure.

"O Azdahak!" cried Dositheus. "Claim now thy servant!"

The oval object leaped from the wizard's hand with such speed that Simon could not even react before it smacked squarely into the center of his forehead!

Instantly waves of freezing pain lanced through him, bringing him to his knees. He screamed—but even as he did so, the pain was already gone. He could feel the thing clinging to his forehead like some giant, cold tick. Horror filled him; he reached up to pluck it away, but found that his hands would not obey his will.

"Rise, Simon," said Dositheus.

He did so. Hate glared from his shadowed, deep-set eyes as he regard-ed the sorcerer. He tried to step forward, but could not. Fury and despera-tion strove within him as he realized that he was completely subject to Dositheus' will.

"Simon!" He heard the girl cry out, saw her run to him with terror in her features, felt her throw her arms about him. *"Simon!"*

Dositheus nodded to the two guards, who immediately strode for-ward, grabbed the girl roughly by the arms, and dragged her, fighting and screaming, from the room. Simon strained frantically against the supernat-ural force that held him—but could not move a muscle.

"Oh, Simon!" muttered Dositheus, sadness and pain now openly ap-parent in his old eyes. "How you must hate me! I can feel your hate, your fury, even as damned souls feel the burning fire of Mazda for their sins. Yet pity me, Simon, for it is a heavy thing that I must do. Would that I could die beneath your knife, rather than that fair and innocent maid, for gladly would I give my life to destroy the Roman tyranny that strangles the world! But such cannot be; only the slaying of a High Soul by its Kindred One can induce the outraged gods to smite the object of worship. Pity me, Simon, for the True Spirit in me, even as in you, goes out to this girl who must die—and though you and she must suffer pain and tragedy, these are honest sufferings that are at last transmuted into other things. But I, for my part in this sacrifice, must finally enter into the Hells and there endure the fires of Mazda for all time." Dositheus' face once more grew stern. "This and much more would I endure to bring Tiberius and his cruel empire down to doom, thereby releasing all the nations from the Roman yoke! Come, Simon—it is the time of sacrifice."

Slowly, inexorably, Simon followed his hated mentor out into the torch-lit corridor, curious and frantic but unable to disobey—

And behind, in the empty room, there was a rustling of feathers as Carbo stirred against the darkness that had rendered him invisible, spread his wings, and leaped from the window sill into the night.

Menander crept quietly through the cellars of the mansion, wondering at the altered aspect of things. More torches were lit than usual, but his effects and those of Dositheus and Simon were not in their accustomed rooms.

Entering the chamber where the altar and the statue had been, he found both these items gone. A square hole gaped in the center of the floor—evidently the altar had hidden it previously. In one corner was a large bundle wrapped up in heavy sailcloth. The lad approached, and saw that atop it rested several squares of parchment held down by a large, yellowed scroll. The latter he recognized, for Dositheus had once told him what it was: the *Sapientia Magorum* of the ancient Persian fire-priest, Ostanes.

He set it and the parchments upon the floor and examined the bundle, untying one of the cords and slightly unrolling the cloth. As he had suspected, it contained more scrolls, plus vials and instruments of divination—Dositheus' accouterments of sorcery—plus garments and a few other items belonging to Simon and himself. He untied it completely—and found that the moneybag he sought was not there.

Hastily he tied the bundle shut again. Evidently Dositheus meant to leave Junius' mansion this very night. As he picked up the scroll it unrolled slightly. He glanced at it, but found he could not read the alien script and rerolled it hastily, placing it back atop the bundle. Dositheus, he remembered, had said that it was a compendium of monstrous, arcane sorcery, dangerous for even adepts to read and attempt to use.

He lifted the parchments to place them atop the scroll, and as he did so he noticed that they were written over in Greek—a language he had been instructed to understand almost as perfectly as his native Aramaic. Immediately, he realized that the writing was Dositheus' own, evidently a translation or elaboration from the scroll of Ostanes.

"Let only the sorcerer whose heart is free of doubt and fear (read the writing upon the topmost parchment) invoke the name of *Azdahak*, that Evil one who of his own perversity did precipitate entity into the chaos of materiality. And then let him sacrifice, before the image of his enemy, one who is his own True Spiritual Counterpart; whereupon the outraged gods shall smite the object of worship with their wrath. Yet let the one who so sacrifices beware, no matter how high his motives; for the performing of the rituals of preparation, given heretofore, shall cause to gather the minions of that Evil One, even as vultures gather to the carrion. Then is the life of the sorcerer in great peril, unless he has prepared for his escape immediately upon the performance of the sacrifice. But if the sacrifice be not consummated after the preparation, then is the sorcerer's peril even greater; for in that event the fire-minions of *Atar*, the right hand of Ahura Mazda, shall come to work their vengeance upon the servitors of Azdahak. In that time and place, all who serve Evil will surely perish. And any innocent ones with them shall die also, unless there be among them an uncorrupted True Spirit who shall fervently call upon the name of *Atar*...."

Suddenly there were footfalls outside the door. Menander hastily put down the parchments, then turned—to see about a dozen men and women crowding through the doorway. He recognized them, for they were all slaves or freedmen of Senator Junius' household. Almost all carried cloth-wrapped bundles.

"Hurry! Hurry!" said the tall old man in the lead, whom Menander recognized as Ambronius, Junius' majordomo. "Down the tunnel, all of you—it will lead you safely to the deserted shrine of Caeles Vibenna. Thence you must make your way to the docks at the Emporium, where your mistress and the rest wait aboard the ship that shall take us all to our master's estate at Antium. Hurry—down. Yet, wait—you two, Guido and Asellus—take up the bundle of the damned foreign sorcerers. It will be in this corner—*ah!*" He started upon seeing Menander standing by the indicated bundle, then hurried forward. "Young wizard, your master is looking for you! He has instructed me, should I find you, to tell you to depart from this house with the others. He will join you later."

"But—where must I go?" asked Menander.

"Through the tunnel, with these people—the last of Junius' household. My master and I will join you soon—if *your* master's evil manipulations do not soon bring about the destruction of us all."

"My master is not evil!" retorted Menander hotly.

"Nor is mine," said Ambronius. "Yet I fear Senator Junius' mind has been fired with a madness which was brought into this house by your mentor, Dositheus."

"Is it mad to hate Rome? Did not Rome make you a slave?"

The old man's eyes blazed with hurt and fury. He drew back his hand as if to strike, but then lowered it.

"Junius is a better man than you will ever know. Had he his way, no man would be master or slave! But why do I stand here arguing with such a whipper-snapper? Go with these others through the tunnel and wait for us on the ship, according to your master's orders. And, speaking of him—he has asked me to bring up *these*."

So saying, Ambronius snatched up the scroll and parchments from the top of the bundle, then hurried out of the room.

Most of the slaves had already climbed down through the black aperture and vanished along the secret tunnel. Only two remained—youths not much older than Menander himself, clad in mauve tunics. Quickly they picked up the sailcloth-wrapped bundle and began climbing down through the opening.

"Hurry, boy," called one of them as he vanished from sight.

Menander hastened to the opening and looked down. The two young slaves had just reached the bottom of a shaft perhaps ten feet in depth, lit by two torches. One of the slaves called up: "Follow us, Samaritan." He lifted a torch from its bracket; then, carrying the bundle between them, the pair vanished into a horizontal tunnel.

"I—I'm coming," Menander yelled down the shaft.

Instead of following, however, he leaped up and ran back through the cellars, toward the stairs that led up to the peristyle, where he knew a monstrous ritual of sacrifice was about to be performed.

Simon stood before the block of stone that was the altar, his naked Thracian dagger clutched in his right hand. Upon that stone sat Helen, facing him; her sky-blue tunic seemed actually dark against the pallor of her skin. Her eyes were wide with fear. A fierce desperation raged within Simon. He wanted, more than he had ever wanted anything before, to spare this girl her fate, to lash out and slay the two brutal-faced guards who held her by her slender arms, to grab his mentor Dositheus by his lean neck and feel it snap under his fingers like a rotten stick—

"Simon, it is the time."

It was the voice of Dositheus—hateful Dositheus, to whom he had once felt he owed a debt. Simon saw the old man advancing; he was holding out a hand, and clutched in it was a heavy pouch.

"Take this, Simon. It is money—as much as you will need. After tonight, you must leave Italy. The survivors of the mob at Fidenae will remember you, and will surely find and slay you if you stay; but with this money and Junius' writ of manumission you may journey freely. I have made arrangements for you to journey to Parthia, beyond the boundaries of Rome's rule, and there study magic under the tutelage of the Magus Daramos in Persepolis." So saying, he leaned forward and tied the pouch to Simon's belt.

"Wait!" growled one of the guards holding Helen. "When do *we* get paid? We have served you well. It took no common skill to kidnap this girl and bring her here."

Dositheus scowled briefly, but then nodded. "Aye. You, too, shall be

RICHARD L. TIERNEY 39

paid—immediately after the ritual."

"No, Dositheus—they shall be paid *now!*"

Dositheus turned to confront the speaker and saw that it was the Senator Junius, standing tall and stern in the toga that was embroidered with the symbols of his office.

"These men shall be paid now," Junius repeated. "I shall pay them myself, and then they shall go their way. I have decided that there shall be no human sacrifice in my house."

Dositheus glared at him. "Are you mad?" he hissed.

"No." Junius shook his head, glanced at the girl who sat on the altar of sacrifice, then looked again at Dositheus. "But I think I *was* mad, when I agreed to this. I hate Rome as much as you; both of us have suffered the loss of loved ones at its hands. But listen: Must we foul our hands to attain our ends, even as do the Augustan tyrants? Must we become like them, taking innocent lives, in order to destroy them? If so, what have we gained?"

"You know not what you say! I've instructed you—"

Junius nodded curtly. "You've told me that dire things may happen if we do not pursue this ritual to its end. I believe you. Yet now I am asking you to call it all off and use your magic to avert any possible ill consequences. Not all Romans are without honor, Dositheus, even in these evil times when the agents of Tiberius cause citizens to spy upon one another and deliver their fellows to the executioner. I know that Roman politics are vile, but now I am learning that sorcery is more vile still. Call this off, Dositheus."

"Would that it were possible!" Dositheus shook his head violently, as if he were in anguish. "I know that your True Spirit goes out to this girl, even as does mine. Yet we must not cringe. It is too late to turn back. Even now the evil minions of Azdahak must be gathering about us—"

"I sense no evil here," Junius interrupted, "save that of the ritual you intend to perform. How can you know—?"

"And how can *you* know that such beings are *not* gathering? Mortal senses are dull. Ostanes was the greatest mage of ancient Persia in his time; he knew whereof he wrote. I know not the nature of Azdahak's minions, save that they are said to be the most vile and wicked beings ever to exist in this world; but I do know they are gathering about us even now. Our rituals have drawn them here, and should the sacrifice not be performed— thereby diverting the wrath of the gods from us to the object of worship— the fire-minions of Lord Mazda shall come to slay Azdahak's servitors, and us with them."

"Then we must all be gone from here as quickly as possible," said Junius. "The tunnel—"

At that instant old Ambronius emerged from the cellar. He walked over to Dositheus and handed him a scroll and some squares of parchment. "Here are the things you wanted, Samaritan."

Dositheus nodded, thrust the scroll into a pocket of his symbol-emblazoned robe.

"Ambronius, go into the house," said Junius, "and make sure that all the lamps and torches have been extinguished. We are all leaving this place immediately." As the old slave left the peristyle, Junius turned once more to the Samaritan wizard. "I am firm in this, Dositheus. My house shall not be a stage for the abomination of human sacrifice. These hired louts shall be paid, and the girl released. I shall take her into my own household if she wishes, to be a handmaid to my wife. And you, Dositheus, shall be paid well—"

"*Fool!*" Dositheus stepped back a pace and lifted his hand, as if about to invoke sorcery. "Do you so easily abandon the overthrow of the Augustan tyranny? Not so shall I!" He raised one of the parchments, holding it out at arm's length before his face. "Hear me, great Angra Mainyu, Lord of Evil! Send to me now thy greatest servitor, even Him who created all the material worlds! I invoke Him by his many names: Achamoth, Azathoth, Aziluth, Azdahak—"

"*No!*"

Dositheus whirled at the abrupt cry—to see Menander standing not far from the opening in the floor that led to the cellars. The lad's face showed fear and concern mixed with determination. Dositheus' brow darkened.

"You insolent brat! Why have you not left this house with Junius' slaves?"

The boy's face registered hurt at the unusual tone of harshness in his mentor's voice—but before he could reply there was a heavy flutter of wings.

"*Cavé!*" screeched the raven as it came flapping down into the torch-lit peristyle. "*Cavé!*" The bird circled the space between the columns and the pool, screeching the word several times more, then fluttered down to rest upon Menander's shoulder.

"Carbo!" cried Dositheus. "What danger? Tell me—!"

At that instant old Ambronius came running into the peristyle. "There is a great mob surrounding the house!" he cried. "They are even now climbing the walls of the garden and hammering at the door of the atrium. They cry out in demand for Simon of Gitta."

Even as Ambronius spoke, all within the room began to hear the rising mutter of many angry voices outside the house—a mutter that quickly swelled to an angry roar.

"I shall see to it," said Junius sternly. "Come, Ambronius."

They left the peristyle, hurrying toward the atrium at the front of the house. Dositheus followed, then paused at the door. "Come, Simon," he said, beckoning. "I may need your fighting prowess. The rest of you stay here."

Simon turned away from Helen and the altar and hastened after his mentor, amazed to find that he could move so freely. Evidently there were no restrictions on him so long as he obeyed the will of Dositheus.

Loud thumpings reverberated within the atrium as the four of them gathered there. Many fists and clubs were pounding upon the outer doors, which were fortunately secured by two massive wooden bolts. Muffled shouts filtered in: "Give us the gladiator! Give us Simon of Gitta!"

"The scum!" muttered Junius. "How dare they assail my house! Do they wish to confront me? Then they shall, and hear my opinion of them."

"Do not open the door," cautioned Dositheus, fearing that his patron's patrician indignation was about to result in unwise action. "If you must speak to them, then at least do so from an upper window, whence you can look upon them and better gauge their temper."

Junius scowled at him, but then nodded. Old Ambronius hurriedly led the three of them from the atrium and up the stairway to the second floor, then around to a window that overlooked the front entrance. Simon, bringing up the rear, tried often to turn back but could not.

At length they all stood before a wide casement. Ambronius threw open the shutters, and they looked out.

"Simon of Gitta!" thundered the crowd. "Simon the gladiator! Simon the sorcerer! Give him to us!"

Simon looked down into the surging mob crowded into the narrow streets and lanes, down into the packed mass of torches and hate-filled faces and upraised, menacing fists. There were hundreds—no, thousands—of them, and more gathering. The mob—the Roman mob—lusting for vengeance, lusting for blood—

"Give us Junius!" they chanted. "Give us the traitor Junius! Give us the traitor, and his nest of sorcerers!"

Simon glanced at Dositheus and saw in his eyes a horror akin to his own. He looked back to the mob—the chanting, screaming Roman mob that waved torches and fists, swords and bludgeons and knives—the same mob that had screamed with glee while he fought for his life in the arenas. He saw, at the fringes of the crowd, knots of men already bursting into adjacent houses to loot and rape and slay—

"They've gone mad!" cried Junius.

The mob, noticing the four peering out the casement, suddenly redoubled its roar. Missiles hurtled into the chamber—stones, arrows, clods of earth. Simon and Dositheus drew back instinctively; Ambronius gripped his master by the shoulders and hauled him away from the window, then hastily closed and bolted the shutters. The sound of many heavy objects reverberated against the protective boards.

"*Give us Simon the sorcerer!*" came the muffled screams of the mob. "*Give us Junius the traitor!*"

"Mad!" muttered Junius, obviously shaken.

"Aye!" A light of comprehension was dawning in Dositheus' face. "Mad—and *evil!* I should have guessed—for what is more vile and wicked upon this earth than the Roman mob? *These* are the minions of Azdahak, unconsciously drawn here by the spells that have been performed. And now they lust for blood and entertainment, even as at the arena. Quickly— back to the peristyle! You, Ambronius, watch the front portals. We must complete the sacrifice, and then escape through the tunnel before this mad horde bursts in."

IV

What if the breath that kindled those grim fires,
Awaked, should blow them into sevenfold rage,
And plunge us in the flames; or from above
Should intermitted vengeance arm again
His red right hand to plague us? What if all
Her stories were opened, and this firmament
Of hell should spout her cataracts of fire...?

— Milton, "Paradise Lost"

As the four of them hurried back downstairs, Simon again felt the desperation of powerlessness. He ached to pluck away the cold, evil talisman that clung to his brow—to plunge his blade into the back of Dositheus. Yet he could do neither. His thoughts were free, but not his physical movements.

In a moment they were again in the peristyle, save for Ambronius. Simon saw that Helen, pale and faint, was kneeling on the floor; her guards, having loosened her tunic so that she was bare above the waist, now hauled her to her feet as Dositheus gestured to them, bending her backwards upon the cold stone of the altar, ready for the stroke of the knife. Behind them stood the gray statue of Tiberius, its face grim and shadowed in the flickering torchlight. Fury redoubled within Simon; he felt his heart throbbing, his head pounding as if about to burst. Without much interest he noticed Menander standing nearby, fear and concern in his young face, the raven a dark shadow upon his shoulder.

"Good," muttered Dositheus. "Now, the ritual—"

"No!" cried Junius. "We must escape through the tunnel. Leave off this madness, Dositheus—let Tiberius and the damned Roman mob do what they will—!"

Dositheus, ignoring the senator, raised his hands and again began to intone the monstrous incantation: "Hear me, great Angra Mainyu, Lord of Evil..."

Junius felt a chill, a paralyzing fear; somehow he sensed that mighty supernatural forces were set against his will, and hung back in doubt. Simon, too, felt it—then felt an even greater horror as his knife arm began to rise. Dositheus was intoning the variants of the dreadful Name of Power, and Simon knew that in another instant he would be forced to drive the blade of the *sica* into the girl's breast.

"...Aziluth, Azdahak..."

Menander, also, felt the horror—but in the same instant he recalled the words he had read upon the parchment. Hoping fervently that he met the requirements, he cried out with all his might:

"Atar!"

Simon felt his arm pause. Dositheus stopped chanting, a gleam of fear in his eyes. An immense tension seemed to charge the air—

Suddenly the raven sprang from Menander's shoulder. *"Atar!"* it screeched, flapping wildly about the peristyle. *"Atar! Atar!"* Then, without warning, it stopped its mad circlings and swooped down, straight at Simon's head. Simon gasped as he heard Carbo's heavy beak clack shut upon the dark ovoid that clung to his forehead—felt it being plucked away like a walnut from its stem. Then he heard the bird fluttering off, heard its raucous caw as it released the thing, heard the thing splash into the pool of the peristyle—

Simon roared with rage. He was free! Instantly he struck the blow Dositheus' will had been impelling him toward—but instead of piercing the breast of Helen, the keen blade of his Thracian dagger drove deep into the heart of one of her kidnappers!

"No!" shrieked Dositheus.

The stricken guardsman flopped to the flags without a cry. Immediately the other one released Helen and leaped back, drawing his Roman short sword. Simon, howling with berserk rage, bounded over the fallen girl and the altar and came at him. The two blades rang together, and sparks flew. The hired kidnapper drew back farther, his eyes suddenly wide with fear as he sensed the caliber of the foe he was up against. Though skilled professionally in fighting, he had not spent two years in the arena striving for life as Simon had. Nor had he ever faced such fury in any opponent.

"Junius!" the guardsman shrieked. "Dositheus! Call off your dog—!"

In that instant Simon drove in past his enemy's guard and the wicked

Thracian blade slashed through belly flesh and grated against the bone of the spine. The kidnapper sprawled heavily to the stone floor, gargling in his death agony, a deluge of blood spilling from his great wound.

Simon whirled and crouched as if expecting another foe, his red knife clutched tensely, poised to strike. Through a haze of crimson he saw the others staring at him in shocked horror: Junius, young Menander with the raven once more perched upon his shoulder, Helen clinging weakly to the altar, and—

"*Dositheus!*"

Simon's voice was a low hiss as he spoke the name. Then, his dark eyes glaring like those of a hunting-beast, he began to move forward—

Suddenly, in that moment, a booming crash resounded through the house. For an instant everyone remained frozen in their postures, their eyes turned toward the front of the house whence the reverberating crash had come. Then came another, mingled with the sound of splintering wood.

Ambronius came dashing into the peristyle. "The mob is breaking in!" he cried. "They've devised a battering ram to smash down the front portal. We must flee!"

"*Cavé!*" screeched the raven. Simon glimpsed it, a swooping black bundle of feathers, just as it dove down through the aperture leading to the cellars. For an instant he stood, indecisive as to whether to run to Helen or smite Dositheus as he had intended. The old wizard was, surprisingly, staring up toward the stars that gleamed down into the open peristyle.

"Carbo knows!" he cried out. "They come—the minions of Azdahak! Hurry, all of you—the tunnel is our only chance!"

Simon, glancing upward, saw near the zenith a cluster of many yellow lights that were brighter than ordinary stars. They seemed to be milling, swirling, brightening, drawing closer. Then he heard footfalls, lowered his gaze, and glimpsed Dositheus and Menander vanishing down the cellar steps. Junius and Ambronius were helping Helen to her feet, hurrying her toward the stairs.

"Simon!" yelled Dositheus as he vanished from sight. "Hurry!"

A splintering crash resounded from the front of the mansion—and Simon knew, from the roaring tumult that immediately followed, that the mob had broken in. Another crash resounded, this one from the short hall leading to the garden at the back of the house. Instantly a motley horde surged through it into the peristyle—wild-eyed looters brandishing rocks, clubs, and knives.

Simon snatched up the short sword of one of his fallen foes, then bounded toward the opening through which Helen and the others had just vanished.

"That's him!" screamed one of the intruders. "That's Simon the gladiator—Simon the sorcerer!"

Simon leaped into the cellar opening, landed on the third step, reached up and grabbed the ring of the heavy trapdoor that rested back against the wall. It creaked slowly forward on its rusty hinges. A thrown brick crashed against it, barely missing his head. With a frantic curse to Baal he flung all his weight into it; the long-unused hinges yielded, and the great slab came crashing down into place.

Simon rolled down several steps, his sword and dagger clattering alongside him on the stones, before he was able to bring himself to a halt. Shakily he rose, gathering up his weapons and thanking Baal that he had not been wounded by their blades. At the foot of the stair he saw the others looking up at him. Above, the heavy slab was reverberating to heavy blows.

"Hurry!" yelled Simon as he joined them. "It won't take them long to find a way to pry up that door. Wait—take all the lit torches as you go. Don't make it easy for them."

In a few minutes they were all gathered in the small room where the entrance to the tunnel gaped. Overhead they could hear muffled shouts and the pounding of countless feet as the mob stormed through the mansion of Senator Junius, looting and destroying. Then the shouts grew louder, took on a reverberating quality, and Simon knew that the cellar door was being forced open.

"Into the tunnel, all of you!" he snarled. "Snuff all the torches you don't need, and take the rest."

They complied quickly, Dositheus going first, then Ambronius, who paused to help Helen descend as Junius let her down from above. After the senator came Menander, but the boy, pausing as he clung to the iron handholds, stared up at Simon with concerned eyes.

"Where is Carbo?"

"He's out the other end of the tunnel by now, if I know him," said Simon. "You'd better get going that way, too. Hurry—the others are already starting—"

"Simon! Aren't you coming?"

"Of course I'm coming. Get going, damn it!"

Menander ducked down the shaft, snatched the last burning torch from its bracket, and hurried down the tunnel.

Simon turned away from the hole, faced the dark doorway that led to the rest of the cellars. The clamor of voices was growing; the mob was evidently groping its way down the stairs. In a moment they would have torches of their own; then they would surge into this place howling for blood, ravening for stores of wine and food, seeking women for the sport of rape....

And they would find the tunnel, for the stone altar that had once concealed it had been removed to the peristyle. They would find it too soon for the others to escape—for Helen to escape—unless he, Simon, stayed behind to defend it. To defend it, and take every damned Roman he could down to doom with him....

The tumult increased, and he began to sense the light of distant torches. Quickly he turned to throw his own torch down the shaft, hoping its light had not already been seen—and found it was shining full upon a grizzled face that protruded from the pit.

"Dositheus!" he gasped. "What in the Hells—!"

"Don't cast your torch away," said the old man urgently. "You will need it. It is a spark of fire in a sea of darkness."

"Get out of here!" snarled Simon. "Would you lead the Romans to the others—?"

"To Helen, you mean. Fear not, for she and the others are all in full flight down the tunnel. I told them I returned for you—but we both know better. There is a chance that we will both perish here."

Simon raised his Roman short sword as if to strike, but then lowered it as he saw that Dositheus made no move to protect his venerable head. The wizard's eyes were sad, concerned.

"Give me your torch, Simon," he said. "It is our only chance to save ourselves—or at least delay our foes long enough for Helen and the others to escape."

Yells and curses rang from the far reaches of the cellar, and Simon realized it was already too late—they had seen the light of his torch. Quickly he thrust it into Dositheus' upraised hand, then turned to face the doorway, drawing his *sica* as he did so.

"You'd better have a card up your sleeve, wizard!" he growled, a blade gleaming ready in each hand.

There came the approaching clatter of many running feet, the shouting of many angry voices. Then the forms of armed men appeared in the doorway, crowding and struggling to surge through. Their eyes glared with fury; behind them roiled a mass of humanity with hate-twisted faces, brandishing torches, knives, and clubs.

"Give us Simon the gladiator!" they screeched madly. "Give us Simon the sorcerer!"

The door was only large enough for two abreast and Simon met the first two with steel, expertly parrying, slashing, stabbing. One collapsed mortally wounded from a sword-thrust in the guts; the other leaped back, suddenly fearful, but was pushed forward again by the surging mob—to die instantly on the point of the *sica*. Simon howled with mad rage, swinging and thrusting; a bludgeon glanced heavily off his left shoulder and a knife-point nicked his flank, but three more of his enemies went down with blood gushing. A pike ripped his tunic and gashed the side of his ribcage; he roared and smote in return, cleaving a snarling face with his sword. Fierce exultation suddenly filled him; if he must die, this was how he preferred it, fighting and slaying Romans to the very end—

"Atar!" he heard Dositheus shriek suddenly. *"Come, O great minion of Mazda!"*

A club cracked against Simon's left wrist, causing him to drop the short sword. Instantly his Thracian knife shore through the neck-cords of his attacker, but the press surged on—

"Come, O minion of Mazda—come with thy cleansing fire!"

Suddenly a burst of glaring white light filled the chamber, spilling out the doorway past Simon. His nearest foes seemed in that moment to be turned to chalk, so intense was the radiance. A shriek went up from the crowd, and they drew back. Simon stole a glance behind him, saw that the torch in Dositheus' upraised hand was blazing with a furious blue-white glare and that the old man's eyes were tightly shut—and immediately turned away again to avoid being blinded. His foes were still drawing back from the doorway. Then mingled with their startled screams he heard many muffled, distant ones, apparently from the floor above, together with a thunderous stomping of many feet, as if a great crowd were stampeding in terror.

"Come, great Atar!" shrieked Dositheus. *"Bring doom to the minions of Az-dahak!"*

Simon sensed a glow of light intensifying in the far reaches of the cellar, beyond the torches and flames and brandished weapons of the mob. It was as if the entrance to the cellars were brightening, like the opening of the door of a great furnace. Yells of terror rose from the back of the crowd, but the foremost began to surge ahead again.

"Step aside, Simon—*quickly!*" cried Dositheus.

Simon instinctively leaped to one side of the doorway. Immediately a white glare shot past him, meteor-like; Dositheus had hurled the sorcerously kindled torch through the door and into the mob. A deafening shriek of fear suddenly welled up from more than a hundred throats.

Simon saw Dositheus beckon to him, then vanish down the shaft. He hurried to its edge, sheathing his *sica*, then glanced back—and saw that the whole cellar beyond the door was flooded with the glaring white light. Every torch in the hands of the mob was blazing, expanding into what seemed to be writhing, monstrous, sentient entities of flame—while beyond, the glow from the cellar entrance had brightened and was flowing down the stairs like a cataract of molten steel. The crowd was milling about frantically, screeching in pain and terror, like damned souls suddenly trapped in the pits of Hell.

Simon leaped into the shaft, hardly touching the iron hand-holds in his haste. As his feet touched the bottom he heard Dositheus scuttling off down the horizontal tunnel and hastened after him. The place was pitch black—doubly so after the glare of flame Simon had witnessed above.

"Hurry—do not stop," he heard Dositheus call back. "We are in great danger from the flame-minions."

"Damn you, we'll stumble and fall in this darkness—!" snarled Simon.

"No. The tunnel is straight and smooth. Junius tells me it was built centuries ago, when the Caelian Hill was fortified against the Gauls and Etruscans. It will bring us to the shrine of Caeles Vibenna—beyond the fringes of the mob, let us hope. Thence we can make our way to the bottom of the hill, and then to the Emporium, where Junius' boat waits to take us all to Antium. But hurry!"

For several minutes Simon groped along as rapidly as he could, touching both walls with his outstretched hands, hearing Dositheus shuffling and wheezing not far ahead. Then it seemed to him that he began to be able to see faintly. Glancing back, he realized that a lurid glow had begun to pervade the tunnel behind them.

"Mazda save us!" gasped Dositheus as he became aware of the light. "Faster, Simon! Run!"

"What is it?"

"One of Atar's fire-minions. It has sought out the place where I summoned it, and now it follows us!"

Simon glanced back again, saw that a great ball of flame was filling the far end of the tunnel. Immediately it began to brighten and grow larger. A strange humming, crackling sound began to pervade the air.

"Hurry!" cried Dositheus.

A few steps more and they were at the tunnel's end: Simon could see it clearly in the menacing glow from behind them. Old Dositheus was gasping, faltering, stumbling.

"I can't climb out of here, Simon. Go up quickly, and push the slab into place. The thing can't come through stone—"

Simon saw that the square opening was level with the top of the tunnel. He leaped and hauled himself up easily; lying flat upon the floor, he reached down and gripped one of Dositheus' skinny arms. The glow in the passageway was intensifying, the humming sound growing louder.

"The trapdoor, Simon!" gasped the old wizard. "It's your only chance. Leave me—"

With a surge of strength Simon lifted his mentor up and dragged him roughly over the rim of the pit, then leaped to his feet. The stone door leaned open on ancient hinges, even as had the one in Junius' peristyle.

White light was glowing up from the pit. Simon leaned on the door with all his weight; below him, he saw the tunnel begin to seethe with tendrils of glaring flame, heard the humming rise to an angry shrillness—

Then the door grated over and fell into place with a heavy crash. Instantly darkness reigned once more. From below came a muffled droning that somehow made Simon think of a trapped hive of monstrous wasps. The stone, upon which his hands still rested, seemed suddenly to grow warmer; hastily he stood up and drew back.

Dositheus was stirring and rising in the darkness. As Simon's eyes adjusted to the gloom he saw that they stood within a shallow, natural grotto whose front had been built up with columns and lintels. Beside them stood a nearly life-sized stone statue of a man clad in Roman warrior garb of an ancient design. Beyond was the night sky, dark, yet lit with a flickering glow.

"Hurry, Simon," gasped Dositheus. "We are not yet out of danger. The thing will go back up the tunnel and out of the cellars, then return here. We must be far away when it does."

They hastened out of the small shrine and down the steps into a narrow street, then away from the flickering glare which, they knew, came from the houses burning farther up the hill. The mob did not extend to this place, but they could hear it not far away—screaming in terror. Occasional flashes of light scattered the darkness, but Simon resisted the temptation to look back. He knew that unhuman things were descending from the skies—beings of fire and vengeance, come to cleanse the earth of evil sorcery and consume the vile servitors of Azdahak.

Down dark, narrow lanes they fled, Simon half-carrying his old mentor much of the time. They met few people, and those few took no note of them, their attention being focused on the spreading fire on the hill.

At last the fleeing pair paused, breathless, in an avenue at the foot of the Pabato line, where they had a view in the direction they had come from—and as they glanced back, both cried out in awe. The entire upper half of the Caelian Hill was wrapped in roaring, boiling flames, and above the area where Junius' mansion had been there swarmed and darted brilliant spheres of light—hundreds of them, swooping and dipping and soaring. New fires were springing up wherever they touched.

Dim with distance, a sound welled up—the terrible sound of thousands perishing as the entire hill was surrounded by flame and engulfed in it. For a moment Simon felt a thrill of horror, forgot his hatred for the Rome that had killed his parents and impressed him into the brutal slavery of the arena. Romans were dying, but not just the angry, opportunistic mob or the brutal sadistic guardsmen he had come to know too well. There were *people* dying—master and slaves, patricians and workmen, merchants and street urchins, women and children—and no matter how good or wicked any of them might be, the fire was destroying them all.

"The fire of Mazda," muttered Dositheus, "cleansing the earth of the vile minions of Azdahak."

Simon turned to him, saw the light of the distant inferno reflecting in his old, dark eyes. Dositheus sensed his apprentice's gaze, faced him, saw that Simon's hand clutched the Thracian knife as if about to draw it.

"You say those Romans are the minions of the Evil One," Simon said tensely. "If so, are we not such minions also—and all the rest of mankind as well? And if that be so, will it not please Mazda, the Lord of Light, to see us vile beings slay one another—as I am minded to slay you this very moment?"

Dositheus sighed. "Smite, then. I care not, for I am weary. I have erred greatly, thinking that one wrong might lead to a greater right—that an injustice to one slave girl might deliver millions from the injustice of Rome. Well, the gods decreed differently, and I and all my plans have been brought low. But before you strike me dead, Simon, reflect on this: Would the Lord of Light have been pleased had you so slain Helen, as I in my ignorance wished you to do?"

Simon sighed as Dositheus had, then shook his head somberly. "Fear not for your life, old mentor. For some reason I can no longer hate you. But what is to become of us now? And Helen?"

Dositheus scowled in thought. "Helen will be safe with Senator Junius in his household at Antium. We will go there also, for a brief time—but then, if you will still have me as your mentor, we must leave Rome and seek refuge in Parthia. Menander and Carbo shall go also, but you must leave Helen behind."

"I can't!" said Simon angrily—but seemed to feel the hand of fate upon him even as he did so.

"Oh, Simon, forgive me!" The old wizard's eyes glowed suddenly with sadness, even anguish. "Once was I also forced to lose one who was a counterpart of my own True Spirit. The Romans slew her. But you—you can leave here knowing that your counterpart still lives and shall await your return in this life, not the next. My misguided magic brought the two of you together before the gods willed it, I fear, and so now you must be parted for a time. For unless you leave Rome, Simon, the vengeful mob will soon ferret you out again. Only the passage of time can make you anonymous here."

Simon sensed the truth of it. Again he glanced back at the Mount of Caelius, where thousands were perishing in the spreading flames, then upward to where the stars shone down indifferently from the black sky. The swarms of shining globes were now vanishing swiftly away toward the zenith, dimming and fading, their work done…

At sight of them, Simon felt a chill creep over him. He knew that he would soon see Helen again, and that before long a life of travel and learning and freedom would be opening up to him—and yet he felt a somberness tingeing all his feelings. Monstrous beings fought for power over the universe, striving to keep True Spirits sundered or to reunite them into the Lord of Light, and he knew that the knowledge would always keep him from ordinary happiness or contentment. He was committed to the Eternal Struggle.

"Come on, then—to the Emporium, and Antium," said Simon, helping the faltering Dositheus down the dark streets. Nor did either of them glance back again to where the towering flames glared vengefully against the blackness of the night.

About "The Seed of the Star-God"

We pick up Simon's trail again four years later. The events of this story (which premiered in *Crypt of Cthulhu* #24, Lammas 1984) occupy the period from the autumn of A.D. 31 until the summer solstice of the following year (A.D. 32).

Through all the Simon stories it is evident that Tierney has taken very seriously not only Derleth's attempt to meld the Lovecraftian Old Ones with genuine gods of far-flung mythologies, but also Lovecraft's technique of gaining verisimilitude by giving the Old Ones' names in linguistically variant forms so as to hint at an ancient transmission of the Elder Secrets along subterranean streams within ancient cultures and religions. In particular, HP Lovecraft sought to give an Egyptian, Hebrew, Arabic, and Tatar-Tibetan ring to several of the names so as to suggest their having been handed down in the sort of documents described by Idries Shah in his *The Secret Lore of Magic: Books of the Sorcerers* (1957).

"The Seed of the Star-god" is a prime showcase for the principle in action. Tierney seamlessly weaves Shub-Niggurath, Lovecraft's fertility goddess, whom he dubs "Shupnikkurat" to give it a Sumerian slant, into the web of Mediterranean mother goddesses. She is seen to be one with Astarte, Isis, Ishtar, Cybele (the Magna Mater mentioned by Lovecraft in "The Rats in the Walls"), etc. Little adaptation was necessary in the first place, since the name Shub-Niggurath is based on Lord Dunsany's "Sheol-Nugganoth", which already contained the Hebrew plural ending so beloved of HPL, "-oth." "Sheol" is the name of the netherworld of the dead mentioned often in the Old Testament and in the Gilgamesh Epic, and this is where Ishtar descends to rescue her lover Tammuz. The many-breasted statue of Artemis described in this story really exists, and what goddess can have needed them unless she had a thousand young to suckle?

But the web of mythic associations surrounding a pair of other ancient names is even more fascinating. The evil sorcerer is striving mightily to call down "Kaiwan" the star-god, and, when he answers the call, the sorcerer calls himself "Sakkuth." These names are derived from Amos 5:26: "Was it to me that you offered sacrifices and oblations for those forty years in the wilderness, O Israel? No, but you took up Sakkuth your king, and Kaiwan your star-god...." Both are Assyrian names for the god Saturn, though "skkth" could be given slightly different vowel points resulting in "booths" or sanctuaries, shrines, as in the Jewish holy day Sukkoth, the Feast of Booths. In this case, the phrase might be rendered "You took up the shrines of your Moloch", a divine title meaning "king." Thus when Kaiwan arrives to consummate a ritual act of planetary sex magic, his human host is appropriately called "Sakkuth", another name of Saturn and a pun for the human shrine of his presence.

The Amos passage plainly verifies what scholars surmised from much other evidence—that during their existence as nomadic herders in the wilderness the people of Israel worshiped the host of heaven, the moon and the stars. Under the influence of the solar, stellar, and lunar interpretations of myth propagated by Max Muller and his disciples, Ignaz Goldziher (*Mythology among the Hebrews and Its Development*, Eng. trans., 1877) demonstrated how numerous biblical tales must have started life as symbolical descriptions of the relative motions of the heavenly bodies, as is still glaringly obvious in the cases of Samson (whose name simply means "the sun" in Hebrew), Helal son of Shahar in Isaiah 14, and some others. Abraham, the "father of a multitude", i.e., of stars, was the moon, who ever seeks to supplant his solar rival Isaac, as we see depicted symbolically in Genesis 22. The Amos passage tells us that the Hebrew nomads also worshiped Saturn, which is a hint as to the origin of the seven-day week among the Hebrews. It was based on the seven planets enumerated by the ancients, with one day per planet, and on each day the god of that planet would be honored. The especial sacredness of the Sabbath, Saturday, Saturn's Day as we still call it, may stem from the devotion to Kaiwan.

Notice that Tierney gives this star-god another name as well: "Assatur", or Hastur. "Karakossa" (Carcosa) appears in the invocation liturgy. So Tierney has gone back beyond Derleth's Hastur the Unspeakable to its source, the Hastur of Robert W. Chambers and, before him, Ambrose Bierce. You may recall that Bierce introduced Hastur as a god of shepherds in his story "Haïta the Shepherd." Chambers associates Hastur vaguely with the Hyades and with the Lake of Hali. Tierney has inherited all these mythemes and more. His imaginary derivation of "Hastur" is as follows: "I suspect that Ha-Set-Ur means something like 'Set is great' in Stygian" (Letter, May 22, 1983). Tierney connects Hastur with Set based on a detail in Robert Graves' historical novel *King Jesus*. "Graves also mentioned that the Hyksos founded Jerusalem, where they worshipped Set as 'God of Shepherds,' so I've jumped to equate Set with Hastur & so incorporate him into the Mythos" (ibid.).

This leaves us with a most interesting pattern. To the student of the relevant mythology, all this has the ring of truth about it. The ancient nomadic shepherds worshiped the moon and stars, in whose gentle silver light they might graze their stock. The fierce, unblinking sun they hated. A shepherd god would be the moon, a star, a planet, the dark night sky, etc. So Set and/or Hastur as shepherd gods would be precisely gods of the night and of the desert (as Set certainly is in Egyptian myth). Why is Hastur, a shepherds' god, associated with a "Lake of Hali" and with the Hyades? The nomads worshiped the Hyades in particular and stars in general, because they imagined that the rain fell from them. A Lake of Hali is an appropriate image, standing for a moon-lit pond at an oasis, the object of the shepherd's quest. But remember that Derleth also says Hastur is prisoned beneath the surface of the Lake of Hali. This is typical narrative allegorizing of a celestial phenomenon, in this case the reflected image of the moon "in" the lake. Thus Hastur and Hali would be two names for the moon god of the desert shepherds, Hali being the proper name, Hastur being either an epithet (the Hidden One, i.e., in the depths of the lake—see below) or an invocation (Great is Set!).

But it gets more interesting still. Tierney is identifying Set with Hastur, and in turn with Saturn, hinting at an astromythical depiction of Saturn's rings under the symbol of the Worm Ouroboros, the world-encircling serpent.

Furthermore, Saturn is of course the Roman name for the titan known in Greece as Cronus. As noted Islamic specialist Pierre de Caprona argued at some length years ago ("A Letter on the Lovecraft Mythos", *Crypt of Cthulhu* #14, St. John's Eve 1983), the myth of Cronus as known to the Arabs through Plutarch had Cronus as a banished titan sleeping away the ages bound in a chamber deep beneath the sea. In his age-long slumber, imposed by Zeus, Cronus occasionally tosses and turns, causing the sea above his confinement to foam and boil periodically. Caprona rejected the possibility that it was mere coincidence that "Cthulhu" turns out to be a good rendering of the Aramaic *ketul-hu*, "He who is imprisoned", i.e., Cronus; R'lyeh "is an acceptable transcription of the Arabic *galiyah* (or *r'aliyah*, since g is a glottal r, sometimes rendered by *r* or *r '*)" which means "boiling", i.e., "the boiling sea." Nor can it be mere chance that the name of the Cabiri (*kabirim* in Arabic) said to serve Cronus means "Elder Ones" and/or "Great Ones," hence "Great Old Ones." His hypothesis was that Lovecraft and Derleth had derived most of this from a translation of some old Arabic text setting forth the myth of Cronus. It was in just the same manner, Caprona reasons, that Madame Blavatsky had quite likely seen a copy of a real *Book of Dzyan* and subsequently spun a web of her own fancy over it. If Tierney makes Hastur the same as Kaiwan/Saturn and Caprona identifies Cthulhu as Cronus/Saturn, mustn't Cthulhu and Hastur both be myth-variants of Saturn? If we equate Hastur and Cthulhu in this way, have we not departed far more radically from the traditional framework of the Mythos than Tierney has? No, because Derleth himself originally pictured Hastur as a great, aquatic, octopoid creature at the bottom of the Lake of Hali, an image quite close to that of Cthulhu beneath the waves of the Pacific. Caprona derives the name Hastur from the Hebrew *has-gatur*, "the Veiled, the Hidden, the Concealed", i.e., beneath the surface of the Lake of Hali. That Derleth made Cthulhu and Hastur feuding half-brothers, hence different characters, need confuse no one who is familiar with the work of Rene Girard. Girard shows how literary twins usually stand for warring sides of the same person or society. The single individual or group is demonized, its evil abstracted, extracted, and cast onto another, who becomes his "evil twin" or "monstrous double." It is worth remarking that Derleth first tried to sell Lovecraft on the term "the Mythology of Hastur" and then, once HPL was gone and Derleth had free rein, he called it "the Cthulhu Mythos" instead, almost as if he thought the two were synonymous. Even the implicit logic of his tale "The Return of Hastur", the final battle notwithstanding, implies that Cthulhu and Hastur are the same entity. This is the key to making any sense of the story at all.

THE SEED OF THE STAR-GOD

by Richard L. Tierney

I. PERSEPOLIS

> I saw thee once—once only—years ago:
> I must not say how many—but not many….
> Clad all in white, upon a violet bank
> I saw thee half reclining; while the moon
> Fell on the upturn'd faces of the roses,
> And on thine own, upturn'd—alas, in sorrow!
>
> — Poe, "To Helen"

The young man stood on the steps of the ruined palace and gazed westward to the distant mountains. Toward those gray, snow-clad peaks the sun was descending, a gleam of white gold embedded in a sky of cloudless azure. A cold wind gusted momentarily, causing the man's black locks to whip about his face, and he drew his dark star-emblazoned robe more closely about his slender form.

"Helen…" he muttered, staring into the sunset.

"Fear not, Simon—you will have word of her soon."

The man whirled to face the white-bearded oldster who had stolen upon him unawares. The newcomer wore a robe similar to that of the young man's and carried a long wooden staff in his left hand; his eyes twinkled as he noted that the man he had called Simon gripped the hilt of a half-drawn blade.

"Dositheus! Don't creep up on me like that—!"

The old man chuckled amicably. "The reflexes you learned in gladiator school are good, Simon. Yet you came here to learn more subtle things. Had your mind and body been one, I could not have come upon you unawares."

Simon sheathed his sharp-bladed *sica*, then looked again to the declining sun, brushing bangs of straight black hair from his eyes. "Your dark familiar is long overdue, O Mentor."

"Only by two days or so. Much can delay the flight of a raven over the enormous distance that lies between here and Rome. Fear not. Carbo is clever; neither storm nor eagle nor the snares of man shall hinder him—so my divinations tell me. If he comes not this very evening, he shall come tomorrow—and then I shall have news from Senator Junius, and you from your Helen."

Simon, his countenance still grave, nodded briefly, then turned and strode down the wide stairway. He did not want to talk to his mentor Dositheus nor to anyone else at this time.

Circling to the north of the great ruined palace complex, he began to climb the first of the eastward hills. His athletic limbs carried him easily up the brown slopes where dried bunch-grasses bent and trembled before the chill November wind. Gaining the first low crest of the range, he turned and regarded the sunset once more. Below him sprawled the magnificent columned ruins of Persepolis, once the palaces and temples of Persian kings, now the abode only of the mysterious hermit-mage Daramos and those he instructed in arcane arts and knowledge. Westward the sun had sunk into a haze over the distant mountains—had become a crimson eye whose heatless rays bathed the wide plain of the Araxes as if with blood. Far to the north rose enormous snowy peaks, red-tinged in the waning light, like cold thrones of the minions of Angra Mainyu, Lord of Night….

Simon shuddered, then shook his head violently as if to fling off the dark mood. He had been having more and more of these heavy flashes of—premonition?—these last few days, and he did not like them. Seating himself in the lee of a boulder, he reached under his robe and brought forth several small scraps of parchment, then bent to read the Greek writing on them in the waning light.

"Helen," he muttered again.

For they were messages from her—the strange, almost supernaturally fascinating young woman he had left in Rome just over four years ago. Woman? No, only a girl of fifteen then, and he a lad going on nineteen—about the age she would be now. A girl, yet with the shadow of eternal mystery in her dark hair and eyes….

The letters were necessarily short, borne as they had been on the wings of a raven across a distance equal to half of the known world. He reread the first one as he had countless times before.

> Helen, of the household of Junius in Antium, to Simon of Gitta in Persepolis, greeting. Let my love fly to you on swift wings! The months since you fled Rome have seemed long, Simon, even though I am very happy here in my new home serving my new mistress. I am treated more like a daughter than a servant.
>
> Would that the rest of our time apart might pass as swiftly as the few weeks we spent together in Antium! Those weeks were the happiest of my life….

Simon looked up briefly, memories erasing the lines of concern from his face. He scanned the second note, which had reached him some months after the first one.

Happy news, Simon! My younger sister, Ilione, has been rescued from
our father's house in Ephesos and brought here, even as was I. My mistress, knowing my unhappiness, prevailed upon Senator Junius to buy
her, and when that failed he hired men to steal her away. Ilione's joy
knows no bounds, for our father had planned the same dark fate for
her that he had earlier for me....

The scowl of concern crept back into Simon's face. What fate could
that be? And what sort of father was it whose daughters had lived in fear of
him and rejoiced at escaping from his house forever? Helen had spoken
little enough about her life in Ephesos, but Simon knew that her father,
Prodikos, had had lustful and unlawful intentions toward her. Also, he was
reputedly one of the richest men in Ionia, and there were those who
claimed that he had used dark magic to help him gain his wealth.

Simon skipped over the two or three other brief missives to the most
recent one, which had arrived over four months ago.

. . . Senator Junius is worried. He tries to hide it, Simon, but gossip
among the servants has it that he fears Sejanus, who was supposedly an
ally of those who wish to restore the Republic. Junius fears that Sejanus, whom Tiberius has put in nearly complete charge of the empire,
is actually conspiring to be emperor himself and may even be using
dark magic to attain that end....

There it was—"dark magic" again. Too much of his life of late, Simon
mused, had been involved with "dark magic". Of course, having grown up
in his native Samaria, he had always known of such things. But not until his
mentor, Dositheus, had rescued him from a Roman gladiator school had
he known of them first hand....

Scowling in thought, he rose and thrust the parchments back into his
belt-pouch, then strode down the windswept slope toward the ruins in the
darkening twilight.

Beneath the pale light of the stars and a waxing crescent moon Simon returned to the deserted ruins and wandered to the few intact rooms that
remained of what had centuries ago been the palace of Darius the King.
Here Daramos the Mage lived in austere simplicity, and so were his few
pupils forced to live also, supplied with necessities from the nearby village
by pious worshippers of the Great Lord Mazda and the fire-god Atar. A
strange place to live, Simon reflected—not for the first time. And yet, the
years he had spent here and in other parts of Parthia had been anything but
dull.

"Simon—is that you?"

He turned to face the torch-bearing figure approaching him. It was Dositheus' young apprentice—a lad perhaps fifteen years of age, wearing the symbol-emblazoned robe common to all who studied under the tutelage of Daramos.

"Aye, Menander? What is it?"

"The Master would speak with you, Simon. He waits even now in his chamber."

Simon scowled in puzzlement. It was not Daramos' habit to seek conversation after the lessons of the day, when he was wont to retire to the solitude of his room or take to the hills in lonely wanderings. "Did he say what he wanted?"

Menander shook his head; his dark eyes seemed to glow with curiosity in the light of the torch.

Simon turned and strode down a long corridor whose roof was largely open to the sky. Near its end he came to a curtained doorway and groped his way inside. The room he entered was large but unfurnished save for a very low table and a sleeping pallet. A single torch gleamed upon the far wall beside the wide, open casement, and in the center of the floor stood the mage Daramos, facing him.

No matter how often Simon had seen the Master, he had never quite become used to him. Daramos was the strangest man he had ever seen— scarcely four feet tall, extremely stocky in build and possessing a curiously wide and flattened head large in proportion to his size. His mouth was wide and lipless, his nose flat, his outsized ears slightly pointed. His skin, usually grayish in the daylight, seemed to possess a slight greenish cast in the flickering light of the torch. Despite his strange, even grotesque appearance, his large almond-shaped eyes shone from the crinkles of his face with an expression of calm wisdom and quiet humor that set Simon immediately at ease.

"Sit down, Simon." The Master's voice was deep, possessing an almost nonhuman timbre, yet strangely soft.

The young man obeyed, sitting cross-legged facing the low table. Daramos sat opposite him, hunching down into the folds of his cloak in a peculiarly boneless way. Simon wondered, as he had often before, if this strange mentor of his were fully human. He had heard a rumor that one of Daramos' ancestors had come up from the depths of the Persian Gulf to mate with a woman of Elam.

"You wished to see me, O Master?"

"Aye, Simon. It is the time. Tomorrow you must begin your long journey back to Rome."

Simon started. "Rome? But, why—?"

"Because there are dark things stirring—things that I have sensed of late. I think you have sensed them, too, Simon. Forces are growing that threaten all mankind, and their center is currently in Rome. Now is the time for you to begin to employ all that you were taught here. You must gather your possessions together tonight and depart in the morning. Carbo will tell you why."

"Carbo? But he hasn't yet returned from Rome."

"He will return with the dawn."

Simon felt an excitement. He thought of Helen—lovely Helen, with tresses like the night, skin like alabaster, eyes like dark pools reflecting the stars of the universe and shining with the promise of more than earthly joys. Had the years made her a dream, or was she truly as he remembered her? Soon he would know!

The eyes of Daramos became lidded, then slowly reopened. "Yes, your Helen," he said. "One day you will see her again."

Simon felt a chill. "How did you know—?"

"It is not hard to sense thoughts of such intensity. You will see her, but much time must pass."

"Yes, of course. It's a long journey to Rome—months…" Simon bent forward, his deep-set eyes glowing more intently in the torchlight. "I *have* sensed dark fears of late, O Master, like the formless fears of nightmare. What are they? Sometimes I feel them like a black wall standing between Helen and me, and wonder if I shall truly see her again. In such moods I fear losing her as I would fear death."

Daramos said, "One can lose only that which one clings to."

"Aye, so you have told me often. Yet, Dositheus has warned me that it may be many more years before the time is right for Helen and me to meet again. It was his magic that first brought us together—prematurely, he claims—"

"And so you fear losing her. Listen, Simon of Gitta: You and Helen can no more lose one another than the night can lose the day. Has not Dositheus told you many times of your true nature?"

"Aye—that Helen and I are True Spirits, destined for one another beyond time and materiality. More, I seemed to *feel* this very truth when I was with Helen—even though I know also that we are only human. Yet, Dositheus believes I must lose her—that our reunion would be dangerous somehow—"

"List not to Dositheus. He has seen less than seventy summers—fewer years than I have seen of decades. You cannot lose your Helen, and your reunion with her will be when it is fated, no earlier or later. As for danger—without it the world would lose much savor in the eyes of the God and Goddess for whom it was made. More, *you* are the One who makes this world, Simon—you, and I, and many another. We are only the transient forms in which One abides. And we create this world for *her*, complete with danger, because that is what pleases her—and us."

"And what of pain and horror?"

"Aye, that too."

Simon rose impatiently, shaking his head. He had heard all this before—concepts hauntingly familiar at times, yet surely insane.

"I shall leave for Rome tomorrow, O Daramos. I hope the Romans have forgotten by now the part I played in the destruction of their arena at Fidenae and the burning of the Caelian Hill—though I doubt it."

"It matters not, Simon. If you practice the arts I have taught you, you shall not be recognized."

"What are my instructions, then?"

"You need none. You shall go to Rome with a purpose that is your own."

Puzzled, Simon bowed slightly, then left the room and strode back down the dark hall to his own chamber to pack his few belongings.

There was a stirring of fear in the heavy, formless stillness—the awareness of an ancient menace reawakening in the shadows of Old Night.

He seemed to stand upon a dark plain. Above him the cold stars gleamed down, and the slim horns of a crescent moon. Then, somehow the stars were the mirrored gleam of lovely dark eyes, celestial and eternal, and the moon was a diadem set upon tresses black as the night, and as vast. He felt terror and ecstasy strangely commingled in his soul.

We meet and we part forever, Simon of Gitta.

He held his breath in the eternal stillness, straining to hear that soft yet cosmic voice within his mind—that voice, so familiar and yet so unlike any voice of Earth:

We part, yet never can we lose one another, for in the fullness of the aeons we shall meet again. Eternal is the promise, and the promise is the fulfillment, forever and through endless changings....

The darkness lifted somewhat, and he saw that he stood by the pool within the peristyle of Senator Junius' mansion in Antium. Yet the stillness hung as heavily as before, and strange shadows and fears seemed to cling closely about him.

Then he saw her, reclining on a couch near the side of the dark pool opposite him. She was as lovely as he had remembered her, yet there was a fainting languor in her posture, and the filmy white garment she wore suggested something of the pallor of the grave. Her whiteness contrasted sharply with the surrounding shadows—shadows that seemed to close ever more closely about her, rustling like monstrous wings. A horror swept through him, and he cried out:

"Helen!"

His voice was muffled, as though he stood within a narrow tomb. The woman's dark eyes were open now, staring sadly up into the descending shadows whose pinions were swiftly enfolding her.

"Helen!"

His own cry awakened him. Simon found himself sitting upright on his pallet within his small chamber. The air was still, and the first light of dawn was filtering in through the open casement. An air of nightmare still clung about him—he still seemed to hear the fluttering of dark wings—

He *did* hear it! Turning, he beheld the form of a large black bird flapping to rest upon the wide, window sill.

"Carbo!" Simon exclaimed. "You have come back!"

Quickly he rose in the chilly air, donned his dark tunic and belt, then lit an oil lamp. The raven hopped inward and fluttered down beside it on the rough wooden table. Simon saw that the bird did not carry the usual small scroll-pouch about its neck. He suddenly felt a prickling of apprehension.

"Dark bird, why do you bear no messages?" Then, in a lower, more intense tone: "Carbo—what of Helen? Speak!"

The raven seemed to hesitate, its right eye regarding Simon like a glittering bead of jet. Then, distinctly, it croaked:

"Morta!"

"Dead...? No! *No!*"

Simon whipped out his gladiatorial knife and slashed furiously at the bird, and only its uncanny quickness saved it. With a deep squawk of terror it flapped frantically back out the window into the gray dawn.

"No!" screamed Simon again, hurling his futile blade after the swiftly vanishing raven. Then, whirling, he suddenly confronted the squat, robed form of Daramos standing just within the curtained doorway.

"It is true," said the mage quietly.

Hate and fury twisted Simon's tear-streaked face. His hands clenched and unclenched and he strode forward a pace, fully intending to tear Daramos limb from limb—but then, looking into the Master's eyes, so calm and wise and sad, he knew he could not. His anger fled, leaving only the icy anguish of mounting grief and despair.

"Now you must go to Rome," said Daramos, "for now your purpose in going is plain to you."

II. ANTIUM

... Never yet there came
Phantasms so foul through monster-teeming Hell
From the all-miscreative brain of Jove;
Whilst I behold such execrable shapes,
Me thinks I grow like what I contemplate,
And laugh and stare in loathsome sympathy.

— Shelley, "Prometheus Unbound"

Ambronius the caretaker rose stealthily from his bed and uncovered the small oil lamp that he always kept burning at night. Outside the deserted mansion he could hear the rains of late spring pattering on the flagstones, while muted thunder growled in the distance.

Cautiously the lean old man stole from his chamber into the atrium, the light from his lamp causing highlights to gleam upon his balding head and within his darting eyes. He lit a wall-bracketed torch and peered tensely around the large, columned space. Something was wrong. Though he had heard no sound, Ambronius had spent enough years in this house to sense when something was amiss.

Suddenly, with a tingle of apprehension, he realized what it was: The sound of rain on the tiles was louder than it should be because the door to the peristyle was slightly ajar—

"Ambronius, do not cry out—it's me, Simon of Gitta."

The old man whirled with a start of terror to see that a dark-cloaked man had emerged from the shadows only a few feet from him. The hood of the damp cloak was thrown back, revealing a youthful but angular face in which deep-set eyes glowed intently.

"Simon! What—how—?"

"I have returned from Parthia, to learn of what befell Helen."

"But—how did you gain entrance? There is a guard at each door."

"To stop me, they would have had to see me. The one at the back gate dozed; I whispered in his ear and made his sleep deeper. He will awaken at dawn, remembering nothing."

Thunder muttered again, and Ambronius shuddered. Evidently Simon had learned strange things in Parthia.

"Come," he said, taking the torch from its bracket. "There are no windows in my room—we can talk there."

Inside, Simon looked around the rather large chamber while Ambronius closed the door and bracketed the torch. "This was your master's sleeping room," he commented.

"Aye, but he will be using it no more. Senator Junius was exiled to Lesbos on a trumped-up charge after his involvement in Sejanus' plot against the emperor became suspected; his household chose to share exile with him. Now Tiberius has confiscated all his property and I, as Junius' chief steward, remain here at Antium only until this mansion is sold."

"The senator was lucky," said Simon. "I have heard in Rome that most of those implicated in that plot were imprisoned or executed."

Ambronius nodded and set his lamp on a table, then seated himself. "I am so sorry about Helen, Simon," he said, laying a hand on the young man's arm. "All of us knew how close you two had become here."

Simon took a chair opposite the old steward. There was no sadness in his eyes, only a grim hardness. "Tell me all," he said.

Ambronius took a deep breath. "You know that Junius kept no secrets from me," he began. "I was with him on some of the occasions when he and a few other prominent Romans met with Sejanus in his mansion on the Palatine Hill. Of course you knew, Simon, of my master's devotion to the cause of overthrowing the cruel reign of the Augustans and restoring the Republic."

Simon nodded. "He spoke of it often to my mentor, Dositheus."

"I remember. Dositheus was even in on the plot once—"

"You *should* remember, for his tampering with dark magic resulted in the destruction of the Caelian section of Rome by fire and necessitated my flight with him to Antium and eventually Parthia. But I came here to learn of Helen. Spare me none of the details."

Ambronius sighed. "Dark magic—it runs like a venom-steeped thread through all our destinies, it seems! For Sejanus, too, came finally to employ the black arts in his conspiracy against Tiberius."

"What! Sejanus—?"

"Aye. My master was disturbed to learn of it—for you will remember how he opposed Dositheus for the same thing. Moreover, he had slowly come to suspect that Sejanus was not interested in reestablishing the Republic at all, but only in setting himself up as emperor in Tiberius' stead.

"It seems that the former empress, Livia, had delved heavily into sorcery and had amassed a considerable library of ancient books on the subject. According to Sejanus, she had employed this dark knowledge to slay certain enemies of her son Tiberius and so pave his way to power. Tiberius, as suspicious and vindictive as Livia herself, repaid her by depriving her of all power of her own and finally confining her to house arrest. Such was typical of his reaction to friend and foe alike. Ironically, he trusted Sejanus alone, delegating to him more and more power and authority, and when at last the mad emperor's growing fears drove him to seek seclusion upon the isle of Capri, it was Sejanus who was left to handle matters in Rome.

"Sejanus boasted that it was his own use of sorcery that had fired Tiberius's fears and driven him to seek seclusion and safety far from Rome—for after Livia's confinement, Sejanus claimed he had discovered her collection of arcane books and set himself to master the sinister arts they explicated. More, he turned them against Livia herself, claiming not only to have caused her terminal illness but also to have trapped her soul in the body of a weasel, which he now employed as his familiar. I myself heard Sejanus expound these things to Senator Junius, and at the time considered the man to have become as mad as Tiberius himself.

"It was three years ago that Livia died, and after that Sejanus' power grew by leaps and bounds. His power in Rome was absolute, his spies everywhere, and a word in the Senate was enough to send any of his enemies to doom, no matter how rich or powerful they might be. More and more his audacious ambition to be emperor became plain, and often I pointed it out to my master; but so deep was the senator's hope to restore the Republic that he continued to delude himself that it was Sejanus' hope also.

"Then, less than a year ago, Sejanus' boastful and confident manner began to change slowly to one of nervous taciturnity. He became more and more suspicious and irritable. Then one day, when my master and I and a number of others were gathered in Sejanus' house, a feeling of gloom and tension suddenly fell upon us, as tangible as a cold mist. I felt terrified, as if some monstrous evil being had come unseen among us, and I know all the others felt that way also. The room seemed to vibrate slightly, so that lamps and statues rattled and swayed—and suddenly a large couch on which several people were seated broke apart and sent them all sprawling to the floor.

"Immediately the tension vanished, and some even laughed as if it were all a great joke, but Sejanus was white as a ghost and soon found pretext to adjourn our meeting. As he was ushering us out of the house, a large gray weasel suddenly darted through our midst uttering sounds like high-pitched laughter. Sejanus became so pale I thought he would faint, and I could not help but remember what he had said concerning Livia.

"We saw less of Sejanus after that, but on a later occasion Senator Junius confided to me his fear that the man might indeed be going mad. It seems that after a dinner party subsequent to the eerie events at his house, Sejanus spoke privately to my master about them. He claimed, with pronounced nervousness informing his every word and gesture, that Tiberius had become suspicious of a plot against him and had hired a powerful sorcerer to discover its nature and combat it. It was that sorcerer's presence which we had all felt in the room before the couch collapsed; moreover, that sorcerer had freed Livia's soul from Sejanus' control and made the weasel his own familiar. And now, Sejanus said, the vindictive empress was working against him, prowling and spying about his mansion at night, scuttling and tittering and giving him no peace."

"All this is interesting," Simon interrupted, "but what has it to do with Helen?"

"I am coming to that. Sejanus told my master that he sent a spy to Capri and thereby learned of the sorcerer that Tiberius had recently hired. Actually, the man had come to the emperor and offered his services. He was from Ephesos, a city as full of dark magic as Egypt is of grain, and his name was Prodikos."

"Prodikos!" Simon exclaimed. "That was the name of—Helen's father...?"

"Aye. They are one and the same."

Simon scowled in thought. "Helen once mentioned to me that he had dabbled in magic, but—a sorcerer?"

"The most powerful in Ephesos, according to what Junius was told. Sejanus was deathly afraid of the man—and with good reason, judging from what ensued.

"My master heard less and less of this matter, for as time passed Sejanus became more taciturn and reclusive. I learned, however, from one of his trusted servants, that Sejanus was performing elaborate magical rites in order to protect himself from dark forces he supposed were being brought against him.

"One day early last October, so my informant said, Sejanus was sacrificing before a statue of himself when suddenly a burst of dark smoke issued from the image. He hastily ordered the head removed, whereupon a huge black serpent darted forth from the hollow interior. It was killed barely in time, and proved to be an extremely poisonous snake of African origin. On another occasion the same statue was found with a strangler's cord knotted about the neck. Evidently someone was entering the house unseen and performing these tricks in order to terrorize Sejanus—and they were accomplishing their goal extremely well.

"Sejanus finally attempted a great feat of magic in an effort to defend himself. Somewhere he had procured an ancient statue of Fortuna that had been made centuries ago in the reign of Servius Tullius, King of Rome, and to this image he performed a dark sacrifice designed to thwart and destroy his enemies."

"Aye—the Tempting of Fortune," muttered Simon, "an extremely powerful and dangerous ritual, and only to be performed by the most skilled adepts."

Ambronius regarded him narrowly. "That may well be, for something evidently went wrong. The statue spoke to Sejanus in a hollow voice, announcing his impending doom, then turned away from him on its pedestal and faced the wall.

"Sejanus was terrified. The very next day he journeyed to Antium and presented the statue to my master as a gift, hoping thereby to avert the doom from himself. Of course we did not know his motive at the time—he described the thing as a family heirloom and expressed the desire that Senator Junius would accept it as a token of his high esteem. It was not till several days later that I was told of Sejanus' monstrous ritual, and by then he was dead. His subterfuge had not kept him from his doom.

"That doom came very suddenly, in the form of a letter of denunciation from Tiberius to the Senate. Without warning Sejanus was hauled off to prison and before evening he had been executed. His corpse was hurled down the Gemonian stairway and allowed to lie in the streets for three days, abused by the mob, before being thrown into the Tiber.

"Swift as was Sejanus' demise, it seems that Tiberius and his hired sorcerer had planned it for some time, befuddling his mind with sorcery and terror while gradually removing his friends from positions of power. And now Tiberius began a vindictive purge of his enemies that was even more terrible than the one that Sejanus had instituted. Scores who had known Sejanus only casually had their property confiscated and sold, dozens suspected of involvement in his plot against the emperor were slain, scores more were imprisoned or banished. Sejanus' entire family was executed, his young daughter first being raped by the executioner because it was not legally permissible to put a virgin to death. And in the midst of all this mad and bloody turmoil, Helen's father Prodikos came one evening with several Praetorian guardsmen to this very mansion, demanding that we turn Helen and her sister Ilione over to him."

Simon gripped the edge of the table. "Why? How did he know—?"

"Evidently the return of his daughters was the payment he demanded of Tiberius for forestalling Sejanus' plot. Many of Sejanus' friends had been here and knew of the two sisters—perhaps one of these people talked. Or, perhaps Prodikos discovered their presence here by means of his own magic. I think he may have been capable of it—I sensed an aura of dark menace about him."

"And—and then—?"

"They forced their way in; we could not stop them, and in any case they had written permission from the emperor. Helen and Ilione were in the peristyle and were taken unawares; I will never forget the look of shock in their faces. Ilione sank to her knee in terror, poor girl!—but Helen, after her first shock, rose and faced her father with a proud anger and cried out: 'Monster, you shall not have your way!' Then, before anyone could move, she snatched up a sharp stylus with which she had been writing and plunged it into her heart."

Simon shuddered and gripped his face in both hands. When at last he looked up again there was a grim fire gleaming within his deep-set eyes.

"Tell me the rest," he said, his voice tense yet even.

"Prodikos took Ilione—two of the guards carried her away fainting between them. He left with scarcely a glance at Helen, who lay dead beside the peristyle pool."

"She shall be avenged," Simon muttered. "Tell me, what do you know about this Prodikos?"

"I know nothing more, save that he is said to have returned to Ephesos with his surviving daughter. Simon, what kind of a father could—?"

Simon rose abruptly. "I thank you, Ambronius. There is yet one thing more that you can do for me if you will."

The old servant rose also, sadness in his eyes. "I will do anything I can for you."

"Good. Show me the statue of Fortuna which Sejanus gave to your master."

Ambronius regarded the young man silently for a moment, then took up the lamp and beckoned him to follow.

They traversed the wide atrium and ascended a stairway to the upper floor of the house. At the end of a corridor Ambronius paused to unlock a door, then ushered Simon into a small, cluttered room. For a moment the old servant rummaged amid a dusty jumble of furniture and trinkets near the back wall.

"Here it is," he said after a moment, pointing.

Simon stepped forward and carefully picked up the thing. It was about two feet long—a robed female figure of austere countenance carved of dark gray stone. He sensed an aura of antique mystery about it—mystery, and perhaps even a touch of menace...?

Simon grinned tautly, almost fiercely, as he gazed down into the face of the image. Dark Fortune. It was fitting. He would go to Ephesos, bearing dark fortune with him.

"Thank you, Ambronius," he muttered, a grim vibrancy in his voice. "I came to Rome seeking a purpose, and now I think I have found it."

"Simon—" The old man seemed hesitant. "Simon, there is hate in your soul. I remember that you once swore, after the destruction of the arena and the Caelian Hill, that you would never again have aught to do with true sorcery "

"That was before." Simon's eyes were shadowed, absent, as if he gazed into distant pits of darkness. "That was before...."

III. EPHESOS

But what is it that stirs in that dim fane?
What sifts the dust and breathes the stagnant air
And groans at night within that frightful lair—
There on that demon-hill obscene, insane?

— Fantina, "Shub-Niggurath"

The white walls and columns of the city were tinged with the red of sunset as the ship's oars moved it slowly up the narrow harbor toward the piers. Simon, leaning on the rail near the bow, gazed fixedly ahead. A warm ocean breeze gently whipped his black locks and the folds of his dark tunic.

Ephesos, its walls tinged red as if with blood—and beyond it, massively grand even in great distance, the multi-columned temple of the great Earth Mother the Greeks called Artemis....

But his thoughts were not on architectural wonders. This was the city of his enemy, the sorcerer Prodikos, father of Helen. Her memory rested more easily on his soul now, after the many long months of travel from Parthia to Italy and finally here, yet he knew another feeling that would never rest until vengeance should be accomplished.

Helen—she seemed almost unreal now, distant enough to be remembered calmly. He wondered what his life would have been like had they been reunited—and found that he could not picture it. What, after all, had he wanted with her? Marriage? Children? No, none of these meaningless things that made up the dismal, eternal whirl of countless human lives generation after generation. His love for Helen had nothing to do with all that. When he had been with her, that had been a perfection unto itself, beyond dreams and goals—and yet, it had at the same time somehow contained a promise beyond earthly things. Where it might have led he would never know....

His musings were interrupted by the sound of the hull coming to rest against the stone pier. Without waiting for the sailors to secure the ship or put out the gangway, Simon grabbed his small bundle of possessions, climbed easily over the rail and dropped the short distance to the quay, then began to stride rapidly away through the wharfside crowd.

"Simon!"

He whirled, and was astonished to recognize Menander hurrying toward him. The lad was clad in a plain Grecian tunic, and close behind him was white-bearded Dositheus with the raven Carbo perched upon his shoulder.

"Baal!" Simon swore. "How—what are *you* doing here—?"

"Daramos told us you would be arriving today," said Dositheus.

"By the gods! And how did *he* know?"

"Need you ask, Simon? Daramos knows much. And now, he wishes to speak with you. Follow us."

"You mean he's *here?*"

"Yes—in a way. Please, come quickly."

Simon shook his head. "I have no wish to see Daramos—ever again."

"He says it is of great importance."

"Not as important as what I have to do."

Dositheus looked narrowly into his former pupil's grim visage. "Then at least come with Menander and me. We must talk."

Simon nodded curtly, shouldered his bundle, and followed the pair up the broad colonnaded avenue that led from the harbor into the heart of the teeming city. Before long they came to an inn that looked reasonably large and comfortable. A servant led them into a curtained back room containing a rough wooden table and several stools.

"Sit down, Simon. We have much to tell you."

Serving-girls entered and began to set bowls of fruit, meat, and lentil soup on the table. Simon realized he was hungry; he took a seat and broke a bread roll without further ado. The others joined him, the raven hopping down from old Dositheus' shoulder to strut and peck among the edibles.

"I know why you came," said Dositheus when the servants had left. "Daramos has divined it. There is great danger in what you intend to do, Simon."

"Daramos lied to me. He said I would see Helen again."

The old adept's eyes narrowed as he bent forward. "You will, Simon. When it is the time, she will come again to you."

Simon snorted impatiently. "Bring wine!" he called out to the servants. Then: "I will tell you what I learned in Rome, Dositheus. But don't expect to talk me into going back to Parthia with you. I have much to do here."

"I think I know what you learned. Tiberius' purge of his enemies is no secret, and Carbo recently brought me another message from Senator Junius, who has been recalled from exile in Lesbos to house arrest in Rome. The senator told me about Prodikos and his daughters, and I have learned much more here in Ephesos."

Simon stopped eating. "What have you learned of Prodikos?"

"Much, Simon, but mainly that in this city renowned for its sorcerers, he is the most powerful and feared of them all."

A serving-girl entered with an amphora of wine, and Dositheus ceased speaking. When she had gone Simon filled his goblet. "Go on," he said.

"Prodikos had several children by various slave women, but all were sons save Helen and Ilione. These sons he long ago sold into slavery, but his daughters he kept—for an evil purpose, as it turns out. Simon, it is no mere incestuous lust that drives Prodikos. He means to force Ilione to join with him in a monstrous ritual that shall release forces this world has not seen since it emerged from the last great darkness of the All-Night."

Simon drained his goblet, set it down and refilled it. "How do you know all this?"

"Daramos divined much of it after you left Persepolis. Believe it, Simon! This was the fate Helen's father planned for her; she escaped in the only way she could, and well for her that she did! But now Ilione faces the same monstrous fate."

Simon resumed eating. "Which is—?"

"The rite of the Impregnation and the Slaying—an act of sympathetic magic that shall cause the seed of the Star-god to unite with the Great Mother, thereby generating a horrendous spawn that will overwhelm this world."

Simon gripped his goblet tensely. His scalp tingled as he recalled reading of just such a black ritual in the *Sapientia Magorum* of the ancient Persian magus Ostanes. "Gods of Hades! How could the girl's own father even think of such perverse madness—?"

Dositheus drew a deep breath. "He may no longer be her true father, Simon. Have you not read of Sakkuth, King of Night, and his evil Master?"

Simon felt the tingling extend down his spine. Sakkuth the King, servitor of Kaiwan the Star-god—both evil beings cursed by the ancient prophets yet still furtively worshipped by sorcerers in his own native Samaria....

"The wizards of Acheron and Stygia and even older civilization cycles knew them by other names," Dositheus went on. "To the nations of primal Attluma they were Kossuth and Assatur. It is said that every thousand years Sakkuth attempts to destroy civilization, and that he succeeds unless powerful magic is used to stop him. It was he who plunged the world into the All-Night after the Atlantean and Hyborian cataclysms. And to initiate such times, his master Kaiwan, who dwells amid the stars near the Eye of Taurus, sends to earth his seed to unite with the Great Mother, thereby enabling her to spawn the Thousand Abominations that will overwhelm the world."

"But—what has all this to do with—?"

"With Prodikos? Listen, Simon: fifteen years ago Prodikos went to Sardis to partake in the festival to Cybele. He was there when the great earthquake struck, killing tens of thousands in the city and the surrounding towns. You were but a child then."

Simon nodded. "I remember. I was eight. There was much talk of it even in Samaria."

"Daramos divined some years later that the event had signified the return of Sakkuth to this world—and not long after you left Persepolis, Simon, his divinations revealed to him that Sakkuth's dark spirit had entered the body of none other than Prodikos of Ionia.

"I have talked with many here who remember the man's change of personality after his return from Sardis. It was then that he sold his sons into slavery. Also, he sacrificed more and more often at the great temple of Artemis—who is, after all, only an avatar of Cybele, the Great Mother—and his fortune began to increase mightily, till in a few years he was the richest man in all Ionia. And finally he became high priest of Artemis' very temple—perhaps the most exalted position Ephesos has to offer. So now, Simon, you see the sort of foe we are up against."

"Not 'we', Dositheus. Prodikos is mine alone."

"Don't be rash! This is a peril the like of which the world has not faced for at least a thousand years. Listen, and I will tell you the rest of what Daramos has learned.

"Ages ago, before the destruction of Hyborios, there fell to earth in the wilds of what is now Sarmatia a fire-stone called *Ajar-Alazwat*—a seed of the Star-god. For many years it was worshipped in a temple built for it by wizards, its baleful power blighting the surrounding lands, till at last benign sorcery managed to destroy its temple and send it back to the stars.

"There was a remnant, however, which was salvaged from the ruins centuries later by Stygian wizards and taken south to a temple atop what is now known as *Saru Yeri*—Star Mountain—in Pontus. And there, during the many-thousand-year All-Night that followed the destruction of the Hyborian nations, it was worshipped by dark adepts and savages and demons.

"Then, over a thousand years ago, Hittite wizards again managed to prevent the return of Sakkuth to this world. The dark adepts, fleeing Star Mountain, brought the *Ajar-Alazwat* with them and established it in a shrine to the Earth Mother in the land of the Amazons near what is now Ephesos. The land prospered, and when King Croesus rebuilt the shrine as a huge temple, his fortunes prospered enormously also. Nearly four hundred years ago a man named Herostratus burned it to the ground, sensing its evil nature. The priests called him mad, claiming that he had done it only in order that his name might be remembered forever, but the book of Ostanes records the man's true and benign motive.

"The Ephesians rebuilt the temple, more enormous than ever, and within it erected a colossal image of many breasted Artemis, in the crown of which was concealed the *Ajar-Alazwat*—and there it rests to this day, unwittingly worshipped by thousands."

Simon scowled thoughtfully. "I have heard the legend that the first image of Ephesian Artemis descended from the sky. Yet it is also said that it came from Jupiter, not the face of the Bull—"

"And is not the Bull an avatar of Jupiter? Believe it, Simon—the thing that fell to earth long ago is the seed of Kaiwan the Star-god."

"But, this is madness! What has the great Earth Mother to do with a star-being?"

"This: that she, too, is originally from the starry voids—from the dark planet Iadit which circles the Goat Star. She and black Kaiwan have been mates for countless aeons, with Sakkuth as their servitor. Long before mankind arose, She came to this world and founded the city of Harag-Kolath in vast caverns far beneath the southern deserts of Arabia—and there She waits to this day, served by her countless demon-spawn and waiting to spawn again."

Simon pushed the food and wine from him. He was no longer hungry.

"This ritual that will unite the star-seed with the Great Mother—when does Prodikos mean to perform it?"

"This very night, Simon. Three hours before dawn, when the Eye of Taurus and the Goat Star are rising, he will open the Gate to Harag-Kolath and perform the Abominable Rite."

"Then I have work to do." Simon stood up, reached into his bundle, and pulled forth a large oblong object wrapped in cloth. "Keep my possessions, Menander; if I do not return, they are yours."

"Simon, wait—" cried the lad.

But before he or Dositheus could say more the young man had dashed through the curtained doorway and out of the inn, vanishing into the dark.

Simon strode hurriedly up the wide avenue in the deepening twilight. The crowds had thinned, and many torches were gleaming along the endless colonnades. Nearly a mile farther on, the avenue ended at a huge half-bowl of a theatre carved from a hillside. Not far from here, after asking directions, Simon found a small library open to the public and went inside.

"We are about to close," a scholarly-looking Greek in a long tunic informed him.

Simon handed the man a few coins. "This won't take long. I wish to consult the *Sapientia Magorum*. Is there a copy here?"

The man nodded and walked away, returning shortly with a bulky yellowed scroll. Simon took it to a table and unrolled it, wondering a bit at the ease with which he had achieved his goal. The ancient book of Ostanes was rare and in many places forbidden. To find it would have been nearly impossible in Italy, and difficult even in Simon's native Samaria, but here in this wizard-riddled Ephesos it was easily available even at a public library.

Quickly Simon found the formula dealing with the Tempting of Fortune and copied it out on a scrap of parchment. Then, handing back the scroll to the watchful librarian, he asked: "How do I find the house of Prodikos?"

The Greek nervously made a sign in the air before him. "His villa is just northwest of the city, on the road to the great temple of Artemis. But why, on this night of all nights, would you go there?"

"Is this night special?"

"Midsummer? Of course. And tonight Prodikos will not be home, for at midnight he is to conduct the first rite of the Great Ripening."

"Perhaps I plan to attend."

"Such is not possible. It has been announced that only a small number of chosen priestesses will attend the ceremony. The public will not be admitted until tomorrow."

Simon thanked the man, handed him another coin and hurried out into the night. The streets were dark now, but the light of a waxing half-moon enabled him to see well enough.

In less than an hour he had exited the city's western gate and in a few more minutes saw the dark bulk of Prodikos' mansion hulking before him. There were no lights burning within as far as he could see, but then the wall surrounding the place hid the lower windows.

Carefully he stole along this wall, keeping within the shadows of trees and shrubbery as much as he was able, until he came to the front gate. There, just within the archway, he spied two dark-robed guardsmen lounging.

Softly as a leopard he crept to within a few feet of them, until he could hear their muttered jests and low laughter. Their spears leaned against the wall of the arch, and there was a faint smell of wine on the air.

Simon waited a few moments to make sure no other guards were around. Then one of the men leaned across and handed a wineskin to the other—and in that instant, Simon darted in and grabbed them both from behind, crooking his arms about their throats.

An instant of pressure—and then they went limp without even a chance to cry out.

Hurriedly Simon dragged them within the gate and concealed their unconscious forms in the shrubbery, reflecting that sometimes his gladiator training was more useful even than the arts his mentors had taught him in Persia. Then he stripped one of the guards of his cloak and iron helmet and quickly donned them—when suddenly there was a soft footfall within the gate.

Simon whirled, snatching out his sharp-bladed *sica*. A slender form, clad in a dark tunic similar to his own, was approaching.

"Simon, don't—it's me!"

"Baal!" Simon hissed, recognizing Dositheus' young apprentice and the black blot of Carbo perched upon his shoulder. "Menander, are you trying to get yourself killed—?"

"No. I want to help you."

"And did Dositheus send you? No need to answer—I see his dark familiar is keeping you company."

"But I *do* want to help! May I?"

"Well," said Simon grudgingly, "I see you've learned some of your skills well—otherwise you could not have followed me undetected all this way. Hurry, put on this other guard's cape and helmet, then take one of those spears and watch the gate. And get Carbo out of sight. I'm going to try to penetrate the mansion."

No sooner had the lad complied, however, than the double doors of the house swung suddenly open and the light of many torches streamed out. The sound of low chanting was heard as a procession of robed figures began to file from the mansion.

"Too late to run," hissed Simon. "Stand at attention—and hope that these helmets hide our faces sufficiently!"

IV. HARAG-KOLATH

> . . . Lo you, there,
> That hillock burning with a brazen glare;
> Those myriad dusky flames with points aglow
> Which writhed and hissed and darted to and fro;
> A Sabbath of the Serpents, heaped pell-mell
> For Devil's roll-call and some fete of Hell.

> — Thompson, "The City of Dreadful Night"

Six black-robed guardsmen bearing spears and torches marched slowly out, two abreast, and Simon tensed as he saw the tall, imposing figure that followed them. The man was slender, yet there was great power in his stride, a kingliness in his mien. He wore a dark robe emblazoned with what Simon recognized as Egyptian and Stygian symbols. His features were lean and dark, his head shaven, his short-trimmed beard jet black—and his deep yellow eyes burned with an eerie light of their own, like dying suns. In his right hand he carried a black staff shaped like a snake, and upon his left shoulder crouched what appeared to be a large gray weasel with eyes as yellow as his own.

Instantly Simon knew this was Prodikos—for even in those sinister ascetic features he saw a touch of resemblance to Helen's own. For an instant he thought of springing forward and driving his spear through the sorcerer's black heart—but something held him back. There was an aura of menace about the man, and Simon sensed that he might be guarded by powers greater than the mere weapons of his soldiers. Besides, he dared not risk Menander....

In that moment of hesitation Prodikos passed through the archway, and behind him came more torch-bearing guards, perhaps a score of them, marching in double file. In their midst walked a slender young woman, obviously a captive. Somewhat shorter than Helen, and blonde rather than dark-haired, Simon yet noted in her features also a slight resemblance to Helen's. She wore naught but silvery high-strapped sandals and a brief tunic, white and diaphanous. Her arms were bound behind her with white cords and her long hair hung down over her bare shoulders in a single golden wave. She walked with a dreamy sedateness, as if under a spell.

"That must be Ilione," whispered Menander. "Gods, she's beautiful! Simon, we can't let them hurt her—"

"Quiet! We'll do what we can. Fall in behind the last of these guards as they file out the gate."

Menander nodded. Just as the last soldier exited, the lad turned and uttered a soft bird call, then followed Simon's order. As they joined the end of the column unnoticed, Simon heard a fluttering atop the wall and knew that the raven would be following them in the night.

The road upon which they slowly marched northward under the moon was as straight as an arrow, and as they proceeded the black-robed soldiers chanted in cadence to their steps, over and over:

"Iä, Assatur! Iä, Shupnikkurat!
Kumat Karakossa ut Arag-Kolat!"

Simon suppressed a shudder as he recognized the chant as one he had once read on an ancient Elamite clay tablet—part of a Mesopotamian ritual calling upon the Star-god and the Great Mother to come forth from their dark abodes.

After perhaps a mile they came upon many more black-robed guardsmen flanking the roadway, and presently passed through a gate in a high wall. Inside was an enormous enclosure surrounding the temple of Artemis, and Simon gasped to see that temple's columned bulk soaring colossally upward into the night. Even seen indistinctly in the dim light of the red westering moon, its grandeur was overwhelming.

In a few more moments they were filing up the wide steps of the platform, nearly twice the height of a man, upon which the temple rested. The chant of the soldiers echoed as they marched between great columns and through the enormous high doorway—and then Simon gasped again at what he saw. Ahead, beyond another huge quadrangle of columns upon many of which bracketed torches blazed, there stretched a great marble-

floored space partly open to the sky—the inner temple, or *cella*—and within the roofed portion of it a grim and terrible statue towered nearly to the
ceiling.

Simon gaped at the thing, incredulous. Never had he seen anything so
overpowering, so—evil.

It was only partly human in form. The face, terrible in its classic Grecian calm, seemed to stare directly down upon the beholder; its arms, half-
extended, seemed to threaten an awful embrace. Up these arms strange
graven creatures seemed to crawl, and the tapering lower limbs appeared
strangely enclosed as if within a symbol-carved Egyptian mummy-case.
Strangest of all, a cluster of enormous breasts or half-eggs covered the being's entire front. Atop its head rested a great cylindrical crown, and just
above its feet was carved a huge bee—symbol of all things that spawn and
swarm. In the flickering light of myriad torches the dark towering eidolon
almost seemed to pulsate as if with life, and Simon knew that he looked
upon the world's most imposing representation of the Great Mother, Mistress of Earth and mate of Kaiwan the Star-god.

The two lines of guards were separating as they marched out beyond
the columns onto the vast floor, arranging themselves along the edge of
the space and facing the looming idol. Quickly Simon gripped Menander's
arm and pulled him back into the shadows.

"Simon, what are we going to—?"

"Wait," Simon whispered back. "Let's see what they're doing."

Most of the guardsmen were taking up positions in front of the columns surrounding the great *cella*, while Prodikos advanced straight across
the wide marble floor, followed by Ilione and the two guards who flanked
her. Simon noticed that the weasel was no longer on the sorcerer's shoulder, and hoped it was not prowling in the nearby shadows. The four
stopped not far from the front of the lofty idol, beside a black-draped altar
that stood between a pair of flaming braziers. Prodikos gestured. Ilione at
once sat on the edge of the altar, then lay back and arranged herself full-
length upon it, all seemingly voluntarily. The two guards quickly lashed her
ankles with more white cord to rings set in the altar's sides, then withdrew
to join their companions near the columns.

Prodikos faced the towering statue, raising his serpent-staff, and began
to chant in what Simon recognized as the ancient Elamite tongue. Obviously, despite what the librarian had said, Prodikos had seen to it that there
would be none of the usual virgin priestesses here tonight. Now Simon
knew why the public was being kept away—for this was no ordinary ritual,
and if Ostanes had written truly it was one that the world had not seen for
at least a thousand years.

"Follow me," Simon whispered; then, when they stood in the deep-shadowed southwestern corner far from the guards: "Now, Menander, stay here at the foot of the stair and watch. If anyone comes, hide and send Carbo up to warn me."

"But—where *is* Carbo?"

Simon looked around in exasperation. "Damn it, if you don't know, I surely don't! I guess you'll just have to creep up and warn me yourself, if it becomes necessary." So saying, he turned and began to hurry quietly up the spiral stairway.

In a moment he reached the top and moved cautiously forward through the shadows of more columns, till he reached the balustrade whence he could look out and down into the great central space. The high floor upon which he stood was a wide ledge that circled the entire temple, but high as it was the half-open roof was far loftier yet, and the head of Astarte's colossal image still seemed to stare down at him from a vast height.

For a moment Simon judged the distance to the chanting form of Prodikos while fingering the shaft of his spear, but finally decided against trying a cast. It was too far, especially in this uncertain light, and he could even hit the girl by mistake. Besides, he again had that uneasy feeling that the sorcerer might somehow be protected by spells from physical weapons.

Carefully he knelt and laid down his spear, then untied the cord that held his long cloth-wrapped bundle to his knife-belt. Unwrapping the cloth, he took forth the ancient statue of Fortuna and gazed at it. It seemed ordinary now, a mere lump of rock in his hands. He closed his eyes and let his mind go blank, the way Daramos had taught him to do—and in a moment felt again that vague aura of mystery and menace that he had sensed upon seeing it for the first time in Antium. It had been used in an attempt to conjure ill fortune upon Prodikos, and though the dark sorcerer had managed to turn Sejanus' own spell back upon him, some of the force of that spell still lingered.

Slowly, keeping in the shadow of a column as much as possible, Simon stood the image atop the balustrade so that it faced toward Prodikos and the idol that towered beyond him. Then, drawing from his belt-pouch the scrap of parchment upon which he had copied Ostanes' ritual, he silently reread it in the dim light. It must now be read audibly, yet not loud enough to be heard by those below. More, every syllable of the archaic Latin must be pronounced correctly, and the final word of the formula—the name of the goddess Fortuna   must be intoned at exactly the right moment.

Simon drew a deep breath. Most of the things he had learned in Persia were mere arts of illusion, and never before had he tried to perform a powerful and dangerous work of true magic such as this. Yet, the attempt had to be made....

But then, before he could utter even the first word of the rite, something flew up at him from the torchlit space below—something long and black that buzzed harshly as it came darting directly at his face.

Menander waited restlessly in the darkness for many long minutes listening to the sound of Prodikos chanting, remembering what old Dositheus had said about this ritual and growing more and more uneasy about Ilione's fate. Finally, deciding that it would do no harm to leave the stair unguarded for but a moment, he crept slowly forward through the rows of columns until he could see clearly into the torchlit central space. Silently he crouched in the shadows, hardly daring to breathe, for the nearest guardsmen were now only a few feet away, just beyond the final row of columns.

Ilione lay motionless, white against the altar's black drapery and the shadows beyond. Prodikos was facing away from her, toward the towering idol, serpent-staff upraised as he chanted loudly, and Menander shuddered as he recalled the little he had heard of this abominable rite—the impregnation of a virgin daughter by her father's seed, followed by the sacrifice that would open the Gate and allow the mating of the Earth Mother and the Star-god....

Suddenly he realized that the great idol of Astarte was undergoing a slight change. The crown above its lofty brow—the crown wherein was housed the ancient star-stone—was glowing slightly. Also, there was a peculiar glow of a different sort forming just in front of the idol's pedestal—a swirling grayish luminescence that expanded slowly.

"Open the Gate to thy world, Great Mother," Prodikos was chanting in Greek. "Come forth from Harag-Kolath, thy caverned city, and witness this rite to thy glory. I ask it in thy many names: Cybele, Magna Mater, Astarte, Ashtoreth, Artemis, Ishtar, Nintu, Shupnikkurat...."

The glow at the idol's base had expanded greatly, and now Menander's spine tingled as he realized that it was a hole in space, a Gate to other realms. He seemed to be looking into a vast cavernous space filled with a dim fungoid luminosity, and glimpsed afar off within it what seemed to be lines and angles of strange architecture. Gods!—was this indeed Harag-Kolath, the fabled underground city where dwelt the Great Mother and her swarming brood....?

Then a black object emerged from the glow—a flying object about the length of a man's hand and forearm that buzzed deeply as it circled about the altar. Another emerged and yet another, and in a moment several of them were filling the *cella* with their harsh buzzings. In the dim light Menander thought they resembled giant wasps. Then—did he glimpse something terrific and dark rising slowly from the distant alien architecture beyond the Gate—?

And Prodikos—surely he, too, was changing! His tall form was seeming to shorten and broaden somewhat, his shoulders to hunch, his ears—

"To thee also do I call, O Star-god," the sorcerer was intoning. "Hear thy servant, even him thou hast appointed king over this planet. Transform me now from thy Dark Servitor into the Golden King, even as thou hast promised. O Nameless One, O Unknown God, I ask it by the Names thou hast made known to thy worshippers: *Kaiwan! Assatur!*"

Instantly, incredibly, Prodikos' dark robe brightened until it became a glowing yellow that outshone the torches. Menander gasped at the sight— then almost cried aloud in horror as the sorcerer threw open his cloak and whirled about to face the altar. Though still recognizable, Prodikos had become a frightening parody of himself—a hairy, swarthy satyr-like being with pointed ears, horns and fangs, and obviously in the heat of lust.

He advanced to Ilione's side and with one clawed hand ripped away her gauzy tunic. In the same instant Menander rose and drew back his spear for a cast. He could not let this happen—

And in that instant a sharp pain lanced his right ankle. He bit his tongue, half strangling to keep from crying out, and whirled to see the thing that had bitten him—a large gray weasel—darting away. The creature paused for an instant and turned to glare back at him with its evil yellow eyes; then, with a high titter that was eerily human, it scurried away between the columns.

Prodikos' familiar! Menander felt weak at the realization that the thing had discovered him. And now it was hurrying out between the guards and across the wide marble floor, straight toward its transfigured master, squeaking shrilly.

Simon whipped out his *sica* and struck, all in one motion, at the buzzing thing that darted at his face. His blade sliced through something like a hard-crusted fruit and he felt a few fluid droplets spatter on his flesh. The buzzing ceased and the thing dropped with a muted dry clatter upon the tiles.

He crouched and glared at it, knife ready—but though the thing still moved its several legs, its body was cut nearly in two and it was obviously dying. Peering closer, Simon realized that it was an enormous black bee, as long as his hand and forearm. Its many-faceted eyes glittered dully in the faint light, and its finger-length stinger thrust itself out in repeated spasmodic jerks from the end of its fat abdomen, as if still seeking to inflict death.

Simon cursed softly. The thing was not supernatural but an actual physical being. That must mean that Prodikos was already opening the Gate to Harag-Kolath and some of the Great Mother's swarming servitors were entering the temple. Rising and cautiously peering down into the spacious *cella*, he saw that it was so—there was a swirling glow forming at the base of the huge idol, and several more giant bees were circling the altar to which Ilione was bound. Fortunately only one of them had detected him so far.

Ignoring the sound of Prodikos' chanting, Simon crouched again in the shadow of the column and made his mind a blank. When he felt sufficiently calm, he found the parchment and held it out in the light, scanned it one last time, then slowly and carefully began to read its archaic words aloud. He knew he could not afford even one slip....

In a few moments he was done, save only for the final pronouncing of the goddess' name in Greek and in Latin. Prodikos' loud chanting had drowned out his own. He glanced up at the statue perched upon the stone railing; it seemed to be glowing slightly. He drew a deep breath. Now was the time—

No, Simon—not yet!

He whirled and faced the shadows. The words had not been spoken aloud, yet they were definitely no part of his own imagining. Now, to his astonishment, he seemed to see dimly before him the squat, glowing form of Daramos the Mage.

"You!" he hissed. "How did you get in—?"

I am here only in my astral shape. Dositheus waits outside, guiding me. Speak not the name yet, Simon, or you will be destroyed even as was Sejanus. Prodikos' guarding spells still surround him.

"Then, when shall I—?"

In a moment the sorcerer will be distracted. Quickly, go look over the balustrade!

Simon did so, taking care not to approach the glowing image of Fortuna too closely. Below he saw the yellow-cloaked Prodikos in the act of ripping away Ilione's white shift. The sorcerer had undergone a ghastly transformation, and now his taloned hands were clutching at her—

Suddenly a gray creature came scuttling across the tiles beneath—Prodikos' weasel, Simon realized. It paused near the sorcerer and sat up on its haunches, squeaking and pointing with one forepaw back in the direction from which it had come. Prodikos straightened and turned—and in that instant a black feathered shape swooped down from the shadows and struck the weasel from behind, sending it tumbling and squealing.

"Carbo!" Simon exclaimed involuntarily.

The raven flapped rapidly upward, cawing loudly. Simon saw it climb past him with frantic wingbeats and finally vanish upward into the starry sky. Several of the black bees zoomed up in hot pursuit, but then buzzed down toward the altar again, evidently unwilling to leave the temple.

Now, Simon—speak the names of the goddess!

But in that instant he heard a youthful voice below him cry out: "Sorcerer, you shall not have her!" And instantly the figure of a black-cloaked guardsman came dashing across the wide floor toward Prodikos, spear leveled. No, not a guardsman, but Menander—with many true guards behind him in pursuit!

Speak the names, Simon. Hurry!

Simon opened his mouth and cried out: *"Tyche! Fortuna!"* Then he snatched up his spear and hurled it down into the *cella*, snarling with satisfaction to see it transfix one of Menander's pursuers. In the same instant he was astonished to see the statue of Fortuna turning slowly on its pedestal. In another moment it had stopped, facing directly toward him and away from Prodikos.

It is done! said Daramos. *Now leave the temple—quickly!*

Simon dashed back through the columns and down the stairs as fast as he could in the semidarkness. He could hear a rising hubbub of cursing voices, and then a woman's scream of terror. In another moment he had reached the foot of the stairway, but instead of obeying Daramos he turned and dashed through the lower tier of columns and into the torchlit *cella*.

"Menander!" he yelled. "I'm coming!"

Then he glimpsed the lad at the center of the converging soldiers, lunging at Prodikos. The sorcerer grabbed the spear-shaft with one hand and wrenched, sending Menander sprawling. The guards closed in, hiding them both from sight.

Simon hurtled into the knot of soldiers full tilt, yelling and slashing. Three of them were down gashed and dying before they knew what hit them. Another turned and thrust but, missing Simon, drove the spear through one of his fellows. Then Simon was in the thick of them, slashing and slaying madly, knowing that he and Menander were doomed against such odds. Above, he heard the menacing drone of the giant bees closing in.

Incredibly, the death blow did not come. Simon's foes seemed strangely clumsy, lurching and stumbling and swearing as they struck at him, smiting one another with uncanny frequency in their bumbling attempts. Then one of them screamed as a giant bee settled upon his helmet and thrust its stinger into his face.

Simon avoided a sword stroke, slashed a foeman's throat, and broke through the circle of guards. More of them were screaming now as the bees attacked them, and most of the rest were beginning to scatter toward the columns, howling in terror. Then Simon saw Menander avoid a clumsily attacking guardsman and run him through with a spear. In the next instant the lad had snatched up a fallen sword and was rushing toward the altar where Ilione, now fully awake, was screaming and struggling madly.

"Get out of here, Menander!" yelled Simon. "I'll free her—!"

But the youth was already sawing at one of the cords that bound the girl to the altar—and the satyrish form of Prodikos was clattering toward him on cloven hooves, serpent-rod extended. With a roar Simon sprang forward, *sica* upraised. The sorcerer spun and faced him, yellow eyes glaring, and then with a thunderous laugh flung down his rod upon the marble tiles. Simon leaped aside barely in time—for instantly the staff had become a living black serpent that coiled and struck out at him with venomous fangs.

The snake whipped about and again struck at him, but this time Simon's knife met it and sent its head flying. Whirling, he faced Prodikos a second time. The sorcerer's eyes blazed with supernatural power; Simon, trying to advance, found that he could not. There was a hypnotic force behind those evil yellow eyes.

"Fool!" howled Prodikos, an unnatural booming quality in his voice. "Though you have turned Fortune against me, you shall die!"

He advanced, and the giant bees came down and circled more closely about him. High above, the crown of the monstrous idol was glowing more brightly. Simon strained frantically, unable to move an inch under his foe's hypnotic glare, knowing he was doomed this time indeed. More of the giant bees were swarming in through the Gate, and far beyond them something was humping up higher amid the alien architecture—something like a pulsating black hill upon which a thousand fires gleamed and flickered....

Then, to Simon's amazement, the bees began to settle upon Prodikos. The sorcerer screamed as they thrust their black stingers again and again into his flesh.

"No! No! I am Sakkuth!" he shrieked madly. *"I serve Kaiwan, your Mistress' mate—!"*

Instantly Simon was free to move. He dashed to the altar, where Menander had just finished freeing Ilione and casting his cloak over her trembling form.

"Run!" he yelled.

Together they half-dragged the terrified girl toward the columns, while behind them the sorcerer's howls rose to a frenzy of agony. Glancing up, Simon glimpsed upon the high balustrade the statue of Fortuna, its glow fading as it faced the shadows. Then the three of them were racing down the main aisle between the columns to the open portal.

As they reached the threshold they paused to glance back—and gasped to see a huge buzzing knot of the bees hovering above the altar. Though no part of his form or even his glowing cloak was visible, the sorcerer's howls still rang out madly from that buzzing knot: *"No! I am Sak-*

kuth—!"

Then the droning black bundle drifted slowly toward the colossal idol and through the open Gate, into the gray luminosity where waited the distant black monstrosity that pulsed and gleamed like a living hill with a thousand eyes. After it flew two final bees bearing between them a writhing bundle of fur that struggled and squealed—the gray weasel. The screams of the sorcerer and the squeals of his familiar grew fainter—then ceased entirely as the Gate abruptly seemed to collapse in upon itself and vanish.

"Baal! The very demon-spawn he invoked have taken him," Simon muttered. "Hurry, both of you—away from this mad fane!"

The moon was down, and the vast courtyard they raced across seemed to be deserted. Evidently the surviving guards had fled the place. But as they neared the outer gate Simon saw a dark-robed figure standing there, and gripped his *sica* more tightly—

"Simon—Menander—fear not! I'm here to aid you!"

He recognized the man's voice, saw the black silhouette of Carbo perched on his shoulder. "Dositheus! How did you get by the guards?"

The old wizard pointed down the wide road that stretched away whitely under the stars. "They have fled. Some came bursting forth from the temple like a dragon was at their heels, and the rest followed them. I admit I cast a modest panic spell to hurry them on their way…."

Ilione suddenly faced back toward the towering fane, clutching her face in her pale hands. "Gods! My father!" she sobbed. "What happened to him? What had he become—?"

"He was not your father," said Dositheus gently. "Your father died fifteen years ago, when the dark soul of Sakkuth returned to this world and took up abode in his body. But you are safe now. Come, we will take you to Ephesos—"

At that instant Simon sensed a gleam of light high over the temple. Looking up, he saw a glowing object rise swiftly into the night sky, then suddenly veer and go streaking away toward the southeast.

"Baal! More devils—?"

"No," said Dositheus. "It is the seed of the Star-god. Released by Sakkuth's spell, it now seeks the Great Mother in order that it may unite with her."

"Then we've failed!" Simon exclaimed. "The thing will spawn again, and its new brood will bring down the All-Night upon the world—"

"Do not fear. The Gate has closed. The seed in its blind seeking will find only the sands of the Arabian desert, which it cannot penetrate, and so will expend its energies futilely."

"It will die, then?" asked Menander.

"Alas, no—the *Ajar-Alazwat* cannot die. But it will remain dormant for at least a thousand years, until Sakkuth again returns to incite men to its worship. The world is safe from it until then. Come, now, all of you—we must return to Ephesos."

V. EPILOG: *AURORA NOVATRIX*

> Not from the stars do I my judgement pluck...
> But from thine eyes my knowledge I derive,
> And (constant stars) in them I read such art
> As truth and beauty shall together thrive,
> If from thyself to store thou wouldst convert:
> Or else of thee this I prognosticate,
> Thy end is truth's and beauty's doom and date.

— Shakespeare, *Sonnets*

"So Daramos was never here with you in Ephesos at all?" Simon queried.

"No." Dositheus took another sip from his wine cup, set it down on the rough table. "Not in the flesh, at any rate. His body remains in Parthia, but on occasion he goes into a self-induced trance and appears to us. He says that no one of his advanced years should be leaving his homeland to voyage halfway across the known world."

"I see. And what about the clumsiness of the guards that attacked Menander and me, and then the attack of the bees on them and Prodikos—Sakkuth—and his familiar? Was all that due to spells cast by you and Daramos?"

"No, Simon, it was due solely to *your* spell. For, once Fortune had been induced to turn her back on Sakkuth and those who aided him, nothing could thenceforth go right for them. Nor—thank the gods!—can Sakkuth try his luck again for a thousand years."

They were once more in the back room of the inn in Ephesos, five of them this time, enjoying wine and fruit and bread, Simon and Dositheus seated at the table with Carbo between them pecking at a pomegranate. Simon looked over to where Menander and Ilione sat on a low divan near the far wall, apparently deep in conversation. The girl now wore a white blue-trimmed kirtle Dositheus had bought from one of the serving-wenches; she looked quite beautiful in the lamplight, though still somewhat tired and haggard from her recent ordeal. Simon sympathized with her. He and all the others were weary, too, but though the night was well spent none of them had yet begun to feel sleepy. That would come later, after wine had sufficiently relaxed them.

"Ilione may have lost a father," said Dositheus, smiling, "but I think that in our young Menander she has found a friend."

"Perhaps more than that. You are taking her with you, then, when you and Menander return to the East?"

Dositheus nodded. "Where else would she go?" Then, after considering Simon's words: "Does that mean that you are *not* returning with us?"

"I have learned much, O Mentor, studying under you and Daramos, but now I feel I must go my own way." He took a final swallow from his wine-cup and rose. "I must wander."

Dositheus rose also. "Tonight? But, surely—"

"No, not tonight." Simon smiled. "I'll stay with you here in Ephesos, maybe even take ship with you as far as Antioch. But after that, I must go my own way. I have much to do."

"I see." Dositheus' eyes were grave. "You will go to Samaria and get your revenge upon the Romans who slew your parents seven years ago. Well, I can understand that, though I shall hate to lose your company, even if only for a time. Good luck to you, Simon."

"Thank you. And now, I'm off to bed."

He bade Menander and Carbo good night also, took Ilione's hand and wished her well, then left the room and climbed the stairway to the upper floor. Instead of stopping at his chamber, however, he continued on up another flight and presently emerged upon the flat roof of the inn. The torches of Ephesos were extinguished; the whole city slept peacefully under the stars. The moon was long gone, the Bull's face and the Goat Star were ascending toward the purple zenith, while in the east the sky was beginning to brighten before the advancing dawn.

"I will wander," he said quietly to himself.

He recalled Ilione's face and the touch of her hand, and a pang went through him. She reminded him slightly of Helen, yet could never replace her in his soul—that he well knew. Yet he would wander, hoping that Daramos' prophecy would come true and that somehow, somewhere he would again meet Helen in the fullness of time. And surely, if that hope was not just an idle dream, his wanderings would increase the chances of that meeting occurring sooner than it would otherwise—

No, Simon, the day cannot be hastened—but it will come.

He turned and saw, almost without surprise, the dwarfish glowing form of Daramos standing near him.

"Tell me, O Master of the Arcane, when will that day be?"

In its own time. It can neither be hastened nor stayed. It will come upon you when you least expect it. Until then, Simon of Gitta, live your life as you wish. Wander far, seek arcane knowledge, slay as many Romans if you will—but seek not for Helen. You will find her when it is the time, for you and she are not such as can ever in truth be parted. One day you will know whereof I speak.

The form of Daramos dimmed and vanished, and Simon, alone under the stars once more, felt his soul lighten somewhat in spite of the sadness that still clung to it. And suddenly he knew again that strange unity with the cosmos that he had often felt before in Helen's presence, and as he turned his eyes eastward he seemed for a moment to see her eyes and the outlines of her face in the expanding dawn.

About "The Blade of the Slayer"

WARNING: Contains spoilers!

The following tale is not exactly a sequel to "The Seed of the Star-God." It is actually a paralepsis; that is, it constitutes an episode having occurred within the time frame of that story but not mentioned at the time. It is not a missing piece of that tale; it is heterodiegetic, a story in its own right. "It is an adventure Simon had while wandering from Persepolis to Rome during the fall, winter & spring of A.D. 31-32" (Letter, November 9, 1985). Elsewhere Tierney narrows down the date to "probably January, A.D. 32."

"The Blade of the Slayer" as it appears here is not the version that originally appeared in *Pulse-Pounding Adventure Stories* #1, December 1986. That was a rewritten version in which the Slayer was revealed as the biblical Nimrod (Genesis 10:8-12), whom legend also associated with the Tower of Babel (Genesis 11:1-9). He is described as a "mighty man", a technical term in the Bible for epic heroes of the past, like Goliath and Gilgamesh. "On digging into Mesopotamian legendry, I found that some scholars think that Gilgamesh might have helped inspire the Nimrod legend [though Nimrod is also identified with the Greek Orion] … [H]e was the first post-diluvian warrior and conqueror. He founded cities, ruled kingdoms and reigned for hundreds, perhaps thousands of years. I suspect that his attempt to storm Heaven, first via the Tower of Babel and then by means of a vulture-drawn sky cart, may have been more successful than the pious records acknowledge, and that he managed to steal a portion of immortality from that which is symbolized as the Tree of Life; at any rate, the accounts of his death are contradictory, indicating wishful thinking rather than fact. He's almost a Prometheus character, implacably defiant of the gods. I figure he was a major factor in finally re-establishing civilization after the Hyborian cataclysm (dimly remembered as the Deluge legend). He's described as of towering stature and powerfully built; I picture him as black-bearded & with cruel Assyrian features, perhaps with a non-human touch of Whateley goatishness (but certainly too tough to be killed by any number of library watchdogs)" (Letter, December 14, 1985).

Quite a character, but not the original Slayer at all. What you are about to read makes the Slayer Cain, the first son of Adam and Eve. Cain, too, was a violent man, a weaponsmith, as his name indicates (it means "forger, metallurgist"), a wanderer, and a founder of cities. He bore the famous "mark", or tattoo, identifying him as one whose death would bring seven-fold reprisals through blood feud. This feature he bears as the mythic eponymous ancestor of the ancient Kenite marauders. He could also be made to represent the Canaanites, who were farmers worshiping Baal and

Anath, whose sacred marriage the farmers would ritually repeat with temple priestesses (priestitutes, I like to call 'em) as an act of imitative magic to fructify their fields. As a symbol for all this, Cain offers a vegetable sacrifice to Yahweh but is rejected. Genesis chapter 4 jumbles together all manner of brief Cain episodes which severally pictured Cain (or Tubal-Cain) in various historical times. This did not mean people believed him supernaturally long-lived like the Wandering Jew; they just had no fixed idea of when he would have lived. Obviously, most of the Cain episodes, which have him marry, found a city, and fear assassination by "who[m]ever finds me", are incompatible with the chronology chosen by the compiler of Genesis, who made him the first son of Adam and Eve, only the third person in the fledgling human race.

But Cain the Slayer does not come to us directly from the Bible. No, Tierney has borrowed Karl Edward Wagner's interpretation of Cain, his series character Kane. The blank verse poem in "The Blade of the Slayer" is taken by paraphrase from the poem in Wagner's "Reflections for the Winter of My Soul." Tierney says, "I figure there were many variants of it developed down the millennia since it was first composed" (Letter, November 9, 1985). After consultation with Wagner, who liked the story, Tierney nonetheless agreed to change the Slayer's identity to Nimrod so as not to risk creating possible continuity glitches with future Kane adventures by Wagner. However, since the tragic death of Karl Wagner, that problem has vanished, and the original version of "The Blade of the Slayer" finally appears here as a tribute to Karl Edward Wagner. The result is a special treat, reminiscent of Robert E. Howard's "Kings of the Night", where the champions Kull of Atlantis and Bran Mak Morn meet to fight side by side against a common peril—only this story brings together the two greatest sword-and-sorcery heroes of the 1980's. To take up our Gnostic thread once more, it is worth noting that "The Blade of the Slayer" reflects the strange mirror-image salvation history of Sethian and Cainite Gnostic sects, both of which regarded Cain as a heroic rebel against the sinister machinations of the Demiurge, just as he is depicted in this story.

For the curious, the alternate version of this story, where Nimrod is the Slayer, can be found at the Pickman's Press website (pickmanspress.com).

THE BLADE OF THE SLAYER
by Richard L. Tierney

… by Heaven, which He holds, and the abyss,
And the immensity of worlds and life…
Homage he has from all—but none from me:
I battle it against him… till the great
Conflict shall cease, if ever it shall cease
Which it ne'er shall, till he or I be quenched!
And what can quench our immortality,
Or mutual and irrevocable hate?

— Lord Byron, *Cain, a Mystery*

A chill wind blew beneath gray skies, stirring the withered grasses and shrubs of the low ridge. Simon of Gitta brought his near-exhausted horse to a halt, gazed back intently eastward for a moment, then dismounted. His pursuers were not yet in sight, though he knew they could not be far behind—but up the slope, only a few hundred yards distant upon the horizon, jutted the silhouette of an odd-angled rock outcropping. With luck he could hide there, then steal away after dark toward the far plains of Sumer which lay hazily to the west.

Simon gave the horse a sharp slap on its right rear flank and it cantered wearily away at an angle, southwestward, down the hill. He began to hurry up the gradual slope, stepping from rock to rock whenever possible so as not to leave a trail, glancing frequently eastward, an anxious tension in his dark eyes.

Scarcely had he gained the rocks of the ridgetop before he saw them—the silhouettes of more than a dozen horsemen topping the horizon to the east. Quickly he eased himself down between two boulders, lips drawn back in an unconscious snarl, and watched them approach. His hand clutched for his sword pommel, gripped only empty air. He cursed softly, regretting that he had ever allowed his bandit captors to disarm him rather than fighting them to the death. True, he had later escaped those captors by means of the near-magical arts his Persian mentors had taught him, but now he was a fleeing animal, the hunters upon his track….

The horsemen galloped closer, their helmets, mail, and spear-points glinting in the late-afternoon light. They drew abreast of their hidden quarry several hundred yards down the slope, then passed—following the trail of his abandoned mount, which had already vanished down into the draw and was, he hoped, hurrying westward in quest of the lush pastures of Sumer. Simon drew a deep breath, brushed sweat-dampened bangs of dark hair from his forehead, then slowly stood erect. Some of his tension ebbed away; his angular features relaxed a trifle, and he even felt grateful for the cold wind that whipped his black locks and the dark cloak that wrapped his tall frame. For a moment he stood in silence, watching as the last of the horsemen vanished down the draw to the southwest, while the dimming light of the west limned his craggy, clean-shaven features.

Shouldering his light pack again, he continued on to the highest crest of the ridge, where the odd-angled rocks clustered most thickly. Here he would sup on the last of his meager fare, then continue on over the slope and down the next draw before his pursuers returned. He hoped the abandoned mount would lead them on a long chase....

Suddenly his musings were shattered as a tall, dark-robed figure rose up from the rocks, scarcely a dozen paces ahead.

"Baal!" gasped Simon, again reaching instinctively for his missing sword. The dark figure began to move toward him. Grimly Simon crouched, assuming a fighting stance his hated Roman trainers had once taught him.

The figure drew closer. Simon, seeing the stranger more clearly, relaxed a bit. It was an old man, tall and white-bearded, clad in a dark greenish robe inscribed with the symbols of the Persian Magi. Yet Simon remained alert, recalling tales he had heard of wizards who lurked amid these western foothills.

"Ho, stranger." The voice of the old man was nearly as thin as the cold wind. "Why do you come here to the site of the First City?"

"The—*what?*" Simon rose from his fighting crouch and approached the old man cautiously. "What are you talking about—?"

"And have you not heard that the spirit of the First Slayer, who founded it, still lingers about this ridgetop, waiting for unwary strayers?"

Simon glanced about at the numerous worn boulders, at the sparse dry grasses blowing under the chill wind. "Aye, I've heard such tales. But, surely, no city ever stood here—"

"The legend is true. No outsider is safe in this place. You must go."

Simon barked a derisive laugh. "Unsafe? Didn't you see that band of cutthroats riding by? They're after my hide, by Baal! I rode here in hopes that the local legends would deter them, but obviously they're not impressed. But don't worry, old man, I won't stay long—just until nightfall. Then I'll steal away down the ridgetop before the bastards return to search for my horse's missing rider. By dawn I should be well on my way toward the western plains."

"Do not delay, stranger. Go now."

"And risk having them return and spot me on the open slopes of this ridge? No! Besides, I need a short rest and something to eat." Simon eyed the old man's robe, noting the numerous mystical symbols emblazoned upon it. "Why are you so anxious to see me gone? Your garb proclaims you a Magus and a servant of Ahura Mazda. Are you and your fellow sorcerers hiding some secret here?"

"No secret that you would care to know."

"Well, I don't care about your secrets, I assure you. Hide me for an hour, and I'll be on my way. Surely you must have a hiding place among these rocks—a cave, perhaps? An old man like you does not live perpetually exposed to winter winds upon a ridgetop."

The mage nodded slightly. "Come, then."

Simon followed him a short distance to a huge fractured outcrop surrounded by many toppled boulders, then into one of its narrow fissures. Just before they entered Simon glimpsed a large vulture, perched atop the outcropping, watching them with a beady eye. Uneasily he wondered why the bird did not fly away, then realized that it was no doubt the old man's familiar—for Simon knew that many Persian Magi kept such birds, sacred to Ahura Mazda, for servitors.

After a few paces the twisting crevice ended at a black hole that slanted shallowly downward. They entered, and Simon noted that the walls and ceiling of this narrow passage, though extremely pitted, were straight and regular as if artificially carved. Beneath his feet were stone stairsteps, so worn and curved in the middle that they formed almost a chute upon whose surface he had to proceed with caution. Then the gray daylight faded, but ahead Simon caught the dim gleam of torchlight. In another moment he and his aged guide had emerged into a small room carved from the living rock and meagerly furnished with a cot, a wooden table, and two stools. Upon the table, gleaming in the light of the single wall-bracketed torch, stood many vials, bottles, and mixing bowls, while beneath it in the shadows rested a box full of scrolls. Nearby stood a brazier upon a bronze tripod, and against one wall a small cabinet whose open door revealed many more bottles and vials.

"Sit, and eat," muttered the old man, clearing a corner of the table. "Then you must go. My spells protect me from the Slayer's spirit, but they will not protect you after darkness falls."

Simon snorted derisively as he set down his pack. "Ha! You *are* hiding something. I'm not an ordinary outlander to be easily fooled by such tales, old man. Look." He let his dark cloak fall open and slip from his shoulders to the floor. "You see   I, too, have been trained in magical arts by Parthia's very own Magi."

The old man peered closely at the red-brown tunic emblazoned with yellow symbols, some of them similar to those on his own robe. The man who wore it was young, tall and lean, hard-muscled. He wore a wide sword-belt, but the scabbards for sword and dagger were empty.

"Aye, I know you now," said the oldster, his manner becoming a bit less suspicious. "You are Simon of Gitta, a pupil of the Archimage Daramos. I saw you several months ago, when I and several other priests of my order visited Daramos in Persepolis. Daramos mentioned to us that you were his most accomplished adept."

Simon, too, relaxed a bit more. "Thank you. But your memory is better than mine. I recall your visit, but not your name—"

"I am K'shasthra, priest of the Order of the High Guardians. At least one adept of our Order is always stationed here to guard the secret that—that for now must be kept from mankind. We have kept guard thusly for nearly two years. So much I may reveal to you, who have already been initiated into many secrets of the Magi. Perhaps I shall tell you more—but only with the understanding that the outer world must never know, until the Order has decided that the time is right."

"I see." Simon placed his small bundle of rations on the table, then sat down and unwrapped them. "And so you have no doubt spread these tales of the 'Slayer' to frighten off unwanted visitors?"

"We did not invent the legend," said K'shasthra, "though I admit that we have revived and enhanced it of late. The Slayer's spirit does not truly prowl here—but we have seen to it that a few venturesome, prying ones have vanished, to turn up later as unmarked corpses near the caravan trails not far from here. Of late we have not had to use such tactics; you are the first visitor to come here for many months."

Simon felt a tingling along his spine. "And had I been an ordinary outlander—?"

K'shasthra smiled thinly. "It is well that you revealed to me your identity when you did." He turned away and rummaged amid a shadowy bundle of blankets near the cot. Simon scowled with dark understanding. He of all people knew what powders and poisons could be used by the Magi to induce death with no apparent cause.

The old man returned and set bread, dried meat, and a flask of wine on the table. "Do not be disturbed, Simon. When you learn more, you will understand why such extreme methods were necessary. What we do is for the good of all mankind."

Simon nodded, but when he ate it was from his own rations, washing down each dry mouthful with a sip from his own waterskin. Not until the old mage had eaten several bites from the loaf and the dried meat, and taken a few swallows from the wine flask, did Simon join him in sampling this more palatable fare. K'shasthra smiled again at the suspicion in the young man's dark, deep-shadowed eyes.

"Have no fear, Simon. I swear by Ahura Mazda, and by his fire-servant Atar, that I intend you no evil. But tell me how you happen to come—and in the cold of winter at that—to this desolate ridgetop?"

"I joined a small caravan journeying from Persepolis to Susa. We were attacked last evening by more than a score of bandits, and I was captured." Simon's gaze became somber, introspective. "They left me bound to die upon a snow-slope in the cold; that was in punishment for having fought them well enough to leave several of their number dead. I had to watch while they murdered all the men and children; then they raped the women and slew them also. But in the night I slipped my bonds and stole a horse from the very edge of the bandits' camp, leaving two more of their guards dead behind me. Too bad I had no time to snatch their weapons!—the rest were instantly after me like a pack of wolves—but at least there were a few provisions bundled in a cloak on the horse. I gave the bastards the slip, but they weren't long in getting on my trail, and ever since dawn they've been slowly gaining. I suppose they know this region intimately—and your 'Slayer' legend doesn't seem to impress them."

K'shasthra frowned thoughtfully. "That would be Gutakh and his Mailed Raiders. I've heard of their bloody deeds, but never have they or any other bandit gangs ventured this far from the caravan trails. I saw but sixteen horsemen pass here, Simon—evidently you thinned their ranks considerably. No wonder they burn for revenge! Daramos has obviously taught you well."

"He taught me escape artistry and many other things," said Simon, his eyes more darkly brooding than ever, "but it was the Romans who trained me to fight and kill. They slew my parents and sold me into the arena, where for two years as a gladiator I entertained them by spilling blood."

"I remember the story now," said the old man. "Your first mentor, Dositheus the Samaritan, helped you escape and brought you here to Parthia to study under Daramos, his own former mentor. That was four years ago, was it not? And why do you now journey toward Susa, braving bandits and these wintry mountains?"

"I go to Rome."

"Ah." K'shasthra nodded. "I understand. You feel that your arcane studies here have given you greater powers, and now you would return and use those powers for—revenge?"

Simon did not reply, but a deep hatred glowered from the torchlight-shadowed pits of his eyes.

"I understand well," the mage went on. "Your feelings make you worthy of our Order's confidence. You shall learn the *secret* that we have not confided even to Daramos or Dositheus—and then you shall learn even greater skills and powers, that you may aid us in our plan to bring benefit to all mankind."

"Aid you?" Simon shook his head. "No, I'm not interested in your secrets and plans. I must go to Rome."

"And so you shall, if you wish—but if you decide to join us in our cause, your power and vengeance can be all the greater. Do not adamantly refuse me before you know what I offer. Come, Simon, follow me."

The old man had risen while he spoke, and now he took the torch from its bracket and moved toward a corner of the room where a tattered blanket hung. Simon rose also, then scowled with surprise as K'shasthra pushed the blanket aside, revealing a tall black aperture perhaps two feet wide.

"Come—follow," the mage repeated.

Simon did so. The blanket fell back into place behind them and the torch revealed a narrow passage. After a few paces they began to descend another stairway, this one longer and steeper but less worn than the last, and curving slightly to the right. After what Simon estimated to be about a quarter-turn, the passage abruptly opened into a large empty space. The light of the old man's torch feebly illuminated a vast chamber which appeared to be circular and domed.

"Wait here, near the wall," instructed the mage, who then began to walk around the huge room, lighting a wall-torch every few yards. As the illumination increased Simon became aware of a wide, circular pit whose edge was about thirty feet in from the wall. It seemed to be filled with dark water nearly to the rim.

"This was the water-storage chamber of the First City," explained K'shasthra as he completed the circuit. "It is all that remains of that place, save for my chamber and the wind-worn boulders you saw atop the ridge."

"Gods!" muttered Simon. How many thousands of years would it take for the wind to thus reduce the stones of—"An entire city?"

"By today's standards, more like a small town. Actually it was a walled fortress, founded by the First Slayer in fear of many who, fired by his example, sought to pursue and slay *him*."

A prickling crawled down Simon's spine as understanding began to dawn. His throat suddenly felt dry. He dared not speak.

"But the Slayer was under the curse of the great world-creator Achamoth," K'shasthra went on, "—the Demiurge who had fashioned the First Men to serve him. For his rebellion a Mark was set upon the Slayer; all who saw it shunned him in fear, and he was cursed to leave his city to his followers and wander forever over the face of the earth, hating and slaying, spreading new hatred and death."

"You mean," gasped Simon, "—this was—the city of *Enoch*...?"

"The legends of many vanished races—all of them more or less inaccurate—have called it by many names. Nowhere but in the centuried book

of Ostanes, once Persia's greatest mage, have there been recorded traditions that are at all close to the source—and even these traditions date
from many centuries after the Slayer began to stalk the earth. Surely you
have read in Ostanes, Simon; do you recall these lines derived from the
impious pre-Hyborian poet Klemg'n-Esch?"

So saying, K'shasthra began to recite in an ancient Persian dialect:

> A primal god in madness sought to build
> A mortal race, fashioned in his own form.
> Blindly, with mighty efforts, did he make
> Low beings that mirrored his smug idiocy,
> To serve his whims in worm-like servitude.
> These fecund worms soon swarmed through all the land,
> Yet one rose up in grim, rebellious hate,
> Vowing that he would serve no god so vile.
> No maggot *he*, in cosmic dung a-writhe,
> But a fell serpent filled with hellish wrath
> At his creator's smug and crooning lies!
> Freedom he chose, defying this mad god,
> Slaying with his own hands his very brother—
> The being's most favored toy and servitor.
> Now in despair the god's mind cracked and reeled
> To see the merciless mirroring of his flaws
> Within his own created, cherished thralls.
> Then the defiant one he cursed in rage
> To bleak, eternal wanderings, and laid
> On him the Slayer's Mark, that all might know—

"Enough!" Simon gestured impatiently. "Yes, I've read it. It's an old
Persian variant of a poem reputed to have been composed many thousands
of years ago in a tongue now forgotten. But surely you can't expect me to
believe that—?"

"Believe only what you see, Simon," said K'shasthra. "Come—let us
look into the pool."

He moved slowly forward behind the wizard, curious yet at the same
time strangely reluctant. K'shasthra stopped at the edge of the pit, held his
torch out, and leaned slightly forward, peering down. As Simon drew near
the edge of the wide pool, which was perhaps forty feet from rim to rim,
he was surprised to realize that the dark substance filling it could not be
water, for it held no reflection at all, neither of the torches nor of the surrounding walls. Moreover, its surface had a hazy aspect, as if it mingled
slightly with the air just above it. Nearby, just beneath that surface, was a

small platform from which a stone stairway began to spiral downward along the curved wall.

"Look down, Simon, and tell me what you see."

Keeping a distance between himself and the mage, Simon knelt and peered over the edge of the pit. Despite the darkness that filled it, he was surprised to find that he could see clearly to the bottom—a depth equal to the height of three tall men. In the middle of the circular floor was a raised rectangular dais of stone—and upon it, pale in contrast to the surrounding darkness, lay the body of a man.

"What do you see, Simon?"

He could not reply. A strange fascination had gripped him. The man on the dais seemed tall, though Simon could not be sure because of the striking massiveness of his build—as if the muscles of three powerful men had been strung upon one frame! Yet it was not the build of a gorilla nor a dwarf; rather, it suggested the solidity of the bole of a mighty oak that had assumed human form. The torso and upper thighs were cased in a sleeveless tunic of tight-fitting Persian mail over which was laced a leathern vest; the mighty limbs were bare, save for stout sandals whose thongs crisscrossed the lower legs. About the waist was cinched a wide sword-belt from which a leather strap looped over the left shoulder, while from behind the right shoulder protruded the handle of a sword that seemed, from the little that Simon could see, to be of archaic design.

But it was the face that held Simon's fascination most intensely—the cruel, rugged, yet strangely expressive features that even in death seemed tensed—or ready to tense—into a snarl of menace. Red shoulder-length hair and a short ruddy beard framed those menacing features—

Simon suddenly felt a strange fear—what if those death-closed eyes should *open?*—and immediately drew back from the pit.

"That is the Slayer," said K'shasthra calmly. "For thousands of years he has wandered over the earth in many guises, spreading his hatred and evil among men. But two years ago we of the Order of the High Guardians, resolving to purge humanity of his curse, drew him here to this region by means of spells and illusions, and then trapped him in this pit."

"But—" Simon found it hard to speak. "How—?"

"Even the mighty Slayer had his human weakness. Once in the dawntime he loved a woman—Luluah by name—by whom he sired the race who built the city he founded; later Luluah was slain for her iniquity by the Primal Gods. By means of magical rites, culled from books far more ancient than even that of Ostanes, our Order was able to project into the Slayer's dreams the ghostly beckoning form of this woman, and so we drew him back to this region—and eventually, with the aid of certain fellow rogues who betrayed him, even into this pit. Then we cast the spells that

bound him, and released into the dry cistern the deadly murk that now sur-
rounds him. Look, Simon." K'shasthra knelt and thrust his torch into the
dark substance that seemed neither gas nor fluid; immediately the flame
dimmed and expired. "No creature can breathe therein—no one can approach nor rescue him."

Simon found his voice. "But—*why?*"

"So that mankind may know peace!" The mage stood erect, eyes blazing. "So that there will be no more murder, no more slaying in war, no
more of the madness of violence which this rebel against the Primal Gods
has brought upon the earth!"

Simon laughed as the fascination that had held him broke. "Such nonsense! Even if this dead man is who you say he is—which I don't believe
for a moment!—what have your efforts gained you? During the two years
you say he has lain here the world has had no relief from violence or murder—from wars, from pillage, from bandit gangs such as the one which
pursues me. Moreover, Rome itself—the greatest center of earthly evils—
has seen two of the most monstrous and murderous purges the world has
ever known, the first instigated by its prefect Sejanus, the second by the
mad emperor Tiberius. During the latter, my own Helen was slain—"

His dark eyes blazed; his fists clenched as he choked on his emotion.
K'shasthra nodded slowly, a knowing sadness in his eyes.

"You will aid us," he said. "You understand. You will help us free the
world of this age-old curse of hate and evil."

Simon took a deep breath, forcing his mind back to calmness. "You
haven't answered me. If the dead man in this pit is truly the cause of evil—?"

"He is not dead, Simon. Nor does he even sleep. He is merely… suspended. Even now, I think, he is aware enough to hear our every spoken
word."

Simon shuddered—then threw off his fear with an angry gesture.
"Aren't you going to answer my question, K'shasthra? *Why is there still violence upon the earth?*"

The old mage shrugged. "The Slayer has spread his evil throughout
the lands for many thousands of years. Can we expect that evil to subside
so abruptly? It may take *many more* years—"

"And another thing," pressed Simon, "why keep him alive at all, if
he's as evil as you say? Is he a god who cannot be slain?"

"No, he is as mortal as any other human, though probably the greatest
fighter who has ever lived. The curse of the Elder Gods against whom he
impiously rebelled has withheld from him the peace of a natural death, but
only his fighting prowess and an instinct for survival have kept him alive
during these long ages."

"Then I ask again: *Why keep him alive?*"

K'shasthra stood taller, eyes blazing fanatically. "So that when humanity finally ends its madness and subsides into worldwide peace, we of the Order may show them the originator of their former wickedness—and enjoin upon them the paths they must follow in the future lest that scourge be loosed upon them anew. And should they choose not those paths, there is a way to waken the Slayer!"

Simon almost cringed at the madness in the priest's rheumy old eyes and rasping voice. "In other words," he said, keeping his own voice steady with an effort, "you and your fellow sorcerers hope to subjugate mankind to *your* will."

K'shasthra scowled darkly. "I sense that you have a false and perverted attitude, Simon of Gitta. I had hoped that you would understand. We of the Order wish only to benefit humanity—"

At that moment Simon heard a scrabbling of claws on stone, a fluttering of feathers—and in the next instant was astonished to see a large vulture, evidently the mage's familiar, come waddling in through the narrow doorway from the stairs. It craned its neck toward K'shasthra, croaking several times while flapping its wings.

"Ormu, my familiar, calls me," muttered the wizard. "I forgot that I'd left an important magical brew fermenting. Stay here, Simon; I shall return very soon."

So saying, the old man hurried out of the chamber, the vulture following him in grotesque, waddling haste.

Simon stood unmoving for several moments, listening to K'shasthra's soft footfalls fading away up the stairs. Suspicion stirred within him; though the old wizard's reason for leaving had been given with quick and plausible smoothness, he could recall nothing in the chamber above that suggested preparations for a "magical brew."

Thus, after the sounds of the mage's ascent had faded entirely, he entered the door and began to creep silently up the dark stairs.

As he neared the top he began to hear a voice speaking in hushed tones—the wizard's—and as he stole along the short passage toward the blanket-draped door Simon began to hear the words clearly:

"... yes, yes, he is here, and you may have him, for he has proved useless to the Order. But you should not have come here. Haven't you been told the rules of the Order often enough to—?"

"Shut up, old rock-lizard!" snarled a coarse voice. "We've followed your rules till now, but there's a limit. The bastard's killed seven of my men, and by Ahriman!—we're going to make sure he takes at least that many days in dying."

Simon's scalp prickled as he recognized the voice of Gutakh, chief of the Mailed Raiders; he did not need to approach the curtain and peer through it to picture the bandit's scarred, sadistic face framed by its bristling dark beard, the narrow eyes that scowled or gloated mercilessly beneath thick eyebrows and steel helm. The soft clinkings of armor and blades told him that several other men must be standing in the small chamber as well.

"Hush, you oaf!" hissed K'shasthra. "I've left Simon of Gitta in the chamber below—"

"And just what else is in that chamber?" growled Gutakh, though in a lowered voice. "Gold, perhaps? Gems?"

"No. And in any case, Gutakh, the Order has well paid you and your outlaws to terrorize this region, to help insure that men will shun it. You have no cause to demand more."

"Oh, don't we?" There was a sneer in the bandit's voice. "I'd say we have good cause indeed. The loss of seven good men demands a great deal of compensation. You must have a lot of loot hidden around here, old wizard…."

Simon backed slowly away and crept down the stairs. Behind him he could hear the voices rising in more animated argument, but he had heard enough. He must immediately find a way out of this place.

Back in the great domed chamber, however, he realized that escape was impossible. The entire wall was one smooth circuit of seamless rock. A glance into the pit quenched the slight hope that he might have overlooked an exit down there. Besides, who could live in the smothering vapor surrounding the pale-limbed, hard-visaged man who lay entombed therein…?

Suddenly a wild yell rang distantly from the stairway door—the voice of the wizard, high-pitched in anger or terror. It was followed by the sounds of strange cracklings and hissings, then the screams of several men. The racket lasted only a few seconds; then silence returned.

"Baal!" muttered Simon, sweat dampening his brow. He realized that the argument in the chamber above must have escalated into violence. Doubtless the wizard had defended himself with some sort of magic before being slain. Soon Gutakh and his bandits would be coming down the stair. Simon cursed again, hate blazing in his eyes as he scanned the torches on the wall. They would make poor weapons. Gods, for a sword!—a blade with which to take at least some of his enemies with him—

Suddenly the memory hit him: the handle of a sword, protruding from behind the right shoulder of the man who lay supine in the pit!

He used a precious minute to take several deep breaths and hold them, letting them out slowly, calming his mind in the way that his great mentor Daramos had taught him. Then he deliberately stepped off the rim of the pit and onto the stone platform perhaps a foot down. The thick vapor swirled about his ankles, imparting a slight chill to his flesh; yet it was not as dense as water, nor even wet—something midway between liquid and airy substance....

Drawing one last lungful of air, he purposefully moved down the narrow stairway, felt the vapor close over his head. Despite the dark quality of the medium through which he moved he could see quite clearly—in fact, the flesh of his arms seemed more pale than usual by contrast. The sound of his feet on the stone seemed greatly muffled, and he wondered if he would be able to hear the approach of Gutakh and his bandits while he was in the pit....

Then he was at the bottom, approaching the man who lay on the dais of carven rock. Surely the man was dead—there was not the slightest sign of breathing or other movement. Perhaps the vapor contained some mummifying property, for there was also not the slightest sign of decay. As Simon drew close the induced calm of his mind was slightly disturbed by an involuntary awe, a tingling fear. Those rough yet far from brutish features, framed by red hair and beard, seemed to connote dignity and intelligence along with ruthlessness and an iron will; the body, though somewhat taller than an average warrior's, seemed at least three times as massive, and Simon uneasily wondered what would happen should those mighty limbs begin to stir and flex....

Snuffing the thought, he gripped the sword's handle and tugged. It slid easily from its sheath despite the weight of the body that lay upon it. Simon noted briefly that it was of an ancient design, having only a small guard and a wide, tapering blade—yet that blade was as bright as the best Persian steel and the entire sword was large enough to be wielded two-handed.

Without pondering these anomalies, he strode back to the stairway and ascended as rapidly as he could without setting his heart to pounding. As it was, his lungs felt near to bursting as he neared the top of the pit. He dashed up the last few steps and exhaled explosively as his head broke the surface, then frantically gulped in clean air as the heavy vapor swirled about the base of his neck.

Immediately he heard stomping footfalls, cursing voices, and the echoing clink of metal. Men were rushing from the upper stairway into the great domed chamber! Simon crouched back, forcing himself to breathe more shallowly, his face barely above the surface of the vapor; he did not dare to peer up over the rim.

"Find the dog!" bellowed the voice of Gutakh. "He can't be far."

"There's no place to hide in here," yelled a man closer to Simon. "Wait—I see stairs going down into the pool. There's a platform just under the rim—"

A bearded face appeared over the edge—a hard, brutal Persian face topped by a steel helmet. Even as the man's eyes widened Simon swung the blade, neatly lopping the head from its owner's shoulders. As the decapitated corpse toppled after its head into the pit, neck arteries spurting crimson jets, Simon sprang erect and leaped into the midst of his foes, roaring with rage. Steel clashed furiously, cries of fear and anger echoed, and another bandit went down with a cloven skull beneath the great blade.

Simon dodged frantically as a dozen blades sought his flesh; one ripped his tunic and gashed his side, but then he was beyond his enemies and whirling, back to the wall, to confront them anew. As they paused he grabbed a torch with his left hand, snatching it from its bracket.

"*Alive!*" screamed Gutakh furiously. *"Take him alive!"*

The crowd of bandits surged in as one man. Simon thrust savagely, the point of his great sword plowing through the links of the nearest bandit's mail-shirt, lodging between ribs. In the same instant another Persian struck Simon hard on the forearm with a stave, numbing his hand. Snarling, he rammed the torch into the man's face, sending him reeling back, howling, with beard ablaze. Then the rest again surged in relentlessly, beating Simon to the ground with fists, clubs, and sword pommels.

"Good lads!" yelled the bandit chief, advancing. "That's right, hold him down—at least four of you. Remember what old K'shasthra said—the bastard's gladiator-trained! Good—now, spreadeagle him."

Gutakh drew a dirk from his belt and stood over Simon, who struggled futilely against the six bandits who held him pinned upon the stone floor. For a moment two pairs of eyes glared hatred toward one another.

"Well, Simon of Gitta," snarled Gutakh, licking his thick lips, "you've now cost me *ten* of my men. But you won't die as quickly as they did, by Ahriman! For a beginning, you're going to find out whether you like the taste of your own gonads."

The dagger point started slowly down. Following its motion with sick fascination, Simon was only vaguely aware of the sight beyond it: the bandit with the singed beard, kneeling at the edge of the pool under the mistaken impression that it contained water. Then the man suddenly cried out:

"Hey, Gutakh, there's someone else—"

The bandit's voice choked off abruptly as a large hand shot up and clamped on his neck, then jerked him over the edge. In the next instant the man's voice shrieked out anew, dwindling down into the pit until it ended with a muffled crunch of bone and a clatter of steel—and in the same moment a hulking form stepped up out of the vapor pool and strode purposefully forward, a Persian sword in its left hand and a dirk in its right.

Gutakh whirled, snarling—then suddenly gasped and paled. "Gods of the Hells!" he shrieked. "It's—"

"So, Gutakh, we meet again!"

The voice of the massive red-haired warrior was a growl of menace, his grin a crooked sneer of hate. And his eyes, blue and glaring—for an instant Simon felt a surge of irrational terror, the terror of nightmare, for never had he seen such terrible hatred as that which blazed from the eyes of the Slayer—

The Slayer, risen anew from the pit, lusting for blood—

"I might have benefited you and your gang, Gutakh. You should not have betrayed me into the hands of the Order!"

"Get him!" screamed the bandit-chief. *"At him—all of you!"*

Four of the men holding Simon leaped up to join Gutakh and the rest; the other two slackened their grips slightly, indecisive. Simon adroitly slipped free from them, driving his stiffened hand into the throat of one while twisting away from the other. The first went down, strangling and gasping; the second drew his dagger and lunged. Simon rolled away, barely evading the blade, and came smoothly to his feet in a fighting stance. Behind him he heard the clash of steel on steel, the thud of heavy blows on flesh, the shrieks and curses of raging and dying men.

"Die!" screamed Simon's assailant, rushing in and slashing.

Again he barely avoided the blow, then charged and grappled the man. They went down together, Simon's hand locked around the Persian's dagger wrist, and for a moment wrestled precariously near the brink of the pit. Simon snarled as he felt the fingers of the bandit's left hand gouging into his face, groping for his eyes. Quickly he achieved an arm-lock and rolled his weight into it; the bandit shrieked as his right elbow crunched and cracked backwards. Immediately Simon broke free and shoved his foe with both feet, sending him howling over the edge of the vapor pool.

Snatching up the fallen dagger, Simon leaped to his feet. The knot of embattled men surged between him and the doorway; even as he watched, another Persian went down screaming, mailed sword arm flopping loosely, half-severed. Four other bandits lay dead already, gashed hideously and staining the stone floor crimson. The remaining few were pressing the Slayer hard, driving him back against the wall.

"Kill him! Kill him!" screeched Gutakh.

Simon rushed forward and thrust, but his foot slipped on the blood-slick stone, throwing him off balance; his dagger point was turned by a mail shirt. Immediately the bandit whirled and swung his sword, but Simon was already beneath the blow, driving forward and crashing together with his foe into the melee, thrusting his dirk up beneath the mail-shirt into the Persian's groin and belly. He heard the Slayer roaring a war cry in an unknown tongue, felt blood spatter on him as more foes sprawled mortally gashed—

There was a final ring of steel, a final shriek of fear and pain—then silence. Sitting up in a welter of bloody carcasses, Simon saw that only two men remained standing—Gutakh and the Slayer. Gutakh was clutching his right wrist, his brutish face twisted in agony; nearby lay the hand that had been attached to that wrist, its fingers still gripping the sword pommel.

"You shouldn't have double-crossed me, Gutakh!" growled the massive warrior. His own sword clattered on the stone, and then his left hand shot out and locked on the bandit's throat. Tighter and tighter clenched the thick fingers of that hand, the forearm muscles bulging to the thickness of a normal man's calf. The Persian's face purpled as veins popped under the skin, and his eyes bulged horribly. Then there came a hideous, grinding crunch of vertebrae and cartilage.

Flinging away the bandit's carcass contemptuously, the Slayer turned and confronted Simon, who wondered uneasily what was to come next. Never had he seen a fighter such as this man! Eight or nine bandits had attacked him, and he had killed all but one. True, his mighty chest now heaved from his great exertion, and some of that blood upon him was his own, oozing from a few slight cuts on his arms and face. That proved him mortal, at least. Yet Simon knew that if the Slayer chose to attack him, he stood no chance.

The massive warrior advanced and Simon crouched into a fighting stance, dirk ready. He felt himself cringe inwardly at the blue glare of hate that still smoldered in the Slayer's eyes. The hulking figure stopped only five feet away, and for a moment the two blood-splattered fighters glared silently at one another.

Suddenly the Slayer grinned, held out his left hand, and said: "Hell, man, put away that sticker! Aren't you going to shake the hand of the man who saved your ass?"

An hour later they sat in the upper chamber partaking of the old wizard's food and wine, having cleansed themselves with his store of water before binding up their slight wounds. In a dark corner lay the wizard himself, a sword protruding from his lean breast, while near him sprawled two of the bandits, their corpses oddly charred here and there.

"The old coot put up a fight," growled the Slayer between mouthfuls. "Evidently he knew a few sorcerers' tricks."

"K'shasthra told me that you were responsible for all the hatred and violence on earth," Simon commented.

The Slayer gestured impatiently and made an obscene sound. "Such crap! When it comes to hate and violence, humans need no help from me."

"He also said that only one thing would revive you, but didn't specify what it was. How did it happen?"

"*You* did it, fellow." The massive warrior held up his sword, the blade of which was now polished to its original brightness. "When you used this beauty to lop off that bastard's head, it snapped me out of the spell just like that! Then I grabbed his sword and dagger, and ran up just in time to save your hide."

"I see. Blood." Simon nodded somberly. "But how did you survive the vapor of the pit?"

"The same way you did, of course. Held my breath."

Simon took another swig of the wine. In spite of the red-haired warrior's casual, even occasionally humorous, manner, he did not feel easy in his presence. The smoldering hatred was always evident in those blue eyes, ready to blaze out again. Suddenly Simon realized the significance of that intimidating glare of hate: *This* was the Mark that had been placed upon the Slayer, that all men might know and fear him.

"Your sword," said Simon, "—its design is ancient, yet it's evidently of superior steel."

The man nodded. "I forged it myself. There was a long period during which mankind forgot how to work iron and steel. But I remembered, and eventually became adept at it." He fondled the weapon almost lovingly, gazing into the mirror of its blade as if at dark memories. "I've had this baby a long time."

Simon's uneasiness deepened. He rose, took a final swallow of wine, then donned a Persian sword-belt and cloak and picked up a bundle of provisions he had prepared. "We'd best be going. The wizard's vulture evidently escaped and will no doubt be bearing news of this night's events to other members of the High Guardians."

The Slayer nodded again, rising also. "I see that you, too, know something about wizards."

They left the chamber, carrying their provisions, and soon emerged from the rock crevice into the cold night air. The wind had ceased, the stars were out, and a nearly full moon was rising above the far-off snowy mountains to the east. Some riderless horses stood about on the ridgetop, grazing on the sparse dry grasses. It took each of them but a few minutes to capture a mount for himself.

"I journey westward," said Simon, "—to the plains of Sumer and beyond, eventually to Rome. Will you come with me?"

"No." The Slayer gazed toward the distant mountains. "I go east. I want to pay a call on a few others of the Order of the High Guardians."

"I see. You, too, seek revenge."

They faced one another, an understanding hanging between them.

"I think that you wander under a bit of the same curse that drives me," said the massive warrior, "and I see some of the same hatred in your eyes…. Well, good luck, Simon of Gitta. May all your enemies know terror and death! And someday, mayhap, one of us may somehow meet the gods that have cursed us, and slay them also."

Again their left hands clasped in a firm, strong grip.

"Good luck to you also, Slayer. But before we part, will you not tell me your name?"

The hulking warrior laughed harshly. "You already know it well, Simon. But since you want to hear it aloud, it is—"

The syllable rang out, harsh as the clash of steel on stone in the cold night air. Again Simon nodded somberly. It was indeed as he had already known.

Then Cain turned away and, mounting, rode rapidly eastward up the slope of the moonlit ridge, into the night.

About "The Throne of Achamoth"

Simon's next adventure takes place only six months after the events in "Seed of the Star God" in the autumn of A.D. 32, still in Asia Minor, although he and his companions have travelled from Ephesos to Antioch. Still mourning the loss of his soul-mate Helen, Simon goes to extreme lengths to see her again—even if it's not on this plane of existence.

"The Thorne of Achamoth" (which first appeared in *Weirdbook* #21, Autumn 1985) is unique among the Simon tales, trading in its usual sword & sorcery action in favor of a more surreal, spiritual vision quest filled with cosmic imagery. It's also perhaps the crucial story for understanding the cosmology behind the Simon of Gitta universe that the other stories only hint at. It explains why Simon's soul is so powerful and unique, and why he and Helen are spiritually linked throughout eternity in a bond so profound even death is only a temporary inconvenience.

This was the first Simon tale that Richard Tierney collaborated on with another author, Robert M. Price. An expert in both the Cthulhu Mythos and ancient Gnostic Christianity, Price fused the two together—although whether it's the Mythos seen through a Gnostic lens, or Gnosticism seen through a Mythos lens, is hard to say. In it, the Mythos' daemon-sultan Azathoth becomes Achamoth, which was the name of the Fallen Sophia, the mother of the Demiurge in some Gnostic systems.

Specifically, Price incorporates Tierney's unique interpretation of the Mythos that forms the background not only for his Simon stories, but also his John Taggart and Red Sonja tales. Tierney reimagines August Derleth's Elder Gods as the "Lords of Pain" who created life in order to psychically feed off pain and suffering of sentient life-forms. Their enemies, the Great Old Ones, want to deprive the Pain Lords of this nourishment—by destroying all life!

To fully understand the spiritual cosmology this story attempts to explain through somewhat psychedelic metaphor, readers may want to reference the sections "Simon the Holy God", "Love Stronger Than Death", and "Know Thyself" in the introduction.

THE THRONE OF ACHAMOTH

by Richard L. Tierney and Robert M. Price

I

Simon of Gitta stood silently upon the balcony outside the window of his high room, gazing toward the full moon as it slowly rose above the city of Antioch. Strange emotions stirred deep within him. He leaned forward, hands on the balcony's rail, staring straight at the moon's orange disc, scarcely aware of the few stars that shared the sky with it at this hour of dusk, nor of the dimming sounds of the great city below. The moonlight made his youthful, high-cheekboned face seem strangely ageless—made black pits of his deep-set eyes, black shadows of the bangs that brushed his wide forehead.

"Luna—Selene—Helen," he muttered, the sound of his voice almost too soft to stir the air. "Where are you this night, my lost love—my only love…?"

"Gone from this world, Simon—but not from you."

The young man turned slowly and faced the dark-robed oldster who had joined him so abruptly and silently. "As always, Dositheus, you come with a sorcerer's practiced stealth."

The old man ignored the younger one's slight tone of resentment. He was gazing upon the newly-risen moon, and in its rays his wrinkled face revealed some of the same rapt sadness Simon's had shown.

"Aye—Luna, Selene," he murmured, stroking his white beard. "To mortals of this world it is a symbol of Her. How beautiful she is tonight!"

Simon shook his head abruptly as if to awaken himself from an unwonted mood. His features were stern as he looked upon his old mentor.

"Are you ready?" he demanded. "Have the preparations been made?"

Dositheus nodded. "They have been. But, Simon, are you sure you want to go through with this?"

"I am. I must see Helen again."

The old mage sighed, strode two paces back into the room, then returned to the balcony, his dark, symbol-emblazoned robes sweeping the tiles with a soft whisper. His face was pensive, even anxious.

"I have warned you, Simon: my powers, though great, may not be adequate to guide you back to this world once you have left it. I ask you one last time: Can you not accept Helen's death—?"

"I must see her again, Dositheus."

The old man nodded. The determination in his pupil's voice, the hardness in his moon-limned features, were not to be denied. For an instant Dositheus again felt the almost unique spiritual force that had caused him years ago to seek Simon out and rescue him from the brutal slavery of the arena.

"Follow me, then." He turned and led Simon into the lamplit room and pointed to a dark, symbol-emblazoned tunic draped over a couch. "Don that, and nothing else. You must not wear bands, belts, or garments that constrict."

Simon quickly doffed his own belt, sandals, and tunic, then put on the other tunic with its planetary symbols over his athletic form. Instructed in magic as he was, he knew the reason for Dositheus' directions: an astral voyage such as he planned could be sustained only by a healthy physical body—at least if he hoped to return to earth—and that body must not be encumbered by binding physical objects, lest the flow of spiritual energy be impeded.

"Now, old wizard—lead on."

Dositheus shook his head sadly. "Once more, Simon, I have to warn you: it is a perilous journey on which you embark. You will see things that may blast your soul!"

"Enough. I thought you'd had done with that. No more excuses. You told me once that you were aided upon just such a spiritual voyage as this by Daramos, greatest of the Persian mages—and I have heard it confirmed from Daramos' own mouth during the years we were both under his tutelage."

"Yet there is a difference, Simon. Though you and I are both True Spirits, sundered from the Lord of Light and trapped in this world of matter by the mad demiurge Achamoth who created it, your being contains a greater portion of the fragmented God-Soul than does mine—perhaps more than any other human's—and therefore the impetus of your spiritual destiny may carry you into dangerous realms where my knowledge cannot aid you. During my own journey, even with the aid of Daramos, I was able only to approach the Sphere of Saturn before my soul retreated in terror, and I feel that I was barely able to defy the Archons of the Primal Gods and return to my living body. What you seek, Simon, lies far beyond Saturn's sphere."

For a moment the young man wavered as he sensed the genuine concern in his mentor's eyes. Deliberately he hardened his feelings and said:

"Lead on, Dositheus—unless of course you are the charlatan I have often half-suspected you to be."

The old man's eyes sparked with a momentary anger, and in that moment the mystical symbols on his robe seemed to glow slightly; but in the next moment the spark and the glow were gone, so quickly that Simon wondered if they had been an illusion.

"Simon, Simon," said Dositheus, his tone startling the younger man by its likeness to that of a mother toward a stubborn child. "Your anger, your bitterness, makes you say what you know is not true. You have seen with your own eyes that what Daramos and I can do is no charlatanry."

Simon shook his head. "Yet, we make a good living, you and I, by fooling the mob with magic illusions. Can you or can you not, Dositheus, enable me to see and speak with Helen, as you claim?"

An almost mystical light, tinged with anguish, replaced the anger in Dositheus' eyes. "You know I can—though now you fight against the truth of it even more strenuously than you once fought your opponents in the arena. You must now make your peace with that truth, Simon—and with a truth about yourself—for that is your only hope of commanding the power that will enable you to return from the voyage upon which you demand I send you."

Simon's features softened a trifle; he sensed his old mentor's true concern. "A truth about myself—?"

"An earthly truth—one to supplement the cosmic truth I have often told you, that you and Helen are perhaps the two greatest fragments of the sundered God-Soul of the universe. Perhaps I have stressed that latter truth too much during the two years since the Romans caused your Helen to die; if so, forgive me, for it was but to assuage your grief. But now the balance must be regained. Tell me, Simon: Who are we?"

"What do you mean? We are wandering magicians from Samaria—illusion-makers, garnering a good living from the gullible mob—"

"Aye. And so, we are human." Dositheus gestured to the wide balcony door beyond which the moon, now silvery and companioned by many brightening stars, was rising above the darkened streets and buildings of the great city. "Out there lie hundreds of thousands of other humans, preparing for sleep, or thievery, or lovemaking, or who knows what else—and beyond them in this wide, nighted world lie millions more. Only a small fraction of them are True Spirits such as we, Simon—yet, who is to judge which those few are? But tonight I ask you to identify yourself with those unsouled millions who wrangle and fight, breed and strive and die only for gain or that their progeny might live. Think of them, Simon, feel for them, make of them an anchor for your soul; otherwise, you might never return…"

Simon looked out over the city to the wide river that lay silvery under the moon, ships moored there in the shadows of buildings, to the angular walls and towers that cast those shadows. He seemed to sense the myriad human lives out there, clustered, festering.

"Why should I care for them? Have you not told me that they are devoid of the Spark, like animals? Have I not sensed that for myself? Do they not themselves constantly prove it to me, day by day?"

"Yet any of them might birth a True Spirit. Cling to this world, Simon, cling to it, lest you be unable to return. Remember that you are one human among millions, that you are in a world of time where multitudes have lived and died. Tell me, Simon: *when* are we living?"

Simon humored him. "We live in the autumn of the eighteenth year of the mad emperor Tiberius, Princeps of Rome."

"Cling to that, Simon. You are a human, in this world and in this time. And now, follow me."

He followed the wizard down the several stairways from their rented apartments to the cellars, which were also rented by Dositheus from the rich merchant who owned the building. On the stone floor of the largest room, which was furnished only with one low couch in the center and a small cabinet against one wall, a pentagram was outlined in bright blue chalk. It surrounded the couch, on either side of which coals glowed within the bowl of a bronze brazier, and at each of its five corners burned a white candle. Beneath the couch and partly hidden by it was a large symbol resembling a seven-headed hydra, also drawn in blue.

"Little enough preparation," Simon remarked, "for so momentous a voyage as you say this is to be."

"Aye, Simon. There is seldom any preparation for death, and it is the journey of death that you must undertake—death before its appointed time. Now, lie down on the couch, my son."

Simon did so—then suddenly realized that Dositheus had never before used that term of endearment while addressing him. He watched as the old man turned to the cabinet, unlocked it, and took forth a bulky yellowed scroll. It was, Simon realized without surprise, the old thaumaturge's most prized possession—the original Persian rendition of the *Sapientia Magorum* that held the arcane secrets of the olden magus Ostanes.

"Simon, before I begin—"

"Spare me, Dositheus. I will not be dissuaded."

The old wizard nodded; the various torch-flames about the walls reflected from his balding pate. "I know. Yet I must instruct you. There is more between you and your lost Helen, Simon, than the love of man for woman—as I have often told you. She is your *syzygy*—your yoke-mate, your other self. If only you would curb this madness of yours!—for you and Helen *will* meet again on this material plane—as you *must*. But that time cannot be hastened."

Simon's eyes were hard. "Yet it was your magic that first brought Helen and me prematurely together. I *will* see her now. You cannot deny me this."

Dositheus nodded sadly, turned and paced slowly to the farthest side of the dimly lit chamber. Simon became aware of strange fumes being exuded by the twin braziers flanking him. His mind felt like it was beginning to float. Then Dositheus turned and faced him.

"The fumes are affecting you," said Dositheus. "Do not fight them. Let them waft you where they will."

"Why—why do they not affect you...?" Simon asked dreamily.

"Partly because I am outside the pentacle, partly because your True Spirit is greater than mine. I have told you that you are one of the High Ones, possessing perhaps a larger measure of the sundered soul of the Lord of Light than anyone on this earth. Thus your destiny is great, as is that of Her whom you knew as Helen. For you and she are mates beyond time and materiality, formed of the Ultimate Source. Now you must realize your destiny, Simon, and accept it."

Simon watched the old man, whose voice was inducing an hypnotic effect. His former impatience was now gone, stilled by the strange mixture of odors from the braziers—odors delightful and intoxicating, yet piquant and tinged even with a trace of foulness—and also by the tired yet firm conviction of his mentor's voice and somber air. Suddenly he wanted to reach out to this old mentor of his—this eccentric old sorcerer he had never completely trusted—but found in that same moment that he could not move. The webs of sorcery he had requested were being woven about him.

Dositheus stepped forward with a small jar of blue paint he had taken from the cabinet and proceeded to daub Simon's forehead with a blue symbol. From the feel of it Simon guessed it must be a sunburst or spoked wheel design.

"This is the symbol of Narayana, the Seven-Headed Serpent—the same that I have drawn upon the floor. It is older than Persia, older than India, older than mankind. The Nagas of primal Mu used it to designate the Seven Aspects of Creation, the Seven Minds of Being; it will aid you to penetrate the Seven Barriers you must pass." The old mage withdrew for a moment from Simon's view, then returned carrying the latter's straight, double-edged sword, which he placed in Simon's right hand. "You may need it—or, rather, its spirit-double—before your return."

So saying, Dositheus withdrew again from the pentagram and stood tall, the ancient scroll held up like a wand in his lean left hand. "There are other weapons, Simon, as you well know—words you will need to speak in order to pass the boundaries established by the Pain Lords. I have taught you only the earthly sounds of these words, but your soul already knows their higher vibrations. They will come to you complete at the proper times."

The old wizard then unrolled the scroll and began to read. His voice, which had already seemed to be fading into distance, now was as the merest whisper, yet Simon was able to understand him clearly. And as reality flickered, the Persian words—already familiar from past studies—seemed this time to take on new connotations never before apprehended:

"O Atar, O Fire-Spirit, waft upward the sundered spirit of thy questing, homeward-returning Master! Awake, Simon of Gitta, awake! Sleep no longer, O Lord Mazda, the sleep of matter! Awake—"

Simon's vision whirled. The ceiling was becoming a dark pool, swirling, drawing him upward...

"Awake, O Lord Mazda, from the sleep of matter..."

II

He emerged from the darkness—not the darkness of sleep, but of non-being. Had he been there for a second, or an eternity...?

He was rising upward, through the walls and floors of the great building, passing through material barriers as if they did not exist. Though the rooms were in darkness he sensed clearly the arrangement of their furnishings, the presence of their drowsing occupants. Then he emerged from the rooftop and found himself wafted rapidly upward above the dark, sprawling city of Antioch—upward toward the stars and the full, gleaming face of the moon.

Luna—Selene—

The city receded beneath him, and as he rose he sensed the animal vitality of the hundreds of thousands who slept in its darkness or crept through its alleys on errands of stealth. For a moment the perception of that seething stew of life-force afflicted him with a feeling analogous to suffocation—but then, his ever-more-rapid ascent bore him out of it. Now he could see, amid that stew of uneasy dreams and red emotions, a few bright sparks, perhaps a score of them—True Spirits like himself, he intuitively realized. For an instant he yearned to swoop down and rescue them from this seething ocean of torment in which they were embedded like diamonds in a dung-heap—but realized he could not. He was being swept up by Destiny—and yet, somehow, by his own will—toward that ultimate region whence, he vaguely realized, all True Spirits had originally come.

And now the speed of his ascent was truly alarming. Antioch had become a vanishing blotch upon the darkness of the vast earth, the Orontes River a vanishing silver thread. The world was expanding to horizons astonishingly vast—dark to the starry east, silvery to the west where the great sea sprawled to the sunset—the returning, brightening sunset...

Then the sun began to rise in the west, and Simon realized that it was due to the great speed of his ascent! Just before its returning light flooded his vision he glimpsed, upon the enormous curved expanse of the eastward earth, perhaps half a dozen brilliant gleams of light—the souls of High Ones, like himself...

Then they had vanished, lost amid the light of the western dawn into which he was rising. The earth's curvature was now apparent—and then the sky, despite the sun's brilliance, began to darken. The stars emerged once more, brighter and more numerous than ever, and Simon suddenly realized what had happened: he had emerged from the *air*, that medium that scattered and softened light!

A momentary terror gripped him. The air, which some philosophers felt pervaded all things, was but a thin blanket about the earth. Nature, far from abhorring a vacuum, appeared to be almost entirely one colossal vacuum extending to the ultimate boundary of space!

But, no, this vacuum was not *quite* empty, for now Simon saw what appeared to be dim, sickly-yellowish wisps or streaks of flame ascending upward from that atmosphere surrounding the earth. His astral vision, and the intuition that accompanied it, told him that these wisps were the life-forces of the myriad humans and animals that were suffering and perishing constantly upon the earth.

He turned uneasily from them and gazed upward—no, *outward*, for to his surprise he realized that for him there was no longer any up or down— and fastened his attention on the moon. It now seemed larger, brighter. To him it was a silvery beacon of promise. Surely here he would find the answers to his burning questions...

Luna—Selene—

Yet his course was not taking him directly toward the moon, as he had first thought, but a bit to one side of it. He tried to correct that deviation by force of will, but could not. He tried other maneuvers, found that he could turn in space and view his body—and was startled to see that it, the tunic he wore, and the sword he clutched were expanded, tenuous, so that the bright stars shone dimly through them. He stole a glance behind—and recoiled in startled awe. The earth was but a receding sphere, marked on its thin sunlit crescent with shades of green and blue and streaked with beautiful swirls of white. Beyond it was the sun, whose light, though more intense than Simon had ever seen it, did not hurt his eyes in the slightest. Near it in the blackness gleamed red Antares and its companion stars of Scorpio, their luster undiminished. And then Simon perceived that the solar disc was less than perfect, despite the contentions of philosophers, for irregular blotches seemed to crawl slowly across its face; and again he felt the horror of new revelations contrary to his early learning...

A fresh surge of awe took him as he turned back to the moon, for it was now huge in his sight and he recognized it for what it was—another world. No longer was it full, but gibbous, and along the line of light and dark Simon saw the stark shadows of what were obviously awesome mountain peaks and monstrous craters. He realized, too, that his speed was increasing or his sense of time slowing down—perhaps both—else the moon's phase could not have changed so quickly.

And now, as the lunar orb grew visibly in size, he realized that it was a far different place from what he and his fellow mortals had thought it to be. No blanket of air surrounded it such as surrounded the benign earth, and its surface was cratered and shattered awesomely. In that moment Simon realized that here had taken place that supposedly legendary battle between the Titans and the Gods, and that he would not find upon this airless and shattered world the answer to his quest. A hopeful humanity had used this orb to symbolize its dream of the Eternal Feminine, but only the darkest of such spirits might aptly be so symbolized: Hecate, Lilith, perhaps even the Elamite abomination anciently called Shupnikkurat....

But then he sensed that this blasted globe was not as lifeless as it had at first seemed. Deep within it, like worms and insects within a rotten fruit, teemed myriads of sentient entities—beings so alien in form and thought and purpose that Simon was glad that his spiritual senses could detect them but dimly.

Now, as he began to pass the moon, so that its gleaming gibbous portion decreased toward the half-phase, Simon sensed something new—a pale nimbus of greenish-gray light, barely visible, that entirely surrounded it. At the same time he saw that the moon was turning more and more rapidly, with a motion that was more than the apparent one caused by his approach. Surely his own rate of time-perception *was* slowing down! And now the nimbus was definitely visible—not a cloud so much as a glowing blob of pallid, sickly greenish light—and it was taking on form. In another moment Simon was able to see that form clearly, even though the light of the distant stars shone unimpeded through it.

For an instant he felt horror. The thing was monstrous—a gigantic, pulsing, toadlike entity, eyeless, and snouted with a cluster of slowly-waving feelers like those of an anemone. Its non-material flesh appeared to Simon's senses as of a blotchy, fungoid texture and color; the moon seemed to him to float at its center in lieu of a heart. He tensed, willed himself to flee—but in the next instant sensed that the monster was asleep, drowsily drifting, orbiting with the moon....

And now Simon noticed that a vast, thin membrane extended out from it in all directions, barely perceptible, curving through space like the concave surface of an unbelievably huge bubble. He glanced above, behind, below, but found no direction in which that bubble did not extend. It enclosed not only himself but all the space surrounding the earth he had left so far behind. Its diameter was equal to the orbit of the monster-enveloped moon as it circled the earth—which that orb seemed to do more and more rapidly as Simon's time-rate slowed down.

Abruptly Simon realized that this colossal being was an *Archon*—only the first of several which Dositheus had warned him of and which he knew he must somehow pass.

He was approaching the vast concavity of the bubble, and now he saw that many of the sickly yellowish flame-streaks accompanying him through the void were plunging into it. Immediately it absorbed them, snuffed them out, stretched them like thin yellow strings in the direction of the monster. The thing absorbed them as it pulsed there, unconscious, corpulent and bloated. Simon shuddered to see it feeding thusly off the radiated life-forces of the myriad fearful, pained and dying organisms of the sublunar world of earth; its sleep seemed to him like the sated dozing of a beast of prey. He felt sickened—then realized that he, too, was fast approaching that soul-entangling membrane, was almost upon it—

"Malevanahkuth!"

He cried out the Name abruptly, almost without intention. It was not a vocal cry, but more—a mental peal that vibrated the blackness. And in that instant, during the cry's brief duration, he had passed through the membrane. The thinness of it surprised him. Had it been material not even the most sensitive thumb and forefinger could have detected it between them. For a tiny moment Simon had sensed the pain and fear of the countless lives caught in that bubble—and then he had burst through it, hurtling with incredible speed into the void beyond.

He glanced back and saw that the monstrous Moon-Archon had not awakened. The Name had protected him—and had protected also, evidently, quite a few hundreds of the yellowish wisps of life which were still accompanying him. These survivors, and the less numerous ones afar off, seemed like dim yellow sparks lost in the immensities, faltering, bewildered, yet pressing onward. Nearly all the other such sparks were now but yellow lines on the vast Sphere behind Simon, millions of them, being drawn toward the pulsing Archon as psychic energy to feed it; only the hardiest, or those lucky enough to be near him, had made it through.

Simon shuddered. Astrologers had long sensed the moon to be a source of emotional influence—and no wonder, considering the cosmic whirlpool of fear and pain of which it was the vortex!

But now Simon, gazing sidewise along the plane of the moon's orbit, sensed a filament of energy extending off into space from the vast bubble. Again his unearthly intuition told him what it must be: the excess psychic energy, not needed to nourish the moon-Archon and sustain its Sphere, was being sent outward into the void, toward the next Sphere, that of—

"Mars!" gasped Simon.

It was true. He was hurtling toward that baleful red planet at an incredible rate. It grew brighter even as he watched—became a disc in his vision—and soon he began to sense an even greater bubble-net extending from it, utterly dwarfing that which had extended from the moon around the earth. In that instant Simon realized two incredible things: first, that the olden astronomer Aristarchus had been right in maintaining that the earth and the other planets orbited the sun; second, that Eudoxus and Aristotle had been right in putting those planets—at least in the astral plane—upon gigantic rotating Spheres. For now Simon could see with his psychic eye that the vast Sphere of Mars extended to include not only the earth and the moon, but the sun and inner planets as well!

The immensity of it overwhelmed him—so much so that he became aware barely in time of his rapid approach to the globe of Mars and the monstrous Archon that surrounded it, pulsing in sleep. He saw only briefly that red planet at the hideous being's heart—sensed its thin atmosphere, its mountains and plains blasted like the moon's, and the monstrous alien life that lurked and slept beneath its surface—that stirred, awakening at his approach....

And then he saw that the Archon was awakening also. This one seemed a bladdery, reddish-purple head, smooth like an octopus, featureless save for two great opening eyes and two writhing masses of more than a dozen tentacles. The eyes, Simon felt, were staring directly at him—the tentacles were reaching in his direction....

"Khamael!"

Again the Name he spoke was not really a word but a mind-cry, full of cosmic connotations extending far beyond the sound he had learned from Dositheus upon the far-off earth. Again he plunged through the bubble of psychic force, felt the brief keening shrill of fear and pain from the beings trapped within it. Then he was through it, but the sound of that keening note continued to ring in his mind—and to harmonize strangely with the higher, more intense note that still reverberated in his soul from his earlier passage through the moon's Sphere.

Harmonize....

Suddenly he realized the significance of it. *This* was the Music of the Spheres that Pythagoras and other exceptionally psychic humans had long ago sensed—but, how naively optimistic had been their interpretation of it! Simon recalled the old tale of the king who roasted his enemies alive inside a hollow bronze bull whose nostrils were fashioned in such a way that the death-screams emerged as lovely, haunting harmonies....

He looked back, saw the Mars-Archon settling again into sated sleep—yet his horror was undiminished. Aye, Eudoxus and Aristotle had

been correct in their intuition of the planetary Spheres—yet how wrong
they had been to suppose them the boundaries of uncorrupted realms of
glory!

None of those flame-wisps accompanying Simon had escaped the
Mars barrier; all were now food for the monstrous Archon. Once again he
sensed the filament of excess energy being beamed out to the next Sphere.
And now, as he hurtled soundlessly onward at ever greater speed, he grew
aware of several scores of brightly-shining specks, far from himself and
from one another, hurtling outward also and increasing in brightness as
they did in velocity. Instantly his intuition told him that these were True
Spirits who, like himself, had known in their souls the thought-words
needed to pass the barriers of the moon and Mars. No longer obscured by
the myriad streaks and wisps of mundane human and animal life-forces,
they shone against the black void with a pulsing white glory that put the
stars to shame. Simon glanced at his form, saw that his transparent flesh
was glowing brightly also; his formerly dark tunic seemed now of the pur-
est white, the planetary symbols upon it shining with a golden radiance,
while his sword-blade blazed with a silvery sheen....

The space from the Sphere of Mars to that of Jupiter took far longer
to cross despite Simon's increased speed and slowing time, for it was far
vaster than the inner ones. He looked back, saw that Mars had already
dwindled to a tiny disc, that the earth was no more than a bright gleam not
far from the sun, which in turn seemed only a quarter of its normal size.
He turned away, again feeling a spiritual shudder at the vast empty immensities through which he plunged. He could still see the far-off gleams of his
fellow True Spirits, for though their mutual distances increased as they
sped outward from the earth, their point of origin, their brightness seemed
to increase also. Ahead Simon saw Jupiter shining, much brighter than he
had ever known it.

Then he sensed, humming in the far distance, the next barrier
Sphere—and watched uneasily as Jupiter, the planet that sustained it, began
slowly to expand to a sinister, banded disc....

III

Simon gasped as that monstrous world swelled and grew in his vision, approaching ponderously yet visibly from his right as it pursued the arc of its
vast orbit. It seemed to rotate once every few seconds, and as it advanced
Simon could see four large moons and a few lesser ones swinging in slow
orbits about it. Appalled to realize how much his time-rate had slowed
down—had his untenanted body died during the weeks or months since he

had left it?—he was yet more appalled by the aspect of this colossal, bloated, whirling thing he had once known of as the planet Jupiter.

It was huge beyond conception; he sensed that more than a thousand worlds like the earth could easily be swallowed by it. Its banded surface roiled and seethed as it rolled, and at each ponderous rotation he saw a great reddish eye-shaped splotch upon its equator, widening or narrowing as it swirled like a planet-devouring whirlpool. This time there was no nebulous Archon surrounding the globe, but Simon sensed that the seething world was itself infused with a monstrous life. Its many-colored bands seemed to pulse as upon the flesh of a spinning jellyfish, its reddish eye-splotch to wrinkle and writhe as if it glowered malevolently....

Then, incredibly quickly, half the looming planet was in shadow as Simon approached the barrier. He heard the membrane's deep note, a throbbing drone, harmonizing with those other Spheres he had left far behind. He needed the name! Dositheus had told him the human syllables: Tzed... Tzadek....

"Tzadakkael!"

Again it had come to him barely in time. Again Simon felt the surge of power tugging at him, far more powerfully than had the barriers of the moon and Mars—heard the brief keening of what he knew to be True Spirits in agony—but then he was through, and the monstrous whirling planet was receding behind him as he sped ever more rapidly outward, the evil harmonies of the Spheres accompanying him....

Suddenly he suspected that he might be alone in the void—the scores of True Spirits that had crossed the spaces with him seemed to be gone—

No, not *all* gone, for now Simon could see a handful of those pulsing white sparks still outward bound like himself, though at an incredible distance from him and one another. Only a half dozen were left out of those many scores! Evidently the forces of the monster-planet were set to capture True Spirits after the inner Spheres had weeded out the lowlier and more abundant life forces.

Now there remained only Saturn, ruler of the outermost Sphere. That puzzled Simon a bit, for the ancient wisdom held that there were seven Spheres—or seven sets of them—and he had crossed only three. Surely this was another confirmation of Aristarchus, who had maintained that the sun, Mercury, and Venus were inside the orbit of the earth!

So great was Simon's speed that by the time he had had these few thoughts he realized he was approaching the Sphere of Saturn. Uneasily he remembered that this was the barrier that had turned Dositheus back in terror. In the same instant he began to hear the deep, menacing thrum of the Sphere's vibration, harmonizing balefully with the tones of the inner Spheres, all of which now seemed, strangely, to emanate at higher pitches than before. Then he saw Saturn itself, swinging in from his right as the inner worlds had done, bringing with it the intense thin beam of spirit-energy projected from Jupiter, and he realized that his time-rate was slowing in a way that caused him to cross each Sphere not far ahead of its oncoming planet. And that must mean that he had been years, not months, upon this impossible voyage!

Saturn, he now saw, was like Jupiter in being immense, banded, and surrounded by whirling moons. It, too, showed no visible Archon but seemed to be imbued with pulsing evil life. In addition it was surrounded with broad, spinning rings—rings which, Simon intuited, served to concentrate the energy of its soul-net more powerfully. The monstrous planet whirled so rapidly that it seemed to buzz; the note of its Sphere rose, and Simon felt his fear rising with it. He saw two of the distant soul-sparks waver and turn back—could barely hear their thin wails of terror and despair—and then the next mystic, Gate-opening Name sprang from within him:

"Ziulquag-Manzah!"

He had begun to say the Name before he was abreast of the planet, had passed the whirling banded globe before finishing it. For an instant searing pain flooded Simon's being. He seemed to hear the shrieks of fellow beings perishing....

Then, as before, he was hurtling outward—but this time there was a difference. A great weariness was falling upon him. He realized that he had lost much energy passing the four barriers, especially the last. His form and sword-blade had lost their brilliance and now gave forth but a dim glow. Looking around him, he saw no sign of those few True Spirits who had accompanied him to the Sphere of Saturn. Had they all perished? Or were some still alive like himself, far off in space, weakened and dimmed?

Slowly his glow began to return, his weariness to fade. But no other spark like himself did he detect in all that vast void. He was alone, hurtling outward at an unknown speed into a cold, empty, star-strewn space, the evil humming of the Spheres fading away behind him. He had crossed the last barrier....

But then, ahead of him, he heard—incredibly, impossibly—another deep, menacing tone that harmonized with those behind.

He was approaching yet another Sphere.

A rising fear, almost a panic, gripped Simon as the evil hum from this unknown barrier increased. Was there to be an infinite series of them? And even if not, would his soul instinctively know the names of their Archons—names whose earthly equivalents his old mentor had never taught him? His fear turned to anger, to rage, took the form of a violent thought:

"Damn you, Dositheus! Damn your incompetence—"

You are wrong, Simon—you have heard the Names.

It was the voice of Dositheus within his mind—and now, dimly, Simon began to see the form of the robed old man, vague and transparent against the starry blackness.

"Baal! It *can't* be you. Many decades have passed—perhaps even centuries—"

Time is no more a barrier than is space to the possessor of Arcana. I sensed your urgency, Simon. But I cannot long maintain the trance that has made this contact possible. Remember the Names; there are but two more of them. Once I read them to you from the book of Ostanes the Mage, who in turn had them from the writings of a sorcerer of millennium-lost Hyperboria. You must remember—

But now Simon was approaching the Sphere. He saw its planet advancing rapidly, huge and ringed and banded like Saturn, though its bands were darker and greenish, and its rings smaller. It hummed menacingly as it spun, rolling insanely on its side along the path of its orbit, its several moons looping vertically about it like a swarm of wasps. Simon gripped his sword, held its glowing blade out before him as he hurtled toward the near-invisible barrier of the nameless planet's Sphere.

Remember the name—

Memory and the voicing of it came simultaneously, barely in time:

"Z'stylzem-Ghani!"

Again the brief but searing pain—and with it, one far-distant yet clearly sensed cry of anguish and despair. One last unseen True Spirit had made it with him to even these remote regions, Simon realized—but only to perish. This time he was truly alone.

Aye, truly alone, for now not even the shadowy form of Dositheus was with him. The madly rolling planet was receding away to his left—but, strangely, it was slowing down, both in its spinning and in the progress it made along its orbit. For an instant Simon again knew terror. Was the thing going to stop, then return to pursue him…?

But, no—for now he realized that the velocity of his own outward plunge was decreasing also. Evidently his subjective sense of the time-rate was reversing. He noticed that the glow of his astral form had again diminished to practically nothing, and this time it was returning very slowly. The weariness he felt was extreme; his very consciousness was dimmed. Apparently the last two barriers had drained all but the last reserves of his spiritual energy….

He seemed to hover there in the dark, colossal spaces for an eternity while sluggish, fearful thoughts drifted through his semi-conscious mind. How long must he drift thus? One century… two… or did it only seem that way? Was he still moving outward, or had he stopped completely, doomed now to drift eternally in these black voids…?

No, for now he realized that his glow was again steadily brightening. And with the returning clarity of mind that accompanied it Simon sensed the deep, evil resonance of the final Sphere that marked the rim of planetary space.

The approach of the last planet, which resembled the previous one in its size and greenish banding, seemed slow and sedate, and Simon realized that his time-rate had indeed speeded up considerably. Again he sensed the malevolent life within its monstrous, world-dwarfing globe....

Yet there was something different about this one, for there was another object out beyond it, looping in from the black spaces—a small, dark world whose enormous oblong orbit would soon cause it to cross the Sphere of the giant, Archon-imbued planet. No—actually *two* small worlds, revolving swiftly around each other....

A thrill of horror lanced through Simon at sight of this double world, for he remembered that Ostanes had written of it also. The larger of the pair was doubtless *Iukkoth*, the slightly smaller one *Chag-hai*—both described as the abodes of sinister inhuman beings, fungoid and crablike and demon-winged, servitors of the monstrous Primal Gods who had formed the material worlds. Those twin dark orbs seemed to exude a menace greater than that of the Archon-planet itself, and Simon wondered if there was any Name that would enable him to pass them....

There is but one way. You must cross the Sphere of the last Archon, and utter its Name, at the same instant the double worlds cross it. Remember the final Name—and use your Will—

This time the voice of Dositheus, more feeble than before, faded quickly, together with the dim visual image that accompanied it. And now Simon saw that the thin beam of spiritual energy, projected to the giant Archon-planet from the inner Spheres, was in turn beamed outward, only slightly diminished, to the dark planet Iukkoth.

Simon extended his bright sword before him and concentrated, found that he could increase his speed but not his direction. His timing must be exact. Swiftly he approached the final Sphere, his outthrust blade gleaming ever more brightly, the eerie harmonies of the Six Spheres droning hypnotically in his soul. Those vibrations must not be allowed to lessen his concentration.... The sinister, black twin-planets were approaching the barrier also—were almost there....

The final Name sprang into Simon's mind:

"*Ksuksa Kluth!*"

Again the searing pain, brief but more intense than ever—and then he was through the barrier, barely conscious and floating in the black immensities beyond the outermost boundaries of the worlds.

Slowly, very slowly, consciousness returned. Simon sensed the eerily beautiful and sinister harmonies of the Spheres fading away behind him.

Turning, he beheld the intense filament of trapped vital and spiritual energies being beamed away from dark Iukkoth into the vast starry space—straight toward that large red star of Orion's shoulder known to Ostanes as *K'lu-vho*. And Simon shuddered at the realization, for K'lu-vho was reputed to be the home of those Primal Gods who ruled the universe and fed upon the pain and fear of all creatures within it.

Then he noticed something even more astounding—that the constellation of Orion, and all the other constellations, appeared to be no larger than they had been when seen from earth. Despite the unthinkably vast spaces he had already crossed, so great that the sun behind him was but a small bright gleam upon the blackness, *the stars appeared no closer than before!* A new terror, greater than all previous ones, gripped him in the face of these cosmic immensities. His energies were gone, sapped to the dregs, his outward progress considerably slowed. This time he was indeed doomed to drift forever....

Simon... Simon, recall now the true Name of Her whom you seek!

Again it was the whispering voice of Dositheus, still instructing him, as the reader of the *Book of the Dead* instructs the deceased at his bedside. The voice was dimmer than ever, and this time unaccompanied by any visual illusion, but it stirred new hope in Simon. The one he sought—Helen....

Yet before you speak Her true Name, remember that you must cling to your humanity, your worldly identity, if you would return. Know that your life on earth, your millions of fellow beings, the other worlds and even the Archons who rule over them, are part of your own material and mundane nature. Cling to that nature as you now make your ascent to the Pleroma of Light, which is an ascent to your own true and greater Self. Remember your material nature—for I can no longer accompany you. And now, Simon, speak the final Name—the Name that you were never taught, that you have always known.

He groped for it. Helen... no, that was her earthly name, even though it symbolized the Light. Instead, the name that suddenly burst from his being, vibrating the void with the last of his fading energy, was:

"Ennoia!"

Instantly it was as if pure light flooded his being, infusing his form and exalting his soul. With a velocity he could not have dreamed possible he streaked onward, outward, into the void.

The stars—the incredibly distant stars—were changing. Those ahead were growing brighter, more bluish, while those behind dimmed and reddened. And then, even as Simon watched, they began to change their patterns and perspectives also; the constellations were shifting, losing their familiar shapes, dissolving more and more rapidly into a gigantic swirl of glowing motes. Simon felt a burst of exultation, of unparalleled liberation, of cosmic power and comprehension. His being, expanding like a burst of supernal light, outshone all the stars—which, he now saw, were grouped by countless billions into vast swirls without number across the boundless cosmos. For an instant he sensed centers of power, several within each star-swirl—abodes of the Primal Gods, Lords of the Archons—and also the frightened and pained souls of trillions of creatures being drawn into them, feeding them. Almost it seemed that one huge groan ascended from the material universe, and Simon felt his exultation fading, turning to horror—

But then, abruptly, as he felt his spirit approach the final barrier—the speed beyond which matter could not go, so that matter-bound beings were trapped within the realm of the Primal Gods—he saw the entire vast material universe simultaneously expand into infinite blackness and collapse into an infinitely small nothingness. Suddenly time and space were not—

And then there was Light—transcendent, blazing, all-pervading radiance—and Simon's mightily expanded soul exulted anew. He had won through the Seven Barriers to the Pleroma, the Fullness, the Realm of Light.

IV

He understood.

Understanding was not like finite knowing. He did not know when or where he was, nor did he need to, for all whens and wheres were gone in that stupendous expansion-implosion, gone into the not-yet and the yet-to-be, which were the same yet not the same and did not exist.

Time there was, but of a higher order than what his tiny—human? —portion had known. Space there was, but of many more dimensions than that which the fleeting dream-human had lived in. What this human named—Simon of Gitta?—had known as time was but one of those lower dimensions, so that all he had known of past and future were as—now.

Now—the eternal, unchanging Realm of Radiance.

And his name was not Simon. It was Mazda, Lord of Light, the One Who Stands Alone, Who Comprises All.

He was All—and yet, strangely, there was the Other also, who shared his realm of light with him. She was the *Ennoia*, the Eternal Thought. They were not human, she and he, but many-dimensioned spheres of the pure Light. They were *syzygys*, the Twin Aeons of the Fullness—twins, but mirrored; opposites, yet somehow One.

But these were strange musings. They came from his dream—his dream of the human he had been, or would be....

Then came to him the questioning thought of the Ennoia: "O Mazda, why do you think of us as 'she' and 'he?'"

"Because I dreamed I was a—man," said the Lord of Light. "His name was Simon. He was—thus."

Ennoia was amused to see the white-and-golden form that stood alone at the center of Mazda's being, clad in radiant tunic, shining sword in hand.

"I see. And I was Helen, and appeared to you like this?"

The form that appeared at the heart of her radiance was the perfection of the feminine, human yet more than human, garbed alluringly in shifting mists of pure whiteness. Though her limbs were fair beyond human fairness, her long hair golden rather than black, her eyes like the blue deeps of the empyrean rather than the depths of dark pools, Mazda yet felt his heart tremble. It was indeed she of whom he had dreamed.

Simon and Helen gazed upon each other while no time passed, while an eternity passed.

"You were All to me," he said with human lips.

"Of course!" She laughed a human laugh, tossed her glowing hair. "How could it be otherwise? But this is a strange dream. I will share it with you."

"No!" he said, a vague apprehension stirring within him.

"I will see you with human eyes as you have seen me. I will know and love you in human ways. We are very lovely. It will be an amusing dream, as are all of our dreams."

Suddenly there was Something Else—something in addition to the All, to the Two who were One. To Simon's human eyes it appeared as a whirling splotch of darkness. It seemed distant, though he found that hard to judge, as there were no objects to use as reference points. Slowly it grew larger, advancing....

"Look!" said Ennoia, laughing and pointing. "Our dream begins. I must go to it—see into it."

"No—we should not—"

But already her fair form was turning, advancing to meet the swirl of darkness, which was now flattening, spreading out upon the universal whiteness like the surface of a murky pool. He who was the Lord of Light hurried after her, his spirit stirred by forebodings.

She knelt beside the pool, peered into it, and its surface began to churn more violently as if the reflected light of her had stirred it.

"Oh, Mazda! I seem to have a thousand forms—a million—all of them shifting and changing—"

"Ennoia—*no!*"

Suddenly with a pealing cry she fell forward and disappeared into the pool, falling or being drawn into her own scattered reflection—and then the light of her and that reflection were gone.

"*Ennoia!*"

The pool's dark surface began to grow calm, but Eternity had suddenly become—an emptiness.

Mazda—or Simon, for he still wore his human form—ran to the pool's edge. It was stilled now, but he sensed a greater turbulence than ever occurring far below the surface.

Suddenly everything beneath that surface appeared entirely different. In place of pure blackness there were now trillions upon trillions of infinitely tiny twinklings of light within darkness—the incipient particles of material worlds, flashing into being and out of it too briefly to be said to exist, lacking the energy for continuity of duration. Simon felt a strange horror, even a repugnance, at this minutely scintillating infinity of impending matter imbued with the potential of scattered and finite life. It came to his human portion like the disgusting sound of a swarm of loathsome insects under rocks or snakes in a nest, hideous in its vitality. It was somehow evil, pregnant and straining to give birth to itself in the form of materiality. Simon experienced this with an odd double reaction: on the one hand, as a human, he was actually relieved to see *something*, a space of sorts separate from himself, to remind him of the material reality to which he was accustomed; on the other hand, as the Lord Mazda, he was repelled, gripped with revulsion, at the sight of that incipient material existence.

Then he heard, mentally, the voice of Helen—of the Ennoia—calling to him, though he could not pinpoint the source of that call. It seemed to come out of that almost-world of nonexistent particles. Deliberately, gripping the haft of his flame-bright sword more tightly, he plunged into that dark, seething turbulence to seek her out.

The twinkling darkness surrounded him on all sides. Though his form still glowed, his light no longer shone afar; the darkness of the swarming particle-void delineated him sharply. Pleroma, The Fullness, had taken on a new and dark meaning. He held up his sword, stared for relief at his face mirrored in its shining blade—and was startled to behold the long-forgotten hydra-head sigil glowing in blue upon his forehead.

Then he saw something else reflected there also—creatures, swarming forth from the void, approaching him menacingly. Even as he whirled to meet them he sensed more springing into existence on all sides, forming out of the swarm of scintillating particles. They resembled in malevolence the Archons who had guarded the Spheres, but came in hundreds of revolting forms, tentacled and winged, eyed and eyeless, writhing like tangles of serpents, buzzing and hissing. Anger filled the Lord of Light as he realized that somewhere a mind other than his own was causing these abominations to form, to attack. With a ringing cry of outrage he hove up his blazing sword and charged at them.

They wavered, then broke and fled before him, unable to withstand his wrath. His blade sundered them by scores and hundreds, causing them to dissolve back into the seething void. Others formed, but as quickly as they did the blazing sword slashed and scattered them also, dispersing them once more into nonexistence.

Then there were but a handful, fleeing before him on grotesque wings and tentacles and articulated appendages. Simon pursued them, smiting them down until there was but one left; then he held back, following the final fleeing monstrosity but not trying to overtake it. *This* foul thought, he determined grimly, should be allowed to lead him to its foul source....

Again he heard Helen calling to him but could not determine the direction of her voice. And then, as the fleeing proto-Archon led him on, he became aware of a slow, deep pulsing or drumming that filled all of space, and with it came thin weird pipings that reminded his earthly portion of something analogous to flutes....

The proto-Archon ceased to flee and faced Simon; its thought-voice boomed out menacingly:

"Stop! You approach the Throne of Achamoth—"

Simon rushed in and swung. His sword clove the monstrosity and sent it back to the void, bellowing as it dissolved. But now, straight before him, he sensed a pulsing mountain of blackness, blacker even than the scintillating void. Then a monstrous voice came out of it in words powerful and deep as rolling thunder, bubbling and viscous as a boiling sea of pitch:

"Who comes to the Throne of Achamoth?"

Simon's human portion recoiled in terror. He had read in Ostanes of Achamoth, the evil Demiurge who had created the material worlds. To the ancient Shemites he had been Aziluth, Creator of Archetypes; to the Stygians he had been Azathoth, to the Persians Azdahak. The Chaldeans called him Tiamat; the Hebrews knew him as Rahab, Monster of Chaos, Lord of the Deeps....

But the Lord of Light knew no fear as he approached the pulsing blackness that was vaster than all the worlds, that bubbled obscenely as it began to create for itself new proto-Archons. Two lesser forms, equally black, flanked it like twin shadows, emitting the sounds of flutes which somehow aided those revolting creations into existence.

"I am Mazda, the One Who Stands. I endure forever. You must return the Ennoia to me."

The blackness boomed harshly, deeply—was it an evil laugh? "I am the First Dream of the Ennoia. I have taken her being and sundered it into an infinite fineness, and from it I shall create lesser beings who will serve me, and material worlds which they shall rule, and creatures upon whose energies they and I shall feed. You will not find her whom you seek, for she is now all this seething void, and the incipient substance of all the worlds and beings that shall come forth from it at my command."

Now Simon realized why he had never been able to pinpoint the source of Helen's calling to him—it had literally come from everywhere. A new, fiercer rage gripped him as he raised his sword of light and charged forward.

"Foulness, you shall not keep her!"

But now the pulsing mountain was shrinking, forming itself into a towering humanoid figure of pure blackness. The silhouette of its massive head seemed to Simon to resemble that of a lion, and he recalled the lion-headed symbol of the Demiurge under its name of Ialdabaoth. In its hand was a sword whose blade was as black as the substance of Achamoth himself.

"You cannot rescue her. The process cannot be reversed. Only by aiding me to precipitate the worlds from her substance, and by plunging into those worlds with her, can you hope to rejoin her."

Neither the Lord of Light nor his tiny human portion hesitated an instant.

"Helen!" Simon cried out as he—as Lord Mazda—rushed forward and swung the sword of light.

The black shape hove up its own sword and the twin blades of light and darkness met with a titanic clash of mighty energy—energy that instantly was absorbed by trillions of the nearest seething almost-particles, precipitating them into realness. Ennoia shrieked as those particles precipitated others into reality also, transforming her substance into the material that would form the worlds. Mazda, too, cried out in anger and amazement, for that flash of energy had for an instant illuminated the face beneath the lion's-head crown of Achamoth—and he knew that that youthful yet angular face, scowling with rage and determination, though dark-haired and dark eyed, was yet the exact reflection of his own!

Then all the void, exploding into Being from the point where those sword-blades clashed, inflated colossally like a many-dimensioned bubble and poured forth as a torrent of enduring and inconceivably numerous particles. And with them went the sundered form of Lord Mazda, mingling with them as equally innumerable bits of light, while the dwindling laughter of black Achamoth seemed to thunder throughout all the worlds that soon would be....

EPILOG

He dreamed that the universe slowed in its expansion, that its swirling matter gathered and condensed to form the countless stars and circling worlds.

They were always together, he and the Ennoia, though sundered and scattered throughout material existence, and together they would always be. They met innumerable times during more than a thousand ages, upon more than a billion worlds, sometimes knowing one another consciously, more often sensing their complimentarity but dimly, always forced tragically to part. But during all that enormous time some of their sparks melded and increased to form larger and larger True Spirits, and eventually a few High Ones, growing ever more and more aware. And always on each world there came to be one of Himself and one of the Other—two Highest Ones—having more than usual awareness of who they were, meeting ever and again in new incarnations, life after life....

Simon awoke slowly from these dreams, returned little by little to bodily consciousness in Dositheus' cellar chamber. The old wizard was standing anxiously beside his couch, watching him closely, relief replacing concern in his wrinkled face. The candles and braziers were no longer lit; their pungent fumes had all but faded away.

"How long have I slept?" Simon asked, sitting up.

"All night, Simon. The dawn is breaking."

Simon rose to his feet gingerly, felt his body as if to assure himself that it did indeed exist, then left the room and began to ascend the dark stairway. Dositheus followed close behind him, saying nothing.

When they had gained their upper chambers and had stood silently for a time upon the balcony, breathing the clean cool air and watching the fading stars, Simon finally said:

"Did I dream it all? Or, is *this* the dream?" He swept his hand outward, indicating the dark buildings and lanes of the awakening city, the hills and the stars beyond. "Did I dream for but a night? Or have I dreamed for a cycle of eternity, returning after many ages to a world very like the one I left?"

"Did you see—Helen?" countered Dositheus.

"Aye. That is, if I did not but dream things inspired by the lore that you and Daramos have taught me."

"And was your longing satisfied?"

Simon shook his head. "If what I seemed to dream was true, then I have learned much. My most burning questions for knowledge have been answered. But, no—my longing for answers may be satisfied, but not my longing for Her. For Helen."

"You have seen her in the Fullness," said the old wizard, laying a hand on his pupil's shoulder, "and the time will come when you shall see her again in this life. When the time is right—the time of destiny and the stars—you will find her. I promise it."

Simon did not answer, but now he felt a small hope, an optimism, beginning to rise in his soul, dispersing his sadness even as the light of dawn was beginning to disperse the darkness beyond the eastern hills. Yet at the same time he realized beyond cavil that his new vision-born knowledge would forever deny him the normal happiness of ordinary and oblivious mortals.

About "The Emerald Tablet"

Simon's next adventure, *The Drums of Chaos*, takes place in the spring of A.D. 33 and fills an entire book. Unfortunately, space limitations prevent it from being included in this collection (although it is also available from Pickman's Press). In it, Simon meets Jesus of Nazareth himself and... well, suffice it to say Jesus is not what exactly what history would later remember him to be, possibly blasphemously so.

Chronologically, the next Simon of Gitta short story is "The Emerald Tablet" (originally published in *Strange Sorcery* #24, Rainfall Books, August 2017), which takes place the winter of A.D. 33 - 34, after the events in the novel *The Drums of Chaos* but before Simon and Meander part ways when Simon sets off on his Egyptian adventures. It's partly inspired (among many other things) by Clark Ashton Smith's famous short story "Ubbo-Sathla", which can be found on the Smith fansite *The Eldritch Dark*. In it, a contemporary Englishman finds the crystal ball of an ancient sorcerer in a curio shop. While crystal-gazing, he travels back through time to the dawn of Earth, where he discovers the source of all life on the planet comes from Ubbo-Sathla, essentially a vast sentient pool of primordial ooze. This actually fits quite well with the text of the Emerald Tablet, which states that "all things have their birth from this one thing." But what exactly *is* the Emerald Tablet?

The Emerald Tablet, though quite brief, is a foundational text for medieval and Renaissance alchemy and retains its importance. We do not hear of it until its mention in *The Book of Balanius the Wise on the Secret of Creation and the Nature of Reality*. That book is a pseudepigraph ascribed to Apollonius ("Balanias") of Tyana. As if the Pseudo-Apollonius were himself a writer of pulp fiction, he claimed to have discovered the Emerald Tablet in the grasp of an ancient corpse on a golden throne, in a vault beneath a statue of Hermes in his home town of Tyana. This is a double claim for the authority of antiquity. The Arabic text stems from somewhere between the 6th and the 8th centuries, while the fictive author, Apollonius, would have lived[1] in the 1st century CE, and the Tablet is supposedly a revelation from Hermes Trismegistus ("Thrice-Great Hermes"), an ancient revealer god. He appears in many Hermetic texts, e.g., *Poimandres* ("The Shepherd of Men").

For the curious, here is Sir Isaac Newton's English rendering from the Latin translation of the Emerald Tablet:

---

[1] See Robert M. Price, "Was There a Historical Apollonius of Tyana?" *Journal of Higher Criticism*. Vol. 13, no. 1,

Tis true without lying, certain and most true.

That which is below is like that which is above
and that which is above is like that which is below
to do the miracle of one only thing

And as all things have been and arose from one by the mediation of one:
so all things have their birth from this one thing by adaptation.

The Sun is its father,
the moon its mother,
the wind hath carried it in its belly,
the earth is its nurse.
The father of all perfection in the whole world is here.
Its force or power is entire if it be converted into earth.

Separate thou the earth from the fire,
the subtle from the gross
sweetly with great industry.
It ascends from the earth to the heaven
and again it descends to the earth
and receives the force of things superior and inferior.

By this means you shall have the glory of the whole world
and thereby all obscurity shall fly from you.

Its force is above all force,
for it vanquishes every subtle thing and penetrates every solid thing.

So was the world created.

From this are and do come admirable adaptations
where of the means is here in this.

Hence I am called Hermes Trismegist [sic],
having the three parts of the philosophy of the whole world

That which I have said of the operation of the Sun is accomplished and ended.

THE EMERALD TABLET
by Robert M. Price

The disciples say to Jesus, "Tell us how our end will be." Jesus says, "Have you discovered the beginning, that you ask about the end? For where your beginning is, there, too, shall be your end. Blessed is he who shall arrive at the beginning, for he shall know the end, and he shall not taste death."

— Gospel of Thomas, saying 18

All that is above is like that which is below, and all that is below is like that which is above. It is thus to bring about the miracle of one single thing, from which everything else derives in an unchanging way. This is the talismanic father of the whole world, whose strength is entire and must be transformed into earth.

— Tabula Smaragdina

I. Hermes Trismegistus

The bracketed torches smokily illumined the dense rows of hieroglyphs, very ancient but mostly still legible, that occupied all four walls and ceiling. The color of the walls was red, lurid in the flickering flame light. A single figure sat cross-legged on a cloth mat at the center of the floor. His attention was focused on a squat green candle in front of him. His gazing eyes looked out, unblinking, over his broad, high cheekbones like men keeping watch over a fortified wall. The nostrils of his small nose occasionally flared as if punctuating his faraway musings. His night-black hair was bound back with a bronze comb. His costume was of a coarse brown fabric, and a dark green cloak draped his muscled shoulders. His body, steeled from a career in the arena, was lithe and seemed eager to spring up to meet some challenge. But for the present moment, Simon of Gitta, whom some called a Samaritan, others a Philistine, was occupied in trance-like meditation.

The guttering candle sat between the man and an unfurled scroll. He was, in the manner of the mystics, pondering what he had read in the *Sepher Yetzirah*, the Book of Creation. Like them, Simon sought to recover the very moment of creation, for this, the ancients held, must be the key to the saving knowledge. Whence the rare True Souls such as his? This, one must fathom in hopes of liberating the divine spark within. To this end, Simon weighed various techniques for psychically penetrating the sealed vault of the past. Simon was a *goetes*, a stage magician who made a bit of money by performing baffling feats for easily impressed yokels. Aye, he knew much of the lore of genuine sorcery, which he often had occasion to put to good use, but it was not wise to be too widely known as possessing such powers; they had a way of attracting danger as often as repelling it. But more than this, he was a philosopher, thirsty for the secrets of Ultimate Being, Ultimate Knowledge. It was this endeavor in which he was presently engaged.

Daring to intrude upon his mentor's solitude, Simon's young disciple Menander padded into the chamber as silently as he could and stood waiting. After several minutes he placed his hand tentatively upon the Gittite's shoulder and softly asked him what he had decided. He had to repeat himself twice, for Simon was slow to reemerge from his cocoon of concentration. When he could, he answered.

"Some of the paths to the past are reputedly very dangerous. All men know the tragic tale of Zon Mezzamalech's doomed quest, absorbed into the Abhoth. He had gazed into an artifact that transported his consciousness down the ages until he beheld the Abhoth, which some name Ubbo-Sathla, the primal stuff of all terrene life. But he never returned. Yet I must ask, how then did anyone know what had happened to him? Someone must have returned to tell the tale. That is, providing it was more than a tale. So there must be a way. I own the crystal of that ill-fated mage of Mhu Thulan. It cost me much both of time and of treasure, Menander. But dare I meet its Medusa gaze?"

He dismissed his fretting disciple and returned to his meditation, sinking ever deeper.

Until, that is, he became aware of a Presence with him in the room. Suddenly the light was different. The candle had altogether expired, but the chamber was brighter than before. Simon lifted his eyes to behold a figure of colossal stature, glowing as if some towering harbor beacon. Its face could not be seen for brightness.

Simon's nape hairs stood up. He shielded his eyes with his forearm, saying, "Who art thou, Lord?"

"I am called the Thrice-Great. I bear the names Hermes, and Thoth, which men know, as well as a third Name which is not to be named by men. I hold the wisdom of the three modes of the cosmos. Verily, I am able to unveil all things. What desirest thou, Simon of Gitta?"

"To behold the source of beings, O divine Hermes."

"Thou shalt be satisfied."

Straightway an engulfing darkness obscured all things roundabout. Simon, moorless, floated amid a steamy chaos, filled with roiling smoke and with echoing thunder. Then a voice sounded forth from the abyss. "Behold the origin of life!" At once chaos began to distill into a rudimentary order, and a lapping sea of viscous slime expanded to fill space as far as Simon could see.

"Dost thou understand what thou hast seen?" quoth the Thrice-Great.

"Unless I am mistaken, my Lord, it is the Great Abhoth, which in the tongue of my nation signifies 'fathers.' "

"Well spoken, Simon! Thou hast seen That which containeth all things in potentiality, enclosing the models of all beings."

Simon bowed his head. "Then grant that I may find the path of souls from which man comes and to which he returns."

"As you wish, my son. Behold, I tell you a mystery!" said Thoth-Hermes, "A seed of light plunges from the Fullness of Light into the turgid world of gross matter. Such are germs of souls. They abide as tenuous vapors in the region of Cykranosh, free from all care, oblivious even of their own blessedness. As they fall like autumn leaves from sphere to sphere, they are coated with the substance characteristic of each, the lower the heavier, as befits their incarnation in that world. As they assume denser bodies they come to forget their heavenly existence. This is the Fall of Souls from the divine ether. They rain down upon the sub-lunar world like hailstones splashing into mud, where their ripples churn the sleeping elements into divers forms."

"So I have heard, Great One, but…"

"If thou wouldst see this for thyself, I charge thee: use not the crystal of Zon Mezzamalech lest thou repeat his fate. Instead, use this."

The Being opened his hand to reveal a strangely wrought box. Simon took it and opened it. It was a many-faceted, strangely angled gem, blood red and translucent with a shifting shimmer inside. "It is a window on all time and space."

The voice was lost in a sudden sound of cyclonic wind, though Simon felt no rush of air. He looked up only to see his visitor was gone, replaced by the returning Menander, who averted his eyes from the gem. Instead, he held out to Simon an equally remarkable relic, a green crystalline plaque. It was inscribed with unfamiliar characters.

"Take it, master. It can protect you even in astral form, or so old Dositheus used to tell us." Simon being now lost in a trance, Menander placed the tablet in a small harness and proceeded to strap it around his Master's abdomen. The effect was much like that of the sacred ephod worn by the High Priests of the ancient temple at Bethel. Wearing this, the divine breastplate, they claimed, they took on the very nature of Jehovah himself.

II. The Pool of Putrescence

Simon dreamt of falling, falling, descending into the past, or perhaps into the lowest bedrock of the sub-lunar world of earthly life. He felt he was *inside* the red jewel somehow. He passed bizarre vistas in which the land extended above the sky and the spires of onyx cities backgrounded the moon, appearing to pierce it like a vast melon. There were unsuspected life-forms with rows of heads joined by amphibious webbing, and ranks of dwarflike figures seeming to ricochet against unseen boundaries as they flawlessly executed fantastically intricate patterns of ritual dance. He beheld the enfolding of events, large and small, whose meanings were bafflingly incomprehensible to him.

At length he verged upon the Abhoth, fissioning and bubbling. Through the jungle ferns shading the lip of the living, protoplasmic pool, Simon beheld what Zon Mezzamalech had anciently sought, and what he himself now sought: the Elder Records, engraved by some unimaginable pre-human hand. These tablets seemed mired in the primordial bog, whose lapping undulations alternately concealed and revealed their inscribed faces. Simon was too far away to discern the nature of the writing. He knew he could not very well bear the Records away, in this astral form, but if he could get close enough to them, he might be able to memorize what was written there, even in a tongue unfamiliar to him. There were spells to enhance a man's memory, and others to make foreign languages intelligible, and he knew them well enough.

So closely was he focused on the objects of his quest that Simon did not at first notice the approach of newly-forming creatures, raw and wet, and red with rapidly branching and connecting veins. The things had not been swimming in the liquid; rather, they were splitting off from it, taking form before his very eyes! Some, with blinking orbs, snuffled with curiosity at Simon's booted feet. Other, larger forms followed in their wake, plainly intending to attack and devour him. Was it their own instincts propelling them, or were they still but appendages of the Abhoth itself, seeking to protect its secrets from the interloper?

Simon reached for his *sica*, which he had been wearing, as always, as he entered the trance. But he hesitated: like his clothing and the ephod he wore, the weapon must be as physically insubstantial as himself in this astral form. Could it be of any use here? A tentative *sica*-stroke told the tale. It dawned upon him that, at this early period, matter itself had not yet congealed into its present solidity. The ancient *Senzar Manuscript* had said as much. Thus his *sica* and his thews were every bit as real as the creatures he now faced. He laid to the task with vigor, happily chopping and skewering the weird creatures now stampeding at him. Many of them had a general resemblance to familiar beasts such as Simon had battled when a gladiator: bears, lions, leopards. But they were still in the process of definition, sprouting fur and honing talons.

It was not long before he saw the futility of his efforts, as the severed and butchered carcasses quickly fused back together, those that did not simply fall back into the quivering bulk of the Abhoth, like raindrops returning to the sea.

Simon thought he heard a whisper. Yes! It was the familiar voice of his disciple and sometime battle companion Menander: "Simon! The Emerald Tablet!"

Simon's momentary confusion subsided as he intuitively felt he must join the power of the ephod with that of his sigil-engraven blade. Here came something recalling the Minotaur of legend. Simon just had time to touch the pommel of his *sica* to the emerald surface on his abdomen, pointing the *sica* at the advancing monster. From its tip flashed a green beam that, striking the minotaur, crisped him to a black and smoking pile of char. As this unrecognizable carcass fell back into the Abhoth-bog, the protoplasmic mass pitched violently, creating arching waves that erupted overhead. As he blasted one after another of these puppets the violence of the Abhoth increased exponentially. The incinerated tissue of its destroyed creatures was not to its taste.

III. The Lost Ghost of the Conjurer

As these spewings of bio-magma splattered on the shore of the Abyss of Abhoth, they quickly withdrew into shaking clumps, enlarging as each regathered more of the loathsome gelatin. Simon thought of candles shedding melting wax in reverse, mounting up and up. What form were they building up to?

Human. The heaps were swiftly assuming recognizably human form. Simon expected to see them bulking out into brawny warriors wielding weapons. But instead, the finished forms were those of stooped and aged, bearded men! One or two had tapered cone-like heads, which Simon took to represent the conical hats some wizards wore. The vague and baggy shapes of some probably corresponded to the voluminous robes they had worn in life. For Simon at once realized these must be facsimiles of the enchanters who, like Zon Mezzamalesch, had become one with the Abhoth in their efforts to glimpse the secrets it sheltered! It was a fate he had but narrowly avoided. Even now he feared the immediate peril of his soul. But so far, none of these awful effigies of the dead had ventured any threatening moves, merely dragging themselves in his direction.

When he saw the hazy primeval sun glinting off some small object clasped by one of the shambling golems, a mad thought occurred to him. Could this be the revenant of Zon Mezzamalech himself, holding the very crystal whose siren charm had led so many into this spider web of souls?

The astral form of Simon flinched as the air about him shook at the sudden shock of an echoing voice. It did not seem to come from any one direction as it clanged like a hammer on the anvil of the ear. Reflexively, the Gittite raised his eyes to locate the speaker, but he saw no one. And yet there was no mistaking the voice's owner: not Menander this time, but the divine Thoth-Hermes!

"Simon! Thou must destroy the crystal of Zon Mezzamalech! Now, or disaster awaits!"

This made sense, as the gem had certainly been the source of much mischief and misfortune. But something made Simon resist the idea. As he paused, thunder built and boomed. And the oozing ghost of the Mage of Mhu Thulan came closer, still holding the stone. It began to speak, and the bizarre tone and timbre of its voice made Simon's skin crawl and his soul to shudder. But he listened.

"O son of the living, hear and heed! Thou must not obey the voice of thunder! I must speak quickly for this form cannot long hold together!" Here he raised the crystal higher. "This ancient stone hath from of old beckoned the souls of seekers and savants. The orb is a sentient entity, and it has dangled the secrets of the Elder Records to lure and trap these superior spirits. It reduced them, *us*, to inert matter, absorbing them into the Abhoth-mass. In this manner did the demiurge Abhoth create its spawn, all life on earth. Oh! Oh, my time grows short!"

The voice of the ancient mage was becoming unsteady, garbled. He hastened on: "These choice souls should never die but pass on from one material housing to another, age after age, until, coming to the knowledge of themselves, they should at last slough off the cloying bands of flesh and mount up to the long-forgotten Pleroma of Light whence once they came. If thou destroy the crystal here at the dawn of life, thou shalt abort the future, including thine own!"

Simon ventured an urgent question. "If this be so, then why...?"

"Know you not the third Name of him who commanded you? For it is none other than *Nyarlatophis, the Creeping Chaos!* Long has he bemoaned the birth of Order amid his beloved Chaos and would have prevented it. And this he wished you to perform..."

Zon Mezzamalech's flesh-phantom lost all cohesion, as is the eventual fate of all material effigies, and the alien thunder rumbled once more, then fell silent.

As for Simon of Gitta, he lost consciousness in one world and in the same moment regained it in another as Menander shook him awake back in the glyph-lined chamber beneath the Great Pyramid in Egypt.

As soon as the two of them made their twisting way out of the subterranean labyrinth and back to their tent, Simon smiled at his faithful apprentice, then fell into a deep, wholesome sleep. His visionary journey had exhausted him, both flesh and spirit. For days he slept, and Menander was at his side when finally he awoke.

"Master, you have averted a terrible doom upon mankind. But, alas, you did not manage to bear away one of the coveted Elder Records!"

"Did I not, Menander?" Withal, he held up the Emerald Tablet, which he had worn as a breastplate. "I did glimpse what was etched upon one of them. It was identical to the writing on *this*. This is one of the Records, perhaps the only one to survive. That is, unless we someday find another!"

About "The Soul of Kephri"

Over the next year Simon travels to Thebes to study under the priests of Ptah, kicking off a whole new set of Egyptian adventures. By the spring of A.D. 34, the first one is thrust upon him in "The Soul of Kephri".

One need not read for long to come upon several tips of the helmet to the great titans of *Weird Tales*, Robert E. Howard and H. P. Lovecraft. When we read of "the sword of the Aquilonian king", we recognize a link between this tale and Howard's Conan story "The Phoenix on the Sword." The phantom sage Epimetrius comes from the Conan tales, too, not only those by Howard but the stories by L. Sprague de Camp and Lin Carter as well. (Note that while de Camp always managed to restrain himself from correcting the spelling of the name as given by REH, "Epemitrius", to a proper Greek "Epi-" prefix, Tierney has given in.) From Lovecraft come both the names of the priest Ka-nephru (from Ka-Nepher, a prehistoric pharaoh HPL contributed to Duane Rimel's "The Tree on the Hill") and the more familiar Nephren-Ka and his divine patron Nyarlat.

At least as great an influence on the present tale is George Lucas's *Star Wars* trilogy. Simon fills the role of Luke Skywalker, while Epimetrius is sort of a Hyborian Obi-wan Kenobi. The dwarfish sage Daramos recalls Yoda. Bubo Festinus' name was suggested by that of the bounty hunter Boba Fett, and the grim Megroth is an avatar of Darth Vader. Tierney admits to the debt, but it's not mere borrowing. The *Star Wars* characters are all intentionally archetypal myth-actants, i.e., less characters than personified generic narrative functions. Lucas, as is now well known, wrote the movies expressly under the influence of Joseph Campbell's theories about the fundamental role of the heroic quest archetype. Tierney's characters echo specific characters in *Star Wars* and *The Empire Strikes Back*, but had he never seen the films, we would surely still have seen a hero with a goal to reach, his wise mentor, a powerful villain, etc. Of course, one might simply see him as taking up a thread left dangling by August Derleth in his early Mythos tales, in which he called the emissaries of the Elder Gods the star warriors!

"The Soul of Kephri" was first published in *Space & Time* #66, Summer 1984.

THE SOUL OF KEPHRI

by Richard L. Tierney

I

Why does it glide to me in pre-dawn gloom—
This grim, gray shade from Aquilonian times,
Whispering of monstrous deeds and sorcerous crimes,
Warning of all mankind's impending doom?

— Muthsa, *The Prophecies*

Thrasyllus the astrologer shuddered as he gazed upon the horoscope he had just cast. The signs were unmistakable: extreme disaster and probable death within one year.

He leaned back and breathed a deep sigh, trying to calm himself. The prognosis was common enough, and it applied to some slight extent to every man, woman, child and animal born at or near the time and place for which Thrasyllus had cast his horoscope. Yet, as he well knew, this casting was not at all common, nor would the reaction to it be a common one when it became generally known—for the probable death forecast in the present configuration of planets was that of Tiberius, Emperor of Rome.

For a moment fear clutched Thrasyllus and he buried his face in his hands, shuddering; then, calming himself, he rose and stood erect. The fear in his dark eyes gave way to determination; he stroked his iron-gray beard with a lean hand thoughtfully.

"Be calm—calm!" he muttered to himself. "I have sensed this before now." He walked to the window of his chamber and gazed out upon a vista of blue sea and sky. "O gods, you know I have sensed it! Help me now to continue to conceal the Emperor's impending death from him—for I know that were he to become aware of it, he would immediately order a purge of all those he considers his enemies, and thus bathe all of Rome with blood."

So saying, the astrologer gathered his dark robes more closely about him and, turning from the casement, strode rapidly from the room.

Emerging from the low, flat-roofed building which Tiberius had given him for an observatory in which to practice his divination, Thrasyllus walked rapidly along the cliff path that overlooked the blue sea far below. He knew he should be grateful for the destiny that had made him chief astrological consultant to the Emperor of Rome, yet of late his position had seemed more and more like a bad dream, deepening into nightmare. For Tiberius, Thrasyllus knew, was mad.

Aye, the Emperor of Rome was mad—and the madness, which had first driven him years ago into retreat upon this cliff-girt isle of Capri, had now expanded from a morbid fear of plotters and assassins into a conviction that safety lay only in usurping the very power and immortality of the gods themselves.

Thrasyllus strode between the white marble columns of the portico of Tiberius' mansion—one of many such mansions built upon the isle. The blank faces of watchful praetorian guardsman, clad in polished bronze and oiled leather, stared after the astrologer in silence.

He strode through halls unlit by any lamp or torch, until at length he emerged into a wide room floored with white marble tiles and flanked by polished columns. A wide balcony opened from the other side of the chamber, approached by a broad staircase of three steps; blue sky and white clouds showed through the wide aperture, and the distant whisper of sea waves sounded from far below. Atop the low stairway, seated in a plain but costly chair, was the Emperor Tiberius. Several slightly clad children stood about him.

Thrasyllus bent low in deference, then stood upright once more. "I must speak with you, O Imperator."

Tiberius turned his eyes upon the astrologer—large, dark eyes, disconcerting in their mystical intensity.

"Speak, then, good Thrasyllus."

"We—we should be alone, if it please you...."

The Emperor cackled a brief laugh, then turned and rubbed the head of a dark-haired lad standing next to him. "Run off, then, my little chickadees. This old raven of an astrologer wants my exclusive attention for a bit."

Thrasyllus watched the group of boys and girls scamper away, their sandals slapping on the tiles. Though most of them seemed perhaps eight to thirteen years old, they gave forth no such noisy outbursts as might have been expected from children of that age group, and their faces seemed uncommonly subdued, even grave. The astrologer shuddered. Rumors of Tiberius' perverse lusts were already whispered abroad despite his seclusion, and Thrasyllus was in a position to know that those rumors were not all unfounded.

"Youth!" the Emperor exclaimed. "All life—all hope of future life—is in them." The last child having exited, he turned and faced Thrasyllus, his eyes suddenly menacing under scowling brows. "And now, astrologer— what do you want?"

Thrasyllus swallowed nervously. In that moment Tiberius seemed to him like some lean hunting spider, crouched to pounce. The Emperor's hands gripped the arms of his chair; his thin elbows stuck out acutely; the lank, white strands of hair that fringed his balding pate trembled, reflecting a suppressed tension born of hostile suspicion.

"I have again read the stars, as you instructed," said the astrologer. "Naught has changed; long life and unchallenged power lie before you."

The Emperor's eyes narrowed still more. "Aye, so you have often said—and it must be true, for I have sworn to you that I will have you thrown from a cliff into the sea should you ever tell me falsely. Yet even so, what matters it that I should have years more of life, if someday that life should end? No, Thrasyllus, it is not enough. I must not die. I must *never* die!"

"But—the condition of mortal man—"

"Mortal man!" Tiberius' lips drew back in a quick snarl of contempt. "You mean, *mere* man! Even as I am no common man on earth, Thrasyllus, so have I determined that I shall be no common mortal before the gods. You are not the only sage I have recently consulted, and now I have garnered knowledge that shall raise me to the level of the gods themselves."

Thrasyllus strove to conceal his surprise. He of all people knew that Tiberius, though publicly scornful of magic and religion, was yet basically superstitious; still, he had not suspected that the Emperor was actually studying necromancy on his own.

"Recently I bought a book for a great sum," Tiberius went on, "from one Diomed of Astura, a collector of antiquities. It was a work by Ostanes, the ancient fire-priest of Parthia—"

"By Hermes!" exclaimed Thrasyllus involuntarily. "The *Sapientia Magorum!* Surely you did not read it—?"

The Emperor laughed briefly, harshly. "I knew you would not approve, good Thrasyllus, and therefore I pursued this study on my own. I have learned much—ha! ha! I learned that the Sacrifice of Youth can preserve the aged a while, if the right beings are invoked in the right way."

Thrasyllus was shocked. "You don't mean—the children—?"

"And I learned another thing," said Tiberius, a sudden menace in his voice. "I learned that you have lied to me, Thrasyllus. I might have died ere now had I not made the Sacrifice of Youth to the Old Gods. Yet even this is only a postponement, as I am sure you well know, for even the years of youth are numbered. Humankind tends toward the grave, and even the vital force of many young lives can only temporarily keep the jaws of death from me. Therefore you must aid me to accomplish an even greater sacrifice—unless you prefer that I should keep my vow and have you hurled from the cliffs of Capri!"

Thrasyllus swallowed again. "What must I do?"

Tiberius leaned farther forward, more spider-like than ever. "Surely you must have already guessed, scholar of old wisdom—for you, too, have read the book of Ostanes. You must capture the Soul of the Dawn and bring it to me."

The astrologer gasped, even though he had sensed the demand coming. It was insane—yet, as he valued his life, Thrasyllus knew he must keep silent and humor the Emperor.

"Aye, the Soul of Kephri," continued Tiberius, his dark eyes gleaming, "—the Phoenix, spoken of by Herodotus and Ovid and many another, but whose true nature only Ostanes reveals—the bird who never dies save in god-sent flame after many centuries of life, and who is immediately reborn from the ashes. You must embark this very day for Egypt, Thrasyllus, and go to the city of Heliopolis—where, according to Ostanes, the Phoenix is due to appear before the next full moon, at the rising of the star Sothis in conjunction with the sun. And when this supposedly fabulous bird appears, you must cause it to be captured and brought to me."

"But—but, why?" stammered Thrasyllus, already knowing the answer.

"So that I may sacrifice it to the Old Gods on an altar of my own devising. For only by offering up the life of an eternal being can I induce the gods to grant eternal life to me!"

The astrologer raised his hands in a feeble protest he dared not voice; shock and sadness vied strangely in his eyes. Tiberius grinned.

"Go, then," he commanded. "I have a bireme awaiting you at Sorrentum; it will carry you swiftly to Alexandria. When you arrive there, you will immediately confer with Aulus Flaccus, Governor of Egypt; he will give you a packet which I have already sent him containing your detailed instructions."

Thrasyllus glanced but briefly into the mad, gleaming eyes of the Emperor of Rome; then he nodded, bowed humbly, and backed with slow caution from the marble-pillared chamber.

In that very hour Ka-nephru, high priest of the temple of Ptah in Thebes, woke suddenly in the night, sweating with fear. The dream he had just experienced was the most intense he had ever known.

Quickly he rose, grabbed a dark robe and threw it about his lean form, then strode from his small chamber into the hall. The still flames of torches and oil lamps reflected in his dark eyes and from the sheen of sweat on his shaven head as he strode down the stairway to the ground floor where the acolytes slept in their cubicles.

Lifting a torch from its bracket, Ka-nephru entered one of these small rooms. As the curtain whispered softly back into place behind him, a young man stirred and groaned sleepily upon his thin pallet—then suddenly started awake and sat up.

"Simon," said Ka-nephru uncertainly, "I have dreamed, and—and I think you have dreamed, also."

The acolyte, a man apparently in his mid- to late twenties, blinked as if bewildered. His eyes, shadowed beneath prominent brows, glinted in the torchlight; his lean face, unusual in its high-cheekboned angularity, gleamed like a pale mask. His form was slender yet smoothly muscular, like that of an athlete. Absently he brushed back the bangs of lank, black hair that hung over his broad forehead—hair whose presence indicated that he had not yet passed even the first stage of priestly initiation.

"Aye, I have dreamed," he muttered. "But—how did you know—?"

"Hush, Simon. I think we have dreamed the same dream. But to make sure, tell me yours—and then I will tell you mine."

The man called Simon shook his head, so that his straight black hair whipped for a moment about his bare shoulders; then he rubbed his eyes. "Such a strange dream! How did you sense that I had it?"

"Never mind. Tell me."

"I dreamed of an old man—a thin old man with a white beard and a dark robe. His eyes were shadowed and grave—oh, so grave! He was standing in a room whose walls were of solid stone, and I sensed that it was far beneath the ground. I had descended there on steps carved like serpent-heads; I remember a great empty sarcophagus, and beyond it a great stone statue like an eagle, and then he—the old man—he said...."

"Go on," urged Ka-nephru.

"He said: 'I am Epimetrius, Protector of Civilization.' "

Ka-nephru drew in a sharp breath. The suspicions he had hoped were not true were confirmed.

"Go on, Simon."

The young man eyed him narrowly, questioningly. "It was not just a dream, then?"

"Go on!"

Simon drew a breath. "The old man said: 'Civilization is in danger; the madman who sits on the throne of Rome endangers it, for he seeks to steal the Soul of Kephri.' Does that mean aught to you, O Mentor?"

"*Go on!*"

Simon wondered at the intensity in his mentor's voice, in his scowling dark eyes. "The old man said: 'They come to abduct the spirit that urges all life upward—the spirit that has raised the human above the animal, and that now urges the human race toward civilization and even greater things.' Do these words have meaning, O Mentor?"

"More than meaning, Simon, for these words were in my dream also. The 'madman who sits on the throne of Rome' seeks to capture the Soul of Kephri in order to offer it up to the Dark Gods in sacrifice. Such cannot be allowed, for then all earth would be plunged into an age of horror and endless Night, with Tiberius its ruler forever."

Simon shook his head again, trying to clear his brain of the haze of dream that still clung to it. "The Soul of Kephri—the Phoenix—but, surely, that is only a myth—"

"No myth, Simon. There are mysteries of which you have not been told, inasmuch as you are yet an uninitiated outlander. But now you *must* be told—for Epimetrius, the mage who has lain entombed for many thousands of years, was once the Priest of the Phoenix. And if your dream was the same as mine, you heard him say that you are the one he wants to fight the dark powers and save the Soul of Kephri, if you can."

Simon shuddered, remembering the words of the gray prophet in his dream. "But—why me...?"

Ka-nephru looked at his pupil closely. "Perhaps you can guess at that better than I. Your life has been a closed book to us ever since you came here half a year ago, seeking to renounce the world. Why did you choose to study here, Simon?—in seclusion, a student of arcane things. For I sense you were a fighter and a wanderer before you chose a scholar's life...."

"Aye!" snarled Simon, his eyes suddenly scowling at dark memories. "I've told you that I studied the arts of the mages at Persepolis, but before that I was trained as a gladiator—sold into the profession by the Romans, who slew my parents in Samaria because they could not pay the taxes imposed on them by a corrupt regime. I escaped, after two years of fighting for my life—of spilling blood for the Roman mob—!"

"I see." Ka-nephru nodded slowly. "A fighter with a hatred of Rome, and also trained in the Persian arts of magical illusion.... Can you think of any other reason why the spirit of Epimetrius might have chosen you for this all-important task?"

"I know not. I seem to have lived under a curse these last twelve years, since my parents were slain." Simon was silent for a space, as if remembering. "I have seen much bloodshed and terror, sorcery and death. I have wandered, and hated, and slain many Romans, and learned many arcane things, but the pathway of my life was always dark to me. Then, several months ago...."

He paused, suddenly withdrawn, scowling as if at more evil memories. "Go on," urged the Egyptian.

"I know not what this means," muttered Simon, "but less than a twelvemonth ago I saw a man crucified in Jerusalem—a man who, though he had done harm to no one, died in agony surrounded by a mob screaming for his blood—"

"Aye, a common enough sight wherever Rome rules."

Simon nodded. "Yet this time the sight maddened me and I drew my sword in blind fury. But in that moment I was hurled from my feet as the ground shook and split, and a voice of doom pealed from the darkening skies. The earth opened and buildings crashed down in ruin. It was a time of madness and terror. Many perished—not a few by my own sword, for an insane rage had possessed me; I felt the gods had come at last to smite Rome for all her cruelties and injustices, and I smote with all my might for their cause. Why I was spared during that mad night of horror I know not, for I seemed then to sense the hand of doom upon all things…. Why *was* I spared, O Mentor?"

Ka-nephru hastily made the sign of the Serpent before his brow. "I have heard rumors of these events. Surely they are but a foreshadowing of what impends—for soon, before many more days pass, the Soul of Kephri shall come winging from the face of the dawn. Not for fourteen centuries has mankind known such an event, and there are many signs and portents of it on earth and in the skies. Get up, Simon; gather your belongings and follow me quickly to the docks. You must embark for the ruined city of Heliopolis as soon as possible, that you may be there to do the bidding of Epimetrius."

The air was cool as Simon followed his mentor out into the gray of predawn, carrying his few possessions in a bundle, his dark cloak wrapped about him. Nearby, the mighty pylons of the ancient temple of Ammon loomed, dwarfing the fane of Ptah from which he had just emerged.

"Why should the wise Epimetrius choose one of our small temples to do his work?" Simon wondered aloud.

"He chooses the best for the task," said Ka-nephru. "Never doubt it. Over ten thousand years ago, when the minions of Set and Apophis threatened to burst forth upon the world, he chose as the world's defender a king who was born a barbarian—and the king was victorious, aided by the sign of the Phoenix which Epimetrius caused to be inscribed upon his sword blade. But now the evil threatens again. No more talk, Simon—hurry!"

Simon, hastening on behind Ka-nephru in the dawn-light, his exertions dissipating the lingering mists of his dream, cursed softly to himself and began to wonder whether he and his old mentor had gone mad.

II

If shape it might be called that shape had none
Distinguishable in number, joint, or limb;
Or substance might be called that shadow seemed,
For each seemed either—black it stood as Night,
Fierce as ten Furies, terrible as Hell….

— Milton, *Paradise Lost*

Bubo Festinus shuddered as the desert wind blew about him, whipping the folds of his coarse, blue-gray tunic. It was not that there was any cooling effect in the wind—quite the contrary, for it carried the heat of the western desert with it, the heat of sands that had been baking under the sun for the last twelve hours. Uneasily he glanced at Thrasyllus, the Emperor's astrologer, who had accompanied him and several Roman soldiers on a boat journey southward from Alexandria to Letopolis near the head of the Nile delta, and thence westward on foot a three-hour trip into the timeless desert.

"You feel it, too," he said accusingly. "Don't you?"

Thrasyllus faced him. "Feel what?"

"Don't dissemble, wizard! Tiberius sent me to accompany you because I'm the best animal-catcher in the Empire; the beasts I've sent to the arenas have given as much entertainment to Rome as have the fighters from its best gladiator schools. Yet I didn't become the top in my profession without having certain skills; I not only know animals, I think and feel like them. And right now, my animal-feeling tells me we are in danger of— something...."

Thrasyllus looked upon the animal-procurer with a disgust he could not entirely hide. He had instinctively loathed the man from the moment he had met him—and suspected that Bubo, with his animal instinct, knew it. The game-catcher had been born and bred a Libyan, yet his features were not typical of any race Thrasyllus was familiar with: They were narrow, angular, vertical features, as if hewn from rock or steel. Those features showed emotion only infrequently—by means of a vindictive glint from the narrowed, dark eyes or a quirk of the lean, rigid lips—and then only during the tellings of how he had captured various animals for the arena, or how he had watched them die in combat.

Thrasyllus nodded. "Your senses tell you truly, Bubo Festinus. We have come to a place where dark things abide. Look." The astrologer pointed a lean finger toward the western horizon, where the sun was just touching the ground and swelling redly, like a huge tick feeding upon the blood of the earth.

"I see only low mounds on the horizon," muttered the game-procurer.

"Since you are obviously fearful, Bubo Festinus, you need not accompany me farther. In any case, it's not part of your job. Stay here and help our soldiers put up camp; I will return soon."

"I fear nothing!" snapped Festinus, his lips twitching, though his features remained otherwise as rigid as ever. "My senses are sharper than yours, especially at night—they don't call me the Swift Owl for nothing. I will go with you. Yet you must tell me why we are here. Why is it, when my job is to capture the Phoenix-bird, that we must first go into this lifeless western desert where I will have nothing greater than sand-lizards to capture?"

Thrasyllus stood silent a moment, remembering his meeting in Alexandria with Aulus Flaccus, Governor of Egypt. The governor had given him Tiberius' shocking written instructions, then had led him to the Temple of Thoth, where the priests had shown him the *Scroll of Thoth-Amon*—a book of ancient sorcery Thrasyllus had heard of but never before seen. Even Ostanes' centuried book was new compared to this scroll, the original of which was said to have been written by a sorcerer of antique Stygia. At first the astrologer had read it with fascinated interest, but then the monstrousness of the thing had made him turn away in revulsion. Now only the fact that Tiberius held certain members of his family under the threat of death caused Thrasyllus to persevere in his dark task—but he was not about to tell that to Bubo Festinus.

"Those mounds," he said, pointing, "are all that remain of the ancient Stygian fane which the Egyptians call Het-Apop—the Place of the Serpent. Legend has it that the great Devourer of the Sun was once worshiped here, long before Menes united the Two Lands."

"The Serpent!" exclaimed Bubo, his narrow eyes gleaming with sudden fear. "Aye—there are legends in Libya. Is this indeed the Place that Confronts the Darkness, even as Heliopolis faces the Dawn?"

Thrasyllus nodded somberly, privately gratified by the game-procurer's obvious fear. He took up a dark, cloak-wrapped bundle and shouldered it. "Go back, Bubo, and help set up camp."

"No—I am not afraid.... Yet I have heard that a servitor of the Serpent still lurks in this place, waiting to be called back into being. His name is Mekharat—"

"Aye." Thrasyllus grew somberly thoughtful, remembering what he had read from the *Book of Thoth*. "But to the Stygians, he was Megroth—the Servitor of Darkness. Nephren-Ka, the Dark Pharaoh, once called him up to do his evil bidding.... Need I tell you more, Bubo Festinus?"

The animal-trapper shook his head violently. "No! Speak no more of this. I—I will stay and supervise the setting-up of the camp—"

Thrasyllus nodded, gathered his brown robe more closely about him in spite of the heat, then strode off across the dark sands toward the low mounds upon the desert horizon. There was a chill in his soul. No longer did he feel even the grim satisfaction he had felt when Bubo Festinus had held back in fear to tend the camp. He was alone on the desert now—and just ahead of him rose the mounds that hid the ruins of Het-Apop, the Place of the Serpent.

Thrasyllus shuddered as a wind sprang up, more chill than the cooling sands should have allowed. The mounds were black against the lingering afterglow.

The astrologer halted.

"I am here, O Set-Apophis," he muttered. "I am here, Great Lord of Darkness."

The wind continued to stir the sands—and Thrasyllus, recalling what he had read in the *Book of Thoth*, suddenly and inexplicably realized how these ruins must have looked more than ten thousand years ago. As vividly as if he had been transported magically back in time, he seemed to see titanic serpent jaws of stone looming against the west—black jaws gaping wide to swallow the red ball of the descending sun, while ebon-robed Stygian priests intoned their adoration to the Dark One and his Servitor, raising their daggers for the sacrifice—

Then the vision was gone—but Thrasyllus, gasping in fear, knew that it had not been *merely* a vision. For an instant he was tempted to flee. Then, remembering his family held hostage in Italy, he steeled himself and drew forth from his robe a small, stoppered vial of fire-glazed clay.

"This is the essence of the Sacrifice of Youth," he intoned, repeating the words Tiberius had uttered to him aboard the bireme just before it had departed from Sorrentum. Thrasyllus had shuddered then, remembering the children he had seen in the Emperor's mansion on Capri; now he shuddered anew as he unstoppered the vial, lifted it briefly toward the dying red light of day, then poured its dark liquid contents out upon the sands.

The wind seemed to stir more vigorously—more sentiently....

"Hear me, Great Lord of Darkness," muttered Thrasyllus, intoning the Stygian chant he had learned from the *Book of Thoth*. "Hear me, O Set-Apophis, Devourer of Light...."

The wind rose noticeably, whipping the astrologer's robes, sending grains of sand stingingly against his face. For an instant Thrasyllus knew panic; then, strangely, his courage was renewed and his voice resonated with new confidence as he continued the chant:

"Drink the essence of life, O King of Death! Stir from thy slumber, Great Serpent. Tiberius, Emperor of Rome, has prepared this libation for thee; if thou art grateful for it, send forth thy Servant—"

The wind whipped the sand more wildly.

"Send forth thy servant Megroth, to do my master's bidding—that thine enemy the Light may be destroyed, and thine aeon-long thirst appeased—"

The wind rose to a shrill wail; the sand stung Thrasyllus' face like a swarm of biting insects. He gasped, fell to the ground with his robes whipping wildly about him, felt himself in the grip of a whirling desert-wind—

He felt a sudden horror at what he had just done—

Then, abruptly, the whirling dust-devil subsided. Thrasyllus rose weakly, hesitantly. Silence hung about him—a silence as profound and startling as the recent buffeting wind.

The astrologer looked toward the west—and gasped. Something was rising from the sand against the last afterglow of the sunset, something tall and black—something vaguely humanoid in outline, yet definitely unhuman....

The instant the river captain gave his passengers permission to disembark, Simon gratefully stepped off the boat that had brought him downriver. It had been many days since he had had his strange dream, and its influence on his state of mind had diminished considerably. At this moment he was wondering how he could have taken it seriously—was wondering, even, if his mentor Ka-nephru might have imparted it to him by hypnotic whisperings in the night for obscure reasons of his own....

No matter, though, for he was now completely in control of his faculties again. Moreover, he was in Memphis, a city he had often wanted to visit—and not only because it contained the great temple of Ptah, the central fane of the order in which he was an acolyte. Simon was already entertaining doubts about the life he had chosen, and now as he strode down the marble pier in the twilight, and into the great city, his doubts grew stronger.

He entered a waterfront tavern and ordered a jar of wine, and while he sipped it he eyed the slender, dark-eyed serving girls and felt the stirrings of half-forgotten lusts. Why, he suddenly asked himself, should he continue his grief-driven retreat from the world? Was it not time that he took some of the world's pleasure to himself, shallow though it might be? What was he doing drifting down the Nile on a riverboat, urged on by a mad priest's fears? Why should he believe that priest's assertion that he alone had been picked somehow to save all civilization from a dark doom? The sunlight, the laughing voices in the tavern, the mundane buzzing of the flies about him—all seemed to belie the reality of dark visions.

And yet the dream had been so real....

He shook his head to dispel the memory, raised his hand to call the serving maid—and suddenly noticed a white-robed figure standing next to him. He turned and regarded the stranger, and was irritated to see that the man was shaven bald and wore the garb of a high priest of Ptah.

"I am Menophar," said the stranger, "a priest of the Great Temple of this city. May I sit with you?"

Simon's irritation was tempered with a certain relief that the plain dark tunic he wore gave no hint that he was an acolyte of Ptah. "Why should a priest of Ptah's central fane wish to sit with a common traveler in a wharf-side tavern?"

The priest took this as an invitation and sat down across the table. Simon observed that he was probably in his late fifties, yet slender and hale, with crinkles about his eyes that suggested that life amused him still. Yet his general expression was one of seriousness.

"You come from Thebes," the priest said matter-of-factly.

Simon started. "How did you—?"

"Never mind," said Menophar, raising a hand. "I have a message from your protector."

"Protector!" Simon felt his skin crawl. He had heard that a few Egyptian adepts were able to cast their thoughts across leagues of space to one another. "Speak plainly, bald-head—what do you want?"

"I had a dream," said the priest. "I saw you in it, and was told to meet you here. The one who told me said that you are in danger—that you must not continue on your journey by boat, but rather that you must disembark on the eastern shore at the apex of the Nile delta and continue to the City of the Sun on foot."

"A dream!" Simon rose, his dark eyes gleaming with anger and concern. "Damn you, tell me—was the one in your dream a priest of your order—?"

"No," said Menophar, rising with him and meeting his gaze. "He was an old white-bearded man with wisdom in his eyes. He said that the mad ruler of Rome has called up powers that endanger all mankind, and that only you can thwart these powers. He did not tell me your name, only showed me your aspect."

Simon sensed the question in the priest's statement. "I am Simon of Gitta, mad priest! I'm not even an Egyptian, just a tormented Samaritan wanderer. If your beliefs tell you that the world is endangered, why should you believe that I am its savior?"

"Egypt is not the whole world," said Menophar, "as we who worship Ptah have always known. Before Khem was Stygia and the kingdoms of the Hyborians, and before them Atlantis and the dawn-nations of Attluma. Throughout all time, since man first set his foot upon the path of knowledge, civilization has warred with the forces of darkness—and now that war has reached another crucial stage. Believe me, Simon, when I say that you are a pivotal force in that struggle."

"You're as mad as my mentor Ka-nephru—who undoubtedly told you to meet me here!" snarled Simon.

"Ka-nephru, of Thebes? You are his pupil?"

Simon glared at the priest, decided that the man's eyes held no trace of duplicity. Fear clutched his heart.

"Tell me truly, priest of Ptah," he said, "—this wise old man in your dreams—did he have a name?"

"He called himself Epimetrius, the Guardian of Civilization—and he said that you are in great danger, and must continue your journey to Heliopolis on foot—"

Simon raised his fist as if to strike Menophar, but then lowered it. The gesture was one of desperation rather than a threat.

"Why me?" he asked finally. "What must I do?"

"Do only what I have told you—disembark as soon as you can upon the east bank and continue to Heliopolis on foot. I wish you well, Simon of Gitta—and if all goes well, I envy you. Truly I do." So saying, the priest turned and hastily left the tavern.

Simon, cursing, wishing that he could disbelieve in the strange destiny that pursued him, pushed aside his half-emptied wine jar and rose, knowing that he would obey the instructions of the priest Menophar.

Bubo Festinus saw movement upon the western horizon—two dark shapes striding toward the camp, faintly illuminated by the nearly full moon that had risen in the east. Gripping his Roman short sword tensely, he cried out: "Who goes?"

"Be at your ease, game-catcher—it is I, Thrasyllus."

But Bubo was anything but at ease as the pair approached. The shorter figure was indeed the astrologer, as his gait and voice indicated, but the taller....

The pair drew close, halted.

"Bubo Festinus," said Thrasyllus, "this is Megroth. Welcome him, for he shall make it possible for you to capture the Phoenix."

The game-catcher felt an obscure, subtly growing fear that caused the hair to rise on the back of his neck. Thrasyllus' companion was a full head taller than the tallest man he had heretofore seen, and broad in proportion; his form was completely concealed by a black robe, and his head by a visored Samnite helmet of dark iron.

"Welcome him," repeated the astrologer tonelessly. "Bow to him."

Bubo Festinus bowed hurriedly, anxiously, as a slave bows to avoid a blow—and even as he did so, he wondered why his keen ears could detect not the slightest sound of breathing behind the visor of the stranger's iron helm.

"And now, Swift Owl," said Thrasyllus, "rise and instruct the soldiers to break camp with all haste. I have received new instructions; we must return to our ship and proceed to Heliopolis as rapidly as we can. Hurry!"

Simon woke early. Someone was shaking his shoulder, and the dim gray light of dawn was filtering into the space where he slept on deck by the ship's rail.

"Get up, Samaritan."

It was the captain's voice. Simon sat up, rubbing sleep from his eyes.

"Up!" the captain repeated. "You wouldn't want to waste the money you paid me, would you? Up, now, and off the ship, as you yourself requested."

Simon rose, gripping the captain's hand, then gathered his dark gray cloak about him, shouldered his meager pack, and strode down the narrow gangway to the shore. Immediately the planks were withdrawn and the ship pushed off and sailed away out into the broad Nile.

Simon blinked, then strode away from the muddy riverbank. Presently he came upon a pathway that led to a road. Surmising that this must be the way to Heliopolis, he shouldered his pack more securely and set out northward....

And the ship's captain, ordering his craft to proceed downriver once more, gave a sigh of relief. "By Amon!" he exclaimed to his pilot, who was steering a careful course into the main channel once more, "—I'm glad to have that dark Samaritan off my ship. I swear, he seemed a bird of ill omen—"

"Then pray," said the pilot, "that this ship approaching is not the ill he has forecast."

The captain glanced westward, then snarled nervously. A ship was bearing down on his own, its oars beating the water to froth in the gray predawn light. Above it hung the full moon, a sinister round lantern, settling toward the horizon.

The ship drew close. A dark-robed figure appeared near the bow. Then a voice rang out: "Heave to, in the name of the Emperor!"

"Who comes?" yelled the captain.

"Thrasyllus and Megroth, agents of Tiberius."

"How do I know this? How do I know you aren't pirates?"

A second figure appeared near the bow—a figure taller than that of an ordinary man—and an inhumanly deep voice boomed out:

"Let us aboard, or you'll *wish* we were pirates!"

The captain hesitated, now seeing the shapes of Roman soldiers lining the rail of the ship as it came round. In another instant the alien vessel scraped against his hull; grappling hooks rattled against the rails, planks were let down—and then two cloaked figures stepped upon the deck.

"Greetings, Captain," said the shorter man of the pair. "I am Thrasyllus, messenger of Tiberius. I must ask you to allow us to make a search of this—"

But the taller figure, shouldering Thrasyllus aside, said in his deep, resonating voice: "You have a passenger named Simon of Gitta. Bring him to me."

The captain suppressed a shudder; he felt a sudden fear and distrust toward this arbitrary servitor of Rome who towered nearly seven feet tall in his black cloak and iron helm. "I have no such passenger," he said.

"You do. I will see him."

"Get off my ship, damn you!" yelled the captain. "You haven't shown me any papers of authority—"

"We don't need any damned papers!" Thrasyllus yelled back, tension making his voice unusually shrill.

The towering man in black motioned back the astrologer. "You will not oppose the authority that determines the destiny of the world," he said to the captain. "You will yield to the instructions of those who come in the name of that authority."

The captain felt his fear and dislike growing. "Go to the Devourer!" he yelled. "Get off my ship! You have no right—"

The tall man strode forward; his dark cloak fell open and a black arm shot out—an arm terminating in a huge, gnarled hand which closed like the claw of a hawk over the captain's head, one talon between nose and eye, the others over the back of the man's scalp—

"No!" shrieked the captain suddenly, desperately. *"No—don't! I will serve you—!"*

The black fingers closed completely. Bones crunched; eyes shot from their sockets; brains squished from between the squeezing talons. Thrasyllus turned away and clutched his face, horrified, then heard the captain's body fall to the deck.

Megroth, his clawed hand dripping with blood, turned to Thrasyllus and the Roman soldiers behind him.

"Search the ship," he commanded. "Bring Simon of Gitta to me. He is a tall man, dark-haired and dark-eyed, with a fighter's mien. Find him!"

The soldiers hastily complied, but in a few moments returned with the report: "There is no man of that description here."

The dark-cloaked figure called Megroth turned toward the southeastward horizon—and both Thrasyllus and Bubo Festinus wondered why they could catch no reflected gleam of torchlight behind the visor of the dark iron Samnite helmet he wore.

"The man has gone north on foot," said Megroth presently in his inhumanly deep voice. "Yet he shall soon know the doom we bring. Back to our ship, Romans, and steer us a course northward—to Heliopolis."

Aboard their own vessel once more, Thrasyllus turned fearfully toward the towering figure of Megroth and asked, "How do you know the description of this man you say seeks to thwart us? How can you know his intent, his destination, his very name, when...?"

He hesitated. Megroth inclined his visored head toward the astrologer.

"When I have lain in the tomb ten thousand years? Is that what you meant to say? Listen, then, Thrasyllus: The tomb is not always death, as you well know, and sometimes dreams can invade even the tomb. The man who seeks to thwart us has dreamed, but my Master has seen to it that I have dreamed also. Ask no more of me now, astrologer; soon you will see how dark dreams can plunge all the world into darkness! But now I must go below, for the sun rises."

Thrasyllus shuddered as he watched the black figure of Megroth descending the stairway to the hold, and once again he silently asked himself whether his service to Tiberius had jeopardized his very soul.

III

They hid it from the light of day;
Ten thousand years and more it lay
Within its nighted tomb—
The sword a king once used to slay
The shadow-beasts of doom.
Now doom-shades have again congealed;
What champion shall come forth to wield
The ancient, broken blade?
Pray he is strong and will not yield,
For the world must have his aid!

— Muthsa, *The Prophecies*

Merit rose from her thin pallet of straw, casting aside her goatskin blankets, and stood shivering in the dim dawn light that filtered into her parents' modest hut. The dream was still uncommonly vivid—the dream of a white-bearded old man telling her of a broken sword with a symbol emblazoned on its blade...

She heard her mother outside, puttering about the cooking-fire. Donning her meager shift, she stumbled bleary-eyed out into the gray daylight.

"Mother—"

The thin woman by the cooking-pot, sensing something amiss, came over to her. "Merit? Are you ill?"

"No—no, mother. But, I had a dream—"

The woman sighed with relief. "Only a dream? Thank the gods! You had me worried."

Merit pouted, sensing with the acuity of a nine-year-old that she was not being taken seriously. "Mother, this was not an ordinary dream! A gray old man came out of a cliffside and spoke to me. His name was Ep—Epimet—"

"Hush, child, and eat your gruel. When you're finished, go help your father and brothers in the field. We must finish work early today, so that we may go to the temple of An in time for the rising of Kephri. Thank the gods you are not ill! Do not frighten me so again."

Merit ate her breakfast in silence while her mother puttered about tending to her two baby sisters and feeding the fowls. The girl suddenly felt a sadness in watching her—not at all for the first time. She had long ago sensed that their existence was precarious; they were not even wards of the great temple of Ra in nearby An, or Heliopolis, as were a few of their neighbors who could prove hereditary connections with that ancient fane. She had heard tales that once the temple had aided the poor in its vicinity, but those days were long gone—gone ever since Cambyses the Persian had sacked and destroyed the city centuries ago....

Then, surprisingly, she heard her mother asking, "What was your dream, Merit?"

Eagerly the girl replied: "He was old and white-bearded, and his name was Epimet! He told me I had been a woman more than a thousand years ago when the Pharaoh Aken-Aton tried to get everyone to worship the Life Force in our land of Khem. He told me that I had then the same name I do now, and that I was one of Aken-Aton's followers, and that evil men slew many of us and destroyed our temples. And then Epimet told me that the Life Force is now in danger again, and that I must do something to help it. He told me that I must—"

"Stop!" snapped the woman, a trace of fear in her voice. "Enough of your fantasies. You had a dream, and that is all."

"But, Mother, you asked—"

"Enough. Go out into the field now, and help your father and brothers."

"But, Mother," persisted Merit, "is it true that I had an ancestor named Merit who worshipped Aton, the Life Force—?"

"Go, girl! Your brothers need you. We must finish our work early today, so that we may go camp by the temple and pray to Kephri at tomorrow's dawn."

Merit went into the fields as her mother commanded; but later in the day, talking to her twelve-year-old brother Ptahor, she reported all the details of her dream and their mother's comments.

"Mother just doesn't want you getting into trouble," muttered Ptahor, staring down thoughtfully into the irrigation channel.

"She says my dream means nothing," said Merit, sitting astride the handle of the irrigation pump, her thin brown legs hanging down. "But I know better. She has told us the old stories—and now, my dream tells me these stories are to be fulfilled. Ptahor, I—I must go find the Sword of the Aquilonian King."

"The—what?" Ptahor was as startled in that moment by his sister's grown-up tone of voice as by the unfamiliar, alien expression.

"It is hidden in the ruin of Het-Epmet, on the outskirts of Heliopolis," said Merit. "I must go there tonight, Ptahor, or all the world may be plunged into darkness. So said old Epimet in my dreams. Please do not tell Mother. I can steal away from the camp after she and the rest are asleep, and be back before they wake—"

Ptahor, feeling the flesh on his neck and arms goose-pimpling, said: "I won't tell, sister—and I'm going with you...."

Megroth and the cowed humans who served him strode into the temple of Ra at dusk. Aulus Flaccus, the Roman governor, met them.

"Your instructions have been obeyed, Thrasyllus," he said. "All the priests of this temple have been taken away under guard to my ship. Yet I am surprised at the degree of popular sentiment this action has aroused! Do you know that this night there are hundreds, perhaps thousands, of Egyptians camped amid the ruins of this city? They say that the bird called the Phoenix is to appear here at tomorrow's dawn."

"Egyptian superstition," said Megroth, tall in his black cloak and iron helm. "Surely enlightened Romans do not believe in such tales?"

"N-no, of course not—" said Aulus Flaccus.

"Good. Then return you to Alexandria. Thrasyllus and I shall stay here and attend to any superstitious insurrectionists. You may release the priests of this temple; neither they nor their followers can now do aught against me."

The governor bowed, then turned and hastily exited the temple with his few retainers.

Thrasyllus, feeling more of the apprehension that had grown upon him since this business had first begun, watched in silence as Megroth made his next move.

"Bubo Festinus," said the dark giant, "set up your nets."

The lean Libyan nodded, then motioned to his men. Immediately they began to unstring cords, throw them aloft, then climb up the pillars of the temple. In a surprisingly short time there was a network of cords hanging from the pillars—and then, a sturdy net suspended in place above the altar of the temple.

Thrasyllus asked, his voice tremulous: "This, then, is the place where the Phoenix will come—?"

"You know it well." Megroth's reply was like an iron note of doom. "But you may leave now, astrologer, for I sense the quaver of fear in your voice. Go—and if your loyalty to Tiberius is as great as you claim, you may one day proclaim your loyalty to me instead."

Thrasyllus, fear clutching his heart, bowed hastily, abjectly, then hurried out the door of the spacious temple and into the night, hoping he could catch up with Aulus Flaccus in time to embark with him for Alexandria.

"Now," said Megroth, bending his dark form toward Bubo Festinus, "are your hirelings prepared to capture the Phoenix when it shall arrive here in the dawn?"

"Aye, my lord," said the game-catcher, his face twitching nervously. "They are very skillful, for I have trained them well—"

"Go, then, into the night, and seek out certain ones who seek to thwart us. If your animal-senses are as sharp as you claim, you will succeed. Do not delay."

"But—the Phoenix—?"

"That is in my hands now. Go—for this Simon of Gitta still pursues us, driven by mandates even he knows not the nature of. You shall stop him. Find him, as only an animal-hunter can, and slay him."

"But, how will I know him, my lord—?"

For answer, Megroth bent forward a bit more—and Bubo gasped as an image sprang into his brain: an image of a young man possessing high-cheekboned features, an athletic build, and dark, determined eyes. Beside him were two Egyptian children, a boy and a girl.

"You will find them near Het-Epmet, on the north road. Slay them all!"

Bubo Festinus nodded energetically, then turned and loped from the temple into the night.

Megroth faced the ancient pyramidal stone that stood behind the flaming altar of the Temple of Ra. "Hear thy servitor, O Dark Messenger! Tomorrow's dawn shall spill its blood upon this altar, a sacrifice to Thee, and never shall this world dawn again!" In a deep tone he uttered words that the earth had not heard since the days of Stygia and Acheron: *"Ra na inkon thu ko ithamus! Ikuta mei, Maknu Nyarlat!"*

And in reply, deep in his inhuman brain, he heard:

Fail me not, Servitor of Darkness....

Simon woke from uneasy, formless dreams, feeling the desert breeze blowing about him. Despite his weariness from having walked all day, he felt restless, anxious to be on his way once more.

Rising, he saw that the moon was far inclined to the west. Evidently he had slept longer than he had realized. He wrapped his cloak about him, strode around the sheltering mound toward the road he had left—then saw that that road was full of human figures walking northward, toward the half-ruined city of Heliopolis.

Instantly he realized who these people were—pilgrims, on their way to the holiest temple in all Egypt, to witness the most holy event in well over a thousand years. For Simon had spoken with a few travelers on that road during the day, and they had told him that the morrow's dawn would bring with it the return of the Spirit that had first brought civilization to the world and hope to all mankind—the Soul of Kephri, whom men had first called Ra and then Aton—the very Spirit of Light, who strove eternally against the Darkness....

Simon turned away, partly because of his natural tendency to avoid humankind, but partly because he somehow knew he must go another way than theirs. He began to stride out across the fieldlands, toward a distant, low mound not far from the ruined walls of Heliopolis, distinct under the light of the full moon. As he walked he cursed himself for his cupidity—for following the instructions of dreams, of mad priests and vague urges....

Suddenly a gray shape shot out into his path from the grasses along an irrigation ditch. Instantly Simon whipped out his sharp-bladed *sica*—but then relaxed as he saw that the newcomer was only a common *binu*-stork.

"Ha!" he exclaimed, laughing. Then he sheathed his blade. "You nearly got stuck, friend! What brings you out at night—?"

Then he suddenly felt cold. What *was* this diurnal bird doing out under the moon? And why was it standing in his path so deliberately, wings spread, hopping up and down excitedly...?

"Ra!" it croaked suddenly. *"Ra!"*

Then it whirled about and ran off down the embankment of the irrigation ditch, looking back and pausing often, as if expecting Simon to follow. Each time it paused it uttered the same syllable: *"Ra!"*

"Damn you!" muttered Simon—but his curse was against his own fate rather than the bird. Hurriedly he followed, and after some time the fluttering stork led him to a clump of shrubbery near the base of the low mound he had seen from afar.

"Cavé!" croaked the stork softly. Simon started, for the avian utterance had an uncanny resemblance to the Latin expression: "Be careful!"

"Careful of what?" he demanded.

The bird thrust its beak toward the mount. *"Het-Epmet!"*

"You idiot bird! Am I hearing words, or just random croakings? Did Epimetrius send you, too, or am I mad—?"

But the stork, suddenly fearful, uttered a soft croak and flapped heavily into the air, then sailed away into a thick patch of rushes. Simon cursed his gullibility again—then suddenly stiffened as he heard a new sound. Peering out of the shrubbery, he saw two small, slender shapes upon the slope of the mound. They seemed to be digging with their hands in the dirt.

Carefully Simon edged closer. He heard their muffled voices—then suddenly realized that they were children, a boy and a girl.

"Merit, surely you only dreamed—"

"No. No, Ptahor. It was too real to be only a—*ah!*" The girl's voice grew suddenly excited. "It is here, Ptahor—even as old Epimet told me! Help me dig—help me—!"

But in that moment Simon saw a lean figure rise up over the other side of the mound—a figure whose supple movements reminded him of a stalking carnivore—a figure with a long dagger gleaming in its hand.

"Look out!" yelled Simon instinctively.

The two children jumped up, saw the figure stalking toward them, and backed away, terrified.

Simon, his *sica* gleaming in the moonlight, rushed forth from the concealing shrubbery and dashed between them straight toward the menacing figure. The children cried out, not knowing whether to consider this new shadow in the night friend or foe.

Simon stopped perhaps three arm-lengths from the slinking figure in the darkness. "Who are you—?"

For answer there was a flash of steel. Simon barely evaded the thrust as he jumped backwards.

"I am your doom!" growled a harsh voice.

The lean figure leaped forward. For a few seconds blades rang upon one another in a furious blur, and Simon staggered back as he realized that he faced a foe more quick and skilled than any he had ever faced before, in the arena or anywhere else. For an instant death seemed to impend, and he rallied all his forces, parrying, countering, thrusting—

Then his enemy drew back.

"You are skillful, Simon of Gitta," said the shadow. "I remember you now, for many years ago you were a gladiator of Rome. You fled the arena, and are now an outlaw. Tiberius will be pleased when he learns that I have slain you, and these two inquisitive children with you. Unlike you, I courageously remained in competition for the imperial favor, and emerged from the arena as the foremost game-catcher of Rome. And now it appears that I may serve a master even greater than Tiberius himself—"

"Die, server of masters!" yelled Simon, rushing forward with his *sica* slashing.

Bubo parried the blow deftly and bounded back, then came to the attack chuckling. Blades again rang together as two superbly skilled fighters
strove under the moon for life or death. Merit and Ptahor, huddled upon
the mound, knew that their lives depended on the outcome—

And Simon, fighting for his life, realized that all his training in the arena had not prepared him to face a fighter of such lightning reflexes as the
one he faced now. Though he strove with all his skill, all his hate for Rome,
all his fury in the face of the Dark Powers, he sensed that the near-
inhuman skill of his foe must inevitably overcome him—that this was the
end....

The lean, animal-like figure was pressing in upon him—Simon's
strength was failing—

Suddenly, there was a raucous avian screech in his ear. Simon sensed a
large bundle of feathers rush past him—and then his opponent shrieked as
a long stork-beak plunged deep into his right eye!

Bubo lashed out with his dagger; the stork's next cry was cut short as
it flopped threshing to earth, minus its head. But in that instant Simon's
curved blade lashed out also—and the head of his foe jerked back, half-
severed. Bubo sprawled heavily to the ground, his neck arteries spurting
blood.

Simon ran to the twitching body of the stork, compassion welling up
in him for a reason he could not entirely explain.

"You—you saved my life!" he muttered incredulously, touching the
slain bird. "Did Epimetrius truly call you, then, as he did me—?"

He felt a light touch on his shoulder. Galvanized, he leaped and
whirled, *sica* ready—and saw only a boy perhaps twelve years old facing
him, and behind him a slightly younger girl. Their faces were frightened—
but they relaxed even as he did.

"Don't be afraid," he said.

"We're not," said the girl. "You're good—or the bird would not have
fought for you."

"Who are you?" asked Simon, wondering if he were in a dream.

"I am Ptahor," said the lad, "and this is my sister, Merit. But who are
you? And what is happening this strange night?"

Simon sighed, sheathed his *sica*, and strode over to the body of his
slain foe. For a moment he crouched in the moonlight and carefully scrutinized the lean, angular face, then rose.

"As I thought, it is Bubo Festinus," he said. "Bubo was the greatest
catcher and trainer of animals in Tiberius' employ. Some said he was half
animal himself, and that he turned his talents against his brothers. Many
thousands of animals and birds have died in Rome's arenas because of
him." Simon knelt again beside the body of the *binu*-stork. "Can it be that

this is the reason the bird was willing to give its life—?"

"Listen!" The girl, Merit, was pulling at Simon's sleeve. "I heard the sage, Epimet, in my dream; he told me that I should dig here for the Sword of the Aquilonian King, and that I should give it to a foreigner named Si-mon of Gitta. Are you he?"

Again Simon felt the flesh prickling on his neck. "I—I am—"

"Then—here!" Merit thrust a rusted, rectangular box into Simon's hands.

Simon took the thing, forced its corroded old edges open with his fin-gers. The thing virtually flaked away in his hands—and revealed a deeply rusted object that might once have been a broken sword.

Carefully he freed it from the fragments of its container, brushing the flakes of corrosion from it. It was obviously a sword, ages old, with per-haps less than a third of its original blade-length left—

"Look at the blade," said Merit. Her voice seemed dreamy.

Simon did so. He saw a symbol graved deeply upon the corroded steel—the image of some bird vaguely resembling an eagle. And—did that symbol seem to glow slightly under the moon…?

"You must take this sword," said Merit, "and go to the Temple of Ra in Heliopolis. And there, you must live or die—and deliver the world, or perish—according to your worth."

Simon looked closely into the girl's eyes; they seemed to be glowing with a faint yellow light.

"What do you mean, girl? What good can this broken relic do me in battle? Tell me more—"

But Merit, closing her eyes, staggered into the arms of her brother.

Ptahor said: "I think she's said all she can, sir. I—I hope you'll take over now. I must get her back to our parents—"

"Aye." Simon leaned forward and shook Ptahor's hand. "You and your sister have earned all anyone could ask. Go now."

As the children walked away to the east under the moon, Simon turned northward and strode toward the ruined walls of Heliopolis, thrust-ing into his belt the broken sword of the Aquilonian King and wondering at the madness of his fate.

It was during that darkest hour before dawn that Nephere, High Priest of Ra in Heliopolis, slowly ascended the wide eastern steps to the portico of his god's temple. Behind him followed a half-dozen more priests, their shaven heads gleaming in the light of the torches they carried.

They paused upon the broad portico of the temple, placed their torch-es in brackets, then turned about and faced the east. The great fane had been built near the edge of the city, and the wide avenue extending from its pillared entrance swept away toward the desert, flanked by obelisks. In an hour or less, Nephere knew, the sun would rise at the end of that avenue—and the most significant day in human history for more than a thousand years would begin.

He noted the many dimming campfires that lined the avenue—the small encampments of the hundreds who had gathered here in the ruins of Egypt's holiest city to witness the impending event. Nephere's heart swelled at the sight, and he felt a constriction in his throat as he realized how many of his countrymen must secretly have preserved the old traditions in their hearts. They knew that this was the last night of the Old Age, and that with the dawn the Soul of Kephri was to come, reminding them that its light would be renewed and handed down the ages....

And yet his heart quailed as he remembered the mighty forces that were gathered against that hope. Why had the Romans briefly taken him and his fellows prisoner? What had they been doing in this temple during his absence? Above all, why did he now seem to sense the presence of a great Evil?—now, on this night that of all nights should seem most holy....

Taking a deep breath, he motioned to his fellow priests, and they all turned and entered into the great temple of Ra.

The place was lit by many torches. Nephere gazed about him in awe, though he had seen the interior of this fane innumerable times before. It was columned with dozens of high pillars which did not support the roof, each of which was capped by a stone hawk-god. The most ancient, most sacred place in Khem—

And then Nephere gasped as he saw that a great net was now strung from the tops of those pillars, and that its center was directly above the pyramidal stone that was the oldest and holiest object in all Egypt—the marker that commemorated the founding of Khem itself. Before that stone was the altar, brilliant with the fire kindled for this event—the altar where, if legend proved to be true, the Phoenix would soon appear in splendor from the dawn, to offer up the body of its parent for cremation.

Too much to believe, thought Nephere, his old doubts rising up in his mind. And yet that net of ropes indicated that someone *did* believe—someone who wanted to capture the Soul of Kephri, to bring it down, to destroy all the hopes it symbolized—

In that moment a dark shape stepped from behind the pyramidal stone and confronted him—a giant, black-cloaked figure whose face was hidden by the dark, visored helm of a Samnite gladiator.

IV

Dark and old are the secrets of necromancy, but there are secrets stranger and older still. These secrets mankind shall one day rediscover, and in that day shall sorcery be overthrown, and the old darkness shall be dissolved in the bursting blaze of new Knowledge....

— Ostanes, *Sapientia Magorum*

Nephere felt a sudden, cold fear.

"Leave this place, priests of Khem," intoned the dark figure in a voice too deep to be human. "Destiny impends here—a destiny far too great to be impeded by the wills of mortal men."

Nephere swallowed nervously. His knees began to shake in spite of himself. "I—I know you, dark one. You are the servant of the evil being whose name may not be uttered—the being to whom the Pharaoh Nephren-Ka once sold his soul. I have had dreams. You are Megroth, the Servitor of Darkness."

"Dreams!" said the dark figure. "They swarm as thick this night as bats in the caverns of Harag-Kolath. Yet you know only a part of them, priest—those sent from my foe, Epimetrius. I know the content of them all. My Master hears all dreams, and informs me of them. Go, now, for you are all powerless against me."

Another priest of Ra strode past Nephere. "You seek to slay the Soul of the Dawn—the spirit that brings hope to mankind—to sacrifice it to the foul ambitions of the Roman emperor—!"

Megroth strode forward, towering above the priest.

"Tiberius?" A deep, hollow boom sounded from behind the iron visor, perhaps an inhuman laugh. "He serves me, not I him—though as yet he knows it not. When his fawning astrologer invoked me from my tomb beneath Het-Apop, he sold Tiberius' soul to me. And to me, not to the Emperor, shall the Soul of Kephri be sacrificed, that I may have eternal corporeal life and rule this world in the endless darkness of the All-Night!"

"*Fiend!*" The priest suddenly whipped a *spada*, or Roman long sword, from beneath his robes. "You'll not have the Soul of Kephri! *Die!*"

He swung furiously—but Megroth, not even trying to dodge, reached out and caught the sword blade with a taloned hand. Incredibly, the tempered steel bent and snapped off short in that supernatural grip. Then the priest shrieked as a second black claw shot forth and gripped him by the neck. His shriek was cut short as Megroth lifted him from the ground. The black talons squeezed shut; bones crunched, eyes popped from their sockets and blood spurted from nostrils and ears.

With a gesture of impatience, Megroth flung the body aside and bent to pick up the handle of the broken sword.

Three more of the priests of Ra yelled their hate, drew Roman swords and rushed at the dark figure. Nephere held back, despite his sympathies, sensing disaster. He was right.

The broken sword in Megroth's dark hand suddenly hummed as if with a strange power, and then a blade shot out of its haft—a blade of pure blackness, longer than the original one!

The first priest met it with steel—and the dark blade slashed effortlessly through his sword, his arm, his body. He flopped to the floor without a cry, his sundered corpse pouring a deluge of blood upon the flags. The two other priests flung themselves forward with desperate shrieks of hate—but fared no better. In another moment their bodies, too, lay sundered upon the floor of the temple.

Nephere and the last two underling priests backed away, aghast. They had not known that their four comrades, suspicious, had come armed for a desperate sortie. Now they saw the giant Megroth advancing upon them, a weird light glimmering behind the bars of his iron helm, the sword of darkness humming strangely in his taloned grip—

Suddenly, a cry rang from the temple portico:

"Stop!"

The black giant turned and faced the man who stood just within the entrance. "You!" he boomed. "Then Bubo Festinus—"

"The Swift Owl is dead," said the man, the curved blade of a *sica* gleaming in his hand, dark eyes glaring beneath dark brows. "But I still live—I, Simon of Gitta, enemy of Rome!"

Nephere and his two fellow priests, backing fearfully away between the pillars that lined the great hall, eyed the newcomer with a fascination mixed with dismay. Though his bearing and his tall, athletic frame proclaimed him a fighter, he scarcely seemed a match for the giant black shape that now advanced upon him.

"Human fool," growled Megroth. "Epimetrius has sent you—but if you continue to obey him, you will be crushed like an insect. Go!"

Simon, eyeing the huge dark form and the humming blade of blackness in its hand, suddenly felt a pang of self-doubt that deepened into a surge of fear. Often had he faced death in the arena, and torture by the hands of the Romans, and on occasion even the threat of black sorcery—but now, he suddenly realized, he faced a foe far more dangerous than any he had ever faced before. Previous enemies had threatened his life; this one, he sensed, threatened his very soul.

"You serve Rome," accused Simon, trying to make his voice seem firm.

"No. Rome is my tool. Rome serves *me!*"

Something in the inhuman arrogance of the voice caused Simon's fear to transmute instantly to a blaze of fury. Seeing red, he charged, knife out.

Megroth hove up his black sword and swung; Simon, with the quick reflexes of a trained gladiator, evaded the blow easily and was under it, slashing. His knife plunged through the opening folds of the dark cloak— plunged into cold, living blackness—

Simon leaped away, barely evading a second sword-swipe; he rolled on the tiles and came deftly to his feet, facing his foe in a crouch. But the *sica* in his hand was cold, cold—too cold to hold on to! Its blade, which had slashed the flesh of Megroth, was coated with frost crystals; its haft was burning with a deadly chill. With a curse he flung it to the stone tiles, where it shattered with a glassy tinkling—

A third sword stroke! Simon barely evaded it again—but this time Megroth's left fist, sweeping around, caught him a mighty blow in the chest and sent him sprawling like a rag doll, to slide halfway across the polished tiles of the great hall.

Simon rose to his knees groggily; a pain in his side told him that at least one of his ribs must be cracked. He saw the dark shape of Megroth striding grimly toward him.

In that same instant he saw another shape—the ghostly, gray-cloaked shape of a bearded old man, standing in the darkness between two temple pillars. Simon recognized the old man as the same he had seen in his dream—the ancient Aquilonian sage, Epimetrius!

Simon! The voice seemed to ring urgently from deep within his mind. *Simon, use the Sword—the Sword of the King—!*

Hardly knowing what he was doing, Simon drew from his belt the ancient, rusted artifact Merit had given him—and saw that the eagle-like symbol on what was left of its blade was glowing brightly. Fighting his pain, he rose to a defensive crouch.

Speak the Name, Simon—the Name!

Megroth was a looming, menacing shadow. Desperately, Simon yelled out the name that sprang into his mind:

"Kephri!"

Instantly the sword hilt in his hands shrilled with a supernatural energy, and a blade of golden light sprang forth—a blade that must, Simon somehow knew, be equal in length to the sword blade when it was first wielded ages ago by the Aquilonian King!

Simon swung the weapon and it met Megroth's blade with a fierce crackle of energy. The black giant drew back momentarily, then surged forward again. Simon ran to meet him, roaring with rage, his pain forgotten in the realization that he had been given a new chance—

But had he? He quickly realized, exchanging blow for blow, that he was still on the defensive. All his gladiatorial training had not honed his instincts for the use of sorcery! Megroth, though momentarily taken aback, was driving forward again, confident in his supernatural power—and now, as he drove Simon back, the visor of his Samnite helmet began to rise slowly, eerily, while a flickering blue light became visible behind it. Simon, suddenly realizing with desperate fear that new supernatural forces were about to be brought against him, seemed to sense Megroth's gloating laughter deep within his brain—

But in that instant Nephere, crouching between two pillars, pointed toward the portico and cried out: "Look! The star, Sothis!"

"Aye!" cried one of the priests with him, "—and with it, the rim of the sun—"

"The face of Kephri!" the third priest exclaimed.

The exclamations of the three priests, tumbling one over the other, seemed to have an effect upon Megroth; at any rate, he drew back. In that same instant Simon's blade glowed even more brightly. He gripped the rusted handle more firmly and ran forward. Megroth drew back still further—then returned to the attack, the menacing light behind his visor brighter than ever—

Instinctively Simon threw himself aside—just in time. A bolt of blue energy shot from the Samnite helmet and blasted a square yard of stone tiles to boiling fury!

Simon rose, the smell of molten stone strong in his nostrils. Once again he saw Megroth advancing upon him, the dark sword humming in his hand, the blue glow building behind his visor—

And in that instant the priest Nephere cried out: "Dark Servitor, behold! Your own servants are abandoning you!"

Megroth turned—to see the Roman hirelings of Bubo Festinus hurrying out of the temple as fast as their feet could carry them, terrified by the displays of sorcery they had just seen.

"*Stop!* You must capture the Phoenix—!"

They did not slow their mad retreat. Immediately a bolt of supernatural energy shot from Megroth's helmet—and incinerated three of them to ashes!

In that instant Simon rushed in and swung his glowing sword. Megroth sensed his attack an instant too late—for as he raised the sword of darkness to parry, the light-blade bit through his black right wrist and his clawed hand fell spinning to the floor—

And instantly the black-bladed weapon it clutched became an ordinary broken sword clattering upon the tiles—while the severed claw-hand began to smolder and smoke.

Megroth bellowed fearsomely, like a dragon within an echoing cavern. His visor opened wide, a cave of menace, glowing blue—lightning about to strike—

And Simon, again crying out *"Kephri!"*, hurled his glowing sword full into that cave, point first.

A roaring blast shook the temple. Megroth staggered back and crashed heavily to the flags, sparks of lightning shooting from him. Simon, reeling away from the mighty concussion, collapsed also and lay still.

Nephere, rising fearfully from the base of the pillar behind which he had thrown himself, stole across the tiles toward the fallen combatants. The body of Megroth was steaming, clouds of dark mist rising from its severed arm and the open visor of its Samnite casque; it seemed to be shrinking, dwindling. The black hand on the tiles seemed to be evaporating also....

And the man called Simon of Gitta writhed on the floor, gritting his teeth in pain as he tried to sit up. Nephere ran forward, knelt beside him, and helped him to rise.

"You have won, enemy of Rome!" he exclaimed with a joy he had long doubted he could ever feel. "You have won, and civilization shall live—hope shall live—!"

But in that instant, as the light of the dawn spread across the world, a strange sound was heard out of the east—a pealing, chiming sound that increased as the rim of the sun began to push above the eastern horizon.

Simon rose slowly, painfully, to his feet, clinging to the arm of the priest Nephere. Surely that delicate, distant chiming was but the ringing of his ears—the aftermath of the blast that had smitten his dark foe....

He turned, and saw that nothing remained of the body of his enemy. On the tiles of the temple, amid the bodies of the slain priests, lay only a rumpled dark cloak, an iron Samnite casque, and two broken swords. The traces of a black mist hung in the air.

"He—he's dead—?" muttered Simon, his spine tingling.

"Megroth?" Nephere shook his head. "Beings such as he do not die in the same way we do. Yet you, Simon of Gitta, with the aid of benign sorcery, have sundered his ties with this world and sent him back to the realm of darkness whence he came. May Ra prevent the spells of evil men from ever raising him up again!"

"Sorcery?" Simon shook his head, released the priest's arm and stood upright. "I employ no sorcery—"

"Yet sorcery has aided *you*, Simon. I saw the shade of old Epimetrius, and heard the words he spoke to you just before you slew the Dark One. Those words helped you to perform a deed whose magnitude you probably do not even now appreciate. You have saved mankind's hope for higher things—a hope that Megroth, with the aid of Rome, would have crushed forever. And the magic is not yet ended. Look—look there!"

Simon regarded the object to which the priest was pointing—the broken sword he had wielded against Megroth. Once again it was a corroded relic of antiquity, but on its time-eaten stump of a blade the bird-symbol glowed more brightly than ever.

"The Sword of the King!" said Nephere. "Our legends speak of it, and now I know those legends were true. Ages ago, when a dark sorcerer called up the minions of Set and Apophis to plague the earth, Epimetrius the sage called upon the King of Aquilonia to combat them, and set the symbol of the Phoenix upon his sword blade that he might successfully do so. It has been written that the broken sword was preserved, but no man knew where."

"It was given to me by two children," said Simon, "—a girl named Merit, who evidently had dreams from Epimetrius, and her brother Ptahor. They found it in the mount of Het-Epmet, just outside this city. For the defeat of Megroth, they deserve as much credit as I."

"They shall be found, and rewarded," said Nephere. "Yet—listen!"

Simon realized that the chiming sound could no longer be dismissed as a ringing in his ears. It came from the direction of the pillared temple portico, beyond which a great light was blossoming in the east—the rising of the sun. Then to Simon's ears came another sound—the subdued outcry of a great multitude stricken with wonder.

Together he and Nephere hurried to the portico, followed by the two other priests of Ra. All four of them stopped by the inner fringe of pillars—and gasped at what they saw.

Out of the east, as if emerging from the very radiance of the sun itself, a great eagle-like creature was winging, growing larger and larger. Yet Simon realized instantly that this was no eagle, nor any other creature of earth. As it approached, the chiming sounds increased. The multitude lining the avenue of the obelisks outside the temple had grown strangely quiet; many had fallen to their knees, arms upraised, but most merely remained standing motionless as if lost in wonder.

"The Soul of Kephri!" breathed Nephere. "That I should be blessed to see it—!"

And Simon, too, felt a strange awe, a wistful melting within his heart, as the celestial music grew more distinct. It was so simple, yet so profound—perhaps a half dozen pure, crystalline notes, yet those notes were surrounded by tinkling chimings of incredible, scintillating complexity. The horror of his distant and recent past seemed to be dissolving from him like insubstantial mists.

As the incredible flying thing came closer, he saw that it was followed by a tremendous cloud of birds—hawks, plovers, terns, *binu*-storks, eagles, and many smaller-sized species—thousands of them, cawing and screeching and trilling in what seemed a fantastic paean of joy!

"The Phoenix!" gasped Nephere, falling to his knees. "The soul of civilization—the hope of mankind...."

As the creature rapidly approached the temple, Simon saw that the multitude of birds accompanying it were scattering and swooping down to the earth, landing amid the human multitude that lined the great avenue. Those humans scarcely noticed them; their eyes, as well as those of the birds, seemed intent only on watching the great, radiant creature that had come winging from the heart of the dawn.

Simon gasped as that creature, appearing huge in its brilliance and nearness, streaked above him between the pillars of the portico. He whirled and watched it swoop into the vast nave, between the hawk-crowned columns and beneath the now-harmless net they supported. He saw a large oval object drop from the being's claws—to fall down into the flames of the altar—

"The embalmed body of its parent!" exclaimed Nephere. "It brings its dead parent to the sacred fire of Ra—!"

The altar flame suddenly rose up to tremendous height, burning away the center of the net, and at the same time the unearthly chiming music rose to ecstatic heights. In that instant Simon felt his soul fired with a wonder, an optimism, a spiritual glory the like of which he had never known before.

The flame subsided as quickly as it had arisen and the supernal music lessened, but Simon knew that he would never forget what he had felt in that moment.

The great bird—if bird it was—had wheeled about and was now settling down, flapping its wide and glittering pinions, coming to rest atop the ancient pyramidal stone behind the flaming altar. It perched there and folded its wings, gazing down upon the flames where—so Nephere had said—its parent had just been cremated.

Simon could only stare in awe. He suddenly realized that he had never known true beauty before. He had seen vast mountain landscapes that had taken his breath away, and many fire-emblazoned sunsets, and had known a number of beautiful women—even one that had shared with him and the fallen gods his own soul-nature. But never, until now, had he felt the presence of the very Soul of Beauty.

Yet, despite the mood that was upon him, despite the lingering chords of celestial music in his heart, he could still see actual, objective features of the being. It *was* about the size and shape of a large eagle, and this fact had doubtless formed the basis of the legends that had surrounded it. But it was no bird, Simon knew—nor any creature of earth or its environs. Those scales or feathers, gleaming like a thousand luminous gems, only slightly *resembled* the scales or feathers of earthly creatures; that gently curved bill, glowing like translucent pearl, only *resembled* something between the beaks of ibis and eagle; the golden spray of filaments about its head and throat only *resembled* the inferior crowns and gorgets of earthly kings and queens. And the great eyes, round and limpid and swirling with obscure colors, bright with transcendent life and supermundane intelligence—these resembled nothing he had ever seen.

"Kephri!" moaned Nephere, prostrating himself in a spasm of religious ecstasy, touching his forehead to the ground. "Hope of mankind!"

Simon, less wondering in spite of his awe, strode slowly forward and confronted the strange being.

"Who—what are you…?"

The being slightly raised its head, and though its eyes were not binocularly arranged like those of many earthly creatures, nor even possessed of pupils, Simon knew that its attention was upon him. More, he suddenly realized that it was somehow probing his mind, reading his very thoughts and memories.

Then a thought came vividly into his brain—a thought from outside:

You have saved this world from the endless All-Night, Simon of Gitta—and I am grateful.

"Grateful?" cried Simon. "Yet you must know how much pain and fear still flourish in this world! Why should it be saved from destruction, when such vile things are still possible in it? What did Epimetrius cause me to strive for?"

Megroth would have destroyed hope.

"Hope!" yelled Simon. "Is not hope but a torture in such a world as this—a device of the Elder Gods, to extract as much pain as possible from us earthly creatures, that they might feed upon that pain—?"

I do not know, was the surprising reply. *I am not a god, as these Khemites seem to believe, but only a finite being even as you, longing to correct the things that lead to horror and darkness.*

"No god?" The question was from Nephere, hurrying up to the altar, followed by his two acolytes. "But—are you not indeed the Soul of Kephri—the Light of the Dawn?"

I am what you humans make me, said the strange bird-like being. *Aeons ago I came to this planet offering the light of knowledge and civilization. The primal kingdoms accepted me, but the mighty empires that followed them gave me only their scorn. The nations of Attluma, Atlantis, Acheron, and Stygia all perished because they rejected my aid—and the nations of the Hyborii also, even though Epimetrius, most enlightened of humans, tried to advise them.*

"And the body of your parent?" asked Nephere. "Is it really *that* which you drop into the fire of Ra's altar? What do you really bring? And why do you bring it only once in more than a thousand years?"

Did you not feel what I brought? I brought you hope! As for my true nature—ask not, humans, for you would never comprehend.

But Simon asked: "And what of Evil, great bird? What of dooms and darkness, and the great shadows that hang over mankind? Megroth may be beaten, for now—but will there ever be an end to such servitors of darkness as the empire of Rome?"

Rome is the harbinger of darkness, said the strange Bird. *It was the last torchbearer of the light of knowledge, but it has turned corrupt and now falters down the pathway to darkness, into regions where no hand waits to receive its sputtering torch. Rome dies even now; soon she shall be as dust, and for a thousand years and more the darkness of the All-Night shall brood over her grave.*

"Then—then I have failed, after all—?"

No! pealed the voice of the Phoenix. *Rome carries the seeds of its own doom, and the impending darkness is in its flower. Yet the Light lives on—and because of what you have done this day, Simon of Gitta, mankind shall one day rise anew from the darkness amid the light of a far greater civilization than any that humans have hitherto known.*

So saying, the great Bird spread its wings and leaped from the pyramidal stone, swooping out the great pillared entryway of the temple, and Simon gasped and shielded his eyes as the morning brilliance gleamed from the patterns of its wings in glowing colors. Then, through a haze of tears, he watched as it vanished away to the east beneath the radiant face of Kephri, while all about him he heard the voices of innumerable birds filling the air with joyful song.

About "The Ring of Set"

Simon spends a few more years studying in Egypt before his next adventure takes him back to Rome in March of A.D. 37. As first published in Andrew J. Offutt's *Swords Against Darkness* #1 (Zebra Books, 1977), "The Ring of Set" suffered the accidental omission of one paragraph, which is restored here.

Robert E. Howard and H. P. Lovecraft both made excellent use of the device of providing a background history of some magical object, thereby setting the whole story amid a vast span of historical, even cosmic, scope. Think of Lovecraft's history of the Shining Trapezohedron in "The Haunter of the Dark", and that of the abhorred *Necronomicon*. Howard painted such long shadows for, e.g., the Fire of Asshurbanipal and the Blood of Belshazzer, both talismanic jewels appearing in the stories of those titles. One suspects that following the close of these stories, the artifacts in question had more adventures as they continued flowing with the Tao along the watercourse way of history. What happened to the Shining Traphezohedron after "The Haunter of the Dark"? Thanks to Robert Bloch's "The Shadow from the Steeple", we know. What became of Howard's Ring of Set, which appeared in "The Phoenix on the Sword"? Though even Conan fans may possibly have missed it, the magic ring appeared again in Howard's own story "The Haunter of the Ring" (*Weird Tales*, June 1934; reprinted in *Black Canaan*, Berkley Books, 1978), one of the handful of stories Howard wrote about occult investigator John Kirowan. And after that? You'll find out in Tierney's "The Ring of Set."

THE RING OF SET

by Richard L. Tierney

I

Patroclus folded his pudgy hands across his fat belly and smiled with satisfaction. The crowd that filled the spacious courtyard was large, larger than he had expected. It was composed of a colorfully heterogeneous mass of people, most of whom had come down from Rome for the day. There was an assortment of costumes and skin tones that bespoke representation from at least a dozen countries: Tall, blond barbarian chiefs from lands beyond the Alps rubbed elbows with lean, sharp-eyed Jewish and Phoenician merchants; Spaniards and Greeks mingled with the proud, robed forms of high-turbaned Persians and swarthy Egyptians. There were even a few ebony-skinned Ethiopians in the crowd, and the mixed babble of alien tongues made a chaotic blend. A strange group it was to be gathered in such a small, quiet town as Astura, Patroclus reflected—but then, this was a rather special occasion.

There was a flurry by the gate, and a small party of nobles in white togas entered, accompanied by a number of Praetorian Guards. No fanfare announced their entrance, but the crowd was quick to make way for their advance, and Patroclus rose to greet them with anxious haste. He knew that the tall, lean, white-haired man in their midst was none other than the Emperor Tiberius, on his way back to Campania after a brief visit to Rome.

"Hail, Imperator," he beamed as the group approached. "Your presence is most welcome. Seat yourself here in the shade, I pray you."

"When does this auction begin?" demanded Tiberius, seating himself in the chair provided. The Praetorians drew up behind him in close order along the marble portico.

"Whenever it please you, Imperator—we awaited only your gracious presence."

"Begin, then."

Patroclus signaled, and the auctioneer mounted the platform. His voice rang out in the courtyard, and Patroclus settled back under his awning to watch the proceedings. His fat face assumed a complacent, doughy grin as he contemplated his coming profits. It was not often that such a wealthy client as old Diomed passed away, leaving a huge estate to be auctioned off. Diomed had been a queer old recluse who had spent his later years collecting odd trophies from far corners of the world. Few Romans had suspected his vast wealth but, judging by the crowd present, he was not unknown in stranger parts of the earth.

Even more rare was it for the Emperor Tiberius to visit the area around Rome. Seldom did the old tyrant venture forth from his pleasure palace on the island of Capri where he amused himself by torturing women and young boys in strange, monstrous ways.

Patroclus stole a glance at Tiberius, who was watching the auctioneer through half-closed eyes. In some ways the Emperor seemed rather striking: His form, though smitten with more than seventy years of age, was still tall and imposing, and his lined face was not yet devoid of majesty. But his lank, thinning hair hung white and straggled about his ears, and his large eyes seemed somehow replete with cold malice. He seemed bored with the auction. Patroclus found that annoying, but dared say nothing. Something about the old man's half-closed eyes struck him as most unpleasant.

The first item to be auctioned off was a young Persian slave girl whose beauty attracted many bidders. After a long haggle she was purchased for a goodly price by Gaius, Tiberius' great-nephew, who sat on the old man's left. He seemed a haughty young man, Patroclus observed, with ugly yet ascetic features and foppish dress. His arms were unusually hairy. He grinned after the Persian girl as his slaves led her away, and the executor noticed that his canines were rather large and wolfish.

As more slaves were led back to the block Tiberius began to fidget impatiently.

"Enough of this," he muttered. "Bring out the gold and gems. I can't stay here all day!"

Patroclus made hurried, obsequious apologies and informed his auctioneer of the Emperor's desires. A large ebony chest was then hauled to the stand by two brawny Ethiopians, who unfastened the cover and turned the whole thing over on its side. A glittering profusion of gold, silver, and jeweled ornaments spilled out, making a considerable mound on the platform. The crowd gasped at the sight, but the half-hooded eyes of the Emperor did not alter their expression in the slightest.

The auctioneer picked the topmost ornament from the pile and held it up for all to see.

"What am I bid?" he cried. "This ring is of excellent craftsmanship, and set with fine gems. Who will bid?"

"Let me see it," said Tiberius.

The auctioneer descended and deferentially handed the ring to the Emperor's guards, who conveyed it to the old man himself. It was a strange ornament, fashioned in the shape of a thrice-coiled serpent gripping its tail in its mouth. The eyes were small, bright yellow jewels that seemed almost to twinkle with an inner life of their own. The Emperor seemed fascinated by the bauble. For a long moment he gazed raptly at it, caressing its minutely carved scales with his long fingers, staring into its yellow eyes as if half hypnotized.

"I'll take it," he muttered at last. "Will two hundred *sestertia* be satisfactory?"

"More than satisfactory," beamed Patroclus, amazed at Tiberius' unusual display of generosity. "Your munificence is most gratifying, O Caesar—"

"Never have I seen such a ring as this," mumbled Tiberius, ignoring his host. "Those eyes—they seem to hold lost secrets." Tearing his gaze away from the ring, he turned to his great-nephew and said, "Gaius, pay the man two hundred *sestertia*."

"I bid three hundred," said a voice from the throng.

Patroclus paled. "What did you say?" he gasped, facing the crowd. "Who said that?"

"I did," replied a tall, dark-complexioned man in the forefront of the press. "I bid three hundred *sestertia* for the ring."

Patroclus eyed the stranger with disfavor. He seemed a man in his mid-twenties and possessed the lithe, compact build of an athlete. Black hair spilled in unruly bangs over his broad forehead, and his deep-sunken eyes glowered from beneath dark brows. The cheekbones were unusually high, the mouth wide and tight-lipped, the chin square and clean-shaven. Patroclus could not decide whether the face was homely or handsome— certainly it was striking. The man's apparel consisted of a long, black cloak and a scarlet tunic bordered with black. At his side hung a curved knife, or *sica*, of a type used by gladiators, and in his right hand he clutched a long, dark staff seemingly carved in the shape of a serpent.

"Fool," hissed Patroclus, "be silent! Do you not know the Emperor Tiberius? The bidding is closed."

The stranger's dark eyes glowered more intensely. "I know the Emperor," he said, with a slight bow of deference in Tiberius' direction. "I also know the law. I am entitled to bid."

Patroclus cringed, expecting an outburst from Tiberius, but the old man only smiled, and his enigmatic eyes narrowed slightly.

"The fellow is right," he said evenly but with a trace of sarcasm in his voice. "I raise my bid to four hundred. What say you to that, young man?"

"Five hundred *sestertia*," said the stranger tensely.

"Indeed! Is the ring worth so much to you? Then I must go to seven hundred. What say you now?"

The man's grip tightened on his staff and his brows knit grimly. At last, with what seemed a physical effort, he said in a low voice:

"A thousand!"

The crowd gasped. Tiberius grinned and touched the tips of his lean fingers one against another.

"Is that as high as you will go, then?"

The stranger stood silent, scowling darkly.

"Then I say eleven hundred," said Tiberius. "Give Patroclus his money, Gaius, and let us be off."

Patroclus clutched greedily at the treasury notes the Emperor's great-nephew handed to him. But the stranger was not to be silenced.

"Tiberius," he said in a firm, quiet voice, "you must not take that ring."

"How say you?" said the Emperor slowly, and the crowd edged back. "Who are you to speak thusly to the Emperor of Rome?"

"I speak not from insolence, O Caesar, but in warning. The ring is not to be worn by any of a ruling line. For any such to wear it is death."

"And how do you know so much about this ring?" asked Tiberius. There was a tinge of menace in his voice.

The stranger shifted his stance nervously. "It is the ring of Set, the Evil God of the Egyptians. A priest of Ptah once told me of its existence and its powers. Several months ago I learned that old Diomed had had such a ring brought from Egypt, and so I came here—only to learn that Diomed had died."

"Your story is a strange one," remarked the young Gaius haughtily. "Why should the ring bring death to the wearer?"

"Because it has been cursed."

A woman tittered in the crowd, and this set off a tide of swelling laughter. Gaius smiled irksomely.

"I do not jest," said the stranger, his voice tense with anger. "The ring is old, older than all the nations of the earth. It was owned by Thoth-Amon, a sorcerer who lived ten thousand years ago in the land which is now called Egypt. The ring was old even then, but Thoth-Amon learned its powers and used them to call up demons to do his bidding. His enemies died with the marks of fangs and claws on their bodies, and for a time none could resist his power.

"Yet the ring was not all-powerful: Once, Thoth-Amon invoked its power to destroy a king—but the king had an ally who was a greater sorcerer than even Thoth-Amon, and the ring's power was turned aside. The king lived, and later Thoth-Amon died, but the curse was still on the ring and has never been lifted. Since then several kings have tried to wear the ring, but each died a terrible death, so that at last the priests of Egypt hid the thing beneath one of their altars—and there it lay for nearly ten thousand years, until Diomed's curiosity brought it to light once more."

The crowd laughed anew as the stranger concluded his tale, but Patroclus noticed that several Egyptians in the crowd remained silent, their faces strangely grave.

"Fool!" snarled the Emperor, his eyes now fully open. "Do you think to frighten me into giving up the ring with this child's tale? Fellow, you stand on the brink of death, so answer civilly: What is your name?"

"Simon, of Gitta."

"Then look you, Simon!" Tiberius rose and slipped the ring on one of his fingers, then held up his hand for all to see. "Behold, I stand unharmed. Let the gods strike me if they will."

The crowd cheered, and Simon flushed at the derision for him in their cries. He turned away, angry and embarrassed, but before he could leave, the high, taunting voice of Gaius lanced the air.

"Hold on there—I've a question!"

Simon turned again to face the portico, his face dark and sullen.

"How came *you* to learn of this ring," Gaius continued, "that lures you across half the world in quest of its power?"

"I seek not its power," Simon retorted. "Its power is a threat of bane to all humankind. My mentor was Ka-nephru, high priest of Ptah in Thebes and hereditary guardian of the ring; he was slain by that agent of Diomed who pilfered it. With his last breath he charged me to search out that ring, wherever it might be, and restore it to its proper seclusion—else, he warned, might all mankind be brought down to doom by the misuse of its power."

The eyes of Gaius were scowling coals glaring down into Simon's own—and Simon *knew* in that instant that his story was believed. But then Gaius turned to the nobles beside him and said loudly enough for all to hear:

"What think you, friends, of a man with a story like this, and with no retinue, who carries a thousand *sestertia* on his person? Do you not find that a bit strange?"

"Did I say I carried it?" retorted Simon. "And is it your business to know how I keep or earn my money?"

"Earn it?" mocked Gaius. "Your profession must be a profitable one. Are you a thief, Simon, or a pimp?"

The crowd roared at the coarse jibe. Simon scowled darkly and answered in a low, even voice: "I am a magician."

"Ah—that would explain your ridiculous cloak and staff. Can you do a trick for us, magician? I suspect you are quite expert at making things vanish—especially from men's pockets, eh?"

"If you dared step down here," said Simon evenly, "you would learn how swiftly I can make a man's head vanish from his shoulders."

"That's all we need," grinned Gaius to the Praetorian Guards. "Take him!"

Three burly guardsmen detached themselves from the ranks and strode down into the courtyard. The crowd moved back. Simon did not stir, but watched in silence as the soldiers advanced with drawn swords. Suddenly he raised his staff and shouted:

"Here's a trick for you, Gaius!"

He hurled the staff, not like a spear, but crosswise. It caught the foremost guard across his breastplate, bending at the impact. Then, abruptly, it was a living, writhing cobra whose coils looped and lashed about the man's form. The black, hooded head darted forward, and the guard reeled and fell to the flagstones, screaming and clawing at his face.

Women shrieked in the crowd. Simon whipped off his cloak and flung it over a second guard like a net, sending the fellow sprawling with a quick jerk. He wheeled and twisted aside just as the third guardsman's sword point tore through his tunic and nicked the flesh of his flank. Whirling, he snatched out his *sica* and sprang: The curved blade swished in a glittering arc that ended in a spurt of crimson, and the guard flopped heavily to the ground, his neck slashed nearly to the spine.

Simon leapt up the steps of the columned porch. Three bounds carried him to the Emperor's chair. The nobles scattered; Gaius backed away hastily, screaming for the guards, his face twisted into a wolfish snarl. The fleeing Patroclus tripped in his haste and rolled down the marble steps. Simon grabbed Tiberius' arm and began to tug at the hand that held the ring.

"Help!" shrieked the Emperor. "Assassin! Help!"

The Praetorians were already surging forward. Simon sprang back to avoid a guardsman's thrusting *pilum*; the thick shaft of another spear cracked sharply against his wrist, knocking the *sica* spinning from his hand.

"Alive!" screamed Tiberius, scrambling out of danger. "I want him alive!"

Simon ducked a *pilum* swung clubwise, darted a lightning-swift chop to the guardsman's face that crushed the bridge of his nose and sent him sprawling. He whirled—but not quickly enough: A heavy brass-studded shield crashed down on his head and shoulder, and Simon reeled and fell stunned to the marble floor.

"A madman!" exclaimed Tiberius, rubbing his hand. "He would have stopped at nothing to get the ring. You were too slow, you fools—he might have killed me, had he tried!"

"Thank the gods who made him mad," drawled Gaius casually, "and trouble yourself about him no more, O Caesar—leave him to me, if you will."

"Remove him from my sight, then," ordered the Emperor. "See that he is crucified. You, Macrobius—kill that snake of his! And as for you, Patroclus," he continued, turning to the cowering executor, "hereafter you will be more careful about whom you admit to your auctions. I'll let you off lightly this time, but the damage to my serenity demands compensation. Guards! Gather up these trinkets and gems, and remove them to the imperial treasury."

Patroclus watched in consternation as the imperial party filed out the gate, bearing with them the chest that contained most of old Diomed's wealth.

"A curse on all magicians and madmen!" he muttered vehemently. "Would that the gods had stifled all such at birth. Slaves! Bring me a flagon of wine—I am ill."

II

"Ho, wretch—here is your dinner. Wake up and eat!"

Simon sputtered back to life as a foul-smelling, semiliquid mess splashed over his face and chest. Opening his eyes, he saw that he lay on the floor of a small stone room whose walls were beaded with moisture. Above him stood a hunched, malformed individual bearing an oily, flickering torch in one hand and a dripping pail in the other.

"What is this place?" asked Simon groggily.

"The dungeons at Circeii," croaked the man in a voice as warped and sloppy as his twisted face. "The soldiers brought you here but a moment a-gone. Eat well, for you'll be fed but once a day."

Simon tried to rise, but found that he was chained to the floor. The crooked man laughed and kicked him in the ribs.

"You'll learn to take life easy here," he jeered. "There's no escaping this place. Lie still now, and eat your bilge."

Simon glared up at the hateful face, wishing he could rise and smash it to a pulp. Certainly that would have improved its appearance. Straggled hair pushed out from beneath a dirty leather cap to hang lankly over an apish forehead, and between the strands peered eyes whose fungus-yellow depths reflected a coarse, brutal sadism. A pendulous nether lip dangled droolingly over a receding chin, exposing a jagged line of rotten gray teeth. The man's garments were nothing more than ragged patches of cloth and leather stitched haphazardly together and held in at the waist by a frayed rope. From this rope hung a bundle of keys on a large, iron ring.

The man laughed hoarsely at the anger in Simon's eyes.

"You'll learn the hard way," he grated. "I know your kind. You think you're tough—but you'll break. Maybe you'll even go mad, but I hope not. The sane ones suffer most!"

He laughed again and spat in Simon's face. Simon surged fiercely against his chains, but his efforts only caused the ragged jailer to laugh the harder. The hunched man gave him a final kick in the side and walked chuckling out of the cell. The metal door clanged shut, and Simon was left in darkness.

How long he lay in that dank hole he had no way of knowing, but it seemed like many hours. Several times he heard the jailer's rough, raucous laugh, always in connection with sobbing cries and muffled blows, and the memory of that unkempt creature made him grind his teeth in futile rage.

At last the tramp of feet sounded from the corridor outside, and a key grated in the massive lock. The door opened, and when Simon's eyes had adjusted to the torchlight he saw that three men had entered his cell. One was the ragged jailer; the second was a brawny, brutal-faced giant of a man clad only in a loin cloth; and the third, dressed in an elaborate blue tunic and scarlet cloak, was none other than the Emperor's great-nephew, Gaius.

"Ho, scoundrel," Gaius grinned. "Do you find your new quarters suitable? No, don't bother to rise—our visit will be both short and informal."

Simon scowled at him darkly, but said nothing.

"Ah, you are angry!" said Gaius, bending over Simon in a cocky manner. "Be not quick to take offense—perhaps I'm not the enemy you seem to think I am. If old Tiberius had had his way, you'd be nailed to a cross this very moment. I had you brought here to Circeii instead."

"What do you want with me, then?"

Gaius turned to the jailer. "Leave us," he ordered, and the repulsive creature shambled out of the cell. Simon glanced uneasily at Gaius' massive companion, wondering what was to follow.

"Don't mind Macrobius," said Gaius, indicating the brutal-faced giant. "He's my bodyguard—used to be a gladiator. I would guess, judging by the way you fought today, that you've seen action in the arena yourself."

"I was trained to use the *sica*," said Simon. "For two years I spilled blood for the amusement of your howling crowds. Some of that blood was my own."

"I can see why you survived, Simon—you are quick as a cat. But what of the man you killed with the snake-staff? You didn't learn *that* trick in the arena."

"The priests of Ptah use serpents in their rituals and have long known how to do many things with them. I was once an acolyte in one of their temples."

"After you escaped from your gladiator school, no doubt," remarked Gaius. "But no matter. Were these same priests the ones who told you of the ring?"

"What is all this to you?" Simon demanded. "Have you come here but to mock me again?"

"I do not mock you, Simon of Gitta," said Gaius, bending forward and speaking in a low, intense voice. There was a strange gleam in his deep-set eyes. "Tiberius pretends to scoff at the hidden powers of magic, but I am not such a fool. Do you know that the Emperor has fallen ill? Aye, it happened but an hour after he had left the auction-place, and though he vows it is but a passing sickness I can see death approaching in his eyes. The ring is responsible, Simon—I know it is the ring!"

"What do you want of me, then?"

"The ring, Simon—and the power to wear it. Old Tiberius has named me his heir, and when he dies I will be Emperor of Rome. Yet an emperor has many enemies—his throne is never secure. With the power of this ring at my command I would never need fear their plots; my enemies would fall to the fangs of demons, and none could ever hope or dare to dispute my rule!"

"But no ruler can wear the ring of Set," Simon protested. "As soon as you became emperor you would die like old Tiberius."

"That is why I can use your help, Simon. You must tell me how to lift the curse from the ring."

"I know not whether the curse *can* be removed," said Simon. "I do not even know the ring's full powers. Yet there is a chance—"

"A chance? Tell me!"

Simon gauged the fanatic gleam in the man's eyes. "And what can I expect in return?" he demanded.

"Your freedom, plus ten times the amount of money that was taken from you. I will even make you head magician of my house should you so desire."

Simon laughed shortly. "Your court buffoon? Not I! Besides, what assurance do I have that you will keep your promise?"

"You have my word."

"Your word!" Simon smiled wryly. "What sort of a fool do you take me for? Your word is nothing."

"Yet for you it is all, Simon—it is all you have. Without my help you might rot here forever—or you might end up hanging from a cross. But neither of these things need happen, Simon, if you will but tell me of the means to lift the curse from the ring. I promise you freedom on these terms—and I have always kept my word."

"Free me, first," said Simon, "or you can rot on your throne before I'll tell you the secret of the ring."

"It is you who will rot, Simon—you are in no position to bargain with me. With or without your help I will learn the secret of the ring. My ways are many and devious, as you have doubtless heard, and my agents are everywhere—they can follow back the trail that led you here, or the one that led old Diomed to send his thief to Egypt. Yet if you will make my path easier, I will do likewise for you. Speak quickly, now—or I shall have Macrobius begin to break your bones, one by one."

"It seems I have no choice," said Simon. "Very well, I'll tell you—but your task will not be an easy one."

"Speak," prompted Gaius, his eyes agleam.

"In the temple of Thoth, at Alexandria, there is an ancient scroll called the *Book of Thoth*. It was first written more than ten thousand years ago by Thoth-Amon, the sorcerer of the ring. Only once have I glimpsed this book, and the priests who guarded it would let me read but a few lines of its faded hieroglyphs—yet I saw enough to know that Thoth-Amon wrote his most dreadful secrets therein. If a spell can be found to counteract that of the ring, it will be found within the *Book of Thoth*."

"Good!" said Gaius, grinning wolfishly. "When I am emperor, those priests shall not dare withhold this book from me. After Tiberius dies I shall journey to Egypt. Until then, you must remain here."

"Liar!" hissed Simon. "What of your word?"

"When the ring is mine and its power will no longer harm me, then perhaps you will go free. Until then, Simon, farewell—and wish me good fortune if you would see the light of day again!"

The pair strode out of the cell and the door clanged shut behind them. Simon cried out after them, rattling his chains, but only the mocking laugh of the jailer answered him. Finally he sank back in frustration, realizing that if he were to escape it must be by means of his own.

Most would have despaired of winning free from such a predicament, but Simon had spent considerable time studying the methods of the Persian escape artists who awed the courts of Eastern kings, and had acquired some degree of proficiency in their arts. Yet a tactile examination of his chains showed him there was little hope of escape. Actually there was but one chain which looped round and round his body, passing every so often through iron rings set solidly into the stone floor. Each end of the chain ran through a metal loop on a locked manacle clamping one of his wrists, and his arms were held out from his sides with only about a foot of slack. With his left hand he could just touch the padlock that clinched the ends of his chain together—a huge iron lock that only a sledge might hope to crush.

There seemed no way out, but his mind would not admit defeat. For what seemed like hours he lay in silence while futile plans spun ceaselessly within his brain. The stone floor was cold and damp, and the chain galled him increasingly. From the corridor drifted occasional muted screams, and Simon knew that a few more hours of this would have him screaming, too.

His hunger had been mounting for some time, and at last he overcame his repugnance enough to try to eat. The swill his jailer had flung over him was now dried to a greasy crust, but many solid and semisolid lumps of food littered the floor round about. Evidently the prisoners were fed on scraps from the soldiers' tables. But when he tried to eat, Simon found that the chain would not allow his hands to reach his mouth.

He cursed, loudly and bitterly. His voice was hoarse and high-pitched, and he realized that he was close to cracking—

Suddenly he quieted, and a strange excitement swept over him. The object he had picked up in his left hand was hard and did not crumble at his touch. It was only the broken drumstick of a fowl, but it brought a wild burst of hope to his soul.

Carefully he shredded away the remaining meat, then worked the slender fibula loose from the heavier tibia, retaining the smaller bone in his hand. Next he rasped the broken end back and forth against the rough stone floor until he had a slender pin of bone not unlike a bodkin. With this feeble weapon, in utter darkness and with grease-smeared fingers, he began to attack the padlock.

Only a madman might have tried such a device, and only an escape artist could have hoped for it to succeed; Simon by now had many of the traits of both. Time lost all meaning as he picked away, steadying the lock with two fingers while working the bone pin into the keyhole with the other three. His mind became concentrated entirely in his left hand, so that he was unaware of the rest of his body or the rest of the world. The cold, the dampness, the stench and the distant cries of prisoners all went unheeded—

And at last there was a click!

Simon hardly dared to breathe. Slowly he pressed up against his chain. The heavy padlock fell off with a dull rattle, the thick chain went slack, and Simon realized he was free.

Free of the chain, but not the dungeon. For a moment he rose and stretched his cramped limbs luxuriously. When he had restored his circulation he lay down again and draped the chain artistically over his body. Then, with the patience of an Eastern mystic, he began to wait.

He did not have to wait long. Presently a light appeared beneath the door, and a key grated in the heavy lock. The crooked jailer entered and stood his oily torch in a wall bracket. In one gnarled hand he carried a rusty bucket brimming over with slop, and Simon realized that he had been confined for a whole day.

"Ho, pig," gargled the jailer, setting down his bucket. "I bring your daily fare. But first, I must give you a taste of the lash—I haven't yet heard you scream."

He uncoiled a whip from his rope belt and crossed the cell with a shambling, bowlegged gait. Simon began to mumble under his breath, making his voice seem weak and half-delirious.

"What say you, wretch?" demanded the hunchback. As Simon continued to babble incoherently, the man bent over him and peered into his face. "Curse me beneath your breath, will you?" he muttered. "By Vulcan, I'll—!"

Simon's right hand shot out like a striking cobra, and his stiffened fingers crunched into the jailer's throat, crumbling the hyoid like brittle cardboard. The jailer reared back and sprawled clumsily to the stone floor, the air hissing in his throat as he tried to scream.

Simon rose and calmly stepped out of his chains as the hunchback writhed and flopped about. The man was strangling to death. His face was flushed to a dark gray, then to a dirty purple, while his yellow eyes bulged painfully and his stubby fingers clutched at his throat. Simon regarded his throes in silence, feeling no pity but only a dark, savage satisfaction. Finally the jailer's contortions came to an end; blood bubbled in his throat as his chest collapsed; his feet kicked the stone flags, and he lay still.

Simon peered cautiously into the corridor, but no one was in sight. He turned and hurriedly unlocked his wrist manacles with the jailer's keys, then began to strip the dead man of his grimy clothes. Peeling off his own filth-splattered tunic, he replaced it with the jailer's rags and knotted the frayed rope about his waist. Finally, removing the corpse's crumpled cap, he placed it over his own dark locks and walked into the corridor, closing the door of the cell behind him.

Within the cell Simon's disguise would have fooled no one—indeed, his tall, compactly muscled frame seemed in ridiculous contrast to the squat, twisted body of the jailer—but no sooner had he stepped into the passageway than his whole form seemed to shrivel and shrink. His shoulders hunched grotesquely, and his angular face warped itself into lopsided hideousness. The same Persian magicians from whom he had garnered his escape artistry had also been masters of disguise, and Simon had not studied their arts in vain. No one would have recognized him as he hobbled along that dank, narrow corridor in the uncertain torchlight.

Once he paused with the idea of liberating some of his fellow prisoners, but a quick glance into some of the cells caused him to change his mind. Gaunt, skeleton-like creatures, white-haired and scaled with festering scabs, glared up at his torch with eyes of horror and lunacy, and he backed away shuddering, knowing that he could do nothing for them. Only death could help those who languished in the dungeons of Tiberius.

The corridor ended at a narrow flight of stone steps, and these led up a long spiral to an iron-barred archway. Simon tried several of his keys on the massive gate and finally found one that fit. The gate rasped open, and he emerged into a wider passage. Through the archway at its far end he could see sunlight on the flags of a broad courtyard.

A guardsman suddenly entered the corridor and strode toward him. Simon had no time to conceal himself.

"Ho, jailer," the guard greeted him. "Have you heard the good news?"

"I hear no news in these foul pits," croaked Simon in what he hoped was a good imitation of the jailer's rasping voice.

"Tiberius has left Circeii. His belly ails him, and he yearns for the fresh breezes of Capri. That means our discipline is relaxed! What say you to that, old toad—?" By this time he had approached closely enough to peer into Simon's face. "By Pallus!" he exclaimed. "You're not—"

Simon's fist cracked sharply on the point of the guard's jaw and the man crumpled without a sound. The magician caught his unconscious body before it could clatter against the floor and quickly dragged it into the dark stairwell. Moments later he emerged from the shadows clad in the polished metal and leather of an imperial guardsman.

Leisurely he strode to the archway and scanned the courtyard. About the walls stood a half-dozen soldiers in relaxed attitudes. The far wall opened onto a public thoroughfare, but the wide entrance was blocked by a massive iron portcullis.

Simon scowled. Even as he wondered how he was to pass this last obstacle, a sharp cry of command rang out and he saw that a group of six or eight soldiers had gathered outside the gate.

"Open!" cried the officer. "We come for a prisoner."

"Which prisoner?" demanded the warden of the gate. "And by whose orders?"

"Orders of Gaius, the Emperor's ward. Here is the warrant with his seal. We are to crucify one Simon of Gitta, who was brought here yesterday."

The warden raised his arm, and two guards began to turn the wheel that lifted the gate. Simon strode from concealment and began to walk casually across the courtyard.

The gate creaked open, and the officer stepped inside and handed his warrant to the warden. Simon hoped his crested helmet was shading his features sufficiently. As the body of soldiers tramped in, he walked unhurriedly past their left flank in the opposite direction, just as the portcullis began to descend—

"You, there!" shouted the warden suddenly. "Where do you think you're going—?"

Simon cast aside his heavy shield and spear and ducked under the closing gate. It creaked to a stop and the soldiers cried out behind him. Simon did not even glance back; a quick sprint, and he was across the cobbled street through a knot of astonished citizens and into a narrow alley. He cast away his helmet as he dashed on, hoping to shake his pursuers in the winding streets ahead.

Circeii was an old town, and its alleys were narrow and twisting. Simon cast off the rest of his armor as he ran. The clatter of pursuit faded into the distance, and at last he darted into a black archway and paused, panting.

No footfalls sounded behind him, and he knew he had thrown off the soldiers for the moment. It would be easy to get out of town once he disguised himself. Discarding the rest of his uniform, he retained only the plain linen tunic, the short broad-bladed sword, and a small leather pouch that jingled agreeably.

"Two *denarii*," he muttered, counting out the coins. "Enough to buy a good meal and start me on my way. Tiberius can't be more than a few hours from Circeii—I can surely catch up with him before he reaches Baiae and embarks for Capri. I've come too far to give up the ring now. So Gaius decided to have me crucified, eh? He must have decided to make sure I wouldn't blab to anyone else about the ring. Well, now I know how he keeps his word. By Baal! I once told him I'd make his head vanish from his shoulders—perhaps someday I'll have an opportunity to prove my word better than his!"

III

As the sun sank behind the hills of Campania a ragged beggar, whining for alms, hobbled along the darkening streets of a fashionable neighborhood at the edge of the seaside town of Misenum. There were few other people to be seen, as the neighborhood was some distance from the market place. As the old beggar approached the high wall surrounding a rather palatial estate, a Praetorian Guardsman strode from a shadowy archway and blocked his path.

"Alms for the needy," wheezed the old man in a thin, cracked voice. "Alms, I pray you!"

"Silence, old fool," ordered the guardsman. "The Emperor lies ill within this house. Would you disturb his rest with your whinings? Begone!"

"Alas that the Emperor is ill!" quavered the aged one. "Yet the gods look kindly on those who do kind deeds; a pittance from one of his good soldiers would fill an old man's belly, and perhaps cause the gods to smile on the Emperor's health—"

"Go, curse you!" shouted the guard, brandishing his *pilum*. The ragged beggar limped hurriedly away, muttering in his straggled gray beard. The clack of his gnarled staff faded into the distance as he turned and vanished down a dark side street.

No sooner had he passed beyond sight of the guardsmen, however, than his bent form assumed an upright posture and his shoulders broadened amazingly. There was no hobble in his step as he strode over to a marble fountain that stood amid a small park-like patch of trees. Here in the shadows he pulled off his beard and ragged garments, and began to count out coins from a leather pouch.

"Ten *denarii* and an odd *sesterce* or two," he grinned. "Not bad for a day's loafing. By Baal, the beggars in this town make as much in a day as I've ever earned in a week of performing!"

With this observation Simon of Gitta seated himself against the bole of a tree and began to wait. It was dark by this time, but he did not intend to enter the estate of Tiberius for several hours, until the streets would be entirely quiet.

From gossip on the road he had learned that the Emperor was now seriously ill and that he had been taken to the estate at Misenum, being unable to continue on to Capri. Rumor had it that he was expected to die, and Simon knew he must act swiftly if this were true. He would have a hard time indeed trying to pilfer the ring from the crafty Gaius; also (the thought set his spine to tingling) nothing on earth would be able to protect him from the most terrible of dooms, should Gaius ever master the secret of sending forth the demons of the ring.

For half the night he sat, savoring the cool smell of the salt breeze and listening to the distant tumult of the market place. About midnight the streets quieted and Simon decided to wait no longer. Clad only in tunic and sandals, the short Roman sword girdled at his side, he set out for the estate.

The moon-cast shadows offered perfect concealment as he crept along the road to a point opposite the wall. The gates, he knew, were heavily guarded. The wall was only ten feet high and could be scaled easily, yet he did not attempt it immediately. During the day he had made a careful survey of the outer environs of the estate; he knew the positions of the guards and was ready to act accordingly.

Presently a sentry clanked by. As soon as he rounded the far corner, Simon dashed across the stone-paved street and sprang lightly up the wall. His fingers gripped the edge, and his lithe, hard muscles swung him easily to the top. For a moment he lay there, prone and silent, listening. Then, making sure there was nothing below to obstruct his progress, he slid down the inside face of the wall and dropped softly to the ground.

The trees threw black, comforting shadows over him, but he moved with the utmost caution nevertheless, hoping no dogs were kept on the grounds. The whole mansion was lit, and through the downstairs windows he could see numerous servants and Praetorian Guards moving about. The second story had a ledge running around it that looked just wide enough for a finger-hold, and there was a balcony at the back. But how to reach it? No vines or trees grew close to the house, and both ledge and balcony were more than twice the height of a man from the ground.

The casement to the right of the balcony was open wide, and Simon thought he saw the means to reach it. Stealing from the shadows, he crept across the lawn and began to shin up one of the two pillars supporting the balcony. It was difficult to climb, being fashioned of smooth marble, and its diameter was such that his arms and legs would not completely encircle it. His progress was slow, and he felt horribly exposed hanging there above the garden, though the balcony shaded him from the moon's direct rays. At length he felt the roughness of the pillar's Corinthian crown beneath his fingers, and a moment later he had struggled up and over the balustraded edge.

After resting flat for a moment, he rose and crossed to the door. It was slightly ajar, and through it he glimpsed a tiled corridor flanked by high mahogany portals. At the nearest door stood two Praetorians, their armor gleaming in the soft light of the hanging lamps. No entrance was to be gained here. He would have to try the open window.

Swinging himself hand over hand along the narrow ledge was easy compared to climbing the column, but again he had to endure the exposed feeling. In a moment he was beneath the open casement. Pulling himself up slowly, he peered into a spacious chamber whose marble walls were partly covered with thick tapestry. A single lamp burned on a small table, beside which an old man in the robes of a physician sat drowsing in a padded chair. Against the far wall rested a large bed, carved of mahogany and thickly mattressed, and Simon realized that the Roman Fates had guided him well—for in this bed, pale and emaciated to a startling degree, lay the wan and failing form of the Emperor Tiberius.

Simon's fingers ached. Cautiously he drew himself over the sill and, making sure no one else was present, slid inside. Neither of the sleepers stirred. Sidling away from the window so as not to be seen from the garden, Simon crept softly to the Emperor's bedside and peered down at his inert form. A thrill of exaltation swept over him as he saw a flash of copper on one of the thin, waxen hands. It was the ring of Set!

Slowly he reached for the thing, gripping it gingerly so as not to touch the old man's flesh. The metal felt strangely warm and smooth beneath his fingertips. He tugged at it gently, but it would not slide off the wizened hand.

Simon scowled. When Tiberius had first donned the ring it had seemed to fit loosely. Now its coppery loops clasped the Emperor's finger with a snug, frustrating preciseness. Yet the finger was certainly not swollen. Had Tiberius ordered his metalsmith to alter the ring's dimensions? That seemed unlikely. Almost it appeared as if the coppery serpent had tightened its coils of its own accord, and Simon could imagine that he saw a wicked light gleaming in its tiny yellow eyes.

He tugged at the ring again, harder this time. Tiberius moaned; his head rolled feebly to one side, and his lips began to writhe strangely. Simon drew back a pace.

"The ring!" groaned Tiberius in a scarcely audible voice. "It will not let me go. Oh, take it from me! Those cursed fiery eyes—I cannot bear them! They glare at me from the darkness—they seek to drown my soul…. Listen!" His voice suddenly altered, tensed. His eyes sprang open, bright and feverish, but Simon sensed that they did not see him. They seemed to look through rather than at him, and his spine tingled as he beheld their weird brilliance.

"Listen!" whispered the voice again. "It is coming. From the blackness beneath the pyramids I hear it crawling. Do you not hear? Do you not *see?* Ah—those cursed fiery eyes!"

Simon started. He *did* hear something, like cloth folds sweeping across a tiled floor. Someone was approaching. Swiftly he crept past the sleeping physician and concealed himself behind a section of the tapestry. With one eye he watched the room, tensed to draw back his head in an instant.

But no one entered the chamber. Instead, the sound grew steadily louder, gathering different overtones as it did so. There was a sinister, rasping quality about it that made Simon think of serpent scales sliding over cold stone. Closer and closer it seemed to come, yet somehow its volume did not increase in the slightest. Strange hollow booms accompanied it, muted and distorted, like thunder echoing down the halls of other dimensions….

A slender wisp of smoke began to rise from the Emperor's bed, and Simon's skin prickled as he saw that the ring had undergone a strange alteration. The tiny coppery serpent had released its tail, and from its upward-gaping mouth issued a thin stream of black smoke that coiled and coalesced into a nebulous cloud above the stricken emperor. Even as Simon watched it thickened and swelled, and its billows writhed like the coils of a monstrous serpent. A form took shape in its murky depths—a form black as the blackest caverns beneath the earth, a form whose lambent yellow eyes leered down like glowing spheres of flame into the eyes of Tiberius.

Simon cringed back, scarcely daring to breathe for fear of attracting the gaze of that monstrous shape. Coil after coil looped into being within the hazy cloud. A colossal fanged mouth gaped wide, and a red forked tongue flickered sinuously in the air above the Emperor's face. The thing was like a serpent in shape, but its black scales reflected not a glimmer of light and its luminous eyes seemed to glare with an evil intelligence. Although it filled only the space above Tiberius' bed, it somehow gave an impression of vastness equal to that of the towering pyramids of Khem; and

Simon knew that he gazed upon Set, the most ancient and evil god ever worshiped by the race of man.

Tiberius' mouth was stretched wide as if in a scream, but no sound issued forth. His eyes stared frozenly into the flaming orbs poised above him. Simon stood petrified. He had seen men die screaming in the arena, and expiring slowly on Roman crosses under the glaring sun, yet never had he seen such awful fear as that which twisted the features of Tiberius. Somehow he sensed that the Emperor's soul was being drawn from his body and into the slitted depths of those hellish eyes. The old man's form seemed almost to shrink, and he quivered like a puppet dangled on a vibrating string. Then, abruptly, his shakings quieted; his strained features slowly relaxed into an expression of vacant, staring idiocy, and Simon knew that he was dead.

Already the terrible form was fading away, dissolving into the murky cloud that was streaming back through the mouth of the ring. Simon did not stir until the last wisp of that unnatural smoke had vanished. Then he eased himself slowly from behind the curtain, hesitating as to whether he should carry out his original purpose or flee from that chamber of death while he still had the chance.

There was a soft clatter on the tile. Simon started, and saw a gleam of metal on the floor by the Emperor's bed. Tiberius' dead hand hung limply over the side, and Simon realized that the ring had dropped easily from his finger.

The old physician stirred in his sleep. Simon hesitated no longer—after all, he remembered, the curse had power over kings alone, and could not harm him. He quickly crossed the room, snatched up the ring, and hurried to the window. The ring appeared to be normal now—it felt reassuringly solid and metallic. Slipping it on his left middle finger, he let himself out the window, hung for a moment from the ledge, and dropped.

He landed in a catlike crouch and was on his feet in an instant. Quickly he sprinted across the moonlit lawn—and almost collided with a burly shape that suddenly emerged from the darkness under the trees.

"Ho, there!" rumbled a deep voice. "What do you in the Emperor's gardens—? Oh, it's you, dungeon-rat! By Hercules, you'll not escape this time!"

Simon recognized Macrobius, Gaius' bodyguard. He leaped back barely in time as the gladiator's iron-knobbed club swished past his cheek. Simon's sword flashed out in time to ward off the second blow, but the impact shattered the broad blade and sent him staggering back. Macrobius bellowed and charged.

Desperately Simon snatched up a heavy marble urn and flung it with all his strength. It smacked full into the gladiator's broad chest and sent him reeling back with the wind half knocked out of him. Simon charged in and grappled his attacker; Macrobius dropped his mace and enfolded the magician in a strangling bear hug. Frantically Simon dug his thumbs into the gladiator's sides below the ribs. Macrobius loosened his grip, bellowing with rage, and as Simon slipped free he delivered a savage chop to the gladiator's thick neck. The blow would have killed an ordinary man—but Macrobius only grunted, shook his head, and charged again.

Simon leaped aside and struck again. His quick footwork baffled the heavy gladiator, but his blows might have fallen against a stone wall for all the effect they produced. In the distance he suddenly heard the voice of Gaius calling for the guards. Then his feet unexpectedly struck the fallen urn, and he fell sprawling to the grass.

Macrobius roared as his thick hands gripped Simon's leg in a bone-breaking hold. Simon strained back frantically—and his flailing hand touched the handle of the club Macrobius had dropped. With all his strength he swung the weapon; its iron head crunched deep into the gladiator's skull, spattering blood and brains about the grass—and Simon's foe went limp and sprawled full upon him.

Pushing aside the dead hulk, Simon rose and glared about the garden like a trapped beast. From both ends of the estate sounded the clamor of approaching guardsmen, and several other guards were dashing from the front of the mansion. There could be no escape this time—unless—

Unless he used the ring!

Yet he knew not the thing's full powers. Whatever came to his call might destroy him as well as his enemies. Yet it was a chance—at least it was better than dying without a struggle—

Even as these thoughts flashed through his mind he knelt beside the shattered head of Macrobius and ran his hand through the sticky hair. The formula called for blood—human blood—and there was plenty of that around. With a shaking finger he smeared a crop of it over the yellow eyes of the ring, and then began to recite the Egyptian words of the single chant he had managed to memorize from the *Book of Thoth:*

"Blind your eyes, o serpent of Set,
"Open them wide to the gulfs of Night—
"Whose shadow falls on the waning light?
"Call him to me, o serpent of Set!"

A dozen Praetorians converged from the house and the garden. Simon leaped up to meet their charge, his club held ready—but even as he rose, the soldiers stopped as one man in their tracks, and their eyes went wide. A simultaneous scream burst from all their throats. Two of them collapsed in a dead faint, and the rest turned and fled in a mad scramble for the house.

Simon shuddered. He felt the presence of something close behind him, but a strange fear kept him from turning around. Some of Set's minions, legend claimed, had shapes that would blast men's sanity, and Simon did not wish to put the old tales to the test.

"Follow me," he muttered, setting out through the trees; and *something* obeyed, for strange clumping footsteps sounded on the grass behind him. The guards at the rear gate dashed away screaming at his approach, and he passed unhindered into the street beyond.

Through the deserted, torchlit lanes of Misenum Simon fled, and behind him the rasping of great claws echoed from the cobblestones. No one pursued him nor sought to bar his way, yet he did not stop until he had left the village behind him and the sands of the seashore whispered beneath his feet.

There beneath the moon he paused, and wiped the crusted blood from his ring. Now was the crucial moment: if the demon obeyed his final command, all was well; if not....

"Go, now," he muttered. "Go—back to the hell you came from!"

The wind sighed along the beach, and Simon felt that he was alone. Slowly he turned around—and was relieved at the sight of the empty seashore in the moonlight. Yet his spine prickled strangely as he saw the line of tracks that paralleled his own in the sand—long, slender, five-fingered prints, like those of a monstrous lizard.

"By Baal, this ring is more than I had bargained on!" he muttered. "Power I would have—but not on these terms. The priests of Egypt were right to keep the thing hidden from the world. Well, it's mine now, for good or ill. I'm for Baiae, and a ship that will carry me to Alexandria; with Gaius in power things will be too hot for me here—yet someday, perhaps, I'll return and pay off the debt I still owe him!" With a brief glance back at the village, he shrugged his broad shoulders slightly, then turned and set out along the beach toward the distant lights of Baiae.

About "The Worm of Urakhu"

WARNING: Contains spoilers!

Fleeing Rome, Simon returns to Egypt and attempts to disappear. Roman officers in pursuit of someone involved in the Emperor's death, however, do not give up easily. Although it takes them several months, by the autumn of A.D. 37 they are closing in on Simon once again.

The germ of this story was a mystery mentioned by Herodotus. He tells of the mysterious disappearance of a Persian army of 50,000 in the Libyan Desert in 525 B.C. Tierney recalls having often wondered what became of these Persians. "[A]s soon as I saw *Dune*, I knew!" (Letter, July 9, 1985). Salutes to Frank Herbert in Tierney's tale are not too hard to spot, such as the use of worm-dust as well as the giant sand-worm itself. The sand-worms of Dune (Arrakis) are called "Shai-Hulud", and Tierney calls his creature "Shai-urt-ab", meaning "the Destiny that Stills the Heart", i.e., Death. "Shai" is a god of destiny mentioned in the Egyptian *Book of the Dead*, while "urt-ab" means "the stilled heart." (Incidentally, all the quotations Simon makes from the *Book of the Dead* are quite genuine.) The planet from which the worm hails, Urakhu, is obviously a variant of Arrakis.

But Frank Herbert is not the only source of inspiration for "The Worm of Urakhu." The influence of Brian Lumley is evident as well. Tierney speculates that Lumley's tentacled worm-god Shudde-M'ell "originally came from Arrakis, whose sandworms were among his minions. (Could 'Shudd' be a contraction of 'Shai-Hulud'?)... No doubt the Worm [Shai-urt-ab] was brought to earth from Urrakos by Stygian sorcerers or their Hyksos descendants to aid in the release of Shuddam-El (Semitic variant), who of course was imprisoned by the Elder Gods aeons earlier. It was this servitor who destroyed the Persian army... and, centuries later, Simon's Roman pursuers" (Letter, March 26, 1985). Brian Lumley proved enthusiastic about the story and even made a couple of suggestions for bringing Tierney's sand-wrigglers into closer resemblance to his own can of worms. I doubt I am the only Mythos fan who would much enjoy seeing a full collaboration between the two mages Lumley and Tierney.

To knit the narrative world of Dune together with the Cthulhu Mythos may seem arbitrary, but it is not. Both have something striking in common. Herbert and Lovecraft alike drew upon Arabic/Muslim lore, couching the remnants of unearthly civilizations in Arabic garb.

I must not neglect the creative use Tierney makes of the Egyptian sub-Mythos of Lovecraft and Robert Bloch. For one thing, Tierney here provides for the first time a niche in Egyptian historical chronology for the Black Pharaoh Nephren-Ka. It turns out his reign was near the close of the

Middle Kingdom, just after the reign of Sebeknefrure (a real pharaoh) and followed by Akhenaten. The implications are that Nephren-Ka's immediate predecessor, devoted to Sebek (see Bloch's Mythos tale "The Secret of Se-bek" in *Mysteries of the Worm*), paved the way for Nephren-Ka's nightmarish abominations, which in turn weakened Egypt to such a degree as to make it easy pickings for the Hyksos conquerors. What better to inspire Akhenaten to inaugurate his short-lived solar monotheism of Aten than the desire to counter his predecessor Nephren-Ka's monotheism of darkness? This is clever: Akhenaten's religious revolution actually was swept away, his name effaced from all monuments, providing the model for the Lovecraft-Bloch heretic pharaoh.

Lovecraft plainly derived the name Nyarlathotep from two Dunsanian names, Alhireth-hotep and Mynarthitep, both of which share the Egyptian-sounding suffix with Nyarlathotep, whom Lovecraft placed in Egypt ("The Haunter of the Dark" and his sonnet "Nyarlathotep"). Tierney seems to be the first to ask what that suffix must imply. It means something definite in genuine Egyptian names in which it occurs, so why not in Nyarlathotep's case? You'll see what he does with it.

"The Worm of Urakhu" first appeared in *Weirdbook* #23/24, 1988.

THE WORM OF URAKHU

by Richard L. Tierney

I

Would but the Desert of the Fountain yield
One glimpse—if dimly, yet indeed, reveal'd,
To which the fainting Traveller might spring,
As springs the trampled herbage of the field!

— Omar Khayyam, *Rubaiyat*

Simon of Gitta gazed westward across the vast, sandy expanse of the Libyan desert. Beyond miles of undulating pale brown dunes the sun was just touching the horizon.

I must go west, he thought. *Farther west, into the land of the dead.*

He shivered slightly, though the air was warm and there was no wind. The land of the dead—that was what the ancient *Tomb Texts* of Ani called this vast arid region west of the Nile, thus using it as a symbol of the dread regions through which the soul must pass to gain the heavenly realm of Amenti, populating it with monsters and spirit guardians which only the proper spells might nullify. The land of the dead—yet to Simon it was the only chance for life. With a price on his head and a band of Roman legionaries on his trail, eastward lurked death indeed!

He glanced back, scanning the terrain from the rock outcropping on which he stood—a terrain of sandy hills and wind-carved stone formations. All day he had passed through that landscape on foot, save for a two-hour rest during the hottest part of the afternoon, and now he must press on. Though no Romans were in sight, he knew they could not be far beyond the eastern horizon. The traitorous guide who had deserted him the night before, taking the camel and most of the supplies with him, would have arrived back at the Great Oasis well before now. Probably he was already leading the Romans westward on Simon's trail.

"Damn you, Anguiculus," he muttered, "you'll not get rich at my expense!"

So saying, he descended to the base of the outcrop and shouldered his pack, his meager food supplies and goatskin of water wrapped in his dark cloak. Then he set out westward. His feet left conspicuous tracks in the sand, and he mentally cursed the lack of wind. Surely these dunes gave evidence that winds were common enough. He hoped a breeze would spring up in the night, wiping out his trail.

The sun had now set. The dunes, formerly pink-tinged at their crests, now faded to undulating dun and purple shadows. Simon could almost believe that he trod the waves of a time-frozen ocean—the ocean which bore souls westward to the land of the dead—

"Damn you, Anguiculus," he muttered again, largely to counter the mood that was upon him. "Perfidious little serpent!"

Doubtless the Romans would slay the traitorous guide rather than share any of Caligula's reward money with him. Simon determined to himself that it would not come to that. No, the desert breezes would come up in the night, as they usually did, and obliterate his tracks. Then he would return to the Great Oasis by a roundabout way, perhaps find refuge and concealment in a temple of Ptah, bide his time until the furor of pursuit died out—

Then, Anguiculus, I swear that your blood will stain the blade of my sica!

For perhaps two hours he walked onward while the sky darkened to a deep rich blue, then to blackness, while the stars of heaven gleamed ever more brightly in the dry desert air. Overhead was the great square of Pegasus, and Simon wished briefly that he might ride that fabulous winged steed to the next oasis far to the northwest. Above the southern horizon glittered the stars of Pisces Austrius, higher than when seen from Alexandria some hundreds of miles to the north; the brightest among them, called Fum-al-Hut by the wandering desert tribes, seemed to Simon almost to glare down on him like a baleful eye.

He snorted, shook his head as if to shake off the dark mood, then set down his pack and gazed back the way he had come. A waning gibbous moon had risen and beneath its rays he could barely see the distant dark line of rock outcroppings on the eastward horizon. Toward them stretched the dunes, wave after wave of them, and upon their moon-silvered crests— the line of his footprints, clearly visible.

And still there was no wind.

Nervously he brushed bangs of black hair away from his shadowed eyes. His angular features, somber enough under ordinary circumstances, now betrayed a grim tension beneath the moonlight. Now he must hope not only for a breeze but also for more outcroppings; it would not do to be caught by tomorrow's glaring sunlight among the unshaded dunes.

He spared a few minutes to eat a bit of his food and wash it down with two small swallows of water from his goatskin. Then he again shouldered his pack and continued on his way. Ahead, the moonlit sand-waves extended to the horizon.

Rabdos of Scythopolis gripped the handle of his short sword more tightly as a short, lean figure emerged abruptly from the shadows. It was only the desert guide, returning from scouting the rock outcropping.

"Well, Anguiculus?"

"He is not there," said the lean nomad. "But his tracks are plain. He has gone forth upon the sea of sand."

Rabdos nodded, sheathed his sword, and turned to face the large mass of soldiers who followed him—over four hundred of them, strung out along the trail they had marched upon for half the night, their armor gleaming softly under the moon. "We'll rest here an hour," he growled to his nearest officers. "Light torches. Set them up in a circle here, behind the rock outcrop—we don't want our quarry to see them. Then bring the prisoner Sepa to me."

In a few minutes it was done. Most of the soldiers of the cohort seated themselves outside the circle of torches and fell to chewing on rations and swigging from goatskins. Rabdos sat down on a boulder and leaned back against a rock face, flanked by the one-eyed Roman commander Laecanius and several of his centurions; he stared scowlingly for several moments into the bearded, dark-eyed face of the guide. The latter seemed uncomfortable under this scrutiny, pulling nervously at his dark beard and glancing often toward the southeastward dunes.

Presently a number of soldiers emerged into the circle of light, hauling a prisoner with them—a tall, dark-robed Egyptian whose shaven head gleamed in the illumination of the torches.

"Well, Sepa, priest of Ptah," said Rabdos, turning his heavy-browed scowl upon the prisoner, "have you found your tongue yet?"

"I have told you all I know," said the man evenly. There was no fear in his level, almond-shaped eyes.

"Do you wish to die under the torturers' knives, as have all of your fellow acolytes?"

"You will learn no more from me than you did from them. Simon of Gitta has returned the Ring of Thoth-Amon to the place from which it was stolen; it is hidden where none shall find it again. Simon told the other acolytes nothing save this, and they did not ask to know more. It is well, for despite your threats the world shall henceforth remain safe from the Ring's awful power."

Rabdos stood up, anger darkening his brutal, coarse-featured face. His armor clinked as he strode forward a pace; the torch flames glimmered upon his polished breastplate and iron helm.

"I know what you're up to, priest," he snarled. "You're holding out for a cut. Well, then, you can *have* one. There's plenty to go around, by Pollux!"

"Your bribes can accomplish no more than your threats."

"And you're a fool, bald-head. I've been told by Aulus Flaccus, Prefect of Egypt, that the Emperor Gaius is frantic to recover that ring and apprehend the man who stole it from him. For its return he has offered a reward that will make every man in this cohort rich."

"I cannot reveal that which must not be known."

Rabdos spat on the ground, then slowly drew a long dagger from his belt. "Caligula has a game he plays with reluctant prisoners. It's called 'the death of many cuts.' I've tried it on some of your acolytes, and I think they'd have told me all—if they'd known anything. But you—you were the head of their temple. *You'll* know."

The Egyptian looked away scornfully and gazed past the torches toward the moonlit dunes. "I will die here," he said. "And you will die out there."

Rabdos noticed that Anguiculus made a furtive sign to ward off evil. There was fear in the guide's eyes.

"Anguiculus knows," continued the captive priest. "He has heard the old tales. Ask him."

"Ask what?" Rabdos turned to the guide. "What's this croaker talking about?"

"An ancient—legend." Anguiculus glanced briefly toward the expanse of dunes. "It is said that Apophis, the Great Serpent, sleeps—out there—"

"Ha!" Rabdos spat again. "Priest, if you're trying to unsettle my men with this talk of dark legends—"

"Legends?" Sepa smiled benignly. "Was it legend that Cambyses, the conquering Persian, sent an army of fifty thousand men into these deserts more than five centuries ago? He hoped to plunder the wealth of the Oasis of Amon to the northwest, but his army never arrived there—and no man of it ever came out of the desert again!"

Rabdos felt a twinge of uneasiness. He had heard the story often before. "Don't try to scare us with serpent tales, priest. Herodotus records that that army perished in a great windstorm."

"Aye. But Apophis is known to you Greeks and Romans as Typhon. And is not Typhon lord of the great winds that come out of the south?"

"Silence!" Rabdos struck the Egyptian savagely on the face with his open hand. "I see your game, but it won't work. You're not going to play on the feelings of my men with your superstitions."

"My lord," said the desert guide nervously, "perhaps we should listen to him. I, too, have heard tales—"

"Shut up, Anguiculus." Rabdos turned back to the priest, a sneer on his broad face. "You can't deter us, Egyptian. Money talks louder than superstition. If you won't cooperate, you'll die the death of a thousand cuts—and then we'll go out into the dunes and bring back your renegade acolyte all the same."

"Aye, and there's another thing," said the priest. "The Emperor must fear this Simon of Gitta greatly, to order an entire cohort into the pursuit with you. Perhaps he is wise, for Simon is no common man."

Rabdos grimaced angrily, for the Egyptian had touched a sore spot. Left to exercise his own judgment, he would have picked a swift force of perhaps a dozen seasoned veterans, certainly no more than a score. But both the Emperor and the prefect Flaccus evidently felt an entire cohort necessary.

"We're taking no chances, priest. We'll drive this Samaritan to his limits, till he collapses in the desert. Then we'll haul him back to Alexandria, where Aulus Flaccus will devise persuasions even more compelling than the thousand cuts."

"Do you know that Simon is a fighting man who has survived two years in your Roman arenas?"

Rabdos laughed heartily. "And I've survived *six* years in the legions, Sepa, and four more on the prison isle of Pontia! I've killed many times more men than this Simon, and I have no doubt I can kill him in single combat if it comes to that. But the Emperor wants him alive.'

"Simon is also a magician," said the priest, "—trained by adepts of Persia and Khem in arts of which you know nothing."

Rabdos nodded, grinned cynically. "Aye, trained by the likes of *you*. But your arts didn't help *you*, did they? And they won t help him. Childish arts of disguise and illusion can't hide your footprints upon the dunes."

"Yet those arts *will* help me, servant of Rome. They will enable me to control your actions."

"What?" Rabdos tensed warily, gripping his dagger more tightly. The guards, who had allowed the priest to stand on his own, now moved in close and gripped his arms once more.

"You see," said the Egyptian calmly, "when you go forth upon the sands you will be exposing yourself to two terrible enemies—the great serpent Apophis and the magician Simon. And one or the other of them will leap upon you when you least expect it—like *this!*"

With a rapid, fluid, yet unhurried motion the priest darted toward Rabdos, leaving his dark cloak in the hands of the startled guards. The cohort commander barely evaded the hands clutching for his throat and drove his dagger hilt-deep into the Egyptian's breast. The priest collapsed instantly, rolled over on his back, quivered an instant, and lay still. Rabdos, bending forward, saw a dark blot of blood on the man's tunic and a fading smile on his lips.

"Tricked, by Pallas!" he snarled. "The wily jackal used my own fighting instincts against me to escape the torture. If this Simon is as tricky as he, we'll need to use caution indeed!" He straightened, wiped his dagger on his own tunic sleeve, then sheathed it. "Come on, men, we're breaking camp and marching west. I want Simon of Gitta before another day passes—and I want him alive."

As the men hurriedly packed their gear and shouldered their bundles, Rabdos noticed that the guide Anguiculus was facing the southwest and muttering softly to himself in Egyptian.

"What's that stuff you're spouting?" he demanded. "Say it in plain Greek."

"It's a chant from the *Tomb Texts* of Ani, Commander. No one enters these regions without uttering it. It is a prayer against Apophis: 'Begone, crawl away from me, O Serpent. Return beneath that Lake of the Abyss to which the Elder One hath banished thee—' "

"Shut up," snapped Rabdos disgustedly. Then, seeing the worried looks of several of his officers: "Don't mind this superstitious camel-prodder, lads! Think of the Emperor's reward instead."

There were cheers and applause from the men outside the circle of torches. Rabdos grinned. These Roman legionaries were hard, practical. Then he felt Anguiculus plucking at the sleeve of his tunic.

"My pardons, Commander, if my prayer invoked doubts. It was but a habit, common among us oasis folk. And now, if you will but pay me the money you promised, I'll be on my way."

Rabdos glared briefly at the nomad, then laughed harshly. "Are you truly afraid of accompanying us farther into the desert, then?"

"N-no—but, the man's tracks are plain. Surely you can follow them unaided from here."

"And what if a wind comes up and obliterates them? How would we find him then without your expertise, little desert serpent?"

"There will be no wind tonight," said Anguiculus.

"And how do you know that?"

The slender guide seemed to sniff the air nervously. "I am desert-bred. I know. There will be no wind."

"Yet you will come. You will be paid when Simon of Gitta is in my power, a living captive and able to talk."

"I will trust you, Commander. When you return with Simon to the Great Oasis, you can pay me—"

Again Rabdos laughed loudly. Then his face hardened. "Come, little serpent—don't waste any more of my time. You'll get your money when the rest of us do. And you'll work just as hard for it!"

The torches were now extinguished; the men were forming into a long line again. Anguiculus, following Rabdos closely as he bustled about shouting orders, suddenly muttered tensely, "Don't have them march in unison, Commander. Let them walk as they will."

"Eh?" Rabdos glared down at the nervous little man. "Is this another of your desert superstitions?"

"Call it that if you will. The nomads avoid crossing this area in large numbers and in marching order, fearing that the rhythmic tread of many might awaken the Great Serpent who slumbers beneath the sands."

Rabdos' laughter was a bellow this time, harsh in the stillness. "Don't worry, little lizard, there's no point in trying to march in these loose sands anyway!"

As the cohort moved out upon the moonlit dunes Anguiculus realized that its commander's laughter had been a bit forced. Even that coarse and brutal man had sensed the vague menace that brooded out here amid the sand and the stars. Knowing that, the desert guide felt again a chill of apprehension and began to mutter an inaudible prayer to Osiris.

Simon's feet dragged wearily as he plodded on across the loose sands. The stars of Pegasus and Pisces had been replaced by those of Orion and Carina. Low in the south burned bright Canopus, its whiteness mellowing to a rich sulfur yellow as dawn began to tinge the sky's blue-blackness.

He paused and faced back the way he had come. Under the light of the dawn's encroachment the trail of his dragging footprints showed plainly upon the smooth sands, hopelessly conspicuous. Cursing wearily under his breath, he raised his goatskin and took a small sip. It was more than half empty. He knew he must find shelter soon, before the sun was far up, or he would be in dire straits indeed.

Continuing westward he now saw in the increasing light a distant outcropping of dark rock—an island in this sea of sand, lying a bit to the south of his western course. He would have to take shelter there. With luck those rocks might shelter a tiny pocket of water—and a breeze might yet spring up to obliterate his tracks….

An hour passed. Canopus and Sirius had faded, following the lesser stars; the sun blazed white above the eastern dunes. Simon felt its heat, removed his cloak, and stumbled on.

"*Anet-hra-ek, itha am Khepera,*" he muttered absently. "Homage to thee who comest as Kephri, creator of the gods. Thou risest, thou shinest, making bright the earth—"

It was the adulation to the dawn from the *Tomb Texts* of the divine scribe Ani, a plea to the Sun against the darkness of death. But Simon knew that there would be no blessings this day from Kephri, the dawning sun.

Another hour, and another. Simon's throat burned. He sank to his knees and took a long swallow of precious water, then resolutely capped the goatskin. The outcrop loomed nearer, its nearly sheer sides of dark stone seeming almost vertical as they rose abruptly from the light-colored sands. Was this dark island in a sea of dunes soon to be his grave…?

There was a flutter of wings. Simon turned to see a black bird to his left, settling down upon the sand. Not a vulture, but a large dove—a pigeon. Now it swaggered toward him, cooing softly, until it was little more than an arm's length away. Simon gazed at it, fascinated. The bird stopped and cocked its head, gazing back at him with an eye that was as deeply blue as the evening sky.

A black dove, with eyes of deep blue—

Simon's fascination broke. Here before him was life-sustaining flesh and blood—

And even as the thought crossed his mind, the bird flapped into the air and was gone—a dwindling black shape winging away toward the dark outcropping to the southwest.

Simon rose, new hope bringing renewed energy with it. A vulture or even a raven might well range this far into the waterless wastes, but—a pigeon? Not likely! Surely its presence indicated that there would be water and perhaps vegetation in the shadow of the outcrop.

Two more hours passed. It was nearly noon when Simon staggered to the base of the massive stone formation and collapsed in its shade. Disappointment had replaced his hope. There was no water here—nothing but sand and stone….

As his strength slowly returned, he noticed something that had eluded his sun-blinded vision during his approach: The spur of rock in whose shade he lay was not natural. It was formed of great blocks of stone which were smoothly carved and fitted closely together without mortar.

Slowly Simon rose. Where the spur joined the base of the outcrop's eastern cliff face a stone stairway angled upward. And at the top of that stairway, upon the spur, stood a young dark-haired woman clad in white.

II

> And here, in thoughts to thee—
> In thought that can alone
> Ascend thy empire, and so be
> A partner of thy throne—
> By winged Fantasy
> My embassy is given,
> Till secrecy shall knowledge be
> In the environs of Heaven.
>
> — Poe, *Al Aaraaf*

"Baal!" gasped Simon, incredulous.

"Come up, wanderer. I have long awaited you."

Her voice was low and thrilling, musical as water bubbling in a cool fountain. Simon forgot his fatigue as he slowly advanced and climbed the stair. The woman was young, beautiful, radiant under the sun in the white kirtle that came to her knees and left both her shoulders bare; her skin was a light smooth brown, her hair a long wave of jet bound with a golden circlet at her brow. Upon her left shoulder perched the black dove.

"Come up, stranger."

He stood before her now, upon the wide platform that formed the top of the rock spur. Her features, despite her dark complexion, were of a straight Semitic type similar to those of Simon's own race; their beauty was melded with an air of aristocratic self-possession, with perhaps a trace of humor about the lips. Strangest of all were her eyes, which were as deeply blue as those of the dark bird on her shoulder.

"I am Thoueris," she said. Then, gesturing toward a narrow opening carved like a door in the face of the cliff: "Enter. There is water within, and food, and cool refuge from the sun."

She turned and walked through the door. Simon followed closely. They entered a torchlit corridor that led straight into the living rock. Though Thoueris seemed to have touched nothing, a heavy stone door swung slowly shut behind them, blotting out the harsh sunlight.

"Follow," said the woman.

Simon did so as she led the way down the corridor, appreciating in spite of his fatigue the way her tall shapely form undulated beneath the sheer white kirtle. The black pigeon on her shoulder gave him some uneasiness, for he was knowledgeable about such things; he had no doubt that it was a familiar and that the woman was a sorceress.

They emerged into a vast chamber which was dim in spite of being lit with many torches and oil lamps—a great arching dome, cut like the corridor from the solid rock. Several other doorways led from it, curtained or gaping blackly, while in the center of the smooth floor stood a great circular dais with steps leading up on four sides. Atop this dais stood a cube of stone perhaps four feet on a side, in front of which stood what appeared to be an upright bar of iron of equal height.

"This is the Temple of the Sixth Pylon," said the woman, "and you stand now within the shrine of Shai-urt-ab, the Worm of Destiny."

"*Shai-urt-ab,*" muttered Simon. " 'The Fate of the Stilled Heart.' Which is to say—death?"

Thoueris smiled. "I see that you are a learned man, stranger. You have read the *Tomb Texts* of the divine scribe Ani."

Simon nodded, then quoted: " 'When unto the Sixth Pylon thou dost come, speak these words: Lady of Light, mighty in the power of thy voice, none knows thy sorcerous reach nor yet thine age. Its like has not been known from the beginning.' "

"You are wise indeed," said the woman. "You studied well as an acolyte in Thebes."

Simon started. "How did you know that? And what did you mean
when you said that you had long awaited me? No doubt that dark familiar
of yours told you of my approach across the desert—"

"Aye, Kuru led you here at my direction, but it was I who dispatched
her with instructions to do so. I have anticipated your coming for many,
many years. Does that disconcert you, stranger?"

"You are a sorceress, Thoueris, as I suspected," said Simon. "But your
powers have evidently not revealed to you my name."

"Which is—?"

"I am Simon of Gitta, a Samaritan."

"Ah." Thoueris smiled knowingly. "And you are a wanderer, and an
enemy of Rome. There was a tragedy in your past, and now you travel over
the earth under a strange destiny. You have slain many Romans, and not
many moons ago you were involved in the death of some great one—the
Emperor Tiberius himself, I think. You have made powerful enemies, and
now you flee their wrath."

Simon unconsciously gripped the haft of his sheathed *sica*. "How can
you know these things—?"

"See these eyes?" The woman stepped a pace closer. "Are they the
eyes of an ordinary mortal? No, and they see much that others cannot.
Much of the past—aye, and somewhat of the future."

Simon gazed into her eyes, noting that they were not as deeply blue as
they had seemed in the sunlight. The irises were green; the "whites" possessed a bluish-green tint. Otherwise, the woman seemed fully human, save
perhaps for her outstanding beauty.

"What else concerning my destiny do those eyes see?" he asked uneasily.

"I know that you are pursued by many enemies who are even now
crossing the desert, following your trail."

Simon felt his spine tingle.

"Fear them not, Simon of Gitta," said Thoueris. "Not even the great
army of Cambyses was able to assail this temple with impunity. You are
safe here, shielded not only by rock walls but also by the hand of Destiny.
Now, come. You must have water, food, and rest."

She led Simon across the chamber and through one of the uncurtained
doorways; they passed into a torchlit corridor and began to ascend a slightly curving stairway. In a few moments they emerged into a wider passage
and finally entered a large, unfurnished room. In its center was a rectangular pool of water contained by a rim of stone a foot or more in height. Up-

on seeing it, Simon hurried forward almost involuntarily, stooping to scoop up the cool fluid in his cupped hands and drink greedily.

"Quaff your fill, Simon," said the woman. "Then fill one of basins and lave yourself, if you will. I go to prepare refreshments in my chambers at the other end of this corridor. Join me there." So saying, she turned and exited the room. Simon took a shallow bronze basin from one of the indicated stone niches in the wall, scooped it full of water and placed it on the floor, then removed his sandals and his red, black-embroidered tunic. He felt an impulse to plunge into the rock pool and soak his burning flesh, but realized that water was not to be so lavishly wasted in this arid region. In any case, the laving from the basin proved refreshing enough, almost ecstatically so.

As an afterthought, he filled his goatskin from the pool and bundled it in his cloak with his few remaining provisions. Then he dressed and strode out of the chamber and down the torchlit, rock-hewn corridor.

Thoueris' rooms proved to be well furnished with thick rugs and cushions for lounging. There was a low table set with food, though no chairs. Torches and oil lamps burned on the walls, while a glowing brazier in one corner gave forth a strange spicy scent which Simon could not identify. At the woman's invitation Simon sat cross-legged before the table and ravenously attacked the food. It was simple fare—dates and other fruits, nuts, and a grain porridge flavored with a spice whose taste was similar to the scent from the brazier—but he ate it with gusto, thinking that he had never enjoyed better fare. Thoueris sat down opposite him and ate more daintily. Simon noticed that the black dove was no longer upon her shoulder, nor was it anywhere in the apartment as far as he could tell.

"I have sent Kuru forth to watch from the summit of the rocks," said the woman, as if she had read his mind. "She will warn us if your enemies approach."

Simon groped for a memory and found it. "Herodotus writes that the Oracle of Zeus-Amon in the northern oasis was founded by a black dove who flew there from Thebes."

"Aye—the fane of Amon, the Hidden One." Thoueris smiled. "It was the last of the Twenty-one Pylons which once stood along this river, marking the stages of the Great Pilgrimage."

"River—?"

"The Styx, which flowed through the land of Stygia more than ten thousand years ago, before even ancient Khem arose along the Nile. The upheavals which destroyed Stygia also diverted the river into what is now the Nile's channel. This Libyan oasis chain is all that remains of the course of the long-vanished Styx. But surely, Simon, you have read of these matters in the *Book of Thoth*."

Simon shuddered. Only once had he seen a copy of that ancient scroll said to have been penned by Thoth-Amon, greatest of the Stygian sorcerers, and the cautious priests who guarded it had allowed him to read only a few lines.

"No, Thoueris. But the Twenty-one Pylons—these are mentioned in the *Tomb Texts* as stations the soul must pass on its journey through the land of the dead."

"Aye." Thoueris' smile was cryptic, deep. "And is Stygia not a land of the dead indeed? The Greeks have placed the Styx in their Hades, so dim is their memory of it, and the twenty-one temples that stood upon its banks are remembered by the Egyptians only as stations in their afterworld. Such is the way of mankind—the facts of today are destined to be molded into the myths and legends of tomorrow."

She filled two golden cups with a dark wine and placed one before him. Simon sipped it, noting that it was slightly flavored with the same unplaceable spice as the porridge. He set aside his empty bowl and began to munch on the dates and nuts.

"But, Thoueris—you say *this* is the temple of the Sixth Pylon?"

She nodded. "This and the Oracle of Amon are all that remain of the entire temple chain. The one at the oasis of Amon is famous now, as you know, but only a few of its priests know its Stygian origin, or of the existence of *this* fane. Not even the great Alexander, who conquered Egypt and braved the desert to consult Amon's oracle, ever learned of the Temple of the Sixth Pylon."

"No doubt these priests of Amon's fane bring you supplies, then?"

"Twice a year they send a caravan from the northern oases. Not even the people of the Great Oasis to the east know of my existence."

"And your water?"

"The same caravans bring it also. It is thus sufficiently replenished for one woman who has no other visitors."

"Then—you live here alone."

"For many years now, save for Kuru. I am the hereditary keeper of this fane, and so shall I and my descendants be until its purpose is fulfilled. But enough of that. I would learn something about the man whom Destiny has sent to me."

Simon hesitated. He wished he could fathom the enigma of the woman's words, her smile, her strange eyes. He felt somewhat light-headed. Was there a drug in the smoke of the brazier, in the strangely scented porridge and wine? If so, the priestess was breathing and ingesting it also—

"It is the Dust of the Yellow Lotus," said Thoueris, sensing his unspoken question. "It is not a drug like any other. Kuru and I have used it for many years, for it enables us to see the past and even the future to some degree. You will soon know what I mean, Simon. The Dust will help you to rest, and it will also allow you to see many things—many truths."

Simon nodded, for he was already seeing it. Her words, her gestures, came to him like echoes of things that had happened a moment before. He set aside his goblet, and every detail of his action was as familiar to him as a recent memory.

"You saw truly, Thoueris," he said. "There *was* a tragedy in my past. Twelve years ago Romans stormed into my family's home in Sebaste, slew my parents, and sold me as a slave. I was trained to fight in the arenas. After two years I escaped and journeyed to Persia, where I studied the arts of the Magi. Since then I have wandered in many lands, studying esoteric things and, as you somehow observed, slaying many Romans. And yes, I *was* involved in the Emperor Tiberius' death, though I did not slay him."

Thoueris nodded. "I know. He was devoured by Set, who came forth from the Ring of Thoth-Amon."

Simon started. "Your vision-sense is indeed sharp!"

The priestess laughed. "I must not deceive you, Simon. My vision only confirmed what the priests of Amon told me three moons ago. They said you returned the Ring to the place from which it had been stolen, then journeyed to that Theban temple of Ptah where you were an acolyte. It was then that I sensed that you might be the one who would soon come here, pursued by those who hope to collect the reward which the new emperor has offered for you."

"Aye." Simon heard his own voice as an echo. "I received warning barely in time when the Roman cohort arrived to raid Ptah's temple in Thebes; fortunately I was across the Nile, studying tomb-writings in the Valley of the Kings. An acolyte found me, warned me that I must flee. I joined a caravan that took me west to the Great Oasis, then hired a guide to take me on to the lesser oases in the northwest. The guide deserted me—he must have heard that a fortune had been offered for my capture." The echo-sense seemed stronger to Simon as he talked; it was suddenly as if he could *feel* small portions of the pasts and futures of which he spoke. "Caligula must be frantic to regain the Ring. But he won't succeed. Somehow I know that."

"You know," said Thoueris. "You are beginning to see."

"Lotus dust...," muttered Simon. The room was expanding, yet remained clear and sharp, immobile. No, it was *time* that swelled and shrank. He could now see vistas of landscape outside—not desert sands, but a wide river with square-sailed boats upon it; in the foreground were palaces and temples of dark stone, surrounded by exotic trees and gardens....

"You must rest now, Simon. Sleep. You will dream—and learn."

He held up his right hand, and the gesture seemed to him one of great symbolic portent. "Lady of Light, it is written of the Sixth Pylon: 'There is a worm upon it, none knows how great. It was born in the presence of the Stilled Heart.'"

"The worm is Shai-urt-ab," said Thoueris, rising, "whom the Egyptians also call Apophis and the Greeks Typhon. Long ago the Stygians worshiped his lord Shuddam-El, known to the Khemites as the Devourer of the Earth. I am the servant of the servitor—and so shall you be also, Simon; for this purpose Destiny has led you to me. And one day, when the stars are right, a child or a grandchild of ours shall summon the servitor, and the servitor shall release his lord. Now rest, Simon."

Methodically she extinguished most of the lamps and torches, then turned and walked from the room. Simon watched her go, while every stately yet supple motion of her body—and the echo of every word she had spoken—stirred far-ranging associations that seemed to reverberate in his mind as visions down corridors of time....

The air shimmered above the heated sands. Rabdos of Scythopolis cursed and wiped his forehead with a perspiring forearm, peered out beneath the large awning beneath which he and a number of his officers sat sheltered. The white sun was more than two thirds of the way down the western sky. Among the dunes hundreds of legionaries sought shade where they could—beneath cloaks and blankets rigged up on spear-shafts, or under the sharp crests of wind-curled sand ridges. Some slept; others munched rations or sipped water from goatskins.

"Hades! Not even a breeze," Rabdos growled.

"Maybe you should thank the gods, Syrian," said a lean officer with a black patch over his left eye. "They say it was a windstorm that destroyed the army of the Persian Cambyses."

"You're a cheerful one, Laecanius Scutula!" Rabdos took a deep swig from his goatskin. "I tell you what. I'll leave you here in command while I take ten volunteers and follow the Samaritan's trail. Anguiculus says there'll be no wind tonight, either, so I guarantee I can have Simon back here alive by morning."

"Sure, you scoundrel." The one-eyed Roman's grin was hard, mirthless. "Only, you won't come this way. You'll have that tricky guide take you back to the oasis by another route, and then you'll collect all the reward for yourself."

"And how would I manage that on this open desert?"

"Easy. Ever try to hunt nomads among the dunes by moonlight? No, Rabdos. If you call for volunteers, you'll get four hundred of them. No man of this troop is going to risk losing his cut."

Rabdos spat on the sand. "That's *crazy*, Scutula! Taking a whole cohort into the desert after one man—"

Scutula nodded. "You have a point. But I take my orders from Valerius Argonius, Nomarch of Thebes. Not from you."

"That fat sybarite? He'd puddle his blubber on these sands before one day's march was out! Easy for him to sit back along the Nile and order us—"

"He takes his orders from the prefect Flaccus. And Flaccus takes his from the Emperor."

"And Caligula put *me* in charge of this expedition, damn it!" yelled Rabdos. "*I'm* in command!"

Scutula rose with a creaking of well worn armor and leather. He stood tall, one hand resting lightly on his sword pommel—a lean, hard veteran, craggy face expressionless save for his frozen grin, his one eye glittering with a sinister light. "You're not thinking of fighting me for that command, are you, Rabdos?"

The four centurions with them also rose to their feet. Rabdos' broad features worked with anger.

"No—of course not," he grumbled finally. "Still, you're an experienced commander. You know I'm right."

The centurions relaxed. Scutula grinned more tightly. "Very well, Rabdos, I've admitted that you have a point. I'll appoint a decan to accompany you. You'll start just before sundown."

"My thanks—commander." Rabdos said it almost like a sneer. "I knew you'd see reason."

"But I don't trust you. I still think Caligula should have left you to rot on that prison isle instead of entrusting you with something like this—"

"He knew I was the best man for the job, by Hephaestus!"

"—so, I'm setting the conditions. The decurion Acilius and eight of his legionaries will go; he's a tough desert man, and also not squeamish when it comes to making prisoners come up with information."

"I'd be better," interrupted one of the centurions—a squat, scar-faced man with his pate cropped nearly bald. "I've collected a lot of taxes for the Nomarch Argonius; I know a few tricks of persuasion I doubt even Caligula has heard of!"

"No, Casca. I want you to stay here and take command of the cohort. I'm volunteering to go with Rabdos and Acilius."

"*You!*" exclaimed Rabdos and the centurion simultaneously.

Scutula's rictus of a grin tightened still more. "How better to keep an eye on this jailbird appointee of Caligula's, eh, Casca?"

"Maybe," said Casca, frowning. "But, then, who's going to keep an eye on you?"

Rabdos guffawed; his narrowed eyes glittered with vindictive amusement. "I see what you mean, Scutula—the whole cohort is going to volunteer!"

Scutula's lean face darkened with anger. "Such lack of trust is not good for morale! Very well, then. Casca, order Acilius and his men to report. Full rations and a full goatskin for each man. We'll make a company of eleven—small enough to steal upon this Simon unawares, as a full cohort could never do. And—oh, yes, you can pay off that guide, Anguiculus. He'll not accompany us."

"But, what assurance do we have—?" began Casca.

"You'll prepare the cohort. An hour after we're gone you'll strike camp and follow us; our footprints will be plain even by moonlight. Fan out and cover more desert if you really feel we'll try to double back and slip past you. I tell you that I won't be a party to any such treachery, and if Rabdos tries it he'll find a *gladius* in his guts."

Casca and the other centurions applauded, and a cheer rose from many of the nearer legionaries who had been listening.

"Good lads!" shouted Rabdos to the troops, a lopsided grin distorting his coarse features. "There's no treachery plotted here. It's good strategy, nothing less, and your commander Laecanius Scutula is wise enough to see it. Trust us, soldiers, and you'll find that the generosity of the Emperor Gaius is great enough to make a rich man of every one of you!"

III

Born in what spring and on what city's tomb,
By whose hand wast thou reached, and plucked for whom?
There hangs about thee, could the soul's sense tell,
An odor as of love and of love's doom.

— Swinburne, "Relics"

Simon rested deeply, yet he did not sleep. His body was totally relaxed as it lay on the thick rugs among the cushions, eyes closed, breathing slowly and evenly.

He could see himself lying there.

His awareness held a strange clarity, yet it brought him no fear. It was something he experienced, yet at the same time something he did of his own volition. There was no contradiction in this.

The details were clear to his vision—the rugs and cushions, the table with its fruits and goblets, the rock walls, his own resting body, all illuminated by the single oil lamp on its pedestal. Yet he knew that it was not sight, for there was an added dimension to it—the dimension of time. His vision seemed to pulsate, to flow, to expand and contract, and he knew these shiftings were his awareness of how this room had looked or would look. He saw himself enjoying his recent meal with Thoueris, and saw also his body lying in true sleep as it would be hours from now....

The time-pulsings grew larger, and at the same time he realized that he could experience what was going on outside these walls in the other rooms and corridors of this ancient temple. Not that he could see through walls; it was simply that his "here" and "now" were more extended than before, and growing. Now he was aware of the desert outside; the sun had just set, the rocks and dunes were softly shadowed in the evening light, the stars were beginning to show in the deepening blue of the east.

Such an old temple, he thought. *Such an old land....*

His vision of the distant past abruptly returned, vividly and effortlessly. Again he saw the palaces and temples, the parks and gardens, the gleaming river beyond. Dark-skinned people clad in strange robes walked the roads and pathways while evening torches were being lit near porticoes and in open squares. It was the past, he knew—yet, strangely, it was all part of his extended "now."

Stygia. So old—older far than Egypt or Babylon....

But this temple appeared new to his expanded vision. Young. He saw it being carved from the solid rock outcropping by thousands of craftsmen and laborers, saw the strange pre-Khemite hieroglyphs being chiseled into its walls, the black dais being shaped. It was finished, and he saw a large image of dark stone being brought into the temple and placed upon the dais—an image like a thick, coiled worm with a cluster of tentacles at one end.

What god was worshiped here?

Thoueris' face appeared before him, large in his vision, framed by twin cascades of luxuriant dark hair. Her bluish-green eyes were level; her lips opened and moved.

"The dawn-time was a strange time," she said. "Know that this was originally the fane of Shuddam-El, Devourer of the Earth, who aeons ago came with his worm-minions to this world from the world of Urakhu. Mighty and terrible was Shuddam-El, for he was one of those Old Ones who warred with the Primal Gods at the dawn of time when the fate of worlds hung in the balance. But though the Primal Gods imprisoned him and his servitors beneath his great underground city of Ka-Harne, mankind did not forget the former power of the Old Ones, nor the prophecy that They would one day rise again. And in Stygia were many temples built to their glory."

He knew that Thoueris was not speaking to him, for he was aware of her lying in sleep in another chamber, so little affected by the lotus-dust which she habitually used that she sensed his visions but dimly in her dreams. No, a deep part of his mind was using her image and voice to tell that portion of himself called Simon of Gitta things which on some primal level he already knew….

"But then Stygia fell to foreign conquerors," continued the voice of Thoueris, "—red-haired invaders from northern lands, whose descendants were one day to found the dynasties of Khem. They slew the Stygians, save for a remnant who fled to found a kingdom to the east, and they overthrew the religions of Stygia and destroyed her temples, hammering the images of Set and Nyarlat and Shuddam-El to dust. Only Shuddam-El's fane survived, though plundered and profaned, for it was carved into this outcrop of living stone and was therefore too massive to destroy.

"Then came the Great Upheaval which destroyed both Stygia and the northern nations. Lands sank, mountains rose, and seas flowed in where none had been before. The Styx ceased to flow, its waters being diverted eastward to become the Nile. The climate changed; rain fell no longer, and the desert crept in from the west."

He could see it all as she spoke: vast, shifting panoramas of invading armies and monstrous cataclysms—earthquakes, lightning, clouds that boiled and thundered like world-destroying gods—a colossal wall of water bursting through a cloven mountain range to form a new sea….

"The dark millennia passed. The civilization of Khem arose along the Nile, and for many centuries the gods of Stygia were forgotten. Then came Nephren-Ka, the Dark Pharaoh, who rediscovered the ancient forms of worship and erected fanes and eidolons to Nyarlat, the Faceless One. The olden practices were revived; Nyarlat was exalted above all other gods and his black altars were made crimson with human blood. It was during this time that '-hotep' was added to the god's name, so that thenceforth he was known as 'Nyarlat the Gratified.' "

He saw dark temples and faceless, sphinx-like idols—black-robed priests lifting curved daggers and plunging them down into shrieking victims.

"But at last the people rebelled at this and overthrew Nephren-Ka. They destroyed the fanes and images of Nyarlat, expunged his name and that of the Dark Pharaoh from all monuments, tombs, and temples. Then Khem worshiped again her own gods, and for a brief time the land knew peace.

"Yet the excesses of Nephren-Ka had weakened the nation, so that soon she fell to conquering invaders—the Stygians, whose fleeing remnant had now grown to be a powerful kingdom to the east. They took Khem with great slaughter and founded their own dynasty, which later became known as that of the Hyksos—the Shepherd Kings. Their greatest god was

Set, whom they worshiped under the name Ah-Set-ur, God of the Shepherds.

"Again were the rites of Stygia revived, this time even more widely and intensely than under Nephren-Ka. Great temples were erected to Set and Nyarlat, and even the worship of Shuddam-El the Devourer was reestablished here in this very place; the fane was repaired and purified, and my ancestor Semati was appointed to be its first priest. Once again were prayers chanted within these walls to the great Worm of Urakhu, and cloaked pilgrims crossed the sands in vast numbers to sacrifice before his restored image."

He could see it: hooded wanderers in sand-brown robes... rows of bearded, dark-eyed guards in black armor and oiled leather, naked bronze swords gripped in their hands... ebon-cloaked priests whose sacrificial blades were strangely curved... bound victims who struggled and screamed before the image of the Worm....

"It was Apop, the first Hyksos pharaoh, who sent an expedition far to the southwest to seek age-lost Ka-Harne, the city built by Shuddam-El and his servitors when in the dawn-time they came down to this world from Urakhu. With the aid of ancient Stygian records the city's ruins were found, and the Hyksos soldiers delved among the stones, returning finally to Khem with a great treasure: three of the Pearls of the Earth, which are the life-bearing eggs of Shuddam-El and his servitors."

He saw more bearded, black-armored soldiers; they were digging amid jungle-entwined ruins of enormous walls and towers of dark stone, uncovering gleaming white spheres of a substance like polished marble, each less than the length of a man's hand in diameter....

"The Pearls were brought to this very temple and one was placed deep in the sand, where it hatched and grew; for this region is very like the world of its ancestors—a desolate, dry world of vast deserts. And as it grew it produced the fertilizing substance that alone can sustain the Yellow Lotus, whose pollen extends life and expands vision in those who use it. For many centuries none but the priesthood of this temple has partaken of the Lotus-dust or known its secret."

A strange uneasiness crept into Simon's vision. There was a dark implication in Thoueris' statement. The uneasiness vanished as her voice continued anew, invoking new visions:

"For a century and more the Worm lived near the temple, partaking in its ceremonies. The priests named it Shai-urt-ab, knowing that it was the Destiny that would one day still the heart of the world—for when the stars are right it will journey once more to Ka-Harne and remove the seals which the Primal Gods placed there to imprison Shuddam-El and his followers."

Simon felt a brief thrill of fear. He had a glimpse of mountains erupting, landslides obliterating cities, the earth's crust shattering as unbelievably vast worm-things writhed up and burst from beneath it....

"But as the Worm waxed great it could not remain in the temple," continued the even voice of Thoueris. "It went into the desert and burrowed deep beneath the sands, waxing greater still and returning only to partake in the most important ceremonies. And pilgrims beheld Shai-urt-ab with terror, and spoke of him with great awe in their homelands, and of the great altar-drum which the priests had constructed to summon him from the desert.

"Yet after two centuries of foreign domination the Khemites rose up and defeated their Hyksos rulers, driving them forth once more into the east. Again were the Nile's gods restored, and Ahmose became pharaoh in Khem; his was the dynasty of Akhenaton, who established a worship of the Light in reaction to Nephren-Ka, whose worship was of the Darkness. And again were the temples of the Stygian gods destroyed, save for this one, which men feared to approach because of the presence of Shai-urt-ab.

"In time the fane of Shuddam-El was forgotten of men, save for those few priests of what became known as the Oracle of Amon in the northern oasis. Pilgrims ceased to come and the priesthood dwindled in number, sustained by supplies sent up secretly by acolytes of the oracle. But Shai-urt-ab waxed huge beyond measure, feeding sluggishly far beneath the sands, awaiting the Time of the Stars.

"A thousand years passed, and then came the Persian Cambyses with mighty armies, ravaging and looting in Khem from Avaris to the southern cataracts. While in Thebes he heard that there were immense riches stored at the Oracle of Amon, and so he dispatched an army of fifty thousand soldiers into the desert to conquer the western oases."

The army that vanished, thought Simon. Uneasiness again tinged his vision. A shadow of fear, gnawing, like a worm....

"The Persians found this temple and besieged it. They broke down the door and slew all the priests but one, who was visiting the Oracle in the north. Then they raged and looted, smashing the image of Shuddam-El and defacing his altar. They found the Pearls of the Earth and, imagining them to be of great value, prepared to make off with them. But a dying priest managed to sound the Drum of the Altar, and so Shai-urt-ab was summoned from the desert. Then did that entire army of Cambyses perish most terribly, save for some few who were within the temple, and these dared not go forth for fear of the Worm. When the priest returned from the Oracle, only three Persians within these walls were alive, all babbling in madness; they died soon after, shrieking in horror at the memory of what they had witnessed."

He could see the vast Persian host sprawled out upon the eastward desert, men like ants, teeming and milling, spears and standards waving aimlessly. A soundless wave of terror seemed to rise from that enormous churning throng. Dust-brown clouds full of wind and lightning were beetling up from the south, and at their base approached something like a great moving hill, a wave of sand—abruptly Simon's vision terminated; somewhere deep in his mind he had decided that he did not wish to see more.

"The lone priest who survived was named Semati," said the voice of Thoueris, "after the first so-named priest of this temple. He took a wife named Thoueris from among the Amonians, and they had a daughter whom they named Thoueris also. From that time the priesthood has been hereditary, each couple having but one child, and every priest or priestess of this temple having the name Semati or Thoueris. Every generation a mate is provided by Destiny for the guardian of the temple, and that person is initiated by means of the Rite of the Dust, in which only the priesthood may participate. Thus is the remembrance and the hope kept alive—until that day when Shai-urt-ab will be summoned and sent forth to remove the imprisoning seals, that the Old Ones may rise once more and cleanse the earth of all evil."

Again the uneasiness. He saw Thoueris and himself, white-kirtled and dark-robed, before the dais and the cube of black stone. With them was a child—a girl—whose features bore resemblances to theirs. They had grown to love one another, and their daughter was solemn in her understanding of the great responsibility that was hers. She was being instructed in the Adoration of the Pearls, taught their purpose. Intelligence shone in her dark eyes, and dedication…. Now she was a beautiful woman, and her dark eyes had become tinged with blue-green like her mother's; her parents were gone, living in Amon or Alexandria, while she—the new priestess—lived alone in the temple, waiting for Destiny to send her a mate….

The uneasiness grew as he saw generation after generation pass, too swiftly to count, until finally—the earth's crust shattering as monstrous things burrowed up from beneath!

The vision ceased, save that he seemed yet to behold the room clearly through his closed eyelids—the still flame of the lamp, its highlights reflecting from golden goblets, tinted glassware—

No! Such a future must not be allowed to happen.

With that thought came the realization—the perception—that it did not have to. The future, unlike the past, was multiple and contingent. He saw that two paths—two series of possibilities—lay before him. One led to the girl and, eventually, the Worms that would devour the earth, the other across the sands to the northern oases and then to misty wanderings beyond. Both branched from a point in the near future, in the great room that housed the dais and the cube. He could not see that point clearly—he did not want to. A horror blocked his vision, like that which he had felt while beholding the roiling Persian hosts.

And now the drug was wearing off, the visions fading....

"You will now sleep, and waken refreshed—my husband."

Thoueris' voice was faint. He could no longer see her face, nor the room around him. His mind was joining his body in relaxation, settling into the darkness of a true and dreamless sleep....

Ravennius Casca surveyed his cohort with satisfaction. All was in readiness for the march. The sun had set beyond the westward dunes and the air was rapidly losing its heat in the gathering twilight.

"It's been about an hour since they set out on the Samaritan's trail," said one of his fellow centurions.

Casca nodded. "We'll start pretty soon. But first, bring me that guide, Anguiculus."

The centurion smote his breastplate in salute, then departed. A few minutes later he returned with the bearded little nomad. The guide locked puzzled, a bit apprehensive.

"What's going on?" he asked. "I heard that Rabdos and a few others have gone to find the Samaritan—"

"Aye, snakelet. They decided they didn't need you any longer."

Anguiculus felt a pang of dread. He did not like the expression on the scarred face of this Ravennius Casca—nor the stories he had heard of the man's brutality. "What—what do you mean?"

Casca grinned; it made his eyes narrower, his features flatter. "Don't look so worried. Commander Scutula says you're to be paid off now." He took a large pouch from his belt and tossed it casually on the ground. It jingled.

"My—my thanks, noble Casca." Anguiculus made a quick, nervous bow, then stooped and snatched up the pouch. "I'm glad I was able to be of service to you. Vale!"

"Wait. Aren't you even going to count your money? We may have cheated you, for all you know."

"I know you would not do that, sir."

Casca chuckled. "I like that kind of trust. You've been a great help to us in crossing this desert, Anguiculus—you and that fortunate star up there."

"Star—?"

"Aye." Casca pointed to the southeast where the stars of Pisces Austrinus were beginning to glimmer against the deepening blue. "The bright one—there."

Anguiculus gazed up. "Fortunate? But, that is Fum-al-Hut, the Mouth of the Fish-monster—"

Casca drove his dagger up beneath Anguiculus' jaw and through the palate, deep into his brain. For a moment the centurion's brawny arm held the corpse upright, like a gill-gaffed mullet, then allowed it to flop to the sand.

"So! That wasn't *your* lucky star, eh, Anguiculus? Well, it goes to show that you never know what Fate will bring next." Casca picked up the pouch and tied it back on his belt. "But we'll see that your money's well spent when we get back to Alexandria, by Bacchus! And now," he faced the ranked cohort, raised his arm and pointed westward, "—now, men, we *march*—for the gold of Gaius Imperator!"

When Simon abruptly woke he knew he had slept for many hours. The lamp had gone out, but the light of a torch in the corridor filtered in through the curtained doorway. He rose and groped his way out of the chamber into the lighted passage. His head was clear, all his senses were alert; the drug had left no aftereffects.

He walked to the water room and cleansed himself. When he returned again to Thoueris' chambers he found her waiting there, tall and slim and beautiful in her simple white tunic and a dark robe. The black dove was again perched on her shoulder.

"Come to me, Simon."

He swallowed, struck dumb for a moment by her beauty. She smiled.

"Thoueris," he managed to say at last, "—did you truly speak to me in my dreams?"

She shook her head. "It was your own mind, expanded by the Dust, that spoke to you. But I shared it, Simon, in my dreams. All of it. The past and—the future—"

"It can't happen," he said firmly. "Thoueris, I can't *allow* it to happen!"

"Yet happen it will, for Destiny has sent you and will not be denied. I can understand, though, why you would hesitate and draw back. That will change, and soon. You will lose fear and know wonder. Was there not a moment in our dream, Simon, when you felt love flow between us?

And the child, he thought. *The beautiful dark-eyed girl who will never exist, unless—*

"Come, Simon, don your cloak and follow me."

He obeyed, and she took his hand and led him into the passage, then turned into a narrower side corridor and finally up a steep stairway that ended at a platform before a blank wall. Little light penetrated here from the corridor, but he heard a small sound of metal on stone, sensed that

Thoueris had moved an empty torch bracket on the wall. A section of the blank wall pivoted open and he saw stars glittering in the night sky. Thoueris stepped forth and Simon followed closely. Sand and pebbles grated under his feet; boulders humped up blackly here and there, and Simon realized that he stood atop the rock formation within which the temple was carved. The gibbous moon was westering, bathing the desert with ghostly light, and in the east the first pale hint of dawn was showing.

"Now, Kuru," said Thoueris, "fly swiftly to the Oracle of Amon. Give to our brethren the glad news that our fane now has a new priest."

The black pigeon cooed softly, then flapped into the air and winged northward, vanishing swiftly in the dimness. Simon shivered slightly.

"Now, Simon, look there."

He turned and gazed southward. The stars of Carina were westering, Canopus outshining the others, a gleaming diamond against the night's deep blue. But Thoueris was pointing to the southeast, where the dim stars of the Hydra's Head were rising.

"Why do you show me the stars, Thoueris—?"

"That star—the Eye of the Hydra. It is fitting that we should behold it at the first dawn of our union, for it is the star of our destiny. It is the sun whose rays bathe the sandy wastes of Urakhu, the world whence come those whom we now both serve."

I cannot serve them, he thought. *She would have me be a part of the world's destruction. Why can I not hate her?*

She held out her arms toward the star as if in supplication. The dark robe fell from her shoulders, leaving her as a slim pale gleam under the moon. Simon could sense no evil in her graceful poise, her calm moon-limned features. Only loveliness.

"*Shuddam, ikris ko Urakh, ne mabele kothumus talai....*"

He understood none of the words she intoned but realized that they must form a prayer, an adulation. Beyond doubt she spoke in the ancient tongue of Stygia, known now only to a few initiated priests and scholars. A sudden urge to flee this place possessed him. He turned to face the brightening east; the sun would soon rise above those far rose-tinged dunes to bake the sands—

Suddenly he gasped in astonishment. There were men out there on the crests of those dunes, distant black shapes against the dawn's light. Soldiers, armor, and weapons glittering as they approached, scores of them— no, hundreds!

IV

But see, amid the mimic rout
A crawling shape...
that writhes from out
The scenic solitude...
Out—out are the lights—out all!
And, over each quivering form,
The curtain, a funeral pall,
Comes down with the rush of a storm....

— Poe, *The Conqueror Worm*

"Simon, what is it—?"

"Romans. Gods, they've sent *the whole cohort* after me!"

Thoueris smiled. "I know. I sensed them in a vision the night before your arrival; you were standing beside me here, just like this."

He could not see his footprints below in the shadow of the rocks, but knew they must still be there. "My trail! If there's been no wind in the night—"

"Don't worry, Simon. A mere cohort will have no such siege equipment as had the great army of Cambyses. They will find the temple impregnable—even should they guess that it is more than an abandoned ruin. Many bands of nomads have passed this way without learning of the secret within the stone."

"Still, my vanishing footprints will make them suspicious."

Thoueris shrugged. "They will not arrive here for an hour, and they will die in the desert if they stay. They are not important. Now, Simon, come within, for there is one more thing I must show you before we consummate our union. You must look upon the Pearls of the Earth."

"Pearls, eh?" boomed a harsh voice close behind them. "By Bacchus, if there's treasure here I'll look upon it too!"

Simon whirled, snatching out his curved *sica*. Men were leaping from behind boulders, rushing forward, the two foremost closing on him rapidly with bared swords. He whipped his cloak into the face of one, smoothly slipped under the other's guard and slashed; his foe went down spilling guts. Simon whirled, plunged his blade into the breast of the other man even as he cast aside the cloak. He heard a hoarse gasp of agony, turned to see Thoueris gripping a curved dagger while a man who had tried to grab her collapsed at her feet.

"*Stop!*" roared a deep voice. "*Surrender, or you're both dead meat!*"

Simon, crouching to meet the next attack, saw that four of the men had drawn bows trained on him and Thoueris—short, powerful Syrian bows that could send a shaft completely through a human body. He froze. Four more men with drawn blades strode forward. Soldiers, all eight of them, judging by their short Roman cloaks and leather tunics, but traveling light, without spears or armor.

"Throw down your weapons—quick!"

Simon dropped his *sica*. Thoueris, after a brief hesitation, began to sheathe her knife in a scabbard strapped to her thigh. Simon noticed that its strangely curved blade was not of metal but of some milky, almost translucent material. A sacrificial knife, shaped like those he had seen in his vision—

"On the ground, woman!"

Thoueris placed the blade gently at her feet, then straightened and stood silently, contempt and haughteur in her features. Simon noted the man who had spoken—tall and lean, hard-faced, a black patch over one eye.

"Well, Laecanius Scutula," said Simon evenly, "you're a long way from your Nomarch's jurisdiction, aren't you? No taxpayers to squeeze and torture out here—"

"He's under my command now." A stocky, brutal-faced man strode forward. "Surely you know me, Simon of Gitta."

Simon easily recognized the man's coarse features in the swelling dawn light. "Rabdos of Scythopolis! Aye, you were Pilate's butcher in Judea whenever he needed a Syrian foreigner to do his dirty work. That is, until he caught you stealing Imperial funds. I heard Tiberius banished you to some prison isle; evidently Caligula is getting hard up for flunkies."

Rabdos laughed heartily. "The Emperor Gaius knew I was the best man for this job, and I've proven him right. See, Scutula, didn't I say we wouldn't need the whole cohort after all?"

"I never disputed that." The hard-faced officer turned to the soldier at his right and snapped, "Search them, Acilius—and use more caution than your three dead troopers did. This Simon was trained as a Thracian gladiator."

The young decurion circled behind Simon and Thoueris, taking care not to cross in front of any of the archers. Simon noted his narrow dark eyes, the handsome features set in a half-smirk hinting at sadism. *Another hard one*, he decided.

Acilius' hands probed lightly and deftly down the sides of Simon's tunic, then Thoueris'. Simon noticed those hands lingering on the woman.

"No more weapons on them, sir."

"Good. Now, bind the Samaritan's arms," ordered Scutula. "The man's a killer even without a blade."

"Right." Acilius drew a cord from his belt, pulled Simon's arms back, and expertly tied them together at the wrists. Simon subtly flexed his forearms, testing. It was a standard tie for binding slaves; his training by Persian mages in escape artistry would enable him to slip out of it quickly at the right moment—if there were a right moment.

"Now, bring them inside," said Rabdos, "and let's find that treasure. I see torchlight down that stairway. Go carefully."

Simon and Thoueris stood in the upper corridor, closely watched by Scutula and two of the archers, while the rest of the men ransacked the rooms and drank deeply in the water chamber. They soon returned, bearing a bundle of items wrapped in a soldier's cloak.

"What did you find?" said Scutula.

Acilius bent and opened the cloak. "A few goblets and oil lamps, sir. I think they're pure gold."

"Ancient, too, I'd guess," said Rabdos. "Bring a pretty good price. But we still haven't found those pearls. Come on—I see there's another stairway going down."

They descended it and emerged moments later into the great central room of the dais and the altar. Simon heard two or three of the soldiers gasp in amazement.

"Light some more of those wall torches," Scutula ordered. This place is pretty dim." As the soldiers hastened to obey, he turned to Thoueris. "Now, woman, you can show us those 'pearls' you spoke of."

The Pearls of the Earth. The thought evoked in Simon a memory-flash of his vision. *The Adoration of the Pearls. Shai-urt-ab is ancient but not immortal. The purpose of the Pearls is to replace him.*

Thoueris stood silent. Her features showed no fear, only a cool, aristocratic contempt.

"Come on, now," said Rabdos, a gloating grin on his broad face. "If you won't say it, we guarantee we can make you scream it."

Still she did not speak. Simon wondered why her vision of two nights ago had not shown their capture by Romans, then suddenly saw the answer: The decision to send a small party ahead must have been made more recently. Decisions could change the future. A strange unease grew in him as he remembered his own vision—sensed that he must soon make a portentous decision of his own, here in this very room—

"Let me work on her, sir," said Acilius, drawing Thoueris' knife from his belt. "I'll tie her up and start peeling away some skin. This blade of hers should do the job—it's pretty sharp."

Simon eyed the knife; its milky translucence was tinged with yellow in the torchlight. He tested his bonds, knowing that he would soon have to slip free. Better that they should both die fighting than by torture—

"That will not be necessary," said Thoueris suddenly. "I will show you where the Pearls of the Earth are hidden."

"The lady has some sense," said Rabdos. "Put away your new toy, Acilius; you can use it on the Samaritan later."

Thoueris crossed the floor and ascended the steps of the circular dais. The Romans followed her closely, forcing Simon along with them. There was plenty of room atop the dais for all to stand.

"Well, where?" demanded Scutula.

Thoueris pointed. "Under that stone cube."

"Ha! And how do we move the damned thing?"

"One man must pull this upright iron lever to release it while several others push hard against this face. The cube is hinged at one corner and will swing aside."

"You three—get your shoulders to that block," said Rabdos. "And you, Acilius—throw that lever over."

Something nagged in the back of Simon's mind. He recalled the vision—the girl that was about to be initiated into the Adoration. This was not the right order; a lever on the far wall must first be thrown, or there was great danger—

Thoueris, what are you planning?

She shot him a glance, moved her head slightly. Simon backed away a pace, wondering again if she had read his very thought.

"Now, lads!" shouted Rabdos.

Acilius pulled over the tall lever; the three soldiers heaved against the cube. It slid aside easily—so easily that the soldiers sprawled forward on it when it came to a sudden stop. Simon glimpsed a small shallow pit in which two white spheres gleamed; they were half-buried in a brown spicy-looking material. He caught a whiff of something familiar—the Dust-drug. Then, abruptly, he sensed an enormous black shadow descending from above—

The concussion shook him and all the others from their feet; the sound half deafened him. The temple and the rock beneath it trembled, echoing the brief thunder beneath its high dome. Echoing—like a giant drum.

Thoueris! What have you done?

It took him but a few seconds to slip his bonds, leap up, and grab a fallen sword. The shadow was slowly rising, and Simon now saw that it was a huge square pillar; it had descended directly upon the cube and was being drawn back upward by hidden mechanisms, dripping blood. The three Romans who had fallen on the cube now existed only from the chest down, their heads and arms having been pulped beneath the pillar's base.

He saw Thoueris rise up, her white kirtle flecked with spattered blood, and approach the fallen Acilius; some of the soldiers, similarly spattered, were rising also. There was dust in the air, slowly settling, and the smell of the Lotus-drug was strong in Simon's nostrils.

"Witch!" howled Acilius, leaping up and grabbing for the woman.

With a fluid motion Thoueris gripped the decurion's wrist and flipped him expertly, whipped her knife from his belt and plunged it between his ribs. A second soldier dashed at her, missed his clutch as the priestess smoothly avoided him.

A trained fighter, Simon thought. *As good as the acolytes of the Magi!*

"Kill her, Lasus!" bellowed Rabdos. "We'll take the Samaritan!"

Again the soldier charged. Thoueris dodged, tripped him expertly so that he fell across the blood-smeared cube. Simon, facing the blades of Scutula's other remaining soldiers, saw the black shadow descending a second time—then felt again the mighty concussion, the echoing thunder. Again blood spattered, but this time Simon retained his balance, as did the others; evidently the pillar had fallen from a lesser height. Simon roared and sprang at the legionary, avoided a thrust, and sent the point of the *gladius* through his foe's neck.

Thoueris yelled in an unknown tongue and began to run toward Scutula, who turned to face her, sword ready. In the same instant Simon saw Rabdos dash down the steps and across the floor toward the exit, one of the great "pearls" clutched in each hand. Evidently the Syrian's odds had been reduced beyond his liking.

Again the pillar fell, this time with still less force, yet enough to make the rock floor tremble. In that instant time seemed to freeze for Simon; the Worm-dust was strong in his nostrils, and with it came a returning flash of premonition. Thoueris could not best a fighter like Scutula, yet if Rabdos made it outside the temple with those spheres—

An instant of vision—wind, and a mountainous shadow, towering.... As before, he could not face it fully. But if the eggs of Shuddam-El were lost, buried in the sands, they would germinate, hatch and grow, and eventually reproduce....

The instant passed. Time was in motion again, and Simon was running down the steps of the dais and across the floor in pursuit of Rabdos.

He charged through the doorway and up the stair, emerged into the upper corridor—and dodged just in time as a white object hurtled past him. He heard the stony sphere smash heavily against the rock wall behind him, realized that Rabdos had hurled one of the eggs.

"Damn you, Samaritan!"

Simon saw him dart into the narrow side passage and guessed which trick the man intended next. Instead of rushing into the passage, Simon paused for an instant so that he was framed in the entrance, then immediately leaped back. The second heavy sphere came hurtling out and smashed against the far wall. Instantly he dashed into the corridor—saw Rabdos scrambling frantically up the narrow stairway that led outside—

Thoueris!

Simon whirled and raced back the way he had come. *Let the man escape,* he thought. *Maybe there's still time—*

He knew better as soon as he entered the domed central chamber. Quickly he crossed the floor, then more slowly ascended the steps of the dais. Two more still figures lay there among the bodies—Scutula, with the sacrificial knife driven through his eye-patch and deep into his skull, and Thoueris, with the Roman's bloodied *gladius* lying next to her. Towering above them was the great black pillar, resting now on the bloodied cube, its motion stilled.

Simon knelt beside the priestess, saw instantly that the great wound in her chest was a mortal one. But her large, strangely blue-green eyes were open—looking up at him.

"Simon," she gasped, "you... are priest here... now."

The eyes closed. Her head turned to one side and she lay still.

Slowly Simon rose. Tears welled in his dark eyes; one trickled down over each craggy cheekbone. *Why?* he wondered. *Why do I give tears for the dead? She meant to use me to bring doom upon the world. I should hate her—but I cannot.*

Slowly he descended from the dais, crossed the room, and climbed the stair to the upper corridor. It was empty. On the floor, directly beneath where the spheres had shattered, lay two walnut-sized things that writhed and squealed strangely. Simon took a torch from the wall and, without looking at the things too closely, crisped them in its flame. Then he went into the side passage, ascended the narrow stairway, and emerged into the sunlight.

His cloak and *sica* lay where they had fallen. As he retrieved them he seemed to hear a distant, faint rumble—or was it a tremor within the rock? Hurrying to the edge of the outcrop, he saw that the entire cohort was now quite close, less than a fifth of a mile to the east. He saw the distant figure of Rabdos hastily approaching them, joining them, then heard distant voices shouting orders. He must escape—

Again, remote thunder. Simon turned, and saw a bank of dust-brown clouds obscuring the southern horizon—wind clouds, with lightnings flashing in the darkness beneath them. They were approaching rapidly, towering higher, the dust of their eastern flank beginning to dim the risen sun.

Thoueris, you sounded the Drum of the Altar!

A breeze was blowing—a warm wind from the south. As the clouds beetled higher in the heavens Simon beheld something moving just ahead of them—a gigantic hill of sand, as if something monstrous burrowed beneath the surface of the desert, leaving a low ridge in its wake.

Typhon, who brings hot gales from the south—!

The rock was now definitely vibrating with a steady tremor. The sun dimmed to a bronze disc as the wind rose. Suddenly Simon heard a new sound, keening above those of the rising wind and thunder—the sound of hundreds of men simultaneously screaming in terror. The legionaries were a cohort no longer but an ant-like swarm, milling in mad fear before the doom they saw approaching. The moving sand-hill was nearly upon them—the wind and thunder drowned out their screams. Simon felt again the presence of a horror he had not been able to face in his vision—the horror that he would now see—

It burst from the earth with an explosive billowing of sand and dust—an immense, dark gray elongation with a burning cauldron-thing for a "face." That cauldron expanded, brightening, until it could have dwarfed many siege towers; dark, stubby tentacles surrounded it like a fringe, lengthening, and from the vast burning heart of it issued a deep rumbling and a hissing as of superheated steam. The wind brought a thin wave of that steam to Simon's nostrils—a strange, hot stench tinged with the exotic scent of the Lotus-dust. He fell to his knees on the trembling rock, screaming, unable to hear his own voice amid the winds and thunderings. And still the creature continued to emerge from the sands, elongating, towering—

Then the cauldron-face swept grandly down, blasting forth torrents of white flame. More than three hundred madly scrambling legionaries burst instantly into puffs of fire, bones calcining and fusing with molten sand. Now the thing had completely emerged, was circling to blast the survivors, and Simon crouched among the rocks in horrified awe. The monstrous entity was at least a third of a Roman mile in length; its back was as high as the outcropping, and between it and the rushing clouds played a constant crackle of lightning.

The wind suddenly rose to gale force, mercifully blurring Simon's vision with billows and flurries of sand. He fell on his face and clutched the base of a boulder, shutting his eyes and praying to all the gods of his childhood, while about him the rocks trembled and the mad winds and lightning raged.

How long he lay thus he did not know, but when awareness returned the desert was again still and silent. Cautiously Simon rose and saw that the clouds had retreated far to the south, beyond the horizon. The sun shone clearly once more, while southward a great swath extended through the desert, dwindling toward those diminishing clouds. Eastward, where an entire Roman cohort had recently been, there was nothing but blackened and fused sand—an expanse of charred desolation devoid of any trace of life.

"Gods...."

Simon shivered, though the sun was already warm upon him. Soon it would be blistering, but he knew he could stay here no longer.

Descending from the outcrop by the easiest declivity that he could discover, he found at its base the provisions and waterskins which Rabdos and his small band had deposited before making their ascent. Silently thanking the gods that he would not need to re-enter the dark temple of Shuddam-El for any purpose, he shouldered as many of the abandoned supplies as he could comfortably carry and strode out upon the desert, northward toward the distant oases.

About "The Curse of the Crocodile"

Simon's Egyptian adventures continue only a few months later in February of A.D. 38. The *Dune* influence had not spent itself with "The Worm of Urakhu": A certain Valerius Argonius in "The Curse of the Crocodile" is not coincidentally reminiscent of Baron Vladimir Harkonnen.

The eponymous crocodile is, not surprisingly, Sebek, an actual Egyptian deity associated with the Mythos in the Egyptian stories of Robert Bloch. In "The Curse of the Crocodile" (first published in *Crypt of Cthulhu* #47, Roodmas, 1987) Tierney ties up another loose chronological end, placing the mad priest of Bast, Luveh-Keraph, in remotely ancient Khem, long ages before Simon's time. One wonders if he were not actually a Stygian.

Lovecraft once remarked that, in order to attain the necessary verisimilitude for his horrors, the writer must engage all the craftiness he would employ if he were actually trying to put over a hoax. So well did HPL manage the feat that even today many readers just cannot be disabused of the notion that the *Necronomicon* actually exists. Richard Tierney has put a new spin on Lovecraft's dictum. Instead of the practical joker, Tierney's model of a hoaxer is the scriptural apologist, the defender of the inerrant accuracy of scripture. In order to try to close the gaps between scriptural assertions and the data of ancient history, apologists employ all manner of special pleading and Rube Golberg hypotheses. They seek to show how manifest contradictions among biblical accounts, as well as between them and outside history, are only apparent, that they can be harmonized if only one will admit a number of speculative possibilities. Mark and Luke have Jesus exorcise only one demoniac at Gerasa, while Matthew has two? Well, maybe there really were two, but Mark saw only one of them, while Luke saw the other. Yeah, that's the ticket! Luke places Theudas the Magician before Judas the Galilean, whereas Josephus shows how Theudas arrived on the scene some fifty years after Judas to challenge Rome? Well, uh, let's see... suppose there were two different guys named Theudas, and one was before Judas, the other after him. Sure!

Tierney finds himself in the same position with Bloch's tales of eldritch Egypt. "Bloch mentions in 'The Secret of Sebek' that the crocodile-god was worshipped by virgin-sacrifice in the 'Inner Temple' in Memphis. As far as I know Egyptians didn't practice human sacrifice (except for some early immolations of servants along with deceased Pharaohs), and Sebek had nothing to do with Memphis, which was the center of Ptah-worship. I hope my story explains these anomalies sufficiently" (Letter, May 18, 1986).

Squaring Robert E. Howard's Stygia with Egyptian chronology presented an even taller order. "I seem to remember that Howard once or twice mentioned that the Stygians, not the Egyptians, built at least some of the pyramids. It's things like this that demand all the weasely skill of an apologist in order to make the Hyborian age seem a plausible precursor to actual history, at least in fiction! I suppose that one would have to argue that the Egyptians were copying the Stygians, whose vaster and more sinister pyramids now lie at the bottom of the Mediterranean, and that Howard didn't literally mean that those at Giza & Saquarra were built by Stygians..." (Letter, June 21, 1986). In fact, the challenge here is exactly equivalent to that of the Mormon apologist, stuck with a fictive prehistory strikingly analogous to Howard's Hyborian Age of Conan, namely the Book of Mormon's imaginary era of the Lamanites and Nephites in North America.

This in turn raises the question of whether Simon of Gitta may not have strayed into the Western Hemisphere for some adventures among the Lamanites. Pondering that question led to another Simon of Gitta short story, "The Secret of Nephren-Ka", found later in this volume.

THE CURSE OF THE CROCODILE
by Richard L. Tierney

Menophar, High Priest of Ptah in Memphis, awoke feeling terror in the night. A hand was shaking his shoulder. There should be no such hand here in his quarters, in the fortified sanctuary of the Great Temple.

"Menophar, wake up! It is I—Simon of Gitta."

The priest rolled over and gazed into the dark eyes of the man who had thus addressed him. The youthful, high-cheekboned face was intent, pale in contrast to the bangs and straight locks that framed it.

"Gods!" Menophar sat up on his cot and rubbed his eyes; the single dim lamp in the chamber elicited fiery highlights from his bald, oil-slicked cranium. "Simon, how did you get in here—?"

The dark-eyed young man smiled grimly. "You should know, old mentor. You once taught me how to slip past guards—yes, and even how to climb these very temple walls!"

"Aye." Menophar was standing now, fully awake, donning his white robe. "I had not thought to see you again, Simon. I heard that you had perished in the western desert and my heart was saddened. I joy to see you alive! But—what brings you here?"

"Valerius Argonius, Nomarch of Thebes," said Simon evenly. "He, on orders from Aulus Flaccus, Governor of Egypt, had me pursued by Roman soldiers into the desert west of Thebes. And Flaccus takes his orders from the mad emperor Gaius. I've hidden these many weeks with the priests of the Oasis of Amon, an imperial price on my head. So, my friend, think well before you decide to aid such a fugitive as I."

Menophar snorted, his eyes blazing angrily. "Nonsense! Any enemy of Caligula is a friend of Egypt. But continue, Simon—why did you leave Amon's sanctuary and come here?"

"Argonius had learned of my whereabouts. The Roman soldiers he had earlier sent after me had perished in the desert, and he was now mad for revenge. I fled from Amon so that my presence would not endanger those who had sheltered me, and after a hazardous trek eastward I came out of the desert and into the fertile basin of the Fayum. There, at Crocodilopolis, I learned from an old priest of Ptah that Argonius himself had preceded me and was even then carrying on secret dealings with the sinister priests of Sebek. Moreover, I learned that the fat Nomarch hopes to invoke to his aid the Power of the Crocodile—and thereby cause himself to be elevated to the rulership of Egypt and, eventually, the entire Roman Empire."

Menophar shuddered. He made a mystic sign in the air before him;

then, fingering the silvery looped cross that hung upon his breast, he muttered a silent prayer. "It is as I feared," he said finally. "I sensed Argonius' intent, but Flaccus would not listen to me—"

"There is little time for explanations," said Simon. "Look out your window and you will know why."

The bald priest glanced in puzzlement at Simon, then ran to the casement and peered down into the wide square before the temple. A score of Roman soldiers was approaching, their helmets and breastplates gleaming in the light of the torches they bore. At their forefront marched half a dozen grotesque figures—tall, white-robed forms, each topped by the long-snouted head of a crocodile.

"Priests of Sebek!" muttered Menophar. "Why do they come here to Ptah's temple—and in company with two Roman decans? Simon, do they pursue you?"

"No. I was aboard their ship, disguised as a sailor. An hour ago they docked at the main quay, and I escaped unseen over the side. I need your help—"

"*Open, priests of Ptah!*" shouted one of the crocodile-masked figures below.

"On whose orders?" answered a priest from a casement somewhere beneath Simon and Menophar.

"Orders of Valerius Argonius, Governor of Upper Egypt."

Menophar gasped. "Surely this is treason!" he hissed, turning to Simon. "Aulus Flaccus would never have granted Argonius that title—"

"Aye, treason. And tonight Argonius hopes to invoke magic that will make his nephew, Fabian, king of *all* Egypt—and himself Emperor of Rome."

"But—how? Obviously he has recruited the aid of Sebek's worshipers, but they are no longer powerful in the land—"

"*Open the gates, priests!*"

Menophar glanced down to see a bald priest of Ptah hurrying toward the Romans; evidently the temple gates had been opened as demanded. One of the crocodile figures held out an unrolled parchment before the priest, who scrutinized it briefly, then bowed and waved the group inward.

"That is Tetu, my immediate underling," said Menophar. "Why did he not consult me—?"

"He has been bribed. I managed to overhear some of Argonius' plottings while aboard his ship. Keep your room well bolted, old friend—you may be slain if you go forth to confront the crocodile priests."

"But *why?* Why do they come here, Simon?"

"To open the way to the Inner Temple."

Menophar paled. His bald pate beaded with sudden sweat. "What can you know of the Inner Temple, Simon of Gitta?" he asked sternly.

"Very little. That's one thing I need to learn about from you—for evidently the rite is to be performed there."

The priest was silent for a moment while the clattering footfalls of the entering Romans dwindled and finally subsided altogether. "I—I should not divulge it, Simon," he said finally.

"You must! Forget your oaths, damn it—this is an emergency!"

Menophar glanced toward the scroll-filled shelves that covered all of one wall of his bedchamber. "It is an old secret. Only the high priest and his immediate underling are supposed to know it."

"Tetu has betrayed it already. Tell me, Menophar! I need all the knowledge you can give me."

The priest nodded. "The Inner Temple is old, older than Memphis itself. It was already here when Menes, the first pharaoh, established the city. Within it, according to the writings of the ancient sorcerer Zazamankh, stood the Eidolon of Sebek—the Golden Crocodile between whose jaws countless screaming virgins were torn. Such sacrifices, dating back to ancient Stygian times, caused Menes to expel the priests of the crocodile god, level their temple, and seal off the nether fane—the Inner Temple—where the Golden Crocodile was housed. Above this site, after many cleansing rituals, the temple to benign Ptah, the Creator, was erected. The memory of Sebek's worship was expunged from the land, and only the highest priests of the temple—and the remnant of the crocodile god's secret worshipers—knew that his golden image lay in pillared halls below."

"That is not possible," said Simon, scowling darkly, "for the image of the Golden Crocodile is even now in the hold of the very ship that brought me here! Argonius and his nephew Fabian, with the help of the priests of Crocodilopolis, discovered it in a hidden chamber beneath the Labyrinth by the Lake of Fayum. They plan to bring it into the Inner Temple this very night. In their madness they have already sacrificed virgins to it, and they intend to sacrifice many more!"

Menophar shuddered, glanced again at his shelves of amassed scrolls. "I see. They plan to return the thing to its original temple."

Simon followed the priest's gaze. "Who was this sorcerer Zazamankh, who recorded such dark and ancient matters? Did he write of how the image came to vanish from its temple?"

"No, for that occurred long after his time. Zazamankh was chief magician to the Pharaoh Seneferu, father of mighty Khufu. His writings have been kept hidden from all but the highest priests, for they tell of the monstrous rituals that were practiced in ancient Stygia and during the long All-Night following the destruction of that pre-Egyptian land. In those times human blood was spilled often and copiously over the altars of such dark gods as Nyarlat, Shuddam-El, and Set—aye, and also Sebek, whose worship long antedates Egypt and who is said to be the Friend of Set.

"For a thousand years and more after the days of Menes the Golden Crocodile lay in pillared darkness, unseen by men, and Sebek's cult was diminished and scattered. But then came the Pharaoh Amenemhet, founder of a new dynasty, who revived and exalted the worship of Sebek, building great temples to him at Crocodilopolis and beside the Lake of the Fayum—though even Amenemhet dared not openly revive the sacrifice of virgins."

"Openly?"

Menophar nodded, pointed to a thick and yellowed scroll on one of the lower shelves. "It is recorded there, in the writings of the mad Luveh-Keraph, priest of Bast, how Amenemhet discovered the Golden Crocodile by sorcerous means and caused it to be secretly taken by night from its Inner Temple here in Memphis. Those who rowed the ship that brought it upriver to Crocodilopolis were young virgins clad only in golden fishnets, and after the image was ensconced in its new underground temple the maidens were all sacrificed to it. In later generations, it is written, the Golden Crocodile was worshiped in like fashion by the dark princess Sebek-nefru-Ra, and even by the insane Pharaoh Nephren-Ka. The cruel, conquering Hyksos also carried on its worship, though they did not discover the secret of the Inner Temple, and after they were overthrown by Ahmose the evil rites to Sebek were again banned and the second temple of the Golden Crocodile was sealed away from men even as the first had been."

"And now Valerius Argonius has rediscovered it," muttered Simon. "Gods! I'd learned earlier that he was delving into Egyptian magic in order to advance his power, but this is utter madness!"

"A more dangerous madness than Argonius may realize. This is the one day of the year, according to Zazamankh, when Sebek himself may appear to his worshipers in the Inner Temple, granting them eternal life; no doubt that is why Argonius has chosen this date. But it is also recorded that should any of the rites be done wrongly, the Curse of the Crocodile will be invoked. Then, woe betide those worshipers!"

"That is the sort of knowledge I need," said Simon. "Rack your brains, old friend! Is there aught else in those scrolls of yours that might help? Some spell, perhaps?"

"Perhaps." Menophar turned to rummage amid his collection of ancient writings. Simon joined him, marveling at the sight of so many works of dark lore—works such as the *Texts of Meidum* by Teta, chief magician of Khufu; the *Mystic Prophecies* of the great pre-Hyborian sage Muthsa; the writings of the even more ancient Hyperborean wizard Eibon; excerpts from the sinister, priest-guarded *Book of Thoth*; and even one aged scroll written over with symbols of the aeon-old Naacal tongue, of which Simon could not read a syllable.

For perhaps half an hour they feverishly read and compared notes, while Simon kept one anxious ear cocked for sounds from below. There were none. Menophar, reading his expression, explained:

"The Inner Temple is far beneath the ground. No sounds can reach us from there. By now Tetu will have shown the intruders how to open the hidden doors, and they will be setting up the preparations for their rites within."

"Then I must go," said Simon, rising. "Pray to Ptah and all other benign gods that what you have told me will aid me to thwart Argonius' evil designs!"

He strode to the casement and peered out. The courtyard was once again dark. Cautiously he leaned outward, found the thin rope he had left dangling from the rooftop, then emerged and hauled himself upward easily, hand over hand. In another moment he had crawled over the cornice and stood upon the temple's flat roof. The stars gleamed brightly down from the eternally cloudless bosom of Nout, the Sky Goddess, while high in the east a gibbous moon waxed silvery.

Simon turned to gather in his rope, found it taut. Menophar was climbing up behind him. In another moment the wiry priest was standing with him on the roof, clad in a dark cloak much like Simon's own. A long staff was held to one shoulder by a looped cord.

"I can still climb at least as well as any of my pupils," said Menophar, his voice betraying no strain from his exertions. "I've brought an amulet or two, and my memory holds a few spells which might prove useful."

Simon nodded, secretly grateful for his erstwhile mentor's aid. "What is that staff you carry?"

"This? Merely an ancient priestly scepter, sacred to Sebek. It has been handed down to my priesthood for many centuries. Some claim that the golden head of it dates back to the days of the Inner Temple."

Simon peered more closely, felt a shiver of misgiving at the sight of the small, toothy crocodile head gleaming in the moonlight. "Do we really want such a thing along with us?"

"It may contain power that will aid us, given the right spells."

"Very well, then. Hurry. We have a few walls to descend, many streets to traverse—and no time for magical experiments, more's the pity!"

Valerius Argonius, Nomarch of Thebes, waddled from his cabin near the poop deck, flanked by two Roman guards and followed by his lean nephew, Fabian. Nearly a score of sleepy-looking sailors, already assembled on deck, blinked in the light of the torches mounted along the rails. As always, they marveled at the contrast between the gross rotund bulk of Valerius and the slim, sinewy muscularity of his athletic nephew.

It took a dozen men to bear the Nomarch through the streets in his ornate litter, whose drawn curtains bulged outward from his enormous girth; Fabian, on the other hand, was agile as a panther and had often fought as a *retarius*-man in the arena against half-drugged criminals. The only characteristics the two showed in common were a certain fixed smile or half-grin—an expression of perpetual bored amusement—and an eye-gleam suggestive of sadistic cruelty.

Tonight the contrast was sharpened, for over his Equestrian tunic Argonius now wore a voluminous toga of imperial purple, whereas his nephew was garbed in only the briefest of breechclouts and his body gleamed with oil like a wrestler's before a bout.

"Listen, you men," said Argonius, "I've decided to give you a few days shore leave—with pay, of course. You may go now."

A tall sailor, evidently the captain, pulled thoughtfully at his beard, then blinked up at the gibbous moon high above the light of the torches.

"Very well, most noble Nomarch, but—"

"Call me Nomarch no longer. As of tonight I am Governor of Upper Egypt—and tomorrow I shall be much more!"

The captain scowled in puzzlement but held his tongue. "Very well... Governor. But why now, in the middle of the night—?"

"Aye—when most of the taverns are already closed," added a sailor impulsively.

"Will you men quibble with a gift?" growled Argonius. "Go!"

"But—our money—?"

"My chief officer, Aemilius, awaits you ashore. He will pay you."

The captain nodded, gestured to his men. They followed him down the gangway from the ship, then along the broad stone quay toward the shore. Some of them laughed, joyed by their unexpected liberty; yet their captain felt strangely uneasy. He saw no Roman soldiers upon the shore, though there were many torches along the quay—torches that had lit the way for the soldiers and crocodile-masked priests who had left the ship almost an hour earlier. Very irregular, this nocturnal dismissal. What was it all about? And what of the dozen or more young women who were held prisoner below decks? The captain's uneasiness deepened. Surely this was the strangest voyage he had ever undertaken! He glanced down at the inky waters of the Nile; they were unusually high, their waves lapping within inches of the stone surface, glinting like fluid jet under the moonlight—

He heard the voice of Argonius droning loudly from the ship. The Roman's words were cadenced, intoned—a chant; they were not Greek words, nor Latin, nor even Egyptian. Something about them chilled the captain's soul. Then came the sound of a flute, high and weird. The sailors turned as one man and saw the broad outline of Argonius on deck, one hand waving in time with his chant, the other clutching an unrolled scroll; beside him stood Fabian, oiled limbs gleaming in the torchlight, a Pan-pipe held to his lips. The inky waters surged against the quay, boiled—

Then from those waters burst a score of monstrous reptilian forms— crocodiles, their spiked maws agape, their tails lashing the waves to foam. In an instant they were slithering upon the wet-splashed stone of the wharf, seizing the screaming sailors in relentless jaws, hauling them off the quay and into the Nile's black depths.

Finally, in less than a minute, the night was silent once more. On the stones of the wharf there remained only a wet slick of water to show that a death struggle had just occurred.

"It is well," said Argonius, carefully rolling up his scroll and tucking it into his sash. "Better that we leave no witnesses among the uninitiated." He turned, faced his nephew and the impassive pair of Roman guards. "You piped well, Fabian."

The youth grinned, his teeth flashing in the torchlight, dark eyes sparkling.

"That I did, Uncle. And yet—did I miscount, or were we one sailor short in our offering to Sebek?"

Argonius scowled, remembering. "Aye—the tall one who called himself Sinuhe! I had not noticed. You are sharp-eyed, Fabian! Guards— search the ship! And if you do not find the missing sailor, bring the belongings of all the men up here on deck."

After a few minutes of fruitless search the soldiers returned and deposited a dozen or more bundles upon the planks. Hurriedly Argonius and his nephew searched through them, throwing each overboard as they discovered only one batch after another of common sailors' items. But in one of the last they discovered a long, heavy-bladed *sica*—a wicked weapon, almost a short sword, of a type used by Thracian gladiators. It was wrapped in a red tunic emblazoned with mystic black symbols.

"The garment of a sorcerer and the blade of a gladiator," said Fabian evenly. "Evidently the man swam ashore in his loin cloth and with only a few light things bundled in his cloak. We should have invoked the crocodiles earlier—I *thought* there was something suspicious about that sailor—"

"You did, did you?" snarled Argonius. "Then why, beloved nephew, did you say nothing to me?"

"I found him prowling about near the aft hold last night while you were performing your—ritual duties—there. The man had a plausible explanation. He said he had heard sounds—thought there might be a stowaway. I taxed my ingenuity convincing him otherwise."

"A *sica*—and a sorcerer's garment," muttered Argonius. "You're a fool, Fabian, for all your sharpness of eye! I remember now that this sailor came aboard at Crocodilopolis at the last moment; he was stooped, straggle-bearded, and slow in speech, so I took little notice of him. But now I know that he was our enemy—a master of disguise and trained as a gladiator. I sent soldiers to the Oasis of Amon to apprehend him, but he had already fled into the desert once more. Surely his wanderings then brought him to the Fayum, where rumor informed him of our doings, and now he seeks once more to thwart us—but by the black gods of Karneter, he shall not!"

"You mean—Simon of Gitta?" gasped Fabian.

"Aye!" Argonius' corpulent form seemed to swell like that of a malignant toad. "That devious Samaritan serpent—the very one who lured our pursuing cohort to doom in the desert." His voice rose to an irate bellow. "He's gone for aid now, no doubt, but he'll return—and when he does, I'll be ready for him. He'll die before these eyes, and he'll know—*he'll know*—that it is I, Valerius Argonius, who has brought him to his doom!" The Roman turned and faced his soldiers with mad, glaring eyes. "Bring up the virgins from the aft hold, then go ashore and summon my bearers and the rest of the crocodile priests. The rites to Sebek shall now begin!"

Bare feet whispered upon the smooth planks of the deck; feminine whimpers of fear rippled the darkness. Valerius Argonius, composed once more, watched sternly with folded hands hidden in his toga while his soldiers ushered a dozen or more black-haired young women up the stairway from the aft hold. The women wore nothing but brief linen loincloths, golden flowers in their hair, and meshes of gold-bright netting that pinioned their arms to their bodies, leaving only their legs free. Fear and sadness shone in their frantic dark eyes.

Behind Argonius stood Fabian, licking his lips, a strange black-bladed knife clutched in his right hand.

"Greetings, brides of Sebek," Argonius intoned.

At his words four white-robed priests wearing crocodile masks strode up the gangway from the quay and came aboard. The women gasped and shrank away at their approach.

"But before you lovely maids are escorted to the Inner Temple, where you will soon meet your immortal Husband and be eternally consecrated to him, a rite must be performed. My nephew Fabian will this night, with Sebek's blessing, be proclaimed Pharaoh of Egypt—subject only to my own benevolent direction as Emperor of Rome. But in order to induce Sebek to bring this about, Fabian must, by ancient ritual, defeat the strongest of you, who are all priestesses consecrated to Isis and therefore enemies of great Set. Moreover, he must do this unarmed while facing a blade of ancient design."

Fabian, grinning, held up his dark-bladed knife and cried: "Free her who is the strongest."

Immediately one of the Romans unfastened the net that bound the most robust of the women—a shapely, athletic beauty as tall as Fabian himself. The girl stood trembling before her tormentors in wide-eyed bewilderment.

"Take the knife!" shouted Fabian, advancing and pressing the haft of the weapon into the reluctant girl's right hand, then jumping back. Slowly her long fingers curled about it. Its blade was black, glassy, its edges tinged with yellow in the torchlight.

"Take it!" repeated Argonius in yelled intonations. "It is the Tooth of Sebek, chipped from the vitreous stone of volcanoes in ancient Stygia. If its blade draws Fabian's blood, however slightly, he cannot become Pharaoh. But if he conquers, then you and all your sisters shall become the brides of Sebek!"

The athletic young woman gripped the knife more firmly, determination flashing in her eyes. Fabian grinned. Denying his carnal lusts had been hard during this voyage with a dozen captive virgins whose condition must not be altered; now, he would at least partially compensate for some of that self-denial with sweet violence. The girl, though built like a shapely Amazon, evidently knew nothing of knife-fighting, for she grimly held the blade high, ready for a downward jab.

"Let the contest begin!" shouted Argonius.

Fabian pranced forward, clutching at the girl, apparently leaving himself open; the girl leaped at him, stabbing downward, shrieking with rage. Adroitly the grinning young athlete leaped aside, gripped the maid's wrist, and flipped her expertly. She landed heavily on the planks, the wind knocked out of her, and the knife went skidding across the deck. All the other women cried out in unison, horrified.

"Bravo, nephew!" yelled Argonius, laughing, while the hard-faced Roman guards behind him grinned their enjoyment.

Fabian strode over to the knife, picked it up, and sheathed it, then returned to the gasping girl and whipped a black sack over her head, binding it loosely about her neck. While she struggled feebly he bound her again in the golden fishnet and fastened it with a small hasp shaped like a crocodile's head.

"Good! Good!" crowed Argonius. "Now, Fabian, take her below and prepare her for the sacrifice to the Golden Crocodile. And you—" he pointed to the crocodile-masked priests and the Roman soldiers—"escort

these other virgins to the Inner Temple, which has by now been readied
for the great sacrifice. Then return here, together with the other priests and
soldiers, that you may bear the eidolon of Sebek to its original temple in
time for its nuptial rites. Meanwhile, I shall perform the final preparatory
sacrifice aboard this ship."

The newly subdued virgin's screams, muffled by the black hood, rang
out pitifully as she was borne down into the hold by the chuckling Fabian.
Hurriedly the soldiers and crocodile priests herded the other whimpering,
net-bound women down the gangway to the stone quay, then shoreward
and into the darkened streets of Memphis.

Simon and Menophar, hastening stealthily through the dark streets and alleys, paused suddenly at the sound of clanking armor and tramping boots
upon the pave. In the distance, down the wide avenue leading toward the
wharves, they saw the glimmer of perhaps a dozen torches.

"Quick—into this archway!" whispered the bald priest.

Simon had no need to be told, and instants later they were hidden
within deep shadows, crouching, watching the approach of the torches. In
a few minutes they discerned the figures of about a dozen Roman soldiers
and four of the crocodile priests. In the midst of these figures a number of
dark-haired young women marched awkwardly, occasionally urged on by
spear shafts and many-stranded leather whips in the hands of the Romans.
Their arms were bound to their torsos by meshes of golden netting and
their dark eyes were wide with terror. Simon ground his teeth; a low growl
of rage rose in his throat. In the same instant he felt Menophar's restrain-
ing hand on his shoulder, and froze in awe and fear—for there were six
great undulating shadow-shapes, three on each side and low to the ground,
accompanying the procession. As these shapes drew abreast of the passage
in which Simon crouched, he saw that they were enormous crocodiles!

A soft chanting was issuing from behind the reptilian masks of the
four priests, and the crocodile escorts seemed to march in purposeful cadence to the rhythm of that chanting. The words were not Greek, Latin,
nor even Egyptian, and Simon, though he could not understand their
meaning, recognized them as belonging to the lost language of ancient,
sorcery-riddled Stygia.

"It is the Soul Chant of Sebek," whispered Menophar tensely, "—a
chant which concentrates the will of wizards powerfully. Tonight it is being
used to control the crocodiles—and later, I fear, it will be employed to
bring Sebek himself to bodily manifestation within his Inner Temple. Monstrous powers are afoot this night, Simon. We must hurry!"

As soon as the weird procession was out of sight the dark-cloaked pair
hastened on toward the wharves. As they approached the main quay they

beheld the glimmer of more torches and, in their light, a number of men standing on the shore in front of a row of darkened buildings.

"Argonius' litter-bearers, and a couple of Roman soldiers with them," growled Simon. "But—what are those things on the quay?"

Silently they stole closer amid the shadows, and Simon could hardly believe his eyes. A row of torches burned on poles set along each side of the stone causeway, and among them were ranged a double row of huge crocodiles, spaced as with military precision, snouts upraised and facing inward, tails dangling over the edge into the dark water. They stood motionless on all fours, tensed, bodies just off the ground, spiked jaws slightly agape. At the end of the quay Argonius' ship was moored, but no man could hope or dare to approach it.

"Baal!" hissed Simon. "What do we do now?"

"You must go back aboard. Argonius and his nephew are surely unguarded now, or nearly so. You must find and slay them before the soldiers return here to convey the Golden Crocodile to its Inner Temple. And pray, Simon, that you are able to do so before the preparatory rites are completed, for then the power of Sebek will have rendered his worshipers invulnerable!"

"Go aboard?" Simon glanced nervously at the ranked crocodiles. "Surely I'd be mad to try!"

"You must." Menophar held up his staff. "There is magic in this. And I, too, know the Soul Chant of Sebek. I shall use it to cause the crocodiles to disperse."

"Are you sure you can manage it? And even if you do, what about those soldiers and bearers ashore? They'll see me—"

"You must swim out to the boat so that they do not."

Simon shuddered. "Those waters may be teeming with more crocodiles!"

"Do you want Valerius Argonius to be Emperor of Rome? He'd be worse than even the mad Caligula who rules now—especially with Sebek's magic to aid him! You must try, Simon—it's our only chance."

Simon nodded grimly, then stole down through the shadows to the water's edge. In the dim light the Nile rippled darkly. If there were indeed more crocodiles in the water he could not sense them. Carefully he slipped off his cloak; then, clad only in his dark loincloth, he moved slowly forward. The cold waters lapped upward over his shins, his thighs, his flanks, his shoulders... his feet lost touch with the muddy bottom and he stroked gently away from the bank, breathing softly, stilling his mind. It would not do to think of hard teeth suddenly clenching upon his ankle—

Suddenly he heard a soft chanting from the shore and glanced back. Menophar was standing between him and the quay, bobbing and gesturing, and the head of his crocodile-staff was beginning to glow with an eerie golden light.

"*Ro ithomu! Inkon ku, Sobok kuthumus, ne imonu hakugu kos...!*"

The crocodiles abruptly stiffened, quivered, as if the Stygian words of the Soul Chant had released them from a spell. In the same instant the men upon the shore spotted Menophar and began to yell excitedly. Simon swam more rapidly, trying to quench the spark of panic that wanted to rise from the core of his soul—

Suddenly all the crocodiles on the quay whipped about as one and plunged into the waters. At the same moment the waves boiled as more excited reptiles surfaced and began swimming frantically away from shore. One monstrous saurian passed Simon so closely that he felt the wash of its wake, yet the beast paid him no attention.

In another minute he had reached the boat. Heart pounding, he reached up and gripped the edge of the deck, then hauled himself over the rail and lay silently amid the scuppers, catching his breath. Between the posts of the rail he glimpsed Menophar making off into the night, half a dozen bearers and soldiers at his heels.

As Simon's mind calmed he heard, over the beating of his heart, the sound of a new chant—the voice of Argonius, intoning from within the forward cabin.

Slowly he rose, forcing his mind to calmness, and stole along the torchlit deck toward the bow. There were no guards, but the door to the forward cabin was unyielding, securely bolted from within. From behind it came the scent of strange incense and the cadenced intonations of Argonius—more words in the sinister Stygian tongue. Simon shivered; evidently the preparatory rite was being performed. He seemed to sense evil powers congealing in the air about him in response to those words. Glancing shoreward, he saw crocodiles once more emerging from the dark waters, arranging themselves watchfully along the quay.

"Baal!" he hissed softly. Time was running out. He felt trapped, exposed. Here he was, alone, surrounded by evil magic, and not so much as a dagger at his belt!

Silently he stole aft and found the stairway to the hold. The door to it was not secured. Slowly he crept down the wooden stairs in the darkness. If only he could find some stores of oil he might be able to fire the ship, then dive away and swim ashore—through the gnashing jaws of the crocodiles

At the bottom of the stairway he sensed a light glimmering ahead. Pushing aside a heavy curtain, he emerged into a large space—and gasped aloud. Several oil lamps were burning along the beam-ribbed walls, and in their faint light there gleamed before him the gaping jaws of a monstrous golden crocodile!

In the next instant he relaxed as he realized that it was not alive but a thing made of gilded bronze. That was well, for the head of it alone was fully eight feet in length. The vast scaly body vanished behind it into the darkness of the hold, and Simon knew that it must end shortly beyond his sight—for surely the ship could not hold the complete eidolon of a crocodile built on such a huge scale!

But the head by itself was horror enough. Simon felt himself cringing inwardly before the almost conscious gleam that seemed to flicker from the great jade-green eyes. The golden scales and plates upon the thing's snout were executed with disconcerting realism; the jaws, half-agape, bristled with glittering bronze teeth.

Then, with a second thrill of horror, he saw the altar lying just beneath the thing's snout—the altar he had not noticed till now because of the Golden Crocodile's overwhelming presence. It was of dark stone, its sides carven with Stygian hieroglyphs, and upon its slightly convex upper surface lay the tall, net-bound form of—a young woman?

Simon hurried forward. Yes, it was indeed a woman, though her bent-back, supine position had so flattened her breasts that he had at first not been sure. He touched her shoulder; she quivered, and a low whimper came from behind the black hood that concealed her head. Simon uttered a low growl of anger. He groped at the metallic mesh, at the cords binding the woman's ankles, at the ties fastening the black hood. All were unyielding. Gods, for a knife—!

"So, Simon of Gitta, my uncle was right. You have come."

Simon whirled at the sound of the soft voice. A lean, sinewy-muscled figure was emerging from the shadows. Dark eyes gleamed above a toothy, sadistic grin.

"Fabian!"

"I'm glad you remember me, Simon." The leering youth held up a black-bladed Stygian sacrificial knife; its transparent edges gleamed yellowly in the lamplight. "You've caused Uncle and me a good deal of trouble. Now you'll pay for it!"

Simon crouched and edged back as the mad-eyed, grinning youth gripped his knife expertly in a fighter's stance and tensed to spring.

Menophar hurried through the darkened streets, a swift shadow among shadows. The shouts of his pursuers, whom he had eluded easily, had long since faded away.

But now, as he approached the temple of Ptah, he heard new shoutings.

Emerging into the square before the great white edifice, he saw that it was crowded with torch-bearing priests and acolytes whose shaven heads gleamed in the light of the flames. At the sight of Menophar, the nearest of them knelt reverently and bowed their heads to the paving-stones.

"Rise!" Menophar commanded. "You, Refnu-Ptah—tell me what is happening within."

"I do not know," said the young priest, trembling. "The Sebek priests and the Roman soldiers are within the Inner Temple. Tetu is with them. They were chanting strange rites in the tongue of Stygia. Then, a few minutes ago, more Romans and Sebek priests arrived with a dozen bound maidens and—and six escorting crocodiles!"

"Where are they?"

"Over there, by the wall. A crocodile priest emerged a moment ago, commanded the soldiers and priests to await a signal, then returned inside with the crocodiles following him. There is strange sorcery afoot this night, O Master! What are we to do?"

"Disregard Tetu's orders! Surround those Romans—and free the virgins of Isis whom they hold captive. They must not enter the temple!"

The Ptah priests and acolytes, heartened by the presence of their leader, hastened to do his bidding. The dozen Romans, bewildered and greatly outnumbered, stood sullenly aside and allowed the freeing of the captive women.

Suddenly an eerie sound burst from the portals of the great temple—a distant, high-pitched wail suggesting the mingled shrieks of many voices down far corridors. Then, overshadowing it, came a sinister rumbling—a deep roar like that of a bull crocodile, but vastly greater.

"Gods of Amenti, protect me!" muttered Menophar. Gripping his crocodile-staff in one hand and his silver looped cross in the other, he dashed across the courtyard and into the great fane. Smoke was billowing up into the main corridor from the passage that led down to the Inner Temple, and with it rose also the frantic shrieks of dying men mingled with the rumbling bellows of a monstrous saurian....

Valerius Argonius lumbered from his cabin, crossed the torchlit deck, and descended into the aft hold with laborious wheezings. It was dim there, for only a single lamp burned. A smirk of satisfaction creased the Nomarch's fat face as he confronted the imposing, upraised snout of the Golden Crocodile gleaming in the faint glow. *Soon, O Great Sebek*, he thought, *soon all your divine power shall be at my service!*

But where was Fabian? Surely a more devoted nephew would have remained to help his venerable uncle down the steep stairway! Doubtless the lad had gone ashore to wait with the bearers. No matter. The important thing was that Fabian had obviously prepared the sacrifice that would inaugurate the conveying of Sebek's eidolon to the Inner Temple. There she was, bound and black-hooded, struggling supine upon the convex altar.

Advancing, Argonius heard an object clatter as his toe encountered it. Bending laboriously, he saw that it was the dark-bladed Stygian sacrificial knife. That was careless of Fabian—the Tooth of Sebek should have been lying upon the altar beside the waiting virgin! With a wheezing effort he picked it up, then waddled forward in the dim lamplight. His thick left hand reached out and clutched the thigh of the struggling victim. From behind the black hood came frantic, high-pitched moans. Fabian must have gagged her—that was good. Her shrieks would not interfere with the final chant.

"Kho thamus immamu-tu!" he intoned, the black-bladed Stygian knife rising in his fat right hand. *"Maknu Sobok, dammu-me potorum immentu!"*

The dark blade flashed down, ripped deep into the breast of the victim. Blood spurted; a final gurgling moan sounded from behind the black hood.

Then, to Argonius' horror, he saw the jaws of the Golden Crocodile begin to open—to gape wider—

"No!" he gasped, backing away. As the opening jaws began to move toward him, his gasps of horror turned to mad, frenzied shrieks.

As Menophar came hurrying down to the wharf, followed by half a dozen of his subordinate priests and acolytes, he found only two figures standing near the shore upon the quay—a tall, dark-haired young man in a loincloth and a dark-robed woman nearly as tall as he. The ranked torches still burned there, but no crocodiles were in evidence. Obviously all the dark sorcery of this strange night was now dissipated.

"Simon," cried the priest as he rushed up, "we have won! Something disrupted their rituals, so that when Sebek materialized within the Inner Temple he destroyed the Romans and crocodile priests rather than granting their wishes. I saw what was left of them; it was horrible! I've ordered the place sealed up again so that future generations may be spared the knowledge of what happened there." He glanced sharply at the tall young woman who stood shivering beside Simon, bundled in his dark cloak. "Is she the one who was meant to be the preparatory sacrifice?"

"Aye."

"Thank the gods that you prevented it! Doubtless that was what caused the rites in the Inner Temple to go awry. I feared for your life, Simon! How did you manage to thwart Argonius and his nephew?"

Simon shrugged casually. "Fabian attacked me, but he was overconfident because he was armed and I was not. He was agile and cocky, but he'd fought only drugged criminals and captive women before he challenged me." The young man grinned darkly. "I disarmed him easily and choked him unconscious, then freed this maid and left him bound in her place upon the altar. Unless Argonius has exceptionally good eyesight, he's performed a sacrifice no god of Sebek's tastes could accept—"

"Sacrifice? Gods!" Menophar turned and dashed down the quay, then up the gangway to the ship. Simon, leaving the trembling girl with the priests, sprinted after him. Together they descended into the aft hold. Only one dim lamp burned there.

Simon heard Menophar gasp.

"Is he there?" asked Simon, his voice hard, almost metallic.

"Aye." The priest pointed toward the altar where the bound, hooded figure lay, the black-bladed knife buried in its breast. "Fabian is slain, even as you guessed. But you worked better than you knew, Simon. Look!"

Simon gasped as he gazed at that which loomed behind the altar.

"This boat must be set adrift," said Menophar grimly, "and burned with fire!"

But Simon did not hear this. His eyes were riveted upon the ruptured carcass of Valerius Argonius—the bloated, burst carcass from which streamers of blood and curdled fat drooled down, together with dangling folds of blue-veined intestines, from between the clenched and gleaming jaws of the Golden Crocodile.

About "The Treasaure of Horemkhu"

WARNING: Contains spoilers!

We continue to explore elder Egypt in "The Treasure of Horemkhu" (from *Pulse-Pounding Adventure Stories #2*, December, 1987), which is set in March of A.D. 38. You will remember how Lovecraft ghost-wrote a story for magician Harry Houdini which pretended to chronicle his adventures in Egypt "Under the Pyramids." (It is the convention of Lovecraft scholars to refer to the story thusly, by the title Lovecraft himself gave it, rather than as "Imprisoned with the Pharaohs", the title it bore when published in *Weird Tales*.) Though nothing in that tale connected it explicitly to the Cthulhu Mythos, everything served to connect it with other Lovecraftian references to Egypt, as in "The Outsider." Tierney has brought Simon the Mage into contact with the same subterrene horrors some nineteen centuries earlier, and quite appropriately, as Simon is a master of stage illusion and escape tricks, just like his twentieth-century counterpart Houdini.

Lovecraft, an unflinching rationalist, was nonetheless quite fond of pseudo-science as fodder for his tales of scientifiction, drawing freely upon Churchward's bogus research into the lost continent of Mu and Charles Fort's tales of extraterrestrials mining the earth. Tierney used to write for *Fate* magazine and *Gnostica News*, even casting horoscopes, all the while as stubborn a rationalist as HPL. In "The Treasure of Horemkhu", he incorporates some of the wild speculations on the Sphinx from Zechariah Sitchin's *The Stairway to Heaven*.

The Roman governor Flaccus is no invention of Tierney. The first-century A.D. philosopher Philo Judaeus wrote a treatise to Caesar complaining about this man's enormities, especially his unfair treatment of Jews. Philo makes him a highly gifted administrator who turned sour after the death of his patron Caligula, when he became haunted by fears of the disfavor of his new superiors. It was then that he began to heed the nefarious counsel of his advisors: that he allow the Jews to be scapegoated. Among the injustices Philo ascribes to Flaccus was his failure to stop an embarrassing affront to Herod Agrippa I, who was returning to Palestine from Rome by way of Egypt, having been newly made king. It seems that the hooligans of Alexandria staged a satirical spectacle along the route of Herod Agrippa's entourage. They grabbed a local halfwit named Carabas and made of him a mock king with a papyrus dunce cap for a crown and a door mat for a royal cloak. He was given a reed for his scepter and was hailed as *Mar* ("Lord" in Aramaic), the title with which Agrippa would be hailed upon his homecoming. This was to show what Egyptians thought of a Jewish "king." One thinks of the Gospel Passion scenes in which Jesus is condemned to death in Barabbas' place, clothed in a purple robe and thorny crown as a mock king, then sent by Pilate to Herod Antipas, who happened to be in Jerusalem for the Passover feast. One wonders if Pilate meant precisely to insult Herod Antipas who, though only a tetrarch, styled himself King Herod, by sending him Pilate's version of a "king of the Jews." Or could the whole of the gospel tale have been borrowed from Philo's report?

THE TREASURE OF HOREMKHU
by Richard L. Tierney

Menophar, high priest of Ptah in Memphis, peered tensely from the casement of his high room as the boots of two dozen Roman legionaries tramped in rhythm upon the flagstones of the courtyard below. The light of early dawn glinted from the soldiers' iron helmets, as it did from the priest's own bald and oil-slicked cranium.

"They return, O mentor," said a hollow voice at the old priest's side, "even as we have expected during this past month."

Menophar turned and regarded the tall, grim-faced young man. "Yet we are not unprepared, Simon. Quickly—don your disguise and leave by the secret northern tunnel. Spend the evening guiding tourists through the tombs of the ancients, as usual. When you return tomorrow, all should be well here."

"Are you sure?" The glitter in the young man's dark, deep-sunken eyes reflected his unease. "These Romans are ruthless—brutal."

"I shall handle them. It is you they seek. Hurry—go!"

The young man bowed slightly, then vanished away into the shadows.

A few seconds later Menophar heard sharp blows resounding from below—sword pommels, pounding against the temple's lofty main portal. The old priest leaned forward and called down from the casement: "What do you want, soldiers?"

Their officer looked up and yelled back: "I think you know well, priest. I am Centurion Aemilius Acer; I come with a warrant for the arrest of one Simon of Gitta, a Samaritan renegade who is suspected of murdering Valerius Argonius, Nomarch of Thebes, and burning his ship. Open at once!"

Menophar scowled, hesitated. Then: "The man you call Simon is innocent. Argonius' own evil brought him to his doom—as you well know, Aemilius Acer, for were you not the mad nomarch's chief henchman when he plotted to overthrow Rome's rulership of Egypt by means of dark magic?"

The Roman officer glanced briefly about the courtyard, empty but for himself and his soldiers, but then responded in a firm voice: "Don't stall, bald-head. Open the gate. My troops here are hand-picked for loyalty to me. Moreover, I come with a warrant of power."

"Whose warrant?"

"That of Aulus Flaccus, Governor of Egypt—and *his* mandate comes from Gaius, Emperor of Rome. Flaccus has empowered me to do anything—and I mean *anything*—to capture this Simon of Gitta. Look!" Aemilius waved a parchment in the air. "Send down one of your priests to read it, Menophar, and you will learn that I speak truly."

Again the old priest stood silent, hesitating as long as he dared, his lean fingers gripping the stone window sill. This was more serious than he had thought. He hoped that Simon, his former pupil, was by now fleeing rapidly north through the narrow alleys of Memphis and beyond them into the desert.

"Don't dawdle," shouted Aemilius. "Yours is a stout temple, but I can order up an entire legion from Alexandria if necessary. Are you prepared for such a siege, old priest?"

Menophar was not. He sent down an underling priest and, when informed that Aemilius' warrant appeared authentic, reluctantly admitted the detachment.

While the troops began to search the temple, Aemilius Acer, accompanied by two of his legionaries, met with Menophar alone in the priest's high chamber.

"Do not fear, Egyptian," said the centurion, seating himself in the room's only chair—a spare but ancient and valuable antique. I want only the magician Simon, not you. Tell me where he is and you will be richly rewarded."

"I do not know where he is. He was here, but now he is gone. Moreover, he is skilled in the art of disguises; you would not find him even were I able to tell you his whereabouts."

"Not even if I should offer you a great deal of money?"

Menophar pretended to ponder for a moment. "How much?" he asked finally.

Aemilius' handsome yet hard features relaxed into a grin. "Name your own price. The Emperor Gaius has offered a huge reward for this Simon of Gitta. Moreover—just between you and me—Governor Flaccus has fallen somewhat from the imperial favor since the death of Emperor Tiberius, who was his friend and patron; he would love to present Simon to Gaius, thereby gaining the latter's indebtedness and so ensuring his own continuance as governor of Egypt."

"No power is secure save that which comes from within," said Menophar, his voice and dark eyes emotionless.

"By Hades, don't pull that mystic tripe on me!" snarled Aemilius, rising. "This Simon whom you shelter had a hand not only in Argonius' recent death but also in the death of the Emperor Tiberius last year. I suspect you know something about that, Menophar, but I won't press it. I'll say only that if you do not turn Simon of Gitta over to me, I am authorized to ransack this temple and slay every priest and acolyte in it—which is exactly what I will do."

Menophar paled slightly, though his features remained impassive. "This is one of Egypt's most ancient and revered temples," he said sternly. "Should you thus profane it, the people of the land would rise in rebellion."

"The people?" Aemilius spat on the tiled floor. "That would be a shame, for then our legions would have to blade them down by the thousands, and that would cost Rome a great deal of money. She might even have to import Syrian slaves to harvest Egypt's grain for herself. Gaius would not like to see Rome incur such an expense, and he is not known for his restraint when he is angered. Nor am I, old priest."

Though Menophar maintained his outward composure, his heart sank. The centurion's hawk-like features were hard, merciless. Menophar read men well, and he knew this one was not bluffing.

"Well, Menophar, which is it to be—Simon delivered to me, or Egypt running red with blood?"

There was but one answer. With an effort that was almost an agony the old priest said, "I will lead you to Simon if I can."

The Roman grinned, then sat back down and laughed. "I think that wrenched your guts a bit, sphinx-face! But you're a wise man, and maybe an honest one. Now that I've declared my official mission, we can relax. Order us some wine, and perhaps we can arrange a bargain more to your liking—one that will endanger neither Egypt nor your precious Simon."

Menophar betrayed surprise despite himself. "There is no wine here—"

"No matter. We'll bargain better clear-headed." Aemilius Acer opened a large pouch at his belt and drew forth a tightly rolled scroll. "The Nomarch Argonius did indeed study dark magic, as you mentioned so loudly in the courtyard, and while assisting him I saw enough to learn that the powers he pursued were not illusions. As governor of Thebes he was able to acquire a number of ancient books containing magical knowledge from Egypt's earliest days. Most of these perished, I suspect, in the mysterious fire that destroyed his ship some weeks ago." The centurion smiled, struck his left palm with the scroll he held in his right hand. "Most—but not all."

Menophar, who had begun to feel a slight relief, suddenly experienced a tingling chill. "What scroll is that in your hand?"

"A partial Greek translation of a work which I think you know well. It was in a box of personal effects which Argonius left in my care the very day before he perished; doubtless he overlooked it. It was written long ago by one Luveh-Keraph, a priest of the cat-goddess Bast."

The old priest's chill deepened. Luveh-Keraph's *Scroll of Bubastis* contained dark and disturbing lore handed down from Khem's earliest centuries and even the forgotten Stygian centuries preceding them. Only the most learned of Egypt's priests were supposed to know of its existence, let alone its contents. Menophar's own scroll-shelves contained a near-complete copy in the original Khemite hieratic script, including the dangerous "Black Rites" section deleted from most copies, but he was disciplined enough not to glance in its direction.

"I—I've heard of the work," he said, allowing a touch of worry to creep into his voice. "If the Nomarch Argonius attempted any of the magical spells within it, he was unwise, and perhaps that is why he and his ship perished in fire. Only an adept would dare to probe such dark things—or a fool."

"That's where you come in," said the grinning Aemilius. "And don't play *me* for a fool. I've no doubt, Menophar, that you have a complete copy hidden somewhere in this place, which is said to be, as you pointed out, one of the oldest fanes in Egypt. Well, I'll leave that copy with you, never fear." Again the Roman slapped his left palm with the scroll he held. "I'm interested only in *this* portion of it, which the good nomarch inadvertently left to me."

Menophar did not doubt that Aemilius had stolen it. Inwardly he shuddered at the thought of such a thing, even in partial translation, in the hands of this ruthless, untutored centurion to whom Egypt's foolish governor had given so much authority. Then a thought struck him.

"How did Argonius, a Roman Equestrian, manage to translate that scroll from Egyptian into Greek?"

"He hired an underling priest of Thebes, who is now dead," said Aemilius. "But now let's get down to business. This scroll says that Egypt's greatest treasure is hidden but a few miles north of here, beneath the great Sphinx. You will lead us to it."

Menophar gasped, his composure shattered. "The Treasure of Horemkhu! But you don't understand—"

"Enough." Aemilius Acer scowled sternly. "Don't try to fool me, priest. Every field-hand in Egypt has heard of the vast treasure that lies somewhere beneath the Sphinx or the pyramids. I used to doubt these tales, thinking them the usual lore of hopeful and ignorant peasants—but now, having read of the treasure in this ancient document penned by one of your land's most learned sorcerers, I doubt no longer."

"You *are* a fool!" hissed Menophar, no longer even trying to maintain his inscrutability. "The blackest secrets of Khem's history lie hid beneath the Sphinx and the Three Pyramids, which were carved and built before the pharaohs, before the Stygians—aye, before even the first man built his first mud hut!"

The Roman laughed harshly. "You're a good actor, Menophar, but I'm not one of your superstitious peasants. Luveh-Keraph writes that the secret of the Sphinx—the secret of Egypt's greatest treasure—is handed down through the highest priests of the land's most ancient temples. That means you, friend—don't deny it. Now, lead us to the treasure and I'll forget all about ransacking this temple and the reward Gaius has offered for Simon of Gitta."

Menophar composed himself with an effort. "You would defy Flaccus, the governor of Egypt, and even the Emperor—?"

"Why not? With the greatest treasure of Egypt, I could bribe Gaius' own legions away from him, and," Aemilius tapped the scroll in his hand, "—with the powers Argonius sought to control, no other armies could stand against me. Or, rather, against *us*, Menophar—for you would be foolish to deny me your aid. We could achieve great power working together."

"You're mad—like so many of the untutored who have delved into ancient sorceries more deeply than was good for them."

The Roman abruptly stood up, his features again hard and stern, and strode to the open window. "Come here, priest, and look outside."

Menophar did so, foreboding in his heart. Below, in the courtyard, he saw the company of soldiers, a score of them, with drawn swords. Nearby, white-robed and ranged motionless along one wall, were all the priests and acolytes who had been on duty in the main temple, some thirty of them.

"Look well upon your underlings, Menophar, for unless you do my bidding you shall see them alive no more."

The old priest swallowed. "What would you have me do?"

"Tonight is the night of the full moon nearest the spring equinox—the night when, according to the *Scroll of Bubastis*, an instructed adept may open the hidden way beneath the Sphinx. A blood-sacrifice is required—"

"You know not what you ask! Forces could be unleashed—"

"Silence! I warned you not to play me for a superstitious fool." Aemilius raised his arm and yelled out to an officer below: "Decurion Sporus, begin your appointed task!"

The decurion saluted, then gestured to two legionaries who immediately grabbed one of the youngest acolytes—a lad perhaps sixteen years of age—and hauled him away from the wall, each of them holding him firmly by one arm. The officer stepped forward, bared short sword gleaming in his right hand. The youth screamed madly as the soldiers tipped him forward, struggling and kicking. Then, expertly, the decurion swung; the blade flashed and the screams abruptly ended as the youth's head spun away and rolled on the stone flags.

Casually the soldiers flung down the body; it twitched slightly while blood gushed from its severed neck.

"How's that for a blood-sacrifice?" snarled Aemilius. "Shall I bid my men continue?"

For a fleeting instant fury blazed in Menophar's dark eyes. In the next instant, however, those eyes had set as hard as the Roman's own and his features had become as expressionless as those of a stone-carved pharaoh.

"No, centurion," he said, his voice level. "Slay no more. I see that you are a commander who must be obeyed. Tonight I shall open for you the way to the treasure of Horemkhu."

Simon of Gitta, ragged-cloaked and with a slender walking-stick in hand, hurried northward with long, smooth strides that wasted no energy. For more than half the day he had hastened thus, the muddy Nile far away across the fields to his right, the cliffs marking the edge of the Libyan Desert close upon his left. His angular, high-cheekboned face, formerly clean-shaven, was now half hidden by a scraggly brown beard, while his dark locks were concealed by the folds of a soiled linen turban.

The trail he followed abruptly led up to the desert plateau, bringing into full view the three enormous pyramids which sat there. Despite their familiarity he felt, as always, a tingling awe at their looming presence—an awe inspired not only by their overwhelming, superhuman grandeur but also by the things he had read of them in Menophar's library of sinister ancient texts. Just to the east of them, apparently half buried in the sands, crouched the enormous lion-bodied, human-headed eidolon of Horemkhu, which the Greeks and Romans called the Sphinx.

Simon saw two men approaching. As they drew near he recognized them as guides who made their daytime living showing travelers the pyramids and reciting to them what purported to be Egyptian history; by night, he suspected, they plied more sinister trades. Both wore soiled linen caftans and turbans not unlike Simon's.

As they drew near, the Samaritan allowed his stride to become slightly shuffling, his deep-set eyes to shift and wander a trifle bewilderedly.

"Well, well, Sinuhe," said the shorter of the pair—a scruffy-bearded man whose beady dark eyes and prominent curved nose made him resemble a rat. "What luck! Kabir and I have been hoping all day to run across you."

"Aye," said Kabir, a man as tall as Simon, lean and wiry, whose stubbly face was both darkly handsome and sinister. "The month is over. Today is the day you must pay up."

"Pay? Pay?" Simon jiggled his head nervously, avoiding the eyes of the two men. "I have hired no one."

"Don't act stupid," said the short man. "I think you're smarter than you've let on, Sinuhe—if that's your true name. We've told you often enough lately that half of your take goes to the Guides' Fellowship. So, take that pouch off your belt and let's see how much is in it."

Simon recognized extortion when he saw it, but he merely touched the pouch with his left hand and said in a trembling voice, "It is mine, Arfad. Please let me keep it, for tomorrow I must travel. I will go away and not return. You and the others will lose no more customers to me."

"No, indeed we shall not." Arfad laughed harshly. "When you first arrived here, Sinuhe, we thought you too addle-minded to be a competent swindler of tourists, but we were wrong. We thought *we* had some tall tales to tell, but yours top them all—and now, every rich sightseeing fool who hires you comes back for more. They come to *you*, who are not even an Egyptian, despite your name! Where did you ever hear such stories, Sinuhe? Like that one, for instance, about the Eater of the Dead who dwells beneath the Sphinx?"

"I—I do not hear these tales. I dream them."

"Ha!" barked Kabir, drawing a long, curve-bladed knife. "You *seem* crazy, you jackal, but your craziness has gotten you a lot of money this last month—more than any of the rest of us has taken in despite all our experience. You're a good actor, whoever you are, but not good enough to fool us forever."

"I—I will leave tomorrow."

"Yes, we know," said Arfad, drawing a knife similar to Kabir's, "for today we learned that the rich Greek, Spargos of Megalopolis, has hired you to tell your tales tonight at a party he plans to hold in front of the Sphinx. Such parties are infrequent, Sinuhe, and they bring in a lot of money."

"Aye," snarled Kabir, "—money that should go into honest Egyptian purses. So, *Sinuhe*, hand over that pouch and we'll let you keep half of what Spargos pays you tonight. That alone should enable you to travel far."

"You—you would *rob* me?" cried Simon, feigning astonishment and indignation, clumsily staggering back a step while shaking his thin walking-stick at the pair like a wagging finger.

"Very well, then," said Arfad, teeth flashing in a wide grin from his stubbly beard. "If you'd rather not travel, you may stay here—forever!"

"Forever!" shouted Kabir.

The pair leaped forward, and in that instant Simon's clumsiness vanished; his short walking-stick, whirled with the expertise of gladiator training, smacked sharply against Arfad's wrist and sent his curved knife flying. Arfad squealed shrilly and leaped back. In the same instant Simon twisted smoothly, barely avoiding Kabir's blade as its point ripped the fabric of his tunic; his left fist cracked soundly against the side of the Egyptian's head, sending the man flopping unconscious to the sand.

Snatching up Kabir's dagger, Simon whirled, crouching—but Arfad was already dashing away among the boulders along the top of the bluff, squealing like a terrified rock-rabbit. Simon hurried after him, but immediately the dwarfish cutpurse vanished over the rim; the sound of his scrambling flight came up faintly from the narrow draw that led steeply downward.

"He runs fast for such a little twerp," muttered Simon to himself. "Well, maybe I've blown my cover, but it's not long till sundown. Arfad's not likely to stop running for awhile, and this other cutthroat will be out for a few hours. I'll hide amid the tombs until after dark, then join Spargos and his party when the moon comes up. With any luck he'll pay me off before midnight and I'll be well on the road to Memphis before dawn."

Menophar and the Romans left the boat as the sun was touching the western horizon. Its rays glinted briefly on the many gold coins that passed from the hand of Aemilius Acer into that of the skinny, dirty-robed captain, after which the boat silently shoved off and drifted slowly downriver.

Uneasiness stirred again in the old priest's heart. Acer had evidently hired the most disreputable crew he could find along the wharves of Memphis to bring his party here, then had paid them well to vanish away. Obviously the centurion wished to leave no trail for other Roman officials to follow, and Menophar doubted that he himself would be allowed to return to his temple in Memphis or even live to see tomorrow's dawn.

They strode westward in silence along the dikes that bordered the fields and canals where brown-skinned *fellahin*, too weary from the day's toil to exhibit much curiosity about the passing military procession, were preparing to return to their huts. The two dozen legionaries kept themselves in a tight formation about the old priest—as much to hide his white-robed form from the laborers, Menophar guessed, as to prevent his escape.

Finally the fields were left behind and the dikes gave way to a rocky ascent—the edge of the Libyan desert where, with uncanny abruptness, the most fertile land within the Roman Empire gave way to the barren bleakness of stone and sand. A few minutes later they topped the rise and saw, looming close in purple-shadowed grandeur against the last red rays of the vanishing sun, the three monstrous pyramids that had towered there for centuries beyond man's reckoning.

The troop stopped there abruptly, spontaneously, without any command from its leader. Several of the soldiers muttered awed invocations to their various gods, and Menophar saw that even Centurion Aemilius was impressed, though the man strove not to show it.

"Evidently you have not visited this place before," said the priest. "The mass to the right is *Khufu Khut*, the 'Throne of Cheops'; the middle one, no less grand, is *Ur*, 'The Great', appropriated by the pharaoh Khephren to be his memorial; and the smallest of the three is *Hur*, 'The Southernmost', which the pharaoh Menka-ra chose for his tomb and protected with his terrible curse."

"Jupiter!" exclaimed one of the legionaries. "No mortals could have built these—these mountains! Surely the very Titans reared them up—"

"Silence!" snapped Aemilius.

"Yet the man is right," said Menophar evenly. "No humans built these gigantic piles; the three pharaohs I named merely took them for their own use and built their temples, cemeteries, and causeways around them. No, they and the Sphinx, as well as the passageways and caverns deep beneath them, were constructed by monstrous beings in ages long past, and their entrances are guarded by mighty prehuman curses."

"Shut up!" repeated Aemilius. "If you're trying to get on the nerves of my men, it won't work. Where is the Sphinx?"

"There." Menophar pointed straight ahead to where something humped out of the sand.

The centurion, gazing beneath his shading hand at what he had taken to be a natural rock formation, realized that he was staring at a distant human face hewn from living rock and cowled with the headdress of a pharaoh—a calm, staring face whose gigantic features, though indistinct in silhouette, somehow chilled his soul. Though it was still about a third of a mile away, Aemilius felt a strange reluctance to approach more closely.

"We'll rest here, men," he ordered impulsively, then turned and confronted Menophar. The sun had set, though its glow still suffused the world with twilight; the round moon had just risen in the east, golden above far desert hills beyond the Nile—and its light, eerily, seemed to encircle the old priest's head like an aureole.

"That stone face up ahead—that's the Sphinx?

"Aye. Its giant form, hewn in one piece from a solid stone outcropping, was carved before even these mighty pyramids were raised. It is the eidolon of Horemkhu, the Dweller Upon the Horizon, whose worship antedates mankind and whose subterranean realm receives all human souls at the end of life."

"Ha! Then why, priest, does it sport a human face?" The Roman turned, pointed toward the distant, looming head then gasped. The light of the vanished sun behind it was less intense, the moonlight upon its face greater—

"Hades!" blurted the decurion Sporus. "Those features—*they're the same as this priest's!*"

Half a dozen soldiers gripped their sword pommels nervously. Aemilius did likewise—for, as he could now plainly see, the decurion's words were true. Those distant stone features, cold and noble and god-like, judgmental and menacing in gigantic grandeur, were the exact duplicates of those of the priest Menophar!

Even as he fingered his sword hilt, Aemilius heard the old priest chuckling softly, mockingly.

"Do not fear," said Menophar. "That face is the likeness of the pharaoh Khephren, who obliterated the original features and had his own carved in their place. Perhaps that is well—for what man or woman could bear to gaze, living, upon the face of Horemkhu, God of Death?"

"Then why," asked Aemilius tensely, still gripping his sword hilt, "—why do those features so strongly resemble your own?"

"Do they?" Menophar shrugged. "Perhaps it is because Khephren was my ancestor and his traits still run in my blood. Though Ptah's temple is open to acolytes of many ancestries, some of us who are of Egyptian stock go far back. Who can fully trace such things?" He looked around, saw uneasiness on the faces of several of the legionaries. "Surely you Romans are not superstitious!"

"Enough!" said Aemilius firmly. "I see your game, Menophar, but you'll do better by far to cooperate with me than to try to unsettle my men. Come on—we've less than half a mile to go."

Menophar nodded. "Very well, centurion. Nevertheless, we should wait here awhile. Sightseers sometimes linger about the Sphinx until sunset to place offerings upon its altar—the worship of Descending Ra has been found to be good for local business. But few linger after dark. In any case, the—the thing you wish me to do cannot be done until the moon is at least halfway toward the zenith."

Aemilius scowled in thought for a moment, wondering if this priest could be trusted. Menophar knew too many ancient secrets. Yet, the stakes were high—Egypt's greatest treasure—

"Very well," he said finally. "Break out rations, men. Eat and get some rest. We'll bide here two or three hours."

Simon woke from strange dreams. He seemed to recall a pharaoh, whose face resembled that of his old mentor Menophar, telling him strange things, warning him of impending evil, asking his aid, beckoning him down to dark realms....

He sat up, rubbing his eyes. He had slept but lightly and the snatches of dream, vague at best, were already gone beyond recall.

Rising, Simon donned the robe he had used as a blanket, then strode away from the half-buried mud-brick tomb in whose shadow he had slept. The sun was down and the last afterglow was vanishing beyond the western desert. In the east, well above the far-off cliffs which lay like a long wall beyond the Nile, the moon glowed full and silvery. Beneath its light, which made his way plain among the tombs and ruins, Simon continued on toward the great Sphinx.

As he drew near the mighty image he saw its moonlit profile which, as he had often noticed before, resembled that of his mentor. No doubt the memory of that resemblance had helped inspire his recent dreams—for, despite Menophar's mundane explanation, the similarity had never failed to inspire Simon with awe.

Now, drawing nearer still, he noted again that the Sphinx was not really half-buried but rested within an enormous squarish pit from which the sand had been largely cleared. East of its front paws extended an open, stone-floored expanse, also freed from sand, and several human figures moved upon it. Sounds of merriment came to Simon's ears—laughter and snatches of song.

Descending by the gentle slope of sand and stony debris that bounded the cleared space on its eastern side, he joined the eight or ten people gathered there. They were clad in Grecian robes and tunics, and some of them held silver goblets. A score of torches, bracketed upon the stony paws of the Sphinx and the altar that stood between them, augmented the moonlight and gave a flickering tinge of flesh-and-blood color to the scene.

"Sinuhe!" exclaimed a lean, short man with a graying goatee. "You are late. Here—you must quaff a full goblet to make up for lost time. Then you must tell us one of your tales." He snapped his fingers at a young fellow, evidently a slave. "Bring wine for our most excellent guide."

"Oh, Sinuhe!" A young, dark-haired woman whom Simon recognized as the short man's wife ran to him, gripped both of his hands in hers. "You came, as you promised."

"Did you think I wouldn't—?"

"Of course not." She lowered her voice in mock conspiracy. "But Spargos wondered if you would. He said I was a fool to pay you a third in advance. I'm glad he was wrong."

Spargos laughed politely. "Well, you did come, Sinuhe," he said, shaking Simon's hand, "just as my little Catella said you would. I'm glad you didn't disappoint her. This so-called party needs enlivening."

"Did you expect me to run off with your advance?"

"Frankly, I wasn't sure. Come, join us."

Simon could detect no sarcasm in Spargos' comments, only honesty. He accepted the goblet from the young servant, took a long swig from it. The wine was of good quality, soothing to his parched throat. Spargos of Megalopolis was evidently no piker when it came to funding a party, and Simon decided he liked both him and his wife; they were frank of speech and, despite a bit of genteel reserve, respectful and friendly toward their guide and even their own slaves—unlike so many of the haughty Roman and Greek tourists he had guided these last few weeks. Moreover, both were genuinely and deeply interested in Egypt's ancient monuments and the stories Simon told of them.

"Yes, join us." Catella tugged at his arm. "Your cloak is sandy—you must have come many miles across the desert, and I can see that you are thirsty. Have you been gathering more tales of antiquity from scrolls hidden in dusty tombs? Here—finish that goblet and have another."

Simon nodded, smiling. When he had first met Catella he had been somewhat taken aback by her forthright manner. He knew by now, though, that the young woman, though little more than half her scholarly husband's age, was deeply devoted to the man. Her enthusiasm was for Simon's tales, not for him—a facet of her passion for mysterious antiquity, nothing more. An unusual woman, pretty and vivacious, yet dominated by scholarly passions akin to her husband's rather than by flirtatious or maternal ones.

"My wife is trying hard to make this a gala occasion," said Spargos, sipping sparingly from his cup. "However, most of our invited guests have not come, and the atmosphere of this place seems less than conducive to a festive mood. How old did you say the Sphinx is, Sinuhe?"

"No man knows. Some say it and the pyramids are older than Egypt, older even than mankind."

"That is scarcely credible," said Spargos, grinning wryly. "Herodotus tells us that the pyramids were built by the pharaohs Cheops, Chephren, and Mycerinus—"

"But there are still older writings," Catella interrupted, "which explain how these three pharaohs merely appropriated pyramids which already existed, adding divers structures of their own. And the Sphinx, which Herodotus strangely refrains from mentioning at all, is described in these ancient documents as being older still."

Simon, halfway through his second cup of wine, felt a slight uneasiness that dampened its glow. "Might I ask, my lady, what those writings are in which you have read such things?"

"Why, very old ones indeed, or so I was told by the Alexandrian peddler who sold them to me. I think they were stolen from tombs, for they have a faint odor of embalming spices and are very yellow and brittle."

"Papyrus is easily scented and yellowed," Spargos commented dryly, "by those who wish to sell them to gullible collectors. Your documents are in Greek, my dead, and so can be no earlier than the Ptolemys. Anyone could have written them."

"I don't think so, husband," countered the lady, unruffled, "for I doubt your average forger has the imagination or the craft to dream up such things. The writings purport to be fragments of such legendary works as the *Text of Meidum* and the *Scroll of Bubastis*—"

Spargos, daintily sipping his wine, noticed that Simon started slightly. Nevertheless, he said only, "Such titles are well known from Egyptian folk tales of magical wonders. Anyone could have used them."

Simon glanced up at the moonlit face of the Sphinx which loomed so near and massively, then sipped his own wine. He had read from those very books in Menophar's library in the temple of Ptah, and now his uneasiness was deepened. Were strange forces weaving strands of destiny about the Sphinx this night?

"This may not be a good time or place to speak of such things," he ventured.

"Why?" Spargos regarded Simon sharply. "I've just noticed, Sinuhe, that the more wine you drink the more sober you become! Your eyes don't dart about anymore and you've lost that engaging yet half-witted grin you used to sport. And you speak a better Greek than you did yesterday. Did you perhaps get these wild tales of yours from old books similar to those my dear wife has collected?—surely none of the other guides hereabouts tells tales half so entertaining. It wouldn't even surprise me, Sinuhe, if it turned out that you can *read*."

Simon shrugged, deciding that denial was not worth the effort. After all, he would be long gone by sunrise.

"You're a shrewd observer, Spargos. It's true—I m not what I seem. But don't ask who I am or why I chose this way of life for awhile. You're wrong about the old books, though. They're authentic. I've read them—not just in the Greek but in the original Egyptian."

Catella's dark eyes widened in astonishment. "You can do that?" She gripped his arm again and dragged him forward. "Oh, Sinuhe—look here! Only today the workmen we hired unearthed this slab of stone which you see leaning against the altar. So far, we have found none who can read it. Can you?"

Simon peered down at the short stela inscribed with closely written Egyptian hieroglyphics. "It is very old, but—yes, I can."

"Oh!" Catella clapped her hands excitedly. "Please, Sinuhe, read it to us in Greek. Please!"

Simon nodded. By the light of the flickering torches, with Spargos and the others looking on in fascinated silence, he slowly read aloud:

I, Khaphra, Pharaoh of Khem, Lord of the Two Lands, Beloved of Horemkhu, cause this to be written that those who shall seek here in later ages may be warned or instructed, according to their natures and the nature of that which they seek. For know, O seekers, that mine eyes are even now upon you and that they read the intent of your souls.

To those who seek the olden wisdom, I say: My dreams shall instruct you as you sleep here upon the sands beneath the moon; and, should you do even as I instruct, you shall attain unto realms of wonder and the gods, even as did I. But to those who would despoil my tomb, thinking to take forth mere treasure for their own worldly aggrandizement, I say: Deluded fools, turn back!—else doom surely awaits you. Your bodies shall be devoured by the Devourer, even Horemkhu, Lord of Death, and your souls shall wander lost in his black domains forever.

For I, Khaphra, like those pharaohs before me, delved deeply into the secrets of Those who of old built the pyramids, even Those who did in the dawn-time descend to Khem from the starry bosom of Nout. And, like those before me, I became Their servant. Yet then, delving still more deeply into olden lore than any pharaoh before me, I learned at last the secret of Horemkhu, Lord of Death, and of those primal ones who carved His image, and the chambers beneath it, before even the Pyramid Builders descended from the stars. And, having sacrificed to Horemkhu in that manner which He had not known since the forgotten days of Stygia and Acheron, I became His Favored One who shall not die as die other men, but who shall guard Khem's greatest treasure in His name for all time.

Therefore did Horemkhu instruct me to replace His olden features with those of a man, even with mine own, that His worship might be resumed the more readily by humankind.

And now, unto those who shall one day seek Khem's greatest treasure, as did I, and seek also to understand its true nature, I, Khaphra, say this: Perform the blood sacrifice and the rites, even those which I have instructed my priests to preserve in the sacred temples of Khem throughout the ages. And then, having performed them, you shall enter....

Simon paused. His hand, gently fingering the graven hieroglyphs, trembled slightly.

"Go on!" cried Catella, gripping his arm. "Please, Sinuhe—"

"I cannot. The last few lines are obliterated—deliberately, from the looks of it. Probably it's just as well."

"How can you think that? I wanted so much to know the ending!"

"You're amazing, Sinuhe!" Spargos cut in. "And that's true even if you were just faking that reading. Strange, how closely this correlates with the things you've told us, and the things my Catella has read in her old documents. And, what about this matter of 'Khem's greatest treasure?' "

"*Aye—the treasure!*" a voice screeched raucously. "*At them, lads—cut them down!*"

Simon whirled at the menacing screech, whipping out his sharp-bladed *sica*. A score of lean, brown-skinned rogues were charging down the sand-slope, brandishing knives and twirling looped ropes, and in the forefront were two Simon recognized—Arfad and Kabir.

"Spargos, rally your servants!" he yelled. "Defend yourselves—!"

Then the rushing rat-pack was upon them, stabbing and slashing.

Spargos' few guests, bleating in terror, turned tail and fled between the paws of the Sphinx; lean, loping figures followed them, knives gleaming, and instants later death-shrieks rang out from the shadows. Spargos and his wife, protected by four of their loyal staff-bearing slaves, crouched back in terror against the stonework of the Sphinx s left paw.

So much Simon glimpsed before a wave of attackers rushed him. He ducked a slash and countered; the curved blade of his *sica*, nearly as long as a Roman short sword and designed for arena combat, shore halfway through an attacker's neck; the man flopped to the sand, throat arteries spurting twin jets of blood.

"Take him *alive*, fools!" shrieked Arfad. "And those rich Greeks, too— they're all worth money!"

A cast noose settled about Simon's neck. Just as it drew taut he severed it, and his follow-through stroke spilled the guts of another assailant. But other ropes were looping toward him and he could not dodge or sever them fast enough. He heard screams, knew that the slaves of Spargos were being butchered. Then two nooses simultaneously gripped him, one about the shoulders, the other about his sword-wrist, and jerked him off his feet.

Instantly the pack was upon him. Simon's left fist smashed the jaw of a third assailant, but he could make no headway against a band of of nearly twenty sinewy barbarians, and in another moment his hands were bound behind his back, his knees bent to their fullest extent and his wrists and ankles tightly lashed together with unyielding cords.

The ruffians drew back, and Simon saw that Spargos and his wife had also been bound, though not as elaborately as he. Their servants lay motionless, blood staining the sand about them, together with the bodies of two of their attackers.

"Good job, men!" said Arfad, swaggering forward. He stooped and untied the money-pouch from Simon's belt. His men were similarly relieving Spargos, Catella, and the slain guests of their cash and valuables.

"You won't get away with this, you—you bandits!" sputtered the little Greek, his goatee bristling.

"Bandits?" Arfad chuckled. "The Romans will not think so when we present your—guide—to them. I think they will consider you guilty of harboring a criminal. No doubt they will pay us a great reward when we turn the three of you over to them."

"You're insane!"

"You think so? Then look!" Arfad gripped Simon's turban with one hand, his beard with the other, then abruptly ripped both away and cast them aside. Catella gasped. The man she had known as Sinuhe was cleanshaven, square-jawed, dark-haired—and younger by a decade than he had formerly seemed. Moreover, she now saw a dark, sinister intelligence in his deep-set eyes which were fixed in hate on the short Egyptian who led the bandit gang.

"Don't you know who this man is?" yelled Arfad. "He is Simon of Gitta, the Samaritan magician on whose head the Emperor Caligula has set a great price. He was clever at disguise, but not clever enough to fool me. Several weeks ago, after committing a great crime in Memphis, he came here pretending to be a guide but refusing to pay his honest fee to the Guides' Fellowship. He posed as a half-wit, yet told strange stories about the pyramids to his patrons—stories which none of us had ever heard. He lived in no local village, preferring to camp in the desert, and every few days vanished away altogether for a day or two. On one of these occasions Kabir and I followed him and found that he went to the temple of Ptah in Memphis, which confirmed my suspicions. Now they are doubly confirmed, for it is said that this Simon is also an escaped gladiator—and indeed he fights like one!"

"Perhaps we should kill him," said Kabir, scowling and fingering his knife. "A sorcerer who also fights like a gladiator is doubly dangerous. Surely the Romans will pay as much for him dead as alive—"

"No, for Caligula has a personal grudge against him and wishes to see him die by torture. But enough of this talk. Lift him up, and also these foolish Greeks who employed him—with any luck, the Guild will be awarded Spargos' estate in Alexandria for having captured Simon. We'll turn the three of them over to the Roman authorities at dawn, unless," Arfad bent closely over Simon's bound form, leering and grinning, "—*unless* they choose instead to tell us the secret of Egypt's greatest treasure."

Simon, straining his bonds, glared up at the rat-faced Arfad. "Fool! There is no such treasure—"

"There is!" Arfad kicked the bound man savagely. "Did not you and these rich Greeks discuss it even as we listened? Don't deny it. Every Egyptian has heard of a treasure hidden beneath the Sphinx, and evidently this woman has discovered ancient writings which reveal the way to it. Well, here's my offer: Lead us to the treasure and we'll let the three of you go, maybe even give you a big cut; refuse, and we'll still get rich by turning you over to the Romans—"

"That won't be necessary!" bellowed a stentorian voice. *"Hack them down, soldiers of Rome!"*

Simon, twisting painfully in his bonds, saw a score or more of sword-wielding legionaries rushing down the slope. *Madness!* This was the second time such a thing had happened within a space of minutes—

Then the two groups clashed. For a moment the mad melée of battle raged—blades rang together, curses and death-screams shrilled. A body flopped on the stone a mere arm's length from Simon, and he saw that it was Kabir, face twisted in death-agony, blood gushing from a great chest wound—

Suddenly the Egyptian rat-pack scattered and fled, leaving at least a third of their number gashed and bleeding on the stone pave. They dashed off around the Sphinx on both sides, and immediately the disciplined Romans split into two groups and pursued them.

As the roar and clash of renewed battle sounded, Simon set to work on the ropes that bound him. Despite his training by Persian escape artists, he could tell that he faced a difficult task. The Egyptian rogues—some of them doubtless amateur kidnappers and slave-procurers—had tied him about as securely as he had ever been tied. This would take time, and he had little of that—

Suddenly he realized that he had no time at all. Four men were standing over him. Two were legionaries, another a Roman official, and the fourth—to Simon's amazement—was his old mentor Menophar.

"Forgive me, Simon," said the priest. "I had hoped that you would be gone by now. I had no choice."

The legionaries had quickly laid hold of Spargos and Catella and cut free their legs, though not their arms. Now they roughly ushered the pair to their commander.

"What shall we do with them now, sir?"

"Why, keep them," said Aemilius. "Did not the rat-pack leader say that the woman had discovered a way to the treasure?"

"He did indeed, Commander."

The sound of battle, which had diminished, now died out altogether. The Romans had apparently driven the bandit-gang into the *cul-de-sac* behind the Sphinx and slaughtered them there. A minute later Simon's suspicions were confirmed as a score of legionaries emerged from the Sphinx's shadow into the torchlight, singly or in small groups, their blades dark with blood. Their number seemed undiminished, a fact which Simon did not find surprising. Roman legionaries were the most formidable troops in the world, and these men of Aemilius' were doubtless hand-picked. Little wonder that they had prevailed unscathed against the undisciplined pack of Egyptian cutthroats.

A decurion strode forward, his right fist clenched in the hair of a human head whose severed neck dripped blood. In the torchlight Simon recognized the head's features as those of the rodent-faced Arfad.

"We've killed all the bandits, Commander Aemilius," the decurion announced, "and executed their ringleader, as you ordered."

"Good, Sporus." Aemilius grinned. "Good. Give it to me." He snatched the head from his subordinate's hand, strode between the gigantic paws of the Sphinx, and plunked it down atop the stone altar which stood there. Then, turning, he cried: "Well, Menophar, how's all *this* for a sacrifice to old Horemkhu? More than twenty rogues butchered and bleeding about his image and the head of their leader gracing his altar! I'll wager he's not enjoyed such a sacrifice since the Pharaoh Khephren revived the rites of Stygia here."

"You may well be right," said the old priest somberly.

Catella, trembling in the grip of two Romans, suddenly cried out: "Gods—that evil priest! *He has the features of the Sphinx!*"

"Nonsense, my dear," said Spargos evenly. "There is some slight resemblance, perhaps, but no more than one might expect in an Egyptian of ancient lineage." He turned to Aemilius. "I thank you, commander, for rescuing us. Would you now be so kind as to have your men unbind our arms? These ropes are most uncomfortable."

Aemilius ignored him. "Decurion Brutus, you and two other men stay here. Guard Simon of Gitta and this rich Greek well—they'll be worth a lot to us if the Egyptian treasure proves to be a fool's quest." Then, turning to Menophar: "All right, priest, lead on. As for this woman, we'll bring her along. If she really has read much in the old writings, she may prove useful."

Menophar nodded, turned toward the Sphinx and made a few brief, intricate passes with his hands, then said to Aemilius: "Follow me."

The Romans, led by the priest, vanished around the northern side of the sand-slope.

When they had gone, Simon set to work upon his bonds. Those intricate hand-gestures of Menophar's, ostensibly directed ritually to the Sphinx, had actually been a sign language which conveyed a message to Simon—one which made him break out into a cold sweat.

For Menophar intended to open the Way.

Then he heard Spargos saying plaintively to the guards: Why did they take my wife? Why have you not unbound us? If it's a ransom you want, I'll see that you are well paid. Free me now, soldiers, and I'll pay you more than you could ever expect to gain by pursuing some foolish Egyptian legend—"

The decurion's fist smacked crisply into Spargos face. The little Greek sprawled heavily to the stone, then lay trembling and twitched for a moment, his face not far from Simon's. His eyes registered shock, blood trickled from his lips and stained his ridiculous goatee.

"My Catella!" he moaned. "Why did they take her? What does the commander intend to do with her—?"

The three legionaries, restlessly pacing, ignored him. Their boots scuffed against grit and pebbles; their shadows grew shorter as the moon rose toward the zenith.

Forcing all thoughts from his mind, Simon focused his attention upon his bonds and continued to work on them.

For perhaps an hour, under Menophar's direction, the soldiers cleared rubble and boulders from the base of an ancient wall. The work was hot and close, for they were within a narrow passageway to which the priest had led them by way of an obscure cleft in the ruins outside, through which only one man at a time might pass.

"What place is this?" asked Aemilius as the work proceeded.

"A temple which once stood in front of the Sphinx. It, too, was built by those who preceded mankind—as you can see by the enormousness of the hewn stones which comprise these walls. After Stygia fell the sands buried this temple for ten thousand years; the Pharaoh Khephren uncovered it, together with the Sphinx, but since his dynasty it has lain buried for nearly three thousand years more."

Aemilius, outwardly calm, felt his inward arrogance shaken. Rome could boast but a few paltry centuries of history.

"Why do we clear this wall?" he demanded. "The recess in front of us seems to be merely one of those many 'false doors' that were carved by the ancients to symbolize gateways to eternal realms."

"Aye, and mere symbols most of them are. Yet the most ancient ones, such as this, are *not* mere symbols. The Pharaoh Khephren, and the pharaohs before him, still knew some of the lost arts the Stygians inherited from Those who came down from the stars in the dawn-time. They knew how to construct gates into other realms, other worlds. Such is the gate which lies before you, Commander Aemilius. Even a legion of your most skilled siege engineers would not easily bring it down, and only an adept of the Ancient Way, such as myself, can cause it to open for you."

"Well, get to it, then," said the centurion impatiently, "for I see that my soldiers have now cleared all the rubble away."

Menophar nodded, then walked forward and settled down, cross-legged, before the lofty recess carved into the rock. From his robe he drew a small bronze brazier and set it on the floor before him, then filled it with what appeared to be herbs.

"Now, Commander," he said, "give me your torch."

Aemilius, wondering, complied. Menophar applied the torch to the herbs, which commenced to glow and smolder. A pungent odor filled the narrow passage.

"What is that substance you burn?" demanded the centurion suspiciously.

"The seeds and petals of the Yellow Lotus. It will enable my spirit to go forth and inhabit the body of Horemkhu, the great Sphinx, whence I may control the opening of this portal. Be silent now, for I must concentrate."

Bending over the tiny brazier, Menophar breathed deeply of the smoke rising from it, then sat erect and gazed intently at the high recess in the stone. For many long minutes he sat thus, motionless as a statue. Aemilius, nervous at first, relaxed slightly. The fumes were not toxic, evidently, or the priest would not breathe them into his lungs in such concentrated form. He felt himself relaxing, even exulting inwardly; soon Egypt's greatest treasure would be his—

Suddenly, without warning, a vertical line of blackness appeared in the wall of stone before the Romans. It widened; the "false door", evidently not false at all, swung inward slowly, almost soundlessly save for a slight scraping of sand particles beneath it—and then a lofty black aperture gaped before the astonished soldiers.

"By Pallas!" gasped one of them. "What magic is this? Has the priest opened the very gate to Hades?"

"No!" cried Aemilius excitedly. "Rather, the gate to wealth, fame, power!" He turned to Menophar. "Get up, priest, and lead us on to—"

But Menophar was no longer sitting upright as if in spiritual contemplation. Instead, he was sprawled on the stone floor as if in death.

"Get up!" yelled Aemilius, leaning forward and shaking the priest's shoulder. *"Get up!"*

"Is he dead?" asked Sporus.

Aemilius rose to his full height. "He seems so, but I suspect not. He is in a trance—a state these tricky Egyptian priests are adept in achieving. But it matters not—he has opened the Way. All we need do now is go forward and find the treasure."

"And leave him here?" said the decurion. "Suppose his spirit causes the door to close behind us, trapping us in yonder blackness for all eternity?

"A good thought, Sporus. We'll carry him with us; then, if we're trapped, he'll be trapped also. In addition, we'll roll that broken column fragment into the aperture to block the door in case it tries to close. Hurry, now, men—I want to find that treasure and I think you do also."

Spargos, having given up his struggles in despair, suddenly felt supple fingers working at his bonds. In a moment, incredibly, he felt them slacken and fall away. Straining to peer back over his shoulder, he saw the guide he had known as Sinuhe lying close to him, back to back, still apparently bound, ankles drawn up close to wrists.

"Do not move or speak," whispered Simon. "I am free. When one of the guards comes near, ask in a faint voice for water—wait! Here comes one now. Do it!"

The Greek's bewilderment lasted but a moment. Hope sparked within him. He moaned as the Roman came close, then gasped hoarsely, "Soldier—I need water."

"Water, is it?" said the guard, bending close. "I'll piss in your face if you don't shut up—"

Simon's right hand shot out, stiffened fingers crunching into the base of the Roman's throat. The legionary went down, wheezing and strangling, and even as he hit the ground Simon whipped the man's sword from its sheath and sprang erect. Instantly the decurion Brutus and the other guard, yelling in astonishment, drew their own blades and charged. For a few seconds steel rang on steel in a flurry too rapid for Spargos to follow, but he saw that Simon was being driven back; the Romans, though taken by surprise, were skilled fighters and had rallied instantly.

"Die, Samaritan!" yelled Brutus.

Furiously, without thought, Spargos dove at the legs of the decurion and gripped them. Brutus roared as he flopped forward upon the stone pavement, then twisted about, glaring furiously at the little Greek. Spargos heard a death-yell, the clatter of another armored body falling to the pave—but then twisted frantically to avoid the stroke of the decurion's rising sword, realizing even as he did so that it was no use—

Then, incredibly, Brutus' mouth gaped, spouting blood; his sword clattered on the stone as the tip of another blade protruded a hand's length from his breast. He pitched sideways and lay still.

"Zeus!" gasped Spargos, striving shakily to rise. "Then it's true, Sinuhe—I mean Simon—that you were trained to fight as a gladiator?"

"Aye." Simon helped the little Greek to his feet. "Romans slew my parents in Samaria, then sold me into the arena—but I escaped, and since then many a Roman has paid for my training with his life. And yet, Spargos, I might have died even now but for your aid."

"And my Catella may still die!" cried the Greek, anguish in his voice. "That mad centurion seems to think that her knowledge of ancient writings may help him in his foolish quest for treasure."

"Foolish indeed," said Simon. "But I have no time to explain more. Stay here."

So saying, he snatched up one of the burning torches and ran around to the north of the sand-slope. In a few moments he found the crevice in the rock wall and glided cautiously within, and a moment later was standing in a narrow corridor and gazing at the monstrous black aperture, propped open by a fragment of a massive limestone column, which gaped in its western wall.

Footsteps sounded. Simon turned and saw that Spargos had followed him. The Greek held a torch in his left hand, a Roman short sword in his right.

"I've practiced swordplay in the gymnasium," he said. "I may not be a gladiator, but I'm not useless—and if I can't help you in rescuing my wife, I'll at least die trying."

Simon nodded, feeling admiration for the man. "Come on, then—hurry!"

They stepped through the aperture and immediately confronted a blank wall. The corridor in which they stood extended to the right and left.

"Which way shall we go?" asked Spargos.

"It doesn't matter. Each way leads to a long descending stairway which ends at a pillared hallway far below. Come—we'll take the north route to our right. And go carefully."

A few moments later they were descending a flight of stairs evidently carved from the living stone—stairs which seemed to descend interminably.

"How do you know of these passageways, Sinu—Simon?" asked Spargos, amazed.

"From ancient books in the library of my mentor Menophar. Do not speak above a whisper—we don't know how far ahead the Romans might be, and these passageways carry echoes far."

The steps continued down, down into the blackness, and Spargos felt a crawling fear as the descent continued. He had heard the tales, told by money-seeking guides, of vast chambers beneath the Sphinx, yet never had he credited them until now.

At last the stairway doubled back upon itself, descended a bit farther—and suddenly ended in a vast hall. The blank wall to their left, Spargos noticed, extended ahead of them to the barely discernible steps of a descending stairway identical to the one behind them; to the right, a double row of lofty stone pillars vanished away into blackness.

Simon gestured, and Spargos followed him westward, between the twin rows of pillars. Their torches illuminated only the lower parts of lofty columns which vanished upward into illimitable darkness.

"This is the Reception Chamber," said Simon, "in which the acolytes of Stygia's ancient priesthood were initiated ten thousand years ago. We are now farther beneath the ground than the Sphinx is in height, and those pillars and the roof they uphold are carved from solid rock."

Spargos' torch trembled in his hand. For the first time he wondered whether mere humans could indeed have constructed the pyramids, the Sphinx, and this monstrous underground chamber. Yet his next question to Simon was a practical one: "Where are the Romans?"

"Ahead, evidently, and proceeding at a rapid pace. Follow me."

The pillared hall led westward for perhaps two hundred feet, then opened into a huge circular area about a hundred feet in diameter. Pillars flanked its walls; its central space was empty and, like the grand hallway, its ceiling was lost in darkness.

"This is the temple," said Simon, "where the ancient acolytes were instructed in the most ancient mysteries of Stygia and Acheron. Beyond this place, say the ancient writings, it is death for the uninitiated to venture."

"Is that true?" Spargos' sword trembled as he gripped it more tensely. "If so, then the Romans must be doomed, and—alas!—my poor Catella with them, for they have all evidently ventured beyond here. Tell me, Simon—are *you* one of the initiated?"

"No," said Simon uneasily. "I know only what I have read in the old books my mentor possesses."

Spargos swallowed nervously. "The same old books, evidently, that Catella was so avid to collect and read." Here in the aeon-old darkness his rational assessment of the world seemed to have left him; he felt the weight of an ancient, brooding menace. "What shall we do, then, Simon?"

"I'm going on. I must rescue my mentor if I can, but I suggest that you go back."

"Not while there's a chance that my wife lives!"

Simon nodded, then led the way onward, his liking for the little Greek augmented. He, too, had once lost a loved woman to the Romans, but had had no chance to fight them in order to save her life. Now, though the chances were against it, he found himself hoping that he might somehow help Spargos and his wife....

They left the great circular temple and followed a short corridor which widened suddenly into a chamber where five black doorways gaped in the west wall. Here they smelled a strange odor, as of naphtha and bitumen mingled with embalming spices, and felt a chill draft of air from the doorways.

"Gods!" muttered Spargos despairingly. "Which way shall we go?"

Simon racked his memory. "The middle three tunnels go to regions beneath the Three Pyramids. It would be death to proceed any of those ways, for beyond them lie the Caverns of Set. The other ways lead to twin staircases that descend to the Lair of the Sphinx. I fear it is death to proceed there also, but we must if we are to attempt to rescue my mentor and your wife, for look—fresh pitch has dripped within the right entranceway. Here the Romans have surely passed in their mad quest for the treasure of Horemkhu."

"Mad," repeated Spargos. "You think, then, that there is no such treasure?"

"There is," said Simon, "yet no man who comes upon it shall live."

The Greek looked into Simon's shadowed eyes and saw no madness there, only grim concern and a touch of fear.

"Let's hurry, then," he urged, "and hope they haven't yet found it."

Simon nodded, then hastened into the right-hand tunnel. This time it was a steeply inclined plane rather than a stairway—a straight passageway carved through the solid rock, smoothly descending, doubling back upon itself occasionally as it led ever more deeply into the darkness of inner earth....

Catella stared about her in terrified awe. She and her Roman captors had descended through pillared halls and endless inclined passageways to incredible depths, until she feared that they were nearing the realm of Hades and would never again regain the outer air. Finally they had descended a long, straight flight of stairs, a cliff-high wall on their right and a vast, columned gulf on their left. Now they stood upon a stone floor amid a ranked forest of titan stone pillars whose tops could not be seen and whose bases were carved with strange and enormous hieroglyphs. The widely spaced columns, each perhaps three man-lengths in diameter, stretched away in ranks farther than the light of twenty torches could reach. The natron-scented wind, which had increased as they descended, now carried an almost charnel odor.

"By all the gods, Commander Aemilius!" exclaimed Sporus. "Is there no end to these chambers and caverns? Where is this accursed treasure?"

"My manuscript does not say. Damn Argonius for not having it translated in its entirety! Woman—you also have read portions of it. What do you know of this? Do not hide anything from us if you wish to see the outside world again."

By now Catella would have done anything to leave this awesome realm of darkness. She searched her memory, trying to recall everything she had read in the Ptolemaic Greek of the yellowed fragments the tomb-robbers had sold to her. "I—I remember reading that one must descend to 'the gulf of pillars and winds', and—and then, 'Egypt's greatest treasure will reveal itself to the seeker.' That's all I can—"

"Well, that's a help. This certainly seems to be a 'gulf of pillars and winds', so we can't have far to go. Here, man—lay this damned old priest down and let's see if we can shake him back to consciousness."

After a fruitless effort of shouting and prodding, the decurion said, "He's still in his trance, if not dead."

"Then spread out and explore this hall. The treasure's here somewhere."

They dispersed, their torches gleaming like scattering fireflies into the immense dark, but in less than a minute one of the men called out: "Commander, there's a big cave here!"

When the group had regathered they saw that the soldier's description was quite an understatement. The aperture before which they stood was one in which the tallest apartment building in Rome would have fitted easily. To its left, along the cliff-high wall from which the cave mouth opened, was the long stairway by which they had descended, its far-off lower end lost in shadow, and to the right was an identical stairway. From the colossal aperture the charnel wind, stronger here than ever, poured up from unknown gulfs, while before it lay a cluttered profusion of objects—skulls, bones, scraps of armor and yellowed linen.

"This *is* the mouth of Hades!" gasped the decurion. "Commander, perhaps we should not stay here—"

"Calm down, Sporus." The centurion strode boldly forward to the cave mouth, deliberately ignoring the noisome wind, and examined the bones. All were human, and most were broken or mashed. The ancient shields and armor fragments, none more recent than Ptolemaic times, were strangely bent and dented. For a moment Aemilius felt that his decurion might have a good idea. Did still more enormous caverns yawn far beneath these? From what unimaginable regions did this charnel wind originate? And what sort of monstrous things might those regions conceal?

Hearing some of his men exclaiming excitedly, he turned and saw that Menophar was now on his feet, motionless, facing away from the wind-belching cave, arms outstretched toward the columned blackness. The priest's white robe fluttered in the flow of charnel air.

"Na ka ku-tho ithumus!" cried Menophar. *"Ku-nokomis inkubu!"*

Aemilius did not recognize the chant but knew that the words were not Egyptian. He ran forward, gripped the priest by the shoulder, and spun him around—then stepped quickly back in shock as he saw that Menophar's eyes were now gleaming with an unnatural yellow luminosity.

"Idiot!" hissed the priest. "You have sought Egypt's greatest treasure—and now you shall find it!"

Even as he spoke a new sound broke through the whisper of the wind—a far-off sound that came from beyond the columned gulf and slowly grew louder. Aemilius felt his spine prickle, for what he heard was impossible: measured and definite sounds like drums, flutes, and sistrums, slowly increasing in volume, suggesting some advancing ritual procession.

"Hades and Persephone!" gasped Sporus. "What *is* that?"

Incredibly, faint glimmerings of light became visible far away between the columns. As they brightened, new sounds became audible—paddings, clickings, slitherings, shufflings, as if of many strange feet advancing to the rhythm of the drums and flutes.

Aemilius drew his sword. "Form ranks, soldiers!" Then, turning to

Menophar: "Who are these who approach? Who dwells down here——?"

"Idiot!" repeated the priest. "Have you not guessed? What is it that the ancient Stygians and Khemites were most anxious to preserve and protect throughout the centuries? For what cause above all others did they labor to rear their mighty tombs and temples? What did they hide within them to be preserved even unto the Second Rising? *You fools! Egypt's greatest treasure is her dead—and now her dead are coming for you!*"

Then moving forms became barely visible under the light of the advancing torches—and Catella screamed.

Simon emerged cautiously from the passageway on to the ledge and peered down into the darkness. The natron-scented wind seemed stronger here. Far below he saw the gleaming torches of the Romans and, in their light, the vague shapes of colossal columns whose tops were lost in the vast blackness above.

The Samaritan shuddered, and not because of the chill of the wind. His worst fears were realized. The Gulf of Pillars truly existed, even as the old writings said, and that gulf was vast beyond all his imaginings. No human engineers could have hewn this monstrous space from the solid rock, let alone the even vaster caverns that were said to lie below. And what of the things that were said to lurk within those caverns and creep upward on certain nights of the year—nights such as this one…?

Abruptly he suppressed the thought and stole back to where Spargos waited with both their torches.

"Stay here," he said. "I'm going down to see if I can free Menophar and your wife. Be ready to run up the passage ahead of us, lighting our way, when we come."

"I'd rather go with you, Simon."

"I know, but the Romans would kill two of us as easily as one. This calls for stealth. Keep within the passageway—those torches mustn't be seen."

Then, before the Greek could reply, Simon hurried away and began to descend the right-hand stairway as rapidly as he could in the darkness, keeping his right hand in contact with the smooth stone of the artificial cliff face. He hoped there would be no pitfalls—the Romans had apparently descended safely before him….

When he reached the bottom he was in almost complete darkness. The distant light of the Romans' torches faintly silhouetted the massive rows of columns ahead of him. Rapidly yet cautiously he stole forward between the mighty bases of those columns—and, as he did so, became aware of strange sounds, faint but increasing in volume: drums, flutes, and sistrums——or something suggestive of them—and then, far off between the massive pillars, beyond the Romans, the dim glimmerings of strange torches, paler than those of the soldiers, like corpse-lights—

Simon halted, his hackles rising. Luveh-Keraph's *Scroll of Bubastis* had evidently told truly of what took place within these aeon-old caverns each full moon nearest a solstice or equinox: the Procession of the Dead to honor Horemkhu, God of Death. The Romans were doomed—and so also was he, Simon, if he did not at once turn back—

Then he heard a woman scream.

Anger partly overruled Simon's fear and he dashed forward, less careful now to hide the sound of his approach. The Romans, he sensed, were intent upon *others* who were approaching them.

In another moment he had reached the last pillar between himself and the soldiers. Peering out from its shadow, he saw that the Romans were drawn up in a double line, backs to him, each man with a torch in his left hand and a sword in his right, facing in the direction from which the strange music, footfalls, and corpse-lights were approaching. Just behind them stood Menophar, arms outstretched, eyes glowing with a weird light, and also Catella, her arms bound behind her, backing away in terror toward the very pillar behind which Simon stood concealed.

Then Menophar began to chant in what Simon recognized as the long-forgotten Stygian tongue to the cadence of the strange, advancing procession: *"Ko ithamu nokomis itu—"*

"Damn you, sorcerer!" yelled Aemilius, whirling from the ranks with bared blade. "Here's your death!"

Simon sprang from concealment, sprinted past the startled Catella, and reached the pair barely in time to interpose his sword blade between that of Aemilius and Menophar's bald cranium. The blades rang together sharply, and then Simon's fist cracked into the Roman's face and sent him sprawling.

Sporus and several others, astonished, whirled and dashed at Simon. With a desperate effort the Samaritan gripped the slight form of his mentor about the waist with his crooked left arm, lifted him, and dashed off toward the shadows of the columns.

"Run!" he yelled at Catella—who, having paused by the nearest pillar, stood gazing horror-struck at the Romans and what was advancing toward them. Instantly she turned and, despite her bound arms, hurried awkwardly away into the darkness between the columns.

Then Simon heard Aemilius bawl: "Stand firm, men! Hack the bastards down! No foe can stand against soldiers of Rome!"

In the same instant, hearing footsteps close behind, Simon dropped Menophar and whirled. Most of the pursuers had evidently turned back at Aemilius' shouted command to rejoin the ranks, but one still came on—

Sporus the decurion.

"Damn you, magician!" shrieked Sporus, lunging. "You and your dev-il-priest shall die for luring us into this hell-pit!"

Simon, reacting instantly with all the skill of his gladiator training, barely evaded the decurion's thrust. He swung his own short sword and its keen blade shore through Sporus' neck, sending the decurion's helmed head tumbling from its shoulders to roll clattering into the shadows; the body collapsed instantly, blood spurting from neck arteries to stain the stone floor.

Simon stooped and hauled Menophar erect. The priest's eyes were no longer glowing but darting about as if in bewilderment. Simon slapped his face, shook him, then ran to Catella and quickly cut the rope that bound her wrists.

"Follow me, both of you," he commanded. "Hurry!"

They obeyed, only half aware of what they did, and as they fled they heard the yells of the Romans rise behind them in tones of rage and hor-ror. Then came the furious sounds of metal ringing upon metal, and of metal chopping into something like dry and brittle wood. And all the while the eerie sounds of drums and flutes increased, together with the measured shuffle of many feet muffled as if bound in layers of linen....

After what seemed a tense and interminable groping through pillared blackness, Simon and his two companions found the foot of the stairway and hurried upward. As they neared the top Simon realized that Menophar had regained full consciousness.

"We must hurry, Simon," gasped the priest. "The drug has worn off and I can no longer control the entrance to this place."

"Don't worry. The door has been jammed with a stone pillar—"

"Hurry!" insisted Menophar.

Then they saw Spargos hastening down the stairs toward them, a torch in either hand—a welcome sight, for as the battle between the Romans and their unseen foes had raged below, the light of their torches had dimin-ished considerably. Howls of rage and terror still rang up from the gulf.

"Catella!" cried the little Greek. "Is that truly you? Praise all the Gods!"

"We're not out yet," snarled Simon. "Hurry—lead us!"

Spargos nodded, turned and led the way up with his two torches.

As they gained the wide ledge at the top of the stair, Simon paused an instant and peered over the edge. Far below the battle still raged, though the torches of the Romans were now few and the corpse-lights of their foes far greater in number. Those foes were unnaturally *silent*, save for the sounds of the eerie drums and flutes, and Simon felt his fears returning— the deep, atavistic fears his anger had temporarily submerged. The Romans, yelling in fury and terror, were slowly retreating toward a point directly below—the area just in front of the now-concealed cavern mouth which belched its noisome wind into the vast columned hall. Both the Romans and their assailants appeared indistinct in the wavering torchlight, but in that instant the forms of the latter seemed to Simon to be something other than human—yellow-eyed, linen-wrapped humanoid forms, a few with heads resembling those of hawks, ibises, and jackals, others headless altogether—

And then, more terrible than all that had come before, a gigantic, clutching, five-branched *thing* suddenly extended itself from the cave mouth below and descended upon the combatants, Romans and gulf-spawn alike. To Simon it appeared yellowish-gray and hairy, and its titanic claws grated upon the stone as it pulled its madly shrieking prey into the bone-cluttered mouth of its lair. Instantly all the Romans' torch-sparks below vanished, and above the shrieks of the legionaries as they were pulled down into tartarean gulfs rose the wild beating of dark drums and the keening of eldritch flutes—and in that instant Simon realized that he had been cursed with a glimpse of the *forepaw* of Horemkhu, God of the Dead, in whose monstrous image the Sphinx had originally been carven.

"Look!" gasped Menophar, pointing to a moving cluster of the corpse-lights. "They're heading toward the stairway. We must run!"

Spargos, lean and nimble in spite of his sixty years, led the way, a torch in each hand, and the other three fled after him up incredible inclined planes, along pillared corridors, and finally up the last stairway that led to the outside.

Here on this final stair, gasping and drenched with the sweat of their frantic and prolonged exertions, the four of them paused fearfully as they heard a new sound *ahead* of them—a slow, resonant *boom... boom... boom....*

"Hurry!" cried Menophar. "I am no longer in control—the Sphinx is trying to close the door upon us—!"

They dashed on, Simon's fear increasing. The very rock beneath their feet was now vibrating to each ponderous boom. Were there also legions of the dead behind them, advancing to the beat of the Drums of Horemkhu—?

They gained the top of the stairway—and stopped, frozen in fear. The lofty stone door, swung back to its fullest extent, slowly and ponderously closed—

Boom!

—then bounded back from the section of limestone pillar that blocked it.

"Quick—through the door!" yelled Menophar. "The pillar is cracking—it won't hold up for long."

Spargos dropped one torch, gripped Catella's hand, and dragged her through the doorway. The great stone portal, swinging purposefully to, uncannily like a living thing, again crashed against the pillar, causing it to crack and crumble.

BOOM!

Again the stone door swung wide, and this time Menophar leapt through. Simon, about to follow, heard a rushing scuffle down the passage behind him, turned—and was horrified to see the linen-wrapped shapes approaching out of the blackness, their eyes gleaming an unearthly yellow. In their left hands they carried strange torches that gleamed with a greenish-yellow corpse-light, and in their lead was a figure, crowned with the high double crown of Khem, whose mummy-brown visage was *the exact duplicate of the face of Menophar.*

Simon, yelling with rage and terror, cast his short sword with all his might. It spun true and thudded solidly into the breast of the charnel pharonic figure. The apparition staggered and stumbled, pierced through— but then *regained its balance and came on, eyes gleaming demoniacally.*

The great stone door was again swinging ponderously shut. Simon leaped through the narrowing aperture with frantic haste, feeling the wind of the passing stone—

BOOM!

The pillar section shattered, crumbled, and was shoved aside, divided in two. Simon, rolling on the floor of the outer passage, heard the door thunder shut behind him. Rising, he faced it, fearful lest it should open and allow the flame-eyed liches behind it to emerge....

But it remained shut, apparently a "false door" once again, and Simon trembled as he realized how close all of them had come to being trapped forever within the dark domain of Horemkhu.

"By Mot, God of Doom!" he exclaimed shakily. "I thought, Menophar, that I saw your likeness, the pharaoh Khephren, and some of his lich-servitors pursuing me like flame-eyed demons—"

"They serve Horemkhu, Lord of the Dead," said Menophar, "and so possess a sort of eternal life. These undead Favored Ones are the 'treasure' which Aemilius and his legionaries so foolishly sought and, to their undoing, found."

"Catella," said Spargos nervously, attempting a smile, "I hope this will be a lesson to you. Henceforth, do not peruse silly old documents—" Then, seeing his young wife's anguished face and outstretched arms, his own countenance dissolved in tearful relief and he gathered her to him, sobbing.

A few minutes later the four of them staggered out of the corridor into the moonlit, corpse-strewn area before the great Sphinx, Spargos and

Catella still gripping one another's hands like new lovers.

"Well, Simon," said Menophar, "you have again proven yourself an adept pupil of mine of whom I can be proud. This time, in fact, I might not now be alive had you not learned well the things I have taught you. But now, let us escort this brave couple whom you have rescued to the shore of the Nile and see them safely aboard a boat for Alexandria—which destination will be much to their liking, I am sure! After that, you may return with me to Memphis, where we shall arrange for you to travel upriver and hide there in one of Ptah's temples—"

"No." Simon glanced up at the moon-illumined face of the Sphinx, so similar to the face of his old mentor, then shook his head violently. "No. I will accompany this honest pair to Alexandria—and then, fortune favoring, I'll take ship thence for lands unknown. I fear Caligula's threat, but I now fear the dark evil of Egypt even more. Khem is a land of ancient terrors, as I have learned repeatedly during these last months, and tonight most of all. No doubt Horemkhu, God of Death, shall one day lay claim to me as he has this night lain claim to Aemilius and all his legionaries—aye, as he lays claim to the souls of all who have been and shall be—but when that day comes I hope to be far from dark Egypt, beneath cleansing breezes and blue skies."

About "The Secret of Nephren-Ka"

Simon's next challenge occurs at some point during A.D. 39, in a story penned entirely by longtime associate of Richard Tierney (and promoter of Simon tales), Robert M. Price. This yarn represents a crossover between two fictive worlds. Richard L. Tierney's stories of Simon Magus are set, like Robert E. Howard's tales of Bran Mak Morn, in a *Weird Tales* version of the 1st century Roman Empire. That's the first one. The second is the imaginary North America of Joseph Smith's *Book of Mormon*.

The basic premise of the Church of Jesus Christ of Latter-day Saints (Mormons) is the revelation to 19th-century religious seeker Joseph Smith of a set of inscribed golden plates chronicling the epic voyage of an ancient Judean family to the Western hemisphere, and their division, years later, into two nations, the pious Nephites and the idolatrous Lamanites. It was the Israelites versus the Canaanites all over again. Only this time the bad guys won! The last surviving Nephites compiled the Book of Mormon and hid it in upstate New York where centuries later an angel revealed its location to young Joseph Smith. Alas, archaeologists have never found a trace of the Nephite and Lamanite civilizations. The Lamanites supposedly survived as the American Indians, but modern science debunked that, too, since none of these people were shown to have even a drop of Semitic DNA.

Both fantasy worlds intersect with the biblical epic. It's like Reese's Peanut Butter Cups: an ideal marriage! What if Simon were to somehow make his way to the land of the Nephites and the Lamanites? It's a natural! And Nephren-Ka, the hierophant of Nyarlathotep? Given Simon's oft-engagement with the mysteries of Egypt, it's surprising he hasn't fallen under the shadow of the Black Pharaoh before now!

"The Secret of Nephren-Ka" was first published in *The Mighty Warriors*, Ulthar Press, 2018.

THE SECRET OF NEPHREN-KA

by Robert M. Price

Dark mage of ancient Stygia and Acheron,
Thine awful thaumaturgies have for thee attained
Great powers, and for many ages thou hast reigned
O'er empires fallen now into oblivion.

Thou didst invoke Nyarlat, that Mighty Messenger,
Who set thee on Khem's throne in cruel and haughty pride
As Pharaoh Nephren-Ka, soon styled Death's Emperor!
With his new Chosen One, Nyarlat is Satisfied.

— Richard L. Tierney, *Dark Pharaoh*

I. Return of the Past

One day, Simon of Gitta knew, there would come a mad prophet (or so many would deem him) who would carry a lit lantern in broad daylight, and would say many terrible things, including requiems for slain gods. He would say, "When you look into the Abyss, the Abyss looks back into you." And that is why Simon often resorted to the invocation to Morpheus so that he might sleep of a night. For often had he gazed into the Cosmic Pit of the Pain Lords, and communed with even worse Beings, and what he had seen was by no means easy to live with. Especially in the long night.

He found himself startled awake by an abrupt shock of plummeting temperature. He could imagine no natural explanation for the phenomenon, and so the discomfort that made him shudder was not of the flesh but of the spirit. Initially he thought it an invading nightmare. His brow knitted in apprehension above the broad planes of his prominent cheekbones. As if having waited for the Gittite to orientate himself, a blurred but rapidly crystallizing image appeared, and a hollow voice was coincident with it, without actually seeming to come from it.

"You know me, or do I underestimate you, O Simon Magus?"

The tall figure could now be seen to be draped in fabrics of sunset crimson. Barely discernible because of their hue against the darkness were a pair of tame panthers who licked the apparition's extended hands. His high forehead was surmounted by the double crown of Upper and Lower Egypt. His mien was haughty in implication, though his face remained in shadow.

As Simon sat up from his sleeping pallet, he replied, not with awe but with a guarded, implicitly defensive tone: "Thou art the Black Pharaoh, known to the few who remember as *Nephren-Ka*. Surely you are he?"

"I am. That, I am. In past ages I ruled forgotten Stygia, and before that, unknown Acheron. In every age my powers waned, atom by atom, until at last the priests of decadent Khem overthrew me."

"Are you his spirit, then? His ghost? Men say they slew you."

"As they do with many things, the priests lied in order to douse the fears of the common folk who must otherwise fear my return someday. Would that I might! But I did flee Egypt in those far-off days. I sent my faithful into exile in divers places, the acolytes of my servant Bubastis I sent to dreary Britain, the hierophants of Faceless Byagoona to Gaul, the minions of serpent-bearded Byatis to Greece. I myself accompanied my chief priests to a vast and unknown land across the seas. They kept my faith alive there with sacrifice and offering. Many belonging to one of the native tribes, awed by the miracles I performed among them by sorcerous means, rallied to me and called themselves Nephites after me. In turn, I protected them from their eternal foes, once come down from snowy Lomar, and called Lamanites.

"But not long ago, my vitality failed, and my life ebbed away. Now my people want for protection against the Lamanites, who, in my absence, have redoubled their persecutions. I have cheated death for so long, I never believed it would overtake me. That was foolish, I now understand. My spirit double can linger upon this plane for but a trifle longer. And before I go off to whatever awaits me, I must needs undertake to deliver my faithful from those who would destroy them. Thus I come to you this night. Only a man of your talents can be of help to me."

Simon, genuinely surprised, both at him who sought his aid and at the astounding journey the mission should entail, replied. "O Shade of Nephren-Ka! Forgive me if I speak my mind. Your worship is shunned and persecuted with good reason! I had thought it extinct and rejoiced at the thought! Black indeed are your rites, foul the deeds you have taught your disciples! Far be it from me to stain my soul by entering thy service!"

The revenant's enigmatic visage split with laughter.

"In truth, I suspected as much! But you have dealt with Dark Powers before. I know you have. But I am past nefarious designs. That is all behind me now. In my present infirmity I cannot so much as move a pebble with a finger, as you see. It is a good deed to which I summon you, Simon of Gitta!"

An eyebrow arching in suspicious surprise, the sorcerer answered him, "What interest can you have in deeds of goodness, your Majesty?"

"You are correct, conjurer. Little good have I done in my many days. But some awful fate awaits me. The Hell of Endless Shrieking, perhaps. Or the Cavern of Ravenous Devourers. Mayhap the Black Dimension." Here the larger-than-life apparition's countenance flickered just a bit, as if momentarily daunted, pained by a conscience long since mummified. But he continued. "Perhaps if I can bequeath my followers a measure of safety as my last deed, through you, I may be able to mitigate my damnation by a farthing."

Simon barked a laugh of scorn.

"But the disciple is no better than his master! Why take the trouble on behalf of the devil's disciples? Best to let your ancient evil die!"

"They were no more than dupes! They served me out of fear! Left to themselves they would be harmless sheep. You must know that. It is always the way with helpless mortals. They feed off superstition and ignorance. But their present fears are quite real. In olden times, the Lamanites fought against the fierce Gnoph-kehs of the Commorian ice wastes. But in defeating them the Lamanites became like them. Furthermore, I have given them reason to take revenge on my flock, and their vengeance upon my Nephites must be terrible. But you can save them."

Simon was standing now, his eyes almost level with the glowing orbs in the otherwise-shadowed face.

"Save them? By myself? How?" He was beginning to reevaluate the situation and, with it, the strange appeal of the pleading ghost.

"Across the vast ocean that swells above the grave of Atlantis lies a land equally vast, verily a different world. There my followers await. Their deliverance lies with a potent talisman which men call the Golden Heart of Quetzalcoatl. It was long ago hidden away by the ancient Jaredites. They sold its power short, and their folly destroyed them."

"But suppose I am destroyed the same way? I know even less of the thing than *they* did!"

"The Jaredites were sages but not sorcerers. They left behind a wealth of bronze plates containing much of their science. But the Heart was a product of a science they knew nothing about. But you and I do. I could bring the amulet to life if I still occupied the body of flesh, but now? It is useless to me, for I myself am become useless. Of all the men of today, you, I judge, are the one best able to awaken and wield the power of the Heart. When you see it you will, I believe, know what to do. My servants will meet you and accompany you to the location of the amulet."

II. The Host of Ekron

Alone again, Simon returned to bed, needing sleep against what lay ahead. He had not asked his visitor how he might gain the far shores where adventure beckoned to him like a man waving from a beach. He already knew how he should accomplish that. Legend told that the ancestors of the Jaredites and, after them, of those now called Nephites had crossed the ocean in strange underwater ships. Simon had not the time for such a voyage if he were to rescue the persecuted Nephites. But there was another, quicker way. There was the Host of Ekron. These were the demon spirits commanded by the oracle of Baal-Zebub at Ekron, one of the pentad of ancient Philistine cities of which Simon's hometown Gath or Gitta was another. The demons ranged far and wide and could ferret out any and all secrets as they invisibly scanned the earth. These secrets they would vouchsafe to the Philistine soothsayers, who made their living passing on desired information to their clients who wanted to know where they had lost an expensive tool or if their daughters would ever get married.

Their whispering had the sound of the chittering of insects, hence the traditional costume of the Oracle: a man-sized effigy of a locust. Simon was no oracle-monger, but he knew how to call down the Host and to make them take him on their swarm cloud to whatever destination he desired, since all the byways of the world were known to them. This he knew from a scroll recording some of the secrets obtained from the demons by the Arab *kahins*, a text called *Kitab al Azif*, "the book of the buzzing." Many centuries hence, a descendant of the book would bring great troubles to mankind.

It was not long before Simon of Gitta stood, equipped with his pouch of magical chemicals and fetishes on one hip, and his gladius, retained from his days in the arena, on the other. He wore a bell-sleeved blouse under a tunic of rusty vermillion festooned with silver-embroidered zodiacal signs. He softly sang the chant that only the Host of Ekron could hear, wherever in the world they might be. By the time he had finished, a purplish mist was spinning around him. And he heard the cachinnation, which seemed a not unpleasant melody of its own. The familiar furnishings of his rented room swiftly faded until naught could be seen but the violet cyclone that bore him along at unimaginable yet unfelt speed. He felt as if dreaming, suspended timelessly until he felt solid ground beneath his feet and stumbled into the ready arms of a circle of robed men, their faces displaying a mixture of fear and awe. They led him, light-headed, to a wooden chair with only a thin cloth pad to provide any comfort.

Simon had reviewed a spell designed to make any foreign language intelligible but now found he did not need it. These people, the Nephites, welcoming him, were speaking a peculiar dialect of Hebrew heavily influenced by Demotic Egyptian. A hybrid tongue, it sounded like a kind of reformed Egyptian, no doubt introduced by the original priests of Nephren-Ka during the long years he had dominated the Nephites. Simon was fluent in both component languages and had little difficulty understanding his hosts.

His new acquaintances brought him more food than he could eat, and with it wine. They shared with Simon what they knew of the danger they faced and what they had guessed concerning the artifact from which their late god-king had promised deliverance should come. They showed him to a great and ornate bed, virtually a horizontal throne, which had belonged to Nephren-Ka. Simon had been largely passive in his magical transit, but somehow it had exacted the price of exhaustion, and he needed to refresh himself. At dawn the Nephites would lead him to the Jaredite ruins.

III. The Catacombs of Jared

The morning sky was intensely blue, the sun blazing. Simon thought himself inured to the hellish furnaces of the Negev and of the Nabatean desert, but this was new to him. He might have employed a meditation to lower his body temperature, but he preferred to endure the hardship and grow stronger for it. His companions, however, seemed little discomfited. Good for them. They had been born and raised in these scorching conditions.

Simon took advantage of the trek to sharpen his command of the Nephite language in conversation with the others. They were polite enough, even deferential, but none could conceal a pervasive unease. Of course, they had learned to keep alert for possible Lamanite harassment. No sooner had Simon asked one of the men about this than stones began to rain down on the party from a ridge above them. Some of the Nephites fled, desperate for shelter. Others raised crude metal shields, quickly pitted and dented by the larger of the pelting stones. The Gittite loosened the sword in his scabbard but quickly realized that none of the feathered and armored attackers were descending from their perch to engage in honest combat. So instead, the Magus extended his arms skyward and swiftly gesticulated, his hands weaving a complex pattern of silver-blue fire.

The hurled stones slacked in pace as the Lamanites found themselves distracted by Simon's fireworks. In another moment they dropped their projectiles and turned to flee. Seeing this, the Nephites started to emerge from their concealment behind some nearby boulders.

"O Magus! How did you dispatch them?"

Simon chuckled. "It was not me they feared, but rather the pack of winged and fanged hounds they imagined were springing for them. It is but a trick of the light, I confess, but the beasts they think they see will seem to pursue them for some time, wherever they go. We need not worry about them returning to trouble us further."

The surviving Nephite elders having given Simon thanks, nonetheless made a hasty departure, licking their wounds. Simon laughed at their timidity as he pursued his way. The directions he had received were simple enough; he would not have requested their escort and did not miss it now. But he found himself thinking, too, about his Lamanite ambushers. He might easily have destroyed them with his magic, like Elijah of old, but he had satisfied himself with simply scaring them off like panicky children.

Why had he shown clemency for these attackers? Perhaps he had sensed something amiss. After all, the hostility of the sons of Lomar had been provoked by the atrocities commanded by Nephren-Ka. Perhaps they did not even realize the Black Pharaoh was dead! In any case, would they not share Simon's own initial assumption that the devil's depravity lived on among his minions? And suppose they were right? Until he could sort this out, he was glad for now that he had not killed the Lamanites. There would always be another chance if necessary.

IV. The Golden Heart of Quetzalcoatl

Simon carefully treaded the labyrinth, having memorized the directions and aided by the eerie glow emitted by his blade, which had more uses than just to butcher men. But his way, he suddenly realized, was not clear before him. An advancing shadow alerted him before a giant of some seven feet lumbered forth from around a stony bend, its towering height all the more remarkable given that it possessed no head! As it lunged toward him, navigating, it must be, by means of some other sense than sight, the thing reached out to seize him and tear him apart like a chicken. Simon's observant eyes saw that each gnarled hand sported six fingers. At once he thought of his ancient countryman, his childhood hero, Goliath of Gath, one of the last of the fabled Nephilim whose number included Nimrod, Gilgamesh, and mighty Ishbibenob. Could this creature have been another? But who had ruined him, transformed him into this hulking juggernaut? Well, there was only one answer to that. It must have been the doing of the Black Pharaoh, posting him here to discourage any who coveted the amulet of power. Had his ghostly ally merely forgotten to call off this monstrous watchdog? Too late for that now!

Simon easily evaded the clumsy, club-like swinging of the massive limbs. He hopped from side to side, assessing the most opportune avenue of attack, quickly making his choice and stabbing at the heart. For a moment he feared his gladius lost, as it protruded harmlessly from the chest of the headless giant. Its animation did not, then, depend on the inner workings of mortal men's bodies, but on dark magic. Simon accused himself for a fool for not realizing that right off. But in a moment he found an opening to clasp the familiar hilt and yank the blade free. But of what use was it against this deadly marionette? He stepped away, sheathed the sword, and undid the draw string of his pouch.

There was no real opportunity to scrutinize the contents of his bag of tricks, so he just shook out all the powders in a random puff of mingled ingredients. What the effect might be, Simon did not know. Both he and the undead sentinel paused in their mutual struggle. In a few moments, his foe, though seemingly impervious to bodily pain, began to burst into flame over most of his huge form, flame shifting between blue and green, yellow to purple, and back again. Most of the rest of him suddenly stiffened into clear ice which shattered with every attempted movement. Inches of the dead flesh here and there began to sublimate directly into the air. As what was left of the thing collapsed with a blood-chilling sound, a kind of grinding groan rose from deep within its rotting torso. Simon gaped in delighted surprise and hoped he would be able to duplicate the recipe he had accidentally created.

The lingering stench was overpowering, abominable. Holding his breath, then his nose, he hastened on down the shaft, half-expecting another monster to bar his way. Accordingly, he was both surprised and not surprised to find himself circled by a veritable flock of feathered, flying serpents. Reflexively, he poised to defend himself, but none of the creatures swooped to the attack. And somehow he knew he must not strike with the sword. But why were they here? What was their purpose? It must be to protect the amulet, surely, a second line of defense in case the deadly Golem should fail. But then why did they not descend upon him? Unless perhaps they sensed danger arising from another quarter. What did they know?

The talisman was *here*. In a sudden, blinding flash of light it made its presence known. The winged serpents moved to circle it, but they made no move to prevent him as Simon extended his hand to grasp it, fearing the possible result. Would he be struck down for his sacrilegious effrontery, as the Jaredites were?

Now he held it in his sweating hand, its light illuminating his features from below, and waiting for the worst. And the worst arrived, though not from any direction he had imagined. Simon recognized a hollow voice and turned to face its possessor. As he now knew to expect, the luminous image of Nephren-Ka loomed above him in its clinging shroud of gloom. So it was, from the first, a trap.

"The goal, O Simon, was always to employ the peculiar power of the jewel, that of effecting soul-transference. My incorporeal shade will pass through it into the body of him who holds the Heart."

"Why me? Why go to such trouble? Surely any of your Nephite stooges would have sufficed, if all you need is a host body?"

"Ah, Simon of Gitta, how you underestimate your value! A soul of great power such as mine would overwhelm and destroy a human form unprepared, unfit to contain it. I required you not to find the amulet but to mediate its power. Your years of occult mastery, your conditioning by the forces of strange dimensions, have transfigured you. Of all men now living, you alone are an adequate vessel for me! And in your image the Black Pharaoh will once again walk the earth, blast it, and rule what remains. You are highly honored, my son!"

To his horror, Simon could feel the process beginning already as the fiend's words seemed to echo within his raven-haired head, as if originating there. The Black Pharaoh was beginning to supplant him. In the moments of shared consciousness, the Gittite suffered horrifying visions of the blasphemous deeds—and knowledge—of Nephren-Ka. Compared with this, a beckoning oblivion seemed a bright hope. It would not be so bad to let go…

But it was not to be. Suddenly pain overtook him as a *third* consciousness intruded. Simon knew, because the Entity knew, its identity. This was Holy Quetzalcoatl! He was a Light both glorious and terrible. Dreadful shrieks rang through Simon's skull (or through the catacomb of the doomed Jaredites, he knew not which) as the Golden Heart of Quetzalcoatl subsumed and devoured ancient Nephen-Ka.

This must be what had happened to the Jaredites so long ago. So Simon mused as in astonishment he beheld the Light of the Heart shrinking back into the gem, which had dulled but now regained its supernatural radiance. If the soul of Nephren-Ka was imprisoned there along with the ancient Jaredites, he would never be free again.

V. The Vengeance of the Lamanites

Unstable from assaults both physical and magical, Simon finally retraced his path through the tunnel and into the merciless sunlight. The long shadows of the waiting Nephite elders folded as their owners bowed before him in groveling reverence. It was obvious they supposed the infernal scheme, to which they had been party, had gone according to plan. Their Master had returned! Or so they thought. They were in for a surprise. Weak as he was, Simon knew he could finish them all. He unlimbered his sword.

But the sound of a small, dislodged stone clattering down from the ridge above them caught Simon's attention, and he turned to see where it had come from. He could see the tops of many helmets. The Nephites' eyes widened in terror as Simon yelled up at their Lamanite enemies. "The Black Pharaoh is dead, never to return. But here you see," he said, with a gesture encompassing the frightened elders now rising to their feet, "the next best thing! Have at it, my friends!"

Not merely rocks but spears and feathered shafts fell like a destroying rain. It was over quickly, and Simon waited for the Lamanites to descend and surround him with raised weapons, hailing him for the deliverance he had won them.

About "The Scroll of Thoth"

Over two years later in January of A.D. 41, Simon once again returns to Rome in search of another ancient Egyptian relic looted by the Roman Empire, the Scroll of Thoth. Worse, it's held by none other than the Mad Emperor himself, Gaius Caesar, better known to history as Caligula.

The *Book of Thoth* is surely one of the most evocative titles to appear in weird fiction. Even Abdul Alhazred cites it in his *Necronomicon* ("Through the Gates of the Silver Key"). An idle reading of it in *The Mummy* raises Imhotep (Boris Karloff) from his millennial torpor. Aleister Crowley produced his own version.

Thoth was the Egyptian god of magic. The Greeks of the Hellenistic age identified him syncretically with Hermes, hence the "Hermetic arts", as well as the *Hermetic Corpus*, a canon of quasi-Gnostic philosophical writings featuring the revealer Hermes Trismegistus (Thrice-Great Hermes), who appeared earlier in *The Emerald Tablet*. Richard Tierney has given a Hyborian flavor to the tome, as we might expect, given the Stygian origin of elder thaumaturgy in the *Weird Tales* cosmos. The Thoth for whom the volume is named is none other than Thoth-Amon, Conan's old foe.

One bit of more mundane magic that figures in this story is ventriloquism. Lest any reader think it an anachronism, let me hasten to assure you that the trick was well known and widely practiced in Simon's period. In fact it formed part of the repertoire of the *goetes*, the charlatan magician, as Jesus, Simon Magus, and Apollonius of Tyana were considered by their enemies. It occurs even in the Bible, when the False Prophet of the Roman Beast (666 = *Neron Kaisar* = Nero) causes a statue of his master to seem to speak (Revelation 13:15). The Seer of the Apocalypse thus marks him as a worker of "lying wonders" (cf. 2 Thessalonians 2:9), i.e., a charlatan who fakes miracles. Jeannie Mills, formerly a lieutenant of the Reverend Jim Jones, once told me how Jones used to fake miracles like walking on the water. Things haven't changed much.

"The Scroll of Thoth" supplies one of the most overtly Lovecraftian statements of Gnostic mythology in the whole Simon canon. We read of the Pain Lords who magnify and feed off the sufferings of human beings and who created them for that purpose. "Maybe they equate with Colin Wilson's 'Lloigor'?" (Letter, August 7, 1984). The Pain Lords may be familiar to you from the Red Sonja books by Tierney and fellow swordmaster David C. Smith. The Pain Lords are the same as the Primal Gods, Tierney's name for the Old Ones. These dark deities are featured prominently also in Tierney's novella *The Lords of Pain* (found in *Nightscapes* #3, September 1997) which contains much else of interest to Mythos buffs. The *Necronomicon* looms large in it, as does the unholy gem from Howard's "The

Fire of Asshurbanipal." It is in *The Lords of Pain* that Tierney first establishes Harag-Kolath (mentioned in "The Seed of the Star-God") as the earthly abode of Shub-Niggurath.

Simon's pursuit of Thoth-Amon's scroll first appeared in Andrew Offutt's (ed.) *Swords Against Darkness* #2, 1977.

THE SCROLL OF THOTH

by Richard L. Tierney

I

"Thrust again!" cried Gaius, Emperor of Rome. "Let him feel that he is dying!"

The windowless walls of the large stone chamber echoed back the prisoner's groans as the torturer bent again to his work. The several spectators by the stairway flinched, though none dared avert his face. The Emperor, surrounded by several burly Germans in the garb of legionaries, stood looking on the scene with an avid grin that exposed his rather wolfish canine teeth; his eyes gleamed, his balding pate was beaded with sweat droplets, and his lean form quivered in what seemed to be near-ecstasy.

"Again!" His voice was a sharp bark, nearly a shriek.

The torturer was another brawny German, naked to the waist, his blond hair hanging down his back in two large braids. In his right hand he gripped a dagger of a sort used to dispatch fallen gladiators. The point of this he applied to the breast of the kneeling prisoner, who struggled and strained in agony between the two stone pillars to which he was chained, blood streaming down his body from numerous wounds. The point entered the skin; the prisoner gritted his teeth and trembled; then, avoiding any vital spot, the blade turned along the surface of the rib cage and showed its gleaming tip some three inches from where it had entered. The prisoner lost his self-control and screamed, loudly and shrilly. The blade was withdrawn.

"Ah! Again—again!" cried the Emperor.

The blade was applied once more—but this time the prisoner failed to respond; something seemed to have gone out of him. When the torturer gripped the victim's hair and lifted up his drooping head, the man's eyes were rolled ceilingward and his breath came in fading gasps.

"He dies!" cried Gaius. "Now, the ointment—quick! Quick!"

The torturer sheathed his dagger and stepped back. An elderly physician, bald and clad in Egyptian robes, strode forward and accepted a small jar which the Emperor held out to him, then hurried to the side of the dying prisoner.

"*Wait!*" shrieked the Emperor. "Have your slave administer it. Your hands must be clean when you handle the Scroll!"

The Egyptian physician beckoned to a tall, turbaned Nubian clad in a somber-hued tunic. The man stepped forward, knelt, and, taking the jar from his master, began to dip great gouts of the greenish ointment onto his fingers and work them into the prisoner's wounds. The captive had by now ceased to breathe and hung completely slack in his chains. When at last the Nubian had completed his work, the physician lifted one of the victim's eyelids, felt his limp wrist but found no pulse, and shook his head.

"This man is dead," he pronounced.

"You hear?" cried the Emperor to all in the chamber. "You hear? The man is dead! Now rise, physician, and come here. Take this scroll, and read therefrom as I have instructed you."

"One last time I beseech you, Gaius Imperator," said the Egyptian, "to reconsider of this. Not lightly are the powers to which the *Book of Thoth* is the key to be invoked—"

"*Read!*" screamed the Emperor. "Read—or you share his fate!"

The physician took the bulky scroll, turned to face the dead man who hung in his chains, and breathed deeply several times to quell his obvious nervousness. Unrolling the scroll to an arm's length, he began to intone the words of a strange language in a high-pitched but steady voice. To the watchers it seemed that the gloom of the chamber deepened suddenly— though none save the Emperor, the Egyptian sage, and his Nubian slave could know that the intoned words were of the forgotten language of dark, sorcery-riddled Stygia, the fabled land which had flourished before even nighted Egypt, oldest of living nations, had risen to rule the Nile lands.

The invocation was not long, but toward the end of it the old man's voice had begun to quaver slightly. Sweat was beading his forehead. When at length he finished, the Emperor snatched the scroll from his trembling hands, rolled it together, and held it out like a wand toward the dead man.

"Now, rise!" he commanded. "*Rise!*"

To the horror of all the watchers, the corpse began to twitch slightly. At first they thought it to be their imaginations reacting to the power of suggestion—but in another moment the dead man's animation was too pronounced to leave any merciful doubt. The eyes opened, revealing only the horrid whites of the upturned orbs. The thing was trying to scrabble to its feet, but apparently lacked the strength to do so. Suddenly, it opened its mouth and shouted in a terrible voice:

"*I live! I still live!*"

—After which, abruptly, it collapsed in its chains and hung there as utterly limp as before. Nor did it stir again.

The watchers, who had been holding their breath to a man, all exhaled simultaneously.

"This is a fell and evil thing that we have witnessed," said a Roman of- ficer, evidently the commander of the few soldiers present. "You have seen fit, O Caesar, to punish this man who offended you, and it is not my place to question your judgment; but to afterward subject his soul to a foul sorcery does no credit, it seems to me, to Roman justice—"

"Fool!" snapped the Emperor Gaius. His tone conveyed self-satisfaction rather than annoyance. "You always were a squeamish and effeminate sort, Cassius Chaerea. You presume to chide me, but you are impressed nonetheless—ha! ha! Your voice betrays as much."

The officer, whose noble deportment belied the Emperor's accusation of effeminacy, glowered and trembled with rage but, with a mighty effort of will, held his peace.

"Ha! ha! You shake in your boots," continued the Emperor. "I know you, Chaerea—full of bluster and patrician strut, but a coward at heart. Yet never forget, though you are a commander of men, that I am a commander of gods and demons! What you have seen this day is but the birth of my power over all things. Long have I labored to achieve what you have just seen—the conquest of death! Long have I garnered the occult wisdom of antique Khem and Mesopotamia, and many are the experiments I have performed in this chamber—and now at last, as you have seen with your own eyes, I have banished Death himself, if only for a moment, from the lifeless clay. Soon I shall learn to banish him utterly—and then I shall live forever!" He surveyed the room with burning exultant eyes, as though expecting a challenge. No one spoke.

"Forever!" he shouted. "Do you hear me? *I'll live forever!*" He strode rapidly twice across the room, back and forth. "Leave me now—all of you. Go—and tell all sneerers and smirkers that I, Gaius Imperator, ruler of all earth and all men, *shall live forever!*"

Without a word, all who had witnessed the strange scene filed up the stone stairs toward the light and sanity of the blessed upper air, leaving the Emperor alone in the dungeon room with only the bloody corpse for company.

II

"He is mad!" said the old physician to his Nubian slave when the two were alone in their quarters in a far wing of the palace.

"Aye, Menophar," replied the other. "He is mad—but shrewd and crafty nonetheless. It will be no easy task to destroy the *Book of Thoth*."

"Yet it must be done, or nothing in this world will be safe from his madness!" The old man sank into a chair. "Pour me some wine, Simon—I fear it has done my soul no good to read aloud from that accursed scroll."

The Nubian complied, then removed his turban and retired to an alcove to wash himself. When he returned a short time later he was scarcely recognizable as the same man. His skin had lightened to an olive tan; bangs of unruly black hair fell over his wide forehead and hung nearly to his broad shoulders. He had the trim, hard build of a fighting man and there was something ruthless about the set of his wide, thin-lipped mouth and deep-set eyes. Altogether he seemed somehow to have grown in stature since doffing his disguise.

"Well, Simon," said old Menophar, "you have now seen the scroll... and have been to the chamber wherein the mad emperor employs it. How are we to come at it?"

"You have been there several times," said the other, "before I came with you today as your 'slave.' Tell me all you know."

"What you saw today was a sacrifice as well as an example of Roman 'justice,'" said Menophar, refilling his already-drained wine goblet. "Behind the room of torture lies another room whose door appears as part of the stone wall. It is a temple to the Lords of the Deep and to the Pain Lords, of whose existence Gaius learned from the *Book of Thoth*. The Emperor once took me there alone; it is a strange room indeed. It is entered, incidentally, by pressing upward upon the right-hand side of the lintel, which resembles a mere rock slab set into the wall; I made careful note of that, though Gaius thinks he concealed his action from me. Within the hidden chamber is an altar to the Deep Ones, and another to the Pain Lords."

"Gaius is madder than I thought," said the man called Simon. "These two powers, though both lust evilly after human souls, are in constant conflict with one another."

"Aye—but in his madness the Emperor hopes to gain the favor of both, and in the end rule all gods as well as all men. The important thing for you to know, however, is that he keeps his chest of potions and poisons in this secret room—and in this chest also is the *Book of Thoth*."

"Continue," said Simon, pouring himself a goblet of the wine. "You have told me how Gaius' agents stole the scroll from the temple of Thoth in Alexandria, but you have not told me how much he has learned from it during the three years it has been in his possession."

"I still know little about that. It was not easy for me to work my way into his confidence, even though I am learned in the ancient Stygian tongue which he seeks to master. Yet I have learned a little through court gossip, and this little has enabled me to guess more. Among other things, I know that Gaius, some weeks after acquiring the *Book of Thoth*, led a military expedition to the north coast of Gaul, ostensibly for the purpose of invading Britain. Upon reaching the coast, however, he did nothing of the sort. Instead, he gave his troops a startling order."

"I, too, have heard that bit of gossip," said Simon, setting down his goblet. "It is said he ordered the legionaries to the beaches in order—of all things—to gather *sea shells!* They gathered up thousands of them, I understand, and all Rome talked of his madness when it was known. Why do you suppose he did it?"

"I am one of the few who know," said Menophar. "I have seen what became of those sea shells. They line the walls and ceiling of Gaius' underground shrine to the Deep Ones and the Pain Lords. You shall see for yourself, if your mission is successful.

"Gaius knows the Deep Ones live for aeons, perhaps forever. The ointment he bade you use on the dying man was distilled by occult means from the flesh of sea creatures unknown to man. Have you not heard the rumors that the Emperor has, on rare occasions, received dark emissaries who come to Rome by night from the waters of the Tiber? Gaius hopes to live forever and has made some strange alliances in order to gain this power. But he also knows that life eternal would be of no value should pain and disease wrack the mortal tenement; thus he seeks also to gratify the Pain Lords, who permeate all the matter of our universe and draw sustenance from the suffering of all creatures. Such was the nature and purpose of the sacrifice you saw today."

Simon shuddered slightly. He had long known of Gaius' madness, yet only now did he realize the full extent of it.

"You were right, Menophar: Whatever the cost, the *Book of Thoth* must not remain in the hands of this lunatic. It is the most dangerous of all sorcerous works, and in Gaius' hands it could make him the most dangerous of all men."

"But you, Simon of Gitta, are perhaps the most adept of all magicians—and that is why you have been chosen for this task."

Simon scowled, then took another sip of wine. "I am not a true magician," he said, "in that there is naught of true magic in anything I do. Yet you are right; I have learned enough to be an accomplished mummer—perhaps the best."

"And a fighter! Your service in the arena may stand you in better stead than even your 'mummery', as you choose to call it. You have seen the situation here; now, consider what must next be done. I think you realize, Simon of Gitta, that the fate of all men may rest on the success or failure of this venture."

"Aye!" Simon pushed away his wine goblet and rose. "No more wine for me—I need a good night's rest. What must be done tomorrow will require a clear mind."

III

"Halt, slave—these are the Imperial quarters. What seek you here?"

Simon halted before the outthrust spear of the Praetorian Guardsman.

So far luck had been with him. Once more he was the turbaned Nubian slave, his skin darkened, an artificial scar on his right earlobe indicating his servile status. Two guardsmen had let him pass unchallenged despite the early hour, assuming no doubt that he was about some errand for his master; a third, who had been negligently staring out a window at the city, had not seen him creep stealthily past, silent as a shadow. Now he found himself obliged to explain his presence.

"Pardon, good soldier," he said in what he hoped was a plausible imitation of flustered deference. "I have lost my way. My master sent me to the kitchens to order him a breakfast."

"You've indeed lost your way!" snorted the guard. "Lucullus must have been blind and deaf to let you stray this far. Get you back the way you came—"

"Ho—*guard!*" The voice, muffled with distance, seemed to come down the corridor from the direction opposite the one Simon had been directed to take. "Guard! Come quickly!"

"Damn!" growled the guardsman. "Someone calls. Get you gone, slave."

He hurried down the corridor and vanished around the corner at its far end. Simon, who had begun to walk back the way he had come, whirled about and dashed through the door at which the guardsman had been stationed. He suppressed an urge to chuckle to himself. Ventriloquism was one of the arts he had studied under the tutelage of the magicians of Persia, and he had learned it well.

Quickly yet cautiously he passed through a couple more torchlit halls, then paused to get his bearings. He knew he was not far now from the stairway that descended to the dungeon-temple he had visited the previous day—

Suddenly he heard the sounds of voices and approaching footsteps. He ducked into a curtained doorway and waited in the gloom, hoping the place was vacant and that the approaching talkers would pass him by. The chamber *felt* empty to his taut, straining senses, but the voices were coming ever nearer. He edged around the wall of the small room till he came to a niche that housed a tall statue of the goddess Pallas Athena; evidently this place was a shrine. He ducked behind the supporting pedestal, hoping it was big enough to hide him if need be.

The voices, Simon now realized, were of two men in earnest conversation. They had paused outside the door of the room in which he was concealed, and their tone indicated that they did not wish to be overheard.

"These halls are no place to discuss such things, Tullus," said one of them—and Simon started as he recognized the voice of Cassius Chaerea. "Come—enter. We can discuss in greater safety here."

"But not for long," said the other. "I am already too long away from my post. If I don't rejoin Lucullus soon, the Emperor may return and learn of it—"

"The Emperor!" snarled Chaerea as the two men entered the dark shrine. "The Emperor is mad—and all of us will lose more than our jobs if nothing is done to stop him. We must strike soon!"

"This I know, sir. I assume you have spoken to others in the Imperial Guard?"

"To all I can trust. Here—let me light a torch—"

"Please, sir—do not. We must not be seen."

"I had not judged you for a coward, Tullus," said Chaerea. "If you would rather sit this out—"

"Nor *am* I!" answered the other hotly. "Nor is it worthy of you to imply it, sir, begging your pardon. No one wishes to see the madman's crimes stopped more than I. I have seen too many good Romans sent to their doom by him; Aesius Proclus, for one, whose only crime was his popularity—and good old Marcus Silanus, who would not put to sea in a raging storm for the madman's pleasure—and Tribune Gallio and his bride, whom the Emperor coveted—and Thracius, who died but yesterday under the torturer's knife merely because his good head of hair put Gaius' balding pate to shame—and—"

"Hush!" said Chaerea. "We'll be here all day if you insist on enumerating all the Emperor's senseless crimes. Accept my apology, good Tullus, for calling you coward. Too often has the Emperor suggested the same of me to my very face, till I am sore put to keep my sword in its sheath!"

"Well do I know that, sir, for I have heard him bait you often. Why do we not slay him this very day?"

"The Praetorian officers still debate as to who shall be emperor next," said Chaerea. "But action shall not be delayed much longer. Before the week is done, I am sure, it will be decided. Until then, keep your peace whatever provocation the Emperor lays upon you. And know this: When he is to be slain, you or whoever else is on guard shall be instructed to answer 'Jupiter' when he asks for the day's watchword. Do not forget it, for it may be I shall have no other chance to instruct you in advance. When you hear that watchword—strike!"

"Jupiter—who slays with lightning," mused Tullus. "May I hear it soon—for on that day lightning shall not be swifter than my sword!"

Simon heard the guardsman smite his breast in salute, then the curtains parting and footsteps receding away to silence. Chaerea waited by himself in the darkness a few moments more, then left and strode away in the direction opposite the one Tullus had taken.

Slowly, carefully, Simon stole from the niche and left the room, his feet making not a shadow of a sound. He cursed his luck, for some time had passed and Menophar would by now have evacuated his quarters in the palace. If his absence were discovered suspicion would arise, and Simon hoped to be gone by then. The Emperor had left the palace to attend a theatrical performance, indicating he would be gone till noon at least. Simon hoped he would keep to his stated schedule....

At last Simon stood before the bronze door that opened upon the stair to the underground temple. It was unguarded—for the moment, at least—but locked. Simon fumbled with his right sandal, withdrew a long copper bodkin that had been concealed in its sole, and attacked the lock. Before a minute had passed his skill was rewarded by a loud click, and the door swung silently inward.

Entering and closing the portal behind him, he groped his way down the stone steps in the dark. After three flights and three landings he stood on a floor which he knew must be of the room of the torture-sacrifice. Carefully he felt his way around the wall to where he knew the stone door was concealed in the chamber's far end. His sensitive fingers, groping delicately, discovered the narrow lintel. He pressed gingerly upward on its right end.

Immediately there was a soft sound of metal sliding on polished stone and a shifting of air currents, and Simon knew that an open space gaped before him in the wall. A strange, fishy odor entered his nostrils and a strange sound whispered around him, like the watery swishing of ocean waves on a beach. Slowly, in spite of a rising sense of fear, he groped his way through the door—

Suddenly there was light—a torch in the room behind him had been lit. Simon whirled and confronted a huge German mercenary—the same he had seen torture the prisoner in this very place. Evidently a guard slept here at all times.

"By Mannus!" roared the German, a dagger glinting in his massive right hand. "If it isn't old Menophar's slave sneaking about. You'll die slowly for this, Nubian!"

Simon cringed back, mouthing a slave-like plea for mercy. The German laughed and rushed at him. Quickly as a cat Simon avoided the charge, grabbed his attacker's wrist and wrenched it back. The German howled as his arm broke with a loud crack under the force of his own momentum, and the dagger clattered to the floor. Bellowing with pain and rage, the German spun about and lashed at Simon with his left fist—but Simon was already beneath the flailing arm, snatching up the dagger and driving it again and again into the mercenary s belly and chest. The man folded, clutching his thick midsection with both arms; his eyes rolled upward, and his massive frame toppled to the floor like a felled tree.

"You died more quickly than your master's victims," snarled Simon, breathing hard. "More quickly than you deserved, I'd say!"

He retreated from the doorway, lifted the torch the German had lit, then returned and stepped over the corpse into the chamber beyond. The strange sound was louder here. He gasped as the light of his torch revealed the room.

It was larger than the chamber from which he had come. Two altars, one to the right and the other to the left of him, stood facing one another against the walls. The right one bore a carved face resembling that of an octopus, its round, staring eyes surrounded by tentacles; on it rested a corpse obviously many days dead, its skin rent with many knife wounds. The altar on the left bore a less recognizable face—if face it could be called, for it suggested an inhuman pattern like an unstable swirl of energy, yet at the same time seemed to represent a countenance filled with the most abominable cruelty. Atop it lay the body of the man Simon had seen tortured to death.

But it was the room itself that most astounded him, for all its walls and ceiling were covered with innumerable sea shells, their pearly concave surfaces facing inward. There were fan-like shells of large scallops, clam shells resembling giant pink ears, snail shells like delicate coiled horns, conical limpets, dark mussels and mottled sea urchins—and from all came a strange, soft roaring sound like the sound of forgotten underground seas!

Simon shuddered. He knew he was in the presence of strange magic, a magic induced by spells from the terrible *Book of Thoth*—an awful necromancy that was generating slowly in this dark chamber, growing in power toward the day when it might come forth and overwhelm all the earth....

Conquering his fear with a mighty effort, Simon walked slowly across the room. Against its far wall, resting on the floor, was the chest wherein Gaius kept his potions and poisons—and the *Book of Thoth*. He tried its lid gently. It was locked.

Kneeling on the stone floor, he brought his copper bodkin into play again. Unseen forces seemed to coil around him as he worked, swirling like cold, unseen winds. Never had he felt such an urgency to have done with a task. Sometimes it seemed to him that he labored at the bottom of a dark sea with strange, round eyes passing slowly by to stare at him from the gloom; at other times he felt himself in the midst of an infinite cold blackness where stars hung like glittering eyes in cruel, swirling faces whose gaze pierced his flesh like torturing needles....

Suddenly he could stand it no more. He picked up the chest bodily, retreated to the outer room, and deposited it by the wall farthest from the echoing chamber. After bracketing his torch once more and standing quietly for a few moments to calm his shaken nerves, he again turned his attention to the chest.

Its lock was far more finely made and intricate than that of the door above. Even so, it was barely a quarter of an hour till it yielded to Simon's practiced fingers. Slowly he raised the lid—and saw before him, as he had hoped, the thick, yellowed scroll of the *Book of Thoth*.

Almost reverently he lifted it from the chest. Now was the time for him to destroy it, as he had been bid. Yet—*should he?* Here was the one book that every sorcerer might well covet. It was surely the rarest work of magic in the world, and its dark secrets might make him the world's most exalted mage. Why should not he, Simon of Gitta, instead of the insane Gaius, be the one to use its power to rule all men?

For a long time he crouched there while a silent inner struggle went on and the sea-whisperings from the chamber behind him crawled horribly along the walls. Finally he rose, slowly shaking his head as reason reasserted itself. The thing was too dangerous for mortal men to use. Besides, he could not run the risk of getting caught with it while trying to leave the palace—in which event the *Scroll* would end up in Gaius' hands once more.

Quickly he unrolled it to its full length, tore in into several sections and wadded them into a pile in the center of the room. Then he set his torch to the pile and, as the dry old papyrus caught and blazed, retreated quickly up the stone stairs.

Smoke rapidly filled the room and eddied up the stairway behind him—and, as it did so, Simon thought he glimpsed strange, monstrous faces swirling within it. Many of these seemed the faces of dead, mutilated men but some resembled monstrous frogs, octopi, and needle-eyed whorls of substanceless energy. All seemed to be glaring after him malevolently, and for a moment his nerves shrieked in silent terror at the threat of them. Then, slowly, they began to fade even as the book whose spells sustained them was consumed, and the supernatural sounds from the temple below faded also and finally died to silence. By the time Simon gained the topmost stair the passage behind him was quiet as a tomb and the faces had vanished altogether.

IV

Smoke was filling Simon's lungs; he could not tarry here. He opened the outer door—and confronted two guardsmen who were standing directly across the corridor. As smoke billowed out the door behind him the pair simultaneously gave voice to their surprise with a loud yell, then lowered their spears and advanced upon him.

"Help!" cried Simon. "Help! Murder's been done in the Emperor's magic room."

"What's new about that?" snarled one of the guards; Simon recognized him as Tullus by his voice. "And what means this smoke? Stand where you are, wretch! You, Lepidus—go down there and see what the smoke's all about. Be quick!"

For an instant Simon tensed for conflict—then decided against it as the footfalls of more soldiers rapidly approaching sounded from both directions down the corridor. He relaxed and lapsed once more into the personality of a servile slave, his very form seeming to shrink as he cringed back from the guards' spear points.

Lepidus, who had snatched a torch from its wall bracket and descended into the gloom, returned in a few moments coughing and wiping tears from his smarting eyes.

"Vindex is dead!" he gasped. "The slave killed him, by Pallas!"

"I'm surprised you'd shed tears over that!" said another guardsman, laughing harshly.

"Silence!" barked Tullus. "You, Nubian—explain yourself."

"I slew him not!" whined Simon. "I found him even as you find him now. He has been slain by demons!"

"This cursed magic of the Emperor's—" growled a guard nervously.

"Shut up! Let the slave tell us why he came here. His story had better be good."

"My master sent me," said Simon, "—at the behest of the Emperor, I am told. I was to perform a minor ritual to prepare for a later one the Emperor intended to conduct this day."

"That rings true," said Lepidus. "This dog is the pet of Gaius' hired Egyptian mage. He was at the Emperor's bloody ritual yesterday afternoon."

"We'll soon see what this is all about," said Tullus. "Go you, Lepidus, and find Commander Chaerea. Ask him to come quickly."

"Commander Chaerea is attending the Emperor at the theater."

"Well, Commander Sabinus, then. Hurry! And roust out this Nubian dog's master while you're at it."

In a very few minutes Lepidus was back, followed by a burly Roman officer. "The Egyptian serpent has fled his hole, Tullus. I have a feeling we'll see him no more. His belongings have vanished with him."

"This situation stinks to the heavens!" growled Tullus. "What are we to do with this dog of a slave, Commander Sabinus?"

"Bring him along," said the officer. "We'll see him locked safely away in the Praetorian guardhouse before we do aught else. The Emperor can then verify the dog's story at his convenience."

The commander strode away, followed by the several guardsmen who had formed themselves into a tight square around Simon. They marched down many corridors and finally descended a flight of stairs, emerging at the bottom from the palace onto its grounds. Simon began to sweat with anxiety. His position was now desperate. Gaius knew him of old; the affair had concerned an evil magical ring of great power which Simon had prevented from falling into the mad emperor's hands. That had been nearly four years ago, but Gaius would nevertheless be certain to see through the Nubian disguise during a close interrogation—and then it would be slow torture for Simon....

They passed beyond the palace grounds and down an arcaded street for some distance, then turned onto a roofed, colonnaded walkway. Simon watched for his chance, but the soldiers also were watchful and tense. Soon he would have to risk all on a quick break for freedom, hopeless as that course of action now seemed—

"Ho—we're in luck!" cried Commander Sabinus suddenly. "Here comes Chaerea and his men—and the Emperor with them."

The two parties drew close to one another and halted. Sabinus and his men all saluted. Simon saw that in addition to Gaius and his guards there were a number of foppishly dressed folk—patrician hangers-on, no doubt—and a few slaves carrying the Emperor's empty litter. Some distance away followed a number of German mercenaries—Gaius' personal bodyguard, whom he was known to trust better than native Roman legionaries.

"Ho, Sabinus!" cried out Gaius suddenly. "What's the day's watchword?"

Sabinus opened his mouth to reply—and, quick as thought, Simon yelled out from motionless, barely parted lips:

"Jupiter!"

"Jupiter, is it?" cried Chaerea, who stood directly behind the Emperor. "Then—*take this!*"

A foot of steel suddenly stood out from the front of Gaius' neck. His frantic shriek indicated that the blade had not severed his windpipe. The steel was withdrawn and the Emperor whirled, face twisted with pain and fear, to confront his assailant. Chaerea swung his sword and Simon heard a distinct "clank" as the heavy blade bit solidly into Gaius' jawbone. Then Gaius was down on the paving stones, screaming insanely. Sabinus and his fellow guardsmen rushed forward, ignoring Simon—but instead of attacking Chaerea they joined him in plunging their weapons again and again into the body of the dying emperor.

"I live!" shrieked Gaius madly, frantic to the last to deny the possibility of his death. *"I still live!"*

Simon dashed away frantically, but none pursued him. Now all the soldiers of both parties had joined in the butchery, and the German bodyguard hastening to the rescue was too far away to do any good. A great exaltation filled Simon's being; the *Book of Thoth* had been destroyed and the world was rid of a dangerous madman. And he, Simon, was free. Just before he darted down a concealing byway he paused, cast off his turban, and snatched a final glance at the group of hate-filled assassins stabbing furiously at their writhing victim—

And in that instant saw—or thought he saw—

"Baal!" gasped Simon.

For in the air above the butchered emperor and his slayers he seemed to glimpse, for an instant, the outlines of monstrous faces—the faces of dead, mutilated men and frog-like beings, of octopi and needle-eyed whorls of energy—faces which seemed to converge with expressions of concentrated malevolence toward the twitching body of Gaius before finally vanishing from sight—

"Let him feel that he is dying!" snarled Simon—and an instant later he had vanished away down the dark, narrow alleys of old Rome.

About "The Dragons of Mons Fractus"

WARNING: Contains spoilers!

Less than a year later, in late autumn A.D. 41, we find Simon on the Germanic frontier of the Roman Empire on a mission of revenge. This quest ultimately takes him up Mons Fractus, a mountain in central Switzerland—known today as Mount Pilatus.

Pontius Pilate has the odd distinction of having become an article of faith in a religion to which he never belonged and which he no doubt despised, for the Nicene Creed requires those who parrot it to affirm not just the death of Jesus Christ, but specifically his execution "under Pontius Pilate." Pilate is a figure of as much scholarly doubt as he is of popular faith. It is fascinating to peel back the layers of legend and dogma to reveal the unstable nucleus of historical fact. There is a good amount of Pilate apocrypha, including the Acts of Pilate (a fourth-century Christian document, also called the Gospel of Nicodemus, designed to provide a "safe" substitute for the court records of Jesus' trial which Justin Martyr and Tertullian had supposed must be extant in Rome and which, as Robert Eisler suggests, may have been destroyed by Christians once they attained access to them in Constantine's time). Others include the Avenging of the Savior, the Letters of Pilate and Herod, the Narrative of Joseph of Arimathea, the Letter of Pilate to Claudius, the Letter of Pilate to Tiberius, the *Paradosis Pilati*, the *Anaphora Pilati*, and the Death of Pilate. (All these documents may be consulted in J. K. Elliott, ed., *The Apocryphal New Testament*, Oxford, 1993.)

Some traditions pictured Pilate converting to Christianity and even being martyred for his faith. In the Ethiopian Coptic Church, Pilate has been canonized as a saint! All this is the *reductio ad absurdum* of a tendency, already discernible in the gospels, to whitewash Pilate and, with him, Roman responsibility for the death of Jesus. This spin control was the result of Christians attempting to curry the favor of Rome, shifting the blame for Jesus' death onto Jews, because they wanted to ameliorate the offense of Jesus having died as an enemy of the Roman state.

It is a further irony that Pilate, for whose reputation such zeal was shown, was apparently not the only or even necessarily even the first candidate chosen by early Christian legend-mongers as the probable executioner of Jesus. Certain early traditions reflected in one of Luke's pregospel sources and in the Gospel of Peter ascribed the execution of Jesus to Herod Antipas. One reference in the Talmud even has Jesus crucified under Alexander Jannaeus a century "before Christ!" All this implies that the death of Jesus may at first have been imagined as ahistorical, like those of some Mystery Religion deities like Attis and Osiris, and only later histori-cized.

Tierney based this tale on two sets of legends: first, those attested in the Death of Pilate concerning Pilate being demon-possessed and, second, those "about dragons living within Mt. Pilatus (Mons Fractus) in Switzer-land. The most recent dragon-sighting is said to have occurred there in the mid-13th century. There is also the tale of a man who fell into a crevasse on Mt. Pilatus and found himself in a cave inhabited by two dragons, who allowed him to overwinter with them there. So now it is revealed exactly how those legends originated" (Letter, February 27, 1984).

"The Dragons of Mons Fractus" originally appeared in *Weirdbook* #19, Spring 1984.

THE DRAGONS OF MONS FRACTUS

by Richard L. Tierney

I

Some have seen corpses long interr'd
Escape from hallowing control,
Pale charnel forms—nay ev'n have heard
The shrilling of a troubled soul,
That wanders till the dawn hath cross'd
The dolorous dark....

— Robert Bridges

"Consuming fire!" cried the dark-robed magician, standing tall and extending his arms aloft. "Can a man of flesh and blood withstand such fire? Watch closely, and see!"

Even as he spoke, a trapdoor opened in the center of the stage and the head and neck of what appeared to be a tremendous dragon emerged, its golden scales glittering in the light of many torches, smoke drifting upward from the corners of its fanged mouth as it glowered down at the man. The thousands of spectators massed in the great semi-circular theater leaned forward as one, hushed and fascinated.

"Fire!" the magician cried again.

The dragon's enormous mouth gaped wide and a torrent of roaring flame rushed forth, enveloping the gesturing figure. For an instant the man seemed a blazing statue, the occult symbols on his robe glaring like bits of white-hot iron. Then the flames increased with an almost thunderous roar, and the magician was lost to view in their fierce intensity.

Abruptly the flames vanished, and the dragon's roar ceased. On the floor of the stage, exactly where the man had stood, there now remained only an irregular, dark patch that smoked and steamed. The crowd gasped—a vast, uneasy whisper of astonishment and disbelief. Slowly the huge dragon head closed its fanged mouth, then withdrew into the dark aperture from which it had emerged. The crowd sat in shocked silence for a moment, then began to rustle and murmur.

"He's dead!" yelled a man suddenly. "Something's gone wrong—"

"They've killed him for sport!" a woman shrieked.

"That fire was real—I felt the heat of the dragon's breath—"

Even as the crowd stirred as if on the verge of an uproar, something moved within the dragon pit—something that rose slowly into view. It was the magician, his arms raised high as before, his robes and flesh showing not the least signs of scorching. In a moment he stood upon the wide stage once more, the section of floor beneath him appearing as normal as the rest.

The crowd burst into thunderous applause; the magician, after many gracious bows and many polite refusals for encores, strode away and vanished behind the curtains at the back of the theater.

"You were magnificent, Simon of Gitta," said the thin, gray-haired man who was helping the magician out of his symbol-emblazoned robe. "Surely this has been the greatest display of magic that the city of Vienna has ever seen—or all the province of Gaul, for that matter. Sometimes even I had to remind myself that you were not using true sorcery."

"I use no sorcery, Nicephorus," he said. "It is all stage illusion—as you, who have aided me so well, should know beyond question."

"Yet you are a master at what you do, Simon, and surely there is a sort of true magic in that. I have learned much while aiding you, as I am sure the rest of my master's household have also."

The magician turned away, brushing the dark bangs back from his forehead nervously. He seemed younger now than when on stage—a man in his early thirties with a lean, athletic build that suggested that he might have seen fighting. Nicephorus wondered about the hint of nervousness in the man's movements, in the glint of his deep-set dark eyes. Could it be that this magician, so able to command the fascinated attention of an audience of thousands, felt awkward about accepting in private a compliment from one of his assistants? Or were there other things on the man's mind to account for his distant and diffident manner?

"You are right," said Simon abruptly. "It was a grand spectacle. I have kept my part of the bargain, and I am sure your master will profit well from the money taken in this night. Now he must fulfill his promise. Take me to him."

"I must supervise the closing-down of the theater. Your stage assistant will conduct you to the house of Coponius. *Gratia*—come here!"

A shapely, azure-eyed blonde woman, clad only in a short white tunic and high-strapped sandals, appeared from behind a curtain and nodded slightly to Nicephorus. Simon noticed again that, unlike most slaves, there was no subservience in her bearing; he even seemed to detect a touch of proud defiance.

"Please, Nicephorus, not that name again," said the woman. "I am Gretchen."

"Spare me, girl—you should know by now that I can't learn to pronounce such an outlandish sound. I presume you are now recovered from being hewn in half by this master of sorcery who stands beside me; if so, convey him at once to the villa of our master."

The girl nodded again. Beckoning briefly to Simon, she led him out a back door of the theater into the night. The stars shone hazily in the air of the still summer twilight; crickets shrilled in soft, insistent monotony.

"Wait here, magician. Nicephorus will send a litter around."

"My name is Simon, and I'd rather walk. Come on."

He set out at a brisk pace, and the girl hurried along beside him. "You know the way?"

"I should. I found the house of your master all by myself, when I first came to Vienna."

"And why *did* you come here, Samaritan wizard?"

The man stopped and scowled at her. "Gretchen, I said my name is Simon. And I am no true wizard, as you well know."

She stared coolly at him. He seemed different now, clad only in his dark tunic, with no symbol-emblazoned cloak and miter—younger, more human.

"*You* can pronounce my name," she said, laughing. "And that was clever, the way you appeared to cut me in half for that crowd's entertainment. I was almost touched, the way they called you a murderer—never have so many cared about my fate! I promise I'll never tell anyone how you did it."

Simon shrugged. "It matters not. Tomorrow we'll be gone from Vienna, to perform in Lugdunum—if your master keeps his promise and tells me what I wish to know."

The girl stared at him levelly. "You're a dark one, Simon of Gitta—I can tell. I'd like to ask you what a Samaritan wizard is doing here in Gaul, working for another dark one like the Roman Coponius, who calls himself my master. But I won't, because I know you wouldn't answer. Come."

You're a dark one yourself, thought Simon, striding alongside the girl in the dusk. *Dark, in spite of your fairness....*

Then his thoughts turned in another direction as they approached the northern edge of town and the villa that loomed black against the starry sky.

"Wonderful!" exclaimed Marcus Coponius as he brandished his wine goblet. "Marvelous! You held them all spellbound, Simon of Gitta."

"How do you know? You weren't even there—"

"But my little Gratia was, and she has just told me all about the crowd's reaction." Coponius took a long swig, then called out: "Gratia! Come fill our goblets!"

The blonde slave girl entered the peristyle where Simon and his host were lounging on couches beneath the stars. Carefully she poured wine from a long-necked amphora, while light from the many torches played upon her bare limbs and golden hair. As she withdrew, Simon sensed a sullen resentment in her blue eyes, though his host seemed not to notice it.

"A beauty, is she not?" Coponius enthused. "And proud, too. I captured her during a trip into the remote Alps three years ago. She's the daughter of a chief—took some taming, I can tell you, but she knows her place now."

Simon nodded curtly. "We have business to discuss, Coponius."

"Right you are," agreed the Roman genially. "You have made me a reasonably affluent man again, Simon. I therefore drink to Hermes, god of magic—for he, through you, has once again made my retirement here tolerable. Caligula paid me well to stay here and mind certain of his—affairs. But since Claudius came to power several months ago, I've been neglected—"

"Let's not mince words, Coponius." Simon leaned forward, setting aside his goblet. "By retirement, you mean exile. And I think your stay here in Vienna has not always been pleasant, if the gossip hereabouts is accurate."

The Roman sighed, swirled the wine in his goblet. "Aye—not at first. But you are here to see that our bargain is kept. You have not changed your mind, have you, Simon?"

"No. You need not fear. You may keep nine tenths of the money my performances bring in. I ask in return only that you tell me where to find the former owner of this house—"

Marcus Coponius stared about him, suddenly nervous, then gulped down his wine. "Gratia!" he called out. "Another!"

The shapely blonde girl entered once more, poured, then left again. This time Simon kept his eyes off her long enough to study the Roman narrowly, wondering about his obvious nervousness, the haunted look that had come into his eyes, the trembling of his hands. Obviously the man drank wine too deeply and too often.

"Tell me," said Simon. "No more delays. Where do I find the man who once owned this villa?"

Coponius nodded, drank again. "Pilatus—Pontius Pilatus, former procurator of Judea. He was the owner of this house after Caligula exiled *him* here. You want to know about him?"

"Aye."

Coponius looked into the Samaritan's dark, gleaming eyes. "And you want to know where he is so you can find him. And you want to find him so that you can enact revenge upon him. Don't deny it—I can tell."

"What's that to you?" growled Simon. "We have a bargain."

"Aye, and I'll stick to it." Coponius laughed and swilled more wine. "But it's not hard to figure out why you're out for revenge. You're a Samaritan, and Pilatus had several hundred of your people butchered for insurrection just before he was recalled to Rome four years ago."

Simon nodded, scowling darkly. "My mentor, Dositheus, was slain in that butchery. He was leading a crowd of my countrymen up to the summit of the holy mountain of Gerizim, in a ceremony of peaceful worship. The people were unarmed—there was no insurrection—"

"And so you have sworn vengeance," said Coponius, waving his goblet drunkenly. "Well, ask me your questions."

Simon drew a deep breath. "I understand this was the house of Pilatus, but that he left here some three years ago and no man knows why nor where. Can you tell me where he has gone, and how to find him?"

"Aye," mumbled the Roman. "Alas, I can. I must tell you—I must keep our bargain, and tell you things I cannot bear even to think of— things I have told no one. *Gratia*—!"

"No!" said Simon firmly, crossing to Coponius' couch and grabbing him by his wrist. "If you drink any more wine, you won't be *able* to tell me. Start talking. Tell me all you know...."

The Roman set aside his wine cup; he seemed pale in spite of his overindulgence.

"I was there," he muttered. "I was in the Emperor Caligula's magic room when he performed his monstrous deed of sorcery."

"Sorcery—?"

Coponius nodded. "Old Tiberius had ordered Pilatus back from Judea to face charges—officially for slaying the Samaritans you mentioned, but actually, I think, for crucifying a Nazorean wizard who claimed to have the secret of eternal life. Well, Tiberius died before Pilatus got to Rome, and when the procurator arrived at last he was thrown into a dungeon cell for a few months to await trial."

"So much I've heard. Go on, Coponius."

The Roman drained his wine cup. "Caligula heard about the affair, and was as disappointed as Tiberius about the slaying of the Nazorean. Like Tiberius, he had a mania about wanting to live forever. So he had Pilatus dragged out of his dungeon and asked him if he'd like a nice, plush retirement in Gaul in exchange for—for—Simon of Gitta, can you imagine anyone crazy enough to want to live forever in a world such as this?"

"Go on, damn it!"

The Roman nodded heavily. "Of course. You're a stage magician— you've never seen *real* sorcery. But *I* have! I was there the night crazy Caligula forced Pilatus and his wife, Claudia Procla, to participate in the ceremony. He berated Pilatus about killing the Nazorean—said that because of that blunder, the procurator was now obligated to atone by aiding in a ritual that might yet gain eternal life for Rome's emperor. And then he began to read spells from some old books he had inherited from Tiberius, and to draw symbols on the walls and floor. The two other guards and myself— well, we were terrified, because the walls in that underground room were roaring as if it were under a waterfall. I can read Greek and Latin, and recognize a lot of other tongues when I hear them, but I never before or since heard any language remotely like what crazy Caligula was reading from those old scrolls. He was bobbing and screaming and sweating, while the rest of us were holding candles in different locations about the room, Pilatus in the very center, all of us scared half silly—

"All of a sudden there was a flash of dark light—if that makes any sense to you. Pilatus shrieked and fell down as if he'd been struck by lightning. But in a moment he got up again, and his face was like nothing I ever saw before—rigid and fish-eyed—dead. And then his eyes started to glow. His wife, Claudia, just fell over dead at the sight—never got up again. Caligula was screaming in terror.

"My two men jumped Pilatus, but he grabbed them by the neck, one in each hand, and squeezed—and that was it. I heard their bones snap, and then he flung them to the ground. I stabbed at him—and I swear the sword just slipped through the man as if he were made of fog! Pilatus came after me then, and if I hadn't been near the Emperor I'd have been done for; because even though Caligula was scared out of his wits and screaming insanely, he'd had the sense to haul out a little charm and hold it up—and damned if it didn't make that demon-possessed lich back off!"

Simon felt his spine tingling. "What kind of charm?" he demanded.

"Here." Coponius fumbled at a cord around his neck and drew from beneath his tunic a small statuette of green jade—an ugly female figure, sinister and grimacing. Simon recognized it as a representation of Hecate, the witch-goddess. "Caligula once bragged to me that it had belonged to his father, Germanicus, and that he had stolen it from him, thereby allowing Germanicus to be slain by the evil magic of his enemies."

"And how do *you* come to have it?"

"The mad emperor gave it to me when he ordered me to—to escort the exiled Pilatus here to Vienna, and it has been my sole protection ever since. I must tell you all, Samaritan, but before I can go on I *must* have more wine."

Simon agreed grudgingly, and at the Roman's call Gretchen appeared so readily with the amphora that Simon suspected she had been listening to them from within the curtained doorway.

"Leave the jug here, girl," said Coponius. Then, when she had left: "Simon, there is sorcery of a sort you have never performed on any stage—sorcery born of Hades. That was the sort I saw that night in Caligula's magic room.

"Somehow we subdued the thing called Pilatus, with the green image to keep it at bay and with spells which Caligula recited from one of his ancient scrolls. Then we sealed it in a stone coffin and, with the aid of several soldiers of the Emperor's German bodyguard, buried it on an island in the Tiber. For the undead cannot cross running water, or so Caligula assured me.

"Then the Emperor fell ill as a result of his fearful shock, and for many days he lay raving in a delirium of fever. When at last he recovered, his mind was left in a state of even more extreme madness than before. His terror began to increase as stories circulated in the city of people who had died crossing the trans-Tiber bridge at night, or whose boats had run ashore on the island in dense fog—people whose bloodless bodies were found next day with their spines snapped as by a giant gladiator. Also, storms seemed to increase in frequency over Rome, and Caligula got into such a state of terror over all this that he would hide beneath his bed on nights when lightning blazed and thunder shook the skies.

"Finally the Emperor could stand it no more, and bade me dig up Pilatus' body and convey it far from Rome, into the heart of Gaul. He gave me much gold and many trusty servants, and also that green jade amulet that had protected him—for by now he had secretly hired sorcerers to devise even more powerful protections for him.

"So I conveyed the—procurator—here to the city of Vienna. On the way a sailor was lost overboard each night, and on one occasion Pilatus came to me on deck and talked to me under the moon. Do not ask me to describe that!

"We buried the thing again, this time on an island in the Rhone, and once again there were storms more frequently than was natural, and ships driven ashore, and many people dying in the night. That was a dark and terrible winter for Vienna. So you see, Samaritan, Pilatus never did live in this villa, even though it was registered in his name to support the rumors bruited about in Rome that he was an exile in Gaul. And soon, to further avert suspicion, I gave out that Pilatus had died, and even had a conspicuous tomb built to his memory.

"But the following spring I felt compelled to move the lich once more, for the citizens of Vienna were suspicious of me in their terror, remembering that the dark happenings had begun just after my arrival. This time I had it conveyed far up the Rhone, even to Geneva, and buried there on a small island where the river flows out of the great lake of Lemannus; but again the thing brought fogs and storms, and wrought much havoc.

"At last, with great toil and expense, I had it conveyed to a wild, remote region far to the northeast, near the border of Rhaetia, and there caused it to be sunk in a tarn near the top of a high and uninhabited mountain."

The Roman paused to gulp more wine, then wiped his perspiring forehead with a sleeve of his tunic. Simon did not know whether he should consider the man's story seriously or take it as the ravings of a drunken lunatic.

"What happened then? More—disturbances?"

"I do not know." Coponius shook his head violently, as if to clear it of dark visions. "We sank the thing before midday, and by evening we were many leagues away. That was over three years ago. I have never traveled in that direction since."

"A map," said Simon. "You must have a map drawn for me."

The Roman laughed shrilly, drunkenly. "You're crazy, Samaritan—crazy as Caligula himself. Yet, a bargain's a bargain. I'll give you a map—in the morning—ha! ha!"

Abruptly, he slid from his couch to sprawl in an unconscious, drunken stupor upon the marble floor.

II

… the terrible chasm
Yawning beneath us, black and deep,
As if, in some convulsive spasm,
The summits of the hills had cracked,
And made a road for the cataract
That raves and rages down the steep!

— Longfellow, *The Golden Legend*

Simon gazed down from the brink of the cliff into the narrow canyon, listening to the rushing of the water far below, then raised his eyes to the many-spired mountain that loomed far off and sinister to the northeast, high and white against the deepening blue of the twilight. Mons Fractus—the jagged mountain—that was what his nervous Allobrogian guide had called it before he had demanded his final pay and hurriedly slipped away westward into the forest, back toward Aventicum….

Aventicum. That was the last place he had seen Gretchen….

Simon sighed. He looked up to where the full moon was just rising over the pines of the eastward ridge beyond the canyon.

Luna… Selene… Helen… How long since the Romans caused you to die, my only love…?

He shook his head. That had been years ago….

Quickly he swung the packsack from his horse. This was a good place to camp. He was on a mission of vengeance, nothing less; he would not be distracted by painful memories.

But after he had cooked and eaten his solitary supper, he sat up for some hours, unable to sleep, staring into the fire while the moon rose. And he could not help but think of Gretchen. She had accompanied him these last several weeks, northeastward into the farther reaches of Gaul, performing as his stage assistant in Lugdunum, in Geneva, and finally in Aventicum—always under the eagle eye of old Nicephorus, Coponius' trusted freedman. And Simon, to his annoyance, had found himself desiring her. It had been a long time since he had had a woman.

Gretchen....

He shook his head, trying to brush away the thought that even now she would be returning to Vienna with the other slaves and old Nicephorus—back to the arms of her drunken Roman master, with most of the money Simon's showmanship had drawn in. That had been the bargain: wealth for Coponius, information for Simon—information that would lead him to vengeance....

Simon rose and began to gather more firewood. Vengeance—he had dedicated his mind and feelings to it; yet what an abstract concept it seemed this night in the midst of this wild moonlit forest, as he sat near the brink of a narrow canyon where dark waters rushed and roared like muted thunder far below. Again he glanced at the thin spires of Mons Fractus glowing faintly in the light of the full moon.

"Are you truly there, Pilatus?" he muttered. "Or has that drunken Coponius misled me for your protection? Well, I'll soon know—and if he's lied, I'll be back to Vienna to wring the truth out of him!"

He was feeling more and more that he had been made a fool of. Surely Coponius had merely concocted that tale of supernatural terror. Yet why? To frighten Simon off? No, for if that were the Roman's purpose—to protect Pilatus—why had he not simply lied about his whereabouts? Why invent a tale of an undead thing that walked the night—?

Suddenly he heard a horse whicker in the distance.

Simon started to his feet, drawing his keen-bladed *sica*. His own horse stood tethered at the edge of the forest, browsing upon the sparse grasses. Quickly the Samaritan darted into the trees, moving cautiously, mind working furiously. Someone had followed him here—had been following him for the last few days. It had not been his impression alone, but that of his Allobrogian guide as well. Neither had been completely sure, but now....

Still, no one had appeared, and at length Simon wondered whether he had been prey to his imagination. Slowly he relaxed, sheathing his blade—

And then a movement in the shadows caused him to start, drawing his knife once more. Someone *was* coming down the forest path, slowly and silently, on foot—a cloaked and cowled figure.

Simon's hackles rose. He forced himself to silence and motionlessness, crouching in the shrubbery till the shadowy form had passed him by—

Then, leaping forth, he threw an arm about the neck of the intruder and hissed: "Don't struggle—I can gut you in a second. Why are you following me—?"

"Let—let me go—Simon of Gitta—"

A woman's voice. Startled, Simon released her and she turned to face him.

"Gretchen—!"

"Yes, I followed you," she said, laughing. "I thought you might need a guide after that dull Allobrogian refused to go farther into the land of my own people. I knew he'd turn back. And I didn't want him carrying tales about me back to Aventicum, so I stayed out of sight."

"But—why sneak up to my campsite like this—?"

"I wanted to surprise you."

"Baal! Do you know how close I came to—"

She laughed again, throwing back the hood of her cloak and tossing her blonde hair. "I feared no harm from you, Simon. You knew me instantly, even in the night. I knew you would. Now, let me bring up my horse, which is tethered nearby."

They prepared some warm broth, then sat close to one another by the fire while they supped, their cloaks wrapped closely about them. The air had grown chill.

"What of old Nicephorus?" asked Simon. "How did you escape from him? Will he not send soldiers to follow you?"

Gretchen smiled. "I paid him gold, to the amount of all I stole from his master over the last three years. Coponius will not object. He desired me at first, but now all he desires is gold and his wine cup."

Simon nodded appreciatively. "And what did you mean, Gretchen, when you said you could be my guide? Do you know this region?"

"Very well. I lived here till three years ago, when Marcus Coponius and his soldiers came and stole me from my people. I am a daughter of a chief of the Allemani; at an early age I was betrothed to Brennus, a chief s son of the Helvetii, and sent to live with them. I grew up near here; my village is on the shore of a great lake, just beyond the southern flank of that mountain."

Simon stared gloomily at the ghostly, moonlit spires toward which the girl pointed. "That mountain is my destination."

"Do you really think your enemy is there, Simon?"

He looked at her. "Gretchen, did you hear the story that Coponius told me?"

"I heard all. I was hiding just beyond the curtain."

"And—do you think he told me the truth?"

The girl shuddered slightly. "I do not know. My people have legends of such things, though—of the demon-possessed, who cannot die but who do not truly live, and who crave human blood...."

Simon, too, felt an uneasiness. He had heard legends of this sort during his travels in far lands, and even in his homeland of Samaria—and now, a girl who had grown up among the remote Helvetii was telling him the same sort of thing. Moreover, there was another disquieting fact: Coponius had not lied about being in this region some three years ago.

"What do you know about the Roman called Pilatus?"

"No more than what Coponius told you," said Gretchen. "If they left the man's body upon the mountain as he said, it must have been just before his soldiers captured me. Yet I think he spoke the truth, for I know the very tarn he mentioned; it lies nearly between those two jagged summits."

Simon nodded, looking to where she pointed. "What else do you know about Mons Fractus?"

"That is what the Romans call it, but my people know it as the *Drakamund*—the mount of dragons—for it is said that dragons live within it, and fly between it and the mountains of Zug across the lake to the northeast. The folk of my village shun the place because of these old tales, but I know there are no dragons because I have explored the mountain thoroughly."

"You have courage, Gretchen. Did not the old tales frighten you even a little?"

The girl laughed. "A little, perhaps, at first. But I had not heard the tales from infancy, as my adopted people had. In the beginning I persuaded Brennus to explore the mountain with me; later, I often went alone. Maybe I'm crazy, Simon, but I always thought that even if the dragons did exist, they'd be friendly toward me—lucky for me. I was so disappointed that I never found any of them! She suddenly grew subdued, even somber. "The only monsters I ever encountered there were Romans—the last time I stole away from the village to explore. They captured me, and—and slew Brennus, who followed them when he heard of my capture."

She was silent for a space, the laughter utterly gone from her like the sun behind a dark cloud.

"Since then, I have been a slave in Vienna—I, who was born the daughter of one chief and betrothed to the son of another! Do you know what it means to be a slave, Simon of Gitta?"

Simon took her hand.

"Yes," he said evenly. "I was sold to a gladiator school by Roman tax-gatherers who slew my parents. I fought in the arenas for two years before I regained my freedom. But my fight against Rome did not end then, and it never shall."

Gretchen returned the pressure of his hand, and for a time they were silent.

"Now I know why you are so fierce in your pursuit of revenge," she said presently. "This mentor of yours—you must have loved and respected him greatly."

Simon studied the backs of his hands. "Aye. It was he who freed me from the arena. We had our differences, and there were times when I even thought I hated him—when he delved into dangerous sorcery in order to fight Rome. But even in those dark moments, I knew he was driven to his actions by hatred for the cruel power that crushes and enslaves all nations."

"And who is this Pilatus, who slew him and so many others of your countrymen?"

"A cruel, rapacious—!" Simon choked briefly on his emotion; then a cold fire glowed in his deep-set, shadowed eyes. "In short, a Roman of the same sort who killed my parents. For ten years my country suffered under his hand, but now mayhap I have tracked him to his last refuge—and soon he shall pay for all his foul deeds."

"Simon!" There was compassion, and also a touch of fear, in the girl's eyes. "I know that mountain well. It is desolate of human life. Only the most devoted ascetic could live there, or—"

She stopped speaking, and Simon felt his spine tingling.

Suddenly the girl laughed again. "No, such things cannot be! Coponius has fooled you, Simon of Gitta, and you have come here for nothing. How sad! I should make it up to you...."

Her manner had become light, vibrant, provocative. Simon found himself smiling at her, his black mood lifting; he suddenly wanted to believe that she was right and that he had come to this place on a fool's errand.

"If you're so sad for me, Gretchen, why are you laughing?"

"But you're laughing too, now, Simon. How nice! I *knew* you could laugh—"

Suddenly, spontaneously, they were in one another's arms, and Simon's blood was aflame as their lips met and he clutched her to him in an almost crushing embrace.

After a moment he felt a hardness against his chest. Gretchen whimpered slightly; he released her, and she turned and settled back against him nestled in his arms, trembling slightly. Simon gently touched her bosom, felt the hard object beneath the fabric of her white tunic.

"Ah, that." Gretchen pulled forth a small amulet that dangled from a cord about her neck. "I stole it for you, thinking you might need it if—if Coponius' tale were true...."

Simon examined the thing, recognized it as the jade statuette of Hecate the Roman had shown him.

"How did you—?"

"I took it from Coponius in Lugdunum, the last night he was with us. He was too drunk to know. As on most nights, he wanted me to share his bed but passed out before he could do aught. I don't know which disgusted me more about him, his lust or his drunkenness. But no more of him! He is no longer my captor, nor ever shall be again. Here, Simon—" She slipped the cord over her head and handed him the ornament. "It is yours."

"Why have you done all this for me, Gretchen?"

For a moment the girl looked pensive. "Perhaps it was that first night, in Vienna, when you performed the trick of dragon magic. The priests of my people are the Dragon Druids, and the dragon is our totem. Or perhaps—I don't know. At any rate, you gave me the opportunity to escape at last. Here, Simon, take the amulet."

He took it and started to put it on, then tied it to his belt instead.

"I thank you, Gretchen, and I'll treasure it as a gift, but I won't let it come between us again!"

They both laughed, and he crushed her to him once more with an almost frantic passion. She returned his embrace and kisses with an equal ardor, and there were no more memories of Romans and vengeances and dark things, only the moon and stars, the fragrant pines and the campfire, the whispering wind and the mutter of rushing water far below in the gorge....

There was a ringing in Simon's ears, high and keen. He knew he was dreaming—no, surely that was impossible—when you're dreaming, you think you're awake....

That keening, like painful music, impossibly high-pitched. If needles were sounds, they would be like that. And there was a feeling of lethargy, and horror—

He forced his eyes open. The fire had burned low. Gretchen lay beside him, wrapped in her cloak, eyes closed, face flushed, lips moving as if she were trying to speak in a fever-dream. And beyond her, at the edge of the forest—

Pilatus!

No, surely it was a dream—for how, in waking life, could one man recognize another who stood many yards away, amid the shadows of trees, illuminated only by the dim light of a dying fire? Besides, it was not quite the Pilatus that Simon had seen on occasion in Judea, pronouncing sentences from the portico of the Antonian fortress or parading through the streets with his legions to intimidate a subjugated populace. True, this figure by the forest's edge wore the same crimson cloak of authority, and scowled arrogantly with the same Roman features—only now, the formerly dark eyes glowed with a faint yellow light. No, this had to be a dream....

There was a subtle shifting of perspective. Now Pilatus was standing directly over Gretchen—bending over her. Her eyes had opened and she was staring up at the figure with innocent, raptured fascination.

The face of Pilatus was a mask of unholy lust. The glow in his eyes intensified till it seemed to highlight the girl's upturned face, causing her lashes and cheekbones to cast shadows. His mouth opened, revealing white fangs; his head descended, his mouth caressed the white neck; his teeth—

Gretchen whimpered.

With a surge of horror Simon broke the spell that held him and leaped up, drawing his *sica*. It was no dream! The thing was indeed crouching over Gretchen—and now it was rising to face him, snarling like a beast, yellow eyes glaring, a trace of blood on its lips—

Simon yelled and leaped, slashing—but the blow had no effect. The knife that had slain gladiators in the arena passed through the body of Pilatus as easily as through mist!

But there was nothing insubstantial about the thing, as Simon realized in the next instant when one iron hand locked about his wrist and the other about his throat. Frantically he struggled, but could do nothing against the strength of his foe. His knife fell from his numbed fingers and clattered to the ground; he could not draw a breath as he was pushed back inexorably to his knees. The face of Pilatus grimaced demoniacally before him.

His left hand, groping wildly for any weapon, closed about the jade figurine dangling from his belt. He tore it loose and smashed his fist into the glaring face. There was a wild, hellish scream. Simon felt his enemy's grip relax. He tore himself away, rolled and came to his feet in a combat stance.

Pilatus was backing away across the clearing, his yellow-eyed face a mask of snarling fury as he stared at the figurine clutched in Simon's hand. Abruptly, he turned and ran, red cloak streaming out behind him—and dove from the cliff's edge into the blackness of the canyon. In the next instant a great bat flapped up from the gorge, wheeled against the moonlight sky, and flew off above the dark pines.

Simon ran to Gretchen. She was awake now, and crying out in fear and horror. There was blood on her neck.

He gathered her up in his arms and she sobbed violently against his breast, her face buried in her clenched hands.

III

> "Oh, whaten a mountain is yon," she said,
> "All so dreary wi frost and snow?"
> "O yon is the mountain of hell," he cried.
> "Where you and I will go."
>
> — Anonymous, "The Demon Lover"

The village by the lake appeared to be deserted. It had been a fishing village, Simon guessed. From the look of it, it had not been lived in for years.

Slowly the two of them dismounted and led their horses between the crumbling huts to the lake shore. Simon stole a glance at the girl, her face was serious, her eyes sad.

"They're gone," she said. "All gone!"

They walked slowly down to the shore, where gray waves were splashing against the rocks. The skies were clouded over, and there was a chill in the wind.

"Where did they go, Simon?" There was a note of desperation in Gretchen's voice. "*Why* did they go?"

Simon glanced to the northwest, where the sinister spires of Mons Fractus were half-lost in the drifting clouds, then put an arm around the girl. "Perhaps they fled from—what we saw last night...."

She shuddered, and Simon knew she was recalling how they had kept their campfire ablaze for the remainder of the night, how relieved they had been at sunrise. Then she had guided him around the south flank of the mountain to the wide lake where her village was—had been—

"Gone!" Gretchen buried her face in her hands. "Simon, they're all *gone!*"

He held her close, not knowing what to say. There was such a change in the girl since the previous night; the laughter, the exhilaration over her newly regained freedom had been replaced by sadness and apprehension. Simon felt a hot anger. She had already suffered far too much these last three years.

And that wound on her throat—small, but inflamed.

Suddenly he tensed as he spied two men on horseback riding toward them from the south, along the lakeside path. One appeared to be a warrior, the other a white-bearded old man. They were approaching at a walk, the wind whipping the folds of their cloaks. Gretchen, feeling Simon's tension, turned to face the newcomers.

They stopped a few paces off; the younger man dismounted, helped the old one dismount also, and then both came on, leading their horses.

Simon fingered the haft of his knife. Yes, the young one definitely was a Helvetian warrior, possibly one of some rank judging by the quality of his scale mail and long sword. His bearing seemed noble but not menacing; his eyes were gray and level, his features framed by hair and beard of a light reddish bronze. The wind whipped his locks, as it did the long hair and beard of the old man.

"Karanoch, the Dragon Druid!" muttered Gretchen, wonder in her voice. "And—Brennus—?"

"You know them?"

"Brennus!" The girl suddenly tore herself away from Simon, hurried forward, and flung herself into the young warrior's arms. "Oh, *Brennus!"*

For a few moments the young man and Gretchen clung to one another, then began to speak excitedly in what seemed to Simon a Celtic dialect. The old man joined them in conversation, displaying similar excitement. Simon suddenly realized, with some chagrin, that the man called Brennus must be the one Gretchen had spoken of as her betrothed. Tired of being ignored, he strode forward.

The old man faced him, suspicion in his eyes.

"Who are you?" he asked in Latin. "A Roman?"

Simon scowled. "I'll consider that insult unintentional. I am Simon of Gitta, a Samaritan, and I have come to this land seeking revenge upon a Roman official."

"Revenge, you say?" The old man grinned slightly, a glint of good humor in his dark eyes, though his manner was still wary. "Are you an enemy of Rome, then?"

"Aye, Druid—even as you must be. The Romans have not been at all kind to your order, from what I hear."

Suddenly Gretchen ran to Simon and gripped him by the arm; her face was white, her eyes wide.

"Oh, Simon—it's truly Brennus! He's alive—my beloved, my betrothed! Coponius lied—told me he was slain—!"

Abruptly her eyes closed; her lips parted and she went limp. Simon was barely able to catch her before she hit the ground.

The moon was just rising above the eastern ridgetops when Simon woke and remembered where he was: in the new village of Gretchen's people, a few miles south of the abandoned one, on the shore of a smaller lake. He sat up and rubbed his eyes, then threw a few more sticks on the dying fire, causing it to blaze up. The clouds were gone, and the positions of the glittering stars told him that he had slept some four hours.

It had been an easy ride up the long valley. Gretchen, having quickly recovered from the shock of seeing Brennus alive against all expectations, had ridden beside the young warrior all the way, constantly and excitedly conversing with him in their Celtic dialect. The old druid had interjected a comment or question now and then, but presently had fallen back and left the young pair to themselves. Only once had he spoken to Simon during that journey:

"I must thank you once again, Simon of Gitta, for having saved the lady betrothed to our chief's son. All our village will thank you also, and welcome you."

Not Brennus, thought Simon. Seeing the old man's eyes on him, he had answered brusquely: "She saved herself. She offered me more aid than I her, I'm afraid. But tell me: Why were you and Brennus in the abandoned village when Gretchen and I came there?"

"I had a dream last night—and when I talked to Brennus, I found that he had had the same dream. I have prayed long to the dragons, and now I think they are awakening. Are you their answer to my prayers, Simon of Gitta?"

Simon found his spine tingling. "That dream of yours—a strange thing indeed. But I know of no dragons, and I repeat that I did not rescue your chief s daughter-in-law. She did that herself, through her own courage and intelligence."

"I heard her tell Brennus you saved her life."

Simon shook his head somberly, feeling a reluctance to talk about what had happened the previous night. He felt a certain guilt—and not about amorous feelings towards Gretchen. Had she not given him the jade statuette out of a desire to help him, she might not have undergone the attack of Pilatus....

They had ridden the rest of the way in silence.

The villagers, as old Karanoch had predicted, received Gretchen's return with joy and thanked Simon profusely. Even the grizzled old chief, Brennus' father, had warmly shaken his hand. Then there had been a feast, such as a modest fishing village could ill afford to give every day, and Simon had enjoyed a better meal than he had had since leaving Aventicum.

Now, as he sat by the cooking-fire he had just rekindled, he suddenly saw the old druid standing motionless not far away, staring at him, white beard seeming to glow in the firelight. Simon rose quickly.

"Karanoch—"

"Sit down, Simon." The old man advanced and seated himself upon a log section. "I have just come from the chief s hut, where Gretchen lies ill. We must talk."

"Gretchen? Ill?"

"It happened just after sundown. She told me all, Simon. You did indeed save her life last night. Now show me the jade amulet she gave you."

Simon did so, and as the old druid fingered it he sat back and drew his cloak around him. The air was becoming chilly.

"Hecate," said Karanoch, returning the object. "Other images will serve as well, so long as they symbolize that which commands the awe and worship of many, and are consecrated by ritual. We of the Dragon Druids used to fashion many such things. Alas, so much knowledge has been lost to us in recent years!"

Simon nodded, remembering that the mad emperors Tiberius and Caligula had persecuted the druids. "You've doubtless heard that Caligula was assassinated last January. Perhaps Claudius will be milder. But—what of Gretchen?"

"She was bitten by the devil of the Drakamund, and soon she must die and become like him—unless he can first be slain."

"Die!" Simon leaped up again. "From so slight a wound—"

"Many of our women died of such wounds three years ago, when the Romans first brought that demon to the mountain and stole our prince's betrothed from us. Gretchen tells me you know much of this matter; you must tell me all you can, Simon, even as she has."

Simon drew a deep breath, stifling his impatience to ask more questions, then proceeded to tell the old druid all that the Roman Coponius had told him. The moon was more than halfway to the zenith when he finished; the village was hushed and still under its rays, as if the very huts were huddled together in fear.

"Evidently the Romans know not the secret of how to slay the dead-who-walk," said the druid when Simon had ceased speaking. "Tell me, what is the name of this undead Roman the Emperor was so anxious to be rid of?"

"Pontius Pilatus, formerly procurator of Judea."

"Aye," muttered Karanoch. "His name is familiar to me; even in these remote outlands he has become known for the enormous cruelties he perpetrated in your homeland. No wonder the demons possessed him so readily, seeing that he was a vessel self-prepared for them!"

"And what of Gretchen?" Simon demanded again. "Must she die like those women you spoke of—"

"They did not die as humans die. They had to be slain at the last by stake and steel and cleansing ritual, lest they should live forever in thrall to the thing the Romans brought to the Drakamund."

Simon felt a chill that was not in the air. He could not speak.

"That was three years ago," continued Karanoch inexorably. At that time many of our young men, including Brennus, went upon the mountain and sought the thing in order to destroy it by stake or steel. Always they failed to find it, save perhaps for some who never returned at all. In the end, we left our village and re-established it here on the northern shore of this smaller lake, where the fishing is not so good but where our women may sleep without the fear of fangs in the night.

Simon recalled the several streams they had forded during the day. "Coponius said it cannot cross running water."

"Such is the druid-lore also. We can defend against the thing by such means as water, fire, and talismans, yet we cannot slay it unless its lair can be found. You say Coponius gave you a map—"

"Damn you, old wizard!" snarled Simon. "Are you saying I'll have to kill Pilatus or Gretchen will become like him?"

The druid nodded, then regarded Simon steadily. "Now it's more than just vengeance, eh, Samaritan? I was right—surely the dragons have sent you to aid us in our need."

"What do you mean—"

"I am full of years and magic, and I sense that you are no common man, Simon of Gitta. You are a man of high destiny, a fragment of the very God-soul that existed before it was trapped in this material universe created by the monstrous Elder Gods. And once, at least, you met and lost a woman who was such a divine fragment also—your counterpart. Is it not so?"

Simon shuddered, glancing up at the rising moon once more. *Luna... Selene... Helen....*

"You are a sorcerer, Karanoch—even as was my mentor, Dositheus."

"Your mentor was a True Spirit—even as are you and Brennus. And Gretchen is your counterpart, even as was the woman you lost to the change we call death. Your mentor must have told you that that change is but the act of two Persons who continually put on and take off an unending series of costumes. You and Brennus are the same, Simon, even as are Gretchen and the one you lost. That is why you love Gretchen so much."

Simon felt his head swimming; it was exactly like what he used to hear from Dositheus. Such dark things—such mad things—

"It's true, wizard—I *do* love Gretchen, and somehow it *is* the same as my love for Helen. They don't even look alike, and yet they *are* alike, somehow. It's in their eyes, I think... yet no—for Helen's were dark, and Gretchen's are blue—"

"Blue sky, dark sky," said the druid. "The earth turns and we see first one aspect of the universe, then the other. You must not resent Brennus, Simon; you and he are as light and darkness, and the one cannot be without the other. Gretchen is the True Spirit that matches his on this small turn of the Cosmic Cycle, even as your Helen matches you."

"Helen is *gone!*" cried Simon, unable longer to hide the anguish in his soul. "The Romans took her from me. Must I spend the rest of my earthly term in living death, like that thing on Mons Fractus? Must I die and be born again before I may be reunited with Her? Is this the fate the Elder Gods have prepared for all mortals—to be tortured with the promise of fulfillment, then denied it?"

Karanoch shook his head. "Not all mortals—very few, in fact. Most humans are only animals with a heightened cunning; they cannot understand nor share in the joys and anguish of those few who are True Spirits—fragments of the primal God-soul, enmeshed in this world of which they are not a part."

"Does that justify the anguish of us few?"

"Things are not justified; things simply *are*. We must do what we can about the possible; beyond that, we can do no more. Tell me, Simon—will you face the wrath of the demon Pilatus in order that Gretchen may be delivered from his power and fully restored to Brennus, her counterpart?"

Simon shook his head violently, as if to break the spell of Karanoch's words.

"I came to slay a Roman fiend, and I shall—that has not changed. You are seeking my aid. Have you any to offer me?"

"Aye." The druid reached within his robe and drew forth an oval stone, dark gray in color and a little larger than an eagle's egg. "This is a dragon-stone—a talisman handed down by my great-grandfather, who claimed to have talked with the very dragons who dwell within the Drakamund. It is the most powerful talisman this village possesses. Take it with you tomorrow as you go forth upon the mountain."

"But—but what can it do—"

Karanoch shrugged. "Alas, so much knowledge has been lost! Take the stone, Simon; I know it can aid you, but you must discover how. Perhaps the dragons will make it known to you."

Simon hefted the object. It was weighty and glinted with a dull sheen, like rich iron ore. There appeared to be a brief inscription carved upon it; Simon recognized the characters as runes, but could not read them.

"The meaning has been lost," said Karanoch in answer to his unspoken question. "The words are: *satha sithra, satha ixcatl.* They are in the ancient dragon-tongue, or so my grandfather told me. Now, you must come to my hut and sleep, Simon, for your journey tomorrow will be an arduous one."

He woke suddenly in the darkness before dawn. There was no transition; his sleep had been profound, his wakefulness was equally absolute. And in his mind still hovered the memory of words just spoken by a woman's voice:

Rise, Simon—you must help me. Hurry.

Helen's voice.

He sat up, hurriedly donned his tunic, belt, sandals, and cloak in the darkness, then stole out of the hut, careful not to wake the sleeping Karanoch. The moon had dipped behind the western ridge and the stars twinkled brightly. The air was chill, the village fires dead but for glowing coals.

That voice. Had he dreamed it...?

Quickly he saddled his horse, mounted, and rode out of the village, down the dark valley northward. The forest path was barely visible under the stars.

Yes, it was better to leave this way, without farewells....

He had ridden less than a mile when suddenly he saw a white figure in the trail ahead of him. The horse whickered, came to a halt. Simon dismounted, said a few soothing words to the beast, then hurried forward. The figure was moving away from him, slowly walking down the trail—not a ghost, as he had half suspected in his first shock, but a slender woman whose light tunic, limbs, and hair glowed weakly under the first faint light of dawn.

"Gretchen!"

He caught up with her easily, gripped her by the shoulders and gazed into her eyes—eyes that seemed to glow softly with a faint yellow light.

"Simon, let me go—*he* is calling me—"

"Gretchen! You're sleepwalking! *Wake up!*"

The girl started. She blinked and shuddered. The yellow glow was gone from her eyes. Recognition dawned in her face.

"Oh, Simon—where am I—?"

He saw again the dark blot of the wound on her throat, and held her close with a tender anguish. "Helen—!"

"Brennus—!" she murmured, returning his embrace.

Realizing what they had said, they drew apart. The gray light of dawn increased above the eastward pines.

"You loved your Helen very much, Simon—"

He nodded. "As you love Brennus."

They stared wordlessly into one another's eyes, saw the stars of the universe reflected there, and the light of the impending dawn. In that moment Simon knew again the truth he had learned years ago from his mentor Dositheus, and from Helen—

Gretchen murmured, her eyes wide and wondering: "Who *are* we, Simon?"

"A man and a woman," he answered. "Nothing more. And yet, somehow I know that you are the reason for all this Creation—for these hills, these stars, this entire universe which the mad gods have unfolded for their pleasure and our torment—aye, and even for those mad gods themselves—"

"And, somehow—*you* create and sustain it all, for me—"

"For you—else it would have no meaning."

She shuddered, drew close to him again. "Oh, Simon—Brennus—how can we rid the world of the evil that pervades it? How can we bring to all of it the knowledge of power and beauty that we now know—"

Suddenly, as if exhausted, she collapsed in Simon's arms. Gently he laid her down on the grass beside the path. The dawn was now a dim gray light. Simon looked again to the wound on the girl's throat.

"The dawn comes," Gretchen murmured. "The spell Pilatus holds over me is gone—but I fear it will come upon me again at nightfall. Oh, Simon—"

"True Spirit," he muttered gently, "the Roman shall not have you. Come, get up; I shall return you to your people."

Suddenly they heard hoofbeats and looked up the trail. In the gray light they saw Karanoch and Brennus approaching. In a moment they had dismounted and were kneeling beside Gretchen.

"She slipped away without warning," said the druid. "The vile Roman lich has a hold on her soul. Here, you two, help her up. I will take her back to the village."

Simon and Brennus obeyed, and in a moment the girl and the old druid were gone. The two men faced one another.

"Karanoch tells me you must go up the Drakamund," said Brennus uneasily, "in order to save Gretchen's soul."

Simon approvingly regarded the tall young warrior who stood before him in the dawn-light. "Aye—that is my understanding.

"I would go with you."

Simon, staring into the man's level gray eyes, suddenly felt as if he were looking into a glass that mirrored his own soul.

"You can't, Brennus," he said, an involuntary sadness in his voice. "Your place is with Her. Surely Karanoch has told you—"

"Aye." The young Helvetian nodded briefly. "But go knowing that we are brothers, Simon of Gitta. Nay, more than brothers—we are somehow one and the same. I know, for there is sorcery in the air this night, and I have had dreams."

Again Simon felt his spine tingling.

"You will take good care of Gretchen."

"Aye—you know it. But you, Simon, must free her soul. Do not fail; all hangs on it."

They clasped hands—and in that moment Simon felt that they were as two gods upon whose actions the fate of the universe somehow depended. Gray eyes and dark, mirroring one another—red hair and black, wafting in the breeze of dawn—and the very reason for the world's existence in some strange way in their hands....

Mounting his horse once more, Simon turned and galloped away down the valley, again feeling perilously human and knowing that all depended upon his speed and the dragon-talisman Karanoch had given him.

IV

I readily believe that in the universe are more invisible beings than visible. But who will expound to us the nature of them...? What is it they perform? What regions do they inhabit?

—   Coleridge

A chill wind was blowing down from the sinister peaks of Mons Fractus. Simon drew his cloak more closely about him, then sought the partial shelter of a rock outcropping and shrugged out of the rope-loops of his pack, letting it fall to the ground. He had been climbing for over three hours, and in spite of his impatience he knew he must rest a bit and eat.

While he lunched on the bread and dried fish the druid had given him, he contemplated the landscape. He had seen mountains perhaps as high in Parthia, but none more impressive. South and east rose enormous snow-capped ranges, dim with distance. Thousands of feet below sprawled the lake, far larger than he had suspected; the abandoned village lay at the end of what was only its southwestern arm. He had left his horse there, untethered; the beast would find its way back to the inhabited village, in case he did not return....

No—he must not allow himself such thoughts.

When he had done eating, he took out the dragon-stone and contemplated its enigmatic runes once more. *"Satha sithra, satha ixcatl,"* he muttered aloud. "What can it mean? And what power might lie in this lifeless stone...?"

It might make a weapon, at least, being so heavy for its size. Carefully he began to knot a leather thong about it, until it was firmly enmeshed in a net of rawhide; in the loose end he fashioned a noose, to loop about his wrist, so that the stone swung on perhaps a foot of thong. Not much of a weapon against conventional foes, but if it had the supernatural forces Karanoch claimed it had, it might subdue Simon's enemy long enough to allow him to plunge home his steel.

Stake or steel through the heart. For that, the druid had told him, was the only way to slay the thing that Pilatus had become....

Simon shook his head. He must not think too much. He must press on. Once more he studied the parchment map that Coponius had had old Nicephorus draw up, then shouldered his pack and resumed his climb. The wind was growing colder, and though the sky was blue to the far horizon there was a cap of gray cloud forming over the jagged peaks of the mountain. Those peaks were not far off now; soon he would be passing through the notch between the nearest two. They looked foreboding enough, Simon thought, actually to be the abode of the dragons the villagers believed in.... Involuntarily he glanced to the northeast where, far across the lake, the dark mountains of Zug arose—the mountains where more dragons were said to dwell—

Suddenly he halted in astonishment. Directly before him, standing in the notch atop the rise, were two people—a man and a woman. And both, despite the cold wind, were dressed only in white tunics.

He hurried upward, and in a few more moments stood before them. His astonishment increased. The man seemed a young Adonis for handsomeness, and the woman was one of the most beautiful Simon had ever seen. Both had skin of alabaster whiteness and long hair that blew in the wind—the woman's raven-black, the man s golden as the locks of Helios. Each wore golden sandals, and about the waist a golden ceinture resembling a serpent clasping its tail in its mouth.

"What are you people doing here?" Simon yelled. "This is a very dangerous place—you must go back down!"

"We appreciate your concern," said the man, "yet we are in no danger. We walk here often. It is a place of great beauty and wonder."

"But—you must be freezing! Believe me, you've got to get down from this mountain before dark; if you start now, you can make it. A demon dwells here."

"We fear no demons," said the woman. "Sithra and Ixcatl protect their servitors from all evil. We heard their names spoken on the mountainside, and so we came."

Simon decided the two were as crazy as their presence and garb implied. Impatiently he strode past them, calling back, "Get off the mountain as fast as you can—I mean it!"

He was almost through the notch when a thought struck him—a connection in his mind—

Satha sithra, satha ixcatl....

He spun about and looked back the way he had come. The pair he had encountered were nowhere in sight. Either they had hurried down the mountain as Simon had advised, or—

"Sithra... Ixcatl...."

He shook his head violently. Doubtless those people believed in the same legends as old Karanoch, and came to this mountain to worship. Obviously they knew the words carved on the dragon-stone, and no doubt there were other such stones carved with the same runic words.

And now Simon knew that two of those words were the names of deities—deities of which he had never heard.

Yet he still had a job to do. The view from the notch afforded him new vistas westward, almost as breathtaking as the eastward ones. He consulted his map once more, then struck off down the rugged slope at as rapid a pace as he could manage. The terrain here was rocky, and made more difficult here and there by large patches of snow evidently left over from an early autumn blizzard. The wind was less strong on this side of the mountain, but the dark gray clouds seemed to hover closer.

Once his progress was impeded by a deep crevasse full of snow, and he had to make a long detour around it. It was just after this that he spied his destination, right where old Nicephorus had marked an "x" on the parchment—a small tarn, nestled in a hollow of the mountain.

Drawing a deep breath, Simon strode down the slope. The water of the tarn seemed almost as black as ink under the lowering clouds.

Carefully he loosened from his belt the thong that held the dragon-stone and looped it around his left wrist, feeling somewhat foolish even as he did so. What was he going to do? Dive into the icy pool and search for the coffin of Pilatus? Is so, he might well freeze to death long before he could find it, somehow pry it open, and drive the blade of his *sica* into the undead Roman's evil heart.

The wind rose, and Simon felt a touch of fear. Until now, his desire for vengeance and his concern for Gretchen had sustained him. But in this moment he suddenly realized how *unprepared* he was, and the realization was unnerving. For an instant he felt an impulse to turn and run—to flee the mountain and its environs before darkness should fall.

"Sithra—Ixcatl...." The names fell spontaneously from his lips— almost like a prayer.

And in that instant he started with surprise. There was a patch of red about halfway between him and the tarn, vivid upon the dark slope. Why had he not seen it sooner...? Then he saw that it was the figure of a man wrapped in a cloak and seated upon a boulder, motionless.

A scarlet cloak—the cloak of a high roman official.

Simon breathed deeply, drew his *sica*, and advanced. The figure rose from its seat and faced him. As he drew closer to the thing, Simon's skin crawled. It wore the robe and toga of a Roman procurator, and its features were indeed those of Pilatus—except for the eyes. The yellow, burning eyes....

He stopped a few paces away from the thing, unable to still the crawling of his flesh. In a voice too deep to be human, it said:

"Fool, your desire for vengeance has led you to doom!"

Simon gasped. "How did you know—?"

Pilatus laughed, and Simon saw white fangs gleaming within his gaping black mouth.

"Fear and hate—these things I know and sense from afar. I devoted my life to knowing them, and ever since my mortal life ended I have been able to sense the source of such emotions, like the glowings of dark stars. For many months I have sensed you, Simon of Gitta, crawling ever closer to me, like a black spider in the dark."

"You slew my mentor," said Simon. "You slew many hundreds of his unarmed followers for no more crime than assembling in public, and many thousands of others for the same offense. And when leaders of the people rose up to cry out against you, you scourged them, crucified them, burned their bodies—"

Pilatus laughed again—dark, unholy laughter, inhumanly vibrant. He strode a pace closer to Simon.

"These were small things, Samaritan—things that merely prepared my soul for the great Destiny that awaited it. The dark gods work strangely. Caligula craved eternal life; he died, but by his actions he gave eternal life to me!"

Suddenly, with unhuman swiftness, Pilatus darted forward, clawed hands extended. Only the reflexive quickness of Simon's gladiator training saved him; he dodged, feinted at Pilatus' face, then lunged for the heart. The animated lich avoided the blow, again with a quickness no human could have achieved, then darted a few paces away and crouched like a snarling wolf, eyes blazing.

Simon advanced slowly, knife ready, a ferocity equal to that of Pilatus gleaming in his dark eyes. "You shall die, Roman. You have come abroad by day, without your full powers, and now you shall *truly* die for your crimes!"

"Fool! I command storm and thunder! I have the strength of more than a score of warriors—even during the daylight!"

So saying, Pilatus stooped and lifted a stone that must have weighed as much as a man, then hurled it. Simon barely avoided it, heard it crunch into the slope behind him. Pilatus rushed forward, fanged mouth gaping. Frantically Simon swung the dragon-stone at the Roman's face; the procurator brushed it aside with a contemptuous laugh, lunged for Simon's throat with groping talons—then leaped back barely in time to avoid the *sica* once more. Simon realized with a sinking feeling that Karanoch's dragon-stone had far less power than the jade talisman he wore around his neck.

Slowly he backed up the slope. The vampire crept after him, hissing venomously. Suddenly it raised its arms and cried out:

"Storm—thunder—aid me!"

Lightning flashed in the clouds between the rocky peaks of Mons Fractus. The wind howled, and icy flakes began to fall, stinging Simon's face. Fear gripped him as he continued to retreat up the slope.

Pilatus snatched up another huge boulder and hurled it, then another. Simon, retreating and frantically dodging, knew he could not last much longer in the face of such monstrous sorcery. He was lost—Gretchen was lost. He must steel himself to make one last charge—to give his life if only he could plunge his *sica* into the heart of the hateful Roman demon—

Suddenly his retreating foot encountered empty space, and he screamed wildly as he fell backwards into the snow-filled chasm he had forgotten about until now—until too late. He felt himself falling and crashing through a brittle snow-crust—and knew no more.

Simon woke in darkness, feeling numbed and chilled. His body ached. Then memory galvanized him with fear and he forced himself up on his hands and knees. He sensed that he had been stunned for only a few moments; surely his enemy was close upon him—

His foot struck an object that clattered—his heavy-bladed *sica*. He snatched it up. The dragon-stone, he realized, was still tied to his left wrist. Slowly, carefully, he crawled away from the debris of snow and pebbles in which he had been lying, wondering why he could not see. Was he blind? A chill swept over him at the thought—

Yet no—the darkness was not complete; a faint yellow glow was filtering into his eyes. He concentrated on it, and slowly realized that it was coming from the end of a long tunnel. He had fallen into a cavern of some sort.

Hurriedly he crawled toward the light, then rose shakily to his feet and hastened on, thankful to know that he had evidently broken no bones in his fall. The corridor became more and more distinct, and Simon saw that it was definitely artificial, carved with uncanny precision from the solid rock.

He rounded a right-angle bend—and gasped. A huge room, lit with pale golden light, gaped before him—a room whose walls were lined with metallic surfaces that hummed and blinked with scintillating lights, whose interior was filled with tables laden with glass vessels filled with many-colored liquids, some of which bubbled through intricate transparent coils and tubes....

Stupefied, Simon pressed his hands to his temples. What he saw here was like nothing he had ever seen before. There was nothing he could relate to, nothing he could describe in words. He felt terror growing in him, like a dark worm gnawing its way up his spine.

And then, the crowning horror—two mottled, reptilian shapes, walking upright like men—walking toward him—

"No!" he gasped, gripping his knife more tightly. "No! Stay back!"

But they came on, staring at him with large green eyes with vertical pupils. They were nearly as tall as himself, and their smooth-scaled bodies gleamed with iridescent shades of green and blue under the golden light that streamed from circular discs set into the ceiling. They were crowned with spines connected by turquoise membranes veined with streaks of scarlet.

Peace, human—we mean you no harm.

Simon relaxed a bit. The voice that had sprung up in his mind was soothing; more, it was familiar. A woman's voice, surely... and now the reptilian forms before him seemed less terrifying—began to seem beautiful, in fact, rather than merely alien—

Then those forms began to shimmer, to transform—

"Baal!" Simon gasped, wonder and fear vying within him.

Two humans were standing before him—the same two he had met earlier upon the mountain. A man and a woman, divinely beautiful, clad in white tunics with gold serpent-belts.

"Fear not," said the man. "We should have assumed these forms sooner, knowing as we do that you humans are disturbed by our true aspect. I repeat, we mean you no harm."

Simon's fear vanished completely. He suddenly felt ashamed at his instinctive reaction.

"Your true forms are beautiful, but—"

"But alien to you, and therefore unsettling," said the woman. "You are the first human in more than a hundred years to come to this mountain with the names of Sithra and Ixcatl on your lips; therefore, we greet you with happiness, and as friends."

"Sithra? Ixcatl? I don't understand—"

"Sithra is the Mother of Wisdom, Ixcatl the Dispenser of it; they handed it down to all mortal beings upon this planet. Your race received from ours the knowledge that enabled you to begin the climb upward from the ape stage."

Simon's skin prickled. "You mean—you're—"

"I am Luria," said the woman, "and this is Issuris. We are the last of the serpent people to dwell within this mountain."

"You!" gasped Simon. "Your race preceded mine upon this planet—your ancestors gave to Eve the fruit that led to the curse of our awakening—?"

"Yours was always a poetic species," said Issuris.

"And a clever one," Luria added. "But for the flaw in your nature that makes you subject to cruel and violent passions, you would by now have voyaged to the stars."

Simon's brain was whirling. He had read in ancient books of the serpent people of Valusia, who had inhabited this region long before even the fabled ancient lands of Acheron and the Hyborians. Yet he had never believed those accounts to be more than myths.

"By all the gods!" he gasped. "Then you're the dragons—the beings venerated by the old druid Karanoch!"

"Alas, Karanoch was never bold enough to visit us," said Issuris, "though we tried often enough to answer his prayers. Human minds are still somewhat unreceptive, I fear, despite our race's past attempt to infuse them with perception. Besides, in the last century we have sensed an evil growing up from the south—an evil greater than any since the sorcerers of Acheron rose to crush and enslave the minds of mankind."

"Aye," muttered Simon, understanding. "Rome—"

"Yet not all humans are evil," said Luria. "We know that you are a true seeker of knowledge, Simon of Gitta."

"You know my name—?"

"Yes. And we see that you carry an object tied to your left wrist. Did not the druid, Karanoch, give it to you?"

Simon nodded. "He claimed that it had power, but it did not."

Luria moved forward and took the stone from Simon, unlooping the thong from his wrist and deftly untying the mesh of cord. "How strange, to see this object again," she murmured. "It was centuries ago that we gave it to the druids of Sarnen; then, over a hundred years ago, Karanoch's great-grandfather carried it with him when he visited us. Now its power has nearly vanished. Wait here, Simon."

She strode across the wide room and laid the stone upon a strange crystalline structure that Simon thought vaguely resembled an altar. Advancing to one of the blinking metallic panels that formed part of the wall, she flicked a small lever. Immediately the stone was bathed in a brilliant blue light, while a strange humming sound shrilled within the room.

The glow vanished and the humming ceased. Luria retrieved the dragon-stone and returned it to Simon. It appeared to be unchanged.

"A present from the dragons," she said. "It will aid you now."

Simon shook his head. "You are not dragons, Luria—Issuris. Karanoch's tribe may worship you as such, but the Parthians have told me that true dragons are enormous monsters that fly on scaly wings and breathe fire—"

Luria smiled. "Some of those beings you describe do indeed live in deep caverns within this very mountain, and within the mountains of Zug as well. But you would not care to meet them, Simon of Gitta—their intellect is as deficient as that of most humans, and their passions nearly as un-ruly."

Simon examined the heavy dragon-stone in his hand. "Can this truly help me now? And how have *you* escaped the undead lich that has prowled upon this mountain for the last three years?"

Issuris laughed, tossing his blond hair. "We've hardly noticed him. He craves human blood, not serpent blood. But now, since he seeks to destroy a friend of ours, he must go."

"Friend—?"

"Aye, Simon. How many humans would have conversed with us for so long, or found beauty in our true shapes? How many would have found fascination rather than horror in our nature? You hunger for knowledge, and we hope you will stay with us for a space and let us assuage that hunger. Snow is falling upon this mountain you think of as Mons Fractus; it would be dangerous for you to descend. Stay with us until spring, and we will teach you much."

Simon, his spine tingling more than ever, remained silent for a space. Then:

"I must slay Pilatus; I have sworn that I shall. A woman of Karanoch's people lies under his curse. Help me, and I will dwell with you as long as you wish."

Luria smiled. "No, Simon, as long as *you* wish. We do not force others to be unwilling guests. But you will learn much if you stay, I promise you— secrets concerning the nature of the universe, such as you have never dreamed of. Please let us, the last of the folk who first taught your race, now teach you."

Simon nodded. He sensed a sincerity from these strange beings that he had seldom known from his own kind. "I will stay. Yet what of the un-dead Roman who still prowls this mountain—?"

Luria smiled again. "I do not sense his thoughts. He sleeps again in his pool, doubtless believing he slew you."

Simon gripped the haft of his knife. "How, then, can I come at him to work my vengeance—?"

"Vengeance?" Luria laughed openly. "No, Simon, you will be doing the vampire a favor by slaying him. Though he lusts for eternal life, his is a pointless existence. He knows nothing of beauty or the delights of the mind, only the blood-thirst that burns forever. You would punish him most by letting him live on. But I see that concern for your friends is up-permost in your thoughts. Therefore I will tell you what to do with the dragon-stone. Listen carefully...."

Simon stood again upon the windy slope above the tarn, his mind still in a whirl. Could he believe what he had just been told? Were the two people he had just talked to what they seemed to be?

Yes, they were. They had touched levels of his mind that were too profound to be discounted. And, incredibly, they had offered him hospitality and friendship.

But there was another being upon this mountain who was the friend of no man, nor ever could be.

Slowly Simon strode down toward the black tarn, until finally he stood upon a limestone ledge at its brink. A tension brooded in the air. Above, dark clouds moved slowly between the sinister spires of the mountain, emitting sparse snowflakes; mist boiled in the air, like dark spirits stirring....

The sun was setting, large and orange in the west beyond the cloud-capped peaks. Simon knew he must act quickly. With firm determination he strode down to the edge of the tarn and detached the dragon-stone from his belt.

"Baal," he muttered, "help me now against my dark enemy!"

He hurled the dragon-stone. It arched up, then down—splashed into the surface of the pond—

Lightning crashed between the clouded peaks of Mons Fractus. Thunder rolled, and a tremendous wind blew up. Simon started in sudden fear. Before his eyes the waters of the pond began to roil with what seemed a supernatural intensity—almost to boil—

Then something crawled out of the pool—a human shape, wrapped in a great cloak, snarling and whining as if in pain. Slowly it crept forward, like a crippled insect, then collapsed upon the rock ledge, twitching and hissing. Simon advanced, *sica* in hand, and glared down upon the thing that looked up at him with vindictive yellow eyes—the thing that writhed before him hissing in fury, like a broken scorpion upon the rocks—

He raised the gladiatorial knife. The vampire snarled at him, hate and terror in its glowing eyes. The glow brightened as the sun's lower edge touched the horizon.

"I had almost thought to give this blow in mercy," muttered Simon, "but such is not in my heart. I give it in vengeance. *Perite Pilatus!*"

The blade plunged down into the Roman's heart. Pilatus screamed hideously; his clawed hand shot out and locked on Simon's throat—but fell away before the vampire could exert his supernatural strength. The glow faded from the eyes; the body writhed a final time, then twitched and lay still.

Simon drew back, knife ready for another blow if need be. The corpse did not stir. Above, the clouds of Mons Fractus began to disperse. Simon gaped in wonderment—for now the body of the procurator was collapsing, deteriorating rapidly into a state of putrefaction. Hastily he stepped forward and nudged it with his toe—

Slowly the corpse turned over and fell from the ledge into the tarn, then sank from sight. A few foul bubbles rose up from it.

Turning away from the pool whose waters were now unruffled by aught but the dying wind, Simon walked slowly back up the slope, knowing that he would accept the strange new offer of friendship that had come his way, and also that he would never divulge to the world the secrets he knew of the dragons of Mons Fractus.

About "The Wedding of Sheila-Na-Gog"

WARNING: Contains spoilers!

Simon continues his travels westward through the hinterlands of the Roman Empire. Less than a year later, he finds himself studying Druidic magic in the part of Gaul that became the French province of Averoigne.

Averoigne was Clark Ashton Smith's cursed "Lovecraft Country" of medieval France, haunted by witches, necromancers, and monsters. Smith, or "CAS" as he was known to his friends, was one of the "Big Three" writers (alongside H.P. Lovecraft and Robert E. Howard) for the famous pulp-era magazine *Weird Tales*. This "Lovecraft Circle" regularly wrote each other to critique stories and share ideas. It was from this correspondence that a version of Averoigne in the Roman Era emerged.

In a January 25, 1937 letter to Fritz Lieber, H.P. Lovecraft wrote, "I have helped CAS give Averoigne a pseudo-history extending back to Gallic days, when the *Averones* trickled in from a sunken western land and brought with them the hellish tome known in later years as *Liber Ivonis* or *Livre d'Eibon*. This dark people set up the worship of Tsathoggua (Sodaqui or Sadoqua) in the region where they settled, so that by the Gallo-Roman period the *Regio Averunum* or *Averonia* was feared as the abode of a black and unearthly sorcery." It seemed only natural to place a Simon of Gitta adventure in this ready-made Roman setting, and the result was "The Wedding of Shelia-na-gog".

But who, or what, is Sheila-na-gog? It is almost certainly a reference to "sheela na gig", a type of carving or sculpture found all over western Europe on churches, castles, and other buildings from the Middle Ages. Sheela na gigs depict a naked woman, often with her legs spread wide, using both fists to hold open an enormously exaggerated vagina. If that sounds like a strange sculpture to adorn the cathedrals of the notoriously sex-negative medieval Catholic church, that's because it is—and that's part of the mystery of these figures. No one is quite sure of the sheela na gig's origins, what the image is supposed to represent, or even what the name means (the phrase seems to have an Irish origin, but doesn't translate into Gaelic as anything except gibberish). Scholars have theorized that sheela na gigs might depict everything from a warning against the sins of lust to a representation of a forgotten pagan fertility goddess.

The authors of this story seem to have opted for the latter option. Given her "Black Goat Druid" worshipers, does that mean Sheila-na-gog is supposed to be an avatar of Lovecraft's dark fertility deity Shub-Niggurath? Perhaps, perhaps. The physical description of Sheila-na-gog, however, more closely resembles Clark Ashton Smith's creator deity Abhoth in his

Hyperborean Age story "The Seven Geases". Either interpretation *could* work, and ultimately it's irrelevant—no sane person would want to marry an evil pool of sentient primordial protoplasm anyway, whatever its literary lineage.

This story is a collaboration between Richard Tierney and Glenn Rahman—a successful one, apparently, given that the pair went on to work together on the Simon of Gitta novels *The Gardens of Lucullus* and *Path of the Dragon*. Although Rahman wrote the bulk of the text, he did an excellent job of capturing the combination of historical fantasy and sword & sorcery with a touch of Lovecraftian horror that define the Simon of Gitta tales. As a bonus, fans of the Cthulhu Mythos should also keep an eye out for what might be Brown Jenkin appearing toward the end of the story.

"The Wedding of Sheila-Na-Gog" originally appeared in *Crypt of Cthulhu* #29, Candlemas 1985, and is set in French Gaul around the summer solstice of A.D. 42.

THE WEDDING OF SHEILA-NA-GOG
by Glenn Rahman and Richard L. Tierney

"Black and unform'd, as pestilent a clod
As dread Sodaqua, Averonia's God."

— *H.P. Lovecraft*

A ruddy glow lit the twisted canopy of the oak grove, casting strange shadows over the wolfish, expectant faces of the warriors squatting in a circle around the fire. All were big men with light eyes and long, fair locks that swayed as they beat their knees with horny fists in rhythm to the Gallic chant. Their garments bespoke a tribal kinship: similar tartans occasionally cut into a tunic of the Roman style, and a more prominent slashed garment with sleeves descending a little below the waist. Only a few seemed to be experienced fighters, and these bore weapons in keeping with their size: long swords hanging from their belts, tall shields, javelins, bows and slings. Several other Gauls, standing and leading the chant, wore full, red-dyed robes—red symbolizing the nature of the ceremony this night.

There was a stir as a few latecomers arrived: a half-dozen cloaked and cowled men who seemed incongruous among the Gauls. Ferchobhar, first among the Black Goat Druids, came to meet them and led them to their places without a word.

Another incongruous figure at the ritual watched their arrival suspiciously—a black-haired man in his early thirties with high, prominent cheekbones and a square, cleanly shaven chin. His expression was controlled, in no way sharing the fanatical concentration of the Gauls, but the dark eyes in his impassive expressionless face flickered with angry fires. He wore the cloak and tunic of a Samaritan, both emblazoned with symbols indicating him to be a wandering magician.

The Samaritan shifted his stare from the cowled figures to an osier cage between the roots of a spreading oak. A tough, woven mesh that might have held the men within it even had they not been bound by heavy cords, it resembled a giant oval bird-cage piled roundabout with tinder and dry faggots. The captives neither begged nor cursed—less from a fear of punishment, probably, than from a stubborn pride that would not give in to futile displays.

They were dark men, the Samaritan observed, yet unlike the elegant Semitic type that he himself represented. Rather, they appeared akin to the Aquitani—the ancient strain which, so the magician had heard, had ruled Spain and Gaul long before the Celts had come conquering from the east. The Romans called them *Arverni*—a corruption of *Averoni*, the tribe's own name for itself. When the Gauls had ruled, so the story went, the Averoni were tolerated as a source of tribute; but now that both races enjoyed a kind of equality—an equally mortifying Roman slavery—a bitter feud raged between them in the mountains of Regio Averonum. Every captured Averoni suffered a fate similar to this one, or worse....

"I am glad to see you have accepted my invitation, Simon of Gitta."

The Samaritan started from his trance of thought. Ferchobhar stood close beside him, bending near—though only a few seconds before, the Druid had been within the circle of firelight. In this proximity the old man's eyes seemed intense, intent, darkly mystical.

"Tonight you shall learn much concerning Druid-lore," Ferchobhar went on in his low, muttering tone, "as I have promised you."

Simon the Samaritan grunted. "I hope your lore is more impressive than the trick you just used to sneak up on me. I've used it on audiences a hundred times, at least. Tell me—who are those cloaked men who have just arrived?"

"Students of our Druid-knowledge, like yourself. They are but recently come to our land. I shall introduce you to them later. But now, you must excuse me. Soon you shall see that not all magic is mere mummery!"

So saying, Ferchobhar stood erect and strode into the circle of men—strode tall and regal, his narrow white beard gleaming in the firelight, a straight oaken staff clutched in his fist. The other Druids ceased their chanting as he approached, then drew to him in a mass, left hands clenched and staffs held upright. When all were gathered close about him, Ferchobhar began to speak alone—to intone a low, lilting song in a tongue unlike the Gallic Simon had been studying for the past few months.

And while the chief Druid chanted, the Samaritan magician thought, pondered, remembered....

For three months had Simon dwelt among the Druids, more than long enough to decide he couldn't hope to learn much from them. He had hoped differently when he had first arrived and admitted to them his name—a name much lauded by all who hated and opposed the tyranny of Rome.

The Druids, too, Ferchobhar had assured him, used their talents to resist the Romans. He had urged Simon to stay and learn from them. And the Samaritan, who was sought by the Romans as a determined rebel, had welcomed the promise of sanctuary and study.

But as the weeks passed, Simon had grown suspicious. Ferchobhar had presented him with little more than the childish mythology of the Gallic gods and heroes, some verse of a ritual nature and a few mechanical tricks, barring him from the important conclaves and mysteries. But whenever the Samaritan had chafed, Ferchobhar had affected the role of the kindest of hosts, cajoling and flattering the younger man with promises of knowledge yet to come.

"Your studies are preparing you," he had assured Simon repeatedly. "When the summer solstice comes, you shall be ready to receive all knowledge. It is not so far away."

Simon might have concluded that Ferchobhar and his Druids were charlatans and humbugs, had he not already seen the uncanny control they wielded over mist and flame during their rituals. Furthermore, they claimed to command strange creatures that haunted the hills and valleys: cloven-hoofed monsters elsewhere considered only the fancies of ancient legend. He'd had the inhuman tracks of these beings pointed out to him, and had been told by nervous tribesmen how the monsters were created and dispatched by the Druids to harry the Averoni and even war with that tribe's own magical agents, the mystical Cats of Sadoqua.

For the Averoni, Simon had learned, worshipped the deity Sadoqua—the immortal enemy of the Druids' goddess, Sheila-na-gog, whose name meant "Lady of the Gods". The Gauls claimed that the Averoni protected Sadoqua's shrines from defilement by conjuring up hosts of demon felines, whose pelts were dark as the midnight sky and whose fangs gleamed as brightly as stars. An occasional cat's cry under the waxing moon, Simon had observed, was enough to turn a Gaul's blood to water....

Suddenly his reverie was interrupted as, like a bolt of heat lightning, the heads of the staffs flamed with a brilliant blue-white light, briefly illuminating the oak grove like noonday. Simon gasped. The cowled newcomers, clearly as taken by surprise as he, lurched fearfully, one ejaculating "Jupiter!" and another letting his cowl fall back from his aquiline features when the light burst full upon him.

Romans!

Simon's mouth hardened with bitterness and apprehension; he'd half-suspected as much when he had earlier glimpsed the legionnaire-style footgear one of the men wore under the hem of his robe. No longer did he wonder where he stood with the Black Goat Druids!

He knew he was in the acutest danger—knew that his own presence had to do with this unnatural alliance. Why else would Ferchobhar entertain Romans in such a secretive manner? The emperor Tiberius had years ago outlawed the druidic religion; it was the duty of the Roman occupation troops to arrest the wonder-working priests and destroy their shrines. He would be lost if he waited until the completion of this sacrifice. Yet, how to escape, surrounded as he now was by Druids and Romans…?

A ready solution came to him. Although not a true magician himself, he had studied at the feet of Persian mages who had taught him many ruses and illusions that had served him well in the past. Not the least of these was a command of the ventriloquist's art.

Without the slightest alteration of expression, Simon threw a piercing wail out of steady lips—a frenzied wail like that of a maddened cat. The Druids stopped chanting as suddenly as if choked by a strangler's knot. Warriors sprang up, groping for their weapons; the Romans followed suit, in even greater confusion. Simon, too, feigned fear, but gave a second cat's cry and then a third, imitating the continuous yowl of a bounding feline pack. The tribesmen were all jabbering panicked appeals to the Druids at once.

"The Cats of Sadoqua!" exclaimed Ferchobhar. "They're coming to save their masters from the flames! Quickly, all of you—into the forest! We will protect you!"

The terrified Gauls needed no more urging to break into a run for the black woods beyond the spot of firelight.

Ferchobhar thrust his weirdly flaming staff into the tinder around the osier cage; the fire took quickly and threw red sparks into the darkness. Then the chief Druid whirled and followed the rout out of the grove, flanked by subordinates and bodyguards.

Simon also pretended to flee. Once out of sight in the shadows, however, he dove into the undergrowth and waited for the last Gauls to stampede past him. He hastened their retreat with several loud feline yowls, convincing the Celts that the cats were close on their heels.

Then, when the hindmost Gauls were nothing but a distant rustle in the dead leaves, the Samaritan sprang from his hiding place and ran back into the clearing. The fire Ferchobhar had kindled had grown rapidly and the trapped men were already choking on the smoke. Simon ran to the osier cage and laid to it with his Roman *gladius*, or short-sword; the springy wood clove asunder beneath his powerful blows and in half a minute he had opened a gap wide enough for a man to crawl through.

"Quickly, come out of there! You're free!"

Although surprised, the imprisoned and bound Averoni took Simon's offer eagerly and wriggled through the breach headfirst, like human worms.

"Come, now!" Simon hissed to them as they emerged. "The woods are full of Gauls and they won't go far once they've regained their wits. Hurry!"

The last of the four prisoners, a short swarthy man, finished squirming out of the cage, his kilts smoldering. Simon grasped his lean arm and helped him to his feet. "Let's be off!"

"Who are you? Why have you betrayed the Druids? They were treating you as a guest."

"The friends of Rome are no true hosts of mine! I will need a haven for several days—and provisions."

"Follow me to my village—you may have all that I possess! But, wait—cut these cords! It is a long walk and the woods are full of the Whore-Goddess's spawn!"

Simon nodded and whipped out his *sica*, or gladiator's knife—but before he could touch its blade to the Averoni's bindings someone shouted behind him:

"Simon of Gitta, I knew you were an enemy!"

The Samaritan whirled, snarling. In the shadows stood Ferchobhar, gesturing histrionically. Beside him clustered four other men—two armed warriors and two Druids of a lower degree.

"Run!" muttered Simon to the Averoni, shoving the closest of them away. "Into the forest! I'll hold them till you get away—!"

"Take him alive!" shrieked Ferchobhar.

Immediately, like unleashed dogs, the two warriors bounded at him, screaming a war-cry: *"Gogmagog!"*

Simon crouched in a fighting-stance, then darted toward the onrushing Gauls, his *gladius* in one hand and the keen-bladed *sica* in the other.

The foremost Gaul bellowed, his bulky frame towering half a head above the more athletic compactness of the Samaritan, and swung his sword. Steel rang and sparks flew in the darkness as Simon parried expertly. Then blow followed blow with incredible swiftness. Ferchobhar, watching from a safe distance and scarcely able to follow the strokes, remembered that Simon had claimed to have spent two years of his youth as a gladiator in Italy. The Samaritan handled himself with such skill that the chief Druid could almost mistake his darting figure in the shadows for three distinct men.

"Beware!" yelled Ferchobhar. "He's arena-trained—!"

But the two warriors, already aware of their opponent's prowess, cunningly sought to busy him while their priestly masters slipped in from the flanks to pierce his unarmored body with their long daggers. With heavy long swords they flailed away at Simon's guard, forcing him back with their greater reach—but always the Roman sword or the sharp *sica* flashed before them, turning the berserk blows, while the Samaritan's lean figure eluded thrusts by the scantest margins with nimble turns and dodges. Never did their opponent set foot wrongly or waste a motion; he was always a menace, even in defense, executing his replies so precisely that the Gauls could not coordinate their attacks properly, but seemed to fight four separate duels.

Desperately Simon leapt and whirled, snarling with rage; sweat trickled under his clothing, which was ripped from the near misses of whipping blades. Just in time he caught the edge of a long sword on his *gladius*, then stabbed in with the knife. The Gaul bellowed at the pain of his wound, then leaped vengefully at the Samaritan. His painful lurch momentarily blocked his companion, giving Simon time to pounce upon one of the circling Druids, knock his ritual-dagger out of the way, and sink the *sica* into his breast—in the deft manner the gladiators knew, so that the blade did not stick between the ribs—

A sudden lull in the fighting. Two Gauls lay moaning underfoot. Ferchobhar looked dubiously from the wounded men to Simon, who was taxed but untouched, and hesitated. He could order his remaining priest and warrior to finish the Samaritan off, but the odds had been changed considerably. If his men did not get lucky, the high priest of the Black Goat Druids knew he might find himself standing alone before a skilled, vengeful enemy....

"Back, men," he called out. "Wait for the others—!"

Simon cursed aloud. "Your treachery is even more despicable than your cowardice, goat-priest! I thought you Druids were men when I sought you, but you've proven yourselves no better than the Roman masters you serve! I leave you to them!"

He spun and ran fleetly into the dark oaks—but even as he did so he heard Ferchobhar cry out after him, like an incantation:

"You have not escaped us, Samaritan. You have belonged to us from the moment you discovered our village. You will yet pay the wage of your treachery!"

Simon made his way through the night, stumbling uncertainly in the unfamiliar forest, finding no sign of the victims he had freed. As dawn broke he recognized before him a range of blue mountains distantly merging into the mists—peaks the Gauls regarded with aversion. There, he knew, was the Averoni stronghold.

The morning air was perfumed by the scent of crumbling rocks and damp gorse. The terrain sloped downward, over crystalline boulders covered by forest and sparse grass. Since the fight with the Gauls, Simon had seen no sign of human life. That was, in a measure, lucky; he knew now that he could expect little friendliness from either Celts or Romans in Regio Averonum.

He grumbled a curse, realizing that if he had to leave Gaul now, he would take little knowledge with him. Least of all had he discovered the nature of the cloven-hoofed forest creatures or the source of the Druid's alleged power over them. Druidic myth connected the beings with the goddess Sheila-na-gog, the most important and mysterious deity of the Black Goats' pantheon. Her symbol was a crone with obscenely exaggerated genitals, as if she were nearly all womb; grotesque, perhaps, but what Simon had seen of her worship was sinister enough. Belief in this monstrous goddess set the Black Goats apart from their brother druidic societies; evidently the Wild Cats, the Beavers, the Rabbits and most other Gallic cults condemned the dark magic of the priests of Sheila-na-gog....

Regio Averonum stretched league upon league, a sea of hills and forests. As Simon wended his way, the woodland floor, rent with ravines and craggy remnants of rock outcroppings, extended before him toward darker groves where pigeons cooed. The sound reminded him of his hunger. A bird might be brought down with a makeshift sling; it might be eaten raw—or roasted, should he feel safe enough to kindle a fire.

Simon picked up a stone from the bottom of a gully and walked softly toward where the pigeons roosted. At his movements the birds stilled their peaceful cooing, and some of them warily changed their position in the branches....

Although intent on his hunting, Simon was suddenly alert to a quick, stealthy sound behind him. He whirled just in time to see a glittering blade lifted menacingly above him, clenched in a gnarled fist— and behind the fist a devil's mask. Then the dagger plunged down.

Reacting with the reflexive swiftness of the trained fighter he caught his assailant's wrist in his left hand and drove his stone-hardened right into a muscular, hairy belly. The creature bleated painfully and staggered back.

It was a wonder that the sudden shock of seeing such a creature had not stunned Simon too much to allow him to fend off the fatal blow. Even in the dim light it could not be mistaken for a man. The face, though coarsely human, had a bestial cast in the crook of its huge nose and the muzzle-like jut of its lips and teeth; the torso, too, was superficially human, though knot-like muscles moved strangely under its sallow skin. But below the waist humanity ended; the creature was a living satyr—manlike above and a two-legged goat below.

And it was big—almost as tall as Simon, and broader. It danced strangely from hoof to hoof, as nimble as the animal whose hind limbs it seemed to possess. Protruding eyes glared into the Samaritan's face, but Simon forced himself to watch instead the curved dagger which the monster rapidly switched from hand to hand, as quick as thought and seemingly to no purpose unless to distract and confuse its foe....

The creature leaped without warning, a hard, sharp hoof aimed straight at Simon's middle. Simon dodged the unorthodox attack barely in time. Landing nimbly upright, the satyr leaped again instantly, like a compressed spring, evading Simon's *gladius* and driving a hard shoulder into his chest. Both crashed into the ground, clawing at one another while rolling across a blanket of dew-wet leaves.

Simon brought up his short-sword skillfully—but the satyr, anticipating him faster than any human could have, caught his sword-arm and stopped it as suddenly as if the air had frozen thick, then began to squeeze the captured limb with the pressure of a cart wheel. The blade tumbled out of Simon's numbed fingers.

Frantically he groped for the *sica* at his belt, but in doing so left an opening through which the satyr's dagger plunged. Simon felt its cold bite in his side, heard its tip grate upon a rib, then saw it flash up into the sky for a second descent—

But instead of striking again, the monster suddenly bleated and lurched forward, blanketing the Samaritan with its hot, reeking body. Simon stabbed it and bucked furiously, throwing it off—but sensed immediately that it was not fighting back. Rolling on top of it, he saw why not: a Roman *pilum* protruded from its broad back. Simon scanned the trees; someone out there had chosen to help him at the last moment.

He spied several figures emerging from the forest. Gauls and Romans!

Urgently Simon tried to regain his feet, but a shot of pain from his wound brought him down flat. The Romans rushed him and beat the *sica* out of his fist. When he was unarmed and held hand and foot by several warriors, their leaders strode up.

"Mailaen," said a short Roman officer, "your monster was told to take him alive! Had I not given the order, the creature would have slain him!"

The Druid shrugged. "Sometimes, Commander Scaevola, the spawn obey their basic nature in spite of their orders. Ferchobhar shall be displeased that you destroyed the satyr. His type is very precious and it required a rare sacrifice to create him."

"Ferchobhar had better concern himself with *my* displeasure! My creatures must obey me *absolutely!*"

Simon had perked up his head upon hearing the Roman commander's name. The Druids were evidently not dealing with simple renegade Romans, for Scaevola—Mettius Aelius Scaevola—was proconsul of Regio Averonum. Simon knew him of old—an agent of Caligula, until that mad emperor's demise, and now, by touch-and-go maneuverings, an officer of Claudius. Whatever the Roman-Druid conspiracy, it obviously reached to the very highest circles of the province.

Scaevola turned away from Mailaen and approached Simon, pompously, as if he considered himself a conquering emperor. He was an ungainly man, plump in the belly and skinny in the limbs. His craggy face was characteristically Roman, but sagging from dissipation. Unlike most Roman officials, he sported a beard—a short, sparse fringe of hair that outlined his pallid face like a wreath of brittle moss. Without his uniform the keenest imagination would not have pictured him as a soldier—but for the last generation many worthless sorts had risen to the high ranks of Roman officialdom on the strength of personal friendship with Tiberius or Caligula.

"Your recapture is a fortunate stroke for me, Samaritan," said the proconsul, grinning at Simon's look of consternation. "Oh, yes, Simon of Gitta, I know you—by reputation. Of course the Black Goats reported your presence to me in Augustonemetum. Ferchobhar knew I needed a man like you."

"What do you want from me?" Simon demanded stiffly. "Apparently you have greater magicians than me licking your boots—and with Caligula groping in Tartarus where he belongs, there can no longer be any great reward attached to my carcass."

"You underestimate yourself, Simon. You are a remarkable man—and the Druids have use for such."

Simon fell silent. He measured up Scaevola as a man who might gloat in his own self-importance for hours without answering a simple question.

"How are his wounds?" the proconsul asked.

A centurion lifted Simon's shirt and examined the gash the satyr had made. "It's not serious if it can be dressed properly."

"Permit me," volunteered Mailaen. "We have skills even your Greek physicians know not of."

"Get on with it," muttered Scaevola, "and spare me your boasting. The wound will not weaken his powers, will it?"

"Physical suffering," smiled Mailaen, "if short of killing, does not diminish one's soul. Indeed, some men's latent powers are enhanced by it. Occasionally—when we believe it will heighten the victim's psychic energies—we employ torture before sacrificing him to Sheila-na-gog."

Wounded, bound and closely guarded by Scaevola's bodyguards, Simon found no means to escape his cage over the next two days. His wardens—ignorant, taciturn underlings—either knew nothing about what it meant "to be given to Sheila-na-gog" or would not say.

Then, on the third morning after his capture, he happened to overhear Scaevola and Ferchobhar arguing:

"I warn you, if I don't get what I want and return safely to Augustonemetum, a legion will burn this place out! Even if you personally escape into the hills, you'll be a hunted dog, without followers to make you feel important."

"Your fear talks," Ferchobhar admonished softly.

Scaevola's eyes flashed.

"No, take no offense," the Druid went on, "for even I have my fears. Sheila-na-gog is mother of all living things, all things upon this world that ever were and ever shall be. Do not, however, imagine we would betray you. Steel yourself! If you do not attend the spawning, you cannot attain power over the beast."

"I will bring my guards!"

"Bring them."

"You agree too easily," said Scaevola, suspicion in his eyes. "What of your precious secrets?"

"Every Roman who enters that place is a traitor to his emperor and his gods. If he is not mad, he will not speak of what he has seen. And if he goes mad, his words will not be believed."

"Mad?"

"There is that danger. But the ends we pursue are great and well worth the risk. You have sworn that you will accuse the Averoni of plotting to rise as they once did under Vercingetorix, and destroy them utterly. In return, you can count upon the Gauls to march shoulder to shoulder with your own legions."

"Perhaps I would do better if the Averoni were my allies. While you Gauls were fawning at Julius Caesar's hem, the Averoni were the only ones that showed him any fight—"

"When all the Caesars have passed away," said Ferchobhar scornfully, "there will still be Sheila-na-gog. Remember, once you are emperor, the laws of the Claudians shall be abolished and a temple of the Goddess shall be raised in Rome."

Scaevola shrugged. "I'll give you your temple. There are worse gods entering Rome every day. What do I care if Sheila-na-gog becomes first among them?"

The two conspirators walked on, still speaking in low tones. Simon watched them disappear behind a hut. So that was it—a double treason, racial enemies embracing for narrow ends!

In less than an hour Simon again saw his foes, this time as part of a procession that was gathering in the heart of the village as the morning sun rose above the surrounding trees. The highest Druids, now robed in black, mingled with Gallic warriors and fully-armed Romans. A number of lowly acolytes leaned upon their staffs, bulging packs of provisions hanging from their backs. Another acolyte, near the head of the assembly, held a stake on which was impaled the severed head of a black goat with large, twisted horns.

Simon was then brought from his cage, chained by the wrists to a Roman on either side. His wound did not pain him much anymore, and he could walk with some confidence. Evidently the healing herbs and ointments of the Druids were as potent as they claimed.

Ferchobhar stepped to the side of the goat-head standard and beckoned the assembly to follow him.

He chose a path leading out of the village toward the volcanic hills. The route rose up through a forest of beech and juniper, over black basalt ledges and boulders largely clothed in a thick carpet of moss. As they ascended the growth thinned, but Simon saw little more; a strange mist had filled in around the group, almost as if summoned by the Druids to disguise the winding route they followed. Occasionally it thinned and the Samaritan could make out a ghostly peak in the distance, a peak he recognized as the dead crater of the ancient mountain Cantal.

The trail continued to climb for most of the day, as if seeking perhaps the very roof of the world, where waited—what? What was the thing called Sheila-na-gog . . . ?

In the gray twilight of evening, Ferchobhar at last motioned the column to a halt on a blasted ridge near the summit of a long-extinct volcano. Only a rare scrub clung here and there to the dark, cracked rocks. The valley below was shrouded in a stratum of mist through which only the evergreens on the highest bluffs managed to break. In addition to its desolate natural appearance, Simon sensed a queer presence in this landscape that chilled him to the quick. His companions evidently felt it too, for a subdued tension was apparent in the experienced Druids, a more open nervous agitation in the novice Romans.

"What is this place, Druid?" demanded Scaevola, a slight tremor in his voice.

"We have arrived," said Ferchobhar simply. "Bring the Samaritan forward."

The guards, seeming even more ill-at-ease than their captive, prodded Simon along between them.

"My warriors shall guard the entry," said the chief Druid. "Let your own men come in with us, Commander Scaevola, if you so desire."

The proconsul nodded nervously and beckoned his bodyguards

with a wave of his hand. "Let's get on with it, Druid."

Ferchobhar deployed his warriors, then led the rest of the procession along a chasm whose walls ran with greenish slime. In places it was gathered into blisterous shapes and where they stepped on it, it clung like pine gum to their boots. At the end of the rift they came upon a pit that sloped downward and gave off an acrid odor. Once it might have been a chimney channeling black lava over the mountain's steep side.

Ferchobhar descended by a narrow path into the pit, followed by Mailaen and the other Druids. The Romans' faces gawked longingly at the light they were leaving behind; then they fell in behind the priests, who advanced more confidently—though even Ferchobhar wore a grave expression on his face. What horror, Simon wondered, could so affect even those who adored it the most . . . ?

The darkness was suddenly banished by the Druids, whose staffs flamed on as if by mental command. Simon, studying the enchanted torches carefully, noticed that the smooth finish at the head of the rods was neither blackened nor consumed.

"What magic is this?" Scaevola blurted. "Those staffs—?"

"A magic handed down to us by the sages of ancient Acheron, who brought our Goddess here from foundering Hyperborea," muttered Ferchobhar. "But, be silent—we approach the sacred presence."

The tunnel ended in a black, hollow space from which puffed a warm and ill-smelling draft. Blowing over the Samaritan's bare hands and face, the breeze somehow made him feel grimy and foul. The Druids, entering first, had the cavity well-lighted before the Romans and their prisoner reached it. The Samaritan, as he entered, drew up sharply in surprise and horror.

Bubbling within the vast cavern was a huge gray pool, some thirty yards across. It churned silently, constantly putting forth gigantic mouths, eyes, pseudopods and animate creatures. These last were the most incredible, swimming across the glistening surface, or flapping above it on clumsy and dripping wings. A few had escaped to the shore and grown somewhat—but even as Simon watched, tentacles or a sucking force from underneath, pulled the rest of them back down. They resembled composites of bats, toads, birds, reptiles and less describable forms of life. Thankfully, the pool dissolved them—but just as rapidly gave birth to more creatures, similar only in their hellishness.

The infant monsters on the scummy bank paid no attention to the intruding men; but the Romans gasped incoherent prayers and shrank back at the sight of those beasts that happened to wriggle inadvertently close.

"Begone!" commanded Ferchobhar, extending his staff toward a small, gelatinous lamia that was squirming toward the Romans. At once the thing dissolved and rilled back into the churning pool.

The chief Druid raised his arms. "Behold the womb of Sheila-na-gog, Mother of Life! Now, in the hour of the Lark, we bring to our Goddess a worthy mate. May his seed conceive in her a child of unsurpassed power. Receive him, O Goddess, into your sacred body!"

Ferchobhar then continued to speak, but in a tongue that Simon did not recognize. The remaining Druids struck up an undecipherable chant in support of him.

And Simon at last understood—and wished he did not! The gelatinous creatures cast off by the viscous pool had very little physical stability to them; the Greeks knew of such things and called them "*khimeras*". Although a few might escape into the outer world, they could maintain a semblance of life only by vampirizing the truly living beings who had already adapted to that world.

But such entities would not suit the needs of the Black Goat Druids, who wanted servitors of dependable physical stability. Apparently a human or animal from the outside world, cast into the pool, would provide the substance of a real monster—such as the satyr he had fought in the woods. And especially so if the victim was animated by a strong life force....

Scaevola turned and grinned wolfishly at Simon. "When you fell into the Druids' power, they realized that you would provide the soul and flesh for what I demanded of them—a servant like no man has possessed before! There are men who must be destroyed and others who must know terror before I dare make my move and overthrow that limping fool who reigns in Rome. Judging from your notoriety, Simon of Gitta, you have great spirit. Surely the Druids' slime-goddess will make of you nothing less than a demon—perhaps a host of demons—and then Ferchobhar's magic shall make your spawn my absolute slave!"

"Mot take you first, madman!" snarled Simon, leaping forward furiously. The guards chained to the Samaritan responded barely in time to restrain him before his hands reached the proconsul's flabby neck.

Angrily, the Roman commander struck him across the face and thrust him back.

"Take off these chains and try that again, Roman slime!" howled Simon.

"See how he fights!" Scaevola trumpeted. "What spirit! Did I not choose rightly? What he generates in union with Sheila-na-gog will shake the throne of Mars!" He signaled his guards. "Give him his wish and remove his shackles."

One of Simon's escorts dug a key out of his pouch. As the guard opened the bracelet around his own wrist, Simon's mind raced. When his left hand was also free, he would make his move. The Romans were ill-at-ease in front of the incredible pool, partly distracted by its heavings and bubblings; he might strike one of them down with his bare hands, then seize a *gladius*, kill as many of his foes as he could before being hacked down—possibly even fight his way up the tunnel. The Gauls waiting outside—little chance to elude them, but better a fighting death than a surrender to Sheila-na-gog....

Suddenly a cat's scream echoed. The Roman holding the manacle-key jerked in nervous surprise and fumbled it; it dropped into the slime underfoot. The Romans and Druids looked anxiously at one another.

"Stay where you are!" ordered Scaevola. "It's only the Samaritan! He made fools of you once!" The echo of his voice thundered between the rheumy walls of the huge cavern.

The wail of the cat was followed by the shouts of the Gallic warriors outside. Scaevola looked askance into Ferchobhar's pallid face. "We *are* being attacked!" exclaimed the proconsul. "Hurry—let's get this over with!"

He gripped Simon by the shoulder and pulled him forward. The soldier still shackled to his left hand lurched behind him, cursing in protest.

"Fool!" roared Scaevola. "Remove that chain or you'll go into the pool with him!"

"It's not my fault!" the guard protested frantically. "Rufus dropped the key into the muck!"

"Then strike off the Samaritan's hand!" barked Ferchobhar, "but in the name of the Goddess, hurry!"

Swiftly Simon shifted his weight, seized the chained guard by the wrist and upper arm, bent forward—and expertly flung the surprised Latin over his muscular shoulders. The man crashed into two more Romans, sending them sprawling also.

"Stop him!" bellowed Scaevola, retreating behind the Druids.

Ferchobhar, showing more spine, thrust his staff flame first at Simon's chest. The Samaritan sidestepped with the agility of a trained gladiator—barely in time, for the brand slid along his side, singeing his woolen chiton. Cursing, he struck out with the heavy manacle that dangled from his right wrist, bringing it down savagely on Ferchobhar's shoulder. The old Druid yelped and slacked his grasp on the staff. Instantly the Samaritan grabbed it and jerked it out of his hands—but then lost his advantage as the chained Roman gave the other shackle an angry tug and pulled him down.

Simon grappled with the man on the scummy cavern floor, while the other Romans began to push through the indignant Druids with swords drawn. The foremost legionary raised his *gladius* over the Samaritan's head.

"No!" shrieked the proconsul. "Take him alive!"

The warning spared Simon a severed neck. Instead, the Latins seized him by the legs and his free arm, controlling him despite a struggle that would have done credit to two men.

"Hold out his hand!" yelled a Roman, his white knuckles clenched upon his sword grip. Two others forced Simon down under their combined weight and wrestled his manacled arm into a position convenient for its detachment.

Suddenly a man howled in pain. The Druids and Romans glanced toward the egress as a Gallic warrior came threshing and stumbling into the grotto. A black cat clung to his bleeding back, biting and clawing his flesh.

"The Cats of Sadoqua!" blurted Mailaen.

The Gaul, seemingly blind with terror, plunged frantically through the startled men and blundered over the edge of the pit into the churning pool, the cat leaping from his back to the bank barely in time. The living muck held the Gaul for an instant, submerged to the waist, like a berry on a steaming porridge; then, as his cries intensified in recognition of his new horror, tentacles formed out of the upper surface and dragged him under.

Frenzied yowls rang down the narrow tunnel. Fear lit up every Druid face.

Ferchobhar alone had the self-control to shout: "Defend yourselves!" and retrieve his staff from under the Romans' feet. He had scarcely done so before dozens of black feline figures gushed out of the tunnel, as nimble as bats.

They rushed and sprang straight into the mass of men, claws and fangs bared, moving so swiftly that Simon, now abandoned by his captors, could make out little of them in the uncertain light and moving shadows. He glimpsed darting, shiny pelts and large eyes gleaming like moons. The Romans and Druids fought them with steel and flaming staves, but were obviously disorganized by the inhuman manner and ferocity of the attack; even those hardened veterans seemed baffled by the smallness of their foes and the supple ease with which they evaded the weapon-thrusts.

The chained guard, forgetful of the manacle in his panic, scrambled to his feet and dodged a rushing cat; the chain brought him up short and threw him off balance. Screaming out in horror, he plunged into the pool of Sheila-na-gog, feet first.

As the man was drawn under, the manacle wrenched Simon's arm with a force that rolled him over on his belly and dragged him toward the pool. Frantically he caught hold of a scum-caked stone with his free hand and arrested his slide, but the bubbling fluid was swallowing the Roman—and Simon, chained to him, was accompanying him down the gullet of Sheila-na-gog!

He strained and held on tenaciously. The edge of the iron wristlet cut through his skin, and some of his blood dribbled into the ichor. Pain shot up his forearm till he feared that his arm would tear off—a severance more painful than the quick cut the Romans had intended for him....

Suddenly the tension broke and the chain sprang slack. Simon lifted the manacle.

"Baal!" he gasped.

The other wristlet hung empty, not a trace of blood on it. The Roman had been swallowed alive and dissolved.

Shaking off his astonishment, Simon scrambled to his feet—to find himself jostled and trampled by the struggling men. Except for himself, every man in the cavern had one or more cats clinging to his clothing and biting his exposed flesh. Blood reddened the black robes of the Druids and rilled down the Romans' limbs as they threshed about. Their panicked shrieks filled the grotto and mingled with the yowling of the cats—which yelling now began to shed its feline tenor and become more like screamed syllables in a forgotten tongue!

The shrill chanting seemed to drive the beleaguered men mad. They ceased to defend themselves and began to run crazily, randomly around the narrow ledge above the pool, jostling one another in their terror, striking themselves senseless against the walls or stumbling blindly into the goddess' fluid mass.

A louder voice penetrated the commotion—Ferchobhar's, invoking a protective spell against the cats' shrill voicings. Bright flashes of flame suddenly lit the cavern—searing blasts from the end of the Druid's magic staff. The fire dissolved the felines it touched in the wink of an eye, but also charred those luckless men who were mingled with them, driving them in blind agony into the clutch of Sheila-na-gog.

Then Ferchobhar made a dash for the exit, and close behind him ran Mettius Aelius Scaevola, the cats no longer barring their escape. Quick as thought, Simon grasped a Druid's fallen staff and threw it between the proconsul's legs. Even as Ferchobhar vanished up the tunnel the Roman stumbled over the staff and crashed to the rocky floor, his armor ringing. Before he could regain his feet, he felt Simon's strong hands upon him.

"Latin dog!" hissed the Samaritan, gripping his foe's throat.

"Spare me!" Scaevola gasped against the pressure. "I had nothing to do with this! I can make you an important man—!"

Disgust welled up in Simon's breast, and hate. It was corrupt Roman officials like this one who had plundered his home in Samaria, slain his parents, sold him into the arena.

"Scum who would rule the world," he snarled, "kiss the bride you would have given me to!"

Then with a surge of rage he heaved the man off his feet—and straight over the brink of the pit into the pool of Sheila-na-gog.

For a moment the Roman stuck like a fly in the surface of the seething paste; then, screaming, he sank down. Simon watched, dark eyes narrowed, feeling no pity for the dying proconsul. Scaevola howled as his mouth filled with the gray, pulsing fluid; then his voice choked off, and his frantic eyes vanished beneath the fetid surface. The depression he left behind slowly filled in with ichor....

Suddenly Simon realized he stood alone in the grotto. The cats had gone and those men who were not dead or senseless underfoot had vanished into the goddess-pool. The Samaritan felt a strange heaviness begin to take possession of him....

Something huffed close by. Turning, Simon beheld a creature heaving itself out of the pasty womb of Sheila-na-gog. It was a small criosphinx—a ram-headed beast with leonine hindquarters and wings still dripping with fluid. Other fetid monsters were similarly rising, most smaller and frailer—amalgamations of all manner of lowly beasts, some possessed of forms that had no known equivalent in Nature. Simon recoiled; here, he realized, were the men who had gone into the pool, now remolded into abominations not of this earth.

He backed away, and turned to retreat up the tunnel—but then he heard men's shouts and footsteps coming from around a bend. Was it the rest of the Gauls? Had Ferchobhar rallied the men outside?

Simon snatched up a Roman sword. Wounded, sickened, he would yet make a fight of it....

The intruders moved cautiously into view. Simon's *gladius* wavered unsteadily. These were not the Gauls, although Ferchobhar's face was in the forefront....

Aye, in the forefront—for in the fist of the first Averoni tribesman dangled the head of Ferchobhar, chief of the Black Goat Druids. Blood and horror had hideously changed the dead priest's face.

"Put down your weapon, Simon of Gitta," said their leader. "We surely have not done all this with the intent of harming you."

Simon recognized the newcomer as the last man he had released from the Druids' osier cage. He nodded, lowered his sword and slumped wearily against the wall.

"I thank you," he said, fighting to keep from passing into a swoon.

Several Averoni nudged past him and began to attack the creatures of the pool with spears, axes and knives, hewing them into lifeless pieces.

"Good," said their chief when the butchery was finished. "Now, let's get out of this foul place!"

They all hurried from the cavern; but as the last two torch-bearing Averoni helped Simon through the exit, he turned—and gasped as he observed a final creature rise from the womb of Sheila-na-gog. It had just surfaced in an obscure corner, near the spot where Mettius Aelius Scaevola had disappeared; it was small and had the shape of a rat, but its pallid, bearded face and handlike forepaws were evilly human....

Then a sudden bubbling of the pool seemed to frighten the risen creature, sending it scurrying into the shadows with a loathsome, piteous titter.

About "The Pillars of Melkarth"

WARNING: Contains spoilers!

Readers may notice a large time lapse between the events of "The Pillars of Melkarth" (spring equinox, A.D. 50) and those of the previous story set in A.D. 42. This is because those years were taken up with the events of the novels *Path of the Dragon* (forthcoming from Pickman's Press) in A.D. 42 and *The Gardens of Lucullus* (Sidecar Preservation Society, 2001) in A.D. 48. Other stories were planned during this time period as well. Richard Tierney intended some German adventures in A.D. 46 - 47, as well as entertaining another collaboration with Glenn Rahman on a pair of novels set on the western Roman frontier, one centered on the Claudian invasion of Britain, the other involving the Picts in Scotland. Sadly, none of these stories were ever written—yet. And so we come to the final Simon tale (and a good one to end on), "The Pillars of Melkarth".

Melkarth is one of many cognate divine names meaning "king", others being Moloch, Melek Tous, Molech, Melchizedek, Milcom. Many of these gods (or local variations on the same god) were also included among the Baals ("Lords"), and Baal Melkarth was the Phoenician deity whose prophets Elijah opposed in the satirical legend of the contest of the gods in 1 Kings 18 (very likely the source for the later Peter versus Simon Magus legends). As Tierney says, Melkarth was a god of fire, which is presumably why Elijah (himself a historicized sun god) challenges him to send down fire from heaven. Moloch received child sacrifice in the flames. In Carthage, the ovens used for such sacrifices themselves came to be called molochs. So where would you guess Melkarth might fit into the Cthulhu Mythos pantheon? Of course he would be identified with Cthugha, the fire elemental created by August Derleth to plug the gap pointed out by Francis T. Laney in Derleth's Periodical Table of the Elementals (the periodical in question being, of course, *Weird Tales*). Though Mythos fans have largely derided the very notion of Cthugha as an unimaginative trope on watery Cthulhu, as uninspired an idea as Stan Lee's creation of the Iceman as a counterpoint to the Human Torch, Tierney shows in "The Pillars of Melkarth" how the whole concept can be rendered convincingly authentic, both the idea of Cthugha himself and the seemingly trite theme of the conflict of the elements among the Old Ones.

Another fire entity mentioned in this story (which first appeared in *Space & Time* #78, 1990) is "Atar, servant of Mazda." Atar was the Iranian name for the Vedic Agni, the fire spirit among the gods, specifically the fire of the sacrifice. When the Prophet Zoroaster restored Varuna/Ahura Mazda to his original primacy, he retained of the other Vedic gods only

Mitra the overseer of oaths and Atar/Agni. The fire sacrifice, though no longer part of an offering of food to the gods, retained its ritual centrality in the Zoroastrian faith, coming to denote the purity of the elements. Thus Simon's reference to Atar the flame lord who is subordinate to Mazda, the Lord of Light. Ku-Thugha is not "friendly fire", however. Among the many infernal aliases Tierney lists for Ku-Thugha/Melkarth you will notice Yamath, Lin Carter's creation, the fire god of ancient Lemuria.

The link Tierney forges between the Lovecraftian cult of Dagon and its ancient Philistine prototype is still more ingenious. Lovecraft implied that the ancient religion was based on half-understood myths stemming ultimately from Dagon and the deep ones, though human worshipers would suspect the true origin as little as believers in the Abominable Snowman would guess that the truth behind their myth was really that of the crustaceans from Yuggoth. Tierney has reversed this. For him, the ancient religion of fishy Dagon was the same cult that spread in later ages to Innsmouth. Father Dagon is not the unsuspected truth behind a pagan cult; rather, he is the explicit object of worship, and ancient Tyre, whose maritime wealth is ascribed by Ezekiel to Yahweh, really owes its success in trade to the deep ones the same way the Marsh Refinery did.

Tierney's treatment of Helen, making her a priestess in the temple of Astarte, is a sound and insightful explanation of the Christian heresiologists' claim that Simon's consort Helen had been a whore fished out of a brothel. Tierney is on firm ground when he notes that the Jewish and Christian charge of prostitution often simply denoted the worship of foreign gods, "whoring after the heathen." On this understanding, the "brothel" of Helen need have been no more than the pagan temple she served.

In Lovecraft's "The Horror at Red Hook" we overhear an invocation to Hecate, Mistress of Black Magic. It includes the words, "Gorgo, Mormo, Thousand-faced Moon, look favorably upon our sacrifice." This chant was not Lovecraft's creation. As he knew, it actually formed part of the ancient liturgy. So did a familiar bit of Lovecraftian glossolalia, the exclamation *Iä!* This cry was that of the frenzied Maenads, the Bacchantes of Dionysus. Lovecraft thought it appropriate for the noxious and detestable orgiasts of the Cthulhu cult. Thus it is especially fitting for Richard Tierney not only to take both the Hecate liturgy and the Dionysiac shout back to their original era, but to bring along their Lovecraftian associations as well.

In this tale Simon has a new apprentice and sidekick, a youth named Nilus. He is intended as the later Gnostic mystagogue Satornilus (or Satorninus), actually a disciple of and successor to Menander, Simon's own disciple. Another fictional transfiguration of Satornilus occurs in Thomas Ligotti's "The Last Feast of Harlequin."

THE PILLARS OF MELKARTH
by Richard L. Tierney

PROLOG

Amran the Phoenician, merchant of Tyre, prided himself on being of a hard and practical nature. His pride was justified, for his shrewd practicality had enabled him to become one of the richest sea-traders of the eastern Mediterranean. Yet now, as he stood before Mattan, High Priest of Melkarth, he felt his hard and stern nature shaken and some of the old fears of his boyhood reawakening. He did not like the feeling.

Not that Mattan was anything less than affable. It was just that the bald, black-robed priest, standing here upon the torchlit roof of his temple, was so… overwhelming. Nor was this merely because the man was a head taller than most and bulky in proportion. No, it was something in the man's face—black-browed, thick-lipped, and heavy-jowled—that hinted at cruelty combined with an unbridled lust for power. Most sinister of all were the gleaming dark eyes which seemed to hold a gloating hypnotic quality, the confidence of a will that felt itself empowered to bend all other wills to its purposes should it so choose.

"You are a gem, Amran!" said Mattan in a deep, powerful voice, beaming and throwing wide his arms in an expansive gesture. "The children you have brought to me are exactly what I specified, and now the sacrifice of them will enable me to obtain more of the same."

The merchant shuddered slightly but strove to conceal it. "Your order was a bit out of line, Mattan. I am primarily a corn merchant, not a slave procurer."

"Be not so modest. Six of the children you obtained have proved to be exactly of the sort I need—temple acolytes, pure and unblemished. Tell me, friend, where did you obtain them?"

"In Sidon," answered Amran, "from the temples of Astarte and Adonis. Even high priests can be corrupted if only the fee be great enough—" He stopped abruptly, as if guiltily realizing the audacity of what he had said.

Mattan strode forward a pace, his large dark eyes gleaming with an intimidating intensity from beneath heavy black brows, and for an instant the merchant felt that childish fear of his intensify. Yet the priest's lips were parted in a grin of amusement, not a snarl of anger.

"You are right about priests," he chuckled. "Most of them are corrupt and so do not deserve to hold their offices. That was the trouble with my predecessor Neleus, who was little more than a Roman flunky. I warned him repeatedly that he was not serving the god Melkarth properly, but he would not listen. And now...." Mattan shrugged beneath his voluminous black robe; his large, pale hands, palms upturned, protruded in striking contrast from his black sleeves.

Amran remembered uneasily that Neleus had died mysteriously a few weeks earlier. His body had been found between the two sacred pillars which stood before the god's altar, charred as if by intense fire. Now this Mattan, formerly of Baalbek and a stranger to Tyre until less than a year ago, was high priest in Neleus' stead. No one claimed openly to know Mattan's origins, but furtive rumors were abroad that he had once studied sorcery in eastern lands and was a practitioner of the darkest arts and an invoker of demons.

"By Moloch!" exclaimed the Phoenician trader. "Are you implying that the god Melkarth himself killed Neleus for his lapses?"

The priest threw back his bald head and laughed heartily.

"No!" he boomed finally, still shaking with mirth. "He died because he defied *me!*" Then, in answer to the shocked expression on Amran's face: "—for of course I am the servant of Melkarth. How apt, Amran, that you, like so many of your race, should still swear by Moloch, god of ancient Carthage. For Carthage, as you know, was founded by an expedition from this very city of Tyre, and her people never ceased to worship Tyre's god Melkarth. In fact, the two gods are at bottom the same: the great Lord of Fire whom the ancient Stygians called Ku-Thugha and who is one of the foremost among the primal Old Ones."

Amran, uncomfortable and uncomprehending, made an effort to assert himself. "Mattan, why have you brought me here to the rooftop of Melkarth's temple? Surely there are no spies within, that we should need this much space about us in order to talk freely."

The priest chuckled throatily. "No. I merely wanted to show you our city—our empire—our world." He leaned one hand on the parapet and swept the other grandly around to include the entire horizon—from the south and west, where the afterglow of the vanished sun still scintillated upon the sea, then north to where the lofty apartment buildings and colonnaded avenues of the nearby island-city of Tyre still gleamed dimly in that afterglow, and finally eastward to the busy ship-filled harbor and, beyond it, the wide mole that connected the city to the mainland. "For, behold! All this—this sea, this city, those eastward hills and the lands beyond them—will soon be ours to rule as we will. Your wealth, Amran, and my sorcery shall, before this month is done, have made the entire world our domain and our plaything!"

Amran was now certain that the priest was mad, yet he sensed also that he must humor the man if he hoped to leave this place with the money that had been promised him—or, perhaps, with merely his very life.

"You doubt my sanity," said Mattan. "Well, I won't blame you for that, Amran. Such a grand claim as I have made must be backed up, and so it shall be. Tonight the stars will be right for the Invocation of the Flame-beings. See, the equinoctial sun has set, and though the moon is yet aloft it, too, shall set before the dawn—and tomorrow, Amran, both shall rise upon a very new world and the dawn of our new empire. Come—follow me."

He beckoned, then led the merchant back down into the temple via a narrow stairway until they reached a much wider one, then down again, finally bringing them into a short corridor that opened into the grand columned nave. Though a bracketed torch burned on every pillar, the place was yet dim and shadowy due to its hugeness. There was no idol to Melkarth present, but at the southern end of the great hall stood a dark stone altar flanked by two thick, high, smoothly cylindrical pillars, and before these stood a silent conclave of bald priests who were wrapped, like Mattan, in black robes whose thrown-back cowls bunched at their necks.

Amran gasped at the sight of the twin pillars flanking the altar. Often had he seen them during previous visits to this temple, when he had offered prayers to Melkarth to watch over his merchant ships at sea; the left pillar was normally an emerald green, the other golden. But tonight they gleamed with an eerie luminescence of their own, the golden one shedding a beautiful amber radiance upon the marble tiles about its base, while within the emerald one there darted and spiraled strange glimmerings of pale blue light whose movements seemed almost like those of living things. Moreover, a deep humming sound came forth from both, steady and vibrant, as if they were filled with great power ready to be unleashed.

"Do not be afraid," said Mattan to Amran. "Stand here beside me, and watch." He then turned toward the northern end of the great hall and shouted in a thundering voice: *"Jag Sodhi, bring in the sacrifice to Melkarth!"*

There was a stir of white at the hall's northern end, and then a small procession filed into the great nave from between the marble columns—six children clad in snowy tunics followed by a black-robed man at least as tall as Mattan. At the same moment there began a sound of eerie woodwinds in strange harmony, and Amran saw that all the priests were facing away from the altar and playing upon dark flutes.

As the children drew closer the merchant observed that they walked two abreast, boys on the right, girls on the left. None was more than nine years of age, yet they advanced in a perfectly disciplined, slowly cadenced unison; their eyes were fixed straight ahead, unblinking, as though held by a hypnotic spell. The man who followed them, tall and massive, seemed taller still because of the large black turban he wore. In his right hand he carried a great curved sword, wielding it as though symbolically to herd his flock of small charges forward. As the group drew nearer Amran heard a strange clopping upon the tiles, as if the turbaned priest wore wooden shoes under his robe. He suppressed a shudder at the sight of the man's eyes, dark and cruel as Mattan's own, that gleamed above his hooked nose and straggly brown beard.

"Who is that man?" whispered the Phoenician nervously when the procession had passed. "He's no priest of any god I know—"

"Jag was a priest in Ku-Thugha's black temple at Ratmissar, beyond the Indus," rumbled Mattan in a low voice. "I studied there for a time, and when I returned to Syria he accompanied me, bearing certain scrolls he had obtained from the temple's library—writings containing the chants that would activate the Pillars of Melkarth and open the Gate to Ku-Thugha's fiery realm. You are fortunate among men, Amran, for you are about to witness that opening, if only briefly. Stay here, and watch."

So saying, Mattan strode out into the middle of the nave and faced the altar, raising his arms so that they pointed toward the tops of the twin pillars. The flute-playing priests had drawn aside, forming into two lines, and between them marched the white-clad children, followed by the tall and turbaned Jag Sodhi. The latter halted between the ranks of the subordinate priests, but the children continued on until they came to the altar and ascended its steps. There they stopped and stood, silent and motionless, directly between the lofty and eerily gleaming pillars.

"*Phun-klui munglu-naph!*" boomed Mattan suddenly. "*Ku-Thugha Fum-al-hut!*"

The humming of the pillars rose to a shrill whine—and suddenly flame burst and blossomed between them. In the split second before he reflexively shielded his eyes Amran glimpsed the children as six black silhouettes and, beyond them, what seemed to be a great fiery vista of a strange world—boiling flame-clouds, towers and avenues of white-glaring crystal, moving entities like columns of fire. The light spilled out into the temple, briefly illuminating every tile and stone with stark brilliance—

Thunder boomed. Abruptly, the light was gone.

Amran rubbed his eyes, then opened them. The children were also gone, evidently swallowed up by that fiery, briefly opened Gate, and in their place now swarmed hundreds of what appeared to be living fire sparks. These quickly dispersed from between the glowing pillars to scatter in the temple's gloom like preternaturally bright fireflies.

"Servitors of Ku-Thugha, obey me in His name," intoned Mattan. "Bring us light."

Immediately the points of light bunched themselves into many small clusters, each cluster then settling down into the flame of a bracketed torch. The flames expanded and heightened; the temple was filled with their radiance as they consumed the substance of the torches at a furious rate.

Mattan turned and strode back to Amran. "You did well, Phoenician. From among those children you procured, these six proved to be True Spirits and so have been accepted by Ku-Thugha into his realm. See, they are gone, and in their place he has sent many of his servitors to us. With their aid I shall obtain more sacrifices, and so our power shall grow."

Amran felt sick but strove to conceal it. "Is that what happened to Neleus, your predecessor?" he asked, glancing toward the altar.

"I spoke the words of the invocation while Neleus happened to be praying between the pillars," said Mattan, grinning, "but Neleus was not a True Spirit and his prayers were offensive to Ku-Thugha, and so he was blasted to ashes where he stood."

Amran swallowed nervously. "And now?"

"Now, my friend, you must send forth your ships to procure many more such sacrifices. You are no longer a corn merchant, Amran, but a gatherer of sacred flesh and souls to feed the fiery hunger of Ku-Thugha. With your wealth you shall procure young victims from Alexandria, from Antioch, and from a hundred other cities—aye, even from Rome itself. And over each city which provides such sacrifices Ku-Thugha shall establish his sway, even as he shall establish it tonight over this great city of Tyre."

"Tonight—?"

"Aye!" Mattan swept an arm enthusiastically toward the eerily flaring torches. "With the aid of these servitors, Jag and I shall this very night obtain more child-acolytes from Tyre's temples, and by the time the star Fum-al-hut rises in the darkness before dawn, our power shall be great enough to invoke the enduring presence of Ku-Thugha himself!

"Go, therefore, Amran, and order all your vessels to sail at the first glimmer of day. By then Tyre shall be firmly under my rule—and after your ships return, so shall the rest of the empire be also. Then shall Ku-Thugha feast as he has not feasted since those days when thousands died in flames before the altars of imperial Carthage!"

Amran nervously bowed in acknowledgment, not trusting himself to answer, then turned and hurried out of that vast hall and across its columned portico to rejoin his servants, who awaited him outside in the night.

And as he and his servants strode rapidly north along the tree-flanked avenue toward the causeway linking the isle of Melkarth to the main island of Tyre, Amran could hear Mattan's laughter booming out behind them from the fire-illumined temple.

I

He stood alone on a dark plain. Fear stirred in the heavy, formless stillness; cold stars and the slim horns of a crescent moon gleamed down.

Then he saw Her, dark-haired and lovely as of old, surrounded by shadows that enfolded her ever more closely. Her white face contrasted sharply with those shadows; her dark eyes stared sadly up into them as they rustled about her like monstrous wings. A horror swept over him.

"Helen!" he cried out desperately. *"Helen!"*

Bare feet pattered rapidly across marble tiles—abruptly, he snapped from the nightmare into wakefulness. Someone was shaking his shoulder.

"Master! Master! *Wake up!*"

Simon of Gitta rolled over on his side and gazed up into the concerned dark eyes of Nilus, his ten-year-old slave boy. The lad was standing beside the cot, his face grim and a bit fearful in the dim light of the solitary oil lamp, his hands still on Simon's shoulder.

"Nilus! What—?"

"I heard you crying out fearfully, Master. Were—were demons tormenting you?"

"No. Not demons." The man threw aside his bedding, rumpled from much tossing, sat up, and wiped his sweat-beaded brow with a trembling hand. "It was a dream—and yet, a dream such as I have not had for nearly twenty years!"

The man grew silent, staring down at the marble-tiled floor as if he could see through it into vistas of past time. Nilus, despite his mere ten years, precociously sensed—not for the first time—that his master was a man burdened with strange and heavy memories. Though he had been in Simon's service for scarcely three months, he was fond of the man, who had been kinder to him than any previous master and had even undertaken to instruct him daily in skills as diverse as the reading of Greek and the arts of hand-to-hand combat. Yet the man was reputed to be a sorcerer—not a common one, either, but the foremost mage in the employ of the Emperor Claudius. Now Nilus was reminded that he knew little of this man who had recently, by the greatest good fortune, rescued him from the life of a street urchin in teeming Antioch.

"Master, you cried out a woman's name—Helen."

"Aye, Helen." Simon's dark, deep-set eyes became even more introspective—sorrowful and haunted. "I knew and loved her long ago. The Romans caused her doom when I was far away in Persia and could not come to her aid, but the night she died I had the same dream that I have had just now! Several months ago, I began to hear her voice in my sleep and dimly see her face, and always she beseeched me to leave Rome and journey here to Tyre...." He paused and stared intently at the youth for a moment. "What can it mean, Nilus? Neither Helen nor I ever dwelt in Tyre."

Nilus shrank back a bit from the intensity of his master's gaze. He sensed that he was being talked to on an adult basis, and on this occasion it made him feel more uneasy than proud.

"I—I don't know, Master Simon—"

"Ha!" the man barked in sudden self-derision. "Don't look so troubled, Nilus—it's not your problem. I forgot myself. I had a nightmare, that's all. Go back to your bed."

The lad felt easier immediately, yet a concern for his new master prompted him to ask, "Do you think, sir, that she really was calling you here to this city?"

"What?" The man stared at him sharply. "Nilus, whatever would make you think of such a question?"

"Because when I was young," said the boy seriously, "I was taken into the household of a magician of Antioch who said that I was not like other children. It was in his house that I first learned the art of reading and thereby many other things, for which I am grateful; but when I found out that he intended to sacrifice me to dark gods on my ninth birthday, I fled again into the streets—"

"And lived there until I found you." Simon gazed intently at his serious-eyed apprentice. "I think I see. This magician who told you that you were not like others—what did he say you were?"

Nilus swallowed nervously. "He said I was a reincarnated True Spirit."

"Ah." Simon nodded. "That is exactly what I sensed you were, and that is why I chose you to be my apprentice."

The lad's dark eyes flashed sudden terror. "You—you don't plan to sacrifice me to the dark gods, Master Simon—do you?"

Simon laughed briefly at the absurdity of it—but then, seeing the genuine concern on the lad's face, he said, "Nilus, of course not! I'm a True Spirit too, and so was my lost Helen. You and I are like brothers, Nilus, even though Roman society makes us technically master and slave for the moment. But I, too, was a slave once—and I predict that you, Nilus, will one day hold a position at least as lofty as the one I hold now."

"But my former master—?"

Simon scowled darkly. "Evidently he was an evil man, one given over to the service of the dark powers. To such, True Spirits are the greatest offerings that can be made, in exchange for power, to the mad gods who created this world. For True Spirits are fragments of the transcendent God and Goddess, who were sundered and trapped in this material world when Achamoth and his evil archons fashioned it—" Simon abruptly stopped speaking. "Forgive me, Nilus, I forget you're just a boy. You're not ready for this level of instruction—"

"But I am! My former master once told me, while in his cups, that True Spirits, unlike other people, are reincarnated generation after generation—and that is why I wonder, sir, if the woman Helen may have called you here." The lad's eyes lit up excitedly at the thought. "Maybe she is living in this very city, born anew!"

Simon scowled incredulously at this precocious apprentice of his. He had himself been haunted by that very same thought for many months.

"Nilus," he sighed, "I've said too much. You shouldn't have to trouble your mind about such things, not at your age. Go back to bed."

The lad nodded and returned to his rumpled blankets in the antechamber.

But his master did not go back to sleep. For some time Nilus listened to the man's restless pacing to and fro upon the marble floor, then finally heard the whisper of cloth and guessed that tunic and cloak were being donned. Carefully he raised his head and peered through the doorway, watched his master fasten on sandals and sword-belt, then pick up a short staff from beside his bed.

Nilus lay back in the darkness and feigned sleep. A moment later he heard the door of the apartment softly open and close and sensed that he was alone.

Instantly Nilus rose, then hurriedly donned his sandals and a dark, symbol-emblazoned tunic similar to his master's. Whipping a cloak about his slight form, he opened the door and hurried out into the empty, torchlit corridor.

At the outer entrance of the apartment building he encountered two Roman soldiers who regarded him inquisitively.

"My master, Simon the Mage, has bid me to follow him with all haste," said Nilus earnestly. "Which way has he gone?"

The guards, recognizing the lad, opened the portal to the street. "To the right," said one of them, grinning. "Hurry. It would not be well for you to earn a great magician's displeasure."

Nilus thanked them, then hurried out into the dark street. Faint moonlight glimmered down and as his eyes adjusted to it he saw his master just vanishing around a corner far down the narrow lane.

Carefully, practicing the techniques of stealth Simon himself had taught him, Nilus followed his master through the complex maze of Tyre's streets: After a short time he saw that they were approaching the dark bulk of the great Temple of Astarte, and in another moment his master had entered the torchlit court before its wide, columned entryway.

Hanging back in the shadows, Nilus watched as Simon strode up the wide stairway and confronted the single white-robed acolyte who stood watch upon the portico. Nilus guessed that the slender, yellow-haired figure was a youth about his own age.

After a brief exchange of words, the magician was allowed to pass inside.

Nilus waited a few minutes. Then, drawing himself up to his full height, he strode forward openly, not doubting that the young hierodule would let him pass even as the Roman guardsmen had done.

Simon entered the great pillared nave and stared up in awe at the lofty, calm-featured eidolon of Astarte—an awe undiminished by the fact that he had already come here each day during the past week. Her stylized, symmetric, even rigid aspect gave her a cold dignity far removed from those seductive, round-limbed forms the Greek sculptors had carved to represent Her under the name of Aphrodite, yet Simon knew beyond doubt that both represented the same... Person.

He bowed briefly in respect, then stood and faced the eidolon squarely.

"Helen," he muttered softly, his tone less one of prayer than of direct speech, "I have felt your presence these many months, and it has drawn me across the seas to this place. I came here as the official emissary of Claudius the Emperor, delegated by him to officiate at the ritual of renaming this ancient city of Tyre as 'Claudiopolis', and I have now fulfilled that mission with all the appropriate pomp and pageantry; yet my real purpose in coming here was to seek You. Give me a sign, O Helen, through this image of stone which the Tyrians have erected as your symbol—aye, even as all have symbolized You through ages beyond reckoning. All mankind know and love You in their deepest devotions, and call You by many names: Ishtar, Astarte, Aphrodite—yet I have known You in human form, as few humans have been privileged to, under your human name and aspect as—Helen."

The face of the eidolon remained austere, unresponsive above the clean unwavering flames of the oil lamps on the altar. Simon gazed down pensively into those flames. He had received no sign, yet somehow he sensed the imminence of a Presence....

A young priestess or acolyte, white-clad and bearing a lit torch, entered the temple from some alcove beyond the altar and began quietly, unobtrusively to light more torches bracketed upon the columns. Simon realized that she was preparing the place for a midnight ritual, for this was the eve of the spring equinox, the time when Astarte, Queen of the World, was on the point of bringing her winter-lost restorative powers back to a hungering earth.

He again raised his eyes to the face of the image and, in a voice louder

than before, intoned: "Come, O Helen! Is this not the hour for great secrets to be bared—the one moment of the year when hidden truths may be
revealed?"

Immediately, to his surprise, the young torch-bearing hierodule hurried toward him across the tiles. As she drew close she asked: "You called
me, sir?"

Simon stared at her, dumbfounded. She was remarkably beautiful. Her
lustrous hair, held at the nape of her neck by a fine silvery net, was as dark
as her large and expressive eyes; her features were as pure in outline as if
hewn from alabaster by the masterly art of a Praxiteles. But it was not
merely her beauty that dumfounded the Samaritan.

"Helen!" he gasped.

"That is my name, sir. How may I help you? If you wish to attend the
rituals, they are soon to begin."

Simon felt his limbs trembling. It was *her*, to every expression of her
lovely features, every intonation of her voice—

"Helen," he said, "it has been so long, so many years—"

"Do I know you?" she said, searching his rugged face, studying intently the high cheekbones, the firm mouth and shaven jaw, the deep-set dark
eyes that reflected the light of her torch with an almost sinister gleam. "It
almost seems to me that I do. Did we once meet in Antioch?"

"No. In Rome."

"That is not possible, good sir, for I have never lived in that city."

"You did, though," insisted Simon, "for I first met you there more
than twenty years ago."

"Again, that is not possible, for I have not yet reached my nineteenth
birthday. My first twelve years were spent as a slave in Antioch, whence I
fled after being sold to brutal masters. Since then I have lived in Byblos,
Berytus, Sidon, and, finally, here in Tyre. I have known no other cities. You
have mistaken me for another."

Simon took a deep breath, let it out slowly to calm himself. "Helen, I
am Simon of Gitta. Do you truly not know me?"

"Simon?" Something moved at the corner of the girl's mouth, a dimpling that hovered between seriousness and an incipient smile. Simon
thrilled. The thing was so familiar to him, so characteristic of her—

"Simon," she repeated musingly. "Your name, like your face, has a
strange familiarity. I am sure we have never met, yet somehow I feel I
know you. Perhaps I have seen you in dreams." She glanced up at the calm,
lamplit face of the eidolon of Astarte. "This is a strange night."

"Strange indeed. And stranger still that you should mention dreams.
Helen, this very night I had a dream of you—the same dream I had the
night you were slain so many years ago."

"Slain?" The girl again looked closely into his earnest eyes, saw no madness there. "You mean, our first meeting was not in this life but in a former one?"

"Aye." Simon's voice grew firm. "Helen, I have prayed for this reunion ever since we were sundered by death more than two decades ago. But you must come with me this very night! I know that that dream of mine was a portent of our reunion, but I sense that it is also a foreboding of doom. The first time I had it, I was far away in Parthia and so could not come to your aid. But now I am here—and this time, by all the gods, no wizard-sent bane nor steel blade shall again separate us!"

The young woman stepped back a pace at his intensity, and Simon feared for a moment that she might think him mad. But there was no fear in her face, only that slight dimpling at the corner of her mouth that indicated a puzzled—perhaps even amused—uncertainty.

"I *should* think you mad," she said, as if echoing his thought, "but, strangely, I do not. Tell me, Simon—oh, how familiar that name seems!— tell me more of this former life of mine."

"There is no time. You must come with me now."

Helen glanced around at the sound of many soft-sandaled feet. A double line of white-clad, torch-bearing acolytes was emerging from behind the statue of Astarte, arranging themselves between the columns along either side of the temple. Simon saw that they were all much younger even than Helen—children ranging in age from perhaps eight to twelve.

"I cannot go with you, Simon, even if I would. The midnight pre-equinox ceremony is soon to begin. I must finish lighting the torches."

So saying, Helen turned from him abruptly and hurried away, flashing back at him a brief enigmatic look, then resolutely resumed her task.

Simon hesitated but a moment, then strode around the altar and the eidolon in the direction from which the twin procession of young hierodules had come. In the shadows he made out a wide stairway leading upward and, ascending it, emerged into a tile-floored corridor whose surface dimly reflected the light of many bracketed torches. At the head of the stair stood a white-robed lad perhaps twelve years of age.

"Quick, boy," said Simon, "lead me to the high priest."

"But—but, sir," stammered the young acolyte, "you may not pass here. Besides, the ritual is about to begin—"

"Do as I say. Great danger impends for this temple—I can sense it. Hurry!"

Overawed by the stranger's intensity, the lad quickly nodded, then beckoned Simon to follow him down the tiled corridor.

Nilus, standing erect on the point of advancing toward the temple portico, suddenly heard stirrings amid the shadows at the far end of the alley. Whirling, he glimpsed a brief movement of black shapes—but then silence returned. He tensed, recalling mention of a rumor that many children had vanished during Tyrian nights of late, but the sounds did not recur. Gradually he relaxed. The streets of all cities teemed with rats and beggars; still, it was a reminder to keep his senses keen and alert, for slave-procurers were also ever a-prowl. Taking a deep breath and letting it out slowly, in the way his master had instructed him, Nilus allowed his mind to become still that his senses might perfectly detect every sight, sound and smell about him.

The night was quiet, breezeless, utterly silent.

Reassured, Nilus strode forward and proceeded down the wide approach to the temple; the gibbous moon, now slightly westering, was dimmed by the torches upon the columns that flanked the way. As he approached the wide, well lit portico he saw that the acolyte set to watch the entryway was not a lad at all but only a girl about his own age. Her golden hair hung straight and loose upon her shoulders; her slight body was formally erect beneath her white tunic; her blue eyes were expressionless as she watched Nilus.

"Who comes to the temple of the Queen of the World?" she intoned as the lad ascended the steps. Nilus sensed that she was nervous.

"You're new at this, eh?" he said. "Well, I'm with Simon of Gitta, the very important man you just admitted. He's Emperor Claudius' ambassador to this city, in case you haven't heard, and I'm his second-in-command."

Instead of being impressed, as Nilus had hoped, the girl merely confronted him firmly and repeated, as if by rote: "Who comes to the temple of the Queen of the World?"

"Didn't you hear me?" cried Nilus. "I'm an important person! My master, whom you just admitted, has commanded me to follow him. If you don't let me in, you'll be in trouble."

For an instant the girl seemed doubtful, but then her face set in determination. "Give me the response."

"What—?"

"I can't let you in unless you give me the correct *response!*"

"You can, too," countered Nilus. "I told you, you'll be in big trouble if you don't."

The girl laughed. "Now I know you're just a silly boy. If the man who just entered is really your master, why didn't he teach you the response? If you want a handout, go behind the temple and wait until dawn, when the cooks will be arriving—"

"Ha!" shouted Nilus, stung to the quick and instinctively concealing the fact by an impulsive display of arrogance. "Do my garments look like those of a beggar? Can you not see that they are similar to those of my master? Let me in, girl——I command it!"

The girl noted the resemblance. "I guess I believe you," she said grudgingly, "but I can't let you in this night unless you give me the correct response. It is forbidden. This is the special pre-equinox ceremony, and only the properly initiated may attend."

"Ha!" repeated Nilus derisively. "And do you think that you, a mere girl, could stop me from attending? My master is the greatest magician in the empire and he has taught me many of his skills. More, he was once a gladiator; he has taught me how to fell an obstinate foe with one kick. Watch!" So saying, Nilus bounded high into the air and kicked the nearest pillar smartly with his heel at the height of a man's head, then dove to the ground and, with remarkable agility, rolled and came erect, poised in a fighter's stance. "There, girl! Try to stop me if you will!"

The slender acolyte, obviously impressed, nevertheless stood her ground. "You would not be such a beast," she said, "—and besides, there are guards concealed at the other end of this portico in case of trouble. And even without their aid the Queen of the World would protect me." So saying, she pulled forth from her tunic a large talisman—a great, round, pearl-white stone set in whitish-gold metal which depended from a silvery chain about her neck.

Despite his injured sense of self-importance, Nilus bent forward, fascinated, to examine the object more closely. He now saw that the stone was not smooth, as had been his first impression, but that its surface was composed of a thousand tiny and precisely identical facets. It seemed to be glowing with a soft inner light of its own.

"What *is* it?"

It was the girl's turn to feel important. "It is the Jewel of Astarte—as you would know, foolish boy, were you the apprentice of a great magician, as you claim to be." She looked down at the glowing amulet, her face suddenly rapt. "I was entrusted with it this night as keeper of the portal—and never have I seen it glow—so brightly—"

Then, abruptly, she collapsed upon the marble tiles.

Nilus, startled, stooped over her—but even as he began to help her up, her blue eyes opened and regarded him with a strange intensity.

"Thank you, True Spirit," she said in a low sweet voice, "but I can manage quite well myself."

Nilus stood back, puzzled, as the girl stood up. There was a panthe-

rine grace, an arcane confidence, a womanly suppleness in her movements
that he had not seen before. His spine tingled. For a moment she stood,
regarding him coolly with level blue eyes, then drew back and sat down
upon the plinth of the nearest column, crossing one leg over another and
thereby exposing an expanse of thigh. Nilus swallowed, and again his spine
tingled. Though the being before him still had the body of a girl, he sensed
that she had somehow changed—profoundly.

"Who—who are you?" he asked, feeling like an even younger child
than he was. "And why did you call me a—True Spirit?"

She tossed her head and laughed—a womanly laugh—then gestured
toward the lofty open portal of the temple. "I am She who dwells within.
But in this body I am called Clarissa. I like you, Saturnilus, for I sense that
you are a True Spirit indeed."

The tingling along Nilus' spine increased. So far as he knew, his master Simon was the only person in Tyre who knew that his full name was
Saturnilus. For an instant he wondered if the girl before him had been possessed by a demon—

"No," said the girl-being who called herself Clarissa, "and you do not
believe that, either. Do I seem to you like a demon?"

Nilus could only stare at her whom he had thought, moments earlier,
to be a pretty but rather ordinary girl. Her eyes, which held his with such
fascination, now seemed sapphirean rather than merely blue; her skin
seemed alabastrine rather than pale, her hair golden rather than yellow, and
her figure almost womanly rather than that of a skinny prepubescent—all
this, and yet she was somehow the same person, unchanged! She was not a
demon, yet neither was she just a girl. She was, rather, a *perfect* girl!

"No, you're not a demon," he muttered finally. "But—who *are* you?"

Again she laughed. "I am the reason for all existence—and you,
Saturnilus, are the One who realized it and brought it all into being for my
pleasure." Then, seeing the lad's face: "I am sorry, my love—it was your
master, Simon, with whom I wished to communicate in my guise of Helen,
but as it happened it was Clarissa who bore the Jewel of Astarte this night.
These things are beyond your understanding, Saturnilus, yet I am glad to
have met you in my guise as Clarissa, for I sense that we, too, may one day
have much to share. Only the Fates know how much."

"What—what do you want of me?" stammered Nilus, now thoroughly
shaken in the presence of this mysterious Being.

A slight dimpling occurred at the corner of her mouth, something in-
dicative of wistfulness combined with amusement. "What have I *always*
wanted from you? A world replete with wonder, adventure and—aye, even
danger!" At this she suddenly became tensely poised, alert, her blue eyes
staring into the darkness beyond the long avenues of torches. "And now

danger impends—for you and me, for Helen and your master. Here, Satur-nilus—take this talisman of Astarte and convey it to your master, who is learned in the mysteries. He will know what to do."

Nilus, averting his gaze from the girl's serious yet somehow—paradoxically—mocking blue eyes, took the glowing moon-colored stone which she handed to him. As he received it its glow vanished.

"Go, now, but do not enter the temple—the greatest danger will be there."

Then the girl's eyes closed and she again collapsed. Nilus caught her and eased her slight body to the stone floor of the portico; again she seemed but an ordinary, even fragile girl—

Then he heard rustlings in the dark, turned and saw many cloaked and cowled forms emerging from dark streets and alleys, advancing down the torch-flanked avenue toward the temple.

Falling flat on his face, he crawled like a lizard to the edge of the por-tico and over its side into the thick shrubbery, hoping against hope that he had not been seen by those who advanced.

The white-robed youth led Simon to a door flanked by two armed and ar-mored guards—the first he had seen within these precincts. As he ap-proached they crossed their spears in front of the portal.

"Who comes?" said one of them.

"This man wished to see Holior," said the youth. "He says great dan-ger is about to befall our temple."

At that moment a man appeared in the doorway and glanced at the youth, then at Simon. He was of medium height, balding and somewhat paunchy, and his face was set in a scowl of mistrust. Like the acolytes, he was garbed in a long white tunic and soft sandals, but in addition a large, silvery medallion symbolic of the waxing moon hung upon his ample breast.

"What's this?" he demanded somewhat pompously. "Who presumes to intrude upon these sacred precincts even as the Ritual of the Burgeoning is about to begin?"

"I am Simon, the ambassador of the Emperor Claudius to Tyre. It is urgent, O Holior, that I speak with you."

The high priest's expression softened; in fact, he beamed an oily smile worthy of a politician. "Ah, excellent sir, this temple is honored—" Then his seriousness returned. "But, as I say, a preparatory ritual is about to commence—one of the most important of the year. I must not neglect my duties. Would you be amenable, good Simon, to putting off our visit until after tomorrow?"

Simon appreciated the man's internal conflict. There was but one way to cut through it. Rapidly he sketched a sign in the air with his right fore-finger. Holior gasped; his face paled more than a shade; then he said to the guards:

"Admit him. And you, Helios, return to your post—that's a good lad."

When they were alone in the priest's chamber, the door having been shut behind them, Holior drew forth a kerchief and dabbed with it at his sweat-beaded brow. "I had heard, Simon of Gitta, that you are a great mage learned in arcane secrets, yet never did I suspect that you were an initiate into the inmost mysteries of the Queen of the World."

"I have sought out her priests and studied her mysteries in many lands," said Simon, "ever since I first met and loved her in human guise more than twenty years ago. Even then, though I was completely uninitiat-ed, I sensed her true nature—and my own. She was slain in Rome during the Terror of Sejanus, and ever since then I have sought for her, awaiting her return."

Holior's eyes grew round. "You mean—you and this woman were True Spirits?"

"Aye. And tonight I have at last found her again here, in this very temple."

"But of course She is here," said the priest, "for this temple is Hers."

"No, no!" Simon gestured impatiently. "She is embodied in one of your acolytes—a girl named Helen."

"*She* embodies herself in many women—"

"But not to this degree. Listen, Holior: tonight a dream of portent and bale informed me that Helen was here in Tyre, and now I have found that the dream did not lie. Now I must take her forth from here immediately, for I sense that if I do not, a great doom threatens her and perhaps all in this temple!"

"I—I do not know." Holior glanced about nervously, unconsciously wringing his hands. "Helen must lead the children in the preparatory rite to Astarte this night—it is very important. How can I call off the ceremony merely because you say—?"

"Time's wasting. Here—I'll *buy* the girl!" Simon tore a large leather pouch from his belt and hurled it upon the marble-tiled floor; from its loosened mouth spilled and rolled a flood of heavy golden coins. "There, Holior, that's far more than the temple paid for her, I'm sure—and if you want more, I can multiply it by ten times."

Holior half stooped, his fingers spread and his eyes wide in avarice and astonishment; but then, recovering his dignity, he stood erect and con-fronted the Samaritan.

"It is true, Simon of Gitta," he said, "that this temple, like others, buys some of its acolytes at the slave-market, but that does not mean that we are unfeeling toward them. Helen was bought several months ago from Benoni the Jew, one of Tyre's richest sea-merchants, along with a number of younger children. Her life before that had not been a very happy one, but she has blossomed amazingly here and is beloved by the children in her charge and an inspiration to them. Much as this temple could use your gold, I cannot sell Helen to you without satisfying myself that her life henceforth would be at least as good as it is here." Holior glanced down at the gleaming gold coins that littered the tiles. "Ironic, your offer of money, for Helen's masters here in Tyre were Jewish followers of Christos—harsh fanatics who denounce our temples as brothels and our worship as 'whoring after false gods.' They sold her cheaply to the merchant Benoni when she would not accept their cruel religion."

Simon, despite his impatience, could feel no resentment toward Holior. The man was obviously not a True Spirit—indeed, like most high priests, he was undoubtedly at core a politician—but it was obvious from the way he spoke that Helen had captured his basically kindly heart as she had the hearts of the children.

"Nevertheless, the money is yours," insisted the Samaritan, "with more to come if you wish. Moreover, Helen shall not leave here with me unless she desires it—but if she does not, she may be in peril." Simon glanced at the door. "Have you no more guards than those two within this temple?"

"A few, but most are off duty, since this midnight ceremony is not one to which the public is invited—"

"Summon them quickly, then, for I sense that with each passing moment the peril impends more closely. Hurry—"

Suddenly muffled shrieks rang out—the voices of many children shrilling in terror. Then came a strange sound as of whirlwinds, and the massive temple seemed to tremble slightly.

"Hurry!" yelled Simon, bounding to the door. He hurled it open and dashed out between the pair of startled guards, running toward the stairs. An intense glare of light was shining up the stairwell from below, together with a deep vibrant hum as of a nest of giant wasps.

Quickly the guards and Holior joined him at the head of the stair, gasping in horror as one man at what they saw—a pulsing, swelling sphere of flame that filled the descending stairwell from side to side, blocking their way.

"By all the gods!" shrilled the young acolyte, who had already backed away in terror from his post at the head of the stair. "What *is* it?"

"A fire elemental," snapped Simon. "Stand back, all of you." From beneath his dark robe he whipped forth a magician's ceremonial knife whose long, symbol-emblazoned blade gleamed silvery in the eerie light of the flame entity. "Atar, servant of Mazda, aid me!" he cried out, then loudly intoned a brief chant which Holior, though he could not understand the words, recognized as being an ancient form of Persian.

The fire-globe, however, responded only by expanding slightly and advancing a foot or two, while its vibrant drone grew a bit more loud and menacing.

"It does not serve Atar, the Flame Lord," growled Simon as he drew back. "Whoever commands it has ordered it to block access to the temple hall from this direction. Quick, Holior, lead us to another approach."

The high priest nodded. "There are twin staircases near the front. Hurry—this way!"

When they neared the end of the long corridor, however, they found that the twin stairwells there were also full of light and sinister humming. An odor of smoke, as of charred woodwork or molding, wafted up to them.

"Baal!" cursed Simon. "Are we trapped up here, then?"

"There is a way outside—the stairway to the kitchens at the back of the temple. Follow me—"

But Simon shot past and quickly outdistanced the unathletic priest, dagger in hand and cloak flowing out behind, praying soundlessly to Astarte as he ran that he would be in time....

II

Nilus paused, panting, and cautiously peered back toward the temple from between concealing shrubs and thick tree-boles. The cloaked and cowled figures, perhaps a dozen in number, had gathered in a group and were striding rapidly and purposefully down the wide pave toward the columned portico. The two in the lead seemed uncommonly tall and bulky.

Then came a clatter of boots as a group of armed and armored temple guards—also numbering about a dozen—trooped rapidly out of the darkness at the portico's far end and ranked themselves along the length of its wide stairs, blocking the way. One of them bent over Clarissa, and Nilus, feeling a certain relief, saw her stir and then rise to her feet.

"Halt!" yelled the commander of the guards. "Who comes to the temple of the Queen of the World?"

The advancing group slowed their pace but did not stop. One of the tall figures in the forefront raised a hand, and at the gesture several of those who followed drew what appeared to be black rods from beneath their cloaks and set them to their lips. Immediately an eerie piping of flutes vibrated the air, rising and falling in unearthly harmonies and dissonances, its rhythm matching the pace of the cowled figures. Nilus felt the air of menace increasing.

"*Halt!*" repeated the captain of the guard, while his subordinates all raised their spears and held them at the ready.

Suddenly the leading figure again raised his arm, this time also raising his face skyward so that his cowl fell back, exposing his features and his gleaming bald cranium.

"*Phun-klui munglu-naph!*" the man suddenly roared in a powerful, booming voice. "*Ku-Thugha Fum-al-hut na-ka-gaa naf-al-thagan!*"

Instantly, to Nilus' terror, many hundreds of tiny points of light appeared swarming down from the sky, circling like fiery bees, occasionally and briefly alighting on the ground or the shrubbery—and wherever they touched, thin flames and wisps of smoke flared and curled upward.

"*Attack!*" boomed the bald sorcerer, pointing toward the temple guards. "*In Ku-Thugha's name I command it!*"

The fiery lights swarmed aloft, whirling and shrilling, then gathered and merged into about a dozen clumps. In another moment each clump had become a pulsing fiery sphere about four feet in diameter.

"*Attack!*"

The guards broke and ran even as the things surged forward—but they did not run far. With preternatural swiftness the fire elementals were upon them, one to each man, and for a few moments wild death-shrieks mingled with shrill buzzings and cracklings. Nilus, cringing in silent terror, caught the smell of burning flesh upon the air. He saw Clarissa turn and flee, a streak of white, into the temple.

Then it was over. Upon the temple steps the blackened bodies of a dozen guardsmen lay smoking and steaming in their half-molten armor. Above them hovered the fire spheres, their buzzings now muted to deeply vibrant drones.

"Enter the temple," the bald sorcerer commanded, "but harm no one within. Block all doors and windows, that none may intrude upon us as I cast my spells!"

The fire beings floated forward between the columns and through the wide front portal of the temple, the conclave of dark-robed sorcerers following while still producing their eerie flute music. Nilus then heard cries of fear from within, together with more deep-voiced chanting from the chief sorcerer. The doors and windows of the great fane suddenly seemed to fill up with fire—for an instant Nilus feared that the building was ablaze within, then realized that the flame entities were merely blocking every possible entrance as commanded. The screams faded away, but the deep chanting of the chief sorcerer continued, accompanied by the weird flute harmonies and the dronings of the watchful fire servitors.

After several minutes Nilus rose, trembling, and began to steal away—

when, abruptly, the flame entity at the main portal left its post and floated upward from the portico into the night sky. Immediately the lad crouched down again, watching fearfully. To his relief the fire globe paid him no attention, continuing to rise up into the sky until it was but a point of light indistinguishable from the stars, then slowly veered away southward.

The eerie flute music grew louder as the troupe of dark-robed sorcerers issued from the temple and descended the portico stairs. In their wake marched a score or more of white-gowned children, their faces blandly expressionless, their eyes staring straight ahead, unblinking. Nilus recognized Clarissa among them, her hair gold-bright under the light of the torches. Behind them came a similarly garbed young woman of great beauty, also obviously spellbound, and then a final pair of the ebon-cloaked flute players. In a few moments the strange procession had traversed the length of the wide pavement and vanished into the shadows of Tyre's high, dark buildings.

The other fire beings issued from the apertures they had guarded and vanished rapidly away into the sky as the first had done.

Nilus stood up, sensing that he was now completely alone. A chilling thought struck him.

"My master—"

Jolted into action by the thought, Nilus dashed across the flagstoned way and, avoiding the bodies of the charred guards, up the portico steps and through the temple's lofty entryway. Inside the huge columned *cella* a haze of smoke hung in the air but, to the boy's relief, he saw no bodies on all that great expanse of tiled floor. Nor, he recalled, had he heard any sounds that had indicated combat.

"Simon!" he called out. *"Simon!"*

His repeated calls brought no answer save hollow echoes from the lofty walls and columns. The temple felt deserted. Nilus' relief did not diminish; to his mind it was now evident that his master, the world's cleverest magician, had sensed the menace coming and had escaped by some other exit. Possibly he was returning to their apartment even now....

Nilus dashed back outside and down the wide avenue. He must find Simon and give him the great gem. Obviously Clarissa and the other temple acolytes had been kidnapped for purposes of dark sorcery. But his master would know what to do, for had not the Perfect Girl told him so—?

Suddenly he heard the far, faint sound of many flutes—sounds that were diminishing in the distance.

The young lad shuddered as he suddenly realized the enormous responsibility that lay upon him. Now he must either follow the procession of sorcerers and their captives, or rush back to the apartment to seek out his master and tell him all he knew—

Nilus' indecision lasted but an instant. Clarissa and her companions could not be rescued unless their whereabouts were known.

Immediately he hurried away from the temple down the wide avenue, then plunged into the maze of Tyre's dark streets and alleys, following the swiftly fading sounds of eerie flutes.

Simon, dashing along the pathways that wound through the parks and gardens surrounding Astarte's temple, slowed his pace as he neared the front of the building. Cautiously peering out from behind a clump of foliage, he saw only the torchlit portico. The flame beings were nowhere in evidence.

Then he saw the blackened bodies of the temple guards smoldering upon the steps.

"Baal!" he gasped, gripping his magician's knife more tightly.

Footsteps sounded behind him, and in a moment the priest Holior and his two guardsmen had caught up, the young acolyte Helios bringing up the rear. All of them gasped in horror even as Simon had done.

"By the bolts of Zeus!" swore Holior, his priestly dignity forgotten. "Simon, did those flame elementals do this?"

Simon held up his symbol-engraven knife almost as if testing the wind, saw that its blade remained bright, unclouded.

"Aye. But I think they have gone. Nevertheless, stay here while I check the temple. There may yet be one or more of them within."

Holior made as if to object, but Simon turned away and hurried up the steps past the horribly burnt guards. As he entered the wide portal the smell of smoke was strong in his nostrils and he saw that a haze hung in the air. Yet the building was not aflame, being built almost entirely of marble and limestone. Woodwork and draperies smoldered here and there, while upon the columns a score of torches flickered weakly, mere stubs in their brackets.

"Helen!" Simon called out. *"Helen!"*

The columned hall echoed back his cries. The place where more than a score of acolytes had gathered for ritual and prayer was now empty and as silent as a vault. Yet there was no sign of bodies either.

Simon dashed back outside and down the steps of the portico. His eyes searched the shadows beyond the column-flanked avenue, but the night was empty and silent also.

"What did you find?" gasped Holior, hurrying to meet him. "Gods! Are the acolytes all slain—?"

"No. They've been abducted—and for a terrible purpose, I fear. No mere slave-procurers could have accomplished this, no matter how well financed. Only a sorcerer of the greatest power could have commanded those flame elementals. Tell me, Holior, does your temple's library contain a copy of the *Sapientia Magorum* by the ancient Persian fire-priest Ostanes?"

"Of course not!" said Holior, apparently shocked by the suggestion. "I would never allow such a monstrous thing within the fane of the Great Goddess."

"Then I must consult my own copy. Hurry—follow me!"

The five of them each plucked a torch from its bracket, then hastened away from the temple and through the dark and winding streets of Tyre. The moon had westered enough that its rays no longer shone straight down between the high apartment buildings, so that despite their torches they were obliged to proceed through the thick shadows more slowly than Simon wished.

"Alas, the moon declines," panted Holior as they hastened along over the uneven cobbles, "and the ceremony to the Goddess remain unperformed!"

"That's the least of our troubles," growled Simon. "If my suspicions are correct, this entire city may be in grave danger."

"You mentioned... sorcery. Of what sort—?"

"I fear that a Gate has been opened nearby. No more talk, Holior—we must make haste."

After a short while they arrived at the tall building in whose sumptuous ground-floor apartment Simon was residing. As they crossed the torch-lit inner courtyard the pair of Roman guards at the apartment's entrance drew aside.

"Nilus!" shouted Simon as he strode through the portal into his quarters. "Get up, quickly, and attend me—"

"Sorry, sir," said one of the guards, "but the lad isn't here. He followed you out when you left—told us you'd ordered him to."

"Gods!" muttered Simon, feeling his fear suddenly deepen. First Helen, and now— "Holior, come inside. The rest of you wait out in the courtyard."

"Beg pardon, sir," said the other legionary, "but there's a man waiting in there to see you."

"What man?" There was a tense edge in Simon's voice.

"Amran the Phoenician—one of the richest sea-merchants in this city."

Simon looked around the court but saw no servants such as might accompany a rich man. "You admitted his slaves as well?"

"He came alone."

"Very interesting." Simon beckoned to the priest. "Come, Holior."

As they entered the spacious main chamber of Simon's suite Amran rose from a couch upon which he had been sitting stiffly. He appeared to be nervous. "Simon of Gitta," he began, "I am—"

"I know who you are, Amran, for we met briefly at the municipal dedication ceremonies yesterday. But I'm afraid I can't do any business with you right now."

"This is not business. I am here not because you are Claudius' emissary, Simon, but because men say that you are a great magician—"

"Nor have I time to cast spells to insure favorable winds for trade," said the Samaritan. "Besides, despite what you may have heard, I do not practice true sorcery, only the mummery of the stage—"

"Simon of Gitta, listen to me! This city of Tyre, and perhaps the empire itself, is in great danger. I need your aid."

Simon saw that the merchant's face—a hard, practical, sensible face—exhibited an expression of deadly earnest. Suddenly he sensed with intuitive certainty that Amran's concern and his own were one and the same.

"Tonight," Amran went on, "Mattan, High Priest of Melkarth, somehow activated the ancient pillars flanking the altar in Melkarth's temple, and then he performed a human sacrifice of a sort that has not been practiced here for centuries. In so doing he invoked demonic servitors to do his bidding." Amran drew a trembling breath; his eyes suddenly held fear. "Simon, you may think me mad when I tell you the nature of those servitors—"

"They were entities of flame," said Simon, "capable of hovering in the air like giant fireflies. They can cause combustible objects to burst into flame."

Amran stared at him in amazement.

"They are fire elementals," Simon went on. "Once before, in Rome, I encountered such beings. That was twenty-three years ago, the night the Caelian Hill district burned and all who lived within it perished. Amran, I want you to tell me in detail everything you know of this matter."

"But—human sacrifice!" interrupted Holior indignantly. "We should take this information immediately to the Roman authorities—"

Simon turned his glowering dark eyes on the priest. "Don't be foolish. You saw what those fire creatures did to the temple guards; they could wipe out a cohort of legionaries just as easily."

"I feared as much," said Amran, nodding gloomily. "Moreover, most of the Roman officials in this city have been paid to look the other way where Mattan's doings are concerned, and I—I'm afraid it was my wealth which helped accomplish that. You see, Mattan promised me great prosperity, even partial governorship over Tyre, should I aid him, and the proposal appealed to me. I knew he was a sorcerer, for he often boasted of his powers, but I had never witnessed an act of actual sorcery—until tonight." The merchant shuddered and his eyes stared past Simon, focused upon memories. "I saw the children sacrificed to the fire god, and the sight has shaken my soul. Once I had a daughter—" His hard face softened. "But let that be. Simon, I will tell you all."

So saying, the Phoenician launched into a detailed account of what he had seen that evening in the temple of Melkarth, Simon occasionally interrupting him in order to clarify specifics. When at last he had finished his account, Holior burst out:

"By all the gods, Amran, what manner of man is this Mattan? Surely he can be no less evil than the very flame-demons he commands!"

"The fire elementals are neither good nor evil," said Simon. "They are merely forces, obeying the will of whichever man or god holds the secret of commanding them." He rose and strode over to a case that held many scrolls, drew forth one of the bulkier ones, and began to unroll it upon a reading stand.

"Is that the accursed book of the fire-priest Ostanes?" asked Holior nervously.

"Aye, and here is what he writes about the matters which concern us." For a moment the Samaritan traced out the ancient Persian text with a slightly trembling finger, then slowly began to translate it aloud in Greek:

First to inhabit the earth was Ku-Thugha, the Flame-born. For, long ere the advent of the other Old Ones from the stars—aye, ages before even Ubbo-Sathla spawned the germs of this our cycle of life in the azoic seas—great Ku-Thugha and his fiery servitors came to dwell within the seething magmatic craters and chasms of a world but newly congealed from the swirling dusts of chaos; and for a thousand aeons the earth knew no rule but his.

Yet during the long kalpas of time, as the smoldering lands slowly cooled and the rivers and seas of molten fire hardened into stone, the Flame-born and his minions betook themselves to regions far within the earth where the mighty heat yet prevailed; and there they dwelt for many aeons more.

Then came that cosmic war in which the fire-god Atar, servant of Ahura Mazda, together with many others of the Primal Gods, did prevail against Ku-Thugha and all the other Old Ones who had ruled upon the earth for countless ages in despite of the Life Force. Thereupon were many of these Old Ones imprisoned beneath Earth's oceans and mountains for aye, they being impervious to death by any means; while others of them retreated to the stars and outer gulfs whence they had come—many of them, however, first establishing Gates in certain places by means of which they plotted one day to return when, under favorable stellar auspices, their earthly worshipers should summon them.

Now among those who fled was Ku-Thugha, who rules at this time upon a cindered world bathed by the flame-waves of Fum-al-hut, that star which marks the Mouth of the Fish-monster in the southern skies; Aquarius pours out his water upon its fires for aye, yet they are not quenched.

And now, although many aeons more have passed since that primal War, Ku-Thugha, like others of the Old Ones, has even to this day many worshipers among men and other earth-dwellers, which worshipers perform sacrifice to him and aspire to one day bring about his return. Among the nations of mankind his names have been many: Yamath, Milcom, Chemosh, Hammon, Moloch, Melkarth, and others too numerous to recount here. His worship is accomplished by the fiery immolation of living victims, most especially of children suspected of possessing True Spirits in addition to the common animal vitality of ordinary humankind.

Now these are the rites whereby Ku-Thugha and his elemental of fire may be summoned wherever there be established a Gate: The aspect of the heavens is most favorable when the star Fum-al-hut rises before the sun and the moon declines—

Simon abruptly ceased to read aloud but continued avidly to scan the ancient scroll, ignoring his two guests.

"A *Gate*," said Amran uneasily. "Mattan used the same term. Surely the twin pillars in Melkarth's temple must be one of those Gates."

"The pillars are indeed very old," said Holior, worry intensifying in his eyes. "It is written that before the founding of Tyre they were placed here by a god—a god who also first brought fire to mankind...."

Simon did not respond to their remarks, and they saw that he was still intensely reading. Presently, however, he rose and put the parchment scroll of Ostanes aside, then took up a dark leather pouch and fastened it to his belt. His face, shadowed in the lamplight, was somber and set in grim determination.

"I must go now," he said. "Do not wait for me. In fact, it might be safer for you to leave the city, for if I fail—"

"Simon!" cried Holior. "Aren't you even going to alert the Roman commanders of the garrisons?"

"Legions could not storm Melkarth's temple this night. Yet it may be that stealth and skill will succeed where armies cannot. Pray to all the gods that it shall prove to be so."

Holior nodded, unable to speak.

"Good luck, Samaritan," said Amran earnestly.

Simon saluted them briefly, turned and hurried from the room, then strode rapidly down the short corridor to the portal and out into the night.

Nilus, practicing the arts of stealth which his mentor Simon had taught him, hastened silently through the inky shadows of Tyre's alleys, keeping the eerie procession of cloaked flute-players always just in sight. That was easier to do now, for a pair of priests had lit torches and were leading the way. As they proceeded, Nilus soon realized that his stealth was unnecessary, for the priests were taking no precautions to see that they were not followed. Moreover, there were no sleeping beggars or prowling thieves in the streets and alleys; apparently all the usual denizens of the night had fled before the eerie sound of the flutes and the sinister procession of cowled night-walkers.

After a half hour or so of winding through Tyre's dark and tangled ways, Nilus saw that they were emerging onto a wide and smooth-flagged street which narrowed somewhat to become the causeway bridging the gap between Tyre and the southern island whereon stood Melkarth's temple. Without pausing, the procession filed through the gate in the city's wall and on down the wide causeway to the avenue on the opposite side. In the distance loomed the temple of Melkarth—a towering black bulk against the moonlit southern sky.

Nilus hesitated. He knew he should find Simon, tell him all that had happened, and give him Clarissa's moonstone as instructed. Yet he must also discover as much as possible as to where the acolytes were being taken and why. No guards were upon the causeway and no torches burned there. That was strange, perhaps, but also fortunate....

His decision made, Nilus dashed like a fleeting shadow down the length of the causeway and in a few moments was concealed beyond the south end of it amid the foliage of the temple gardens. Creeping stealthily, he continued to follow the procession as it proceeded southward down the wide moonlit avenue toward the looming fane of Melkarth.

Suddenly, at a shouted command from the chief priest, the marchers halted as one man. The bald sorcerer raised his arms and, facing skyward, bellowed: *"Na-ka-gaa naf-al thagan!"*

Instantly Nilus saw perhaps a dozen points of light glowing in the sky, brightening as they descended, and realized that the fire beings had accompanied the procession all along, hidden aloft among the stars. For an instant he feared that they were aware of his presence, and was greatly relieved when they paid him no attention. Instead, six of them ranged themselves along the causeway he had just crossed, while the others dispersed around the shores of the temple-island, moving slowly along the beaches as if on patrol.

Nilus' relief turned to anxiety as he realized that he was now trapped upon the island. He could not hope to return to Tyre either by the causeway or by swimming.

The procession was now ascending the steps of the columned portico at the end of the avenue, filing into the temple. Nilus took a deep breath and slowly let it out, calming himself. After repeating this exercise several times, he began to steal around toward the side of the temple. Evidently he was safe from the fire beings as long as he kept to the shadows of the trees and shrubbery and stayed away from the shore. Surely the things could not stand watch here indefinitely! The night was more than half gone; at dawn many people would be arriving to attend the equinoctial ceremonies and then Nilus could safely mingle with them and escape. In the meantime, he could perhaps contrive to find another way into the temple and learn as much as possible.

In a short while he found a servants' entrance at the rear and, after listening carefully for several minutes, cautiously tried the door. It was unlocked. Entering quietly, Nilus found himself in a torchlit hall adjoining the kitchens. There were no guards or servants; the place was silent, deserted, and Nilus began to suspect that there was no one in the temple except the priests and their captives. Apparently they wanted no witnesses to what was happening this night. Nilus shivered at the thought. He might not have until dawn—might not be able to find Simon before something awful was destined to happen to Clarissa and the other acolytes. If so, how could he rescue them unaided?

Slowly he stole down a long, unlit corridor that led toward the front of the temple. It was a slow grope in the dark, seemingly interminable, but eventually he saw light ahead and soon came to the corridor's end. Peering out carefully, he beheld rows of stone columns beyond which lay the vast main hall of the temple, dimly lit by a few bracketed torches. In its center stood the group of white-clad acolytes, while about them the robed priests sat cross-legged upon the marble tile, their now-silent flutes held in their laps. In the forefront of them all sat the chief priest, his bald head gleaming in the flickering, eerie light of the two huge and uncanny pillars which he faced.

Fear stirred deep within Nilus' heart. He knew there was nothing natural about the faint glow that oozed from those twin pillars—especially the emerald one on the left, which flickered and pulsed as if serpents of pale light swam within....

He looked away, resisting an almost hypnotic effect from the things. Children and priests alike were staring fixedly at them, motionless as statues, silently waiting for... what? The time appropriate for some ritual, no doubt. Nilus noticed Clarissa's golden hair gleaming amid the group of mostly dark-haired children, saw the tall young woman whose lustrous black tresses were gathered in a silvery net—

Suddenly, with a chill, he realized that someone was *not* present—the tall, black-turbaned priest with the great sword!

He turned barely in time to see a huge dark shape rush at him with clacking footfalls from the shadows. The shape had a bearded face and glaring eyes—snarling lips that bared fang-like teeth. Then the great curved sword blade flashed toward him.

Instantly Nilus leaped high into the air, heard the sword blade whip by just beneath him, then kicked out savagely, feeling his foot connect solidly with the priest's great nose. He dove for the floor, heard the sword go clattering, rolled to his feet in a fighting stance—then gasped. The bearded priest, staggering to keep his balance, had lost his turban as well as the sword, and from his shaggy forehead curved *a pair of sharp black horns!*

The feral dark eyes fixed malevolently on Nilus; the fanged mouth opened wide, emitting a loud, almost reptilian hiss.

Nilus whirled and dashed off into the dark corridor as fast as his legs would carry him. Behind him he heard the clang of steel on marble as the sword was snatched up, then the voice of the chief priest bellowing: *"Kill the intruder quickly, Jag. The time approaches!"*

Nilus darted down a side corridor——one of many he remembered passing. He was in pitch darkness now and so had to grope his way along the wall slowly and carefully. Before he had gone far he heard rapid footfalls clattering in the outer hall, then saw the faint gleam of approaching torchlight. Something about those footfalls made him shudder; it was as if his pursuer had two wooden feet.

He felt a door under his hand, found it unlocked, and slipped through, closing it behind him as softly as possible. Unfortunately there was no lock or bolt, but the narrow passage in which he now stood was faintly lit. At its end, near the head of a descending stairway, gleamed a small oil lamp upon a stand. Nilus frowned. That lamp indicated that the priests probably intended to come this way later on, perhaps as part of their ritual. Still, he must go on—he had no choice.

Taking up the lamp, he descended the stairs and found himself in another long corridor, this one lit by several more lamps spaced at intervals. It sloped downward at a very gentle angle, and as Nilus hurried along it he noticed that the masonry of the temple had given way to smooth and seamless stone. He was within the bedrock of the Isle of Melkarth. Then, ahead, he heard a strange droning—

The long tunnel suddenly opened into a huge room, and Nilus gasped at the sight of the towering things that occupied it—huge geometrical shapes of metal and crystal, cylinders and pyramids and cubes intricately interconnected, some of them glowing with an eerie luminescence that reminded him of the Pillars of Melkarth. Surely they must be somehow connected with those pillars—perhaps this huge chamber lay immediately beneath the main hall of the temple—

He froze as, above the strange low droning sound that filled the room, he heard again the approaching clatter of hoof-like feet upon stone.

III

The wide, column-flanked Avenue of the Market ran interminably south-eastward, its smooth flagstones pale under the westering moon. As Simon jogged along it his senses were keenly alert. Often he glimpsed huddled sleepers or skulking prowlers amid the twin rows of columns and the closed and bolted shops behind them, but no prowling robber ventured to approach him. In Tyre an armed athletic night-runner was not unusual, nor safe to accost.

Ancient, brooding Tyre!—founded thousands of years ago by a god who had brought fire to man, if legend could be believed. What dark secrets lay hidden in crypts beneath her lofty, looming apartment buildings where human dregs plotted dark things—in her ancient fanes to gods older than human memory—in her wharfside warehouses which contained the mercantile spoils of a thousand lands? Simon knew that there were many legends other than that concerning the fire god....

Near the end of the long avenue he turned south into a maze of narrow streets and lanes and finally, in the very shadow of the city's southern wall, arrived at the portico of a small, squat temple of dark stone. A solitary bracketed torch flickered upon one of the portico's columns. The doorway, open and unattended, gaped like the black mouth of a mausoleum.

Entering, Simon saw a dim light at the end of the corridor and strode forward. He emerged into a moderately large pillared hall, saw an altar of black stone at its far end. Two oil lamps flanking the altar gave barely enough light to reveal partially the monstrous eidolon, part fish and part man, that loomed behind it. The image was decked with gold and silver ornaments of strange and exotic workmanship, and crowned with a high tiara of whitish-gold metal sparkling with inset gems of many colors. That such a treasure stood open and unguarded even in this squalid section of Tyre did not surprise Simon.

A priest suddenly emerged from the darkness behind the altar and strode forward. He was short and squat; his ornate robes, strangely decorated with stylized images of fish, snails, and octopi, entirely concealed his arms, hands, and legs. His eyes bulged slightly and their expression was somehow both sad and sinister.

"Who comes to the temple of Philistine Dagon?" The priest's voice was deep yet also soft; the words were uttered with a strange lisp. Simon suppressed a shudder and answered:

"I am Simon, a Samaritan. It is very important to you, as well as to me, that I now perform a ritual here."

Interest showed on the priest's flat, pudgy face. "I know you—you're the magus who came here to Tyre as the Emperor's emissary! And now you come to sacrifice to Father Dagon?"

Simon knew that Philistine Dagon was little worshiped anymore in Tyre, unlike the Semitic corn god of the same name whose grand temple drew in enormous numbers of gift-giving worshipers. Yet, judging by the jewelry adorning the fish-god's image, this fane was in little need of donations.

"No, not sacrifice. Rather, a conjuring. I must counteract powers that threaten to overwhelm the world this very night if left unchecked. Mattan, priest of Melkarth, has made preparations to open the Gate between the stars at the hour when Fum-al-hut shall rise before dawn. And you well know, priest, what shall become of you and all your watery kinfolk should the ancient Lord of Fire and his elemental servitors surge over the earth."

The priest looked up closely into the man's grim and sinister face. "You are not of our kind. How do I know that what you say is true?"

"Allow me to meditate here awhile," said Simon, "and I shall soon produce a kinsman of yours who will verify what I say."

The priest regarded him steadily, suspicion lingering in his sad, protuberant eyes. "It is said, Simon, that you are a mighty sorcerer."

Simon smiled slightly. "Mostly a trickster, rather—a public performer of illusions. But I do know something of true magic, and though long ago I swore to avoid its use, this is a time when its dangers must be risked to prevent a danger far greater."

"The danger of fiery Melkarth?" The priest's expression became introspective and, Simon thought, a trifle resentful. "How great Melkarth's temple is, and how lavish, surpassing all others in this city! The people have forgotten that Tyre's prosperity is due primarily to our Father Dagon, whose servitors many centuries ago brought to these waters the *murex*-snails which make possible the industry of purple Tyrian dyes.... Very well, Samaritan, you may meditate here and summon your witness, if you can—and should your tale prove true you shall have all the aid which Dagon's servitors can give you."

Simon nodded, then slowly walked forward and sat down cross-legged on the stone floor in front of the altar. He breathed deeply at first, then more and more slowly and shallowly, until after a time his mind was still and without thoughts or imaginings. The twin flames of the oil lamps were pure and bright, mirroring the stillness of his mind and faintly illuminating the eerie ichthyic face of the eidolon of Dagon.

After a further time, when the moment was right, he reached beneath his cloak and took from his pouch a large round medallion, like a giant coin, whose metal shone with the same yellowish whiteness as the tiara that rested upon Dagon's brow. On one side of it was an image of the fish-god himself, on the other an ancient symbol representing the Queen of the World Incarnate.

"O Powers of Earth and Water," he softly intoned, "enemies of Air and Fire, send now to me my mentor, your servant Daramos, that I may confer with him."

The air above the altar seemed to shimmer slightly. The shimmer took on a greenish glow that gradually brightened, like an image slowly coming into focus—and, suddenly, a man stood atop the altar!

Simon heard the priest gasp and come hurrying to his side.

The man on the altar—if man it was—was shorter and squatter than the priest, even dwarfish, and his skin possessed a grayish-green cast that seemed faintly phosphorescent. A plain shapeless robe concealed his form. His features, though similar in some ways to those of the priest, were also different in prominent respects, his large pointed ears contrasting with the priest's near-earlessness and his eyes, though large and prominent, being lidded and not bulging outward. Those eyes, deep and calm as still pools, seemed to reflect strange wisdom.

"O priest of Dagon, this is my witness," said Simon, "—the phantom of Daramos the Mage, my former mentor and your kinsman. His sire was one of those sea-servitors of Dagon who do not die—even as was one of your own forebears, I suspect...."

The figure on the altar slowly closed its eyes, then opened them again.

Simon, I know why you have called me here from far Parthia. It is the time when things once sundered are to be again unified.

The priest of Dagon gasped slightly. The wide lips of the dwarfish being on the altar had not moved; its statement had been entirely mental and its form was undoubtedly an insubstantial astral projection.

"I have again found Helen," said Simon, "even as you foretold so many years ago, O Mentor. But now she has been captured by the servitors of Ku-Thugha, who plot to open the Flame Gate to him this very night. I will not abide her loss again, Daramos! Aid me in her recovery, or I swear that I shall invoke against her abductors the powers this servant of Dagon serves—for if I lose Helen again, what care I if the earth be destroyed also?"

I cannot aid nor hinder Destiny, said the phantom of Daramos, its expression of benign calm unchanged. *Worlds without number arise and die in their due time. I sense that this night is a time of reunification—whether of you and Helen, or of Ku-Thugha and his ancient domain, who but the Primal Ones can know? Yet perhaps I am permitted to give you a clue. Behold!* He gestured, and the metal disc in Simon's palm glowed briefly with an inner light. *That medallion, which I gave you many years ago in order that you might summon my presence in direst need, was sundered many centuries ago from its complementary part—aye, even at that very time when the walls of Troy were sundered and Helen was first separated from her Lover upon this world. You know of this mystery. Now, know also that when the medallion and its complementary part are reunited, so also shall be Helen and her Lover.*

Simon, feeling befuddled and angered by this riddle, could think of no reply. But the priest beside him now spoke up.

"I have heard of you, O great Daramos, and I see now that you are as great a sorcerer as you are reputed to be. I am Petrilor, high priest of Dagon in Tyre and kin to him who is reputed to have sired you. Why will you not aid us against the elements of Fire which threaten this very night to overwhelm the entire earth?"

The phantom again closed its eyes, as if in deep thought, then reopened them. *Though my sire was a Denizen of the Deep, even as was yours, my mother was half human and half rock-oread. I have not beheld the ocean for many centuries; my destiny is here upon the high plains amid Parthia's snowy peaks. Yet, my brother, I have even now aided you as much as I have been permitted by Destiny. Ponder well what I have just told my former pupil Simon.*

"That disc he holds," persisted Petrilor, "—it bears the image of our Father Dagon. Surely that counterpart of which you speak can be none other than—"

I can say no more. I sense vast forces impending. Fare you well, Simon— Petrilor—

The figure on the altar abruptly vanished. Simon rose and confronted the priest of Dagon. "I had truly hoped for more. Tell me, Petrilor: What do you know of this medallion's... counterpart?"

"I will tell you on the way. Needless to say, Simon, I now believe all that you have told me. Quickly—follow me."

Nilus hurried across the huge room between the eerily droning and glowing geometrical shapes that loomed there, careful to shield the flame of his lamp with one hand so that it would not be extinguished. The sound of clattering footfalls grew louder—soon his inhuman pursuer would burst forth from the corridor, sword in hand. Ahead, in the far wall, Nilus now saw three more black doorways gaping, evenly spaced. The middle one was closest and so he dashed into it.

He found himself in another smooth-walled corridor and took the first side branch. From then on the footfalls behind him faded and, as he continued to choose each branch corridor he came to, finally faded out altogether. Yet he did not dare to slow his pace and so continued on for some time.

At length he paused and listened carefully, gasping for breath. The sound he at first feared might be a renewal of pursuing footfalls was but the frantic beating of his heart. For a while he stood there in silence, letting his heartbeat subside, breathing deeply, then letting the breath out slowly in the way that his mentor Simon had taught him....

His inner being finally stilled, he began to return the way he had come, his every sense alert. Much as he trembled at the thought, he must do what he could to rescue Clarissa and her companions, and to deliver the strange, many-faceted gem to his mentor as that strange girl had instructed him to do.

He soon found that he was not on the return path. The tunnel he was following narrowed until it was too small for even his slender young body to squeeze through, though it continued on as a narrowing crevice. Nilus shuddered. The passage was still evidently an artificial one, but what beings had it been designed for?

He backtracked and made another attempt, again without success. This time the tunnel he chose became gradually more and more rounded, like a wormhole, while at the same time gradually sloping downward at a greater and greater angle. Nilus turned back before the angle of descent became too great to insure sound footing, shuddering at the thought of sliding down its curved smoothness into the black abyss of Hades.

The third attempt was no more successful. The passage remained level yet endless and featureless. Evidently the bedrock beneath the Isle of Melkarth was honeycombed by a maze of tunnels, and Nilus again shuddered at the thought that no human civilization could have been responsible for such an engineering project. He had heard Simon speak of millennia-lost empires such as Atlantis and Acheron, and of the pre-human empires before them. Upon what strange ruins had antique Tyre been built...?

On and on Nilus wandered in that featureless stone maze. It seemed to him that he had been wandering thus for at least an hour or more but he had no way of measuring time—and now he saw that the level of oil in his lamp was getting low.

At length, after groping through a long narrow passage just wide enough for the passage of one man, he emerged into a large, low-ceilinged room in whose center was a circular pool of dark water. There was a salt smell in the air. The water's surface seemed to swell slowly, gently, and Nilus guessed that he must be near the sea. Surely there must be an underwater passage from here to the outside.

Several torches were bracketed around the wall. Nilus applied the flame of his lamp to one of them and, though the pitch was so old and dried as to be brittle, it took fire readily enough and burned with a slightly crackling flame. Relieved, Nilus lit another, then blew out his lamp and set

it down on the stone floor. There were two other doorways leading out of
the chamber, but he was reluctant to explore them until he had ascertained
whether the pool offered him a quick means of escape from the maze. If
the underwater passage to the sea was not long, he could swim through it
and thereby avoid the dark priests as well as the fire beings which patrolled
the island.

Taking one of the torches with him, he approached the pool and
peered down into its depths. Yes, he had been right—there on the far side,
only a few feet beneath the surface of the gently heaving water, gaped a
black circular hole—surely the entrance to the tunnel that led outside!

Then, to his surprise, he saw a dark form come swimming out of that
hole, followed immediately by another—

There was a roiling and splashing of the water near his feet. Terrified,
Nilus drew back—and screamed as great webbed hands appeared upon the
stone of the pool's rim, followed by a huge dark-scaled head whose bulging
green eyes stared up at him with all the baleful hypnotic effect of a Gor-
gon's.

Simon and the priest Petrilor stood upon a low promontory of Tyre's
southern shore. Each now wore only a loincloth and weapon belt, having
just emerged from a watery tunnel that led from Dagon's temple into a
narrow natural cleft in the rock which had in turn opened upon the beach.
Behind them towered the city's lofty wall, and again Simon marveled at
Tyre's mysterious antiquity and the secrets she concealed. How many other
underground passages and chambers were known to her priests and sorcerers...?

Across the water, perhaps no more than a quarter of a mile to the
southwest, lay the Isle of Melkarth, the temple in its center bulking darkly
against the stars. Simon tensed as he saw that its shore was being patrolled
by slowly moving spheres of flame. To the right he saw more of the fire
elementals ranked along the short causeway that linked Melkarth's isle to
the city.

"As we feared," said Petrilor, "the flame beings are on watch. We
must swim out and enter the temple by means of the ancient tunnels I told
you of."

"How do you know these tunnels are not guarded also?"

"The priests of Melkarth lost the knowledge of them centuries ago,
and it is not likely that the newcomer Mattan has rediscovered that
knowledge. Only the priests of Dagon know of them."

Simon nodded. "That may give us the advantage of surprise, but will
even that give the two of us enough of an edge?"

"We shall have allies." Petrilor drew from his belt-pouch a strangely shaped object and held it up. In the darkness Simon could not make out its exact shape, but it glinted dully in the moonlight as would a relatively lusterless metal, perhaps lead.

"When we reach the deepest part of the channel," the priest went on, "I shall release this into the depths. Then Dagon's servitors will know of our need and come to aid us."

Again Simon nodded. The plan made him uneasy, yet with Helen in peril he would not balk at invoking even such allies as these. As he followed Petrilor down to the shore and into the water he observed the man's form more closely. Even in this dim light he could see that it was strangely hunched and misproportioned, reminding him somewhat of a huge frog, and the feet were abnormally long and long-toed. Where the man's thick neck joined his shoulders appeared several horizontal markings suggestive of gill slits.

Rapidly they swam out into the bay. Above the promontory to his left Simon could barely see against the night sky the masts of ships clustered in the Egyptian Harbor, while to his right the moon was declining westward, pale beyond the glow of the fire beings who patrolled the causeway. Simon felt a sense of urgency. In perhaps another hour the star Fum-al-hut would rise beyond the southeastward hills...

Midway across, Petrilor suddenly stopped swimming and uttered a brief, low-voiced chant in a tongue Simon could not understand. Raising the strangely shaped leaden object in his right hand, he let it fall back into the water, after which the pair resumed swimming without comment. Simon now found that he had trouble keeping up. Though a powerful swimmer himself, he could not begin to equal the speed of the priest of Dagon in the watery element. Again and again Petrilor was obliged to slow down and wait for the Samaritan to catch up—

Suddenly a chorus of yells burst out upon the still night air—the roar of men rushing into battle. Simon turned in the water and saw that about a score of shield-bearing legionaries were hurrying from the city's gate out to the causeway, their iron helms and sword-blades gleaming in the torchlight. Even as they charged a cluster of fire globes floated and converged toward them.

"That fool Holior!" muttered Simon. "He's alerted the garrison in spite of my orders—"

Battle cries abruptly turned to shrieks of agony as the fire beings rushed upon the soldiers. Those in the front rank held formation for less than a second, then dropped red-hot shields and swords with involuntary haste and staggered back against their comrades. The crackle of sizzling flesh came distinctly across the water. The surviving troops turned in mad rout, dashing back through the gate or plunging off the causeway into the waves to escape the pursuing flame beings.

"Aye, they were fools," said Petrilor, "yet the distraction may aid us. See—some of the fire guardians are moving along the island's shore toward the causeway. Hurry—swim faster."

As they began to near the shore of Melkarth's isle Simon became aware that there were *other* swimmers accompanying them. Some were dolphins, but others were not, and Simon felt a twinge of fear as he suspected the true nature of the latter.

Slowly and silently they approached the island at a point where a low cliff came down sheer to the sea. The dolphins and the *others* had vanished beneath the waves. For a few moments Simon and Petrilor bobbed motionless as the light of a fire elemental drifted past them atop the cliff.

When it had gone they moved in close to shore and Petrilor said, "Now, Simon, we must dive deep. Follow me and stay close."

The priest abruptly submerged. Simon drew a deep breath and dove straight down. He found himself in pitch darkness and for an instant felt near-panic. How in Hades was he to follow if he could not see—?

Then he sensed a faint bluish glow beneath him near the cliff s face and detected the motion of Petrilor's swimming silhouette. The glow came from an opening in the rock and Simon saw that dolphins and *others* were swimming into it. The priest swam in also and Simon forced himself to follow, glimpsing as he did so a dark being floating just within, hovering near one wall and clutching in webbed hands a large globe that glowed with weird bluish phosphorescence. Then came a long tunnel that led southwestward, straight into the island's bedrock. Other light-bearing beings were swimming down it ahead of Petrilor.

Just as he felt that his lungs were about to burst Simon emerged from the tunnel into a large circular space and saw light overhead. Following the priest upward, he broke the surface and gulped in a great breath of air. The light came from two torches, one bracketed on the wall, the other—

A scream rang out. Simon saw a bulky shape clambering out of the pool ahead of him—a scaled, web-fingered shape with flaring gill-slits, yet roughly humanoid in outline—and beyond it, a young boy clutching a torch, eyes wide in terror, backing away toward a black doorway gaping in the stone wall. To his astonishment, the lad's face was familiar.

"Nilus!" he called out, hauling himself up on to the pool's brink.

The boy faced him, terror vying with the shock of recognition. "Simon—Master! Is that really you—?"

Simon skirted the hulking scaled being, who was now standing motionless beside the pool, and ran to Nilus. The lad rushed to meet him, gripped his hands and gasped: "Master, don't let them hurt me!"

"They're friends, Nilus. Calm down. How on earth did you manage to turn up in this place?"

"I—I got lost in the tunnels after I followed the dark priests and the captive acolytes to Melkarth's temple. I hope you're not angry, Master. Clarissa told me to come straight to you with the medallion, but I didn't know where to find you, and I had to learn where she and the others were being taken—"

"Clarissa? Who in Hades is Clarissa?"

"A girl—one of the acolytes of the Goddess. Only, she's *not* just a girl. I—I can't explain, but she told me to give you this." Nilus drew the medallion from beneath his tunic and slipped the chain over his head. "Here, Master—she said that you with your learning would know what it was and what to do with it."

Simon took the thing and peered at it closely. The great milky ovoid of a gem reflected the torchlight eerily from its myriad facets, and its metal setting gleamed with the same golden-white luster as the disc in Simon's pouch. Simon felt a strange sensation at sight of the object. What was it that the phantom of Daramos had said to him? *It is the time when things once sundered are to be again unified....*

Petrilor came hurrying up to the Samaritan's side. "Do you know this child, Simon? Who is he and how did he come to be here?"

"He's Nilus, my apprentice, and he says he followed Mattan's priests to the temple and then got lost in the tunnels. He also says that one of the acolytes from the Goddess's temple asked him to deliver this amulet to me. I think it's the—"

"Lord of Arlyeh!" croaked Petrilor in astonishment, his eyes bulging even more than usual as he peered closely at the milk-white gem with its myriad facets. "Simon, do you know what this stone is? *It is the Thousand-faced Moon!*"

Simon nodded. "I suspected as much. Daramos told me of its existence many years ago, when he first gave me the disc which was once its component part. Look." He turned the amulet over and pointed to the large circular indentation just behind the jewel. "The talisman I carry originally fit there. But by what strange good fortune have these components now been brought together again, after all these centuries and in this unlikely place?"

"Not fortune, Simon," said Petrilor excitedly, "but Fate! Destiny! Surely the Great Goddess has somehow contrived to bring this about, that we may thwart her enemies. Bring the components together now, that the affinity of Earth and Water may again be manifest and that each of them may augment the powers of the other."

As Simon drew forth the giant coin-like medallion he saw that several more of the gilled and scaled water beings had joined the first. They moved forward and clustered about him, their lipless fish-mouths agape, their great round eyes fixed on the gem in what seemed to be fascination, even reverence. Behind them, the heads of several dolphins were visible above the pool's rim, and these creatures, too, seemed enthralled at sight of the jewel.

Simon carefully fitted the disc into the circular depression so that the image of the Queen of the World lay against the great jewel. The fit was snug and precise. Immediately the soft radiance from the Thousand-faced Moon increased to a fiery diamond-bright luster.

"Iä! Iä!" cried Petrilor, bowing in adoration before the shining gem, then reverently extending his hands to receive it. As Simon passed it to the priest of Dagon he seemed to feel a surge of energy from the talisman. "Iä!" repeated the scaly beings in deep frog-tones, eerily accompanied by shrill squeaks from the dolphins, "Iä!"

Was it Simon's imagination, or did the water in the great circular pool that connected to the ocean seem to be rising slightly…?

"Good!" exclaimed Petrilor, passing the great gem back to Simon. "You are a True Spirit in the body of an Earth being; in your hands this jewel will guide us to the Queen Incarnate." He gestured to the dolphins in the pool and said something in a strange guttural tongue. Immediately the creatures vanished beneath the water. Petrilor then took Nilus' torch from him, snatched the other from its bracket on the wall, and cast both into the pool. Instantly the room dimmed, lit now only by a bluish glow emitted by great sapphirean gems on the ends of wands carried by many of the scaly fish-men, as well as by the diamond-white sheen of the Thousand-faced Moon.

"Thus perishes Fire in Water," said the priest, "and so shall Ku-Thugha's servitors perish before us. The dolphins shall guide more allies here to aid us. Now, follow me, all of you. The Thousand-faced Moon shall lead us to the Queen upon whose breast it once hung—and if need be, our great Father Dagon shall send the very ocean to Her aid and ours!"

IV

The enormous interior of Melkarth's temple blazed with the light of several fire beings who hovered, buzzing faintly, near the tops of the high columns that flanked its main hall. Weird music echoed within its walls as a dozen cowled priests played on dark flutes. Mattan smiled with sinister anticipation. The preparatory rites had been long and complex but had been performed flawlessly. They had been necessary—this would be no mere transitory summoning of Ku-Thugha, but the opening of a great permanent Gate between this world and his—a Gate through which would surge the cloud-vast Lord of Fire himself, accompanied by many thousands more of his flaming servitors.

Already the outline of the Gate was forming between the twin pillars of gleaming gold and blazing emerald—a thin white circle, bright as the rim of an annular eclipse. The white-robed children stood facing it, eyes closed and two abreast, still as statues. In a few minutes they would be marched into that fiery circle and it would blaze like the sun—

But first the final and climactic rite must be performed: the two-staged ceremony of the Humbling and Sacrifice of the Queen.

"Are you ready, Jag Sodhi?"

The tall goat-faced sorcerer, his black turban again in place, nodded and grinned broadly, licking his teeth.

"Then accomplish the Humbling of the Queen. Take one of these girl-children—that one whose True Spirit is greatest—and do with her up-on the altar that which you know will please your great Master, the Guardi-an of the Gate. Meanwhile I will take this woman Helen to the roof and there perform the Sacrifice of the Queen—for I would watch as the very skies open and blaze with fire as I give to Lord Ku-Thugha the spirit of her who is the very incarnation of the Queen of the World."

"*No!*" cried the dark-haired woman suddenly, her eyes wide with ter-ror. "You won't—you can't. *They* won't let you!"

Mattan snarled. Something was wrong—the spell should have kept her entranced until the moment of sacrifice. Yet this Helen was a High One, possessing a greater portion of the spirit of the Goddess than most True Spirits. Had she sensed some influence...?

Quickly he snatched out a locket that hung around his neck by a gold-en chain and flicked open its cover, revealing a great glowing ruby within. Its light pulsed rapidly, fading and brightening alternately.

"Enemies approach," growled the high priest, "—or at least some in-fluence antagonistic to our cause. Perform the Rite of the Humbling, Jag, while I take this Helen to the roof and perform the Sacrifice—stop your struggling, woman! Look at me—look into my eyes. Look deeply—"

But though Mattan bent upon her all the power of his sinister dark eyes, Helen only struggled more fiercely. "*They* come," she cried out, "and the Moon of Glory comes with them!"

Exasperated, the priest struck Helen sharply across the face with his heavy palm, then lifted her half-dazed form easily and carried her out of the great hall, vanishing between the marble columns and into the shadowy arch of the stairway. In a few moments his ascending footsteps had faded entirely.

Jag Sodhi turned and walked to where the golden-haired Clarissa stood at the head of the line of children. His feet clacked strangely upon the marble, sending echoes throughout the vast hall. He extended one hand toward the girl's white-clad shoulder and raised the other as if in salute to some high dark god.

"*Iä! Ku-Thugha!*" he boomed in a voice more like that of a great bull than a human being.

At Jag's touch Clarissa suddenly started awake, her scream of terror following close upon his bull-bellow. The turbaned priest gripped her by one frail arm and began to drag her around the side of the golden pillar, toward the altar, again bellowing: "*Iä! Ku-Thugha!*"

The twin pillars brightened, their deep vibrant humming intensifying. Then twin shafts of radiance, one green and one golden, shot straight up from their tops and held against the high ceiling like columns of light supporting it.

Clarissa screamed again in the grip of the monster-priest, sensing an unspeakable intent in his gloating bestial features as he dragged her toward the altar—

Abruptly, a fire elemental darted from a shadowy colonnade and soared into the nave, circling erratically while pulsing and emitting a shrill buzzing. Clarissa felt a strange sensation in her mind and somehow realized that the being was sounding a warning. Immediately the other fire beings began to dart and buzz also, and the cowled priests ceased their eerie flute-playing. Clarissa heard the other children cry out in fear as the spell over them was broken. At the same time, incongruously, she thought she caught the smell of the sea—

Then came the sound of many strange feet or paws slapping against marble tiles, and Clarissa screamed a third time as a horde of scaled and fish-eyed beings, some bearing silvery-golden blades and tridents or glowing sapphire-tipped wands, hopped and loped monstrously from among the columned shadows, surging toward her.

They had passed through the room of the great droning shapes of metal and were now proceeding down the straight corridor which Nilus informed them was the one leading to the temple. Simon marveled at the way the glowing Moon-gem hung forward from his hand on its silvery chain, leading him along almost as a leashed dog. Unerringly it had guided them through the maze of ancient tunnels—seeking, as Petrilor explained, the Incarnate Queen of the World—and at every juncture Nilus had excitedly verified its accuracy. Now, as they neared their goal, it stood out almost straight on its chain, pulling against Simon's hand as if with the eagerness of a living thing.

As they climbed the stairs leading to the temple the passage ahead was suddenly filled with light and a harsh, shrill buzzing smote their ears. A spherical fire being pulsed angrily just ahead of them, nearly filling the ascending corridor from side to side, and Simon realized that it must have been set there as a guardian after Nilus' escape.

"Back, fire-slave!" barked Petrilor imperiously. "Dare you to oppose the Thousand-faced Moon?"

The thing receded abruptly, then vanished around a corner at the top of the stairway. Its light rapidly dimmed and faded away. Simon and his companions followed the priest of Dagon upward. As they neared the top Simon noted an odd fact—he could once again smell the sea. Then he heard the sound of water swirling in the corridor below. Pausing upon the landing to glance back, he saw, beyond the hunched scaly beings and their sapphire-glowing wands, a surface of rippling dark water gradually ascending to cover the first stone step—then the second—

"By Poseidon!" gasped Simon. "The sea itself follows us—"

"Aye, and with it shall follow *others* to aid us," said Petrilor, "—minions of Him who is Arlyeh's lord and whom even Father Dagon serves. Hurry, now, for you and the lad must be clear of the tunnels before the waters ascend."

They traversed the remaining stairs and corridors quickly, now hearing the sounds of bellowed chanting and weird flutes. Simon saw light beyond the corridor's end, the silhouettes of great stone columns. And then he heard a girl scream.

"The rites are culminating!" croaked Petrilor. "We can't wait for the others—we must disrupt the ceremony now. That flame elemental will have alerted—"

Again the girl screamed. The flutes ceased their piping and the angry buzzings of many fire beings became audible. Then, as Simon and his companions burst charging from the corridor, Nilus cried out: "Look—it's Clarissa! That monster-priest has her!"

"Nilus, stop!"

The boy was already dashing forward. Simon thrust the Moon-stone into Petrilor's hands and raced after Nilus, drawing his symbol-emblazoned knife as he ran. At his heels immediately charged Petrilor and his squad of Deep-denizens, brandishing their weapons and wands.

Instantly the fire beings swooped down to attack. Jag Sodhi bellowed something in an unknown tongue, and in an instant more of the flame elementals were streaking into the temple from their posts and patrols outside. The great hall was filled with their light and the children were shrieking in terror. The cowled priests threw down their flutes, whipped out their ritual daggers, and charged to meet the attacking Deep-denizens.

"Simon!" Petrilor managed to grab the Samaritan's arm. "Don't follow the boy. You've no protection without the Moon-stone—"

"I have my own protection," snarled Simon, wrenching away and dashing across the flags. Behind him he heard the buzzings and deep croakings, then the sizzling of scaled flesh. A cowled priest raced to intercept him, curved dagger slashing; Simon feinted expertly, slashed in return—and the priest, no match for one who had been gladiator-trained, fell back with blood spurting from both neck arteries.

Clarissa, cringing in terror, suddenly felt her arm released, then was astonished to see the boy Saturnilus charging, in advance of the frog-fish beings, straight toward her and the towering Jag Sodhi. Behind him the cowled priests were engaging the beings in battle while the fire elementals swooped down on the fray from above.

"Clarissa, I'm coming! Run!"

The girl stood paralyzed with fear. Nilus completed his dash with a high leap and, reversing himself in midair, kicked out savagely—but this time Jag Sodhi, prepared, moved with inhuman swiftness and caught the boy's hurtling body about the middle with one hand.

Nilus gasped as he felt that monstrous hand tightening, squeezing the breath out of him. Jag Sodhi laughed—a deep, rumbling bellow.

Suddenly the glow of the gigantic twin pillars began to flicker and dim, and loud cracklings and hissings burst from them. Jag cast Nilus aside and whirled to face them, his face a feral mask of consternation.

"The sea water is at their bases!" yelled Petrilor. "It is sapping their energies—weakening the Gate!"

Nilus, gasping on the floor, saw a fish-man smite one of the fire beings with his sapphire-tipped wand. Immediately the elemental burst into scores of tiny flamelets which dispersed and shrilled about for a moment as in confusion and fear, then darted in a swarm toward and through the ring of light between the crackling pillars. Others were sharing its fate, for the nave was now full of the frantic little fire-bees, all of which seemed to be seeking escape back through the Gate. The Deep-denizens, though now withdrawing in slow, bunched retreat toward the columns, were holding the fire beings at bay; moreover, the elementals seemed disinclined to approach the Dagon priest and his glowing Moon-stone. Several black-robed priests lay about the floor, slain by the Deep-denizens, while a few of the fish beings lay dead also, hacked and charred, bleeding a greenish ichor.

Then Nilus saw Simon dashing toward him.

Jag Sodhi whipped out his great sword. Simon halted a few feet away, watching warily as the black-turbaned priest danced oddly before him, cloven hooves clattering on the tiles. Nimbly the satyr-like being tossed the sword from one hand to the other, occasionally spinning it and catching it like a juggler, all with superhuman quickness, while never taking his gleaming eyes off the Samaritan. Simon had met his kind before—servitors of the Gate-Guardian—and knew that few men could hope to best one in combat. Then he saw Nilus begin to crawl determinedly toward the being, rise and crouch as if to spring.

"Damn it!" Simon tossed his own knife from right to left hand, crouched as if to fight—but instead drew a dark five-pointed object from his pouch and hurled it, all in one smooth motion. The thing spun true, swift as a darting bat, and thudded solidly into the chest of the turbaned priest. Jag Sodhi bellowed in pain and staggered back, smoke and flame erupting from where the object had embedded itself in his flesh, then fell heavily to the floor, his great sword clanging upon the flags beside him. For a moment his hooves clattered against the stone as he twitched in death-spasms.

Simon ran forward. "Nilus! Are you all right—?"

"Look out!" cried the golden-haired girl.

Simon whirled, glimpsed a fire being darting down toward him, and snatched another iron-dark star from his pouch. Barely in time he hurled it; the fire elemental flared up and shrilled uncannily, then vanished as abruptly as a burst bubble, leaving behind nothing but a rapidly dispersing haze of pale smoke.

Nilus and the girl ran to him. "Simon!" gasped the lad. "What *are* those things?"

"Star-talismans, fashioned from meteoric metal by sorcerers of ancient Mnar. They are sovereign against servitors of any of the Great Old Ones. Here—take one, each of you, and none of the fire elementals will approach you. I have two more in my pouch—"

The pillars of Melkarth crackled and hummed more loudly. Simon saw that more and more of the fire beings, both fragmented and whole, were streaming into the wavering ring of light that was the Gate back to their world. He heard Petrilor yell exultantly, turned to discover that all the cowled priests were slain and the rest of the fire elementals were in retreat before the Deep-denizens. Then he saw something stranger still—a dark sheet of water spilling from among the columns and spreading rapidly across the marble floor. Again the sea scent was strong in his nostrils.

A few minutes later most of the flame beings had vanished through the wavering Gate that still hung between the eerily pulsing pillars. Petrilor and the Deep-denizens surged forward to join Simon, then stopped short and gazed in horror at the objects which he and the two children held in their hands.

"Star-stones!" croaked the priest of Dagon. "Had I known that you carried them, Simon, I would never have permitted you among us."

Simon quickly pocketed his. "They'll not be used against you and your friends, Petrilor. But tell me, where is Helen? Why is she not here? We must make haste to find her!"

The priest glanced at the Moon-stone, which now hung limp from its chain. "The stone still glows, so she is alive. Perhaps she has been taken somewhere aloft." He glanced at the other children, who were now huddled trembling together in a quiet group, then at the sea water which was rapidly spreading over the entire temple floor. "You and the children must leave this place, Simon, for soon the Temple of Melkarth will be inundated and all air-breathers remaining within it must perish. The minions of Great Ku-Tulu are coming to confront him who kidnapped the Mistress of the Moon-stone, and with them they bring the sea itself."

Simon turned to his apprentice. "Did you hear the man, Nilus? You and these others must leave immediately. I'm putting you in charge. Hey, all you kids—come here!" As the children gathered around him, Simon continued: "You're out of danger for the moment, but must leave this temple at once. This is Nilus, my apprentice—he'll lead you back across the causeway to Tyre and safety. Do as he says, and may the gods go with you."

"Simon," said Nilus uneasily, "aren't you coming too?"

"I'll join you shortly. Just get yourself and these others safely back into the city. And be sure that you and your friend—Clarissa, is it?—keep those star-stones visible. There may be a few fire elementals still lurking about, but with those talismans you bear they won't dare bother you."

Nilus nodded, saluted his master in a smart military fashion, then shouted to the children: "Follow me, all of you. The water's rising!"

They obeyed, trotting along after him across the tiles through the ankle-deep sea water. Clarissa ran at his side, casting back occasional anxious glances at the other children, holding her star-stone high, and despite the terror of his recent ordeals Nilus felt a glow of pleasurable excitement. For now, he knew, the girl must realize that he was as important as—as he had wanted her to believe he was!

Simon watched them as they raced in splashing strides toward the temple's main entrance. When they had vanished beyond the columns of the portico, he turned to Petrilor and said: "Give me the Thousand-faced Moon. I must find Helen."

The priest blinked. "Are you sure, Simon? Even we, who can breathe underwater, are in peril now. If we fail to rescue the Queen in time, you will surely perish with her. No human can hope to—"

"You must know that I am no ordinary human," said Simon, "I am the Enduring One—the Consort of the Queen. Is that not why the gem leads me, and no other, to Her?"

Petrilor blinked again. "I guessed it from the words of Daramos. Aye, it seems that Destiny has chosen you to restore the gem's missing component that you may attempt to succor the Queen Incarnate. Lead on, then, O Enduring One, and we shall follow!"

Helen, half-dazed, realized that she was lying on a stone surface beneath the stars. Twin pillars of flickering, fading light flanked the low altar on which she lay, rising from the temple's roof and vanishing interminably upward into the night sky. Their radiance eerily illumined her white tunic— and the bald, gleaming cranium of the black-robed man who towered over her.

Terror gripped the girl. She strove to rise, only to find that her wrists and ankles had been bound.

"Fum-al-hut has risen," intoned the dark priest. "Now, O Queen of the World, your great spirit shall feed my lord Ku-Thugha, and then he shall reward me beyond the dreams of all men and demons."

Helen realized that the priest must be mad; certainly the light in his glowering dark eyes implied it. Mad eyes, yet set in a heavy, calm face whose expression connoted great power and confidence—

"I am no queen of this world, nor of anything else," she protested fearfully. "I am but a temple acolyte—"

The priest chuckled gutturally. "Do you, in your incarnate ignorance, presume to know more than I? For I am Mattan, formerly Priest of Baal in that olden time when the Hebrew prophet caused me to be slain after he stole my secret of calling down altar-fire; in another time I was that very Prince of Tyre who walked gem-clad amid the fiery stones. Like you, I am a High One—but *I remember.* Even as your incarnate destiny is of Earth, so is mine of Fire—and through fire I shall rule all things! I am the Adversary of Man, even the foe of that Enduring One, your consort, whose blunder in the beginning caused the creation of the worlds. Like you and he, I am incarnated from age to age—but now, my sorcery has caused me to recall the cosmic drama of which you and he remain largely unaware. I would have you know this before you die, O Queen of the World, for that knowledge will increase the anguish of your soul—anguish whose energy will feed Lord Ku-Thugha and cause him to elevate me closer to the throne of *his* lord, even the Throne of Achamoth, Lord of All Things. And some-day I, Mattan, shall no longer be merely Priest or Prince or Adversary, but shall sit upon that Throne and rule all the cosmos!"

Helen trembled. Madness beyond measure—and yet, the man's words woke strange visions in her soul—visions that were like memories. She suddenly seemed to glimpse a far-off Realm of Light—how far off and long ago!—from which she had been hurled in exile by cosmic misfortune. A cosmic spirit, trapped in matter, imprisoned in the grotesque bodies of complex organisms generation after generation—

"You *see!*" growled the priest, leering down at her. "You *remember!*" He turned to the southeastern sky and raised his hands toward a bright amber star not far above the horizon. "It is the Time. Come, great Lord of Fire! *Phun-klui munglu-naph! Ku-Thugha Fum-al-hut na-ka-ghaa naf-al thagan! Iä! Ku-Thugha!*"

The cloudless sky thundered, and for an instant Helen glimpsed above the twin flickering pillars of light a faint fiery brightening.

"He hears!" yelled Mattan. "He sees! *Phun-klui munglu-naph....*"

As the second enunciation of the outlandish chant was completed, the sky-brightening recurred, this time lingering for a space, flickering soundlessly like heat lightning. But now Helen's unearthly visions, stimulated by Mattan's remarks, were increasing in intensity. Whether cosmic memories or hallucinations, they were expanding—and linking up with impressions she'd had earlier in the temple below—

"*They* are coming to aid me," she cried out, "and you cannot stand against them!"

Mattan chuckled. "I know that enemies approach, for I sense them. Do not enemies eternally beset the Adversary? But soon all my enemies shall be no more, for at the third recitation of the chant Ku-Thugha himself shall come in all his power to destroy them. *Phun-klui—*"

"*Helen!*"

Both the girl and Mattan turned at the shout. Helen gasped as she saw the man who stood near the western parapet of the temple roof, the man she had seen in the Temple of Astarte—a tall, dark-haired man holding a great luminous gem in his hand. Somehow in that moment she equated him with that Enduring One she had just glimpsed in her strange vision. Behind him stood several hulking, dark beings who seemed to resemble frogs or fish more than humans.

Mattan's heavy-featured face twisted in a snarl. "*You!*" he growled. "Had I known *you* were among those who opposed me... but it makes no difference, for I sense that you are still more than half mired in ignorance. Stand back, you who are called Simon of Gitta, or I shall blast your soul down into Hades."

Simon, puzzled but still more angered, drew his dagger and advanced—but even in that moment he sensed that this Mattan was no ordinary human. Nilus' description had not prepared him for the aura of pure superhuman evil that seemed to emanate from the hulking priest' glowering dark eyes—

Then he felt the barrier between himself and the priest—a seemingly physical barrier, invisible and frictionless, unyielding—and sensed that it emanated from the sheer power of Mattan's mind. Not even the point of his symbol-inscribed dagger would drive through it! Petrilor and his fish-men were now also attacking the invisible barrier with their tridents and sapphire-tipped wands, but with no greater success.

"Fools!" Mattan swept his hand toward them—and Simon, Petrilor, and the Deep-denizens all went sprawling back, tumbling and clattering to the flags as if bowled over by an invisible ocean wave. Slowly they groped to their knees and shakily rose.

"Fools!" repeated the bald priest, laughing deeply. "Helpless, flesh-bound mortals! Now I shall complete the chant that shall summon the Lord of Fire, and then you shall watch as I rip the living heart from the breast of the Queen of the World in sacrifice to Ku-Thugha."

He turned back to the altar and raised his right hand aloft. Simon, again straining furiously against the barrier, saw that there was no knife in that upraised hand.

"Phun-klui munglu-naph!"

Mattan's right hand began to metamorphose, to darken and elongate into a scaly reptilian claw with great curving talons. Helen shrieked in terror.

"Ku-Thugha Fum-al-hut na-ka-gaa naf-al-thagan!"

The sky was rumbling—or was it the temple trembling beneath? The claw descended toward Helen's breast. Suddenly Petrilor cried out:

"Simon, don't fight the barrier. Speak the Goddess's primal name, then release the Thousand-faced Moon!"

Instinctively, without pause for thought, Simon cried out the word: *"Ennoia!"*

The straining gem leaped from his hand, silvery chain trailing, and darted through the air straight toward Helen, passing the barrier as if it did not exist—

"Iä! Ku-Thugha!"

Thunder answered from the sky, which was suddenly filled with a fearsome amber glow. Thousands of tiny pinpoints of light appeared above the temple and Simon yelled in a rage of frustration. He had failed! A Gate was opening in the heavens and Ku-Thugha and his minions were streaming through—

The Moon-stone darted to Helen and settled upon her bosom. The taloned hand of Mattan, descending to rend open the woman's chest in sacrifice, closed upon the great gem instead. Instantly Mattan bellowed in agony and staggered back, his claw-hand disintegrating in a furious white-hot blaze that threw off sparks brighter than the fire elementals themselves!

The sorcerous barrier was down. Simon rushed forward, crashed into the reeling priest, and drove his dagger deep into the man's midriff. Mattan bellowed again and struck out with his left hand. The forearm caught Simon across the chest and sent him sprawling. He scrambled erect in time to see the priest pull the knife out of his body and toss it aside, then begin to advance, his left hand now a reptilian claw as his right had been, his dark eyes glaring with rage.

"Flee, Simon!" yelled Petrilor. "You have won—don't try to fight him—"

Simon, however, whipped a star-stone from his pouch and hurled it at the bald priest; Mattan, evidently no mere servitor of the Old Ones, caught it and tossed it contemptuously aside. At sight of the five-pointed talisman clattering on the tiles, Petrilor and his fish-men turned as one and ran to the temple's western parapet, then leaped over it in a mad scramble that looked to Simon like suicide. A moment later he was surprised to hear their bodies splash into water not far below.

At the same time, the myriad fire-sparks above the temple also fled, streaking up into the sky.

But he had no time to ponder these things, for Mattan was advancing upon him, right wrist-stump smoldering, left claw groping. The bald priest's head was darkening, sprouting black horns, and his form was expanding so that it filled the voluminous black robe entirely. His unseen feet now clopped upon the tiles in a way reminiscent of Jag Sodhi's, only even more loudly and with an iron ringing; his eyes, formerly dark, now glowed an eerie sulfurous yellow.

Simon darted away from him toward the altar—then stopped, astonished. Helen stood upright upon it, tall in her white tunic, her raven hair now streaming loose. There was something regal, imperious, even superhuman in her great dark eyes and the set of her face. At her feet lay the sundered white cords that had bound her, and upon her breast blazed the great Thousand-faced Moon.

"No—!" bellowed the thing that had been Mattan.

Helen extended her right arm. From her fingertips streamed a vivid shimmering radiance, a shaft of humming force that struck the monstrous priest and hurled him backward. Mattan howled as he was battered and tumbled across the rooftop, like a frenzied aurochs in the grip of mighty rapids, until he crashed into the northern parapet with a force that shook the temple and jarred loose great blocks of stone.

"I would sunder you from your devil-flesh now, spawn of Ahriman," cried Helen in a voice too grand and vibrant to be that of a mortal woman, "save that I deem it more fitting that you now face the being you invoked but whose sacrifice you have failed to perform."

Then the light faded from the Moon-stone and the girl abruptly fell to her knees, staring about her as if suddenly bewildered. Her expression had none of its former grand imperiousness, and Simon realized that the Goddess had withdrawn. The amber light from above was increasing, and as he glanced up he saw a great glowing cloud advancing, its billows writhing like living things, blotting out most of the southeastern sky—Ku-Thugha, expanding through the Sky-gate from his fiery domain on Fum-al-hut—

Again the temple trembled, and this time Simon heard something like thundering footfalls from below—wet, squelching footfalls of something gigantic coming up the broad stairway by which he had ascended to the temple's upper story—and next, a sucking sound and an uprushing vile stench, as if a giant sea-slug were oozing up through the last narrow stair-well—

Simon snatched up his fallen star-stone, then ran to Helen and lifted her off the altar. Careful to touch neither of the giant vertical beams of flickering light he raced for the eastern parapet with the girl in his arms, while again the temple trembled and the fire-cloud boiled nearer.

Glancing back, Simon saw Mattan rising to his knees, huge and dark under the tatters of his cloak, yellow eyes blazing.

"He can't harm us," gasped Helen, "as long as I wear the jewel. Yet we must flee, for I sense vast powers converging—"

"No exit-way on this side." Simon peered over the parapet, then cried out in astonishment. Under the sky-glare he could see than an unnatural tide had humped the sea up around the temple in a huge, gently sloping mound. Not a ripple stirred its glassy surface, which was less than twenty feet below and rising. The rest of the great fane was submerged beneath it.

Simon leaped atop the parapet and helped Helen up after him. He glimpsed something huge, tentacled, and gelatinous begin to ooze and expand upward from the aperture on the other side of the roof; at the same time he felt heat radiating from the amber-flaming sky.

"Water and Fire," muttered Helen, her eyes wide in mystic awe, "converging to do battle—"

"*Jump!*" yelled Simon, grabbing the girl with one arm about her waist.

They leaped and plunged down, striking the water feet first, then paddled furiously upward and away from the temple. As soon as they broke the surface they found that their progress away from the wall was increasingly rapid, more rapid than a swimmer should normally make. They were sliding eastward down the slope of that great mound of water and gaining greater speed every second. Twice they just missed the upper foliage of trees projecting above the water mound, and then they were shooting beyond the edge of the island faster than anyone could hope to swim.

"Go with it, Helen!" yelled Simon. "Dive with it!"

A wild bellow of terror rang out behind them—the voice of the thing that had called itself Mattan. Simon snatched a glance back, saw the dark and horned figure trying to scramble over the parapet—but before it could leap a pulsing green mountain of a being loomed up behind it and enfolded it in huge glistening tentacles. Then the vast fire-cloud descended upon the temple roof with thunderous roarings, even as the sea seemed to grope upward to meet it....

Simon drew a deep breath and extended his body as if in a dive, shooting eastward down the water slope at an incredibly high speed that to him, in his terror, felt like a snail's pace. Behind him sounded growling thunder, together with vast and uncanny ululations like the battle chants of Titans, strangely *vocal* yet too enormous to be natural.

Simon became aware of early dawn-light. Half dazed, he realized that he was swimming with powerful strokes. His speed had gradually declined, and now he saw that he had passed beyond the foot of the sea slope. Helen was swimming not far ahead. The eastward shore, which had originally been over a mile distant, was less than half that now. Dawn was breaking beyond far hills.

Suddenly he sensed a jolt, a shock wave such as an undersea earthquake might make. Turning, he saw that the fire-cloud above the temple was dimming, vanishing away with incredible speed in the direction of the star Fum-al-hut, and in its declining light he saw also that the sea-mound was subsiding rapidly down the glistening sides of the temple. No longer did the twin beams of radiance shoot upward into the sky. The Gate had closed and the sea water had finally quenched the strange energies of the Pillars of Melkarth—forever, Simon hoped.

Then the nearer waters began to hump up toward him in a wave.

"Stop swimming, Helen!" he cried out. "We mustn't be near the shore when it hits there!"

The water rose higher and higher, and then Simon felt himself being lifted up with it. Just before he reached the top of the wave it began to crest, and for a few moments he felt himself churned violently about; then he broke through the surface and watched as the great wave swept grandly on to crash at last against the distant shore.

When at length the sea had calmed he swam on and finally waded ashore, looking anxiously about for Helen. To the northwest he could see the masts of ships still swaying amid high waves within the protected Egyptian Harbor of Tyre. Nearby he saw the squat, hunched form of Petrilor approaching him along the sandy beach.

"Ku-Thugha has fled back to his fiery domain," croaked the Dagon-priest, "and those few of his minions who did not flee with him are scattered and destroyed. Now may your folk and mine—the folk of earth and water—continue to live yet awhile upon this world. And much of the credit for that must go to you, Simon of Gitta."

"But what of Helen?" said Simon anxiously. "I must find—"

"She is there. Did you think the Goddess would let Her incarnate form again perish, after all these perils?"

Simon turned to where Petrilor pointed—and felt a great relief as he saw Helen wading ashore, her long wet tresses glistening, her white tunic clinging to her slim and supple form. In that moment, with the swelling gray light of early dawn full upon her and her eyes alight with joyous relief as she advanced toward him, she seemed to Simon the very incarnation of Aphrodite emerging from the foam of the sea.

VENGEANCE QUEST
by Richard L. Tierney

Black vultures soared above the mists, the sun rose redly burning
When Simon the Mage to his ancient land returned with a vengeance-
    yearning.
Adown the Empire's endless roads he'd wandered the provinces o'er,
Steely of eye and with steel in hand, to settle an age-old score.

Beside the road in silence grim he paused upon his way.
His comrades quailed to see him draw his blade, then hear him say:
"The Romans slew my kith and kin, now vengeance I have sworn."
A cold wind moaned among the trees like the sound of a hunter's horn.

"They placed me in a cage," he said, "and bore me off to Rome.
For two full dark and bitter years the arena was my home.
They trained me for the buckler and the wicked Thracian blade.
I've sent to Hades' echoing halls full many a wailing shade.

"Two years I entertained the howling crowds with deeds of death,
Till one day came a centuried wizard who, with his last breath,
Uttered unto the Great Old Ones a dreadful vengeance-spell.
Full twenty thousand perished when that great arena fell.

"An aged magus rescued me and hid me in his lair.
I watched him cast mad spells invoking Powers of Fire and Air.
I saw great globes of flame descend from out the midnight gloom;
Upon the blazing hills of Rome, ten thousand met their doom.

"I've crossed the peaks of Persia where the ice-winds whine and wail,
Fleeing a score of bandits who rode hard upon my trail.
They would have killed me but for One I summoned to my aid—
The primal killer Cain, who slew them all with his great blade.

"And once I fought in Ephesus a wizard dark and fell
Who offered up his daughters to the awful Queen of Hell—
Shupnikkurat, who reigns in realms where nighted chasms yawn.
I'm proud I sent his soul to dwell amid her thousand spawn.

"I've slain full many a Roman and freed those they held in thrall,
And once in dream I crossed all space to confront the Lord of All.
I fought him on his darksome throne where he bubbled and blasphemed."
The mage's eyes grew somber as he pondered what he'd dreamed.

Then to his friends he turned and said, "Good comrades, I must go.
My sword is eager for the feast, I hear the death-winds blow."
He faced the east and raised his blade to the glaring crimson sun
And swore an oath of vengeance in the Name of the Ancient One.

"Oh, leave us not!" his comrades cried. "Why would you seek your doom?
Journey with us to safer lands and spare your soul from gloom."
But Simon the Mage in steely rage strode off with sword in hand.
They watched him vanish in the mists of that grim and god-cursed land.

About the Author

Richard L. Tierney (1936 -) is a poet, author, and editor of adventure fiction, mainly in the realm of dark fantasy. Since his mid-teens, he has been both a fan and scholar of H.P. Lovecraft, Robert E. Howard, Clark Ashton Smith, and other great names from the pulp fiction era. In 2010, he was nominated for the Science Fiction Poetry Association's Grandmaster Award.

In 1961, Tierney earned a degree in Entomology (Iowa State College) and served for many years with the U.S. Forest Service in several of the western states and Alaska. A haunter of archaeological ruins by instinct, he has traveled widely, especially in Mexico, Central, and South America. Many of the ideas and images that he has employed in his stories have been inspired by his extensive travels. His major works include *Collected Poems* (1981, Arkham House), *The House of the Toad* (1993, Fedogan and Bremer), *The Drums of Chaos* (2008, Mythos Books), and *Savage Menace and Other Poems of Horror* (2010, reprint 2021, P'rea Press).

Richard is currently enjoying his retirement in his house, "the hermitage," in the Corn Steppes of northern Iowa.

OTHER NOVELS BY RICHARD L. TIERNEY

The Winds of Zarr

The House of the Toad

The Drums of Chaos

WITH GLENN RAHMAN

The Gardens of Lucullus

The Path of the Dragon (forthcoming)

WITH ROBERT E. HOWARD

Hawks of Outremer

Tigers of the Sea

WITH DAVID C. SMITH

For the Witch of the Mists: Ban Mak Morn

Red Sonja Series:
> The Ring of Ikribu
> Demon Night
> When Hell Laughs
> Endithor's Daughter
> Against the Prince of Hell
> Star of Doom

POETRY COLLECTIONS BY RICHARD L. TIERNEY

Dreams and Damnations

Collected Poems: Nightmares and Visions

The Blob That Gobbled Abdul and Other Poems and Songs

Savage Menace and Other Poems of Horror

MORE BOOKS FROM PICKMAN'S PRESS

THE AVEROIGNE ARCHIVES

For the first time in paperback or ebook, all of Clark Ashton Smith's weird tales of Averoigne—the sinister, monster-haunted province of medieval France—are collected into one volume. Werewolves and satyrs stalk the dark forests, witches and necromancers lurk in the swamps, and gargoyles and giants terrorize the cathedral city of Vyônes.

THE AVEROIGNE LEGACY

Over two dozen new stories and poems set in Clark Ashton Smith's world of Averoigne. Revisit Vyônes and Périgon, meet Luc le Chaudronnier and Azédarac once again, as tales of harpies and vampires, ogres and giants, changelings and cockatrices await you!

CORPORATE CTHULHU

Just like the Great Old Ones, corporations are powerful but unseen entities we have no control over, yet subtly manipulate our lives and our world—and we don't even realize it. Who needs a Cthulhu Cult when you've got Cthulhu, Inc.? Endure twenty-five Mythos tales of bureaucratic nightmare, but remember: it's nothing personal—just business.

Paperbacks available from Amazon, Barnes & Noble, and Lulu.

eBooks available from Amazon, Barnes & Noble, Google Play, Apple iBooks, Kobo eBookstore, Drive Thru Fiction, and Lulu.

Printed in Great Britain
by Amazon

2d893c0c-217b-49e3-b675-5050a22def68R01